The Venetian House

Mary Nickson has three children and a host of grand-children. She lives in Yorkshire.

MARY NICKSON

The Venetian House

arrow books

Published by Arrow Books in 2006

5 7 9 10 8 6

Copyright © Mary Nickson 2004

First published in the United Kingdom in 2004 by Century

Arrow Books
The Random House Group Limited
20 Vauxhall Bridge Road, London, SW1V 2SA

Random House Australia (Pty) Limited
20 Alfred Street, Milsons Point, Sydney,
New South Wales 2061, Australia

Random House New Zealand Limited
18 Poland Road, Glenfield
Auckland 10, New Zealand

Random House (Pty) Limited
Isle of Houghton, Corner of Boundary Road & Carse O'Gowrie,
Houghton 2198, South Africa

The Random House Group Limited Reg. No. 954009

www.randomhouse.co.uk

A CIP catalogue record for this book
is available from the British Library

Papers used by Random House are
natural, recyclable products made from wood grown in
sustainable forests. The manufacturing processes conform to
the environmental regulations of the country of origin

ISBN 0 09 946632 5

Printed and bound in Great Britain by
Bookmarque Ltd, Croydon, Surrey

Specially for Susannah,
with love as always

Acknowledgements

Many friends have been generous with their time, help and expertise and I am deeply grateful to them all – any mistakes will be mine, not theirs.

I would particularly like to thank: Angela Papageorgiou, George Harewood, Dick Temple of The Temple Gallery, Robin Sheepshanks, Mrs Lascari, Bishop Michael Mann, Sheila Robertson, Patricia Cookson, Rosie Campbell, Karol Farnham, Pamela Nicholson, David Noble and Christopher Sykes.

I am grateful to the islands and islanders of Corfu and Paxos for many happy family holidays over the years. I have taken some liberties with the geography of Corfu: The island has many beautiful and historic Venetian houses, but Vrahos, the house in this story, is imaginary as are also the town of Kryovrisi, Aghia Sophia, the villa Petradi and the little island of Helladonia.

I owe a special debt to my long-suffering daughters and daughter-in-law for giving me unstinted encouragement and criticism – and to my son and sons-in-law for putting up with even more telephone calls than usual.

Last but by no means least I want to thank my wonderful agent Sarah Molloy and also Sara Fisher at A. M. Heath & Co, and my wonderful editors Kate Elton and Georgina Hawtrey-Woore at Century for their patience and for having faith in me.

I found three books especially helpful:

Corfu – The Garden Isle presented by Spiro Flamburiari
Noble Families of Corfu by Despina Paisidou
Icons by Richard Temple

Prologue

❧

To start with, the track from the house to the sea wound gently down through the olive grove, a pleasurable and easy amble that anyone could manage, but then it suddenly became steep, stony and narrow – not a walk suitable for elderly ladies, thought Evanthi Doukas wryly, as she picked her way carefully over the loose stones and shale that made it dangerously easy to lose one's footing. Years before she had skipped down that same path as lightly as her granddaughter, Victoria, now did, but somehow the lissom, black-haired girl she had once been – as sure-footed as the goats that roamed over the mountain of Pantokrator – had turned imperceptibly in late middle-age into a statuesque woman with slightly swollen ankles and a tendency to puff.

She paused to catch her breath and listen to the laughter of the children from far below as they splashed and shrieked, their voices amplified by the rock-face above the bay. Nafsica would be there with them, supposedly keeping watch while they swam, but actually sitting on a rock dozing in the late afternoon sun like a lizard in a state of suspended animation; what good she would be if any of them actually got into difficulties one couldn't imagine, but they were all three as at home in the water as young dolphins. Though Nafsica had been born and bred on the island she had never learned to swim; nor had she ever shown the slightest desire to do so, and combined both the wholesome respect for the power of the sea with the unsentimental disregard for its attractions of someone who has lived by it all her life and can take its changing moods for granted.

We are both on the verge of getting old, thought Evanthi with astonishment – ageing seems to have crept up so stealthily. How tiresome it is that there is absolutely nothing we can either of us do to stop this relentless, unacceptable march of time; but

1

Nafsica will cope with old age better than I shall, when it eventually comes, because it is not in her nature either to question or repine. She will sit sunning herself in an open doorway on an old wooden chair dressed in her black dress and headscarf – content to watch the world go by and become as much a part of the landscape as the tall cypress trees, the scarlet geraniums and the stray cats.

But I, thought Evanthi, I will not be content to do that.

Together the two women had packed for the many journeys in Evanthi's roaming life as she had followed her international lawyer husband round the world – not that the maid often joined her mistress on these travels. But one day even stay-at-home Nafsica will be forced to travel, said Evanthi to herself. There will be no choice in the matter for either of us – we shall both have to face a journey that will require no carefully packed trunks of clothes or household possessions. She gave herself a little shake. She certainly did not intend to set out on that particular expedition for a long while yet: there were far too many things she still wanted to do; too many people who needed her – and one in particular now, of course. Whatever else happens, I must see Victoria launched in life, decided Evanthi; perhaps I can prevent her from making the same mistakes that I made. But in truth she doubted this. One could only watch helplessly as the drama of other people's lives unfolded; and she thought with sadness of her own son, Constantine, Victoria's father, who would never see his child grow up. Dear God, prayed Evanthi, let me live for a long time yet.

It was perhaps more of an instruction than a supplication, for Evanthi Doukas could be imperious and all her life, in the most charming way possible, had been used to issuing commands to everyone she dealt with. She saw no reason why she should make an exception for the Almighty.

When she had made her way down to the little bay which could be reached only by the rocky route she had just taken, or by boat – thus making it a virtually private beach for the Doukas family – the two boys were still swimming, but Nafsica was rubbing Victoria with a towel, clucking over her like a broody hen and muttering in Greek. Nafsica could in fact speak perfectly adequate English, and often did, but she certainly wasn't going to do so to Victoria. She disapproved of the fact that Constantine's daughter would now be brought up in England by her aunt, Evanthi's daughter Spiridoula – Toula, as she was known to her family – who had had the bad taste to marry an Englishman, something about which Nafsica held strong opinions.

'Well, my little one, did you have a good swim?' asked Evanthi.

'Mmm . . .' Victoria went and leaned against her grand-mother. She had always been a grown-up, rather self-possessed little girl, but since her parents' death in a plane crash the year before, she had become uncharacteristically hungry for the reassurance of touch. Her grandmother stroked her wet, dark hair and thought how heart-rendingly like her father she looked. 'The boys have taught me to jump in holding my nose. And, Nonna, I swam underwater for miles and miles. But now they're having a Lilo-fight and said I couldn't be in it.'

At seven years old Victoria looked like a baby bird, all big eyes and fragile bones and – so the boys would have said – a mouth constantly open, squawking for attention. Her legs were so skinny it seemed possible they might snap. She liked to tag along after the boys – her cousin Guy, Toula's son, and his friend Richard – wherever they went; she was their camp follower and sometimes also their torment, though on the whole they were tolerant: two benevolent dictators, or rather one dictator, for Richard usually went along with Guy's suggestions too, as most children were apt to do. They patronised but protected her and sometimes she was even useful – particularly with the dramatic performances the boys were endlessly putting on; Guy, of course, as director and usually playing the star part too – though Richard, surprisingly, was the better actor – and Victoria, doubling up as scene-shifter and general dogsbody was, occasionally, allowed to play minor parts as well.

'Well, never mind, darling,' said Evanthi now. 'Boys are silly about fighting and, anyway, I've come to call you all in. It's time for tea and the *papas* is calling today. He would like to see you all.'

The boys pulled gloomy faces when they heard this bit of news. They thought the black-clad village priest a dreary old bore and couldn't understand what Evanthi saw in him. 'He stinks too,' muttered Guy, wrinkling his nose disdainfully, but he took care that his grandmother did not hear this particular comment.

After they had all climbed up the steep hill, a good twenty minutes' walk for even the fastest walker, they had tea in the dark dining room that had changed little since Evanthi's own childhood. The shutters were half closed against the throbbing heat of the sun and the room seemed muffled in quietness; outside, crickets sang continuously, filling the air with their monotonous, high-pitched drone. Nafsica brought in the heavy, ornate silver tray with its matching teapot, jug and sugar basin, and placed it carefully on the white embroidered tablecloth. There were plates of small sweet biscuits and little cakes, and a tiny cup of thick sweet coffee for the old priest, who had not been converted to the cosmopolitan Doukas family's habit of drinking tea. The children sat up straight and polite, for their grandmother was a stickler for manners and would never tolerate what she considered the sloppy deportment of typical English children of the seventies.

At nearly thirteen the two boys were uneasily perched on the narrow shelf that lies between childhood and adolescence. Next year, Evanthi thought, they may no longer be content to spend three weeks of the summer holidays with so little social life and be completely happy in such unsophisticated surroundings. Two middle-aged women and one small girl will not be sufficient company to keep them amused. She was sure that Guy in particular – restless, talented, mercurial Guy – would soon need new experiences and more challenging surroundings to cut his teeth on; she was less sure about Richard, who was something of an enigma to Evanthi – though she tolerated his presence because it was much easier to keep two boys occupied than one on his own.

'So,' said Father Theodoros, his accent as thick as his coffee, 'and what are you boys going to do when you grow up?'

4

Guy, never one to be over-burdened by modesty, said at once that he was going to be a successful writer. 'I shall travel to distant places and then write about them – and I shall be amazingly famous.'

Richard, more cautious, said he thought he might be a farmer, or something in the city – or perhaps both, like his father.

'Boring,' said Guy scornfully.

'And Victoria?' asked Father Theodoros

'I shall marry Guy and have eight children, all boys.'

'You can't do that. I'm your cousin – almost your brother. We'd have batty children and, anyway, I shan't ask you to marry me.'

'Then I'll marry Richard instead,' said Victoria. 'He's much kinder than you – and we can still all do everything together so it won't make any difference. So there.'

Everyone laughed. 'Oh, Victoria,' said Evanthi, 'you *have* got it all carefully planned! But childhood friends are not always the right people to marry. You must have a great, great romance. You must wait till you meet someone who strikes you like a bolt of lightning!'

'Were you struck by lightning, Nonna?' asked Victoria, round-eyed.

'Believe it or not, my darling, yes, once, a very long time ago, I was.'

Guy looked at his grandmother in disbelief. He remembered his aloof Doukas grandfather as a chilling presence – as unresponsive as the great stuffed eagle in the library downstairs, which gazed out from expressionless glass eyes and had terrified him as a small boy. He certainly could not imagine his daunting grandparent in the role of romantic hero.

But Evanthi Doukas had no intention of enlarging on the situation and turned away from the children to talk to the old priest in Greek.

Chapter One

❧

The church bell could be heard from miles away. Victoria felt it reverberate through her whole being and knew it would become part of her memories for the rest of her life so that she would never again be able to hear the tolling of a bell without recalling this particular moment.

The sound floated over Holt Wood and up to the top of Lark Hill. It penetrated through the windows of the houses at the north end of the village, and could be heard at Manor Farm, where the Cunninghams lived, which stood surrounded by fields to the south. In the village street the insistent clanging stopped people in their tracks – spreading news and conveying a message, as it had done in times of joy and sorrow for centuries.

Mrs Banham, proprietor of the Baybury general store, pulled on her fur-fabric hat and prepared to shut up shop for the afternoon – out of genuine affection and respect for the Cunningham family, certainly, but also because she considered it her duty to give her customers a first-hand account of proceedings. She knew that local gossip was one of the few advantages the small shop still had over the supermarket, and, in any case, gathering information was as important and natural to her as collecting pollen is to a bee. No detail would be missed.

Half an hour before the service was due to start, the church was already crammed with people. Only the pews at the front, which had been reserved for family, were still empty and it was clear that new arrivals would not only have to stand but might not even be able to come inside. Those who had arrived early enough to get a seat were squashed up in their thick winter coats, arms clamped to their sides in an effort to take up as little room as possible. The vicar had never seen such a congregation at St Luke's and couldn't help thinking how good it would be to

7

have this sort of turn-out for an ordinary Sunday service. The narrow lane leading to the church was congested with cars, the verges on either side churned up by spinning tyres and the grass a sea of mud. A nearby field, which was being used as an extra car park, looked more like a bog, and though bales of straw had been humped in and spread to help prevent vehicles from becoming stuck, it was clear that getting the cars out again was going to be a nightmare. People wearing boots were the envy of anyone foolhardy enough to have turned up in fashionable shoes, and the London contingent stuck out from the locals as they picked their way gingerly through the sludge. Mrs Banham regarded her own stout legs, snugly encased in Derri Boots, with approval, while Peter Mason, chairman of the City solicitors Mason, Whitaker & Ziegler looked down with dismay at his expensive tasselled black loafers, which were already caked in mud. Luckily the rain had stopped, but the cold February air was raw and uninviting. Only the snowdrops for which the church was famous added any note of brightness.

It wasn't that long since the Christmas decorations had been taken down; the tired-looking holly removed from windowsills, and trails of wilting ivy unwound from the old stone pillars to join the tree – denuded of its glitter and shedding needles everywhere – on its way to the bonfire behind the church. Richard and Victoria Cunningham, together with six-year-old Jake, had been part of the team who had volunteered to banish the last signs of the festive season, pack away baubles, dismantle the crib and clean the church. Afterwards everyone had trouped back to Manor Farm to down the hot and alarmingly alcoholic brew that Richard and Victoria had concocted earlier, and to demolish the last mince pies of the season.

Richard had recently been short-listed as a prospective Conservative candidate for the local constituency and many congratulations were coming his way; though Victoria, the least politically minded of women, was privately not keen on this venture she put on a show of enthusiasm for his sake. The kitchen had been full of warmth and laughter. Jake, fortified by illicit swigs of spicy wine, got thoroughly over-excited and silly.

Victoria's cousin Guy Winston had been staying – fascinating, enigmatic Guy, a magnet to all ages and both sexes who could be guaranteed to enliven any gathering – if he chose to turn on his charm. Victoria, who had been partly brought up by Guy's parents and liked to explain that Guy was more like a brother than a cousin, often teased him about the crowd of glamorous people by whom he was usually surrounded: she called them Guy's Glitzy Groupies, though when he came to stay at Manor Farm he nearly always came on his own.

'You think we're too boring for your smart friends,' Victoria would mock, but she delighted in the fact that she and Richard and Guy made as happy a trio together now as they had in their childhood.

That evening Guy's special magic had sparkled as beguilingly as the fairy lights had done at the midnight service on Christmas Eve – lights that had just been carefully checked, coiled up and packed away in a cardboard box till next year. Back at the house, Richard made sure that glasses were kept topped up and no one felt left out, so that an evening that had started out as a chore ended up as a rattling good party.

By the time everyone finally departed, the task force, mostly members of the PCC, appeared overflowing with peace and goodwill towards each other – which was by no means always the case.

As she and Richard waved their guests goodbye Victoria felt enclosed in a bubble of security. She linked arms with her husband and cousin. 'Well done, us!' she said. 'Guy – what on *earth* did you say to get Mrs Banham simpering like that? Don't tell me it was only the mulled wine that made her so flushed!'

Guy laughed. 'I'm not a journalist for nothing. It always pays to keep in with the purveyor of local news and our Mrs Banham is certainly that! But thank God they've all gone at last. Remind me not to come and stay next year until that little ritual's out of the way – though I suppose trekking up and down the belfry stairs is good training for climbing mountains. I'd be bored out of my mind if I had to do that sort of thing too often. Don't you ever get fed up with your uneventful life, little cousin?'

'Don't be so condescending,' said Victoria. 'Our village life is a hotbed of intrigue and drama – and now I'm just about to sit down to supper with my three favourite men. What could be more exciting than that?' And as she looked at her cousin, her husband and her small son she had thought to herself: I must remember this moment. It isn't the big occasions that are the necessarily the happiest, but the unclouded, ordinary ones like this – the ones that are only too easy to forget. I shall take this evening out and look at it again sometime when I need cheering up.

Richard and Guy were leaving for an expedition to Nepal. They often went on sporting or exploring trips together, as they had done all their lives; sometimes Victoria went with them. This time she had decided to stay at home with Jake and keep an eye on the farm in Richard's absence. Besides, Victoria worked part time for the local branch of Chalmer & Fenton, the fine art dealers, and there was a sale coming up that she knew her boss wanted her to attend.

That had been nearly a month ago, and now the church had been decorated again and this time it spilled over with fresh flowers and foliage. In that month Victoria's whole life had been turned upside down and could never be the same again – and she remembered painfully her childhood vow to marry Richard.

The scent of flowers would have been overpowering in a smaller building, but here it blended comfortingly with the whiffs of dusty hassocks, candle-wax and treated woodwork that hang about old churches. A band of the Cunninghams' friends had arrived the day before, armed with clippers, Oasis, extra vases – and an overwhelming desire to help. From their gardens they brought armfuls of greenery, baskets of snow-drops and moss, but because February is such an impossible month for home-grown flowers, they had also purchased great bunches of early daffodils, branches of forced blossom and sheaths of more exotic flowers – lilies, carnations and freesias – from the florist in nearby Toddingham. Victoria insisted on doing some of the arrangements herself, though she looked so exhausted that everyone begged her not to. Most of the time she felt as though she had been switched on to automatic pilot and went through every physical action in a detached state as though her real self was completely absent from her body and she could watch it being driven by remote control from some faraway place. Is there something wrong with me? she wondered. Shouldn't I be reacting differently? After her first wild scream when Jeff, the Cunninghams' farm manager, had come hurtling into the house to fetch her, she had been unable to cry at all. A terrible sound that scream had been, Jeff told his wife, Violet, later – like an animal caught in a trap.

When Richard's father came down to the church to meet the vicar, he looked round in a bewildered way:

'You don't think all this looks a bit over the top?' he asked. 'We've never been much of a family for display. I wonder if people might feel it's all a bit ... unsuitable? More like a wedding than a funeral?' Unsuitable was a favourite word of Bill's.

'How can anything be *suitable*? It shouldn't be happening at all,' said Victoria. 'Richard loved this church so I want to make everything look as wonderful as possible, and I don't much mind what anyone thinks – except you, of course, Bill,' she added, seeing her father-in-law's face. 'I do mind if it's not right for you. If you don't approve we'll scrap it.' But Richard's father had shaken his head. He thought Victoria looked threadbare, so thin and tightly stretched she might rip apart at any moment – and heaven knew what might spill out then.

'No, no,' he said at last, after a painful pause, 'I suppose you're right. There's no suitable way. Do what you want.' And they stood bleakly together in silence, achingly aware of the black hole that had opened up in their lives with such appalling suddenness, but unable to comfort each other. Existing from one moment to the next was as much as they could manage – even breathing seemed an effort.

Victoria thrust her hands deep in the pockets of her fleece and hugged it tightly round her, clenching her teeth in an effort to stop them chattering. Though the church, despite the heating having been turned on, was a little chilly, it wasn't really cold – but temperature didn't seem to make any difference to her at the moment. She had been shivering for a week.

Bill Cunningham, normally a well-preserved seventy, looked as if he had aged ten years.

*

The tolling of the bell came to an end at last as Victoria and Jake, together with her father-in-law and Richard's two older sisters filed into the front pew.

Jake, who had clutched Victoria's hand for most of the previous night as he fought for breath with one of his asthma attacks – the worst for a long time – refused to hold her hand now as they entered the church, and walked beside her, hollow-eyed but fiercely independent. His grandfather had tried to stop Victoria from letting him attend the service, thinking the child too young to be put through such an ordeal and also dreading lest there should be a display of emotion, but on this she had been adamant.

'I wasn't allowed to go to my own parents' funeral – I want him to remember today and know he's been a part of it,' she said and Bill hadn't argued for fear her unnatural calm might suddenly snap.

Victoria had had a terrible night with Jake: despite his puffer he had coughed so badly she thought it a wonder he hadn't broken a rib.

'Daddy never said goodbye,' he'd whispered in between paroxysms.

'I know, darling,' she answered rocking him in her arms. 'He didn't say goodbye to me either. But how could he? We'll say our own special goodbyes to him at the service tomorrow – if you're sure you want to come, that is. You absolutely don't have to, you know.'

'I do want to come,' said Jake, 'but it won't be any good because he won't be able to hear me.'

'Yes he will,' said Victoria firmly, wishing she felt as certain as she sounded.

'How will he hear?'

'I don't know, darling. Not in the way we're used to, anyway. We must try thinking things to him in our heads – more like praying. It'll probably take us a bit of practice – like twiddling to get the right programme on the car radio when the automatic setting's got wiped out, or getting stuck with the computer. You know how hopeless I am at that.' What an absurd thing to say to him, she thought wearily, but Jake, who at six was already gently scornful of Victoria's antipathy towards instruction manuals, seemed to accept this explanation as all too likely.

Just as he was at last drifting off to sleep he'd said: 'It's horrid when people don't answer.' And Victoria had thought bleakly of the many questions she would have liked to ask Richard herself – questions that were piling up alarmingly. When Jake eventually fell asleep she was afraid to withdraw her hand in case she woke him again, and had lain beside him, her left arm gradually growing numb, waiting for the morning. Painful memories of her own early childhood loss resurfaced to haunt her, and the knowledge that a similar darkness might now fall across Jake's hitherto sunny security seemed unbearable. Despite the turmoil of her thoughts, in some ways she was relieved to stay awake – at least it saved her from the agony of having to remember afresh the events of the last week after the treacherous oblivion of sleep had temporarily blotted them out.

Victoria glanced across the aisle at Guy, who was one of the ushers, as he slipped into the pew beside his parents, Anthony and Spiridoula Winston. She saw that Toula looked dramatic as always, in black from head to foot, with a chimney-pot of a hat, which reminded Victoria of the old village priest in her grandmother's native Greece – it was extraordinary what details one noticed even under the greatest stress. Guy gave Victoria a long look and made the secret sign that had been their private signal of communication since they were small children, and she knew he was sending her a message of love and support – but she was startled to see that Francine was also sitting with the Winstons. How stupid I am, she thought, of course Francine is there. She will be a fixture now and I must get used to it. Guy had given no indication that he was expecting her to come – but then Victoria had not thought to ask him.

Of all the Glitzy Groupies Francine Magee, an ex-model turned freelance fashion journalist, had always seemed the most gilded of the lot – all tossing tawny hair, clanking gold jewellery and sun-bed-kissed skin. In the company of Richard's two sisters, Meriel and June, she looked as unexpected as a tiger lily that has accidentally been planted in a clump of daisies. Guy, the expert gardener, had once described Meriel and June as 'useful ground cover', something Francine most decidedly was not.

Victoria, who had never particularly liked her, hadn't realised how deep Richard's antipathy to her had been until he returned from Nepal with the astonishing news that she and Guy had decided to get married – would indeed already be married, even as he spoke, since Guy had flown straight to New York from Nepal to attend his own wedding. Was it really only ten days ago? Though Richard had arrived home nursing this riveting piece of information, Guy having apparently told him at the start of their trip, it had been an unbelievable twenty-four hours before Richard had mentioned it to Victoria – and that was on the day the announcement was in the papers anyway.

Despite his tanned face Richard had looked unwell on arrival home – withdrawn and uncommunicative, and so unlike his usual equable self that Victoria thought he must have picked up a bug on his travels and be sickening for something. He'd brushed her concern aside and insisted he was all right: just a bit exhausted: 'Don't *fuss*,' he'd said with unwonted irritability. When he'd finally told her about Guy and Francine, there had been little chance to discuss the news because he dropped the bombshell as he was leaving the house after breakfast. She had stared at him in disbelief.

'Guy *married* – he can't be. Don't be ridiculous. He would have told me.'

'See for yourself if you don't believe me,' he'd said, shoving the paper across the table at her. 'It's in *The Times* today which is why I couldn't put off telling you any longer,' and he'd left abruptly to attend a meeting with his father about the farm, a venture in which they were partners, slamming the front door so that the whole house shook. Even in the face of this extraordinary news she'd been astonished by his vehemence – Richard, who was so even-tempered! And why had he not told her the moment he got home?

She grabbed the paper to find the 'Births, Marriages & Deaths' announcements – and there it was: 'Mr G. S. Winston and Mrs F. M. Magee'. Victoria was not aware that Francine had been married before and realised how very little she actually knew about her. It had never seemed important before. 'The marriage has taken place quietly in New York between Guy

Stavros Winston of London, and Francine Mary Magee of Philadelphia,' she read.

She felt bitterly hurt that he had not told her himself, but much worse was her reaction to the news itself. She realised with shock and shame that what so devastated her wasn't the fact that Guy was marrying someone whom she didn't much like but that he should be marrying anyone at all. I shall lose him, she thought – and it seemed unbearable.

She had immediately tried to ring him but there was no reply from either his London house or his mobile. She left what she hoped sounded a deceptively light-hearted message on his answering machine to say she would try to ring him again later and what did he think he was up to, taking such an important decision without consulting her first? Then she had telephoned his mother.

'Toula? What on earth's all this about Guy and Francine? Is it true? Are they actually *married*? Richard's only just told me – but apparently he's known about it all the time they were trekking. He seems very upset, so he can't think it's good news. What's going on? Guy never breathed a word to me before they went off – and he was staying with us, for God's sake. I take it *you* knew, at least?'

Toula sounded agitated. 'Oh, Victoria! Darling, I've been expecting you to ring ever since Richard got back. I've been absolutely dying to talk to you. Isn't Guy a monster? He tossed the news at us in the most casual way imaginable just before he went off – almost over his shoulder as he left the house – but then swore us to secrecy. Said he wanted to tell you and Richard himself. We were stunned. I'm trying to get used to the idea but I'm not at all sure about Francine, though Anthony thinks she'll be all right. Of course she's been around at the edges of Guy's life for a long time but we don't feel we really *know* her. What do you think?'

'I don't know what to think. Why the rush and why the secrecy? I thought Francine was supposed to be having a raging affair with that extraordinary artist who exhibits the contents of people's dustbins in trendy galleries. I've never thought either of them had the slightest interest in getting married, let alone to each other. D'you suppose she's pregnant?'

'Surely Guy would have told me that. I know he's always adored children but I can't see him falling for that as a pressure to get married. To be fair, I can't see her playing that card either. They're both far too sophisticated. Of course, I've always hoped he'd marry one day – but Francine's not what I had in mind as a daughter-in-law.'

Victoria privately didn't think the powerful Spiridoula had a daughter-in-law in mind at all, except perhaps in the distant future as a sort of baby machine with herself in charge of the nursery.

'Well, I shall put Richard through a real inquisition as soon as he gets back. He must know more than he's letting on but he's been in the most peculiar mood since his return – not like himself at all. I'm quite worried about him actually. I shall have a lot to say to that cousin of mine when I get hold of him.'

Toula suggested that Victoria should come over as soon as possible so that they could not only pool information but pin out Francine's reputation on the specimen board of their shared opinions and dissect it thoroughly, and it was agreed that Victoria should go over for lunch in a few days' time.

But before that day arrived a far more shattering event had taken place. When Victoria had finally managed to speak to Guy – who had just got back from New York – it had not been to quiz him about his marriage but to break the dreadful news of Richard's accident.

Guy had driven down from London immediately. He had looked terrible. He and Victoria had hardly spoken about Francine. When she raised the question of his marriage Guy brushed the subject aside, saying they could talk about that another time, and she'd been too preoccupied with her own horrendous news to pursue it. Perhaps his reticence was rather odd but then she was used to the fact that Guy seldom pinned his feelings to his sleeves.

He had been endlessly helpful over the awful formalities a sudden death entails, coping with whatever he could to spare her, and accompanying her to give moral support when she had to be directly embroiled. But they had clashed over choices for the funeral service, and they were without Richard's emollient presence to smooth things down between them – to try to extract the sting out of Guy's occasionally poisonous verbal arrows and soothe her own ruffled feelings. It seemed a terrible irony that Richard should be needed to mediate between them over his own funeral service – but he had understood so well the complicated relationship between his wife and his life-long friend, compounded as it was of adoration, resentment and old nursery rivalries. It had been part of the childhood of all three of them.

Normally she would have expected to approve of Guy's musical or literary suggestions since they shared more tastes than she did with her husband, but therein lay part of the trouble.

'No, no,' she'd objected at one point, feeling totally exhausted by all the decisions that were required of her, but all the same resenting Guy's assumption that he should automatically take charge of the proceedings, 'that might be what *you* would like but it wouldn't be Richard's thing at all. He's never read Dylan Thomas or Philip Larkin, and he was bored to sobs by Wagner – and, anyhow, Bill would feel uncomfortable with most of your suggestions.'

'What makes you think you knew Richard's tastes so well?' Guy had asked. 'The Richard you lived with was largely a product of your imagination.'

She had been winded with shock and outrage.

He had been instantly penitent and apologised profusely – pleading his own grief and shock as an excuse – but even though she accepted his apology, and they had eventually agreed on compromises to produce readings and music that they hoped would be acceptable to the Cunningham family, the incident had left a bitter taste in her mouth. She was used to being tormented by Guy when one of his dark moods overcame him, but that he could deliberately cut into her at this particular time was a wound too far. What made it worse was the fact that she discovered a certain uncomfortable truth in his accusation; Guy had always had a deadly accurate hammer for hitting nails dead centre.

What had her husband really been like? She was finding it disturbingly difficult to bring him back into focus. Richard had been a comforting presence in her life since childhood – but try now to define his individuality, paint a portrait of his passions and preoccupations and he seemed to elude her.

As the congregation finished singing 'Immortal, invisible, God only wise' Guy went to the lectern to read the passage on friendship from *The Prophet*: '"Your friend is your needs answered",' he read, his face expressionless, his voice taut, clipping the words as decisively as though he were snipping off dead-heads in the garden. '"He is your field which you sow with love and reap with thanksgiving."' Well, thought Victoria, clutching at a little comfort, that is true anyway. That's what Richard was . . . my needs answered. What a lovely thing to be. But then Guy's voice continued: '"When you part with your friend, you grieve not; For that which you love most in him may be clearer in his absence, as the mountain to the climber is clearer from the plain,"' and she suddenly wanted to scream, *No! No!* It's not like that at all. He has gone and I can't see him. Oh, Richard, where are you? Why did you go?

Her mind flipped back again to the day Richard had told her of Guy's engagement. Was it really only just over a week ago? She felt that she had gone through so many experiences and emotions during those few days that it seemed more like a lifetime.

A few days after he'd got back from Nepal, Richard, who still seemed strangely withdrawn, had come home early on a windy February afternoon and announced his intention of going out again to shoot pigeons.

'Have a mug of tea first before I collect Jake?' she had suggested, but he'd said no, the light would be gone if he delayed and he wanted to catch the birds as they flighted in to roost.

'Jeff says they've been murdering the winter rape in the big field.'

She had opened her mouth to protest that it couldn't be urgent at this time of year but something in his expression stopped her. She had a ridiculous feeling that he was trying to avoid her. He'd whistled for Teal, his old spaniel, and a few minutes later she had heard the Land Rover rattling over the cattle grid and down the back drive.

It was pure chance that Jeff Burrows had found Richard before he'd even been missed.

Jeff had gone to check on a fence that was supposed to have been mended, and was surprised to encounter Teal running loose, whining and obviously in a frantic state – placid, professional Teal, who was so rock-steady he could be guaranteed to sit at Richard's side marking where birds fell without attempting to run in. Jeff had followed the old dog – and found Richard lying in a pool of blood with half his head blown off, and immediately rung the emergency service on his mobile for an ambulance, though his fingers shook so much he could hardly punch in 999. Incredibly Richard still had a faint pulse at that stage but he died without ever regaining consciousness soon after the ambulance got to the hospital. It was already dark and Victoria had just been beginning to wonder why on earth Richard was so late, when Jeff had burst in with the news. Jeff's wife, Violet, had been summoned to stay with Jake, and Jeff had then driven her at breakneck speed straight to the hospital, telephoning to Richard's father as they went.

But like Victoria, Bill Cunningham arrived too late to be with Richard before he was pronounced dead.

The coroner's verdict had been Accidental Death. The cause was a twenty-bore cartridge, stuck halfway down one of the barrels of Richard's twelve-bore shotgun, which must have exploded when he reloaded and fired another shot from the same barrel. After arriving in the wood it was thought he'd roamed about for a while because four or five dead pigeons were found lying in various places, proving that the accident could not have happened immediately. The rogue cartridge must have got into his pocket by mistake, though everyone on the farm knew how particular he was that the two different kinds should be kept well apart – the hazards of mixing up twelve- and twenty-bore cartridges being well known to anyone with a knowledge of firearms. In fact, he very rarely used the smaller gun, only occasionally finding it useful for shooting vermin – rabbits or squirrels in the garden, or rats in the yard – and was keeping it for when Jake was old enough to learn to shoot. When questioned, no one could actually remember when he'd last used it, but both Victoria and her father-in-law had expressed astonishment that Richard – meticulous Richard – could have made such an elementary mistake and been so lethally careless. It was quite out of character. At the inquest Victoria could only reiterate her suspicion that Richard had been sickening for something and felt unwell. It was the only explanation she could suggest.

After the congregation had sung 'Praise, my soul, the King of Heaven', Peter Mason, who was Richard's godfather as well as being the family solicitor, gave an appreciation. He stressed how tragic the loss was and looked round as though daring anyone to disagree; he told the congregation that he had first seen Richard when he was a week old and that in all the thirty years of their acquaintance since he had never had cause to feel anything but proud of his godson. He told a few unremarkable stories about Richard's schooldays, mentioned his fondness for sport and said what a useful cricketer he was – a good all-rounder; dependable. And as in sport so in life, he said impressively: Richard had been a valuable – and indeed he knew he could safely say a valued – member of the community: a respected man of business; an excellent farmer, and if things had turned out otherwise – who knew? – possibly a future Member of Parliament too: the loss was the community's. He had been a good husband and father. If there was one word that summed Richard up – Peter Mason paused to give his audience time for anticipation and then brought the word out as triumphantly as a rabbit out of a hat – it was *sound*. Richard Cunningham had been thoroughly sound.

Victoria felt a terrible hysteria rising in her throat and for one awful moment thought she might scream. Then she was afraid she might faint. She clutched Jake's hand, not so much to give as to get support and, by focusing her mind on her son, managed to hold herself together as Peter Mason stepped down from the pulpit. It had been a polished performance: bland and complimentary but somehow unsatisfactory. Under different circumstances she would have enjoyed catching Guy's eye since they both thought Richard's godfather was a pompous old windbag, of whom Guy did brilliant impersonations, catching perfectly not only his fruity and portentous tone of voice but the cliché-encrusted contents of his speech; he and Victoria sometimes talked to each other in what they called 'Masonese', vying to produce outrageous examples of how Peter Mason might have described some person or event, never using one word if six could be crammed in. Anyone hoping for special insights into Richard would be none the wiser, and she felt passionately that it should have been Guy giving the address.

It was out of character for Guy to refuse a challenge, but he had been adamant. 'Please don't keep asking me, Vicky,' he had said with great intensity. 'I'm really sorry – but I just couldn't do it,' and he'd looked so tormented that she had said no more. When Bill Cunningham – who had ambivalent feelings about Guy anyway – suggested Peter Mason instead Victoria felt she had no choice but to agree.

The vicar paid his own brief tribute, which was somehow much more moving than Peter's rolling cadences had been. He was new in the parish, he informed the congregation, and said he was sad that he had not had time to get to know Richard better but had much appreciated his unobtrusive kindness and his straightforward help as vicar's warden. He talked about the difficult questions that a tragedy like this brought forward and the impossibility of trying to explain them away. All we can do for Richard now, he said simply, is to remember him with love, to pray for his soul – and give our practical and ongoing help and support to Victoria and Jake. Before giving the final blessing he had used a shortened version of the bidding prayer from Newman's *The Dream of Gerontius*:

Go forth upon thy journey, Christian soul.
Go in the name of God the omnipotent Father
Who created thee;
Go in the name of Jesus Christ, our Lord,
Son of the living God,
Who died for thee;
Go in the name of the Holy Spirit
Who hath been poured out on thee;
Go in the name of Angels and Archangels,
In the name of all the saints of God;
Go on thy course,
And may thy place today be found in peace;
Through Jesus Christ our Lord.

Those are powerful words, and words are mysteriously powerful things, thought Victoria as she walked down the aisle with her son and her father-in-law to follow Richard's coffin out to the churchyard. If I can let Richard go on the tide of those words perhaps he will be all right – wherever he is – but how will we learn to live without him?

Chapter Two

After the funeral service, tea was provided at the house for anyone who wanted to come. The dining-room table was laden with plates of sandwiches, home-made cakes and biscuits and thin-sliced bread and butter. Mrs Banham and a team of helpers from the village had slipped away before the rest of the congregation and were busily boiling kettles, filling teapots and whisking cling-film off plates. Though there was much goodwill towards the Cunningham family in the neighbourhood and genuine distress for Victoria in particular, the occasion also provided fertile ground for seeds of umbrage not only to be planted but to take root and put on rampant growth since Mrs Banham's tendency to take control of any function she attended was not always appreciated by all members of the community.

'I think I'd better just give this teapot a quick rub,' she said to Violet, whose particular pride and pleasure it was to keep Richard and Victoria's silver in gleaming condition at all times. 'We wouldn't want any of those Londoners thinking it's kept in the safe most of the year.'

Victoria, who had done nothing towards the preparation of this feast and was luckily unaware of the sweet-and-sour exchanges of the Baybury ladies, thought she had never seen so much food in her life. She felt as though she was entertaining for some completely different occasion – a major charity function perhaps – and even now, more than a week after the terrible events that were so indelibly stamped on her mind, she still half expected to discover it had all been a grotesque mistake and that any minute Richard might suddenly walk in and start offering everyone drinks.

Toula and Anthony Winston had whisked her and Jake straight home after the interment, leaving Bill Cunningham and Richard's sisters to stand at the door of the church and shake hands with everyone. Victoria felt she should have done this too but the rest of the family had insisted it was too much for her, that no one would expect it, and she simply had not had the energy either to argue or try to explain that what she did or didn't do really seemed to make very little difference at the moment because of the extraordinary bubble of unreality by which she felt surrounded.

'You go and take your things off,' said Toula, 'and come down when you feel ready – or not at all if you can't face it. We'll hold the fort here.'

It was a relief to get out of the raw February air. Standing by the grave had chilled her to the marrow physically and mentally so that she felt as if splinters of ice had pierced her heart, as sharp as the splinters from the devil's shattered mirror in Hans Andersen's 'Snow Queen'. She wondered if her heart would ever completely thaw. Anthony gave her a great hug that was better than any words.

'Let me take your coat,' he said. 'You're absolutely frozen! Would you like a nip of something potent before the onslaught? Brandy might do you good.' He was deeply fond of his wife's niece and regarded her as the daughter he and Spiridoula had never had.

Victoria let herself relax against his reassuring bulk for a moment. 'No, thanks. Actually I think brandy might finish me off completely. I'd better try to stay upright till everyone's gone.'

'Chin up then.' He held her away from him looking down into her drawn face and searching it anxiously for clues as to the best way to help her. 'You will survive this, Victoria,' he said. 'You may not think so at the moment, but you will. Partly because there is no choice but also because you are that sort of person anyway – a survivor.'

'How do you know? I don't feel like one. Oh, Uncle Anthony, I don't really know what or who I am . . . I just feel so strange . . . as if I might drown in my own thoughts.' She put her hands over her face as though to protect herself from an unbearable sight.

'Trust me. You don't realise it yet, but I know it – you have enormous inner strength. I always thought so when you were a little girl and first came to live with us after your parents were killed. You had terrible things to come to terms with then and you survived triumphantly, and now you have your son to think of. You will keep going for him.'

'Thank you,' she whispered. 'You've always been such a comforting person Uncle Anthony. And you're right – I'd better go and see to him now, then I'll come and join you both.'

He nodded and went back to the dining room to help Spiridoula chat up the helpers and wait for the guests while Victoria went in search of Jake, who had disappeared. She found him communing with Teal, who had been shut up in the boot room while they went to church. The small boy and the ancient dog were curled up together in Teal's tatty old basket.

'What would you like to do, darling? Do you want to face everyone or would you like to hide away?' she asked, wishing she could do just that herself. Dealing with Jake seemed the one stabilising thing in an upside-down world.

'Could I watch a video?'

'Of course. Shall I come and put one in for you? An old favourite, perhaps?'

'I can do that myself,' said competent Jake, and then added: 'But could you come and watch it with me?'

'Oh, darling . . . I'm sorry. I don't see how I can with all these people coming back for tea.'

'When will they be gone?'

'I don't know. But I can't think anyone will stay very long. Shall I see if Violet would come and keep you company?'

Violet Burrows had helped Victoria in the house since before Jake was born and was much beloved, but Jake shook his head. 'I only want you,' he said.

Victoria looked at her son and felt helpless to do the right thing. Jake was not a clingy child, which made this appeal doubly hard to withstand.

'Listen,' she said gently, 'I have to look after all these people who've come today – some of them from quite far away – because they all loved Daddy too. I think it's what Daddy would have wanted me to do and we must do our best not to let him down now. You go and tuck yourself away in the playroom with Teal – you might let him out first, that would really be a help – and then I'll get Violet to bring you some tea and promise I'll come just as soon as I possibly can. All right?'

'All right.'

As she watched his proud little figure walk off towards the playroom she felt her throat constrict. I mustn't let myself play the card of 'doing what Richard would want' too often, she thought: it would be so horribly easy to let it become a habit and use it as a sort of blackmail.

She heard the sound of voices and knew that people were beginning to arrive. Don't let me cry now, she prayed desperately, because if I start I might not be able to stop and I need to be alone before that deluge begins. She stood for a moment leaning against the wall beside the door that led from the passage into the hall, trying to summon up strength to go into the dining room; trying to summon up strength just to move. A huge wave of sound met her ears as she stood outside the half-open door. This is bizarre, she thought – it's turned into a party, and she felt quite unprepared for the social chit-chat that is the reaction that often comes after the highly charged emotions of a harrowing service, a desperate sort of papering-over of threatening emotional cracks.

To her dismay Francine was the first person she saw. Victoria had hoped to avoid her but as she was hovering just inside the doorway there was no escape. Normally exuding social self-confidence, Francine looked as alarmed as if she would like to make a bolt for it and had no idea how to greet her hostess. Why did she have to be here? thought Victoria. She must have known she'd have to meet me if she came back to the house – but ingrained social training came to her rescue. 'Hello, Francine,' she said politely. 'How good of you to come.'

After hesitating a moment the other woman made no attempt to embrace Victoria, though she was normally very free with social kisses to people she hardly knew at all.

'Victoria . . . I just don't know what to say to you.'

'I know. It must be very difficult for everyone. Don't say anything.'

'You must absolutely hate me.'

Victoria was taken aback. It was not what she had expected from Francine and she thought it a very inappropriate moment to be forced into a discussion about her own personal feelings over Guy's marriage.

'Hate you? You mean because of you and Guy? Your marriage was certainly a great surprise – perhaps it shouldn't have been but it was – but why should I hate you?'

'I meant because of Richard.'

'Because of *Richard*? What on earth do you mean?' Victoria was dumbfounded.

'His reaction to our news – Guy's and mine. He'd tried so hard to stop us getting married once before and seemed so terribly upset . . . I just thought . . . I just wanted to say . . .' Francine looked acutely uncomfortable, clearly having said more than she intended, yet leaving things unsaid, which nevertheless hung in the air like menacing clouds before a storm.

What does she mean, 'he tried to stop us *before*'? wondered Victoria, and it occurred to her that Francine seemed privy to more information that she was herself. She had a sudden sensation that she was walking over a minefield and that at any moment she might be blown apart.

'Let's not talk about Richard at the moment or I might not be able to cope,' she said. Then, trying to turn the conversation, added stiffly: 'I'm afraid I haven't even congratulated you yet. Normally I'd have written, of course . . . but nothing's normal at the moment. I had no idea you and Guy had thought of getting married before.'

'Oh God!' Francine looked desperate. 'We . . . we finally decided this was the right time but we didn't want a wedding over here. We thought it would save a lot of trouble if we just presented everyone with a *fait accompli*. And, of course, Richard's . . . accident was a coincidence . . . a terrible coincidence . . . it had nothing to do with . . .' her voice trailed away. Her burnished glamour seemed temporarily to have deserted her. Instead of looking sleek and beautiful she looked almost plain – jaundiced rather than golden – and older than Victoria had always presumed her to be. The two women stood and stared at each other, surrounded by people, yet locked into a private moment.

An extraordinary conversation that she had overheard earlier in the day started to bang and clatter round and round inside Victoria's head like a mad bird desperately beating its wings against a windowpane in an effort to get out. No! she thought, oh no – this I can't face!

'Francine,' she said, 'I must talk to you – but not here, not now. Perhaps I could come up to London. If I asked some difficult questions, would you tell me the truth? There are things I need to know.'

There was a long pause, and then Francine said: 'Oh, Victoria, what a terrible mess. I wish I'd kept my big mouth shut. I guess I'd do my best to answer you – but I don't think it's a smart idea. I'm pretty sure Guy won't approve and I'd much rather not because—'

Francine broke off suddenly and Victoria saw that Guy had come up to join them. She had no idea how long he'd been there or how much, if any, of their conversation he had heard. He wore the shuttered look she knew so well: not so much a look of being closed in on himself as of deliberately barricading other people out. It was the expression she had always dreaded as a child, when Guy, her hero and mentor, the person above all others whom she most wanted to please, would suddenly become inaccessible to her. She had been too proud as a little girl to give him the satisfaction of seeing how much she minded these unaccountable withdrawals – though, of course, he knew – and she had never tried to hang round him or ingratiate her way back into his favour. Rather she had learned to withdraw too, outwardly occupying herself with independent ploys and inwardly waiting for the sun of his approval to shine again of its own accord – as it invariably did. Perhaps that was what Anthony had meant by her inner strength? She thought that only her Greek grandmother had ever truly understood her as a child, and she found herself longing passionately for her company, but Evanthi Doukas had gone down with one of her bouts of pneumonia at Christmas and had not been well enough to travel over for the funeral. As soon as I can get away I will go out to Vrahos and stay with Nonna, she promised herself; I could talk about things with her that I can't talk about to anyone else.

She thought Francine looked surprisingly agitated for

someone normally so collected, and it occurred to her that Guy's wife might be more vulnerable than she had imagined. I might have grown to like her once if I'd known her better and things were different, Victoria thought in surprise. She turned to Guy and said: 'Francine's been telling me about your wedding. I still can't believe you didn't tell me about it yourself.'

Guy gave her an unfathomable look. 'You had rather a lot of other things on your mind,' he said drily, 'and of course I would have talked to you about it eventually. But now I've come to take my wife back to London. I don't think I can do much for you at the moment. I wish I could – but I can't. Later, perhaps.' There was great misery in his eyes. Suddenly he stooped down and enfolded her in a tight embrace. 'Don't give way, Vicky,' he whispered. 'I'm so desperately sorry about everything – you can't know how sorry – and I'll be in close touch. Good night.'

For a brief moment they clung together, then Guy straightened up. 'I think we should be getting back, Francine,' he said. 'Let's say goodbye to my parents and be on our way.'

Victoria watched them go, and question marks seemed to dance before her as though they had been hung in front of her eyes on some irritating mobile, too flickering to pin down yet defying her to ignore them. I can't take any more shocks at the moment, she thought, and, anyway, I'm probably over-reacting – imagining things.

I won't think about it now, she decided – and she determined to blot the nagging uncertainties from her mind.

Chapter Three

After the departure of Guy and Francine other people started to leave too. Victoria stood near the door so that she could say hello as well as goodbye.

Meriel Hawkins, Richard's elder sister, made her way purposefully over to Anthony and Toula. 'We need to talk,' she said in what was meant to be a low tone, though unfortunately that particular register had always been missing from her voice. 'What are we going to do about Victoria?'

'In what particular way?' asked Toula. She couldn't stand Meriel but had promised Anthony that she would try to keep her aversion in check. 'Do try to be civil to the Hawkinses,' he had said as they had left their own house for the family lunch at Manor Farm before the funeral.

'I'm always civil,' she had protested, 'not perhaps friendly but certainly civil – and really, Anthony darling, I can't suddenly start to *like* Meriel because Richard's dead.'

'But you could try to disguise your feelings a bit better. This whole affair is dreadful for her too, remember.'

'I do feel sorry for her – really I do – but disguise isn't my best thing.' Toula had rolled her magnificent eyes and thrown her arms in the air. She was always gesticulating about something or other. Anthony maintained it was like living with a windmill and said it was a waste that his wife's whirling gestures could not be harnessed to the National Grid. 'I'm not letting her browbeat Victoria and turn her into one of her dreary good causes,' said Toula, 'but if it makes you feel safer, you old pacifist, I will try to avoid her as much as possible today.'

This, however, was no longer an option. Meriel had a way of pressing very close to anyone she was speaking to, thrusting her face into theirs and blocking escape routes with her considerable bulk; people were apt to back away rapidly if they saw her advancing, but today she had succeeded in penning the Winstons in a corner with all the skill of a prize-winning contestant on *One Man and his Dog*.

'We must discuss Victoria's future,' she announced 'and Jake's too. I'm very concerned about them both. I'm sure you'll agree they can't stay on here. It's far too big.'

'Don't you think it's a bit soon to think about that? Victoria needs to recover from the appalling shock she's had – and so, of course, will you,' said Anthony diplomatically. 'You can be sure we'll do all we can for her. She and Jake are bound to need time before any major decisions are taken. And you've got enough on your hands looking after your father. How much longer are you staying with him?'

'Only tonight. Junie's going to stay on for another week. Fortunately she hasn't got as many commitments as I have. That's why I thought we should talk now – I've had an idea.'

Anthony could see Toula's nostrils flaring. She looked like a Stubbs painting of a particularly dangerous horse that may lash out at any moment.

'Oh well, I'm sure you'll be coming to see your father again soon,' he said hastily. 'I know how devoted you are to him. Bring him to dinner with us next time you're down, when we've all had time to think things through more calmly and tried to assimilate the effects of this awful tragedy. In the meantime we'll make a point of doing what we can to keep an eye on him. We're very fond of Bill.'

'That's really kind of you,' said Meriel, not to be diverted, 'but perhaps I should tell you my idea so that you can be brooding on it. I shall talk to Victoria, of course, but I thought you could help me get it over to her. She's so impractical and I'm afraid she's going to find it specially hard now because Richard always looked after her.' She took a deep breath, which swelled her bosom so alarmingly that Anthony flattened himself even further against the wall.

'Well,' continued Meriel, 'I've been talking to Peter Mason about Richard's affairs. I don't think things are going to be easy for Victoria financially. That's one problem. Then, as I said, this house will be far too big for her – she and Jake would rattle about in it. Stafford and I both think she'd much better make a break. My father's going to be dreadfully lonely because he and Richard were so close, and he's not getting any younger either, so that's another difficulty. Funnily enough I was talking to Richard about it the last time we saw him and telling him it was high time Daddy had someone to live in, for all our sakes.' She paused.

'So-o-o,' said Toula pulling the word out like a thrush with a worm, 'so-o-o, Meriel, you've hit on the idea that Victoria and Jake could move in with your father?' She eased herself sideways by moving a chair, and shot Anthony a look of triumph as she managed to break away from the wall. 'Umm. I can see that could be convenient.'

Meriel looked gratified. She had not expected to have an easy time with Spiridoula Winston over any suggestions she might make. An overbearing woman at the best of times, and – worse, in Meriel's book – so flamboyant; but of course one had to remember she was *foreign* and make allowances for that Mediterranean temperament. Meriel was always aware that despite her English education her sister-in-law was a foreigner too. She had never been able to understand Richard's affection for that disconcerting Greek grandmother of Victoria's, who looked like an unfriendly old tortoise, though apparently, according to Meriel's father, she'd been a renowned beauty in her day. Hard to imagine that now. And that awful gloomy family house in Corfu that Victoria was so mad about! Not Meriel's idea of a holiday villa at all. She remembered how she'd hated it when she'd been sent to fetch Richard home from one of his many childhood visits, and how much of an outsider she'd felt – a sense of being the only onlooker when everyone else was inside a charmed magic circle. She'd tried to persuade her father that it was bad for Richard to spend so much time with Guy and Victoria and old Mrs Doukas, but it had suited him to have Richard occupied. A pity Jake had inherited Victoria's dark looks, she thought, instead of Richard's Anglo-Saxon fairness, but there it was. Her own children were all most satisfactorily fair-skinned – she'd always had to use an extremely high factor sun cream on them.

'Yes,' she said now, giving Toula a nod of surprised approval, 'yes, that's exactly what I had in mind. My father's always been *really* fond of Victoria,' she made this sound quite an achievement, 'so I'm glad you think it's a good plan.'

'And what have you planned for this house?' asked Toula.

Anyone more sensitive than Meriel Hawkins might have felt the ground beneath their feet quake a little, but she crashed on comfortably confident that she had everyone's best interests at heart.

'Well, it just so happens that we might be able to take it on ourselves. It's owned by the family trust, you know – it didn't belong to Richard. With four children and all their friends it would be just the right size for us so I thought that might suit everyone.'

'Except perhaps Victoria?' suggested Toula, silky sweet.

'But it's Victoria that made me think of it.' Meriel looked puzzled. 'As I told you . . .'

'Well now, let *me* tell *you* something.' The glitter in Toula's eyes was more than enough to act as a warning signal to anyone who knew her well, and at this point her husband deemed it strategic to create a distraction by knocking over a small table and spilling his tea. In the kerfuffle that followed, with Mrs Banham and Violet both rushing to help, cloths and dustpans to be fetched, mopping-up operations undertaken and apologies made, the awkward moment was broken – as well as several of the borrowed Parish Room teacups. Money well spent, thought Anthony, as he insisted to Mrs Banham that he must pay for replacements.

Luckily Stafford Hawkins came up at this moment to collect his wife and say that June Cunningham thought their father needed to go home.

'Goodbye, Meriel,' said Anthony. 'So sorry about my clumsiness. I do hope it hasn't marked your dress. We'll certainly think over all you've said, but it might be wiser not to mention it to Victoria just yet. Give her time.' He watched the Hawkinses leave with a sense of having averted a crisis – for the moment.

Victoria, still standing in the doorway, could hardly bear the look of despair on Bill Cunningham's face as he left. They looked at each other wordlessly as they kissed. There was nothing of comfort to be said.

When Peter Mason said goodbye to Victoria he gripped her

by the shoulders and massaged them with his thumbs. He'd always thought his godson's wife a damned attractive girl – bit thin for his own personal taste perhaps, but definitely a looker with a certain indefinable something about her, though he was never quite sure what.

'Well, young woman,' he said, 'we'll have to have a business session soon. Come up to London and I'll give you lunch. Sorry about all this – bad business – that goes without saying.' Victoria made a mental note to save this last utterance to tell Guy: Peter Mason had never let anything go without saying a great deal too much about it. She wondered if she would still be able to share private jokes with Guy without upsetting Francine. She couldn't imagine how his marriage was going to affect her relationship with her cousin, something she had always taken for granted. She noted with astonishment that it was still possible to find things funny even though her world had crashed. How strange it all is, she thought.

She extricated herself from Peter Mason's clutches, managing to give him a polite kiss and retreat out of range in one skilful movement. 'Thank you so much, Peter,' she said. 'I do need to come and see you. I must know exactly how things stand for Jake and me. Give me a few days to sort myself out and I'll give your secretary a ring and make a date. And thank you for your address this afternoon. Now don't delay because you've got a beastly drive ahead of you and apparently there's going to be a blizzard.' She hadn't the faintest idea what the weather forecast was but this prediction certainly did the trick. She could hear Peter's voice in the hall warning other departing guests of the snow hazards ahead, and caught her uncle's eye. Anthony gave her a surreptitious wink and made a thumbs-up sign.

The vicar had slipped off early, promising to be in touch and saying that his wife had left a cottage pie and an apple crumble in the kitchen for Victoria and Jake to have sometime when they were on their own. 'Catherine particularly said to tell you they're fresh so it can all be frozen if you want,' he said, and Victoria was touched by such practical and unobtrusive kindness. Farewells were said to Mrs Banham and her team of helpers and much gratitude expressed for all their hard work. Violet was appeased about Mrs Banham's attitude to her silver cleaning, and Jeff and the men from the farm thanked for managing the car parking so efficiently.

It was a relief when everyone except her aunt and uncle had finally gone.

'Usual clutching from Peter Mason?' asked Toula. 'Shocking old lurcher.'

'Lecher,' murmured Anthony. His wife's idiosyncratic use of English still gave him enormous pleasure after forty years of marriage.

'Oh, Anthony!' Toula rolled her eyes. 'I wish Peter wasn't Richard's lawyer. Poor old Bill looked dreadful I thought. How he and Julia – who used to be so pretty and such fun – came to have such deadly daughters I'll never understand.'

'Oh, come on,' said Victoria, 'June's all right. She doesn't exactly fill the air with sparks but she's awfully kind. At least she means well.'

'More than can be said of Meriel,' said Toula darkly, lighting one of her Balkan Sobranie cheroots. 'Meriel's a real pain in the nose but I can't help admiring one attribute – it takes talent to spend as much money as she does on clothes and still manage to look such a frump. I know June buys her things at that charity shop but she still doesn't look as dismal as Meriel.'

'Oh, Toula – I do love you!' said Victoria, laughing.

'What about that strong drink now?' asked Anthony. 'What would you both like?'

'What I'd really like would be a huge mug of boiling tea, but I'd better check on Jake first.'

'You do that, darling,' said Toula, kicking off her shoes and dropping her enormous pearl earrings into a Meissen vase where she would certainly forget she had put them. Anthony quietly tipped it up and put them in his pocket. Toula blew out clouds of smoke like a fire breathing dragon. 'Go and see how Jake is and we'll have tea ready for you. I'll read *Harry Potter* to him, if he likes.'

She thought Victoria looked absolutely done in.

Jake was fast asleep in front of the television, thumb in mouth, something he had almost grown out of except at times of illness or stress. Victoria turned the video off, but he still didn't stir.

She touched his cheek gently and decided to leave him. The rings under his eyes looked like bruises against his white face. Sleep would probably be the best thing for him. Poor little boy, she thought, when you wake up you'll have to remember all over again what's just happened to us. And she looked at her young son with foreboding.

Violent death sends shock waves through a family that go reverberating down the generations, she thought sadly; Jake would never be quite the same carefree child again, and she wondered what other long-term effects the last days would have on him.

Teal, in his basket whined and thumped his tail at her as though to give comfort but didn't move. She turned the thermostat on the radiator up and picked a piece of paper off the floor. Jake had obviously been making one of his lists before he nodded off: his pencil box had fallen open and there were felt pens scattered over the carpet. He had a passion for the written word and was a compulsive compiler of lists – of things he liked or didn't like, of places and people; of books he'd read, and birds or animals he'd seen; of ideas – of which he had a great many – and new expressions he'd discovered. Sometimes there would be illustrations, sometimes not; often there would just be columns of words in several different colours. Victoria wondered if he would become a journalist like Guy.

She looked at this latest example, all in big black letters.

'BANG,' she read, 'DEAD BANG BANG GUN PIJINS WOOD KARTERDJES BANG DADDY EGSPLOJUN BLUD DEAD DEAD DEAD'.

There was a drawing at the bottom of the page of two figures and a dog. Underneath was written, 'Mummy, Me, Teal.' The lack of the fourth figure in the picture hit Victoria like a blow to the face.

She walked slowly back to the drawing room. Toula was pouring out tea.

'Here you are – a real bricky's brew,' she said, 'and Anthony's laced it with whisky. For heaven's sake sit down and have a bit of a collapse now. You look like a ghost.'

Victoria took the steaming kitchen mug Toula held out to her and put it carefully down on the table at the end of the sofa, but instead of flopping down and curling up, feet tucked under her, in the way she usually liked to sit, she just went on standing there.

'Victoria? What is it? Is Jake all right?' Anthony gave her a sharp glance.

'He's crashed out – but no I don't think he's all right at all.' Her voice which had been so controlled up to now, came out first as a shaky whisper, and then rose in a crescendo of despair. 'What am I going to do?' she cried. 'Whatever am I going to do?' She thrust the piece of paper at them and then collapsing on to the sofa as though her legs would no longer hold her up, she buried her head in her hands.

Anthony and Toula read Jake's list and then looked at Victoria. They had been expecting her to crack for the last ten days – indeed, had been concerned that she had not done so before – but now that it seemed as if the moment had come at last they felt acute anxiety.

'Oh, *agapi*.' Toula was by her side in a flash, crouching beside her, holding her; rocking her. 'Let it all out. Cry. Scream. Thump the walls. Don't hold back.' Then reverting to the nursery language of Guy and Victoria's childhood: 'Toula's here, *chrysso mou*,' she murmured. 'It's all right – Jake will get over this, I promise. Children are much stronger than one thinks.'

She shot Anthony an agonised look over Victoria's dark head, remembering how the loss of Victoria's parents had affected her niece. Evanthi always maintained that Victoria's determination to marry Richard Cunningham had been a direct result of the traumas of her childhood, stemming from a longing for what she perceived to be security – some security that had turned out to be, thought Toula, though she supposed one could hardly blame poor Richard for the tragic way things had turned out. Evanthi had been very much against the match, though most people thought it wonderfully suitable. The boy next door and the two families such good friends – how delightful! The childhood sweetheart – how romantic! But Evanthi did not think it nearly romantic enough.

'Victoria is like the sleeping princess,' she said, 'and Richard is *not* the right prince to wake her up.' She complained that despite his kindness and apparent reliability she wouldn't trust him with Victoria. 'He will let her down,' she prophesied darkly. At the time Toula, who had encouraged the match in every way and was enchanted at the prospect of having Victoria living so close by – still under the sphere of her own influence – thought her mother was being terribly unfair. 'My mother suffers from Predictions,' she would say excusingly when Evanthi made one of the forecasts that sometimes turned out to be unnervingly accurate.

'It'll all be all right,' she repeated now, murmuring the words over and over like a litany. Rocking. Rocking. But even as she spoke she was desperately aware that she was no longer dispelling childish nightmares, kissing everything better and banishing bogies that would be forgotten by the morning: for Victoria and Jake it couldn't possibly be all right – or not for a very long time.

Victoria let out a great wail of despair and then she began to cry at last, great racking sobs, and all the tears that had been bottled up inside her since the day of Richard's death seemed to be wrenched out of her in an outpouring of grief, bewilderment and fear.

It was the appearance of Jake, bleary-eyed from sleep, that eventually brought the fit of weeping to an end. Victoria held out her arms and he ran into them.

'Don't look so worried, darling,' she said. 'I'm just having a good cry about Daddy and I shall be much better for it. Toula's been telling me to cry for days and she's right as usual. Come and mop me up.'

Anthony gave her an approving nod. He thought she was absolutely right not to shut the little boy out of her grief, which would have sent Jake a confusing message about how he was supposed to deal with his own muddled feelings of loss and anger.

After they had put Jake to bed, and Toula had read to him, they had supper in the kitchen, heating up some soup Violet had left and making scrambled eggs. After the accident Toula and Anthony had wanted Victoria and Jake to come back with them to Durnford House, the house where Victoria had spent so much of her childhood and which she still partly regarded as home, but she had steadfastly refused, feeling that it would only make it harder to face Richard's absence when she eventually came back to the farm again. 'I'm like a dog,' she said. 'I need to go to ground in my own basket,' and they had perfectly understood and not pressed her. Violet had been coming in to sleep in the spare room, so they knew Victoria was not alone in the house.

'You ought to go to bed. What time's Violet coming?' asked Anthony now, looking at his watch.

'Not till I ring her,' said Victoria. She did not tell her aunt and uncle that she had told Violet not to come tonight unless she telephoned. She felt a desperate need to be on her own, to face some dark corners in herself and examine some questions that she had so far succeeded in pushing to the back of her mind.

'You wouldn't like us to stay with you tonight instead of Violet?' asked Toula, giving her a sharp look.

'Bless you both, but no, thank you all the same. I think I'd rather be ready for bed before she comes, though – she's lovely, so tremendously kind, but you know how she can talk when she gets going. And there are one or two things I want to do first. It's only half-past nine. I promise I won't be late.'

She managed to push them gently towards the hall, knowing that if she wavered they would refuse to go.

It was with a sense of relief that she finally closed the front door after them and heard Anthony's car start. She stood listening until she could no longer hear it as it disappeared down the drive.

Then she turned back into the house to face her demons.

At Vrahos, Evanthi Doukas lay propped up on pillows in her great carved wooden bed, struggling for breath and listening to the rain lashing the windows.

She had always enjoyed a storm – but not from the safety of indoors – and she longed to be standing on her favourite viewpoint, high above the sea, watching the waves crash against the rocks below, while the olive trees round the house became dervishes and tore their silver hair in a frenzy of whirling dance. Even the stately cypress trees would be bowing and swaying to the music of this wind, thought Evanthi. She stared up at the coffered wooden ceiling, which had fascinated her when, as a small child, she used to be brought to visit her own grandmother in the mornings while she was having breakfast in this very same bed – as years later Victoria had visited Evanthi when she came to stay, and as Jake still loved to do now. Each of the square coffers on the ceiling was painted with a motif of flowers and fruit, and they were all different – a feast for contemplation indeed. From the central beam hung an ornate brass light fitting – originally made to hold candles and only converted for electricity in the nineteen thirties by her grandmother. She could still remember the flickering candlelight and the strange shadows they cast. Now she imagined herself walking outside, buffeted by the gale as she took the track along the cliff top. But I shall never scramble up that rough path again, she thought, to stand on my viewpoint and look across to the island and the little cove where we used to swim – and where we said such a momentous goodbye all those years ago, though we didn't know it was goodbye at the time. In her mind she saw a tall figure, poised to dive, standing on the distinctive rock that jutted out into the sea like a crouching dragon: and she was once again swimming beside him in the kingfisher water. The whole of a long-ago Indian summer was illumined in her memory with colours as brilliant as the page of a medieval book of hours: azure and turquoise and green; scarlet and silver and gold.

There were many small coves that were only accessible from the sea along that bit of coastline, but she always thought of this particular one as sacred to her and to him. They had exchanged the kiss that sealed their betrothal there – and oh! their last kiss too. They had lit a fire of driftwood and cooked kebabs of swordfish skewered on spikes of rosemary and eaten them with ripe tomatoes, Feta cheese and hunks of crusty bread; then, like the Owl and the Pussycat, whose creator had so loved Corfu many years before, they had danced by the light of the moon.

She could not have borne to be there with her husband and had taken care only to go there with her children or grandchildren. She knew they thought they had discovered it for themselves once they were old enough to go out in a boat on their own. Perhaps they had their private memories of it too.

She longed to feel the wind blowing through her hair again

and the sun soaking into her bones. Somewhere one of the old shutters must have broken free from the metal fastening that normally latched it back to the wall and was intermittently beating against the flaking pink plaster of the house. Bang, bang, it went. Pause . . . and then again bang, bang, bang. She considered ringing to ask Dora to attend to it, but it seemed too much effort to reach for the bell pull – and if I don't even have the energy to do that, thought Evanthi in surprise, how many other things are going to remain unattended to? She did not want to think about the deterioration of her beloved home and she opened her eyes again to blot out the inner visions of the past that were so much more vivid than the present; she moved her head on the starched white linen of the big square pillows so that she could look towards the window and watch the water cascading down the glass.We are both becoming decrepit, she thought, the house and I. There was nothing she could do to halt the ageing process in herself, but she was uncomfortably aware that there were things she might be able to do to preserve the house for posterity.

She had been born in this bed, and it seemed likely that one day, in the not-too-distant future, she would die in it too – unless Dr Salvanos broke his word and carted her off to the hospital in town; something she would defiantly resist so long as she had enough breath left in her worn-out lungs for argument. She had thought a lot about death lately and it seemed a terrible irony that she was still alive after her latest encounter with pneumonia, when only just over a week ago Spiridoula had telephoned to tell her the news of another death – the shocking loss of someone in the prime of life. The demise of the old can cause real sadness but there is also rightness about it – the completion of nature's inevitable circle. But the sudden death of someone young is against every fibre of our being. She agonised at the thought of the anguish that would follow Richard's untimely ending.

When Toula had rung from England to tell her of his appalling accident, all Evanthi's thoughts had been of Victoria, and she bitterly resented the fact that her failing health prevented her from getting on a plane and flying to England to be with her today, the day of his funeral – though she knew that

Toula would in many ways be relieved she could not do so. It was common knowledge in the family that Evanthi had never liked Richard Cunningham . . . but, she told herself, she had not actually *disliked* him either. That was the trouble she thought – she could not sufficiently justify her misgivings to Victoria. One of her objections to the marriage had been that she had no idea what Richard felt about any of the things she was so passionate about herself. It was impossible to inveigle him into argument – confrontation was not his thing – and to Evanthi he seemed like a walking compromise: good-looking in a conventional sort of way though not strikingly so; kind and pleasant with excellent manners; competent and apparently quite successful – but what was he really *like*? Evanthi had known him since he was a schoolboy, first as a sort of appendage to Guy and then to Victoria – and she was none the wiser. In her view, Richard had simply been *there*. And now, of course, he wasn't there any more and his violent end seemed extraordinarily out of character.

I must not die just yet, decided Evanthi; there are still things I need to do for Victoria and for myself. But what a strange disguise old age is, she thought. How many different faces inhabit this worn old husk of a body – which is all other people can see when they look at me now. They do not see the dark-eyed child picking scarlet poppies under the olive trees, paddling in the sea with her white dress tucked into her knickers and her long hair tied back with a wide blue ribbon; they do not see her riding her beloved donkey, Lambrini – companion of so many childhood expeditions – up the steep Corfiot paths, through the rock and scrub of the herb-drenched hillside, accompanied by Socrates, the old gardener; nor do they see the clever schoolgirl longing to be allowed to go to university on the mainland but frustrated by her father's old-fashioned views about educating women; and they certainly do not see the passionate young woman who fell in love with a tall young man and exchanged vows on a moonlit beach below this house and thought that nothing could ever part them.

But they are all still there, those parts of me, she thought. Locked up inside I am still that child and that young woman – but where are you, my darling, and shall we meet again in some other existence, and get it right next time? Have you gone on ahead of me? She thought not – for surely she would have sensed it? – and she sent her lost love a message in her head. Think of me today if you are still alive and send me back a communication before it is too late, said Evanthi. I need you to forgive me.

Later in the day the rain stopped, the wind dropped and the sun came out, transforming everything with its Midas touch.

When Dora brought up her tray of tea, Evanthi was asleep. Dora moved softly round the room, tidying and straightening, twitching cushions and aligning books – she could never understand how anyone needed so many books. Sometimes she opened their pages to make sure that no dust lingered inside the covers, but she never tried to read them. Not because – unlike her grandmother Nafsica – she couldn't read, but because the books were mostly in foreign languages with unfamiliar alphabets. She had just spent a depressing half-hour inspecting all the buckets that she and her husband, Yannis, had put out to catch the drips under the many places where the roof leaked, but she looked at Evanthi, and was cheered to notice that the old lady's breathing seemed easier.

Dora was just wondering whether to wake her or take the tea away when Evanthi stirred and then opened her eyes.

'Nafsica?' she asked, and then: 'Oh, no, how silly of me! Of course . . . it's you, Dora. I think I must have dropped off to sleep. What time is it?'

'It's half-past four. I've brought your tea. Shall I help you sit up a little?' She heaved Evanthi into a more upright position and deftly rearranged the pillows.

'You look better,' said Dora with relief. Although she was genuinely devoted to her autocratic employer, she could not help also feeling anxious about the future of her own family when anything happened – as in the nature of things it must do – to old Kyria Doukas. It was common gossip that when the old lady died the crumbling house and unprofitable farm would almost certainly have to be sold. The increase in tourism to the island had brought undreamed-of prosperity to some Corfiot families, but it also meant changes in a way of life that had hitherto gone on almost unaltered for centuries. Even the olive harvest – once that staple of the island economy – was under threat.

'Thank you. I think I do feel better.' Evanthi gave Dora one of her perspicacious looks. 'It seems you may be able to stay on at Vrahos a little longer after all, Dora,' she said drily but with a gleam of amusement. Then she put her hand for a moment on the younger woman's arm. 'You are very good to me. Don't worry about the future. Things may *change* – but I will try to see that they go on, and that you and Yannis and Angelo, and of course Nafsica too, are provided for. I promise you that. Now I think I feel well enough for you to do my hair for me, please.'

Dora collected one of the tortoiseshell and silver hairbrushes from Evanthi's big mahogany dressing table, which was covered by a starched white runner edged with coarse cotton lace – one of the island's specialties – and gently started to brush her long hair. Though silver now, it was as thick as it had always been.

'I think you should air Victoria's room and the little dressing room and make up the beds. I feel certain we shall be having visitors soon,' she told Dora. 'And perhaps your grandmother might like to pay me a visit this evening, if she's up to it? I should love to see her.'

It struck her that Nafsica was the only person, apart from herself, who knew of the existence of someone who had once seemed more important to her than life itself – and yet they had never talked about it. She felt a great longing to talk about it to someone, but when Nafsica came to visit her they did not speak of him.

Chapter Four

Patrick Hammond folded the newspaper in half and shoved it across the breakfast table to his wife. 'Take a look at that.'

'Where?'

'Funerals. Under Cunningham.'

Rachel looked. 'Doesn't mean anything to me,' she said. 'Should it?'

'Well perhaps not . . . .but I'll tell you who I think it is, in fact I'm pretty sure of it. I think that poor chap was the husband of Evanthi Doukas's granddaughter. You know, darling – the owner of The Venetian House at Vrahos.' Rachel looked blank, and Patrick thought ruefully that three years ago she would have known exactly what he was talking about.

'The house I want to photograph for the book,' he said patiently. 'I was hoping to see her when I go out to Corfu; suss out the house and do a preliminary interview with her. By all accounts she's an amazing old bird with quite a past, and the house is reputed to be stuffed with treasures, but I've also heard on the grapevine that she's not in good health, so I'm anxious to see her as soon as possible in case anything happens. However, if there's been a family tragedy it can't be a good moment and, even though it could delay things, I thought perhaps I'd write to her – see if she's still prepared to go through with a preliminary meeting or wants to postpone. What do you think?'

'Oh, I don't know . . . wait and see, I should think. If she wants to put you off presumably she will.' Rachel's mind was running on other things and, as so often nowadays, she was guiltily aware that she wasn't really interested.

Patrick sighed and shot her a quizzical look. 'This new book could be very important to us.'

'So what's happened to the Cunningham man then?' asked Rachel, trying to make an effort.

'It was in the paper a few days ago. An awful shooting accident – he slipped, I think. Anyway his gun went off. He was only in his thirties with a young wife and child. Very sad. I was hoping you might come out to Greece with me on my next trip. There are one or two places I'd like you to see . . . help me decide what to include and what to leave out. You've always had such a good eye. Give me some inspiration.' He smiled at her.

'Oh, Patrick! You know it's difficult with Posy at the moment. I really can't.'

'It never stopped you coming away when the other two were that age.'

'I had more help then.'

'You've got Yvonne now. And you could have her much more if you wanted to. It would do you good to get away. It would do *us* good,' said Patrick pointedly, 'to get away together for a change.'

'It'd be an awful time of year to drag Posy out there. It can be as wet and cold as it is here.'

'I wasn't suggesting we took Posy. That would rather defeat the object.'

'And what do you suggest I do with her?'

'Yvonne would jump at the chance to earn some extra cash and sleep in for a few nights. She's very reliable – and you know she's always offering – and Sophie would be here to keep them company.'

'Sophie!' Rachel snorted. 'Much use she'd be! Anyway, it's too short notice. I'm sorry but I've got too many things on at the moment – there's the Save the Children meeting coming up next week, and various other commitments too.' Patrick thought she made him sound like an importunate child.

'Last time I asked you to do something with me you said you couldn't possibly plan so far ahead.'

'Oh please don't go on at me, Patrick.' Rachel's face took on the closed-up look Patrick had begun to dread – it was like watching someone drawing down all the blinds in a house for fear of exposing anything to sunlight.

'There was a time when you liked to get away with me. When you played a vital part in all my projects. When we had *fun* together.' He came round the table and put his hands on her shoulders. He could feel her tensing up, resisting him. 'Come *on*, Rachel,' he said, rocking her gently. 'One week? Is it a crime to want my wife to myself occasionally? What's happening to us?'

She was saved from having to reply by the sound of a piercing yell. She shot out of the room and Patrick heard her voice soothing the furious wails of their younger daughter. 'It's all right, darling – Mummy's here. What a nasty bump! Poor Posy! There – kiss it better.' Then another voice joined in and there were sounds of an all-too-familiar altercation.

'God, what a storm over nothing!' Sophie Hammond, her gelled hair sticking out round her head like a Gorgon's snakes with rigor mortis, stomped into the kitchen and banged a pile of books down on the table, sending a spoon skidding on to the floor and causing her father's coffee to slop into the saucer. 'And by the way,' she went on, 'there's nothing whatever wrong with darling little Posy, in case you're worried – except that she'd nicked my best pen *again* and I happened to take it back from her. I had to prise her thieving little fingers open. But it's like the roof had fallen in the way Mum carries on!'

'I don't suppose you were exactly gentle with Posy,' said her father mildly, giving her an amused look and carefully pouring the coffee back into his cup.

Sophie grinned. 'Too right I wasn't! Then, of course, she falls over, doesn't she? On the rug, naturally – you'd never catch Posy casting herself on the stone floor – and Mum's like "What have you done to her this time, Sophie?" So now Mum's giving her a little comfort snack *right there* in the passage and ugh – yuck! – that really has to be *the* ultimate turn-off!' Sophie gave an exaggerated shudder. 'Mum's boobs are in danger of getting as saggy as an old chimp's in a wildlife documentary. Sam says he doesn't like to bring his friends home any more in case Posy's groping down her shirt for a drink. Posy's *two* now, for heaven's sake! Honestly, Dad, can't you put a stop to it? It's embarrassing.' Sophie ran her hand dramatically through her Medusa locks and slumped on to a chair.

Patrick considered his elder daughter. He felt a good deal of sympathy for her.

'If I asked you to do something for me how would you react to a little bribery?'

'Would the rates be good?'

'Could be. It depends.'

'And what would the task be?'

'To keep Yvonne company if she came to live in for a week – and promise not to murder your sister; that would definitely be part of the bargain. I want Mum to come to Greece with me. Interested?'

'We-e-ll . . .' Sophie gave her father a calculating look. 'I might be. There are a few things I want, as it happens . . . and, of course there's my gap-year fund.' Sophie was always chronically short of money and the gap-year fund seemed to have a permanent leak in it. 'But I can tell you now,' she volunteered darkly, 'that you haven't a hope, because Mum wouldn't go.'

'What do you think might persuade her?'

'Nothing,' said Sophie crushingly. 'Ab-so-lutely nothing. Posy's all she thinks about – Posy and that Bronwen woman who practically seems to live here now, not to mention her horrid child.'

Sophie got up and gave her father a kiss on the cheek. 'Poor old Dad,' she said. ''Fraid you're on to a loser there. Join the club of neglected Hammonds. But cheer up – Sam and me'll look after you in your old age, help you totter about on your Zimmer and take you for little drives in the car. Drives! That reminds me – must dash! Got a lesson ten minutes ago. Mr Thing from the motoring school would be really *fit* if he wasn't such a midget. He can hardly see over the steering wheel, poor little man, and you wouldn't believe how seriously he takes everything. I'm working on his sense of humour, but it's a struggle. Bye, then – wish me luck! He's picking me up at the end of the drive and we're going on the dual carriageway today.' And she breezed out, humming.

Patrick opened his mouth to call after her to shut the door but decided he'd be on to a loser there too, so he got up and closed it himself. He hoped profoundly that he would not be called on to give his daughter extra driving practice over the weekend. He thought her instructor deserved a medal.

After Sophie had gone he helped himself to another cup of coffee and brooded about his family. He desperately wanted to get his relationship with his wife back to the way it had been before the arrival of Miss Posy Hammond had altered everything.

Patrick and Rachel had met at university. Patrick maintained that for him it had been love at first sight when he, in his second year, was introduced to Rachel, a first-year student, at a party. Certainly there had been an instant attraction for them both, followed by a friendship born of shared interests and shared friends who did a lot of things together and had a great deal of fun. Their relationship had never wavered, so that by the time they came down from Oxford – to the horror of Patrick's family, who thought him far too young at twenty-two to tie himself up, and had reservations about Rachel anyway – they had got married. Other university friends had exchanged partners as often as if they were shuffling a pack of cards – later some had shuffled wives and husbands too – but Patrick and Rachel seemed to have hit on a formula for constancy and their marriage was the envy of many. They would have insisted that they worked at their marriage, but now, faced with a disturbing deterioration in their relationship, Patrick wondered if they'd really had the faintest idea how much effort working at a marriage could be when it was going through a bad patch. What made it worse from his point of view was that he felt the effort to be so one-sided: Rachel refused to discuss the problem – which did not mean that she was unaware of it. She would have had to be very obtuse to think all was well, and no one had ever called her that.

Early in their acquaintance he had discovered that beneath Rachel's cool elegance, so deceiving to those who did not know her well, lay hidden an insecure character who depended on him far more than most of their friends realised. He had loved her the better for it: she brought out all that was most tender and protective in Patrick. With the arrival of children only Patrick understood how difficult Rachel, the winter-flowering product of ultra-conventional parents, found the hurly-burly of family life. Coming himself from a large and uninhibited clan, whose members were a cheerfully argumentative lot who enjoyed nothing better than noisy get-togethers, Patrick thrived on the family gatherings that his wife found so threatening. When

Rachel became pregnant he looked forward with unalloyed delight to being a father.

Rachel's reaction was less enthusiastic. She had never been one of those women who feel themselves in danger of snatching unattended babies from prams. She dreaded being offered a cuddle with the newborn infants of friends. Nerve-racking little bundles wrapped in shawls activated in her the 'ugh' rather than the 'aah' factor they seemed to evoke so easily with most women. It was a source of embarrassment only to be admitted as a sort of joke. 'Rachel pretends she doesn't like babies,' friends teased, and she would be able to reply with a laughing grimace: 'Horrid little things – can't stand them till they're walking and talking,' in the reassuring certainty that she would not be believed. It had not helped that she was miserably unwell for the whole nine months before the arrival of her first-born. She found the actual labour a nightmare of undignified mess, pain, and the fear of feeling out of control of herself. When it was over Rachel regarded her squalling son with horror. Everyone told her he was perfect – a beautiful baby – but Rachel was not only terrified of Sam but secretly revolted by him too. It was Patrick who, when he first proudly held the baby, could hardly bear to put him down while Rachel lay in bed and stared out of the window, overcome with misery, fighting a sense of panic, and shrinking from physical contact with this threatening stranger.

As soon as she and Sam came home from the hospital she engaged a nanny – the first of many – to help her with the uncongenial task of child-rearing. With Sophie's arrival two years later Rachel felt she had more than done her duty – had she not been so in love with Patrick she would never have contemplated going through the miserable process a second time. Though Patrick would have relished the happy chaos of a large brood, he accepted that it might endanger the personal happiness he and his wife had together – and that must not be put at risk. They agreed there would be no more babies. Patrick was delighted with his son and daughter and told himself that he had all a man could possibly wish for: a beautiful wife, two healthy children and, increasingly, a flourishing career as an author and photographer.

Once baby days were over Rachel overcame her physical distaste for the children, and any success Sam and Sophie achieved became a source of satisfaction to her – though she was not so good at accepting failures. She felt no one could accuse her of being an unconscientious parent: she took an interest in their ploys, was ambitious about their results at school and organised family life with the efficiency she brought to everything she undertook. To the outside world she appeared the perfectly assured wife and mother – catwalk elegant and enviably slim – only her bitten nails and over-washed hands betraying any inner turmoil.

All had been going smoothly in the Hammond family, at any rate on the surface, until, three years ago, Rachel discovered she was having another baby. At first she thought her symptoms were due to the premature onset of the menopause and tried to ignore them. When she eventually went to see her doctor she was horrified when he asked if she thought she might be pregnant and utterly appalled when it turned out to be true – by which time she was already over four months into the pregnancy. Patrick's first reaction had been one of amazed delight quickly followed by anxiety for his highly strung wife. An abortion was discussed and he was relieved when Rachel – taking the high moral ground in a martyred sort of way – decided against it.

Sam and Sophie – once they had got over their astonishment that their parents could actually achieve such a thing at their advanced age – had been thrilled. Since then attitudes had altered all round.

Rachel assumed that the debilitating sickness she had suffered all the way through her first two pregnancies would naturally afflict her this time, especially in view of her age, but quite soon she started to look and feel exceptionally well.

She continued to protest that she did not want the baby but seemed to consider the pregnancy entirely Patrick's fault although she had not told him she had given up taking contraceptive pills some time ago, fearing long-term effects and deeming them no longer necessary. He began to feel that after twenty years of marriage, he was living with a stranger. Active, intelligent Rachel had been replaced by a hostile, stay-at-home bearer of grudges. All will be well once the baby is born, he told himself: be patient, make allowances, it's only due to hormones. He already had experience of the havoc that could be wreaked by these mysterious message-carriers of the brain: two teenage children in the family were evidence of that.

When a beautiful baby daughter arrived with the minimum of trouble he was not only deeply relieved that his wife had come through the actual birth so well, but that this time, with the help of therapy, she had fallen in love with the baby too. Patrick was prepared for upheaval in their lives – indeed, in many ways was looking forward to it, promising himself that at forty-two he would relish this autumnal return to nursery days. He had enjoyed being a hands-on father to the older two on the occasions when the current nanny was away, but what he had not bargained for was that though Rachel's hitherto hostile attitude to babies had vanished, it had been replaced by an obsessional fixation on their new daughter combined with resentful feelings towards himself. He felt increasingly bewildered that his wife could be so enchanted with the product of their love and yet manage to bear him a grudge because of his part in her conception when once – it now seemed a long time ago – she had appeared to enjoy that as much as he had.

Nor had he bargained for the change in her attitude to Sam and Sophie. Though they made jokes about it to each other – rolled their eyes and mocked at their mother – Patrick knew that they found Rachel's total absorption in their little sister, not to mention her irritation with their own concerns, deeply wounding.

And then there was her friendship with Bronwen Richards. Sophie, who loathed her, insisted darkly that she was a lesbian with predatory designs on their mother.

'Don't be ridiculous!' Patrick had said sharply when she mooted this provocative theory.

'She's got all the signs.'

'What signs?' Sam, who secretly thought Bronwen unnervingly sexy – though he would have died rather than admit it – looked up from the football results.

'Shaggy armpits,' said Sophie promptly. 'Honestly, Dad, they're like Punch's fetlocks. And when she wears those sleeveless tops you can see them all hanging down. Yuk!' Sophie pulled a revolted face. 'Ellie says that's always frightfully suspicious. The German teacher at school has hairy pits and she's notorious. I really think you should warn Mum. Ellie says—'

'Ellie is extremely silly, and so are you.' Patrick had flung the paper down with uncharacteristic vehemence and walked out of the room, shutting the door with an angry precision that was far more expressive than if he'd slammed it. It was not often that his offspring managed to disconcert him.

'Wow! Bull's-eye!' said Sam. 'Poor old Dad, you really rattled him. Better lay off that one, Sophe.'

'I certainly shan't. Looks like I've found an effective wind-up. Desperate situations need desperate measures and we have to goad him into action. We've got to get rid of grotty old Bronwen, for all our sakes – but it's no good talking to Mum. Apart from Posy and Bronwen all she thinks about are diets, detergents and disinfectant.'

Bronwen had arrived, three years ago, to live in a converted old chapel on the outskirts of the village. Rachel, newly coming to terms with unwanted pregnancy, tense as a highly tuned violin and constantly turning the keys of her anxiety to tighten its strings, had seen her advertisement in the window of the local health-food shop: 'Yoga and Relaxation classes. Counselling. Spiritual insights. Problem-solving a speciality. Your opportunity to go on an inner journey of personal exploration with safe and sympathetic guidance. Expect change!' On a whim Rachel had picked up the telephone and made an appointment.

Bronwen had been right about one thing, thought Patrick wryly: Rachel had certainly changed.

Chapter Five

❧

Patrick took his empty coffee cup to the sink and, Rachel and Posy not having reappeared, started to unload the dishwasher before clearing away the remains of breakfast. He had intended to work on the text of his book for the rest of the morning but remembered that he'd half promised to go over to see his uncle before lunch. He glanced at the clock on the wall – a large mahogany-cased affair that he and Rachel had salvaged from the now-defunct village school. Its unforgiving tick reminded Patrick that he had better get a move on. It also reminded him of a time when he and Rachel used to enjoy going to sales and prowling round antique shops, bargain-hunting for things for the house. It seemed a long time since they had done anything like that together and Patrick longed to put the clock back to how things used to be between them. Tick-tock went the heavy black pendulum, remorselessly swinging the seconds away; tick-tock.

It was now nearly ten o'clock on Saturday morning and though the old man was the least demanding of elderly relatives, Patrick knew he would be looking forward to a visit. Before he left he stood in the stone-flagged hall, with its elegant staircase curving down in front of the long Venetian window that gave the house such a feeling of light and space, and listened. He could hear Rachel talking to Posy upstairs and, rather against his better judgement, he called up to her. 'Darling? Just going over to see Uncle Hugh. Want to come? He'd love to see you and Posy.'

But predictably the answer came back: 'No, thank you . . . afraid I can't. I've got Bronwen coming for coffee. Could you pick Sophie up from the Marshalls on your way back? She's going over to see Ellie after her driving lesson and it would save me fetching her. Bye then – give my love to Hugh and don't be late back.'

Patrick went to get the car out in a state of suppressed irritation. He had no idea what to do about Rachel.

He drove through the early February countryside, noticing the small signs of spring that could be so deceptive but were none the less encouraging: a few catkins in the hedgerows, the reddening of willows, a sort of hazy look about the larches in the wood, as though smoke had been blown through them, and, most cheering of all, as he turned into the drive of Hugh's house, a few brave aconites were shining their small torches among the roots of the dark old yew trees that lined the drive.

The front door had been left unlocked – something he was always begging Hugh not to do – and he walked in. He found his uncle in the long room at the back of the house, which bore more of a resemblance to an upmarket junk shop than a country drawing room. It was stuffed with an eclectic mix of items that Hugh had gathered on his travels all over the world. African tribal masks and fine English watercolours jostled for position on the walls along with some of Hugh's own powerful oil paintings of animals; a Tang horse champed its bit on the grand piano beside a small Henry Moore bronze of a reclining figure; an ostrich's egg made an unlikely neighbour to a Louis XV1 clock, and Hugh's valuable collection of Egyptian shabti over-flowed everywhere, along with piles and piles of books – on most of which, it had to be said, there was a thin bloom of dust. It was a nightmare room to clean and Patrick was always terrified that the unequal struggle might overwhelm Mrs Parkes, Hugh's long-suffering housekeeper. In some ways, he thought sadly, it was perhaps a blessing that her eyesight was beginning to fail so that she was not as acutely aware of the growing deterioration around her as she would once – vociferously – have been. Luckily the charm of the owner was as strong as that of the cluttered room, and though she was always threatening to retire, Mrs Parkes continued to put up with her magpie of an employer in an atmosphere of mutual affection and exasperation. She had been with Hugh for years, and her age was a closely guarded secret, but Patrick thought she must be well over seventy herself.

During the winter Hugh had taken to working in the drawing room rather than his studio at the bottom of the garden. This morning he was at his easel – a good sign. His arthritic hands often made it painful for him to wield a brush, and a couple of years previously he had fallen in the garden and broken his hip on the side where his leg had been blown off in the war. The hip had been successfully operated on and pinned, but there had been problems refitting his artificial leg and though the old man made light of it Patrick knew he was always in discomfort now, and often in pain.

'You're working. That's wonderful. Am I interrupting?' asked Patrick. Hugh Marston turned round, nearly over-balancing in the process and beamed at his nephew.

'My dear boy, how perfectly delightful! Good of you to come – I did hope you might turn up. Give me your opinion on this. I'm rather pleased with myself.'

Patrick came and stood beside him. 'So you should be. You've lost none of your touch. That Prince Haroun's lot?'

'Mmm. The Haroun Stud – mares and foals. In particular the one in the foreground – Moonlight Flit. Do you remember her spectacular win at Ascot a few years ago? He asked me to do it last summer. Too far for me to drive myself now so he sent a car for me and I went over to lunch. I've always rather liked the little man, though we must look pretty funny together – the long and the short of it. I made some notes, did some rough sketches and took a lot of photographs but told him I couldn't promise to manage such a big canvas any longer. Still, he's very persuasive and I suppose I'm susceptible to flattery nowadays. He really should get someone younger but he hasn't set a time limit . . . and my new quack has produced some bloody good pills so I think I might get it finished now. But I've done enough for this morning. Can't stand for too long. Bloody nuisance.'

At eighty-four, Hugh Marston was still magnificently distinguished-looking with his shock of silver hair, enormous height and the unconventional clothes – unconventional for his generation, that is – which he wore with an elegance many younger men might have envied.

Patrick was devoted to his mother's only brother who had been like a father to him since his own father had died when he was a schoolboy. Hugh had always taken a special interest in Patrick, considering him from an early age to be by far the most congenial of his nephews and nieces.

'Not too early for a drink, is it?' Hugh asked now – a rhetorical question – as he lowered himself into his special chair by the fire. 'Give me my usual, will you, and fix yourself whatever you like.' He poked dangerously at the log in the grate with his walking stick so that a spray of sparks spat out on the rug, adding to the existing rash of blackened threadbare little patches which were the despair of Mrs Parkes. 'You'll have been cremated long before your own funeral,' she would prophesy with gloomy relish.

Patrick went over to the drinks tray and poured a generous slug of the fearsomely dry sherry that was his uncle's preferred pre-lunchtime drink into a large tumbler, filled it with ice from the ice-bucket which Mrs Parkes always kept filled, and then helped himself to a lager. Hugh boasted a head like cast iron and in all the years he'd known and loved his uncle, Patrick never remembered seeing him appear even remotely the worse for drink though his consumption of it was prodigious. Both Mrs Parkes and his doctor tried endlessly to get him to cut down on alcohol and tobacco with absolutely no success; the cigars he smoked were as much a part of his appearance as the colourful silk handkerchiefs that cascaded out of the breast pocket of his paint-daubed Breton smock, or the red or green silk socks he favoured – often wearing one of each colour like port and starboard signals.

'How's the book going?' he asked, taking the glass from his nephew in a hand that Patrick noticed for the first time was beginning to shake slightly.

'I'm still at the planning stage, but I'm getting quite excited about it. I've found some interesting families to write about and some marvellous houses to photograph. Your contacts have all been wonderfully useful – literally opened doors for me. It's certainly an advantage having such a famous relation!'

'If this book turns out to be half as successful as your last one you'll be far better known than I ever was – and I'm an old has-been now. Still, I'm not putting up my brushes yet. How's Rachel?'

'Oh, busy. Tired. You know what a perfectionist she is about everything she does and Posy makes big demands on her. It isn't easy having such mixed ages in the family. She needs a holiday but she won't go away.'

'Hmm.' Privately Hugh thought Rachel was tiresome beyond belief, and had always been astonished at how Patrick had protected and spoiled her over the years. He shot his nephew a beady look under his jutting white eyebrows.

'If you ask my opinion, what Rachel needs is not a holiday but a shock.'

'And what do you suggest?' Patrick asked frostily so that Hugh could tell he had hit on a jumpy nerve.

'Oh, I wouldn't presume to give specific advice, dear boy. After all, what does an old bachelor like me know about women?'

'A hell of a lot more than most of us!' said Patrick, grinning and waving his hand at the elaborate silver photograph frames displaying misty Lenaire Studio portraits in black and white of famous beauties wearing off-the-shoulder evening dresses, some of whom had sat for Hugh – and a good many of whom, thought Patrick wryly, had certainly lain down for him too. Since he'd become famous for painting animals – horses in particular – he seldom accepted commissions to paint people, and as a result his early portraits had shot up in value and become collectors' pieces. He had hung on to a few of them – known in the family as 'Hugh's Harem', and there was one hanging in his studio that he had always refused to part with. But if he no longer painted portraits, then his reputation as a collector of pretty women was still considerable. He'd always been a wonderful raconteur and over the years Patrick had frequently been entertained with hilarious Don Giovanni-type stories of Hugh's escapades while fleeing the vengeance of irate husbands or trying to extricate himself from the clutches of ladies who looked for a greater commitment than he was prepared to give.

'And you really weren't ever tempted into marriage with *any* of that lot?' Patrick asked now, more to get his uncle's attention away from the subject of Rachel and back on to the safer topic of his colourful past than because he expected any new disclosures. 'Though I suppose I ought to be thankful you never did get married and have a family of your own. If you'd had children yourself you'd never have been such a fantastic uncle to all of us.'

To his surprise the old man did not immediately reply with one of his light-hearted confections of storytelling, but sat thwacking at the logs and gazing into the fire. Patrick had to leap out of his chair to stamp on a particularly large ember that flew out on to the carpet adding the smell of singeing wool to the richer one of lilies and cigar smoke that habitually hung in the air.

'Funny you should ask me that today,' said Hugh at last, not looking at his nephew.

'I've asked you often enough before. What's different about today?'

'Just that a piece of my past has been very strongly on my mind.'

'Want to tell me?' Patrick tried not to look as curious as he felt.

'Perhaps. I must be growing soft. It's one of the penalties of old age along with the need to drink more whisky and pass more water. But, yes, there was someone once – the reason I never married. This morning I suddenly came across the original sketch for a portrait I once did of her, which I thought I'd lost when I moved here – the sketch, I mean, not the portrait. It went through all the war with me, folded up in the pocket of my battledress, and it kept me sane when I was in the POW camp. I keep a photograph of the finished portrait in my wallet always, but I haven't clapped eyes on the original sketch for ages and suddenly it turns up in a box of stuff I could have sworn I'd looked through a hundred times before. The funny thing is I was just thinking of her when I found it – not the other way round. Gave me quite a shock.'

'What went wrong between you?'

'Oh, nothing very unusual. We fell in love and . . . . let's just say the war interfered with our plans. Many of our generation were faced with the same thing.'

'But you survived the war . . . just. So what happened to her, or don't you know?'

'She survived too. I found that out afterwards.'

'Didn't you get back together? Were you ever engaged?'

'Oh yes! We were determined to marry.' He hesitated and Patrick had the feeling he was not going to be told the full story. Hugh went on: 'It's hard to convey the atmosphere of uncertainty there was at the outbreak of war. Terrible things were happening in Europe, and she was half Italian, which didn't make it easy. Separation was inevitable at the time and I knew I'd wait for her – for ever if necessary – but she was only nineteen. We had one idyllic summer in each other's company – then I returned to England to join up and fight Hitler and she remained in Europe. You know what happened to me then.'

Patrick nodded. He'd been brought up on family stories of his uncle's distinguished war record for which he had been awarded an MC – sacrificed a leg and spent the end of the war in Colditz.

'Surely you tried to keep in touch?'

'Communication was difficult,' said Hugh vaguely and Patrick now felt sure he wasn't getting the full story. 'All these e-mails and telephones the young use nowadays – don't tell me they can take the place of love letters! As soon as the war was over, the first thing I wanted to do was to go and track her down and find out what had happened. I thought she might have been killed. But she was married to someone else by then.'

'That was pretty faithless of her,' said Patrick, feeling a grow-ing anger against this unknown woman who had obviously caused such terrible heartache. 'You were probably well shot of her.'

His uncle threw him a blistering look. 'You didn't know her or you wouldn't say such a damn silly thing,' he said shortly. 'She had compelling reasons – a difficult war and a lot of family pressure. There were problems.'

'And you never met again?'

'No. It would have been terrible for her to have to choose between me and someone else, and she had a baby by then too. I did go out but I turned round and came home again and never saw her. No one else has ever come even close to measuring up to her and I'd given her my word. There . . . I've said more than I meant to. I don't want to talk about it any more.'

Patrick had never seen his uncle look so moved, clearly in the grip of a very powerful emotion. He longed to ask more, but now was clearly not the moment.

'Can I see the picture?'

'It's on the table,' said Hugh, giving the fire a particularly vicious poke.

Patrick got up and went over. Among all the working sketches of particular horses, done in charcoal with bold strokes and covered with pencilled notes and dabs of colour, there was a scruffy torn-out page, folded in four and rather stained, which Patrick had never seen before – but he recognised immediately that it must have been the working sketch for a picture he knew very well. He glanced up at it now, on the wall to the right of the fireplace. It had hung in his uncle's house for as long as he could remember: an oil painting that looked as fresh as if it had been done yesterday. Against a background of dark cypresses and umbrella trees, a girl was sitting on a curiously shaped rock at the edge of sea that reflected all the colours of a kingfisher's wing. She wore a large straw hat and her feet were bare – so vivid was the impression of personality and place that as a boy Patrick had always expected to see her wiggle her toes. Looking at it now he could almost feel the heat of the sun and smell the aroma of wild Mediterranean herbs. He had always thought her face was one of the most arresting he'd ever seen – better than beautiful. There was something about the directness of her gaze, a quality of intensity and joy that the painter had captured, which forced you to look again – and again.

'Yes,' said Patrick, 'oh yes. I do see. Are you going to tell me more about her?'

But Hugh shook his head. He suddenly looked very tired and drawn. 'I've talked enough. Think I'll pack it in for the rest of the morning,' he said gruffly. 'Good to see you, Patrick, but it's time you were off. Tell that naughty Sophie of yours to come and pay me a visit soon – she always takes my mind off my aches and pains and makes me laugh. I might paint *her* one of these days – got good cheekbones. Don't know why I haven't done it before. She's got a future, that child – though I tremble to think what it may be.'

Patrick grinned. 'Oh, Sophie's all right really. Drives us crazy sometimes but she's great value. I must go and pick her up right now. She's been having a driving lesson – God help the other road users. Come and have Sunday lunch a week tomorrow when Sam will be home for the weekend too. They'd both love to see you.'

'Yes, I'd like to do that. Thank you.' Hugh held out his glass. 'Pour me another one of these before you go, there's a good chap. Need refuelling – don't do much to the gallon nowadays.'

'Did you ever?' asked Patrick, laughing. He handed him another beaker of sherry but took care to put a great deal of ice in it.

On the way out he looked into the kitchen. A rich smell of wine and garlic assailed his nostrils. Mrs Parkes was making a casserole.

'Morning, Mrs P. I'm afraid I may have tired Uncle Hugh out. He was in splendid form when I arrived, but he doesn't look so good now and I've got to go and collect Sophie. Don't tell him I told you, though.'

'I'll go and look in on him as soon as you've gone. I'll take him a cup of coffee and check he's had his pills. Don't you fret. He's a creaking gate as'll swing a while yet – and he does love your visits. He's been working too long again and he tires very sudden nowadays. A painkiller and forty winks will put him right.' Mrs Parkes gave a cackle of laughter. 'I expect he'll have had a fair bit of that there paint-stripper he drinks while you were with him – nasty stuff.'

'Thanks, Mrs P. What would we do without you?'

Patrick went out to his car thinking what a lot there must be of his uncle's life about which he knew nothing. He couldn't get the picture of the girl on the rock out of his mind.

What a waste, he thought – all Hugh's love and loyalty over so many years! No good pretending the old boy had been a saint. He'd had a rip-roaring life . . . but all the same . . .

Patrick found himself intensely moved – and deeply curious.

Chapter Six

❖

Three weeks after the funeral, Victoria went up to London for the day. She had made an appointment to see Peter Mason in the morning but managed to decline his invitation to give her lunch. Then she had rung Guy's house. He had spoken to her several times since the funeral, telephoning on his mobile from wherever he happened to be and keeping her informed of his whereabouts in case she should want to get hold of him, but not ringing from home. He had been full of concern for her and yet there was a constraint between them. She chose a day when she knew Guy was definitely going to be away before she dialled his number. Francine answered the telephone.

'Oh – hi, Victoria! How are you?' Francine's husky voice sounded cautious.

'Fine, thanks,' said Victoria automatically, and then, 'Well, no . . . not fine, exactly. But sort of OK, I suppose. Coping, I think.'

'God – what a stupid question. How could you even be *sort of* OK at the moment? I'm sorry. Look, I guess you want to talk to Guy but I'm afraid he's not here. Can I get him to call you when he's home?'

'Actually it's you I want to talk to.' Victoria could almost hear Francine's heart sinking. 'Can I come and see you? I'm coming up to London on Friday.'

There was a pause. Then Francine said: 'Sure . . . if that's what you really want . . . if you think there's any point. I guess you already know Guy won't be here?'

'Yes. Yes, as a matter of fact he told me. I'm seeing Peter Mason at eleven.'

'Shall we meet somewhere for lunch then?'

'I don't know how long I'll be and, anyway, I'd rather come to the house if I may. Easier to talk – but you don't have to give me any lunch. I'm not much good at eating at the moment.'

'I'll fix us a sandwich or something. Just turn up when you're through with Peter. Rather you than me – I've always thought he was a real drag.'

'Me too. I'm not looking forward to it. But there are things I need to know from him about how Jake and I are placed financially. And there are other things I need to know from you.'

'Well, I hope you're right. Look, Victoria, I'm truly sorry for you. I know how devoted Guy is to you and I sure don't mean to stand between you, but I can't think a lot of poking around in the past is going to help you. Suppose it makes things worse?'

'They couldn't be much worse and I think skeletons are more scary when the cupboard doors are locked. Please, Francine.'

'Well, OK, then,' said Francine, a shrug in her voice. 'See you Friday. I may not be able to help you with whatever it is you want to know.'

But Victoria was sure that she could.

She took Jake to school on her way to the station.

'I feel sick,' said Jake as they drew up outside the PNEU school in Toddingham. He had said this every morning. Victoria had agonised about when to make him go back to school but felt that the sooner his life returned to some sort of normality the better. She also knew that the longer he stayed at home the harder it would be to go back, but the first morning of his intended return he'd been so miserable and complained so much of pains in the tummy that she had turned the car round when they reached the school and driven straight home again – where he had forgotten all about the sickness as soon as he got out of the car, and had gone off round the farm with Jeff Burrows and been perfectly all right for the rest of the day.

The following morning he'd been picked up by Romie Constable, a neighbour and friend with whom Victoria shared the school run, and she had hardened her heart and made him climb, clutching his stomach and protesting pathetically, into the Constables' car. The other children had all fallen silent at the sight of him – quite unable to handle their parents' stern instructions to be 'specially kind to Jake'. Victoria had felt terrible seeing his white face pressed against the window, gazing reproachfully back at her as Romie roared off down the drive. She had rung Victoria later to say he had perked up soon after they had turned out of the drive, but Victoria had worried about him all day. It seemed awful to take such a firm stand with him so soon after a terrible trauma, but everyone kept telling her it was the right thing to do.

'My tummy really hurts. You don't understand how sick I feel,' said Jake in a whiny voice. It was unlike him to make a fuss, she thought: he had always coped so gallantly and stoically with his asthma.

'I do understand, darling,' she said now. 'It's a horrid feeling but it will wear off – and you know you have to go.'

'When will you be home?'

'Before bedtime. Toula's going to pick you up from school and take you back to tea with her. You know you love that. I'll collect you on my way back from the station. Now come on, darling, do buck up.'

Jake gave her a martyred look and got very slowly out of the car, deliberately managing to spill all the contents of his satchel on the pavement. Victoria picked everything up, and carried it into the school herself while Jake trailed behind, kicking the path.

'There – well done. Off you go,' she said as they got to the school door. She could see Mrs Atkinson, his kind form mistress, waiting to scoop him up. 'Bye, darling – quick hug,' she said, but Jake stalked silently past her and went inside without saying goodbye.

She sat in the car for a few moments, leaning her head against the steering wheel, struggling with tears and quite unable to see, before wiping them away, starting the engine and driving slowly to the station. By the time she had parked the car and bought her ticket she felt absolutely shattered, as though she had already done a hard day's work, and wished she had accepted Anthony's offer to drive her up to London, or listened to Toula's advice that it was far too soon to push herself into any outside activity. But once she was on the train she felt thankful to have time to think, without the concerned eyes of loving friends and family monitoring her every move or change of expression.

She thought again of the conversation she had overheard just before the funeral. After the lunch party, organised by Toula, for family and friends who'd come from a long distance Victoria had escaped upstairs to have a few minutes on her own and get ready for the service. Despite the wintery weather and her own permanent state of chill she felt suffocated by having so many people in the house and the effort of talking to them, and had opened her bedroom window and leaned out. Two old friends of Richard and Guy's from university days, who'd come to be ushers at the church, were standing on the terrace beneath her window having slipped out of the dining room for a quick smoke.

'Bloody awful business,' she heard one of them say. 'Awful thing to say but I can't help wondering if it can really have been an accident – it's just that the timing's a bit suspect. You don't suppose he meant to do it, do you?'

'You mean because of Francine getting engaged to Guy?'

'Yes.'

'God, what an awful thought! Have to say, though, the same idea had crossed my mind. Relief to hear the verdict was accidental . . . all the same, that engagement must have been a body blow to poor old Richard.'

'Wonder what Victoria thinks.'

'Think back to Cambridge. Don't forget what a wonderful actor Richard always was. Imagine he could fool anyone if he needed to.' At this moment someone had called the two speakers to go down to the church and she heard no more. Victoria stood staring out at the garden and terrible ideas, not previously thought of, whirled round her head. *Richard and Francine?* It was simply too ridiculous. He hadn't even liked her. Then she thought, but what if that was just an act for my benefit?

She leaned her head back against the seat and closed her eyes. I have to know, she thought. However painful, I must face the truth – whatever it is – before I can start to mourn Richard properly; and she determined that she would not be put off by evasions but would press Francine to fill in for her the missing pieces in the nightmare jigsaw puzzle of the last few weeks.

She arrived at the elegant offices of Mason, Whitaker & Ziegler in Fetter Lane at a quarter to eleven. She had only been there once before, with Richard, when they first got married, though she had often met Peter Mason with her father-in-law on social occasions.

'Good morning, Mrs Cunningham, how nice to see you,' said the receptionist, a tailored young woman with immaculate make-up and beautifully cut hair. She had never met Victoria before, but had obviously done her homework well. 'Mr Mason is expecting you. May I take your coat?' and she smiled with just the right mix of impersonal friendliness and discreet sympathy. Victoria half expected her to offer to take her bleeding heart as well, and hang it tidily behind closed doors in the cupboard. 'Please come this way,' she said. 'Mr Mason won't keep you too long,' and she showed her into the waiting room.

It was like a stand at a very prestigious antique fair – no reproduction furniture for Peter Mason – or the drawing room of a grand London house but without any of the reassuring clutter of a personal home: small Dutch oil paintings: cows, canals and ships; Derby and Chelsea figures: sexless milkmaids and shepherds; a bureau-bookcase displaying leather-bound volumes that had never been read. Victoria felt the glossy art magazines and expensive coffee-table books displayed on the library table in the window had probably been drilled like guardsmen to keep their lines straight and imagined they might automatically leap back into place when they heard the next client coming. She fought the temptation to rumple it all up, kick her shoes off, put her feet up on the huge sofa covered in a muted Colefax and Fowler chintz and go to sleep. Instead of which she perched on the edge of a chair with her ankles crossed and picked nervously at her fingernails. Everything in the room gave out a message: not the place to give in to a wild impulse, start singing or play Racing Demon on the floor.

At ten past eleven the door opened and Peter Mason appeared, a whale of a man with alarmingly small feet.

'Victoria! How splendid to see you. I thought I'd come down to collect you myself.' He held her away from him appraisingly. 'You are looking more beautiful than ever,' he said, giving her a lingering after-shave-drenched kiss on each cheek. 'Now, come along with me and I'll try to make everything as painless as possible.'

Victoria wondered if this was what he said when seducing virgins.

As they got into the lift Peter took a small gadget out of his pocket and started speaking into it: 'I am just on my way to the North Boardroom,' he said, for all the world as if he were making a solo crossing of the Atlantic and needed to have his position constantly tracked. The gleaming mahogany table could have seated twenty people and at each place there was a well-sharpened pencil and a fresh notepad. Peter pulled out a chair for Victoria and sat himself down in the one next to her.

'Coffee or tea?'

'Coffee would be lovely, thank you.'

He pressed a buzzer and a tray of coffee and biscuits was instantly produced.

'Now,' said Peter, after he'd told her several long stories about the ingenious financial arrangements he'd made for various other clients, most of whom seemed to own castles in Scotland – it was clearly meant to be reassuring, 'I'm sure we could enjoy chatting away to each other all morning,' and he twinkled with self-conscious cosiness over the top of his trendily narrow half-spectacles, 'but . . . to business.'

Quite soon Victoria felt her attention start to fog over with the same blanketing feeling that often overcame her when she listened to complicated route directions or rang National Rail Enquiries. Competent Richard had always marvelled at her ability to blot out useful information but retain a grip on the most inconsequential trivialities. Her head started to throb and she groped in her bag for some paracetamol, which she swallowed furtively with the dregs of her cold coffee. Funny, she thought, how some people with a particular expertise, be it in medicine, law, science or engineering, can give you a clear – if necessarily shallow – understanding of their subject, while others, like Peter Mason, manage to wrap up what ought to be perfectly simple in such a cat's cradle of waffle that it becomes completely incomprehensible.

'Look, Peter,' she said, drowning in the flow of technical and financial Masonese, 'I know I'm being particularly stupid at the moment but could you just tell me – in a nutshell – if Jake and I will be all right for money?'

Nutshells, however, were not Peter's forte. 'If there's anything you don't understand, we can easily go over it all again,' he said. 'Now let me see – where were we?'

After an hour and a half, Victoria tottered out of the building having been reassured that on the one hand she was not to worry her head about money – but on the other hand she couldn't be too careful: things were not *that* rosy. With regard to the house she need have no immediate concerns about staying on there – though it would naturally behove her to consider other possibilities for the future as it might prove too large and expensive for her to run now that circumstances had so sadly changed. One shouldn't make important decisions too soon after a bereavement, but on the other hand one mustn't let the grass grow *too* long – Manor Farm was, of course, owned by the Cunningham Family Trust, and there might be other claimants for it – but, there again, Peter Mason was the chief trustee and he would naturally have Victoria and Jake's best interests at heart.

Above all, both he and Bill would be there to help her with Jake and advise her about his education. So difficult for a woman on her own to bring up a son – and particularly for her he implied: he didn't actually spell out that her Greek nationality was a drawback, but the inference was plain that despite her English education this was an undesirable hazard. Alarm bells went off in Victoria's head.

'And let me emphasise,' Peter said impressively, 'that if you are in any doubt about anything, you can always come to me for clarification. I would always make time to see you. We'll have to have a valuation done for probate and I'll let you know when I need to see you again. No, no – please don't try to thank me, this is all part of my job and it's been a great pleasure to see you. Next time we'll have that lunch and then we can really enjoy each other's company. I'll just let them know downstairs that you're leaving and someone will get you a taxi.'

She had intended to go on the underground to Gloucester Road station and then walk the short distance down to Guy's house in The Boltons via the Old Brompton Road, but as things turned out she was thankful to be driven door to door courtesy of Mason, Whitaker & Ziegler and deposited directly outside number forty.

There were forsythias out all round the oval, and an almond tree blossoming in front of a neighbouring house. New beginnings everywhere, thought Victoria – but can I cope with them? And she went up the stone steps to the front door, took a deep breath and rang the bell.

Chapter Seven

❧

It was a strange feeling to go to Guy's house where Victoria had so often acted as his hostess and find herself there as the guest of his wife. She half expected everything to be completely altered, though she knew there could hardly have been time for Francine to change much.

Just as she was beginning to wonder whether she should ring the bell a second time, Francine opened the door. She was wearing beautifully cut trousers in supple caramel suede and a paler cashmere sweater. Her mane of tawny hair was casually pulled back by two tortoiseshell combs and her face was so perfectly made up that the uninitiated might have been fooled into thinking that her skin was *au naturel*. The look was impeccable, understated and very, very expensive. She has put on her armour, thought Victoria. If she imagined she had seen some chinks in it when they last met, they were certainly not apparent today.

'Hi, Victoria. Come on in.' This time Francine gave her the statutory social peck on the cheek.

Unlike the perfect receptionist at Mason, Whitaker & Ziegler she did not immediately offer to take her coat, and Victoria, who would normally have flung it on one of the hall chairs without thinking, was somehow inhibited from doing so. It was a long straight coat, rather military, made of a heavy navy-blue cloth; it had been one of her best purchases the year before and normally she felt good in it; now beside Francine's slinky softness it felt hot, restricting and just plain wrong.

'Oh, by the way, did you want to leave your coat?' Francine asked as an afterthought as they went upstairs, but, perversely, Victoria chose to keep it on despite the warmth of the house, as though it were a sort of armour. She had expected to go down to Guy's huge basement kitchen – a brilliant place for informal entertaining – but Francine led the way to the drawing room on the first floor.

'What would you like to drink?'

'I'd love a glass of white wine if you've got one.'

'We certainly have.' Francine opened the drinks cupboard in the wall and took a bottle of Sancerre out of the fridge. She poured out two glasses and handed one to Victoria. 'So how was the inflatable Peter Mason?' she asked.

'Oh well, you know what he's like – fine if you enjoy being eyed-up I suppose. I always feel he's appraising me like a vegetable at a local show.'

'And did he award you a medal?'

'Not even a commended – I'm a big disappointment to him. I make good resolutions to try to like him better but in one minute flat he's always rubbed my fur the wrong way. He probably means to be kind in his heavy-handed way, but I've always found him a creep and he's not only Richard's executor, but my father-in-law thinks everything he suggests is set in stone so it's all a bit difficult.'

'I can imagine.'

'And, of course, boring old Clutterbuck kept coming in and out as usual.'

'Run that past me again – who on earth is Clutterbuck?'

'Oh, hasn't Guy told you about him? Well, you're bound to meet him sometime – he's Peter's particular pal. Whenever he wants to illustrate some important point to financial dimwits like me, he always says, "Now, take my friend Clutterbuck, for example." Guy and Richard and I always have . . .' she corrected herself painfully. 'I mean *had* . . . terrible trouble if we caught each other's eye when Clutterbuck turned up. But today of course,' she added bleakly 'there was no one's eye to catch so I got by all right. How's Guy?'

'Still devastated, of course. In Milan at the moment to write a piece on that controversial *Ballo in Maschera* production at La Scala – but I'm sure you know that.'

'Yes.'

An awkward silence fell. Victoria went over to the window and looked down on the enormous garden below. Gardening, together with music and travel, was one of Guy's passions and he had a monthly column in *Capability*, the prestigious American magazine for high-powered horticulturists, which was officially about English gardens, but was actually a vehicle for him to write about more or less any topic he wanted. It had a huge following and a good many people read it just for Guy's provocative, pithy prose.

'The bulbs look fantastic already,' she said.

'Don't they just? Guy's really pleased with them,' said Francine.

'I've always loved this time of year. Lots of promise but no weeds yet. It's amazing to find so much space tucked away behind the house, isn't it?'

'Yes, it's a great part of London altogether.'

'How much time do you plan to spend here?'

'We haven't decided yet.'

Oh God, thought Victoria, this unnatural formality – here of all places – is bizarre; she's not going to make it easy for me. She didn't want me to come today. She's being polite because she's sorry for me, and open hostility to new widows is a no-no. However tough she is she can't be happy about what I'm going to ask her. Aloud she said, 'I suppose I'd better come to the point.'

'Have something to eat first. I've got some soup and sandwiches for you.'

Victoria saw there was a tray on the table beside one of the armchairs by the fireplace, with a small Thermos, a plate covered in foil and a place setting for one. She sat down and opened her coat but still didn't take it off. 'Is this all for me?' she asked. 'What are *you* going to eat?'

'Oh, I hardly ever eat lunch – and anyway, I've had what I want. I didn't know what time you'd get here. Please . . . help yourself.'

Victoria had felt hungry earlier, but now all inclination to eat left her. It was as though some regulator on her whole system had been blown by Richard's death, so that she either felt deadly sick or ravenously starving, freezing cold or stickily hot. She felt her hands start to tremble – another of the unwelcome after-effects of shock, she supposed, and thought in a panic: I shall slop soup on the tray-cloth and drop crumbs on the carpet, and Francine in those immaculate suede trousers will sit and watch me. She forced herself to unscrew the Thermos top and cautiously poured a little of the contents into the soup-cup without mishap. It smelled delicious – clear chicken broth with a little rice and tiny pieces of carrot. She wondered if Francine had made it, but thought it unlikely.

Francine shot her an amused look. 'No, I didn't make it. I don't do cooking,' she said, and Victoria felt herself flushing. Am I so transparent? she thought.

She took a few spoonfuls, nibbled at one of the smoked salmon sandwiches but found she could hardly get it down. She put the tray on one side. 'This is really kind of you but I'm sorry – I just can't. I can never eat before any kind of confrontation.'

'And are we going to have one?' Francine raised an eyebrow.

'It depends what you have to tell me. I don't want to get into a fight with you, Francine, but we need to clear the air.'

Francine went and sat in the chair opposite and lit a cigarette, looking at the younger woman over the flame of her lighter and blowing out a cloud of smoke.

'When we were kids my father always told us one should never go into battle on an empty stomach but if you're sure you want to go down this road you'd better fire away.'

There was an uneasy pause, while Victoria marshalled her thoughts, and then, not looking at Francine, she said: 'Up to a few weeks ago my world looked so secure I never questioned it but now suddenly it's not only disappeared but it seems it may not have been real in the first place – and I can't get my head round that at all.'

'Do you need to try? You've had one hell of a time by any standard. Seems to me you've gotten more than enough to cope with just facing Richard's death without stirring round looking for more trouble.'

'I'm beginning to wonder if Richard was the person I thought I knew so well.'

'Are any of us quite what we seem?' asked Francine. 'Most of us mean different things to different people. Look, Victoria,' she suddenly sounded curiously intense, 'if the Richard you loved made you happy then nothing else matters . . . if you found your marriage good, then OK, it *was* good. Accept it. Why beat yourself up?'

'But if I'm to find out why all this happened – and that's my only hope of finding any peace – then I must know who Richard was to other people.' Victoria felt more than ever convinced that Francine was hiding something. 'What did *you* feel about him, Francine?' she burst out desperately.

'Oh, Victoria – does it matter what *I* felt? I didn't know Richard that well.' Francine spread out her elegant hands, made more delicate-looking under the weight of the rings she wore, in a dismissive gesture, but Victoria thought she looked wary. 'Well enough to know he was a nice guy and that you and he seemed happily married. What else do you want me to say, for God's sake?'

'But were you surprised at the news?'

'Surprised? *Of course* I was! Horrified.'

'But did you . . . did he . . . ?' Victoria looked at her with misery, anger and challenge in her eyes. Francine looked away. Victoria blurted out: 'You asked me after the funeral if I hated you because of Richard. That seemed an extraordinary thing to ask. It still does.' She paused. 'Were you having an affair with him, Francine? You must tell me.'

Francine stared at Victoria. There could be no doubting the astonishment on her face, but this was quickly followed by something almost like relief. 'What *are* you talking about?' she asked. 'Of course we weren't . . . Richard and *me*? For heaven's sake, Victoria – wherever did you get that idea? You have to be joking!'

Victoria twisted her hands unhappily and gazed at the floor. 'I overheard Victor Stirling and Tony Thwait discussing Richard before the funeral,' she said in a tight voice, only just under control. 'They were talking in the garden below my window. I couldn't help hearing and I desperately wish I hadn't, but I can't get what they said out of my mind. They seemed to think your engagement had the most terrible effect on Richard . . . and they were speculating as to whether, because of it . . . it wasn't an accident at all and he . . . he shot himself on purpose.' She could hardly bring herself to say the words and went on in a rush, 'It all just goes round and round in my head and it's driving me crazy. It was such a shocking thing to hear and then when you suggested Richard had tried to stop you and Guy from getting engaged before, I couldn't help wondering if you, if he ever . . . ?'

Francine stubbed out her cigarette, got up, walked over to the window and stood looking out for what seemed an age to Victoria. It was as though she was making up her mind about something. When she turned round and came back to the fireplace her face was unreadable.

'Look, Victoria,' she said, 'I was *not* having an affair with your husband. Beyond that I can't help you. I have no idea what Richard had in mind on that dreadful day but it certainly wasn't love of me. I'm truly sorry – I can see you're in a terrible state at the moment, how could you not be? – but you have to try to forget that stupid conversation or you really will go crazy. People speculate on absolutely anything, and Victor and Tony were clearly talking a load of rubbish.'

'But do you think Richard meant to kill himself?' Victoria asked, her voice scarcely more than a whisper, eyes wide with horror. 'Because the awful thing is that if he did, I don't think I can forgive him – not just for doing it to me, but to Jake. I am so angry it frightens me.'

Francine shook her head. 'You'll never know. The coroner didn't think so – hang on to that. I don't know the technicalities about firearms but maybe something made him momentarily careless. That can happen to any of us over anything. Think of driving. A momentarily lapse of concentration is all it takes for horrendous accidents to happen. It's a ghastly waste of a life, and your loss is truly terrible but at least you have nothing to blame yourself for.'

Victoria should have been reassured but she didn't feel it. 'There has to be something I'm missing,' she said obstinately. 'Nothing makes sense. It's like struggling with that awful Rubik's cube thing and not being able either to leave it alone or work it out.'

Despite the double glazing there was the sound of a plane flying overhead. When it had gone the house seemed unnaturally silent. The grandfather clock on the landing outside struck three o'clock very slowly. Victoria had never even noticed that it chimed before, though she must have heard it countless times. She had a sensation that everything in her life was now changed – like unexpectedly catching the reflection of a hitherto familiar place or person in a mirror and finding it distorted.

She got up, fearing her legs might give way beneath her, and was relieved to find they still appeared to be working normally.

'I must go. I have to pick up Jake from Toula, and anyway I've taken up enough of your time as it is.'

Francine rose too. 'That's OK – Friday afternoon's always an awful time to leave London so I won't try to delay you. Give my love to Anthony and Toula – if you think they'd like it, that is. I guess she's having problems accepting me as a daughter-in-law.' She pulled a face and gave a little shrug. 'I'm sure Guy'll be in touch as soon as he gets back. I'm sorry I haven't helped, but I hope I've put your mind at rest over one thing at least. I can promise you that if anyone was having an affair with Richard it wasn't me.'

But as Victoria walked out through the front door she was convinced there was something Francine was not telling her. She realised how little she knew about Francine – or indeed about her friends or family. If she wasn't having an affair with Richard herself, she thought, I think she knows who was.

Chapter Eight

❧

Victoria only just made the train at Paddington, so that by the time she had pelted down the platform, hurled herself on to the last coach and walked down the crowded train looking for a seat, she was exhausted. She closed her eyes but immediately felt imprisoned with such a disturbing jumble of distorted images and conflicting ideas that she thought she might indeed be going mad. As so often over the past weeks she found herself going over and over the last days of Richard's life, rerunning every scrap of conversation, searching for clues to some understanding of his state of mind; continually asking the question 'Why?'. She remembered how Jake – not only a compulsive list-maker but also a dedicated composer of stories and poems – had once put his hands over his ears when he had a high temperature and screamed at her to 'make the words in my head *stop*', and she longed for someone to do that for her. She felt as though she must be marked in some physical way by her inner turmoil and glanced at her fellow passengers to see if they were giving her curious looks – but they all appeared quite uninterested, reading their papers or talking into their mobiles. And then suddenly she fell heavily asleep, and woke only just in time get off the train at Toddingham. She had no recollection of it stopping at any of the other stations on the route and for a moment wondered where she was and how she'd got there. She snatched up her bag and almost fell out on to the platform as the train started to move again.

It was nearly six o'clock by the time she reached Durnford House. She found Jake playing mah jong with Anthony and Toula in the little book-lined sitting room next to the big drawing room. Anthony, an expert on oriental art, had picked up the set in the Far East on a buying trip for his antique business years ago, and Guy and Victoria had often played with them as children. Victoria remembered how smoothly satisfying she had found the feel of the small bricks and how fascinated she had been by the strange symbols on their ivory surfaces and the whole mystique of the game.

'Hi, Mum,' Jake said now, the morning's misery apparently forgotten. 'Look – I've got a cong of Red Dragons – my favourites – and I'm winning. We needn't go home yet, need we? We must finish our game.'

'Now, Jake,' said Toula, 'Mummy's tired. Remember what you promised me? No fuss! We'll just finish this hand and add up the scores and then you can get the box and put all the bricks away in their little drawers.' Jake gave his great-aunt a speculative look, but despite the fact that she could be amazingly indulgent if the mood took her, Toula was not someone to tangle with lightly and once the game had been cleared up he reluctantly agreed to go upstairs and have a bath so that he would be all ready for bed when he and Victoria eventually went home.

'It's Saturday tomorrow – no school – so you don't need to rush off,' said Toula when she came downstairs, having left Jake in a froth of bubble-bath, playing with Guy's battered old flotilla of boats which had that special magic that only toys that have been much loved and played with by another generation ever acquire.

'Bless you both. No . . . I suppose it doesn't much matter what time he goes to bed tonight. Perhaps he'll sleep better if he's later than usual – he's had awful nightmares for the last few nights. How have things been today?' asked Victoria.

'Absolutely fine. Mrs Atkinson said there was no trouble at all at school.'

'Thank God for that – I felt dreadful leaving him this morning. I nearly didn't go.'

'But you did – and that was good. Now, how was *your* day? Fill us in about everything.'

Victoria hesitated. She didn't want to tell Anthony and Toula too much about the uncertain prospect Peter Mason had painted for her, knowing they would immediately offer to help out financially and feeling that she had taken enough from them in that respect already. And she most certainly didn't want to tell them about the overheard conversation that had caused her to go to see Francine. She thought Toula was capable of being a difficult enough mother-in-law as it was without any trouble-making on her own part, and she desperately did not want her to guess any of the disturbing doubts she was having about Richard and start one of her inquisitions. Once Toula got her teeth into any sort of mystery she was like a terrier with a rat.

'Well,' she said, cautiously, 'nothing very conclusive but I'm glad I've got it over for the time being. You know how old Peter waffles on and wraps everything in professional jargon. I gather it'll be some time before things are sorted out and I know precisely how Jake and I are placed. There seem to be lots of complicated Cunningham trusts with funny clauses and things. Peter suggested I should take time before making any big decisions – just what you said, Uncle Anthony – but my heart rather sank because I don't want always to have to ask Peter or my pa-in-law before I take even small decisions about our lives, let alone big ones – and they seem to be very much in control. Fond as I am of Bill, I don't want him telling me exactly what I have to do about Jake and deciding which schools he's to go to. Anyway, after I'd seen Peter I had a bit of time left so I dropped in on Francine – just thought I'd pay her a goodwill call.' Anthony shot her a sharp look, but said nothing. 'I must say it was very peculiar finding her installed at The Boltons. It will take a bit of getting used to.'

'Victoria! I wish you'd told me you were thinking of doing that.' Toula was agog. 'I could have met you there and then we could have discussed it afterwards. Anthony could have arranged to fetch Jake from school. How did she seem?'

'Sickeningly glamorous, as always, and very much the hostess, but OK – perfectly friendly.'

'And why wouldn't she have been friendly?' demanded Toula, who had no intention of letting Francine get false ideas about the pecking order of the Winston women.

'She sent you both her love, by the way – pretty guardedly, I thought,' said Victoria, laughing.

'Love! She's certainly not going to have *my* love unless she earns it. I shall tell Guy to bring her down as soon as he gets home so that we can all get to know her better and you and Jake must come too, *agapi mou*. Don't just come over – come and stay the night. It would do you good. I must find out what their plans are at Easter – it's early this year – we could all have a lovely long weekend together then.'

'Well, actually . . .' Victoria hesitated for a moment, 'Jake and I might not be here at Easter. I feel I need a complete break from everything to get my head straightened out. I thought we might go out and see Nonna. What do you think?'

Toula, who had only got back from seeing her mother just before Richard's death, looked doubtful. 'Oh, darling, is that wise? I'm worried about Nonna and I don't think it would be a good idea to take Jake out there just now. She might not be up to it and the atmosphere there wouldn't be right for either of you at the moment. Not exactly cheering, with the house falling to pieces too. Why not wait to see if Nonna gets a bit better before you make a plan?' She didn't say that Victoria might be exposing herself to the possibility of another death by visiting her grandmother, but her face said it for her.

'I don't *want* cheering,' said Victoria. 'How *can* I be cheerful at the moment? I just need time to think. And I haven't seen her since the summer.' Her eyes suddenly filled with tears. 'Richard and Guy were both there then,' she said shakily. 'We all had a heavenly time together – and Nonna was in such good form. It seems a world away already. Do you realise this Christmas was the first time Nonna hasn't been with us whichever house we've all gathered in? If you're seriously worried about her that's all the more reason for me to go. I don't exactly have a crowded diary any more. It's only filled with Richard's engagements – things that don't apply now – or things that I couldn't bear to do without him. I know what you're thinking, but if anything happened to Nonna it would be quite different from what's happened to Richard and I'd want to be with her anyway. What do *you* think Uncle Anthony?'

Toula gave him a warning look and shook her head at him, but Anthony said, 'I think it might be a great idea. It would certainly do Evanthi a great deal of good to see you – you've always been so close. You might even be able to persuade her to do something about repairs – consider selling the Ritzos icon for one thing. Now that would be a positive step. But I agree with Toula. Don't take Jake. Why not leave him with us? We could easily have him, couldn't we, darling?' He turned to his wife.

Victoria shook her head doubtfully. 'I feel Jake and I need to stick together at the moment. I'm all the security he's got. But I promise I'll think about it. I'll ring Vrahos tomorrow and speak to Dora. She'll tell me what the form is and then I'll make a plan. We should be getting back now. I'll collect Jake and we'll be off. Thank you both more than I can say – for everything.'

Toula and Anthony tried to persuade her to stay the night, as they had many times over the last weeks, but she was adamant that she and Jake must get back to Manor Farm. She was afraid that if she let everyone go on cosseting and protecting her for much longer she might never manage to become truly independent at all – and this seemed vitally important. 'Don't worry – I shall be fine,' she said, giving them a brilliant smile as she shepherded a dressing-gowned Jake into her car.

They watched her go with anguish.

'She may be brave but I wish she wouldn't be so pig-headed!' said Toula, her anxiety making her sound fierce. 'She should let Violet stay in the house with her or come here, and I don't think she should go off anywhere by herself yet – especially not to Vrahos.'

'I think you're wrong. What Victoria needs is to find her own way and it doesn't matter *that* much how she does it. She's got to experiment. Try things out. She's let Richard run her entire life up to now – drifting along in a sort of dream – and I've often wondered what would happen when she woke up to her own capabilities. Your mother feels the same. The best thing we can do is to encourage her to make her own decisions and support her whatever those are.'

Toula looked unconvinced. Encouraging people to take their own decisions did not come naturally to her and there had always been a tension between her and Evanthi over Victoria: not only did they have different visions of what Victoria was like, but Toula had always been a little jealous of her mother's influence over her granddaughter.

'I don't feel happy at the thought of her alone in Manor Farm at night,' continued Toula, 'but still less do I like the idea of her leaving the house empty – even for a week – and giving that grasping Meriel Hawkins the chance to rush in and claim it for herself and her brood. I shouldn't be surprised if they moved in the minute Victoria's back's turned. And as for that pompous husband of Meriel's – I don't trust him a yard! Give any politician an inch and he'll take an elephant. You shouldn't have encouraged Victoria to go away, Anthony,' she added accusingly. 'It was so stu-u-pid of you.' Toula had a way of drawing her words out and her Greek accent, not very noticeable normally, always became much stronger when she was excited or upset.

'Oh I don't think the Hawkinses are actually likely to *seize* Manor Farm,' said Anthony, amused as always by his wife's dramatic ideas. 'That wouldn't suit Stafford's sense of dignity at all. Can you imagine the headlines: "Member of Parliament in Illicit Squat – 'Swampy' Stafford Hawkins Digs in. Widow and Orphan Turned on to Street" – or even possibly, "Widow's Aunt Knifes Politician"?'

'Don't be silly, Anthony,' said Toula crossly. 'It's not funny and that's not what I meant at all – but I shall keep my eyes pricked sharply for trouble all the same.'

Anthony gave his wife an affectionate look.

Despite Victoria's brave words, the house looked dark and unwelcoming to her as she and Jake drove up to it. It was comforting to hear Teal barking as she unlocked the back door and he gave them a rapturous welcome. One of Richard's caps was still on the oak chest in the passage – it had always been a dumping ground for dog leads, secateurs and unopened post. His coats still hung from the row of pegs along the wall. There was a growing collection of unopened farm or garden cata- logues and a pile of dreary-looking brown-enveloped letters and bills addressed to him, which Victoria had not got around to dealing with. The letters of condolence addressed to her, which had flooded in for the first three weeks, had slowed down now, though a few still trickled in from people who had missed the original announcement and only just heard the news. The letters were a comfort but also a tyranny, Victoria thought, and though many of the writers begged her not to reply she had started by trying to answer a few each day. Over the last few days, however, this good resolution had come to a temporary halt and she found she both dreaded further batches of letters and yet felt curiously let down and empty if there were none – part of the ever-shifting weather vane of her conflicting emotions.

'You sort of feel Dad might still be here don't you?' said Jake in a wobbly voice, echoing her thoughts exactly as they went upstairs together. 'Can I sleep in your bed again, Mum? Please.'

'Just for tonight then,' said Victoria. Jake had looked so cheerful and normal at the Winstons', but the sight of his white anxious face now tore her apart and she hadn't the heart to refuse him, despite the advice of various well-meaning friends that she shouldn't let him start a habit that might be hard to break later.

She had asked Dr Kirk about it when she'd rung him up to consult him about Jake's terrible nightmares and he had been reassuring. 'Follow your instincts,' he said. 'I have great respect for mothers' intuition. This is not the time to have a big battle over it. He'll kick the habit in his own time once the need is gone. If you can get him back to his own bed once he's dropped off to sleep so much the better.'

'How would you like to go out to Vrahos for the holidays?' she asked Jake now as she tucked him into the big bed. 'I thought we might pay Nonna a visit.'

'Just you and me?'

'Just you and me.'

'Cool,' said Jake. 'When can we go?'

He was asleep before she left the room.

She went downstairs and stood in the hall, knowing there were endless things that needed to be done, but feeling too unsettled to decide what to do next. The house seemed to echo round her so that she felt as though she could hear it breathing. Funny, she thought, how when you are alone you become conscious of noises that you never notice when someone else is with you: a clock ticking, the creak of old woodwork expanding and contracting with changes of temperature; noises from the central heating and the intermittent whirring from fridge or deepfreeze; little rustles that might be almost anything. Imagination could all too easily blow such mundane sounds into the stuff of terror. She was aware of a faint rhythmic beat which puzzled her . . . until she realised it was the thumping of her own heart. She gave herself a mental shake. Stop it! she said sternly to herself – do something – *anything*! At that moment the telephone started to ring and it was with relief that she went into the drawing room to answer it.

The call was from Milan.

Her first reaction was one of joy to hear Guy's voice, but she could tell from his tone that this was no ordinarily solicitous call. She thought he sounded uncharacteristically hesitant.

'I hear you went to see Francine today,' he said.

'Yes I did . . . she kindly gave me lunch.' Victoria was conscious of feeling anxious. Francine must have spoken to him after she left. Perhaps this should not have surprised her but it had not occurred to her that Guy and Francine would keep in such close touch. It spoke of an intimacy between them that she had not expected and did not want to face. I'm jealous of her, thought Victoria with dismay. I've been fooling myself . . . at this moment when I should only be minding about Richard, I'm jealous about Francine's relationship with Guy.

'Did she tell you what we talked about?' she asked.

There was a silence on the other end of the line.

'Guy? Are you still there?'

'Yes. I'm still here. And yes, Vicky . . . she did tell me why you went to see her. I gather you were full of questions that Francine felt she couldn't answer. There are things you're going to have to hear that I hoped you didn't need to know.'

'What things?' Her heart started to hammer again.

'Not things I want to talk about on the telephone.'

'Will you come down here and see me then?'

'I don't want to discuss all this at Manor Farm. It's too full of Richard. Vicky . . . Mum's just told me on the telephone that you might be going out to Vrahos. She doesn't think that's a good idea but I think it might be just what you need. Why wait till Easter? I could easily fly over to Corfu for a couple of nights. I'd have to come back here to Milan again afterwards – there are people I still need to interview – but I want to see Nonna anyway and tell her about Francine in person and I think it would be the right place for you and me to talk – our special place. How about it?'

'Oh, Guy – could you really do that? That would be wonderful. I want to go there so much.'

Where else would they go for important discussions together but to Vrahos, she thought, the house on the rock – often referred to locally as The Venetian House – which meant so much to them both? It seemed the perfect answer, and she thought how in tune they still were. Guy had always been able to read her thoughts.

'Good,' he said. 'I thought that's what you'd say.'

'Give me a day to make plans and book flights,' she said. 'I'll bring Jake and meet you there next week. Shall I tell Anthony and Toula you're going to go there too?'

'No,' he said, and again she thought he sounded wary. 'No, don't mention it yet. I often turn up with Nonna unannounced. She seems to like that and Dora always leaves my bed made up ready. No need to bother Mum and Dad. You know how Mum always wants to interfere – bless her! We don't want to have her making extra dramas at the moment.'

'Will you tell Francine?' She hated herself for asking.

'I already have,' he said. 'She thinks it would be an excellent plan. It's partly her idea too.'

Victoria winced.

'Ring me on my mobile tomorrow,' Guy said. 'Night then, Vicky darling. See you very soon – God bless.'

Victoria went on standing in the drawing room for several moments after she heard the click as Guy rang off. Then she put the receiver back and went upstairs to bed. Perhaps I'm going to learn the truth at last, she thought – but she also wondered with foreboding if she might come to wish she hadn't started asking questions in the first place.

Chapter Nine

Sophie's driving lesson started really well. The emergency stop – Sophie's favourite exercise – had been very satisfactory, and she'd done the most professional three-point turn, proving how hard she'd practised in the stable-yard at home since the last lesson. Disappointingly, Brian Swayne, her instructor, hadn't seemed *that* overwhelmed by her skill. He really did need to lighten up a bit – though he had his own little routine stock of witticisms, delivered deadpan with no change of voice or expression. Sam, who had been through the Brian Swayne experience two years before, had bet Sophie five pounds that she wouldn't be able to make him scream. Amazingly she had not yet achieved this goal, though not for want of trying.

'Let's drive on the near side not the suicide this morning, shall we?' he suggested as they swung excitingly wide round a bend, narrowly missing a tractor coming from the other direction, before they headed for the open waters of the dual carriageway, which was to be the route of this morning's adventure.

'This is wicked – it's so cool being able to forget about oncoming traffic,' Sophie said chattily, treating the accelerator to a burst of pressure as they zoomed along towards Knighton. 'Aren't I getting good at the driving jargon, Mr Swayne?'

'Drop your speed, please, Sophie.' Mr Swayne was unimpressed. 'This is a fifty-mile limit.'

'*Boring*. Oh, do look in that field! Lambs *already*!' She pointed out of the window and the car swerved alarmingly.

'Please keep both hands on the wheel and your eyes on the road, Sophie, and . . . SLOW DOWN!' Sam's fiver nearly qualified for a transfer.

'Sorry, sorry. Oh, hello, kerb!' said Sophie brightly as the car bounced against the edge of the road.

'That would have been extremely dangerous if you'd been overtaking a cyclist.' Sometimes Mr Swayne wondered why he didn't try for a less stressful job.

'But there weren't any cyclists! If there had been I *swear* I'd have seen them.'

'You didn't see the kerb.'

'Bikers aren't that low on the ground – unless they're midgets.'

But Mr Swayne, like Queen Victoria, was not amused. 'Start decelerating for the roundabout and change down now, please,' he said woodenly.

Sophie sighed. It was uphill work trying to bring a little levity into Mr Swayne's life.

They were both relieved when they arrived an hour later at Sophie's friend's house and Sophie managed to negotiate the rather narrow entrance to the Marshalls' drive without scratching the car or knocking down the gatepost.

'Thanks so much for dropping me here – you're a star, Mr Swayne. When do you think I should apply for my test?' she asked hopefully.

'You've a long way to go before I could recommend attempting that.'

'You don't have much faith in me – and nor does any one else. Mum says I'm hopeless. She doesn't think I'll ever pass and doesn't really want me to anyway.' Sophie looked so tragic that Brian Swayne – who was not as immune to her charms as she imagined, even if she did manage to make herself look outlandish – softened a little.

'You'd be all right if only you'd concentrate, Sophie,' he said earnestly. 'I've known worse – believe you me. I could tell you some tales! We could try the next lesson in your parents' car, if you want to take the test in that rather than mine.'

'No dual control? Wow! Would you really risk it? Does Mrs Swayne get worried sick about you?'

'I haven't noticed it keeping her awake nights,' said Mr Swayne drily. 'But you'd better ask your mum if she thinks it's a good idea first.'

'She won't. She'll think it's a terrible idea – I can tell you that without asking her. She won't even practise with me any more because she says I'm "completely irresponsible and a liability to myself and everyone else – and not just with driving".' Sophie had got her mother's brittle tone off to a T, but Brian Swayne was surprised to see her eyes suddenly fill with tears. Not quite as impervious to her mother's opinions as she liked to appear, perhaps.

'Well, ask your dad then,' he suggested. Privately he thought Sophie's mum was a snooty cow – you got to be a pretty fair hand at summing people up in his profession, and Mrs Hammond always made him feel as though his presence somehow offended her, but that she was managing to rise above it. Sophie's father, on the other hand, seemed a really nice chap.

'Hmm. That's a thought.' Sophie brightened up. 'I'll work on him. Thanks, Mr Swayne. See you next week then.' She blew her nose, gave him a wave and disappeared round the side of the Marshalls' house.

She and Ellie had already texted each other twice that morning but there was still a lot of catching-up to do about each other's lives because they hadn't actually spoken since the night before, and there was the crucial question to be discussed of whether Ellie's new boyfriend had e-mailed her yet or not.

The pervasive smell that greeted Sophie as she entered the house told her that Ellie had already got preparations underway for the leg-waxing session they intended to have while Ellie's mother was safely out shopping. For some obscure reason Mrs Marshall didn't like Ellie melting leg-wax in the microwave – although she did it herself – and had complained about the sticky little blobs of hairy wax that seemed to have got all over the floor last time Ellie and Sophie had turned the kitchen into a beauty-parlour. Despite this unfair attitude, Sophie thought Maggie Marshall was a pushover of a parent compared with Rachel, and was deeply envious of the relaxed relationship between mother and daughter.

'Hi there, Ellie! It's me.'

Ellie emerged from the kitchen, wet hair wrapped in a towel, dressing gown flapping open to reveal her ample curves bulging out of an extremely skimpy bra at the top and an excruciatingly uncomfortable-looking thong at the bottom.

'Oh, hi, Sophe. De-dum!' Ellie struck an attitude. 'Look at me, all stripped for action – lucky it's only you. I thought I might brave a bikini wax while we're about it. Ready for the torture? The boiling oil's just about done.'

'Oh, great. God, do I need it! Just look at my legs – I feel like a gorilla.' Sophie unzipped her skin-tight jeans and started to struggle out of them. They were a recent extravagance, disapproved of by Rachel, with which Sophie was particularly pleased. Unfortunately the enormous fringed flares on the legs – which gave her the look of a mermaid with a double tail – had been a hazard while driving and at one moment her right trouser leg had got hooked up on the accelerator – though naturally she had no intention of admitting this.

With much giggling the two girls set about coating their shins with the hot liquid, and then, once it had set, ripping it off to the accompaniment of blood-curdling shrieks.

'So how was the driving?' asked Ellie.

'Oh, brill,' said Sophie. Then she added: 'Well . . . actually it wasn't. I really messed up. Mr Swayne wittered on as usual about "ease up on your gas now" and something called "clutch bite".'

'Clutch bite? Sounds like a sexually transmitted disease.'

Sophie giggled. 'He's got this little dirge which he keeps chanting that goes "Forty . . . forty . . . maximum forty . . . keep it at forty . . . on the dot forty." It's hilarious.'

They pounded round and round the kitchen table chanting it, arms going like pistons, in a sort of Red Indian war-dance. Mr Swayne would have been very surprised.

The dance was brought to an end by the simultaneous appearance of Ellie's mother, staggering under the weight of many carrier bags after a trip to Tesco, and Patrick arriving to collect Sophie.

'What on earth are you two doing?' demanded Maggie Marshall. 'Oh no! Not the wax! Ellie, you are a fiend. I absolutely banned that and . . . darling! For goodness' sake, do your dressing gown up!'

'Oh, whoops! Sorry Patrick.' Ellie hastily tied the sash of her bathrobe. 'We were just inventing a driving dance for Sophie's instructor. Shall we give you a demo?'

'I think I saw enough to get the general idea, thank you,' said Patrick, laughing. 'I do hope you're not proposing to perform it for poor Mr Swayne, especially dressed – or rather undressed – like that. He has enough to terrify him already. Sophie, could you please put your clothes on? We must get back or we'll be late for lunch.'

'Oh, don't go yet. Can't Sophie stay a bit longer? We haven't begun to talk about half the things we need to discuss.'

'It continually amazes me how you never seem to run out of things to say.' Patrick gave the girls an amused look. 'I keep thinking the flow must dry up sometime but I don't suppose it would make any difference how ever long you had.'

'You're welcome to stay and have a snack with us here if you like,' suggested Maggie. 'Won't be proper lunch – not up to Rachel's standard – but we've got some soup and lots of bits of rather dubious cheese that need finishing up. Phil's playing golf but he said he might be back. He'd love to see you.'

'Oh, please, Dad,' begged Sophie and the two girls looked at Patrick hopefully. He felt tempted to stay on in the relaxed and friendly atmosphere of the Marshalls' happy-go-lucky household but the thought of the tension this might spark at home made him resist.

'No, I'm sorry. It's a lovely idea, Maggie, but we really must be getting home. I've got work to do and Rachel's expecting us back for lunch.'

'Oh, well, give Rachel my love. I hardly ever see her nowadays,' said Maggie. 'We make arrangements about daughters on the telephone but I never seem able to persuade her to come over for kitchen lunch or to meet in Knighton like we used to do – and I don't think she's been to the book club since before Posy was born. Where does she hide herself? We miss her.'

'I miss her too,' said Patrick – and then wished he hadn't.

Maggie shot him a sharp look. She thought Rachel Hammond was very foolish to neglect her husband. There were plenty of women around who would be only too happy to take him off her hands if Rachel didn't want him and there were rumours that she was giving him a hard time.

'Poor old Sophe,' said Ellie to her mother as Patrick's car

disappeared down the drive. 'She's awfully down at the moment – I'm really worried about her. I think her mum's absolutely foul to her – specially with her AS levels coming up this summer. She works *so* hard too – her dyslexia makes it even harder, and she never gets any encouragement.'

'Not even from Patrick?'

'Oh, well, yes – he's lovely. But she's worried sick about him too. She says he tries to stick up for her mum and make excuses for her but you can see he's getting fed up about Rachel's fixation with that weird counsellor lady she goes to *and* the fact that she can't think of anything else except that spoiled brat Posy. Sophie says it's really boring. Mum . . . can I ask you something?' Ellie sounded so serious that Maggie wondered what was coming.

'Hmm,' she murmured cautiously. 'You can always *ask* me anything – I don't guarantee to answer.'

'Do you like Sophie's mum? I mean I know Patrick's an old friend of Dad's . . . but how much do you actually like *Rachel*?'

'I used to,' said Maggie, rather sadly, 'but I'm beginning to wonder if I really know her. When you were little we used to have fun together. Apart from being so smart and pretty, Rachel's very bright, you know – she could have had a good career in publishing but she just gave it all up the moment she got married. She's always been a bit highly strung and Patrick smoothed her path and protected her – I used to feel quite envious sometimes. We used to talk books and things but now I don't seem able to make contact.'

'She always makes me feel a nuisance if I go there for a meal,' said Ellie. 'As if one extra was a huge amount of trouble. Not like you, Mum,' she added affectionately. 'That's why Sophe loves coming here so much.'

Maggie was touched. 'Well, I have to admit Rachel wouldn't be my first call if I needed help,' she said drily. 'I can't really answer your question, darling, because I don't know myself. Must be a bit difficult for Patrick.'

'Sophie says life at home's becoming impossible,' said Ellie. 'She doesn't know what to do about her parents. Any suggestions? We're trying to think of helpful plots to sort them out.'

'Well, *don't*,' said her mother, quite sharply for her. 'It's very unwise to meddle in people's marriages – even if they're your own parents. Lots of marriages go through tricky patches and they'll have to sort it out for themselves.'

Ellie looked unconvinced.

Father and daughter thoroughly enjoyed each other's company on the drive home. Sophie made Patrick laugh by regaling the perils of the driving lesson and he told her about Hugh Marston's lost love.

'Wow,' breathed Sophie. 'How romantic! I wonder if she's still alive? Do you think Uncle Hugh would tell me about it?'

'He might – he's always had a specially soft spot for you. You'll have to ask him. All these years and he's never said a word about her before! But suddenly I think he needed to tell someone – and it must be one of the best portraits he's ever done. Why don't you ride over tomorrow and pay him a visit – good exercise for you and Punch. Give him or Mrs Parkes a ring first though. By the way . . . he said he might like to paint you sometime. How about that?'

Sophie went pink with pleasure.

When they got back home there was a note propped against the fruit bowl on the kitchen table: 'Posy and I've gone to Bronwen's for lunch,' it read.

'Well, really!' exploded Sophie. 'Talk about double standards! Now if she'd got lunch ready and we hadn't turned up there'd have been *mega* trouble. Why does everything *we* do have to be such a big deal with Mum – but she can always do what she wants? We could have stayed at the Marshalls after all. Sometimes I do think she's . . .' Then she looked at Patrick's face and swallowed the words back.

'Never mind, Dad,' she said, conscious of a lump in her throat. 'Shall we have a fry-up and send our cholesterol levels through the ceiling? It's just what I feel like.'

She had every intention of leaving the kitchen in a terrible mess. She would really enjoy the row that this would certainly engender with her mother later and would give her the chance to vent some opinions, which were only partly connected to immaculate kitchens, and calorie-controlled food. Sophie

93

savoured the knowledge that this time she would almost certainly go much too far.

'What a very good idea,' said Patrick, smiling at his daughter. 'Isn't that lucky then – because a fry-up is just what I feel like too. Let's have fun.'

He suddenly felt very angry with Rachel, and a small iron filing entered his soul and lodged there.

Chapter 10

When Rachel had first arrived on Bronwen Richards' doorstep, two and a half years ago, she was already regretting the impulse that had led her to make the appointment. It was a day of drenching rain and had she not been feeling so desperate about her pregnancy she might have turned tail and bolted straight home again; as it was, she hesitated in the porch outside the Old Chapel House, trying to make up her mind whether or not to wield the huge wrought-iron knocker on the nail-studded door – there didn't seem to be a bell – when it was flung open and the option to flee was no longer there.

'Hi,' said the tall woman who stood there. 'You must be Rachel Hammond. Come on in.' She stood aside to let Rachel into the house. 'I don't bite.' She raised a quizzical eyebrow at her visitor.

'Oh,' Rachel was disconcerted. 'Well . . . thank you.' She stepped cautiously inside, not knowing what to expect.

Her first impression was one of space and light. Except for the stone surrounds to doors and windows, the walls were plastered and painted white. Halfway along the high-ceilinged room, the level had been split and curved wooden stairs led up to some kind of gallery. Sleeping quarters presumably, thought Rachel. The wooden floor was sealed in a pale finish and a large white rug in the centre of the room – where pews might have been – was rolled back. Small mats were laid in a circle round the edge of this space. She imagined a yoga class had been taking place.

It had been one of those cold, wet summer days when, despite the unseasonable temperature outside, some people are unwilling to turn the heating on, but to Rachel's relief the house was pleasantly warm. At the far end of the room, in the place where an altar must have stood, a wood-burning stove crackled and hissed – the original altar-rails making a convenient sort of club fender round it. Two sofas, covered with coarse cotton throws patterned in earthy colours of ochre, rust and green, looked invitingly squashy. There were evergreen plants in terracotta pots, and a bowl of roses mixed with sprays of philadelphus filled the air with the scent of summer; there was also a distinct smell of incense – which Rachel thought must make the long-gone Methodist ministers spin uneasily in their graves.

On the walls hung an assortment of old keys of every size and shape, from huge old iron ones, which might have opened the medieval doors of castles, to modern Chubb and Yale ones. They were brilliantly arranged in circular and fan-shaped patterns and made an arresting decoration – but there was something disturbing about them all the same. Left to herself Rachel was not an adventurous interior decorator but she had not lived with Patrick for twenty years without acquiring an eye for the interesting and unusual. Their own house reflected his taste more than hers and until recently she had gone along with this, enjoying the results of some of his more innovative ideas – though he was meticulous about consulting her first. She didn't know if she liked this house or not, but her first thought was that Patrick would find it interesting and might want to photograph it. Apart from his increasingly successful books, he sometimes did articles for glossy interior-decorating magazines and was always on the lookout for new projects.

'I must have driven past this place loads of times,' she said, looking round, 'but I hadn't realised it had been turned into a private house. I believe I've seen you somewhere before too.'

'You have – several times – but you didn't seem very receptive to smiles from strangers.' Bronwen looked amused. 'No doubt you've heard about me too – I seem to have given this village something new to talk about. I had terrible trouble getting planning permission – not because I wanted to do anything architecturally outrageous, but because someone put about a rumour that I'm a witch!' She laughed uproariously.

Her long dark hair was streaked with grey, though her face, unadorned by make-up, looked quite youthful. She could have been any age between thirty and fifty. She wore a gaudily patterned dress that reached to her ankles, a long cardigan with silver acorn buttons and a great many silver chains and bangles. On her feet were the kind of heavy leather sandals much advertised in mail-order catalogues for camping clothes. She had strong hawk-like features and a tan that could not have been caused by the recent weather in England. If a feather had been stuck in the brilliant yellow scarf that was bound round her head, Minnehaha might have sprung to mind. She did not look like Rachel's kind of person at all.

Rachel had first noticed the newcomer when she was exercising the dogs down by the river but until now had not made a connection between the advertisement in the health-food shop and the arresting woman in front of her. Had she done so she would certainly not have booked the appointment. She had imagined an efficient-looking professional, of a vaguely medical nature, wearing a crisp white coat – a sort of cross between a beauty therapist and a nurse; someone who would be eager for her custom, perhaps even a little deferential, certainly sympathetic. When she had seen her on the walks, the woman had sometimes been accompanied by a man, occasionally by a child – once by a goat.

She had also noticed her on a Sunday morning, coming out of church when the Hammonds and the rest of the congregation were on their way in. There was nothing particularly unusual about that: the church of Kirkby-Wytherton, with its medieval tower, famous crusader tombs and beautiful setting by the river Wythie was a well-known tourist spot and often attracted summer visitors; it was more that this woman was extra-ordinarily noticeable, with her wild hair, bright, eccentric clothes and strong, fierce face. Rachel had found her eyes following her as though drawn by a magnet, and been disconcerted when the woman caught her gaze, raised an enquiring eyebrow and nodded at her. Not given to casual greetings with strangers, Rachel had given her a tight little smile and turned hastily round to face the altar and busy herself with her hymn book. But she'd had the greatest difficulty in preventing herself from looking back.

'So,' said Bronwen, looking at Rachel and giving the uncomfortable impression that she was assessing what she saw, 'tell me why you've come to see me?'

'Because,' answered Rachel, 'I made an appointment with you on the telephone. We spoke last week.'

'We did and I'm expecting you. But why did you make the appointment?'

'You advertised in Sutcliffe's window in Lower Knighton.' Rachel was beginning to feel threatened. She knew her voice sounded unfriendly as it often did when she was faced with unfamiliar situations. 'It said—'

'Oh, I know what I put in the advertisement. What I want to know is what made you think you need my help. You were adamant on the phone that you weren't interested in joining any of my weekly classes and wouldn't want to be part of a group. What is it you hope I can do for you on a one-to-one basis?'

There was a silence. Bronwen didn't appear at all bothered by this and just stood there letting the silence grow and grow around them as though it was something tangible, enclosing them in a bubble of glass.

Rachel felt panicky. What on earth *had* made her come here – she who took care never to wear her heart anywhere near her sleeve and was always uneasy about attempts to breach her reserve? She, who considered herself to be so sophisticated and accomplished at dealing with surface small talk and making dinner-party conversation; who liked to feel in control of social situations, was struck dumb. She stared at this confident woman like a hypnotised rabbit caught in the headlights of an oncoming car.

'I don't know,' she said at last.

'Was it perhaps,' asked Bronwen, 'that you were desperate about something and knew you needed help? Was it that you thought you might feel safe talking to a stranger?'

And Rachel, to her own astonishment, had found tears pouring down her face.

That had been the first visit.

Bronwen used her living room for group meetings or classes. Opening off it on one side was a kitchen, and on the other a small therapy room – perhaps the vestry of the old chapel – where she gave individual counselling sessions and various treatments. On that first visit, this room had seemed less threatening to Rachel than the main one – more what she had expected – with its black leather reclining chair, treatment couch, book-lined walls and stereo-system.

Bronwen had seated herself at a business-like desk and asked her a great many questions while making copious notes. What foods did Rachel like? Was she afraid of thunder? If she sat on a bench would she choose to sit in the middle or at the end? Did she dream much? What was her earliest memory? Did she mind heights? How did she react to spiders? To begin with Rachel felt sceptical about the relevance of these queries but after a bit she began to feel as though, inadvertently, she was giving away an extraordinarily revealing picture of herself. Bronwen then suggested Rachel should tip the chair back, and close her eyes and she and Bronwen would go through some relaxation exercises.

She switched on some music full of the sound of waves breaking on a beach and birds singing in some echoing forest; bells chimed. Rachel found herself overcome with drowsiness – the suggestion that her eyelids felt heavy was only too true. It seemed easy to follow Bronwen's other suggestions and visualise herself walking down a narrow, twisting path that led to a special place of her own choosing – a sunlit place; a beautiful place; above all a safe place that nobody could enter except by Rachel's express invitation.

When – it seemed only moments later – Bronwen's voice announced that she should take some long, deep breaths, gradually become aware again of the room and the everyday world, and that on the count of five she should then open her eyes, she had felt loath to leave the idyllic garden that she had invented for herself. Nevertheless, on the count of five her eyes sprung open as though they had been operated by a switch.

'Goodness.' Rachel blinked in surprise, feeling as though she had returned from a long journey. 'I never normally sleep during the day but I think I might have dropped off for a moment or two. I do apologise. What time is it?'

'It's half-past three. You've been here for over an hour. Now I'll give you a tape to listen to at home and I'd like you to practise the relaxation exercises on it – just for fifteen minutes – every day until I see you again in a fortnight. And please drink at least eight glasses of water a day. Could you manage that?'

Rachel said she could.

On about her third visit, in response to Bronwen's casual questions she had found herself suddenly back again in the terrible time after Sam was born, sobbing uncontrollably with terror and shame at her inability to love her child.

'That was terrible,' she said afterwards.

'Yes. But I think we're getting somewhere,' said Bronwen. 'Next time we'll go further back.'

To start with Patrick was impressed with the effect that her latest therapist was having on his wife. He often felt that his protectiveness in their early married years had been partly responsible for encouraging her neuroses to get out of hand and was pleased that this time she seemed to have sought help from someone who sounded effective. He thought some of Rachel's previous health gurus had been extremely dubious – not to say cranky. Sam would have been surprised to know that he was not the only one to find Bronwen sexy – his father found her disturbing too. He had first met her when Rachel asked her round for supper one evening and had thought her intriguing company. Bronwen had travelled as widely as he had, and was knowledgeable about some unlikely topics. They had argued enjoyably about religion and art and each found the other a worthy adversary. He was pleased that Rachel – normally more conventional about friendships than he was – had gained the confidence to branch out a little beyond her usual tight social circle.

'I'm intrigued by your new friend, darling,' he said. 'She's unusual.'

To his surprise, Rachel had not seemed particularly pleased at his approval.

It was difficult to learn much about this newcomer to the neighbourhood because she was sparing with information about herself and could be tantalisingly evasive if questioned directly. Trying to put her life story together was like doing a colourful jigsaw puzzle and discovering that a great many pieces were missing.

Bronwen confirmed the village gossip that the man Rachel had first seen with her was her current lover – though, apart from this strenuous role, she did not volunteer any information about what his other occupation might be. No one seemed to know much about him. Yvonne, round-eyed, said she'd heard he was connected with the IRA. What he was not, apparently, was a fixture in Bronwen's life, and she seemed amazed at any assumption that he might ever become one.

'*Marry* Milo?' she replied in response to a query of Rachel's. 'What on earth would I want to do that for?' He was certainly not the father of her daughter – eleven-year-old Hetta – a self-possessed child who was sometimes in residence at the Old Chapel House. In answer to Rachel's cautious probing Bronwen replied vaguely that Hetta mostly lived with her father and his other children – older and younger than Hetta – in Spain. She seemed casually pleased when the child came to stay – completely unfazed when she left.

'What about her schooling?' asked Rachel, herself the dreaded grand inquisitress of her children's teachers, who liked to know exactly how Sam and Sophie's education was progressing.

'Oh, her father sees she gets enough of that,' replied Bronwen, as though she were talking about eating fresh vegetables. 'The schools in Spain are supposed to be quite good.'

'Is Hetta's father Spanish then?'

'Partly – among other nationalities.' Bronwen was not in a communicative mood.

The calm casualness of the relationship with Hetta astonished Rachel too. 'Don't you feel the need to go and check the school out?' she had persisted. 'I would.'

'Yes, I'm sure you would.' Bronwen looked amused. 'But it's not compulsory to put yourself on the rack over every detail in order to be an adequate mother.'

The goat, on the other hand, *was* a fixture. It lived in a shed in the patch of garden – once the graveyard – at the back of the house. Bronwen said it helped to keep the brambles down. It sometimes accompanied her on walks and occasionally – to Rachel's horror – was allowed in the house. Bronwen sold its milk at Sutcliffe's Health-food Shop, which was run by a member of her meditation group.

*

It was only gradually that two things started to dawn on Patrick: one was that though Rachel was apparently losing a few of her long-standing anxieties, she seemed to be exchanging them for a new set of obsessions. The other, and infinitely more disturbing thing, was that she no longer appeared either to want or need him.

Initially, he was delighted by Rachel's involvement with the new baby – something he had not dared to hope for – and gave Bronwen full credit for this development. But he had taken it for granted that he would still be required to play the part of a hands-on father himself. He was taken unawares when it first became obvious that Rachel not only did not require his assistance with Posy, but resented him having anything to do with her at all.

The first time he became alerted to this state of affairs was when Posy was only a few weeks old and Patrick had staggered out of bed to go to her in the night as he had often done with Sam and Sophie. He had just picked his squalling, furious daughter out of her cot, when Rachel appeared like an avenging fury and snatched the baby from him.

'Don't touch her,' she had hissed. 'Leave her to me.'

To say that Patrick was astonished would have been an understatement, but he told himself this unbalanced reaction would soon right itself and was anyway a huge improvement on Rachel's previous horror of small babies. She was actually breast-feeding this baby – something she had never done before. However, as the months went by, Rachel's possessiveness got worse rather than better. She was still going for counselling sessions every few weeks, and as Bronwen had apparently brought about the change in her attitude to childbearing, it seemed obvious to seek her advice about the way the pendulum had swung too far the other way, since Rachel herself refused to discuss the subject with him.

When Posy was about nine months old he chose a day when his wife had gone to visit her elderly parents and rang Bronwen up. He was relieved that she answered the telephone herself because he didn't really want to leave a message on her answering machine.

'Hello there, Patrick.' Bronwen had an attractively husky

voice and the musical lilt in her speech hinted at Welsh ancestry. 'What a nice surprise to hear you. What can I do for you?'

'I wondered if I could possibly come and see you sometime?'

'Well, wouldn't that be nice? Of course you can.'

'When could you manage to fit me in?'

'How about coming round straight away? No time like the present.'

'That's extremely kind of you.' This was far more helpful than he'd dared to hope. 'Actually, it would suit wonderfully well. Rachel's gone to see her parents but I never imagined there'd be any chance of you being free at such short notice. What a bit of luck.'

'Oh, I'm free,' Bronwen had said.

Patrick drove the four miles to the Old Chapel House feeling relieved that help was at hand. Perhaps he ought to have talked to Bronwen weeks ago? He felt uncomfortable about going behind Rachel's back – he'd never had secrets from her – but then it had never been so impossible to communicate with her before. No doubt Bronwen would advise him what he should do.

He parked the car outside the house and walked briskly up the path. Bronwen must have been looking out for him because she was standing in the doorway. She was wearing the most extraordinarily voluminous garment that reminded Patrick of a Bedouin tent in an old Hollywood movie. He would not have been surprised if Rudolph Valentino had stepped out from under her skirts, and he thought he must remember to tell Rachel – though shared amusement had not been on the menu lately.

'How good of you to fit me in . . .' said Patrick, holding out his hand to her and coming straight to the point. 'I need to talk to you about Rachel – I'm very worried about her.' Bronwen raised her eyebrows and did not shake his proffered hand. 'Oh,' she said. 'And I thought you'd come to see round my house? Houses are one of your . . . passions . . . aren't they? Or perhaps we could continue one of our interesting discussions? Am to take it this is not a social call then?'

'Well, no . . .' Patrick was taken aback. 'That is, of course, I'd love to see your house – I know Rachel was most impressed by it the first time she came to see you – but perhaps I should have explained on the telephone. I'm seeking your help in your professional capacity – and it goes without saying I shall expect a bill, no nonsense about that, please. I wouldn't dream of presuming on your friendship . . . I'd hate you to think that.'

'What a pity.' Bronwen looked him up and down. Patrick started to feel uncomfortable.

'The thing is I want your advice about Rachel.'

'I'm sorry, I'm afraid I don't "do" advice.' She gave him an enigmatic smile. 'I do lots of other things,' she said, 'but not advice.'

'But you advise Rachel,' he'd protested. 'You've done wonders for her.' He smiled at her. 'She's always quoting you at me.'

Bronwen shrugged. 'Too bad. I'm afraid I can't help that. I assure you I don't tell Rachel what to do. I hope I enable her to think for herself.'

'But she's changed so dramatically – she's really quite different.'

'And you don't think she needed to change?'

'Well, yes . . . perhaps in many ways she did. Don't we all? I'm sure I do too.' Patrick wondered how he'd managed to antagonise Bronwen so quickly. Perhaps she thought he was meaning to criticise her treatment of Rachel. He certainly hadn't intended to.

'Don't think I'm not grateful,' he said. 'You've helped her enormously over the baby . . . it's just that along the way something seems to have changed in our own relationship . . . something precious has gone missing. She doesn't enjoy doing any of the things we used to do together.' Even as he said this he realised that more could be read into this than he either intended – or meant.

Bronwen stood looking up at him. She was a tall woman but Patrick was taller. As she moved a shaft of sunlight struck her and Patrick felt absolutely certain that far from having Rudolph Valentino disguised beneath her robe, she had nothing beneath it at all.

'*We* could enjoy ourselves together – you and I,' she said softly. 'I think we could have a lot of fun.'

Patrick froze. What a fool he'd been! 'I'm sorry but I'm afraid I don't "do" that kind of fun,' he said icily, flinging her own words back at her, and added emphatically: 'Especially not with my wife's friends.'

The uncomfortable knowledge that her invitation excited him made him furious with himself.

'Suit yourself,' said Bronwen lightly, challenging him – mocking him. 'But – you may regret it.' She held the door open for him, and as he walked out Patrick knew he had made an enemy.

He made a complete mess of telling Rachel about his encounter with Bronwen. The more he tried to explain, the worse it got. She had been incandescent with rage that he should have encroached on her privacy in this way.

It was after this that Bronwen had started to become so indispensable to Rachel that hardly a day went by without them meeting.

Chapter Eleven

Jake leaned heavily against Victoria and twiddled a strand of hair at the top of his head so that it stuck up on end like his hero Tintin's quiff – always a sign he was over-tired.

'I'm thirsty, Mum,' he said.

Victoria groped in the backpack for a carton of juice. Sod's law, she thought: Jake would almost certainly fall asleep just before their flight was called and then she would have a struggle to wake him up. 'Here – drink this. It'll keep you going,' she said encouragingly. 'You've been such a good boy, darling. Not long now.'

'That's what you said in London.'

'I know, and it's been an awful day but hang on a bit longer because we really are almost there. I'm sorry, darling. Perhaps I shouldn't have brought you after all.'

The flight to Athens had been delayed for hours at Heathrow, causing them to miss their flight to Corfu – the direct flights to the island not yet having started for the tourist season. Now they were stuck at Athens airport and she knew it would be well after midnight before they arrived at Vrahos. She hoped Dora's husband, Yannis, had checked with Olympic Airways before setting out to meet them in Evanthi's battered old car and would not have been waiting at Kerkyra for hours. She had tried to ring Dora to warn her of the delay but had not been able to get through – the house telephone system at Vrahos being unpredictable.

'Would you like me to read to you again?' she asked. Jake shook his head and tucked his hand into hers.

'I'm all right, Mum,' he said. 'I'm still glad we came.' Victoria felt the tears pricking her eyes.

No one thought it a good idea when she'd decided to bring Jake with her to Corfu straight away and not wait till the school holidays. Had she not been so newly bereaved that everyone – except Toula – felt they had to treat her as if they were wearing kid gloves, she knew she would have encountered even more opposition.

'Oh, Victoria, do you think that's wise?' kind Mrs Atkinson had said doubtfully. 'Jake's only just beginning to settle back at school – it does seem a pity to disrupt him so soon unless you have to. I gather your grandmother's been ill but I know from Mrs Winston that she'd be only too pleased to have Jake to stay . . . and the holidays start in a couple of weeks anyway. Couldn't you wait till then? It isn't that his work matters – Jake's very advanced for his age – but it will be harder for him to start next term if he breaks with all his friends now. Routine is the best thing for children when they're disturbed.'

Victoria had nodded and smiled and listened – but remained adamant. How could she explain to Toula and Anthony, who had so unhesitatingly taken her in and always treated her like their own child, that the memory that haunted her most about her own childhood loss was of being parted from her grandmother so soon after her parents were killed? It still gave her a hollow feeling in the pit of her stomach to remember the wrench of saying goodbye to Evanthi when Toula had come to fetch her. Evanthi had wanted to accompany her and stay with her in England for the first few months, but had been overruled. It must have been extremely difficult for the Winstons to say no to Evanthi at the time – herself utterly grief-stricken at the loss of the son she had adored and passionately wanting to cling on to his only child, but with hindsight, Victoria understood the stand they had taken. Evanthi would have queried Toula's every decision, and Victoria have continued to turn to her grandmother rather than her aunt.

The terms of Constantine Doukas's will, however, had been clear: he had appointed his brother-in-law, Anthony Winston, as the sole guardian of his daughter – and it had turned out to be a wise choice. She thought it said much for Anthony that he had managed for all those years to act as referee between his wife and mother-in-law – and retain the respect and devotion of them both. All the same, remembering her own bewildered anguish, there was no way she was going to inflict any parting, even a very short one on Jake at the moment.

'I think you're being very selfish, darling,' said Toula, who had never known how to beat around a bush, though Victoria found her directness a relief, bringing some normality back to her disrupted life. 'Go yourself – though I can't see what all this rush is about. Nonna seems to have weathered the latest crisis. Don't drag Jake out with you.'

'Oh, Toula,' said Victoria, 'first you didn't want me to go until Nonna was better – now she's better and you still don't want me to go.'

Toula waved her arms dismissively. 'I don't see why it has become urgent for you to go immediately.'

'I just need to go – I can't explain it.'

She did not mention Guy's telephone call.

Her reminiscing was interrupted by the announcement that their flight was being called at last.

'Come on, Jake – last lap. Let's pick up all our bits.'

The new Athens airport – so much more glamorous than the old one – was all blue and silver, with huge expanses of slippery floor that made Jake pretend it was a skating rink and go skidding towards the escalators with their trolley to the danger of other travellers, his energy miraculously restored. They made their way to the departure gates on the lower level and out to the small plane for the short flight to Corfu.

Yannis was waiting for them outside the airport – practically deserted now in contrast to the usual summer pandemonium. Jake, who adored him, launched himself like a missile into Yannis' muscular arms, winding his own bony little legs round Yannis' stocky bulk in a rapture of greeting.

Yannis' soulful black eyes filled with tears as he gently put Jake down and clasped both Victoria's hands in his, making grunts of sympathy and muttering incoherently about Richard and guns and the strange ways of the Almighty. *O The' mou!* He and Dora have never been so shocked! And Kyria Doukas too! But Victoria has done the right thing to come home – one should always be with one's own people in times of trouble. Nafsica, his wife's grandmother (Yannis rolled his eyes and shrugged at the thought of her), had, of course, seen this death coming when she read the tarot at Christmas – everyone knew that Nafsica had 'The Sight'. But now that she was back where she belonged, he knew Victoria would recover. It might take time, of course, but she'd see how much better she and Jake would start to feel soon. Dora had some good *avoglimono* waiting for them in the kitchen and they'd be home in no time now – trust Yannis to see to that! Knowing his adventurous driving of old, Victoria could believe this all too readily and hoped they were not about to beat all records round the hairpin bends and sheer drops that were an inevitable part of the excitement of arrivals at Vrahos.

'How are Dora and Angelo?'

'Well – very well.' Dora was looking forward to seeing Victoria, and Angelo to playing with Jake again. Angelo had started at the village school now that he was six and was doing well. 'He is clever. A fine boy – very handsome, like his father!' said Yannis modestly.

'And how is Nonna?'

Yannis took both hands off the wheel to demonstrate that his employer was only so-so, 'like this and like that', but would doubtless be better for seeing Victoria. Yes, Nafsica was all right too – old, of course, and suffering from the rheumatics, but her tongue was as sharp as ever, more's the pity. There were too many dogs as usual, but Kyria would keep taking in strays. One of the cats had died, but they had rescued a new one with her litter of kittens and Jake could choose one for himself. He turned round to wink at Jake over his shoulder, only just managing to wrench the car to the right in the nick of time to avoid an oncoming car – both drivers indulging in a hugely pleasurable exchange of insult-by-horn.

After turning off the main route out of Kérkyra, the road started to rise dramatically and snake its way along the coast, the occasional dilapidated metal barrier providing scant protection from the sheer drop on the right-hand side of the road. Even Yannis had to slow down as they passed through the villages en route, where there was little enough room for one car, let alone for two, to thread its way between ancient houses that leaned towards each other like eager lovers from either side of the road.

The turning to Vrahos came unexpectedly in the middle of a fearsome bend, so that it was easy even in broad daylight to miss the overgrown stone pillars that marked the entrance, and which bore the arms of Evanthi's mother's family, the Grammenos. Despite detailed maps being drawn for them, visitors usually overshot it and had to go several kilometres further down the road before they could find a safe turning place and retrace their route – which then involved a hazardous left-hand turn across oncoming traffic. Yannis, of course, knew the route like the back of his work-roughened brown hand. Victoria felt the familiar lifting of her heart as he turned the car in past the open wrought-iron gates – battered by age but still beautiful like so much at Vrahos – and started rattling along the rutted, mile-long track that led to the house. To call it a drive would have been a misnomer.

Arrivals, thought Victoria – that's what I have to concentrate on now. I've had this bewildering departure forced on me and I have no choice but to learn to live with its consequences, try to unravel its mystery, free its matted threads of tangles – and rewind it into something worthwhile for myself and Jake.

She suddenly remembered Evanthi's stories of the hardships of war after the German invasion of Greece: the nagging daily fear, constantly counter-balanced by small acts of courage, that became the daily lot of an exhausted and bewildered people; the hunger and the shortages; the cold of a harsh winter and how every outworn woollen garment had been laboriously and carefully unpicked; the wriggling snakes of unravelled wool wound into skeins, then washed and dried, before being rolled into balls and knitted up again into something different – new socks or scarves made from old, threadbare sweaters; children's jerseys created in variegated stripes from all sorts of odds and ends. She had once shown a small Victoria, who had been supplied by Nafsica with a bag of leftover wool and was engaged at the time in trying to knit a coat for her teddy-bear, how to fray the ends of two different lengths of wool, place them on the palm of her hand, spit on them and carefully roll and roll them together till the join was invisible and – hey presto! – soon you had a wonderful rainbow ball of who-knew-how-many different shades of wool with which to make a thrilling coat-of-many-colours.

'Nothing was ever allowed to be wasted in those days, you see,' Evanthi had explained, 'and it made us all wonderfully resourceful. We surprised ourselves, not only by learning how to do things we wouldn't once have thought of attempting, but by becoming extremely skilled at all sorts of unlikely occupations. Sometimes we had to become devious too. We dissembled in order to survive.'

I will survive, vowed Victoria, as Yannis brought the old car to a shuddering halt. I will dissemble if I have to – to protect Jake from the truth until he is older – but I will unpick, and repick and make a new life for myself and for him. Perhaps it will be a life of many colours.

Chapter Twelve

Victoria woke the next morning and momentarily wondered where she was as she opened her eyes to see the barred stripes of light and shade on the wall opposite where sunlight filtered through the shutters. Then she remembered, and lay savouring every familiar sensation of the room in which she had so often slept since she was a little girl.

She fingered the heavy white cotton cover, and its coarse weave felt as reassuring to her touch as it had when she was Jake's age and used to rub it between finger and thumb before dropping off to sleep; she knew exactly what sound the enormous, creaky old bed would make if she turned over and she reached a hand above her head to feel the satisfying slender curves of the antique wrought-iron bedstead. As a little girl she had thought this was the most wonderful bed in the whole world – a bed for a princess in a fairy tale – and still found the elegant designs of gilded flowers and fruit on the lacquered tin cut-outs at the head and foot, both beautiful and unusual. Unlike Evanthi's dark and fascinating bedroom, with all its treasures and clutter, this room was white and sparsely furnished – even the wooden ceiling was painted white – and the effect of its tranquillity was like a soothing balm for overwrought emotions; a cool compress on her bruised and battered spirit.

I've slept the whole night through, she thought in astonishment and felt rested for the first time in weeks.

She got out of bed and flung the shutters open. Far below lay the sea, the intensity of its colour a shock after the greyness of English winter – like opening one's eyes to the windows of Chartres after closing them on the plain glass of a Scottish kirk, she thought. Though it was a breathlessly still morning, she could see little flecks of white on the stretch of sea that lay between the island and the rugged, forbidding coast of Albania.

There must have been a stiff wind during the night for those galloping white horses to be visible from this height, she thought, and saw that the Albanian mountains, standing this morning against a Madonna sky, were still snow-covered – a reminder that despite the warmth of the sun now pouring through the windows, winter still had the high places in its grip. She looked at her watch and was relieved to see it was not yet eight – she had been afraid she might oversleep – and she padded barefoot into the little dressing room next door to see how Jake was, expecting him still to be dead to the world and intending to leave him to have a lie-in. But his bed was pulled back and he was no longer there. He must have gone out through the other door that led on to the landing.

Victoria unearthed a pair of jeans, a clean T-shirt and a jersey from her suitcase – she had been far too tired the night before to contemplate unpacking and had done no more than pull out her own and Jake's night-things before falling into bed.

She had not expected to see her grandmother till the morning, but Dora, clucking round Jake, had laughed at her as she dished out soup to them both in the kitchen. 'Do you think she would forgive me if I didn't let you see her tonight?' she had asked, speaking in Greek as she usually did to Victoria. 'She will be listening for you and I wouldn't dare face her in the morning if she hadn't seen you! I will get Jake into bed. You go on up and see Kyria.'

Victoria had gone upstairs and opened the bedroom door very softly. As she poked her head round it her nostrils were assailed by the familiar delicious smell she associated with her grandmother. Evanthi had worn the same scent as long as Victoria could remember – it was specially made up for her by a perfumer in Grasse and the mix of ingredients was a state secret. Somehow it never smelled as delicious on anyone else and was always a disappointment to the privileged few, such as Toula and Victoria, who had been allowed to try it. Evanthi was propped up against a pile of pillows, wide awake, her beautiful hair lying over one shoulder of her silk dressing gown in a long plait, the pointed nose of Tomasina, the little Italian greyhound, who was stitched to Evanthi's side like Peter Pan's shadow, just visible under the covers at the foot of the bed.

'*Agapi!*' she said, holding out her arms. '*Chrysso mou!* You are here at last!' and Victoria had kneeled by the great high bed and buried her own dark head against her grandmother. She had talked for ages, pouring out not only the horrors of what had happened but voicing some of the fears that haunted her now – the agonising suspicion that Richard's death might not have been an accident after all, though she had not elaborated about this or told her grandmother about her visit to Francine. Evanthi had not said much, apart from asking the occasional, prompting question, and certainly hadn't volunteered her own opinions; she had just given her granddaughter the sympathetic, focused attention that is perhaps the most valuable gift to the bereaved – and listened.

'Oh, Nonna – it is *so* wonderful to see you,' said Victoria at last. 'You don't look half as bad as I feared you might – and I always forget how beautiful you still are – but what a selfish monster I am! You've been so ill and now I must have worn you out. It's two o'clock in the morning!'

'But I'm not ill any more, my darling – I am much, much better.' She gave Victoria one of the brilliant smiles that had captivated many hearts in her younger days and still had the power to transform her face so that age seemed immaterial. 'I found I wasn't quite ready to leave you all yet, despite what everyone predicted! Besides, it doesn't matter what the time is – one of the few advantages of age is that one doesn't require long stretches of sleep any more and I can doze off as much as I need tomorrow. When is Guy joining us?'

'Oh, good – he did ring you then. I hoped he would. It's a shame he can't stay longer, but it will be lovely to see him.' Victoria hesitated, then said: 'He says he wants to talk to me about Richard, which I suppose is only natural – and I certainly want to talk to him about his marriage . Were you as stunned as I was about that, Nonna? But we both wanted to see you anyway, so when Guy suggested it would be easier to talk about difficult things here than at home I jumped at it. We knew you wouldn't mind.'

'You know you can always come any time – it is what this old house is for. A place for family. If you want to talk to me afterwards about what he has to say about Richard . . . well, you know you can do that any time. But I shan't keep asking you questions because you may not feel up to them, and that's all right too.' She looked anxiously at Victoria. 'This talking it over with Guy – I don't expect it will be . . . easy . . . for you, *agapi*.'

'No. No, I do realise that. I'm not looking for comfort from Guy,' Victoria said bleakly, 'but he and Richard were always so close – he probably knew Richard better than anyone except me.' She wondered whether to tell her grandmother about the nagging suspicion, which would not go away, that some hitherto unsuspected mistress was about to emerge from the woodwork of Richard's past life like a sinister worm. She added painfully: 'Guy actually knew him almost better than I did. He may be able to throw some light on his state of mind and a few things that are puzzling me.'

Evanthi got the impression that she wanted to say more, but then changed her mind. She did not think it was the right moment to press her. 'You must go to bed now, *agapi*,' she said. 'You look exhausted.'

'I'm sure I will want to talk it all out with you after Guy's gone,' said Victoria, getting up. 'You've always been my guiding star, Nonna.'

After Victoria had kissed her good night and gone upstairs to the peaceful white bedroom where she crashed out almost immediately, Evanthi had lain awake for a long time, turning over old anxieties in her mind, inspecting old prejudices – and liking none of them. It was perhaps lucky there was no one to see the troubled look on her face or read her thoughts.

Now Victoria went down the stone stairs that led to the first floor where many of the main rooms of the house were situated, and followed the smell of freshly made coffee into the dining room. On her way she couldn't help noticing how decrepit everything was looking, how paint and wallpaper were peeling in places, revealing ominously damp patches on walls; how threadbare the curtains had become. There were several actual holes in the once-valuable old rugs in which she thought it would be dangerously easy for Evanthi – or anyone else, come to that – to catch a foot and have a nasty fall. If she had been pleasantly surprised that her grandmother had not looked as bad as she had feared, the same could not be said of the house. Although it was only six months since she had last been there, it seemed to have deteriorated considerably, or perhaps, thought Victoria, it was more that she had never really noticed the state of the house before.

Jake was already seated at the big mahogany table – covered now by one of the huge white cloths that had her great-grandmother's crest and initials embroidered in one corner – tucking into a bowl of yoghurt and honey. Victoria felt certain there would soon be some tell-tale blobs of jam or honey on the snowy expanse – the wipe-down surfaces of modern kitchen-eating habits not being good training for immaculate table-cloths in grand, old-fashioned dining rooms.

'Hi, Mum.' He beamed at her, all traces of yesterday's exhaustion vanished from his face. 'Dora said I wasn't to wake you, and I didn't, did I? Can I go and play with Angelo? Dora says I can if you say so. He hasn't gone to school this morning because it's a saint's day or something.'

'Yes, of course you can, darling – as soon as you've finished breakfast. Nice to see you tucking in for a change.' Neither of them had felt like eating for weeks, and one of her many worries had been that Jake – a skinny child at the best of times – had lost so much weight since his father's death. Dora had been shocked at the sight of him.

'I'd forgotten how yummy the bread here is,' he said now, dolloping Nafsica's home-made apricot jam on to his plate.

'Mmm – the best in the world,' agreed Victoria, sitting down beside him, cutting a hunk from the long crusty loaf and helping herself to coffee.

'So can I go *now*? He's going to show me the kittens – and there's all the outside dogs to see too.' Jake slipped an illicit titbit to Rocky, the hound-like brown mongrel who was lurking under the table and was allowed the run of the house.

'Yes – if you've had enough. Take your fleece if you're going out, though – it can still be chilly, and be sure to do whatever Dora says. If you see Nafsica remember to say hello nicely and give her a kiss.'

Jake wrinkled his nose in distaste. 'I don't like her moustache – it's all scrubby. Like an old witch.'

'Well, tough!' Victoria laughed at him. 'Aim for her cheek or something and perhaps you'll miss the bristles. And don't call her a witch to Angelo – remember Nafsica is his *yiayia* – his great-grandmother. You wouldn't like it if anyone said that about Nonna.'

'Nonna hasn't got whiskers.'

'All the same . . . you must be careful about people's feelings. Dora wouldn't like it either.'

'Oh, *Mum* – Dora would just think it was funny.' Jake rolled his eyes at the fussiness of mothers. 'She thinks *everything's* funny.' He thought for a moment. 'Why don't you call Nonna Yiayia?'

'Because she's Italian as well as Greek and that's what Guy and I called her when we were little. You can go in and see her when Dora's taken up her breakfast. But you mustn't stay long and tire her with too much chat. I'm going to meet Guy at the airport. I might not be back for lunch . . . will you be all right without me for a bit?'

'Course I will,' Jake came and leaned against her briefly, rubbing his cheek on her arm. 'I like being here,' he said. 'It isn't such a Dad place as home, is it?'

'No,' said Victoria, and as she watched him dart out of the room in search of Angelo she felt she had made at least one right decision.

She was late arriving at the airport. The drive took longer than she expected partly because she got stuck behind a water-tanker and partly because she'd forgotten what a frightful old rattle-bones the Vrahos car was to drive – Yannis must keep his foot flat on the floorboards to get up so much speed. She thought she might arrange to hire a car for herself sometime during the next week – something smaller and a good deal nippier. Independence would be important.

She spotted Guy's unmistakable figure as soon as she drove up alongside the arrivals entrance. He was lounging against the wall, smoking one of his American cigarettes and reading a paper. He wore dark blue chinos and an open-necked shirt; a linen jacket was slung across his shoulder, his wide-brimmed hat was tipped over his nose and very Italian-looking dark glasses hid his eyes. But it wouldn't matter what Guy wore – she felt the familiar pang of pride and admiration: he always looked effortlessly elegant. Despite the dark glasses, he'd have made a rotten undercover agent, she thought, because you couldn't help noticing him wherever he was, whatever he was doing.

'Well, well – I like the shades, very fetching,' she said, drawing up beside him and opening the car door. 'You in disguise or something?'

'Vicky!'

She got out, leaving the engine running and lifted her face for his kiss, and it seemed so normal to see him standing there, to be with him and about to go together to the house they both loved so much that she felt as if the events of the last month must be a terrible dream from which she was just about to wake up. Perhaps she was wrong to have been feeling so apprehensive about this meeting with her beloved cousin. Perhaps Guy would weave a magic spell.

Somehow when she had shaken off the nightmare, Richard would still be there in both their lives. Somehow Francine would not be.

Chapter Thirteen

❧

Guy held Victoria away from him, scanning her face, but his dark glasses being of the disconcerting kind that allows the wearer to see out but no one else to see in, all she could see when she looked up at him was the reflection of her own anxious face. He touched her cheek.

'Wonderful of you to come to meet me – I expected Yannis but it's so great that it's you. You've become a remarkable woman, little cousin. Did you know that?'

'Don't feel very wonderful or remarkable at the moment.'

'Well, you are. I'm telling you.' He threw his bag into the back of the car. 'Where shall we go?' he asked. 'Ought we to go straight back to Vrahos?'

'Not unless you'd rather. Dora's looking after Jake, and Nonna seems better than I dared to hope so there's no need to hurry back. She hadn't surfaced when I left but I was amazed how good she was last night. I thought we might just take off somewhere like we used to do – Dora's made us a picnic.'

'Couldn't be better,' he said. 'Any ideas?'

'How about Angelokastro? I haven't been there for ages because the whole area's been closed while conservation work was going on. Dora says they've been making it safer for the summer hordes but apparently you can get right up to the top again now. You know how impossible that road gets once the tourist season starts, but I thought we might have it almost to ourselves this early in the year. Remember our wonderful picnics there with Nonna? It's so clear today the view should be stunning. We could climb to the summit and look out to sea while we eat our lunch. What do you think?'

'Fine. Would you like me to drive?'

'I'll drive there – you can drive us home.'

The brave, optimistic mood was already fading and the sense

119

of dread that was becoming horribly familiar to Victoria returned like the nagging pain from a sensitive tooth. The sudden mood swings of bereavement still took her by surprise. She had felt her usual surge of joy at seeing Guy, but whatever he intended to tell her surely wasn't going to be pleasant: she thought she might not feel like driving on the way back.

Guy shot her a searching look. 'Right. Good thinking,' was all he said as he climbed into the passenger seat beside her, shoving it back as far as it would go to accommodate his long legs.

Having left the airport and skirted round the town, they drove along the coast road and then forked inland at Tsavrós.

'You don't want to go into Paleokastrítsa itself, do you?' she asked.

'No, it's far too long to walk from there and a stiff climb at the end. I shouldn't think you feel up to that at the moment – you still look pretty fragile, Vicky – hardly surprising, of course. Let's take the turn to Lákones and Krini and wiggle our way along there.'

By unspoken mutual consent they did not talk of Richard or Francine but reminisced about the island and old expeditions in their shared childhood, sparking memories and making each other laugh. How odd it is, she thought, not for the first time, that things can still seem funny even when you feel as if you're bleeding inside.

'Do you remember when Nonna was going through a botanical phase and had one of her educational blitzes on us – "widening our horizons", I think it was called – and made us go orchid-hunting up Pantokrator for some rare species, and the car broke down and we had to walk all the way back to the main road?'

'I certainly do.' Guy pulled a face. 'You didn't have to walk, I seem to remember. You got a lift part-way on a donkey – girl's perks. Bloody unfair, I thought at the time! Nowadays we'd have had a mobile, or someone would have come zooming past on a scooter and sent for help. I got a frightful flea in the ear from Nonna for complaining that it wasn't worth it for a boring old orchid!'

'Girl's perks indeed! I was five years younger than you – you always forget that. Anyway, the orchid hunt must have seeded something – look at you now: a distinguished writer about plants, no less. Who'd have thought it!' She paused. 'Oh, Guy, what a lot we owe to Nonna. She lit a lot of fires for us, didn't she?'

'She certainly did.' He laughed. 'Do you remember all those "train your eye" jokes?' He imitated his grandmother's deep velvety voice, her accent: '"You must train your eye to *look* at everything, children, no matter where you are." I'm still grateful for that habit she ingrained in us.'

'And we used to say, "Oh, look – train your eye – there's the public loo," or the bus stop or whatever, and think we were being really witty. What pests we must have been – how we used to tease her!'

'Ah, but she loved that! Still does. What she can't bear are people who don't stand up to her. I always thought—' Guy broke off. He'd been about to say he thought one of the reasons his grandmother had never liked Richard was because he'd tried too hard to ingratiate himself with her – but he bit the words back. Time enough to talk about Richard later. 'Better keep our eyes skinned for that right-hand turn,' he said, and then went on smoothly: 'Not only "train your eye" but "train your ear" too – it was Nonna making me listen to all her old records of Rosa Ponselle that first got me hooked on opera.'

'We'd better not talk about cars breaking down,' said Victoria, changing down to second gear with a grinding noise as they went round a particularly sharp bend, 'or this frightful rattle-bones might conk out completely. Can't you persuade Nonna to get a new one? She always pays more attention to what you say than to anyone else. I know the house is falling to pieces but it's so stuffed with treasures, surely money needn't be *that* tight. The thought of her batting round hairpin bends in this old relic – if she ever gets back to driving at all – fills me with horror.'

'I know – relics all round. Everything's in awful condition. It's going to have to be flog-the-icon time soon, I'm afraid, whether she likes it or not – but whenever Dad or I suggest it she bites our heads off and tells us to mind our own business.'

Guy laughed, but there was a slight edge to his laughter. 'She's so hooked into that old legend about the icon that she won't hear of parting with it. It's ludicrous.'

'I don't think it's really the legend,' objected Victoria. 'I think she partly uses that as an excuse to cover up how much it means to her personally – devotionally. As long as I can remember she's used it when she prays. When she moved it from the chapel, it wasn't really because of its value, as she told everyone, but because she wanted it by her bed once she started to find it difficult to get up and down the steps to the chapel. I think she feels it's inviolable and that any thief would instantly be struck down by the hand of God if they tried to take it!'

'I don't think any insurance company would be very impressed by that theory,' said Guy drily. 'But I'm afraid it's a question of choices. Something's going to have to be sacrificed or there won't be anything left to save.'

It had always been assumed that Victoria would inherit Vrahos one day. Everyone in the family – even Toula – agreed this would be the right thing to happen. Fair-minded Anthony felt especially strongly about it. 'Guy will have plenty coming to him one day – unless I suddenly make a complete cock-up of everything – but Victoria's got nothing,' he said. 'And Vrahos is not only a rock in name – it *is* her rock.' But no one knew how the estate would be left for certain. Evanthi occasionally asked for opinions, but that had never been any guarantee that she would act on advice.

Guy went on: 'I don't know if it's my business or not – or yours, or Mum's or a cats' home, come to that – but I should hate the roof to crash down about her ears or the Greek part of our family history to crumble away into the sea. I have a nightmare of Nonna buried alive in bits of flaking gold leaf. Vrahos is so special – but have you seen the obstacle-race of bowls and saucepans that Dora has to put out down the long passage when it rains?'

'God, yes! I nearly tripped over a bucket last night – a leftover from last week's torrential rain I gather.' Victoria sighed. 'I noticed a whole lots of things this morning I've never really taken in before – frayed carpets, damp patches, peeling paint – everything badly in need of attention, and therefore, I suppose, frighteningly large injections of cash. But I'd hate Nonna to feel pressured to part with the icon when it means so much to her. Oh, look – I think that's the turning.'

She was relieved to change the conversation, not feeling up to embarking on discussions about the future of Vrahos at the moment. Guy could be unpredictable on the subject of property – wildly generous one moment and dauntingly acquisitive or resentful the next, and she had enough problems without going into dangerous areas like inheritance. Under their pleasurable reminiscences of a shared childhood, they were both acutely aware of tension.

They bumped along the narrow road, winding their way through olive groves and talking about the changes to the island, and the tourist economy that was altering an ancient way of life – both for better and worse – and the terrifying proliferation of building all along the coast.

'Every time I come back, whole crops of new villas have popped up there like mushrooms. It's going to get spoiled if they're not careful – Prospero's magic island – *our* island,' said Victoria. 'Talk about killing the goose that laid the golden egg . . .'

'There's still a lot of magic left, though – you just have to search a bit harder. It's not exactly built up in the middle yet, thank God. Look at that!'

Victoria stopped the car. They had come through the hamlet of Krini, where the so-called road ended and had started down the rough track, which dropped vertically in a giddying plunge. Ahead and above was the rocky crag to which the ruins of the old Byzantine fort straggled and clung – and beyond that lay the sea. They got out. The air smelled of fresh herbs.

'Dare we take the car any further down?' asked Victoria. 'I'm not sure if we can turn at the bottom and even if we could, we might not make it back up again. Dora says they've built a café down there now but I don't suppose it'll be open before Easter – if then – so I shouldn't think there'd be anyone to help. I wouldn't fancy being towed up here anyway! Let's walk.'

Guy slung the old rucksack, which for years had been used for family picnics, over his back and they set off downwards, slipping and sliding on the shaly path. Near the bottom a sort of wooden bridge with rope handrails had been placed across to the opposite hill, like a drawbridge across a moat, cutting out the steepest scramble both down and up again. On the other side, the now renovated path zigzagged up between rocks and traces of old fortifications, with occasional little walkways, and handgrips – easy walking compared to the old days but, even so, quite a climb.

When they reached the summit they stood and gazed. 'Wow!' said Victoria, awed. 'I'd forgotten how stunning it was.'

'Paradise Lost,' said Guy. She glanced at him, disturbed by his tone – half sad, half mocking – but his face gave nothing away.

'So much blue,' she said: 'The sky, the sea – and the land – all those little anemones everywhere. I didn't think they'd be out yet. I can't remember which they are?'

'*Anemone blanda.* They're always early.'

They found a place where they could sit with their backs against a rock and look out to sea while they ate their lunch. Dora had put together some of her delicious *tiropitakia* – little cheese pies in filo pastry; there were hard-boiled eggs and cold chicken; there were tomatoes and black olives, a dip of *tzatziki* and a loaf of fresh bread; a bottle of wine in the cool-bag was still wonderfully cold, and the sweetness without which Dora would have considered no meal complete was provided by a slab of rose-pink Turkish delight – or Greek delight as it was now more politically correct to call it, she had informed Victoria. They ate in companionable silence. The tragic events of the last weeks seemed unreal and had it not been for the cloud of anxiety hovering around her, Victoria thought this would have rated as an idyllic picnic – one to add to a bank of happy memories.

'Well, what a banquet!' She licked icing sugar off her fingers, and put all the remnants carefully back in the rucksack. Then she looked at her cousin. Both knew that the moment had arrived that could no longer be postponed. Both were desperately conscious of the ghost at the feast.

'So . . . can we talk about Richard now?' she asked, surprised at how normal her voice sounded.

Guy lit a cigarette, and flicked the match over the cliff. There was no breath of wind. He didn't answer immediately, but drew on his cigarette, watching the smoke hanging like a memory on the air. They were both thinking of Richard.

Guy and Richard had first met at prep school, but the friendship had really been cemented in the holidays. Anthony and Toula had recently bought Durnford House and were introduced by mutual friends and neighbours to Richard's parents, the Cunningham family having long been established in the area. Guy being an only child and Richard very much younger than his two sisters, it suited both sets of parents that their sometimes exhaustingly energetic little boys got on so well together and could share occupations and amusements. They soon became inseparable companions: restless, mercurial Guy and the more stolid Richard had proved to be a wonderful foil for each other. They were both good games players and crazy about all sport. If Guy was the more graceful athlete, given to flashes of outstanding brilliance, he was also the more erratic and temperamental; Richard might look less elegant in action but he had a dogged quality that brought him almost as many victories as Guy in their numerous contests: Anthony, amused at their very different attitudes to life, had christened them the Hare and the Tortoise.

As they grew older and went to different public schools, the friendship not only survived, but also strengthened. Richard was the better footballer; Guy was a more distinguished tennis player. Later, Richard rowed for his school and Guy, a demon fast bowler, captained the first XI at Harrow. They sailed and skied together. They made a formidable men's doubles partnership in local tennis tournaments. They went to the same parties, shared many of the same friends and were much in demand socially. And, of course, through much of this time Victoria had been their devoted acolyte, first considered a bit of a bore, tolerated and teased, though protected by them both, then, as she blossomed into an enchanting young woman, they had still teased her, still protected her, but adored and admired her too, and been proud to have her along with them.

Guy said abruptly, 'I'm afraid I'm going to ruin your day for you, Vicky.'

'My days are ruined already,' she said sadly, leaning forward and hugging her knees. 'The fact of Richard's death is terrible enough to cope with – but I've racked my brains these last weeks wondering whether he killed himself on purpose, despite the coroner's verdict. It didn't occur to me to start with – I was too shocked even to think, I suppose – but I overheard something that started these nightmare doubts, and now I can't get rid of them. They go round and round in my head and drive me crazy. Did Francine tell you?'

'She did . . . yes. She also told me you suspected her of having an affair with Richard. I don't know what put that into your head.'

'I couldn't really believe it – Richard wasn't a womaniser; actually I didn't think he'd ever looked at any woman but me – but all my certainties about everything have been turned upside down. Francine promised me – she swore – I was wrong but I didn't know whether to believe her or not. I'm in a desperate muddle about everything.'

Guy watched his cousin as she struggled with her words. He could see a small pile of bones strewn on a grassy ledge below them on the cliff's face – perhaps a bird had been dashed against the rocks by a winter storm. He thought Victoria's fine-boned face looked as white and desolate as the small, broken skeleton.

'Go on,' he prompted.

'Francine did seem astonished at the suggestion,' admitted Victoria, 'but I got the feeling she was hiding something all the same. I keep asking myself why Richard should have been quite so upset about you and Francine getting married. *I* might have minded. I *did* mind. I *do* mind. I couldn't believe you could sneak off like that and get married without telling me. That was so cruel of you.' Guy said nothing. 'Now you're going to tell me you think Richard shot himself on purpose – I just know you are,' she said. 'But what I don't know . . . is *why*?'

Guy sat very still.

She blurted out passionately, 'He had *everything* to live for – if in some crazy, inconceivable moment he'd even *contemplated* such a terrible thing, how could he do that to Jake and me? *How could he?* He'd never suffered from depression – I'd have known. There has to be something really serious that I've missed. Had he been told he'd got some dire disease and couldn't face telling me? Was he going to die?'

'No – nothing like that.'

'What happened in Nepal then? Something must have. I thought he must have picked up a bug or something when he got back – he was so unlike himself. He was really short with me. I wouldn't have thought anything of it if it had been you – we're all used to your filthy moods – but Richard didn't have moods.'

He answered her with questions of his own: 'How well do you think you really knew Richard, Vicky? I mean knew about how he ticked, what his passions were?'

She looked astonished. 'What an *extraordinary* thing to ask me! I've known Richard almost as long as you have . . . since before I came to live with Toula and Anthony and you . . . most of my life. We were the proverbial childhood sweethearts – you know that. I've been *married* to him for nearly eight years. What are you suggesting? Richard wasn't brilliant and tricky and unpredictable like you. You couldn't really quarrel with him – he'd walk away. OK, so perhaps I didn't share his involvement with politics as much as he'd have liked, but we didn't fall out about it.' She grimaced. 'He got more than enough encouragement from Bill, anyway, not to mention Peter Mason and the Hawkinses – Stafford and Meriel were always egging him on. I wouldn't quite have described politics as a *passion* anyway.' She plucked at the turf beside her, sifting bits of grass through her fingers, and then said reluctantly, as though the admission was forced out of her: 'Perhaps Richard was always a bit short on passion. I admit I used to goad him about it sometimes – but he was just so kind and loving . . . so . . . so ordinary, if you like.' She let out a sudden wail of anguish: 'He was my *husband*, for God's sake!'

There was a long silence. Then Guy said, 'Richard had a talent for not showing his feelings. But you're right about one thing – he never looked at another woman. I can absolutely promise you that. But all the same there was someone else. Only it wasn't a woman he loved.' He stopped for a moment, looked away from her and then looked back. 'Vicky, darling Vicky . . . did you never even *wonder* if Richard might be . . . gay?'

She stared at him. '*Richard?* No! Never! Don't be *ridiculous!*'

She instinctively clapped her hands over her ears in a futile attempt to blot out his words. 'Richard and I had a good marriage,' she shouted at him, as though he was the one who couldn't hear. 'We had a child together. We had a great life. We were *friends*. What are you talking about? Are you trying to tell me he didn't even love me? I don't believe you.'

'No, of course not. He *did* love you, Vicky – very much in his own way. And he adored Jake too . . . but he was desperately unhappy with how things were and that wasn't your fault – or his. *He couldn't help it* – it was how he was *made*. You have to accept that.'

'No! No – I won't! Why should I?' she asked passionately. She leaped to her feet then, suddenly feeling as if she was about to faint, had to sit down again on a rock and put her head between her legs until the dizziness passed off. After a long moment she looked up at him. 'You're making it up!' she said fiercely. 'How can you be so cruel? Why are you telling me this . . . this sickening rubbish?'

'Because if I don't tell you someone else will. Believe me, I'd much rather not.'

'Oh *please*!' she burst out. 'Don't give me that old "this hurts me more than it hurts you" stuff! You're making me sick.'

Her scorn was blistering. Guy desperately wished he hadn't embarked on the subject and struggled with a temptation to retract what he had told her, but he had gone too far to stop now. He went on, speaking softly but with deadly clarity: 'Lots of old friends knew the score but a conversation – a row – we had in Nepal was overheard by the wrong person, and . . . well, word has got round. I thought you'd better hear it from me.'

'Go on then,' she said, at last. 'But for God's sake tell me everything *now*. Who are you suggesting he loved?'

'Oh, Vicky,' said Guy. 'Don't you see? It was *me*.'

Victoria opened her mouth but no sound came out. Her throat felt as though a hand was squeezing it and she might choke.

After what seemed an interminable moment Guy put out a hand to her, but she shook him off as violently as though a scorpion had settled on her arm. 'Don't touch me!' There was a drumming in her ears and she felt as if she was going to explode. She thought she might be sick at any moment. Then she leaped to her feet and stumbled off down the narrow path that ran along the top of the cliff – anything to get away from Guy. Guy her childhood hero; Guy her betrayer.

He watched her go, deeply disturbed: unsure whether to follow her or leave her alone. After what seemed an age, but was probably only about ten minutes, he couldn't bear it any longer and decided to go after her. She was standing at the edge of the cliff, the far side of the rope that now ran along the edge of the path, facing out to sea, gazing over the sheer drop that overhung the rocks below. He thought she was perilously close to the edge and was afraid of startling her, horrified by the fear that the tussock on which she stood might suddenly give way.

'Vicky,' he called urgently. 'Vicky? Please come back. I am so, so sorry – but we have to talk about it. Please hear me out.'

She turned at last, and to his infinite relief came slowly back towards him. She looked up at him and shook her head in a baffled sort of way as though she had met someone vaguely familiar and was trying to remember who they were. Then she gave a tormented little cry – far more upsetting to Guy than angry accusations – and walked slowly back to their picnic spot. The stunning view, the beauty of the day, all seemed a mockery. There was a long silence.

'You . . . stole . . . my . . . husband,' she said at last, and her voice, in her own ears, seemed to come from very far away, as though it was someone else's voice and she was merely hearing it. 'You of all people who I've always thought so special – closer even than a brother; my soul mate. You'd better tell me everything now. I couldn't stand any more uncertainty. If I discover later you haven't told me all you know . . . or *think* you know . . . then I'll never forgive you. Never. How could you do this to me? You . . . you absolute shit, Guy. You *traitor*.'

She sensed him wince, but his face wore again the inscrutable look she knew so well.

'It was the other way round,' he said quietly. 'When you married Richard, you took him from me.'

It was as though cataracts had been removed from her eyes and lenses implanted that enabled her to see with appalling new clarity, and what she was being forced to examine was horribly disturbing. She would have given anything to return to the comfort of her hazy vision.

'Dear God! I must have been incredibly stupid,' she said.

'Never stupid. Innocent perhaps, naive probably. Certainly unwilling to probe. But you must have realised I've always played it both ways? I've had affairs with men and women. You *did* know that really.'

'*You* perhaps,' she said at last. 'Yes, I suppose so . . . there were always wild stories . . . about you. But Richard . . . never.' Then she whispered, 'When . . . when did the sex between you start?'

'It was at Cambridge,' said Guy. 'It just seemed part of growing up to me . . . experimenting. . . exploring sexuality. It was all too easy and, well . . . it happened. I was devoted to Richard – you know that – but I knew I'd never feel the same way as he did. But Richard wasn't bisexual like me. He knew he was gay quite early on but could never face acknowledging it publicly. Perhaps his political ambitions came into it later, but you know what the Cunninghams are like too – born with a load of prejudices set in concrete. Can you imagine what his father's reaction would have been? Or Meriel and June's? Richard wasn't promiscuous – I don't think he was ever in love with anyone but me. Frightening, really.'

'Well, don't expect me to be sorry for you,' she flashed. 'How *could* he marry me if that was how he felt? How could *you* let it happen to *me*?' It was a cry of anguish. 'Did it go on after we were married? *Did it?*'

Guy looked acutely uncomfortable. 'We never meant it to – but . . . well . . . occasionally. Not lately.'

'You stabbed me in the back, both of you. You've turned my whole marriage into a sham. I can't bear it.'

Guy lit another cigarette from the tale-end of the first one. His hands were shaking.

'When we were children you always used to say that Richard was much nicer than me and you were right,' he said. 'I've always been a selfish bastard – you've told me so yourself often enough. But Richard always adored you. I swear that's true, Vicky. You were the only woman he could ever have married. Think how well you got on together – far better than lots of married couples we both know. Richard loved family life . . . and children . . . and being *accepted*. You know how he minded about convention and what people thought of him – unlike me. I'll never have another friend like him, but I couldn't feel for him what he felt for me. I couldn't give him what he craved, any more than you could. I wasn't prepared for the sort of relationship he really wanted – totally committed . . . yet secret.'

'So you're trying to tell me he married me as a sort of camouflage?' Victoria burst out. 'How deeply comforting! How nice to know I've been such a convenient cover story for you both! Did you laugh together about it?'

'Stop it, Vicky. Of course not!' Now Guy's voice was raised too. Then he said more quietly: 'Richard would never have done that, or me either, for God's sake. I may be every sort of shit – I'm well aware of it – but not that bad. But let me ask *you* something. Who's idea was it to get married? Yours or Richard's?'

Victoria looked away.

'Well?'

'I don't know,' she answered with sudden weariness. 'I really . . . do . . . not . . . know. We were *always* going to get married. I suppose it started as a sort of joke when we used to support each other if you were being foul. It sort of evolved.' She buried her head in her hands. 'We'd lasted eight years,' she said wretchedly. 'I longed for another baby but after that miscarriage it didn't happen. It would have been good for Jake – and Richard would have loved it too. He was a marvellous father. That was a sadness to us both, but apart from that I thought we were happy. How could I have been so wrong?' Then she asked, 'Why did you marry Francine?'

Guy gave her one of his enigmatic looks. 'There are loads of reasons. We're amazingly well suited, for one thing. We share lots of friends and interests; we never bore each other. We both want children. Francine's thirty-eight and she longs for a baby too, and we both wanted to be married for that.'

He looked at Victoria's expression: 'All right – you don't see her as the maternal type and you think I'd make a lousy father . . . well, I hope you're wrong.' He surprised her by adding quite fiercely: 'You think Francine's just a brassy socialite but there's much more to her than that. I think she'd be a brilliant mum.'

Victoria felt a tormenting stab of jealousy. I shouldn't be feeling this now, she thought, horrified at herself. 'And is it true what Francine started to say – that Richard had tried to stop you marrying before?' she asked.

'We nearly got engaged soon after you were married, if you must know. Richard put terrific pressure on me not to marry her.'

'What sort of pressure?'

'Oh, Vicky, leave it. Don't rake over all that now. He's gone. We've both lost him. Nothing will bring him back.'

'Did he threaten suicide?' she asked, suddenly certain.

Guy nodded. 'But I never for one moment thought he meant it. I didn't take him seriously.' He added bitterly, 'How disastrously wrong I was.'

'You took him seriously enough not to get engaged.' Her voice was cutting.

'There were other reasons – selfish ones as usual. I told Francine it was entirely because of Richard but that was only partly true. I've always shied away from commitments and I haven't exactly been wearing the willow these last few years.'

'And now? Don't tell me you're *in love* with Francine! All these years you've been my hero but you're weak and destructive . . . and you don't even know what love means.' She spat the words at him.

Guy took a long time to answer and Victoria watched him, this cousin she'd always idolised. What was it that made him so intriguing to women? How strange – how terrifying – that it should turn out to have been the less charismatic Richard who was the one with the dark secrets.

'Since you say I don't know what love means I can't answer that,' he said eventually and she could see her shaft had gone home. He went on: 'You've always thought Francine was tough, and she is in a way – thank God. It's a huge relief that I can't hurt her too easily. She has no illusions about me, she's amusing and sexy and strong-minded, and though this may surprise you, she's also something I'm not – genuinely kind. I don't suppose we'll always be faithful but we won't ever *bore* each other. We both think we can make it work.' He added with difficulty: 'I

132

feel more for Francine than I thought I could possibly feel for anyone.'

'How touching. How idyllic,' said Victoria. 'So did you paint this romantic little scenario to Richard?'

'Francine made it a condition that if she married me I must absolutely break off any relationship with Richard, but . . .' Guy weighed his words as carefully as if he were handling a dangerous substance and feared an explosion, 'but Richard wouldn't . . . accept that.'

'Did he threaten suicide again?'

'Not in so many words.'

'What was the conversation someone overheard?'

'It was that little shit Toby Parsons,' he said reluctantly. 'Richard insisted on inviting him on the trip. I've never trusted him and that's not good when you're climbing. He's good enough technically but he's a troublemaker and he always had a fancy for me. One night I told Richard – what he really knew already – that Francine and I were serious this time. Toby heard Richard say that if I'd agree to chuck Francine he'd come out about being gay . . . even if it meant breaking up your marriage. I couldn't believe he meant it and I made a terrible miscalculation. I thought if Francine and I got married as quickly as possible he'd accept the inevitable and it would be better for everyone. I didn't think anyone – especially you – would ever need to know about it. Then this terrible accident happened – if it was an accident. We'll never know for sure, but Toby's been trying to blackmail me and means to tell you. Somehow I have to live with my part in all this, but I shall never forgive myself for what it's done to you. If it's any consolation to you, Richard and I haven't had a physical relationship for ages – not since Francine came back into my life seriously.'

'Oh, wonderful – bloody marvellous. You gave Richard up for Francine but it was fine to muck about with *my* husband before that,' Victoria said. 'It obviously didn't occur to you to give him up for *my* sake when we got married. How dare you talk about consolation?'

For once there was no mistaking the misery in his face. 'What can I say except I'm sorry – so dreadfully sorry? I'd give anything to put the clock back and play things differently. Look,

Vicky, I realise you must be in a terrible state of shock but . . .'
He couldn't finish his sentence.

She looked at him with blistering scorn. 'Shock doesn't begin to describe what I feel. I don't know if I can ever forgive you, Guy, but I can't talk about it any more now. I don't think I could stand it. Take me home.'

'It's a God-awful mess,' he said. 'But Richard did love you and at least, unlike me, *you* have nothing to reproach yourself with, Vicky.'

'Only blindness,' said Victoria bitterly.

They drove home without speaking, each locked into a separate world.

Chapter Fourteen

Jake had spent a thoroughly happy day. Though his Greek was rudimentary and Angelo spoke no English, they managed to communicate together without the slightest difficulty.

Despite its dilapidated condition, Vrahos, both outside and in, was a paradise for children. Its courtyards and terraces and the apparently haphazard layout of its many different levels – often reached by outside stone staircases – made it perfect for bloodcurdling games of hide-and-seek. The cavernous arched cellars, which housed wine and olive oil, also acted as a store for garden machinery and tools – some of them dating back generations since nothing at Vrahos ever got thrown away – and were officially out of bounds to Jake and Angelo, though that naturally made them irresistible. Having visited the latest litter of kittens, Jake, after agonising indecision, chose a bold ginger tom to be his own. The place was always overrun with cats, Evanthi – who did not have the chore of caring for them herself – being a sucker for the waifs and strays that proliferated on the island.

Dora took him to say good morning to Evanthi when she carried up her breakfast tray. Jake's face lit up at the sight of her as though a hundred-watt bulb had been switched on inside him, but he hung back shyly, not sure how to treat his great-grandmother after so many warnings that he mustn't exhaust her. But Evanthi looked reassuringly as he remembered her and when she held out her arms he walked rather cautiously into her embrace – and then suddenly the barriers were down and he snuggled up to her, information about the long journey, the late night arrival and, best of all, his chosen kitten, all pouring out.

'Come and sit on my bed, *agapi mou*, and tell me all about him – be careful not to sit on Tomasina, though. Now let's think of

135

suitable names,' said Evanthi. 'You can leave Jake with me, Dora. Victoria can collect him when she gets up.'

'Mum got up *ages* ago,' said Jake. 'She's gone to meet Guy at the airport.'

'How is this, Dora?' Evanthi's voice was sharp. 'I particularly asked Yannis to go.'

'I know – and he would have gone, of course, Kyria.' Dora looked anxious. 'But Victoria insisted she must go herself. I think she wanted a chance to talk to Guy without . . .' Dora indicated Jake with a movement of her eyes. 'I said I would look after Jake. I think they meant to go off somewhere and not hurry back. I am very sorry, Kyria.'

'This is just what I wanted to avoid!' Evanthi had been about to ask Dora to see that Guy came straight up to see her the moment he arrived. There were things she had intended to discuss with him before he got a chance to talk to Victoria alone. 'Well, it's too late now.' She looked very displeased but then relented. 'It's all right, Dora – I know it won't have been your fault and I don't suppose Yannis could help it either. But let me know as soon as they get back. I'll send Jake down to you shortly and then I shall want you to help me get dressed. I've been an invalid far too long.'

Dora went down to tell her husband that Kyria was definitely better – wanting to have her finger on the pulse of every activity again, but still not back to her usual self or they would not have got off so lightly for failing to interpret her wishes correctly.

After much discussion, Sotiris, meaning 'saviour', was chosen as a suitable name for a marmalade kitten that had undergone a miraculous rescue. It would be very distinguished for his kitten to have a special name of its own, thought Jake, since most of the cats at Vrahos did not have individual names and were referred to indiscriminately as Psipsina. Without appearing to ask questions, Evanthi managed to gather more in a few minutes about Jake's anxieties over his father's death than anyone else had done in the last few weeks. She thought that despite the best endeavours of all the grown-ups concerned, he had picked up more about the uncertainties surrounding Richard's accident than anyone had realised.

'Do you think Daddy wanted to die?' he asked suddenly, apropos of nothing, twiddling a tuft of his hair so that it stood up on top of his head like a unicorn's horn. 'Is that why Mummy seems so cross with him all the time?'

'Oh, I shouldn't think so,' said Evanthi easily, thinking that Victoria would be horrified to know that her anger was so apparent to the little boy. 'If Mummy's cross it's only because Daddy can't be with her any more and she misses him so much. I often feel cross if the people I love can't be with me – don't you?'

'Even if it's not their fault?'

'It doesn't make much difference if it's their fault or not. Perhaps it ought to, but it doesn't. If I'm missing someone badly I just feel cross that they're not there – which is why I feel specially happy this morning because it's lovely that you're here with me now.'

'Did you feel cross when I wasn't here before then?'

'Furious,' Evanthi pulled a ferocious face. 'Like a tiger.'

Jake giggled. 'And now you're not?'

'And now I'm not.'

He got off her bed and wandered round the room, looking at all the cut-glass bottles on Evanthi's dressing table, fiddling with a silver baby's rattle hung with coral bells, which lay on a chest of drawers and which he had always loved, opening and shutting the ornate candle-snuffer that worked like a pair of scissors. Evanthi watched him. She never told him not to touch things – he had always been a careful child and she thought he had an eye for precious objects.

'So it's all right to feel angry with people – even if they're dead?' he asked.

'Of course,' said Evanthi firmly. 'Why would God have given us frowns if he didn't mean us to use them? I frequently feel very angry with God himself – when he doesn't do what I want, which I have to say is rather too often.'

'I think it was horrible of God to take Daddy away.'

'Have you told him so?'

'I didn't think you could.' Jake's eyes grew round at the enormity of such a suggestion.

'Oh, you most definitely can.' Evanthi believed in handing

out certainties to children. 'I should give him a good telling off. Try it next time you say your prayers.'

'Will it make any difference?'

'Well, it won't bring Daddy back – that's not the way it works. But you'll feel much better for getting it off your chest.'

'It's in my chest it always hurts when I can't breathe,' said Jake, much impressed by this idea.

'There you are then,' said Evanthi. Feeling the conversation had gone far enough for the moment, she added briskly: 'Now it's time for you to run along downstairs because I must finish my breakfast. Angelo will be waiting to play with you – and you might need to check on Sotiris too. Ask Dora if she'd come up to me in about half an hour. Off you go, *agapi*.'

Jake whizzed off, arms outstretched in aeroplane mode, and she heard him making cheerful vroom-vroom noises all the way down the passage.

By the time Guy and Victoria returned a chill had invaded the late afternoon air and a few warning clouds were hovering over Albania. The snow-capped mountains, which earlier had looked so radiant floating in the distance, were suddenly dark, threatening and close, boding a change in the weather. Victoria got out of the car and walked indoors without a backward look at Guy.

Guy found his grandmother, a white cashmere rug over her knees, sitting in the Grand Salon, which took up a large part of the ground floor. Her hair was piled up on her head, as though for a formal occasion and her face was expertly made up. He knew she had chosen to receive him here – rather than in the cosier small drawing room on the first floor – intending the surroundings to convey a message and a warning: she was not pleased with him.

'Ah . . . Guy. Come in, *chrysso mou*. You may kiss me.' Evanthi graciously held out her hand.

'Thank you, Nonna,' said Guy meekly, a sardonic glimmer in his eye, thinking how surprised and put out she would have been if he'd shown any hesitation about doing so. He swiftly raised her hand to his lips then bent down and kissed her gently on each papery cheek, remembering as Victoria had done, the delicate, delicious scent that recalled his childhood so vividly. He thought she looked frail, and though she was sitting as ramrod straight as ever he had detected a tremor in the long fingers when they rested on his, as though they could not support the weight of all the rings she was wearing. The rings too were a signal.

'You get more beautiful every time I come back,' he said. 'Full war paint, I see. I am honoured. I thought you'd still be in bed.'

Evanthi looked scornful, refusing to be beguiled by flattery – though she was never quite immune to Guy's wiles. She looked at her most patrician and aloof, but though he respected his grandmother – and was deeply fond of her – Guy had never been among those who were intimidated by her.

'Where is Victoria?' she asked. 'What have you done with her?'

'I haven't done anything with her. I think she wanted to find Jake – let Dora off the hook and see about his supper. I've come straight to see you.'

'And what have you done to her?'

'Ah, that's more to the point, I'm afraid,' he said soberly. 'Ruined any peace of mind she hoped to find for a very long time, I fear – and made her even more unhappy. I have just told her that I'm sure Richard committed suicide.'

'How could you be so *stupid*, Guy?' It was not lost on her grandson that Evanthi chose to accuse him of the one quality he was most likely to object to – he might admit to being selfish, even occasionally cruel – but stupid never. 'Why did you need to tell her things she need never have known about?' she went on: 'If you have reason to think Richard killed himself what was the point of telling her? You should have come to see me first.'

'It wasn't only about suicide. I have just had to tell Vicky that Richard was a homosexual because she was going to find out in a very unpleasant way otherwise and I had to forewarn her. I was being blackmailed about it. Surely you don't think I should have given in to that?'

'Naturally I don't. That would have been absolutely distasteful.' Evanthi, at her most imperious, looked at though such an idea was quite beneath her notice. 'Blackmail is so middle class,' she said sweepingly. Under normal circumstances Guy would immediately have wanted to share this Evanthi-ism with Victoria, but today things were far from normal. He gave his grandmother a curious look. 'We've never discussed it in so many words – but did you know about Richard, Nonna?'

She hesitated, then said slowly, 'I didn't know. I've sometimes wondered. I did my best to stop the marriage. But I had no effect.'

'And you didn't explain to Victoria then?'

'I didn't spell it out, no . . . what good would that have done?' She threw him a scathing look. 'I had nothing to go on except a hunch – your mother would have called it one of my unjustified prejudices. Victoria seemed so happy and determined and I hoped for her sake it wasn't the truth. And I assumed,' she said, giving him a piercing look, 'that you would certainly have told Victoria yourself if you suspected it, and told your father too.'

Guy said nothing.

Evanthi went on: 'Victoria's so loyal she'd have refused even to admit the possibility on just a vague hunch of mine. The marriage would have gone ahead despite anything I said, but I would have spoiled her vision of Richard. It's easy to get deceived by Victoria's sweetness into thinking she's malleable, but you and I both know how determined she can be – she would have stuck to him anyway unless I had any proof.' She said sadly: 'I have been tormented ever since I heard the news of his death by the idea that perhaps I should have tried harder to put her off. Was she aware of it?'

'She had absolutely no idea,' said Guy. 'I'm afraid she's devastated. I thought she might have had an inkling and chosen to ignore it, but it obviously came as a complete bombshell.'

'Perhaps they'd always been too close to each other – a case of the wood and the trees – and she was such an innocent when she first got married. At least while it lasted I suppose it was a good enough marriage – in its way,' said Evanthi. 'I had one confrontation with Richard before they got married. I told him I thought he was completely wrong for Victoria temperamentally and emotionally . . . but that didn't get me anywhere,' she admitted. 'He told me he loved her and would look after her and I couldn't budge him. I was quite surprised because he'd always seemed rather nervous of me and I thought I could wear him down easily. I have to say he went up in my estimation.'

'What an extraordinary person you are, Nonna!'

Guy had an inclination to tell her the whole story, including his own part in the tragedy, but told himself that such an act of confession would be an indulgence on his part, a seeking for an absolution he didn't deserve and she couldn't give. He would have to live with his own conscience and if Victoria chose to tell their grandmother the truth, then that was her right, and he would face the full force of Evanthi's wrath if need be – but he couldn't help wondering what she thought about his part in it. 'You never told me that,' he said.

'Of course not! I'm perfectly capable of keeping my own counsel. He tried to convince me he could make Victoria happy. It seemed he was right in a negative way because I have to admit I don't think he actually made her *unhappy* – until the awful horror of the last month, that is. But I've always hated the idea she should have such an unexciting marriage. She's worth more.'

'Is that because your own marriage was so unsatisfying?' asked Guy. 'I remember you telling us as children that you had once been struck by lightning and I always longed to know who it was – surely not Grandfather Doukas. Who was your great love, Nonna?'

Evanthi spread out her hands and gazed at them as though she was considering something. For a moment Guy thought she was about to make a revelation, then she seemed to change her mind.

'You are trying to side-track me,' she said. 'I want to know what you have told Victoria.'

'I've told her about how Richard was,' said Guy, deciding a half-truth was all he was prepared to admit to his redoubtable grandparent. 'I also told her that I think he probably intended to shoot himself because of it – and I'm pretty sure he did mean to, though we can never know for certain.'

Evanthi said angrily, 'I am very displeased with you, Guy. You know what this information will have done to Victoria, don't you? Absolutely destroyed all her confidence in herself as a woman. That's extremely sad.'

'It had nothing whatever to do with her attractions as a

woman,' said Guy. 'That's the whole point. It was something Richard couldn't help. Like being tone-deaf.'

'Exactly!' said Evanthi scornfully. 'Imagine if you were a musician – a composer, say – and that you suddenly discovered that the person you'd been living with for years was tone-deaf. They'd constantly told you how marvellous your music was, and you'd believed them, and then you find it can never have meant anything to them at all because they simply couldn't hear it properly. What would that do for your opinion of yourself as a musician?'

'I don't think that's a fair analogy,' said Guy, who saw all too clearly what she meant.

'No? Well, I suggest you think about it.' Evanthi knew her grandson too well to get into an argument with him – she had made her point. She fixed him with her penetrating gaze.

'And what did you tell her about anything else – your marriage for instance? She was deeply hurt you didn't confide in her about that. How could you have done that to her, Guy? It was unforgivable. Are there any further shocks in store for her, poor child?'

Guy got up and started pacing about the room. Then he came and stood in front of his grandmother. His habitual look of self-assurance seemed to have slipped. She thought with surprise that he suddenly looked . . . almost . . . vulnerable.

'Yes,' he said. 'There is something else. We did talk about my marriage and how Francine and I want a family. And of course you're right – she's terribly hurt. And I do feel very badly about that.' He seemed to be searching for words – also unusual for Guy, she thought. Then he said: 'But there's one thing I haven't told her yet. I've been cursing myself all the way home in the car. I should have done it, of course, because she'll know soon enough and it would have been better to get it over – for both of us – but I missed the opportunity. Oh, Nonna, I so nearly did . . . but by then she looked utterly done in and was in such a state of distress, I just funked it.'

'At least that's unlike you. And what was it?'

'Francine is going to have a baby,' said Guy quietly. 'I just can't tell you how pleased we are. Absolutely thrilled – even at this time of tragedy; perhaps especially so. But I cringe to think what Victoria will feel. She so desperately wanted another baby herself – and then I've always known . . .' He didn't finish the sentence and something acknowledged but unsaid hung in the air. He continued: 'Francine's been dreading Vicky finding out. It's nothing compared to everything else she's had to face but I'm terrified this extra thing will tip her over an edge. She'll be generous about it – but I'm afraid she may be distraught.'

'Yes,' said Evanthi. 'Yes, I'm afraid she will be – and we both know why. Richard was only ever a substitute for you. A protection against being hurt – she who had been so wounded as a little girl: her way of settling for the possible rather than the desired – never a good idea. The irony is that she thought Richard seemed so safe.' She looked at him severely, though she could hardly contain her joy at his news. 'I am still *very* upset with you, Guy,' she said. 'I think you have been uncharacteristically inept. I think you should somehow have avoided telling her all this.' Then she suddenly held out both her hands to him. 'But oh, *agapi*, my darling boy, I am so very pleased for you about the baby. It will be hard for Victoria, especially now, but it will be the making of you. And you know it may even help her to move on. This marriage of yours is a *good* thing. I hope I live to see your son.'

'You're more generous than I deserve, Nonna,' said Guy. He was acutely conscious of the coals of fire she had just heaped on his head. He looked down at her and said with a glimmer of amusement: 'It may be a daughter, you know – we would both be just as pleased.'

'Of course – but it will be a boy all the same. I know these things. And you will call him Constantine after my son and Victoria's father.'

'I'll tell Francine,' he said, smiling at her. 'Who needs scans if they've got you? And if you're right – and you usually are – he shall be Constantine Doukas Winston and we'll bring him here to Vrahos to be christened in the chapel.'

Grandmother and grandson looked at each other for a long moment. Then Guy took a deep breath as though he'd been swimming underwater and was just coming up for air. He said, rather abruptly, 'Bless you, Nonna. I'll come and see you again later. I must go and say hello to Jake, and see if Vicky's surviving – and then if the water situation's all right I'd love a bath.'

He turned to go. Victoria was standing in the open doorway. He had no idea how long she had been there.

Chapter Fifteen

The following morning the sky looked cloudy as if the weather had not made up its mind what sort of mood to be in and though the stained-glass brilliance of the previous day had vanished, the storm that had threatened the evening before had not yet materialised.

Guy came down to find Jake had already finished his breakfast.

'Can we go in the boat this morning?' asked Jake, adding quickly, 'because you *promised* last night.'

'I certainly didn't. I said we'd go if the weather was right, and if it is – then we will. Anything to do with boats depends on the conditions, as you know perfectly well – unless you've forgotten everything your father and I taught you last summer.'

Jake gave him a speculative look, seeing the trap and unwilling to admit that he'd forgotten anything.

'When will you know?'

'When I've finished my breakfast – not at all, if you badger me.'

Guy selected an orange from the fruit bowl and helped himself to coffee with maddening slowness before opening yesterday's *To Vima*, the newspaper Evanthi took.

Jake considered his options. On the one hand he had learned a wholesome respect for Guy's intolerance of childish scenes and badly wanted his good opinion. On the other hand it had not been lost on him that his bereaved status seemed to make grown-ups unusually reluctant to thwart him, thus providing unwonted opportunities for extra treats.

'Yes, I know . . .' he began in a tragic voice, trying to look interestingly soulful, 'but I would feel very sad if we couldn't go . . .'

Guy shot him an amused look over his coffee cup. 'No buts!

Don't pull that pathetic stuff on me, Jake,' he said, cutting him short in what Jake considered a thoroughly unfeeling way, 'because it won't wash.'

'Can we go in Daddy's boat?'

'No, that we really can't do. The *Aphrodite*'s been laid up for the winter. I'll take you out in her in the summer. We'll have to go in Nonna's old *pilotina* if Yannis isn't using it.' Guy and Richard had always shared a sailing boat, but during the winter months they kept it down at Gouvia, the island's original, fortified, safe harbour, which had been so strategically important to the Venetians, and was still a wonderfully sheltered bay. The ancient Vrahos *pilotina* was a utilitarian craft with a tiny cabin, a faded old canopy for the sun, an antiquated outboard engine and no pretensions to elegance.

'So how's Mum this morning?' Guy asked casually, though he felt far from casual inside.

'Dunno,' said Jake. 'Dora said she might take her up her breakfast in bed so I wasn't to wake her. And I didn't,' he added virtuously.

'Quite right. Give me twenty minutes and we'll take a weather-check. You scoot off and find Angelo, and I'll call you when I'm ready.'

He was still not sure how much Victoria had overheard the evening before because Evanthi, without a second's hesitation, had said: 'Oh, Victoria, you've come at just the right moment! Guy has been telling me such lovely news – which he's somehow managed to keep from you all day because he wanted me to be the first to know – Francine's having a baby! Isn't that wonderful?' Guy thought that whatever toll old age might be taking on his grandmother's body, there was absolutely nothing wrong with her wits.

'Guy doesn't seem very keen on sharing his news with me himself nowadays,' said Victoria in a tight little voice. She gave her cousin a blistering look. 'First his wedding . . . now this. Well, many congratulations then, Guy.' And she had turned and walked out of the room.

Guy started to go after her but Evanthi laid a restraining hand on his arm.

'Leave her,' she said. 'She's too upset. Give her time. Now, will you help me upstairs? I need to rest first if I'm to dine with you both.'

They had met again for the simple dinner Dora had left prepared for them. It was a tense meal with none of the teasing – or even fierce argument – that normally took place in the dining room at Vrahos when there was a family reunion: usually everyone spoke at once with the noise levels rising on gales of laughter. Now an icy distance on Victoria's part and an awkward silence on Guy's that was quite foreign to them both replaced the cousins' customary ease and delight in each other's company. Evanthi, suddenly looking old and exhausted, had made a few sporadic attempts at conversation and then lapsed into silence herself. As soon as they had finished eating she retired to bed, and Victoria had gone up with her.

'Can I look in on you to say good night when I come up, Vicky?' Guy had asked, hoping to break through the electric fence she had put round herself, but she had looked at him with a distaste that turned him to stone and said no thank you – she just wanted to be left alone and go to sleep. She had left him to telephone his wife and drink rather more whisky than he intended in his grandfather's library under the baleful eye of the stuffed eagle that had once frightened him so much as a small boy.

But upstairs in her white childhood bedroom, more desperate and confused than she had thought possible, her thoughts in a turmoil, Victoria had not slept all night.

A rising wind was whipping the olive trees when Guy went out on to the terrace. It would not have made him hesitate if he'd been going on his own, but it was sufficient to make him think twice before taking two small boys too far out to sea. Storms could blow up with alarming speed, and apart from the safety angle he had no desire to cope with seasick children. He'd hoped to go down the coast beyond Aghia Sophia and out to the uninhabited rocky little island a mile offshore – the scene of countless expeditions when he and Richard and Victoria were children – a place of entirely happy memories. He was seized with a longing to go there now – to face some private demons, make some resolutions for the future and try to lay ghosts from the past – but perhaps the weather was doing him a favour. For that particular purpose it would be better to go alone. The island hadn't been inhabited for years, except by visiting swallows, who built or renovated nests in the stone ruins of what must once have been an old house – a welcome and very exclusive summer resort after their journey from Africa. Last summer he, Richard and Victoria had taken Jake there and spent an idyllic day swimming and sunbathing; making a driftwood fire on the beach and barbecuing *souvlaki*. They had come across the remains of the rough wooden playhouse that Nafsica's husband, Socrates, had put up for them years ago when they were going through a camping phase. Jake had been enchanted, spent a blissful time making a den in it and had been longing to revisit this paradise ever since. Guy was thankful he hadn't mentioned it last night. 'There's too much wind to go down the coast,' he said. 'How would it be if we went along to the harbour at Kryovrisi for an ice?'

'Cool,' Jake beamed at him. Any boat trip was a treat.

'You could fish off the jetty for a bit, so get some bread for bait and put your life jackets on, I'll get the lines and hooks and we'll see if Dora wants any shopping done.' It occurred to him that if the wind really got up before the return trip he could telephone Yannis and ask him to come and pick up the boys in the car while he brought the boat back on his own.

Dora was in the kitchen, just about to take up Victoria's breakfast. Nafsica was sitting at the wooden kitchen table – scrubbed almost white over the years – mumbling her way through a bowl of bread and milk. She owned a perfectly good set of teeth, made by the dentist in Kérkyra and paid for by Evanthi, but she regarded them in much the same light as her best dress – only to be worn on special occasions. She was dressed in her habitual black, her face as brown and wrinkled as a walnut. She was a couple of years younger than Evanthi but the fierce Mediterranean sun is not kind to women's complexions unless they are protected and cosseted. Nafsica had looked sixty when she was in her forties, whereas Evanthi had looked much younger than her years until she was over seventy. Nafsica greeted Guy with doting affection – and what Victoria considered the maddening reverence she accorded to the male sex. Victoria always claimed that Nafsica had ruined Guy when they were children by encouraging all his most outrageously arrogant attitudes. Evanthi had already told Dora the news about Francine's pregnancy when she called her with her morning tisane, so Guy was forced to delay the boating trip while Nafsica insisted on filling him up not only with a celebratory glass of Metaxa – not his chosen drink at that hour of the morning – but also with dire tales about every conceivable disaster that could occur in childbirth.

He was gulping down the last of the fiery Greek brandy when Dora returned with the breakfast tray. 'That was quick,' he said, and then seeing that nothing on the tray had been touched asked: 'She hasn't eaten a thing – is she all right?'

'She wasn't there,' said Dora. 'I don't know where she is. She's not with Kyria because I checked.'

'Probably gone for a walk then,' said Guy lightly. 'I expect she's at the viewpoint – you know how she loves to go there. We'll meet her on our way down to the bay. Come on then, you two.'

'I'll come down with you and bring the spare petrol can,' said Yannis, appearing in the kitchen. 'I think it's running low. We'll put some in to be on safe side and then you could get more and also refill the can in Kryovrisi.'

There was no sign of Victoria on the way down. The boys ran about whooping and laughing; pushing each other over and rolling downhill like a couple of puppies, but Guy and Yannis strode quickly down the track, each keeping a sharp lookout for her. When they got to the bay, the sea was more than a little choppy, the wind definitely getting up – and there was no boat tied up to the landing stage.

'Where the hell . . .?' started Guy, and then: 'Oh my God!' He and Yannis looked at each other.

'Victoria – she can't have gone off by herself? In this weather?'

'Looks bloody like it. Where else could the boat be – or her? How much petrol was there?' asked Guy.

'Enough to get to Kryovrisi. Not enough to go much further.'

149

Yannis' normally cheerful face was creased with anxiety. Black clouds were rolling overhead and a few drops of rain were now falling.

Though Victoria was reasonably competent with boats, they had never been a passion with her as they had been with the boys and she was inclined to be a nervous sailor; she enjoyed expeditions if someone else was in charge of the boat, and was prepared to take it out herself in good conditions to do the shopping in Kryovrisi or take Jake to a nearby bay on a lovely day, but she certainly wasn't given to taking solo trips for fun. All the same, under ordinary circumstances Guy would not have been too concerned – but circumstances were anything but normal at the moment. He had told his grandmother the night before that he felt afraid of tipping her over an edge after all she had already been through. He thought of her standing too near the edge of the cliff at Angelókastro – and suddenly the memory didn't bear thinking of.

He felt in a pocket for his mobile. 'What's Petros' number?' he asked urgently, then: 'Shit! Shit! I'd forgotten there's no bloody signal here. I'll have to go straight back up to use the house telephone. Anyone else who could lend us a boat if I can't get hold of Petros?'

Yannis looked doubtful. 'Petros is the best one.'

Petros Kaloudis was the entrepreneur of Kryovrisi. His father had been a local fisherman and from small beginnings Petros had started hiring out boats in the tourist season, a business that had rapidly grown into a flourishing concern. He and his English wife now owned the popular Harbour Lights bar and there were not many local pies in which he did not have a finger. Guy and Victoria had known him all their lives. He and Guy were old sailing companions.

'What's happened to the boat? Where's Mummy?' Jake's voice wobbled dangerously.

Guy squatted down and took him by the shoulders. Jake seemed all delicate bones. It was like holding a bird between his hands. 'Looks like Mummy's stolen a march on us, old boy, and nabbed the boat before us. We won't half give her a piece of our minds when she gets back – spoiling our trip! But I must get petrol to her right now and I need you to be a grown-up chap and not make a fuss. You and Angelo can stay with Yannis and I'm going to find her.'

'She won't have got shot will she?' asked Jake in a whisper.

'No, of course not.' Guy felt his throat constrict. 'But she'll need help with the boat in this wind and the best way *you* can help is to stay with Angelo and let me go to her. OK?' Jake nodded. 'Good man.'

Guy spoke rapidly to Yannis in Greek, who agreed to stay on the landing stage in case there was any sign of Victoria while Guy went up to the house to telephone Petros and try to borrow a boat. He would send Dora down to collect the boys.

It was a good thing he was in training. He ran all the way up the steep path.

Petros had just walked into the bar when Guy rang.

'*O The' mou!* Where's she gone?'

'God knows. But she might have headed down towards Aghia Sophia.' Guy had the strongest hunch that Victoria, like him, might have wanted to go to the island.

Petros said he'd come straight down to Vrahos in his speed-boat and pick Guy up: 'Quicker than you coming here by car – and if she's between Kryovrisi and Vrahos I'll see her before I get to you. I'll send Spiro and Nikos out the other way.'

During the summer season Petros could be seen in his speed-boat every evening patrolling the coast to make sure none of his clients had got into trouble and that all the hired boats – about which some of the holiday-makers knew absolutely nothing – could be accounted for and were properly anchored. If the weather looked really rough he would send his brothers to collect the boats and take them back to the shelter of Kryovrisi harbour till the wind settled again.

'I'll be on the landing stage.' Guy rang off.

It was only about ten minutes before Petros roared up in his powerful boat and he and Guy set off to the south, looking anxiously out to sea as well as scanning every small bay along the coast. They passed Spilia with its famous cave, and the pretty little harbour of Aghia Sophia with its two rival tavernas – until recently only accessible by boat, but now joined to the main road by a steep track. There was no sign. Guy had no idea how long Victoria had been missing – or what her intention might have been, but as they headed out towards the island, known locally as Helidonia – the island of swallows – he hoped desperately that his hunch was taking them in the right direction.

At five o'clock in the morning Victoria had abandoned hope of sleep – or rather decided she couldn't face the possibility that after eight hours of aching insomnia she might suddenly drop off just as morning was approaching only to have to wake again in a couple of hours and face afresh her turmoil of misery. She opened the shutters and leaned out of the window. She felt terrible. The first glimmerings of dawn streaked the sky and everything seemed extraordinarily still – as though the whole island was holding its breath, waiting for something to happen. She felt desperate to order her thoughts before she faced anyone: Guy, Evanthi – even Jake – but most especially Guy. She had no idea how she was going to cope with all her conflicting emotions about him. The sea had always been her source of help and healing – she would let herself out of the house, walk to the viewpoint to watch the light creep over the mountains, look down on the sea, and think.

She tiptoed into Jake's room. She'd left the landing door ajar and a light burning all night and could see that he was sleeping peacefully, one arm flung over the pillow the other clutching the ancient rabbit that was still a necessary night-time companion. She stood looking at him, anguishing for his present and trembling for his future.

Victoria shivered, and closed the door softly as she went back into her own room. She dressed swiftly, took her trainers in one hand and padded softly along the passage and down the stairs in her stockinged feet; as she went through the salon with its treacherous, creaking floor-boards she felt as if she must have roused the whole household – but all was silence. She inhaled the familiar scents of the room: the pungent smoky smell of olive-wood fires mixing with the heavier fragrance of lilies; the smell of old leather books blending with the fainter trace of Evanthi's own distinctive scent. Normally all these smells would have been reassuring, but this morning, to her distraught mind, they were reminders of a world that seemed to be crumbling round her.

Opening the huge double doors was a noisy business, and after she had managed to raise the heavy iron bar, which latched across them, and then turned the vast key in the lock, she was relieved to get out on to the top terrace, put on her shoes and walk noiselessly over the flag stones and down the outside steps. Cocks were crowing and a donkey brayed raucously from the olive grove, all sounds evocative of her childhood – though donkeys were growing obsolete as beasts-of-all-work nowadays and those that had simply been abandoned and turned loose were becoming a real problem on the island. The idea of culling wild donkeys filled her with horror.

When she reached the viewpoint a breeze was beginning to feather through the olive trees, turning the leaves from green to silver and back again against the grey beginnings of the new day. Albania had disappeared in cloud and the sea looked leaden – the view was not at its beautiful best. She decided to get nearer to the sea and go on down to the bay, memories flooding her mind of many expeditions with Richard and Guy as she walked down the rough path between the scrub and holly oaks.

When she saw the boat she didn't stop to think at all, but on an impulse hauled on the mooring rope, pulled the boat in and clambered aboard. She lowered the outboard engine into the water and it started at the first pull on the cord.

To begin with she had no particular destination in mind and was only conscious of a liberating sense of escape as she headed out to sea, relishing the taste of salt on her lips and the feeling of wind blowing through her hair. It wasn't until she passed the point at Spilia that the idea of going as far as the island took hold of her. Then it seemed an absolute necessity to get there – as though if she could only reach it she might find magic solutions to all her problems, as though she might recapture and rewrite the past. With some part of her mind she was aware that the weather was deteriorating fast, that the sea was wilder – waves slapping the bows with increasing fury – and that she had never been by herself in such rough conditions before. But wrapped in a curious detachment, to her none of this seemed to matter. It was as though she was protected from reality and as the island came into view she felt triumphant.

Waves were pluming above the rocks, sending up great fountains of spray when it suddenly occurred to Victoria that she would have considerable trouble landing. Worse – what if she managed to land but hadn't the strength to moor the boat properly? It was as though an electric current had been passed through her, giving her such a jolt that she literally jerked – and came to her senses.

But with sense came fear. What a fool she was! What on earth had possessed her? No good even attempting to get on the island today – the sooner she turned for home the better. Perhaps she could get back before anyone discovered that in her unbalanced state of misery she had attempted such a pointless and foolhardy expedition. She knew it would be much slower and more difficult going back with a head wind, rain and the sea becoming rougher by the minute. As she struggled to turn the boat against the waves she wondered if Jake was awake yet, had perhaps pattered into her room to snuggle into her bed as he often did if he woke early – and found her gone. Jake! Have I gone completely and utterly mad? she thought, in horror. How could I have done anything so reckless? Real terror now took over.

She became aware that the engine seemed to be firing unevenly, stuttering and then racing, but she had no idea what this signified or what to do about it. Dear God! Don't let the engine fail, she prayed desperately. Help me! Save me! Save me for Jake. And she started to bargain incoherently with the unknown deity whose very existence she had so recently started to doubt. She thought of the Vrahos icon and found herself babbling all the childish prayers she had been taught by Evanthi years ago, desperately invoking the two saints depicted on it – both famous miracle workers – repeating their names over and over again. She was already soaked to the skin and she was quite oblivious to the tears that now poured down her face and mingled indistinguishably with the rain and spray that lashed her cheeks.

It was at this moment that the engine cut out completely.

Chapter Sixteen

It was a terrible moment when Guy sighted the Vrahos *pilotina*, bucketing drunkenly about in the open sea at a terrifying angle, the stern already awash. There was no one in it.

'Did she have a life jacket on?' asked Petros.

'God, I hope so.'

Guy knew that Yannis kept one stowed away on the boat but whether Victoria knew this, or in her present state of mind would have put it on, he didn't dare to think. He trained his binoculars on the bay and then handed them to Petros.

'Look,' he said. There was definitely something orange on the one small beach where it was possible to land. Neither of them spoke. As they got closer they could make out a figure in a life jacket – but it was impossible to tell what sort of state it might be in. As Petros brought the boat in as close as he could, Guy flung himself overboard and waded ashore. The water felt arctic.

'Vicky!' he shouted as he ran up the beach. 'Vicky! We're here. It's all right.'

Victoria was slumped against a rock, absolutely still with her eyes shut. There was clotted blood on her forehead and she made no movement. Although she must have been conscious enough to drag herself a short way up the beach at some stage, for one awful moment he thought she was dead. Then he detected a faint pulse. He held her to him, chafing her hands, rubbing her back and speaking urgently to her. He didn't think the wound on her forehead looked deep, but she was like a block of ice and quite as unresponsive.

'Come on, Vicky, come *on* – speak to me,' he said urgently. 'Wake up. Can you hear me?'

She let out a moan and her eyelids flickered. Then she opened them and stared at him.

'Jake?' she asked faintly. 'Jake?'

'Jake's fine. Are you hurt?'

'D-Don't think so – don't know. I c-can't remember.' She seemed thoroughly confused, closed her eyes and appeared to drift off to sleep.

'*Wake up*,' said Guy again. 'Try to tell me what happened?'

She opened her eyes but for a moment looked quite blank. Then she seemed to be making an effort to concentrate. 'I th-think I hit my h-head trying to crawl ashore. I couldn't – couldn't land – then the engine f-failed. The boat f-filled up with water and I th-thought it was going to s-sink.'

It didn't seem the moment to remind her of the golden rule that you should stick with your boat until it actually sinks. Her teeth suddenly started to chatter violently – a good sign, Guy knew. The relief was overwhelming. Together Guy and Petros got her into his boat, wrapped her in a blanket and forced some brandy down her throat.

'Better go to Kryovrisi,' suggested Guy. 'We'll never get her up the path to Vrahos if we go to the bay.'

Petros nodded. 'I'll run you home in my car. It will be quicker.'

Guy suddenly felt furious with Victoria – all his pent-up anxiety surfacing now that the crisis was over.

'What the hell did you think you were playing at?' he demanded, only just restraining himself from shaking her. 'You bloody, irresponsible little fool. How could you do such a stupid thing?'

'Sorry,' she whispered. 'S-So sorry. I must have been m-mad.' She closed her eyes again and leaned against him. 'I feel a bit muddled,' she murmured.

'It's all right,' he said gruffly, the anger draining out of him as he looked down at her. 'We'll talk later – but oh, Vicky don't ever, ever give us a fright like that again.'

Later Guy came to say goodbye to Victoria before Yannis drove him to the airport to catch an early evening flight to Athens. He thought she looked very slight and fragile in the great bed, her face as white as the big square pillows against which she was propped, her dark, almost black hair and eyes emphasising the pallor of her skin.

The doctor had been earlier and checked her over, dressed the cut on her head, which luckily, he said, was not deep, but added that since she had obviously lost consciousness for a short time and must have been concussed, she should stay quiet in bed. He announced that he would look in again the following day to check on her. Dora had packed hot-water bottles round her and Victoria had drifted in and out of sleep most of the afternoon. Now Jake was curled up beside her like a puppy.

'I must say, you two look very cosy,' said Guy with an attempt at cheerfulness that he did not feel. 'Jake, Nonna wants you to go down to have tea with her in the little drawing room.'

'Can't I stay and have it with Mum?'

'I think Nonna would be disappointed – she wants to play spillikins with you after tea. She says you beat her on your last visit here before she was ill and now she's so much better she wants her revenge. You can come back to Mum later. I'll come and see if you're winning before I go. Off you go – there's a good chap.'

'I'm very, very good at spillikins so I expect I'll win,' said Jake modestly, climbing off the bed. Then he suddenly turned and clutched Victoria in a violent bear hug that made her wince. Her head throbbed and she felt dreadful. She stroked his cheek. 'Run along then darling,' she said. 'But come back and see me later.'

'You won't go away again, will you?' he asked from the doorway.

'I promise,' she said, horribly conscious that she had multiplied his insecurities.

Guy closed the door after Jake and came to sit on the edge of her bed in his place. They looked at each other in silence for a minute, both conscious that there were many things that might be said, but neither of them wanting to be the first to speak.

Then Victoria said in a low voice, 'When the boat started to sink I absolutely willed you to come and rescue me – and you did. How did you know where I'd gone?'

'Because I'd wanted to go there too,' he answered. 'To look for answers and try to make sense of things. Call it a sixth sense or a lucky guess but all that matters is that you're all right.'

'Yes,' she whispered. 'I must have been crazy – completely out of my mind. What you told me came as such a terrible shock. I'm haunted by how desperate Richard must have been to do such a terrible thing, and yet I still feel so bitter with you both. I don't know how I'm going to come to terms with it.'

'Have I lost you, Vicky?' he asked abruptly. 'Will we ever be able to get back to how things were?'

'I don't know,' she said. 'I just don't know, Guy. I'm truly thankful to you for saving me but that's as far as I can go at the moment. I can't take in that Richard was really someone quite different from the husband I thought I knew so well – I simply can't get my head around that at all. Last night I went over and over our marriage, trying to look for signs that should have warned me – trying to bring Richard back. Wondering when it all went wrong and why I didn't see it years ago. But all I could focus on was that Richard wasn't real – that our relationship, all our years together, were a fake *and that you knew it all along*. But I hate myself too. It doesn't bear thinking of that I risked what blighted my own childhood happening to Jake – losing both parents!'

She put her hands over her eyes as though to blot out an unbearable sight, then moved her head on the pillow and winced again. She said, 'I've been lying here trying to dredge up every detail about my mother and father – something I hardly ever do now. When I was Jake's age I used to conjure them up every night before I went to sleep, although it was almost too painful to bear. I was always terrified that one day I might try to take them out of the private place in my head only to find they weren't there any more, and had faded away like watercolours exposed to too much light. It was a horror I could never tell anyone – not even Nonna. Now I can't find Richard in my head and even if I did, I wouldn't any longer know what was real and what was my imagination. It's a nightmare.'

Guy took her hand but it lay, limp and unresponsive in his. He didn't trust himself to speak.

'How well do *you* remember my parents?' she asked.

'Oh, very well. Don't forget I was nearly twelve at the time of the crash. I suppose I didn't see them *that* often but they made a huge impression whenever they came over to stay with us, or if we all overlapped here. Your mother was wonderfully pretty and I was as susceptible as most small boys to charm. And Uncle Constantine always seemed incredibly dashing and funny. I longed to be like him – I clearly remember that.'

'You're very like him to look at now,' said Victoria. 'You even smile and move like him. I know you do because just before Christmas last year when we'd gone over for Sunday lunch at Durnford, Toula had been turning out the attic and come across a box of old cine films – oh, of lots of things, like her and Uncle Anthony's wedding, and you when you were little, and suddenly there were Pappa and Mamma with me as a baby. Jake was watching the film with us so I pretended I was thrilled to see it all, but afterwards when we'd got home I started to cry and simply couldn't stop. Richard was awfully bothered but I couldn't help it. Of course I'd seen ordinary photographs before, but it was different to see them moving and laughing and waving . . . and, and *holding* me. It was the most extraordinary shock.'

Guy could see she was reliving the moment. The drowsiness must be wearing off, he thought, because the words now seemed to be pouring out of her in a feverish sort of way – but at least she was speaking to him again.

'D'you know what I still mind most?' she asked. He shook his head. 'That I never said goodbye to them. Isn't that strange after all these years? And now Jake and I couldn't say goodbye to Richard either.' She gazed at him with a haunted look in her eyes.

'When do you mean to come back to England?' he asked at last. 'I don't imagine you'll be up to travelling for a bit. Will you stay out here for Easter?'

She pleated the sheet between her fingers. 'I might not come back this summer at all,' she said. 'Not just because of what happened this morning but because of lots of other things too. I suppose you could say I'd be running away.'

'No, of course not. I think it might be right for you. Nonna would adore it. Look, Vicky – you can't escape from what's happened wherever you are, so you should be in whichever place helps you cope best. Stay out here all summer – and then review the situation.'

'I'm not sending Jake back without me.'

'Jake's half Greek anyway. What's wrong with him living in this country for a bit? I think it would be good for him – a break with the past, but in familiar surroundings. Why don't you send him to school in Kryovrisi with Angelo for the summer? He'd pick up the language without even trying – children do. We did. You don't need to take any long-term decisions yet.'

'The Cunninghams won't like it. Can you imagine what Meriel and June will say – they've always been darkly suspicious of my "foreign blood". I might come from Mars, as far as they're concerned. They never thought I was the right sort of wife for Richard – Meriel didn't, anyway – but while he was alive they had to accept me. I dread all their criticism now. And what about poor Bill?'

'The ugly sisters will have to look after him. Poor chap, he has to cope with his grief in his own way too – we all do. With the best of intentions you mightn't be much help to each other at the moment. And it's not as if you're proposing to keep Jake away from him for ever. Bill could come out and see you both here, if he wanted to.' He looked at his watch. 'I hate leaving you,' he said reluctantly, 'but I have to go. I daren't miss this flight because I have that big interview to do first thing tomorrow.'

'I know you do,' she said dully. 'You told me.'

He wondered sadly if the precious, almost telepathic, bond there had always been between them would ever return.

'Will you still come and stay with me . . . with us . . . in London?' he asked.

'I don't know.' Then, with an obvious effort she said: 'Give . . . give my love to Francine. And, Guy?'

'Yes?'

'Tell her I'm pleased for you both about the baby.'

'Yes,' he said, 'I'll do that. That's very generous of you. One day, you and Francine might even get to like each other better than either of you thinks possible now.' He added wryly, 'You're the only person I know who makes her really nervous. Quite an achievement.' She gave him an unfathomable look.

He got up. 'I must say goodbye to Nonna before I go. Forgive me if you can, Vicky.' He bent over to give her a farewell kiss but she did not respond. 'Take as long as you need to lick your wounds – and then start living again. I think the wind is going to change for you.'

She watched him go. At the door he turned, hoping for her usual smile – but she turned her face away. Then she heard him running downstairs and a few minutes later the slam of a car door. The wind had dropped as suddenly as it had got up earlier that morning, and the house seemed strangely quiet after the racket of the storm. She wondered from which direction the next wind would blow and whether she would welcome the changes it might bring.

She thought it was typical of Guy to dash off and leave so much unresolved. She lay straining her ears to hear the sound of the car driving off – taking Guy away from her. Taking him back to his wife.

Chapter Seventeen

Patrick reread the letter on his desk, took a decision and picked up the telephone. Then he went to look for his wife.

She was in the drawing room writing letters and he stood looking at her for a moment.

'Darling?'

'Mmm?' Rachel turned round, her pretty face marred by the look of discontent that his presence seemed to invoke nowadays.

'I've just made a plan. I hope you'll approve.'

'What sort of a plan?' Rachel immediately looked defensive.

'A plan for a holiday. I can't go on putting off this trip to Greece much longer, but more importantly I think we all five need to get away together for a break. I think we could combine the two things. How about taking the Marshalls' house on Corfu for a week over Easter? You know what fun we had there when we went with them – one of our most successful holidays with the children.'

'Oh, Patrick! It's far too short notice. Anyway, I shouldn't think for a moment it would be free over Easter.' Rachel was at her most dampening.

'It *is* free,' said Patrick levelly. 'I've just rung Maggie on the off chance – they're not going there themselves till June and by great good luck the people they'd let it to for Easter have cancelled.'

'You've talked to Maggie about it without asking me first?'

'I'm asking you now. You wouldn't come with me on your own five weeks ago so let's all go together and make it a proper family holiday. I could go on to mainland Greece and possibly Italy later but it's this old Venetian House on Corfu I really want to see first and I've just heard from Winterton's that they've got permission for me to photograph it – but Saphira thinks I ought to buck up and get on with it because old Evanthi Doukas, who owns it, is pretty frail.' Saphira Winterton was Patrick's agent. 'What do you say?' he asked. 'Saphira says the old lady's agreed to give me an interview provided she's well enough. It seems such a marvellous opportunity.'

'I'll have to think about it. I'm not sure it suits my plans. Anyway what makes you think Sam and Sophie would want to come? It was great when they were younger but they'd probably rather head off somewhere with their own friends now. We can't expect them to keep on wanting to go on holiday with us.' Coming from Rachel, who always made endless objections whenever any of her young wanted to branch out and do something in which she had no hand, Patrick thought this was a bit rich.

'Actually they both think it's a great idea,' he said, an edge to his voice. Then not wanting to be unnecessarily confrontational, he added on a milder note, 'Sophie informs me she desperately needs a chance to "chill", as she calls it – which is certainly what she'll do in a bikini in April – and Sam can't wait to see all the boozy local friends he made when he worked in that bar in Corfu town for a few weeks last summer. He thinks he's an authority on the island.' He gave his wife an amused grin but there was no answering glimmer.

'You mean you asked them before you asked me? I don't believe what I'm hearing.' Rachel's face was tight with anger. 'Has their opinion suddenly become more important than mine?'

There was a silence. Then Patrick said coolly: 'It never has been before – as you very well know – but yes, Rachel. This time I think it is. And you're not in a strong position to expect me to put your wishes before everyone else's. I'm fed up with having a wife who never wants to do anything with me, who always puts one of our children before the rest of us. I've had enough.'

'Meaning?'

'You know perfectly well what I mean. We can't go on like this – living together almost like strangers, worse than strangers because of all this hostility. No joint discussions. No sharing – no *fun* any more.'

'And if I say no?'

'Then Sam and Sophie and I will go,' said Patrick decisively.

'Posy can come too as far as I'm concerned, though I'm well aware you wouldn't like that. Think carefully, Rachel. It would be much, much better if you came too – I can't tell you how much I hope you will – but it's up to you and I'm not going to go on asking.'

Rachel shook her head. 'I can't possibly give you an answer off the top of my head. There are other plans to consider.'

'I'm afraid you'll have to decide now.' Patrick's voice was quiet but there was an anger in it that Rachel was unused to hearing and she was taken aback. 'I need to let Maggie know – and Olympic Airways will only hold provisional bookings till lunchtime. There's no problem about which day we'd come back but the flights going out are very booked up before Easter. So will you and Posy come or not?'

Rachel didn't really like the idea of them all going off without her – but some demon prevented her from agreeing to go too.

'You're being quite unreasonable. I can't possibly come at such short notice,' she said. 'I'd made a provisional plan to do something with Bronwen over Easter – she's got Hetta for a week then – so I'd need to talk it over with her first.'

She expected Patrick to argue, but he just raised an eyebrow and said: 'I see. Pity.' And then quite briskly: 'Right then. I'll get on with organising it for the three of us.'

And he turned on his heel and left his wife staring after him.

The Marshalls' house, up in the hills above Kryovrisi, was reached by a winding track that bore more resemblance to the bed of a stream than a road.

'I notice roads more now I'm learning to drive,' announced Sophie, 'but gosh, I'd like to know what little Mr Swayne would make of this one. It seems to take ages to get anywhere here. It can't be that far in distance.'

'You're in Greece now – time and distance have different meanings,' said Sam loftily. 'You'll have to get used to it.'

Sophie punched him on the arm. 'What worldly wisdom – oh, thou who art so widely travelled,' she mocked. 'It wasn't *that* long ago when we all came with the Marshalls. Look, Dad, isn't that it? It looks just the same as I remember – oh, I do love coming back to places.'

Patrick parked the hired car at the side of the house, where a big ilex tree provided welcome shade in summer, and they all piled out. Sam and Sophie had been wonderful company on the journey. He'd been touched and amused by their solicitude; he suspected they had made some sort of pact to try to make up to him for Rachel's absence, and even though – he thought wryly – it made him feel positively geriatric, it warmed his heart. He'd been entertained by their high spirits and light-hearted sparring – which not very long ago would quickly have deteriorated into bickering – and was struck by what good companions they had become. He realised with a guilty shock that he felt carefree for the first time in ages without the oppressive company of his wife. He decided he would try to forget his worries about the state of his marriage for the next week and enjoy the break. When he returned, he and Rachel would have to make a serious effort to sort things out.

'I'm absolutely starving,' announced Sam. 'It must be nearly three and we haven't had lunch. What's the form about food, Dad?'

'Let's locate the key first and then we'll forage. Maggie said she'd get old Lefka to leave basic supplies but I expect we'll need to stock up before tomorrow – specially knowing your capacity, Sam.'

The key had been left under a plant of small-leafed basil in a terracotta pot at the back door.

'Marvellous! First place a burglar would look – we could never do that at home,' said Patrick as he fitted it in the door.

The Villa Petradi – like the jewel from which it took its name – nestled in a silver setting of olive groves. Phil and Maggie Marshall had converted the house out of an old olive press and they had been careful to preserve its original charm, using the old stone and curved roof tiles that were so much a feature of local buildings. The walls were stuccoed a pale apricot and the shutters were painted green. A wide terrace, partly covered overhead, ran round three sides of the house, which consisted of two ground-floor wings on either side of a central hall. One wing contained two small double bedrooms and a bathroom; the other wing was taken up by a large comfortable sitting room with an eating area up one end and a kitchen and utility room opening out of it at the back. Phil and Maggie's own bedroom in the centre of the house was the only upstairs room and was reached by an outside flight of stone steps at the back of the house.

They stepped from the bright sunlight outside, into the cool dimness of the hall. During the summer months this was often a relief, but now the house struck rather cold. Patrick knew from Maggie that they were the first guests of the season, and though Lefka, the caretaker, kept the house aired and would have made up beds for them, Maggie had warned Patrick that they would probably need to light a fire in the sitting room and turn on the electric heaters in the bedrooms. Despite the chill there was a relaxed, lived-in feeling to the whole house that made it instantly welcoming.

'Oh, the hats! I'd forgotten all about the hats,' said Sophie. An old wooden hat-stand in the entrance hall was hung with a selection of battered straw and Panama hats, baseball caps and children's sunhats, some belonging to the Marshalls, some left behind by visitors, but always borrowed by anyone renting the house. Sophie took down a sombrero, tipped it over her nose and struck a pose.

'Glamorous student Sophie Hammond relaxing at her sunshine retreat after the rigours of her hard-working term,' she announced. 'Read her fascinating story in *Hello!*'

'*Glamorous?* Dream on, Sophe!' Sam snorted derisively. 'I'm off in search of food.'

Patrick was reassured to find Petradi as delightful as he'd remembered – unpretentious enough not to be an anxiety for guests with children and very much a home too, with family possessions lying about and leaving clues to the various interests and tastes of the owners. There were bowls of shells and stones collected over the years, family photographs and shelves of books to cater for a variety of tastes; a big painted wooden chest in the hall was full of board games and packs of cards; tennis racquets and golf clubs were stuck in the umbrella stand and at one end of the terrace there was a rather dilapidated ping-pong table. He sent grateful thoughts to Maggie Marshall and felt well pleased that so far his idea seemed to have got off to a good start.

Inside, the house was painted white throughout, but vivid watercolour paintings of the island and a collection of colourful pottery in the strong greens and blues that look so good in the clear Mediterranean light, prevented it from looking too stark. In the sitting room there were two big squashy sofas positively inviting teenagers to sprawl across them, several deep comfortable armchairs and a couple of beanbags.

Sam headed straight for the kitchen and opened the fridge, where he was greatly relieved to find a supply of eggs, cheese, butter and bread. A second fridge on the terrace was stocked with beer, Coke, Fanta orange and mineral water; a couple of bottles of local wine had thoughtfully been provided too, and Patrick immediately opened one. Though the air was cool the midday sun was satisfyingly hot and they sat down at the table outside to eat huge plates of scrambled eggs, and then filled in the corners with fruit and cheese. Patrick raised his glass to his son and daughter. 'To a good holiday,' he said. 'It's great having you with me. And to Mum and Posy. Wish they were here too.'

Sam and Sophie exchanged looks and Patrick suddenly wondered just how much he really meant this.

Much later, when they had unpacked the car and Patrick had carefully unloaded his photographic equipment and taken it upstairs to Phil and Maggie Marshall's big bedroom, Sam and Sophie decided to go off to Kryovrisi to visit the Harbour Lights bar, where Sam had enjoyed several drinking sessions in his time off last year. Their own unpacking had consisted of hurling their backpacks on to their beds. Sophie, squirrelling in hers for a pair of shorts, managed to pull most of the rest of the contents out as well and as she surveyed the general chaos, thought with some satisfaction how much it would have irritated her tidy mother.

'Come *on*, Sophe – move it! What *are* you doing?' yelled Sam from the terrace.

'Coming.'

Father and son exchanged resigned looks. 'Girls!' groaned Sam. 'Bet she's decided to wash her hair or text Ellie Marshall or something.' Sophie always found a variety of things she absolutely *had* to do just as everyone else was ready to leave.

'At last,' he said when she finally emerged ten minutes later having exchanged her jeans for the shorts and then changed back again. 'Come on then – I'll take you for a drink when we've stocked up with provisions, and introduce you to Petros, the proprietor. I don't know if he'll remember me, but he's a great guy – the local fixer of everything round here. You'll think he's really cool, Sophe – but don't go falling for him because he's married.' Sophie gave him a pitying look. 'Can we take the car, Dad?'

'I'm afraid not. You have to be twenty-one to drive a hired car in Corfu. I'll take you down, we can all do the shopping together and then I'll come back here. You can ring me when you're ready to be collected. But don't expect Kryovrisi to be humming with people like it was in the summer,' warned Patrick. 'Maggie says quite a lot of places don't open till May – and some just open up for the Easter weekend and then close again.'

'Oh, Harbour Lights will be open,' said Sam confidently. 'I'll treat you to an Aphrodite's Aphrodisiac, Sophie – it's Petros' special concoction. All the girls go wild over them.'

'Now, Sam,' said Patrick, 'you're not to get Sophie drunk.'

'Yeah, yeah, yeah. She's just a little girl.' Sam grinned provocatively at his sister. 'Cool it, Dad! We know. You needn't come and fetch us, though – we can pick up a scooter while we're there.'

After they'd stocked up with necessities at the small local supermarket, Patrick dropped them at the main square of the pretty little fishing town of Kryovrisi, so named because of its cold spring – fresh water having always been a much-prized commodity on the island – and resisted the temptation to stay and drive them safely home again, which he knew would spoil their fun. Sam had been all round the island on a scooter the previous summer, but the thought of him taking Sophie pillion round the alarming Corfiot bends secretly filled Patrick with dismay. However, he was anxious not to dampen their enthusiasm so he managed to restrain himself to saying: 'Make sure they give you crash helmets – they're compulsory now, thank God – and don't forget about driving on the right.'

Sophie came and planted a kiss on her father's cheek. 'Don't *worry* so, Dad. We're very responsible. The question is – will *you* be all right? What will you do while we're gone?'

'I think I'll manage to survive for a short time,' said Patrick, grinning at his son and daughter. 'I'll probably have a snooze – very boring and middle-aged. I also need to do a bit of work on my notes. You can have drinks on me this evening. Have fun then. See you.'

As he heard the shrieks of laughter with which they set off down the street he reflected that Rachel would certainly disapprove of him for not staying with them. Rachel! He knew he ought to let her know they had arrived safely – once it had been the first thing he thought of on arrival anywhere when he was on his travels. Now he felt disinclined to ring her up. When he got back to the house he fetched his mobile and dialled their home number – only to hear his own voice on the answering machine telling him that neither he nor Rachel could come to the telephone at the moment.

'Darling – it's me. Just thought you'd like to know we had a good journey and everything here is fine. Sam and Sophie have gone off to look round Kryovrisi and they're in great form. Give Posy a kiss. Hope you're both all right. Bye then.'

He did not end the call by saying 'Love you', as he usually did – and hoped that Rachel would notice the omission. But what she would feel about this now, he no longer had any idea. On an impulse he punched in the Marshalls' number and was absurdly pleased when Maggie answered.

'Maggie? It's Patrick. Just thought you'd like to know that we're happily installed at Petradi and everything's perfect. I can't thank you enough for all you've done. No, we haven't seen Lefka yet but she's obviously been here and left everything we could possibly want.'

They chatted away easily for a few minutes. Maggie, sounding as warm and amused as usual, was full of enquiries about their journey and instructions to let her know if there was the slightest difficulty over anything. Patrick felt a pang of envy for Philip Marshall. He wondered if Maggie would see Rachel and mention that he'd rung her. He very much hoped she would.

*

When Sam and Sophie returned nearly three hours later the light had already gone and Patrick had begun to wonder whether any mishap had befallen them when he heard the sound of the scooter roaring up the track. He winced at the treatment its engine must be getting but was relieved when they appeared a few moment later in tearing spirits, lugging carrier bags of additional treats, some of which were beginning to ooze in an ominous way.

'Oh God! We got some ice cream but it's turning to mush. I forgot all about it,' shrieked Sophie. 'It looked so yummy I thought we could really pig out on it and – oh dear – we saw these yummy prawns as well, but they seem to have gone a bit soggy too. Will we die of what's-it poisoning if we eat them, d'you think, Dad?'

'No doubt we'll find out soon enough. Try putting the ice cream in the freezer compartment to firm it up a bit and then if we have it straight away perhaps the bugs won't have time to get going,' suggested Patrick, not really sure himself. 'But I don't think we'd better refreeze any fish so let's eat the prawns tonight too. Sounds a good enough menu to me. How on earth did you manage to clutch all that on the scooter? You have done well. So – was it fun? How was the Harbour Lights?'

'It was cool. Rather an exciting drive home – don't think you'd have enjoyed it much, Dad – the poor brother hasn't quite got the hang of the Corfiot bends yet – but Petros pretended to recognise him. And guess what? He's going to hire us an RIB – one of those rigid inflatable rubber dinghies with a whizzy engine. Now we can be completely independent if you want to do something different.' Patrick wasn't at all sure he liked the sound of this.

'Oh, by the way, Sam's fallen madly in love with an *older woman*,' went on Sophie. 'You should have seen him coming on to her. Embarrassing.'

'Oh, yes? A local lady, I take it.'

'English, actually,' said Sam, staggering up from the car with a crate of lager, where Patrick had left it earlier. 'She was really *fit*, Dad – even you'd have approved. Much too young for you, though, so don't get excited.'

'*Young?*' Sophie rolled her eyes. 'She was quite old – her child must have been at least six.'

'And was this elderly Aphrodite on holiday here then?' asked Patrick.

'I'm not sure. I think she might live out here. She seemed to know Petros very well anyway – she was having a drink with him.' Sam dumped another bag on the table. 'I said we might take her little boy out in the boat sometime,' he added casually. 'He was fishing for tiddlers off the landing stage.'

'Huh! Greasing up,' said Sophie. 'You were just *so* obvious! But then we all know how susceptible you are to older women.'

'You really do talk a load of crap sometimes, Sophie.' Sam made a lunge at his sister but she skipped deftly out of the way.

'What about lusting after Beastly Bronwen then?' she teased, taking care to stay the far side of the table.

'That's not even worth answering. You're pathetic sometimes – piss off.' Sam gave her what he intended to be a withering look – but he had gone rather red all the same.

'Well, you do seem to have had an eventful trip,' intervened Patrick, disconcerted by Sophie's insinuation and not at all wanting to be reminded about anything to do with Bronwen Richards – especially in connection with his son. 'No hope of there being any change left out of the money I gave you, I suppose?'

''Fraid not, Dad. We bought a few extra things and there was just enough left for drinks,' grinned Sam.

It was quite dark by now. While the others were gone, Patrick had found a stack of olive-wood logs – rather wet – out at the back and had laid a fire in the sitting-room grate. With the help of a packet of fire-lighters and much puffing from an enormous pair of bellows, he managed to get a roaring fire going and opened a bottle of wine for the three of them. With much arguing and hilarity they got supper together. Sophie made a very creditable Greek salad with tomatoes, cucumber, black olives and Feta cheese to go with the soggy prawns; the ice cream was voted delicious if a bit sloppy, and Sam topped the whole thing off with three Shredded Wheat drowned in long-life milk. After they'd cleared away Sophie put one of the

Marshalls' CDs of Greek music on the stereo, and curled up with the latest romance bought at Gatwick. Sam rootled in the big games chest and dug out a backgammon board and challenged his father to a game. When they finally went to bed they all agreed they'd had a thoroughly satisfactory first day.

'Night then, Dad. Sleep well.' Sophie yawned widely and gave her father a huge hug. 'Will you be all right?' she asked again.

'Of course. Good night, my darling. Good night Sam.'

Patrick climbed the outside steps to the upstairs bedroom. But as he lay alone in the Marshalls' enormous double bed, sleep eluded him. He had often travelled without Rachel on the assignments that were part of his job, and though this particular week was supposed to be partly a working trip as well as a break, it seemed strange to be in any holiday situation without her. He thought about his marriage and how it had changed – especially the last three years. Had it changed beyond recall – and if not what should he do to reverse the decline? Rachel had certainly changed; there was no doubt about that – but he was beginning to wonder if he had altered as well.

His thoughts were in turmoil.

Chapter Eighteen

Saphira Winterton had made a provisional appointment for Patrick to visit Vrahos two days after his arrival in Corfu.

'But I said you'd telephone and confirm it when you get there,' she had said. 'I gather Mrs Doukas has a married couple who look after her and apparently the wife speaks reasonable English. They should be able to help you as far as taking photographs is concerned, but not, of course, for an interview. If the old lady's well enough she'll see you herself – I believe she's fascinating, and her daughter, Toula Winston, told me when we first mooted the idea that she's still very much on the ball mentally – but if she's not up to it then I gather they could arrange for a neighbour, who's a local historian, to talk to you about the house and the family history. Toula was quite surprised her mother even agreed to contemplate the idea. Apparently there have been approaches before and she's always been dead against any publicity.'

Patrick really hoped he would be able to see Mrs Doukas. It made all the difference to catching the flavour of a place, not only in what he might write, but in what he tried to capture in the photographs he took – and it was for his brilliant evocation of atmosphere that his pictures were so greatly prized – so he was pleased when Evanthi Doukas answered the telephone herself. She had clearly forgotten all about the appointment for the following day, but remembered the original correspondence.

'Ah – it's all coming back to me now. You must forgive me. I've had a stupid illness and been *hors de combat* for some weeks. I believe you are a friend of my son-in-law, Anthony Winston – is that right?'

'Well, no, it's actually my agent, Saphira Winterton, who knows your daughter – but I did meet your son-in-law once when I had to photograph a big exhibition of oriental art for the

Royal Academy a few years ago and he had loaned some of the exhibits. He was extremely helpful and interesting. He did get in touch with me again to see if I could help with illustrations for a catalogue he wanted doing, but I was embroiled with my last book and had a deadline to meet so I couldn't help him. I've heard what a wonderful house you have.'

'Ah – the house is an old lady now – like me. We are neither of us quite what we once were. You mustn't expect too much of us, but I would be pleased for you to see it. So – where are you now then?'

Patrick explained.

'Oh, then you are really quite close – as the crow flies, though humans tend to take a little longer than crows to get around on Corfu. But you won't be more than about twenty minutes away by car. Would you like to come to lunch?'

'No, no. I wouldn't want to put you to any trouble. Besides, I have my son and daughter with me so I'll probably meet them for lunch somewhere. If I could just come over tomorrow morning and have a preliminary talk with you that would be wonderful – and I promise not to stay too long. Then perhaps I could arrange to come back later and take some photographs without having to bother you?'

'You can certainly do that, of course – but do come to lunch. You can bring your family with you. I can't get about much myself any more but I like young people and I have my granddaughter staying so it would be fun for her to meet you all.'

'Well, that's really very kind.' Patrick wasn't sure how much Sam and Sophie would welcome this suggestion but felt he could hardly refuse. He gave Mrs Doukas the Petradi telephone number in case she should want to put them off, and she suggested they should arrive about twelve so that she and Patrick could talk before lunch. 'I'm under doctor's orders to rest in the afternoons.'

Sam and Sophie groaned when he told them.

'Oh, Dad, no! It'll wreck the whole day!' said Sophie tragically. 'Can't you ring back and say Sam and me are doing something else? She can't really want us any more than we want to go.'

'She says she does. She particularly wants you to come

because she's got a granddaughter staying and thinks it would be nice for her to meet other young.'

'Worse and worse! I know that scenario.' Sophie rolled her eyes. 'Mrs Thing'll go "Now do let's get all our young things together again,"' she put on a social voice very reminiscent of her mother, 'and *you'll* go, "Well, that's extremely kind of you," and be all polite like you always are and *we'll* get clobbered with having to *do* things with this random granddaughter, who'll probably be really *sad* and want to tag along all the time – and then there'll be awful plans and it'll spoil *everything*.'

'How old is she, anyway?' Sam enquired, looking equally gloomy. He didn't think it would enhance his cool image with the Older Woman to have some teenager hanging around who might be mistaken for his girlfriend. He intended to grill Petros about the identity of his goddess whom he was determined to track down again.

'She didn't say,' said Patrick. 'I think she has a grown-up granddaughter whose husband has just been killed, but it doesn't sound as if it's her. Sorry, guys – you'll have to be human sacrifices in the cause of my work. Just for lunch tomorrow – and I'll guarantee to protect you from any future involvement. If there's even a sniff of more plans I'll say I know you've got a hectic social schedule and can't fit in anything else at all. Deal?'

Sophie sighed dramatically. 'Oh, well, OK then – just for you, Dad – but we'll hold you to that promise.'

'Thanks. Really sorry to inflict this on you, but you never know – you might even enjoy it,' suggested Patrick, laughing at their disbelieving faces. 'And I think you might be interested in the old house.' As compensation for having landed them with an unwanted social engagement, he agreed to go with them to Kryovrisi straight away to take delivery of the boat Petros had promised to hire them.

To Sam's disappointment, neither Petros nor the goddess was anywhere to be seen when they got to the harbour and it was Petros' younger brother, Spiro, who was in charge and produced a rubber dinghy for them, but they spent a happy day roaring along the coast, stopping at various little bays they remembered from previous holidays. The heat of the sun tempted fair-skinned Sophie to cast off shorts and T-shirt and, defiantly bikinied, she rapidly became a dangerous lobster pink and then announced she was going to swim.

'Rather you than me. Lucky you've got all that blubber to keep you insulated,' said Sam.

'Just because you're so weedy and look like a toast-rack yourself . . .' Sophie dipped her hands in the sea and sent a scoop of icy water over her brother, who retaliated with interest.

'I really wouldn't swim, Sophie – it's only April,' said Patrick, dodging out of the way of the water fight. 'You're going to burn dreadfully as it is but the sea will be really cold.' He had hitherto left the sun-cream-and-cover-ups versus wellies-and-waterproofs fussing to Rachel on holidays and now felt reluctant to take on the role of spoil-sport, which she had always played so readily – but he didn't want to lay himself open on their return to a catalogue of reproaches for irresponsibility either. However, Sophie only got as far as standing up to her thighs in the freezing water before deciding that even her brother's derisive mockery was better than death by hypothermia.

'I've lost all feeling in my legs,' she moaned. 'Can you die of gangrene if the circulation stops?'

'They're looking purple already – bad sign. But I expect it'll only be amputation rather than death if it's caught early,' said Sam cheeringly. 'Not much of a loss, in your case.'

Sophie's legs were not her best feature.

They stopped at Aghia Sophia for lunch, where one of the two tavernas was already open for the season. They sat at a table under a rickety beach umbrella, eating mounds of tiny fresh sardines, fried to a crisp and served with delicious bread and Greek salad.

The following morning was brilliantly clear again. The grass under the olive trees, long, green and luscious, was starred with wild flowers, and though the delicious scent of baked Mediterranean herbs, evocative of barbecues and leisurely meals eaten on terraces, was missing, everything smelled incredibly sweet and fresh. Patrick loaded up the car with his photographic equipment and they set off down the track. They found the turning off the main road, as described on the instructions Patrick had scribbled down, but a huge water-tanker driving close on their tail made it impossible to turn in so they had to go on and turn round, as people usually did on a first visit to Vrahos.

'I'd like to take a shot of those wonderful gateposts later,' said Patrick. 'That'd make a good picture – though it'll be tricky to find a vantage point to shoot from without getting mown down on that bend. Perhaps I can scramble up the rocks on the far side of the road. Did you notice those odd stones sitting along the top of the wall? I'm pretty sure they're carved antique heads off some much older, possibly classical, building. I must ask about them too.'

The long driveway seemed to go on for ever. 'D'you think this is really the right place?' asked Sophie but at that moment an imposing house came into view.

'It looks pretty crumby to me,' said Sam, looking at the flaking stucco of its mottled crushed-raspberry-coloured walls, and indeed there was an air of dereliction about the whole place.

'You feel a sort of Greek Miss Havisham might live here – jilted by her lover years ago and dressed only in cobwebs and a shredded wedding dress. How spooky! D'you think Mrs Doukas will be crazy? Is this what you expected, Dad?'

'More or less,' said Patrick, laughing at his daughter's dramatic expression as he brought the car to halt. 'But I don't think Mrs Doukas will be mad – she sounded very *compos mentis* on the telephone. I'm not sure we've come to the right bit of the house, though. Let's go exploring.'

It was difficult to know where the main entrance was. There appeared to be no door, only a series of small, square windows, heavily barred, slightly above eye level. Somewhere in the distance they could hear a dog barking. Sophie began to feel rather nervous and mentally plotted the quickest line of retreat in case they were attacked by savage hounds, but eventually round a corner they found an archway that led, through a tunnel in the thick walls, to a large courtyard paved with old flagstones on which several cats were sunning themselves. Grass grew through cracks in the paving, ancient vines and bougainvillaea clung shakily to the flaking plaster of the house, and trailing plants tumbled out of huge terracotta pots. Patrick thought the colour combination of all this greenery with the dusky pink of the plaster, the grey stone and brilliant blue sky above was quite stunning and could hardly wait to get his camera out.

On the far side of the courtyard shallow stone steps led up to imposing metal-studded doors beneath a stone pediment, and below the steps an old woman in black was sitting on an upright wooden chair snoozing in the sunshine. Beside her lay an equally ancient dog whose varied ancestors might have included wolfhounds. It raised a grey, whiskery nose and thumped its tail in a lethargic greeting but to Sophie's relief showed no immediate inclination to attack. Obviously not the distant barker – which meant there must be other hidden dogs still to be encountered.

'*Kalimera* – good morning,' tried Patrick politely, but there was no reaction. Patrick cleared his throat several times on a rising crescendo.

'Cough a bit louder Dad, why don't you?' suggested Sam with a grin.

The old woman stirred slightly and then suddenly woke with a start, her eyes snapping open in her walnut-shell face.

'I'm looking for Kyria Doukas. Have I come to the right place?' asked Patrick in halting Greek, smiling down at her.

She stared at him silently for a moment, jaw dropped, displaying toothless gums, then her hands flew to her mouth and she let out a stifled scream. '*Panayia mou!*' she gasped, and crossed herself. He could not have had a more dramatic effect if he'd been wearing a silver space suit and stepped out of a flying saucer. She gazed at him in horror, looked wildly round as though for a rescuer, and then without another word got to her feet and scuttled off across the courtyard as fast as her bent old legs could carry her, putting on a turn of speed she probably hadn't achieved for years. They half expected her to disappear down a hole and vanish from sight like a sand-crab on a tropical beach.

'Hmm. Friendly type,' remarked Patrick. 'Did I say something offensive?'

'Somehow I don't think she took to you, Dad,' grinned Sam. 'Not the sort of reaction you're used to getting from the ladies, was it? Left your famous charm in England?'

'I don't think I like it here. They can't be expecting us – you must have got the day wrong,' said Sophie, and added hopefully, 'Couldn't we just go away again?'

'Certainly not. Let's give this a try – and hope I don't strike quite such terror into anyone else.' Patrick gave the wrought-iron bell-pull a yank, and they could hear a distant jangling echoing through the house. Nothing happened. After what he considered a decent interval, he pulled it again, and then for good measure tried one of the two lion-mask door-knockers too. They were just about to give up when they heard footsteps inside the house and the sound of heavy bolts being drawn back.

'Lo, Miss Havisham cometh. Beware her spectral touch,' whispered Sam in Sophie's ear, but when the doors opened a pleasant-looking young woman in a blue dress and white apron greeted them.

'Is it Mr Hammond and family? You come to see Kyria Doukas?' she asked in careful English, smiling at them.

'Yes, I'm Patrick Hammond – and this is my daughter Sophie and my son Sam.'

'Please to come in. Kyria is expecting you. I am her housekeeper, Dora.'

They followed her across a large hall, its walls hung with fearsome-looking swords and ornate long-barrelled pistols, then through some double doors into an enormous reception room with a high, coffered ceiling and imposing-looking antique furniture – mostly a mix of French and Italian, thought Patrick.

'Wow! What a room!' said Sam, impressed in spite of himself. He liked to mock Patrick's passion for architecture but was secretly enormously proud of his father's knowledge and had picked up far more himself than he chose to let on.

'If the young lady and gentleman will stay here, I take you upstairs to Kyria Doukas,' said the housekeeper to Patrick. She smiled at Sam and Sophie and said, 'Kyria's granddaughter will come to you here to entertain you. Please to sit down.'

Sophie mouthed, 'Don't be too long' at her father before he followed the housekeeper up another staircase and down a long corridor hung with oil paintings in battered gold frames, which were all so badly in need of cleaning that it was impossible at a cursory glance to make out what the subject matter was. Finally she knocked at a door at the far end of the passage. Clearly the house was a rabbit warren, thought Patrick. He hoped he would be given a chance to prowl about on his own at some stage. It would take time to discover all the fascinating treasures with which he felt sure the house was stuffed. Already ideas were running through his head about how to present The Venetian House and whereabouts in the book he might place this particular chapter.

A voice he recognised from the telephone the day before called, 'Come in' and he opened the door.

The owner of Vrahos was standing before an open fire, a small elegant dog at her side. He had half expected to see a chair-bound invalid, but though Evanthi Doukas had an ivory-handled stick in one hand for support, she held herself very upright and was much taller than he had expected. Her abundant silver hair was knotted behind her head and tied with a purple chiffon scarf, and she wore a simple black suit, which Patrick realised from its cut must once have been extremely expensive. The immediate impression she gave was one of great distinction. She held out her hand to him, and it was only as he took it that he noticed how frail she really looked, what deep shadows lay under her enormous dark eyes and how papery-white her finely lined face was.

A face that has known love and suffering, he thought: a lived-in face – a face that would be wonderful to photograph.

Then something disconcerting happened. For the second time that morning a stranger gazed at Patrick with a look of stunned shock.

'Mr Hammond – forgive me. I must sit down.'

Evanthi Doukas felt for the chair behind her and lowered herself into it, never taking her eyes off his face.

'Are you all right? Is something the matter? Can I get you anything?'

'No – no, thank you. So stupid of me – I'm so sorry. I felt a little faint. Just give me a moment and I will be perfectly all right. Perhaps you would like to get yourself a glass of wine?' She indicated a tray and glasses on a table by the window. Not a woman to run squawking across the yard, this one, whatever the cause, thought Patrick. He went over to the table, deliberately turning his back to give her a chance to recover. He felt as if he must suddenly have sprouted some strange disfigurement – grown a second head or taken on the appearance of a monster, but if so, whatever the problem was, it had not been apparent to Sam or Sophie. He poured himself a glass of white wine. 'This looks wonderful. May I bring one for you?'

'Please.'

He took as long as he could before turning round and carrying the two glasses back towards the fire. When he did, Evanthi Doukas had recovered her composure. He wondered if any explanation would be forthcoming, but apparently she had decided not to refer to it – at any rate for the time being.

They chatted politely about trivialities for several minutes, but all the time Patrick felt himself to be under veiled but acute observation and was puzzled by something in the old lady's manner of . . . anguish, almost, he thought but also of extreme curiosity: as though she both had something to hide but also wanted to discover something. There had been no hint of this when he had spoken to her on the telephone the day before. What could it be about his appearance that had caused such a strong reaction? Patrick was intrigued.

'This is a very charming room,' he said, hoping he would be able to do justice to its fading grandeur when he tried to capture it on film. Like owner, like house, he thought. 'Is this the one you use the most?'

'Yes – it's known as the little drawing room. You came through the Grand Salon on your way up here. We really only use that for formal occasions – not that there are many of those nowadays. Do go and look out of the window,' she said. 'There is a spectacular view from here and you will see how the house is perched on the cliff.'

He did as she suggested. The long windows in the centre of the room – rounded at the top, Venetian style – opened on to a small balcony with a curved wrought-iron balustrade, painted, though certainly not recently, the same blue-green as the shutters of the house. Patrick leaned on the rail, now rusted with age, and flakes of dry paint came off where he touched it. He hoped it wouldn't give way and felt as though he were clinging to the mast of a tall ship, hanging over the water. Far below, the Ionian Sea looked so dark it appeared almost navy blue, and all along the coastline the woodland was a glossy mass of brilliant green, punctuated by darker cypress trees; across the narrow stretch of water between Corfu and Albania, snow-clad mountains made a dazzling backdrop.

'That's sensational! What a place to build, though!'

'Yes,' she said. 'Now you see where the name comes from: Vrahos: Rock. It's the house on the rock. Originally there was an old fortress here. A good vantage point for defence against invasion. Once there was a monastery – we still use the chapel. If you look to the left you can see its bell tower. Very Venetian, very Corfiot.'

He could hear laughter floating up from a long terrace down below which must open out of the Grand Salon, he thought, and he recognised his children's voices. He looked back over his shoulder. Evanthi Doukas was still watching him. He came back into the room and sat down opposite her again.

'My family sound very happy down there,' he said, smiling at her. 'They are obviously being well entertained.'

'Good.' She had a deep, attractive voice and spoke almost perfect English.

'So,' she said at last. 'Tell me about this book of yours – what it is you want to do and why it is in particular that you are interested in Vrahos?'

'I did a book a couple of years ago for The Eagle Press on Great European Houses, which was quite well received,' said Patrick. 'It was the first time I'd done both the text and all the photographs, so I was particularly pleased when Eagle approached me about a second commission – the subject to be of my own choosing.'

'It was very interesting, your book – wonderful photography – but I liked what was written too.' Evanthi pointed to a table beside her chair. 'As you see, I have a copy.'

She's done her homework, then, thought Patrick, impressed.

Evanthi smiled faintly, reading his thoughts: 'I didn't get it specially just because you were coming. I had the book already, Mr Hammond. My son-in-law, Anthony – whom you have met – gave it me for Christmas the year before last,' she said. 'If I hadn't liked it so much, and liked the way you wrote, I would not have agreed to see you when your agent first approached me. We have never sought publicity for Vrahos. Now, sadly, things are changing.' She added with obvious reluctance: 'I may have to sell things and I have to be practical. A book might help with their value.'

'Yes,' said Patrick. 'I can see that it might. I appreciate your frankness.'

'We do have a few valuable things, one in particular, our special "jewel in the crown". It's a fifteenth-century icon by the Cretan master Andreos Ritzos – a triptych – and it's signed, which adds to its monetary value, but its value to me has nothing to do with money and I would hate to have to part with it, so if enough interest could be aroused in some of the other things I would be relieved. What particular angle do you wish to take? The houses in your last book were not falling to pieces like this one. They were very grand, very well preserved. They were famous houses owned by seriously wealthy families.'

Patrick considered for a moment. 'Two things in particular interest me,' he said. 'The fact that it is *not* well known – much more exciting to write about – and the fact that it's still in your family after many generations. That gives enormous individuality. Trying to capture the *feel* of a place in photographs is something I specially enjoy.'

'My family have been here for over four hundred years – latterly through the female line. This house is not a Doukas house – it came to me through my Greek mother, who was a Grammenos. My husband's family came from the mainland. My father, a diplomat, was actually Italian – but though we travelled quite a lot, this was where I spent most of my childhood. Vrahos was always home to me. I spent a lot of time with my maternal grandparents and then after the war I came back here to live. My children and grandchildren have spent a lot of time here too. So yes, it is very much a family house.'

'What happened to it in the war?'

'Corfu had a bad time in the war. The town was heavily bombed, as you probably know. This house was commandeered by the Germans for a short time.'

'Being half-Italian – did that make things difficult for you? Were you here?'

'I was here – yes. I was under house arrest for a bit even though I was married to a Greek. I was confined to a few rooms.' She stared into the fire and started turning one of the rings on her still beautiful hands. 'Yes, it made things . . . difficult,' she said. 'My parents were in Italy and were both killed in a direct hit.'

She suddenly seemed to withdraw from him, and there was a long silence. Patrick had a feeling that the war was not a welcome topic. He thought he would try to return to the subject on a later visit and steered the conversation back on to safer ground now.

'I take it that's you and your husband?' he asked, looking above the fireplace at an oil painting, very formal, and to his critical eye not particularly well painted, of a saturnine-looking man with a thin aquiline nose and impressive dark moustaches standing behind a gilt chair on which sat a young woman in evening dress. He thought it looked vaguely familiar and wondered if he had seen the picture before – in some exhibition perhaps?

'Yes,' she said, glancing up at it. 'It was thought to be quite a good likeness at the time but I never really liked it. It's too stiff – but my husband was pleased with it. After he died I thought of taking it down, but somehow I never did.'

'You were certainly very beautiful.' He did not add that he thought the portrait made her look lifeless – almost bored – not at all the impression she now gave.

'Thank you,' she said politely. She gave a little shrug as though dismissing the picture as unimportant. 'Tell me more about your interest in Corfu.'

'I've always been interested in the Venetians and the huge influence they had on the architecture here during their four-hundred-year rule,' he said. 'That's an added attraction for including Vrahos in the book. Also, old family houses gather personalities of their own – as though something of all the different people who have lived in them rubs off and creates a special atmosphere – and I can see this one is no exception. I would love to be able to present a portrait of what *you* consider to be the particular character of this house.'

Suddenly she smiled at him. 'Then I will do my best to help you find it,' she said, 'and I think my granddaughter, Victoria Cunningham, may be able to help you even more. She too has spent a lot of her childhood here and loves the house as I do.' She made a rueful face. 'Also she is a good deal more agile than I am,' she said drily, 'and would make a better guide. As I think I told you, she happens to be here with me now, which is why I wanted you to bring your children with you. She doesn't want to meet people at the moment – I have to admit she would have liked me to put you off – but it is not right for her to be too dependent for company on an old invalid like me and it would be particularly good for her to get involved with a project which interested her.'

She hesitated for a moment and then continued, 'She is out here for the summer to try to come to terms with a devastating personal tragedy. Her husband was killed in a shooting accident recently. She has her six-year-old son with her – and again I think it would be good for him to meet your family. Luckily he has my housekeeper, Dora's, little boy to play with but I thought it would be a civilising influence for him to mix with your somewhat older children. I hope Victoria and Jake are both looking after your young people now.'

So the 'random' granddaughter was not a teenager after all, thought Patrick, and then remembered Sophie's description of susceptible Sam's Older Woman at the Harbour Lights who had a little boy. Ah . . . perhaps they would not be so averse to getting involved with future plans after all, he thought with amusement. As far as he was concerned it would be very convenient to have an excuse for further visits and also the chance to research the family history in more depth, but he couldn't imagine that his exuberant son and daughter would be the most helpful companions for a recently bereaved widow seeking solitude just because they were nearer to her in age than her grandmother was, and as for either of them being a civilising influence . . . Patrick's imagination boggled at the idea. He thought resentfully that Rachel should have been here to help him – but then ruefully acknowledged to himself that easing situations had never been Rachel's forte. She had always been too engrossed in her own neuroses to have much spare sympathy for the troubles of other people.

'I'm so very sorry,' he said. 'I believe I read something about that tragedy in the papers. It must be dreadful for you all.'

Evanthi Doukas rang a bell beside her chair. 'Let us have lunch now,' she said. 'My wonderful Dora, whom you have already met, will go and find Victoria and Jake and your son and daughter. The dining room is on this floor so we have not far to go but I'm afraid I am very slow at the moment. Come.'

She got to her feet with some difficulty but Patrick resisted the temptation to help, feeling it might be regarded as impertinence. She gave him a wry look. 'It goes against the grain not to be independent,' she said. 'Growing old is very hard but at least there is no choice about it – but choosing to grow old gracefully is quite another matter – that's really difficult.'

'I think you do it beautifully,' he said, and meant it. 'Am I allowed to offer you an arm?'

'Thank you,' she said. 'Yes, that would be kind – you may take me into lunch.'

As they walked slowly towards the dining room together, the tiny greyhound pattering along beside them, he couldn't help wondering whether the sight of him would have the same curious effect on Victoria Cunningham as it had on both her grandmother and the old woman outside the front door.

Chapter Nineteen

❖

Whether his offspring were a civilising influence or not, it was clear to their father that Sam and Sophie, far from having had the dreary morning they had forecast, were enjoying themselves.

They were out on the terrace when Patrick and Evanthi came into the dining room. Sam was good-naturedly engaged in arm-wrestling with a thoroughly over-excited small boy, and Sophie was deep in discussion on the all-important topic of clothes with a young woman who could have been any age between twenty and thirty: definitely Sam's goddess, Patrick thought appreciatively, judging by the look of her. He could see immediately why Sam had been so smitten, but she had clearly made a big hit with both his offspring because Sophie was hanging on her every word too.

'There's a wonderful shop in Theotoki Street, off the Liston, in town, where they have suede trousers to die for,' he heard Evanthi's granddaughter say. 'I'll take you there if you like – but the snag is that though they're marvellous value, they are still quite expensive.'

Patrick, whose photographer's eye automatically took in whatever anyone was wearing, noticed with some relief that she herself was casually dressed in dark jeans and a white T-shirt with a scarf knotted round her neck. Spendthrift Sophie, who was always chronically short of money, shot him a meaningful look as he stepped outside.

Before they came out to Corfu he had laid down a few unwelcome ultimatums to his daughter about learning to live within her allowance, but earlier that morning there had been problems about what Sophie should wear to accompany her father out to lunch with an unknown and possibly rather grand old lady. Patrick had eyed her frayed jeans and scuffed trainers with disfavour and said he would like her to wear a skirt. However, when presented with the choice between a trailing and transparent ground-length garment – somewhat muddied around the hemline – or a microscopic and revealingly tight little bandage, which Sam referred to as 'Sophe's pussy-pelmet', he had reluctantly agreed that jeans might be the better option. 'But surely you must have a tidier pair than those,' he had objected, and Sophie had replied tragically that as she was *completely* broke, she couldn't afford a spare pair. He could see that he would now be in a much weaker position to argue against the purchase of amazingly desirable new leather trousers.

Though Sophie frequently wore unsuitable clothes in order to flout the wishes of her elegant and ever-critical mother – Rachel had never mastered the art of not firing till she saw the whites of her children's eyes – Patrick felt a certain sympathy for his daughter because he knew that under the bravado she had much less social confidence than she liked to make out. He guessed that though she would have died rather than admit it, she had probably been in an agony of apprehension about looking wrong and gave her a reassuring wink.

They all got up as Evanthi and Patrick came into the dining room, and introductions were performed. The distant barker they had heard earlier was revealed as a large brown mongrel, which seemed perfectly well disposed and was stretched out peacefully in the sun.

'Nonna, Nonna,' said Jake. 'This is Sam – you must feel his biceps.' Everyone laughed and to Patrick's relief Victoria Cunningham, unlike her grandmother or the old woman in the courtyard, showed no unnerving signs of shock at the sight of him.

This time it was Patrick who got the jolt.

He was immediately conscious of a feeling of recognition when Victoria shook hands with him, although he was certain he had never met her before. He was used to meeting glamorous women in the course of his career, but this reaction was something much more than automatic admiration for a pretty face and a good figure. Certainly she had an unmistakable elegance, more due to the way she moved than the clothes she was wearing today, he thought, and wondered if she had ever trained as a ballet dancer. But the impact she made on him had as much to do with her expression as to any physical characteristic and suddenly he knew with absolute certainty why she seemed both so fascinating and so familiar. It was as though the missing piece of a jigsaw had unexpectedly fallen into place.

Evanthi seated herself at one end of the table and placed Sam and Sophie either side of her.

'You go the other end, *agapi*,' she said to Victoria, 'and we'll put Mr Hammond on your right. Jake, you can sit on Mummy's other side.' Sam had secretly hoped he would be sitting next to Victoria, whose attractions he felt would be wasted on his father, but decided to make the best of things by launching a charm offensive on her grandmother and hoped it would not go unnoticed by the object of his admiration.

'I'm sorry not to be eating outside, which I'm sure you'd both prefer.' Evanthi smiled at her young guests. 'As it turns out it would probably have been warm enough but we thought it might be too windy and I'm not supposed to get cold. Also because I'm lucky enough to live here all the year round, I don't feel I have to be outside every moment the sun is shining like visitors do. Enjoying the shade is one of the few luxuries of old age – but not something I expect either of you to appreciate for a great many years yet. I do hope you don't mind being in here.'

'Oh no. It's nice for us to be able to see your dining room,' said Sophie politely. 'Dad will go absolutely crazy about your house – it's so old and romantically tumbledown and shabby and . . .' She stopped suddenly, scarlet with confusion. 'Oh, I'm sorry. I didn't mean *shabby* exactly,' she said. She shot her father an agonised look, but he gave her another reassuring little wink and everyone laughed.

'Don't worry – we know *exactly* what you mean, Sophie,' said Victoria, quickly, 'and it's very discerning of you to feel the charm behind the dilapidation. It's what antique dealers call "distressed condition". Forgers are always trying to fake the look successfully, but we've got the real thing without trying!'

Sam added, 'Sophie's right about it being just Dad's kind of place and he really does take the most wonderful photographs of old houses.'

'Yes, indeed,' said Evanthi, liking them both and approving of their family loyalty and friendly manners. 'I've seen some of them and I'm hoping he's going to take pictures of Vrahos for me. Now tell me what Victoria and Jake have been showing you while your father and I were talking. I hope you saw the chapel? We're very proud of that.'

The dining-room table had been formally laid for the six of them with heavy silver, fine Venetian wine glasses on tall, slender stems and plates from a dinner service that had been used by Evanthi's own grandmother. Evanthi was not of the school of thought that believed her own standards of living should be lowered to accommodate the changing customs of a different generation. Above the two heavy mahogany sideboards on either side of the room, narrow-faced ancestors with bony features and shrewd clever faces looked down at them with lofty self-assurance from walls where the dark blue-green paint was blotched with damp in places. Dora came in and started handing round a big dish of moussaka, which turned out to be absolutely delicious and a far cry from the tough-meat and wallpaper-paste sauce that sometimes passed in tourist hotels for this Greek cousin of shepherd's pie.

'Thank you for rescuing Sophie,' said Patrick, smiling warmly at Victoria. 'That was very understanding of you. And thank you also for looking after them both. I hope it hasn't interfered with other plans?'

'I've enjoyed their company actually, and your son is definitely Jake's new hero – the funniest person he's met for ages. It's been great to watch Jake giggle like that. Where did they learn to be so good with children?'

'They have a small sister.'

'Lucky her.'

'I think they find her a perfect torment most of the time,' admitted Patrick. 'But I suppose they're pretty tolerant on the whole.'

'Well, they were certainly very sweet to Jake. Actually, it turned out we'd already met briefly down at Kryovrisi the other evening. Petros, who owns the bar and the boat-hire business, is a vital part of life for everyone on this part of the island and I'd gone down to thank him for something he'd done for me.'

'I know,' he said, looking at her with an amused twinkle in his eye. 'I'd already heard *all* about you. It must have been a very nice surprise for Sam and Sophie to see you this morning.' He laughed. 'They were convinced you were going to be a tiresome teenager who might want to "tag along" and spoil their fun. Now I fear it may be the other way round. You mustn't let them be a bore.'

'Oh, I won't.' Victoria smiled at him, disconcerted by her own pleasure at the implication of his words. 'Now tell me how you got on with Nonna – she must have liked you or she'd never have let you take her arm and bring her in to lunch. You don't know what a mark of favour that was!' she said, aware that she was no more immune than her grandmother to Patrick's attraction. I shouldn't be reacting like this at the moment she thought, horrified at herself.

'I want to know all about this book you're doing,' she said. 'We were all very surprised she agreed to see you. The slightest whiff of publicity has always sent her into siege mode in the past – doors and windows barred and drawbridge pulled up.'

'We don't have a drawbridge, Mum,' objected Jake.

'An invisible one perhaps?' suggested Patrick. 'All houses should have one of those to keep the enemy out.'

'Boiling oil might be good, poured over the cliff.'

'That would certainly keep unwanted photographers away,' agreed Patrick laughing. 'I can see I'll need to be careful. Perhaps you could think of a secret password to give me next time I come?'

Then, seeing Jake turn back to Sam to regale him with an account of the latest *Harry Potter* book, he said to Victoria, 'Your grandmother says you might show me all the places she can't get to any more. But I particularly don't want to intrude on you because I know you've had the most terrible family tragedy and I am so very, very sorry.'

'Thank you,' she said simply, liking his directness and thinking how charming he was. 'Yes – it's . . . it's a difficult time.' She made a rueful little face and added, 'But I bet my grandmother told you it would be good for me to have a project.'

'She did actually.' He gave her an amused and sympathetic

look. 'But please don't think she committed you in any way. I'd hate you to feel under any pressure to be involved.'

Victoria shrugged. 'She's probably right about me – she usually is. Anyway, I love this place – it's in my bones – and I adore my grandmother. She's one very special lady to whom I owe a great deal – so if it's what she wants, then anything I can do to help would be a pleasure.'

'Tell me about the house then.'

They chatted away easily about the history of the house and its contents – about which she was clearly knowledgeable – and about her childhood memories of the island, and Patrick was aware that he was enjoying not only her beauty, but her conversation and her company in a way he hadn't done with any woman for a long time. She definitely had a look of her grandmother, he decided. They had the same eyes – unforgettable eyes – he thought, and Evanthi's silver hair must once have been as dark as Victoria's; the older woman was statuesque now and, judging from the portrait in the drawing room had probably never been as slight as her granddaughter, but there were definitely similarities: the high cheekbones; the distinctive, rather heavy, eyebrows; a way of looking at you with great attention as though everything you said was extraordinarily interesting and then the giving of a sudden brilliant smile that was like a floodlight being turned on.

Whoever had painted Evanthi Doukas's portrait when she was a young woman had not captured this vivid intensity, or perhaps the sitter had deliberately withheld her personality from the artist . . . and Patrick thought of another portrait he knew where this had clearly not been the case.

The moussaka was followed by home-made ice cream and then cheese. When Dora came to ask where they would like coffee, Evanthi suggested it should be taken out on the terrace.

'But I think I must leave you all now and have my rest,' she said. 'Dora will help me upstairs. Goodbye, Mr Hammond. I shall look forward to seeing you again soon. Victoria will make arrangements for you to come and take photographs and show you anything you want to see.'

They all got up and said their goodbyes, and she made her exit leaning, only very slightly, on Dora's arm.

'We must go too,' said Patrick, not at all wanting to leave but feeling they had stayed long enough for their hostess and that it would probably be better to come back another day. He thought Victoria suddenly looked exhausted too. She had given such an impression of vitality when she was talking that the contrast was all the more marked – it was as though a dimmer switch had suddenly been activated by an unseen hand, and he couldn't help noticing that her face in repose was full of sadness.

'You can't go yet,' objected Jake. 'Sam could stay and play football with me and Angelo.'

'The ultimate treat,' said Victoria, rolling her eyes. 'Do you want to make a date to come back now, Mr Hammond, or would you rather ring us when it suits you? How long are you here for?'

'Oh, for goodness' sake, call me Patrick – and only a week altogether, I'm afraid. I can take the interior shots any time, but what I'd really like to do is get some outdoor pictures soon to try to catch this marvellous freshness and all the spring flowers, and then come back again later in the year – say in early autumn – for the olive picking. But the inside pictures would be the most disruptive for all of you, so you must say what suits you best. I'll try to be as little in the way as possible. I would also very much like to see the icon your grandmother was telling me about.'

'Let me talk to Nonna first then. Can I give you a ring?'

'Of course.' Patrick pulled one of his cards out of his wallet and scribbled down the Petradi address and telephone number. 'We're staying in a villa belonging to some friends of ours. My mobile number's on the card too but I have to say I don't always have it switched on out here. It's nice to get away from it. I'd get a message, though.'

'Oh, I've noticed that house,' said Victoria, looking at the address. 'I've always thought it looked lovely but didn't know who it belonged to.'

'Dad – why couldn't Victoria and Jake come and have lunch with *us*? Then she could look at Petradi and I can give Jake his game of football,' suggested crafty Sam, who had no intention of letting his father monopolise Victoria with long photographic sessions that did not require his own presence.

'Yess-sss!' Jake made a clenched fist gesture and punched the air. 'Can we, Mum?'

Victoria looked doubtful. 'Oh, darling, I don't know. I expect they're busy.'

'No we're not,' said Sophie. 'We haven't got a thing to do – have we, Dad?'

'No – do come,' Patrick, highly amused at this volte-face on the part of his son and daughter, could see what was expected of him, and was only too happy to oblige them. 'We'd all love it. Come any time.'

'Oh, well, um . . . thank you then.' Victoria looked a little hesitant. 'That would be lovely. What about the day after tomorrow?'

'That would be fine. Do you play tennis, Victoria? We had thought we might try the court at the Krokalia Beach sometime, which the Marshalls say is quite good – and it would be much more fun with four.'

'Well, I do play . . . I'm not exactly the Williams sisters' standard, but I love it.'

'Fantastic!' Sam was enchanted.

'Some hotels outside the town aren't open yet, but the Krokalia often starts up early. Their court's very good, but you'd need to check if they're open.'

'It's probably better to play in the morning, isn't it?' suggested Patrick. 'We'll drop in at the hotel on our way home and see if we can book the court for Monday morning and then you and Jake can meet us there and come back afterwards for a very scratch lunch. Would he be bored by that?'

'I should think he'd be thrilled – the hotel has a children's play area near the tennis court with climbing frames and things which he adores.'

'Right,' said Patrick. 'We'll give you a ring and confirm a time. Come on, you guys – time we departed. We've stayed quite long enough. Thank you so much – and please thank your grandmother again. She's a very remarkable lady – it's been a privilege to meet her.'

They said their farewells and Victoria and Jake waved from the top of the steps as the Hammonds walked across the courtyard.

*

After the visitors had departed, Victoria went in search of Dora to see if Jake could spend the remainder of the afternoon with Angelo. Patrick had been right. She felt utterly drained: overwhelmed with the sudden exhaustion that is such an unpredictable part of bereavement – as though all her energy had been tipped out of her and seeped away into the ground like spilt water.

Contrary to her expectations she had enjoyed meeting the Hammonds, but now she longed to be alone. She half wished she had not accepted their invitation, but told herself they were so kind and friendly that she would have been churlish to refuse. She was secretly unnerved to discover how much she wanted to see Patrick Hammond again. It made her feel restless and uneasy. Perhaps I am emotionally unbalanced at the moment, she thought.

Dora was in the kitchen emptying the dishwasher, and a very bored Angelo, furious at not having been allowed to join Jake for lunch, was lying on the floor repetitively running his toy tractor into the back of her heels. Dora, who usually had a seemingly endless supply of patience, suddenly turned and yelled at him and smacked him sharply – and Victoria thought deservedly – on the leg, whereupon Angelo, unused, like most Greek sons, to any intolerant treatment from his mother, bellowed with rage. It was not a peaceful scene.

'Go and find Jake and take your cars out on the terrace, Angelo, and leave your poor mother alone,' said Victoria.

Angelo switched off his roars immediately and sped off to find his playmate.

'That was a delicious lunch, Dora. I don't know how you manage to do so much in the house and cook like that too.'

Dora heaved a sigh. 'It is getting difficult,' she admitted. 'My grandmother still helps a little with the cleaning but she can't do much, and the house needs far more doing to it than Yannis and I can manage. We worry about it.'

'I know. I do too. I mean to try to talk to Nonna about it all. But is there anything else the matter? You look upset.'

Dora sat down heavily on one of the wooden kitchen chairs. 'It is my grandmother. There is something wrong with her.'

'You mean she's ill? Should we telephone the doctor?'

Dora shook her head. 'She says she isn't ill and she won't see the doctor. It's the *papas* she wants. She's desperate to make her confession.'

'Heavens!' said Victoria. 'What on earth's brought that on? I didn't think guilt was something Nafsica ever suffered from. She's always so wonderfully sure she's right.'

Dora spread her arms wide in a gesture of total bewilderment. 'I don't know. She came rushing in here before lunch, looking as though she'd seen a ghost and sat in the kitchen all the time I was trying to cook lunch, flinging her apron over her head and wailing that she'd be judged and there would be a curse on her. I couldn't make head or tail of what she was saying.'

'Have you told Nonna?'

'I asked Yiayia if she wanted me to fetch Kyria and that made her worse. She begged me not to tell her.'

'Where is Nafsica now?'

'She's taken to her bed. You know she never does that – but I was thankful to be rid of her.'

'Would you like me to go and talk to her?'

Dora hesitated and then shook her head again. 'No – not yet. She'll kill me if she knows I've said anything. She just wants Pater. I suppose I'll have to ring him and see if he'll come over.' She sighed deeply. 'It's all I need! You know what he's like – he'll stay for hours. But at least he may get out of her what's the matter. I certainly can't. I'd better go up to her now.'

'Oh, Dora, I'm so sorry.' Victoria put an arm round her and gave her a hug. 'Will you let me know what he says? We can't have both grandmothers being ill at the same time. I'll keep an eye on the boys and give them their tea and send Angelo over to you before bedtime.'

When she went back to see what the boys were up to they were in the middle of a game that involved tearing round the house shooting at each other with pretend guns – the cause of his father's terrible death obviously not having impinged on Jake yet, she noted. She wondered what on earth could have happened to upset old Nafsica and wished Guy were here to discuss it with her. Guy – still in Nafsica's eyes the treasured male child – would have winkled whatever was troubling her out of the old lady in no time. She took her book out on to the terrace, but felt too restless to read and sat gazing down at the sea, her head full of questions and memories, watching the colour turn from lapis lazuli to pewter, and thought its changes reflected her own unpredictable moods.

Her mind went back to Richard and to childhood. She vividly remembered the first time Richard had come out to stay at Vrahos. It was soon after her mother and father had been killed but before she had been given a permanent home by Guy's parents, and she had been counting the days to Guy's arrival – the big cousin whom she so much admired. She had been dismayed when Evanthi told her Guy was bringing a school friend with him.

'Why does he want a friend when he's got me?' she had asked, scuffing the sun baked grass with the toe of her sandal.

'Well, sometimes boys do want other boys to play with,' explained Evanthi, aching for her orphaned, hero-worshipping, little granddaughter. 'Sometimes boys need to do the sort of things that they enjoy doing best with other boys – like sailing and playing cricket and things like that – just as you sometimes love to play at dressing-up with other little girls.'

'I like boys better than girls and I can sail and play cricket too,' insisted Victoria, who hated both occupations. Sailing filled her with apprehension, though she would have died rather than admit it, and she had learned about cricket because her father had taken her to watch it played on the gravelly, dusty Spianáda in Corfu town – cricket being one of the idiosyncrasies the islanders had picked up from the British, along with a taste for ginger beer – and she had thought it both alarming and boring at the same time, an opinion she had not changed when she was graciously allowed to spend long hours bowling and fielding for Guy.

She had expected that Richard would be a clone of Guy but when he arrived she thought he looked disappointing – a polite, fair-haired boy with none of Guy's dark glitter and moody excitement. Sure enough her misgivings had soon been realised as the boys became totally wrapped up in each other, and though she trailed doggedly after them she might just as well have been invisible for all the attention they paid her. Then one day when she had been sent by Nafsica to tell them that lunch would be ready in half an hour, she had found Richard alone on the beach, gloomily throwing pebbles into the water.

'Where's Guy?'

'Dunno,' said Richard, shrugging. 'Haven't seen him for hours.' And he threw another stone with great force.

'Shall I look for good duck-and-drakers for you?' she asked. 'I know what they ought to be like.' She had found two wonderfully thin flat stones, one round, one long and presented them to him. He sent the first one skimming across the bay and they counted together as it rebounded satisfyingly across the calm surface of the sea. 'Eight, *nine, ten . . . ELEVEN!*' chanted Victoria admiringly.

'It was the stone you found,' said Richard generously. 'Best I've had all morning.'

They had sat together on a low rock gazing out to sea. 'Sometimes,' said Victoria carefully burying one of her feet in the soft shingle and sharing the wisdom of her seven years, 'sometimes Guy's the sort of person who goes off without you. When he gets like that I pretend I don't mind.'

'He can be really foul sometimes,' muttered Richard.

'But if you wait long enough he always gets nice again in the end,' said Victoria, who couldn't bear those she loved to be at odds with each other.

They had formed an unspoken bond, and it was the first of many times that they had supported each other through Guy's black moods and unexplained absences.

She recalled a teenage dance to which she had only been invited because the hostess had not realised that she was five years younger than her cousin – Victoria being a child who gave a false impression of sophistication. Guy had promised his mother he would look after her, but soon after their arrival he disappeared to the local pub, not to be seen again till the end of the party. None of the boys had asked her to dance, none of the girls spoke to her. She might have been made of air for all the impression she made, though standing shyly amongst the crowd she felt herself to be horribly obvious, as if she had an illuminated sign over her head with the word 'Failure' written in neon lights. Richard had rescued her and saved her from the public ignominy of languishing as a wallflower all evening. At a later stage, most of her girlfriends had been in love with Guy and some of them had slept with him. Richard and Victoria would watch him setting out to make a new conquest and automatically turn to each other for companionship until Guy decided to notice them again, but they never discussed it. He seemed to attract both sexes equally, though as far as his own preferences were concerned Victoria thought now that what had always attracted him most was the challenge of the chase rather than the gender of the prey – especially if there was a whiff of taboo involved. Flying too close to the sun was the thing that turned Guy on.

To set against those memories were ones of the many times when they had enjoyed doing things as a threesome, both before and after she and Richard had married; or rather I enjoyed them, thought Victoria painfully. I had the safety of Richard and the excitement of Guy – but had Richard enjoyed any of their marriage? Was I always the encumbrance I had often been as a child – the intrusion on his longing to be alone with Guy? Did my femininity never mean anything to him?

She went over and over her marriage, looking for retrospective clues that might have alerted her to the true state of affairs. There is nothing I can do about it now, thought Victoria, but she couldn't stop herself looking for signs that she might have picked up if she had been more observant . . . and the more she looked the more she found Today she had been acutely aware that someone had unmistakably reacted to her as a woman and the contrast to Richard's response was very marked.

Had marrying Richard been an attempt on her part to hang on to the magic of their shared childhood, she wondered – a way of ducking several issues because she knew she could never marry Guy? It was not a comfortable thought. Victoria shivered and went into the house to fetch another jersey.

But she felt as though the chill came from inside her heart and spread through her entire being and that no amount of extra cardigans would make any difference.

Chapter Twenty

❧

Guy and Francine lay in a state of post-coital contentment that might or might not flare again at any moment into urgent desire.

Guy's flight from Milan had been on time and Francine had met him at Heathrow and had driven him back to number forty The Boltons in the yellow convertible BMW he had given her for Christmas. They'd had dinner at the little Italian restaurant in the Fulham Road that they both liked, where the proprietor possessed a ready wit but knew when not to apply it, there was no canned music and the atmosphere was conducive to easy conversation and the enjoyment of good but simple food. Then they had walked home up Gilston Road, both ready to make love.

Now Guy sat up and lazily wound a lock of Francine's tawny-coloured hair round his finger. He looked down at his wife.

'This is the bit of being an old married man that's getting to be quite addictive,' he said. 'Coming home from a trip and finding you still here – and no fear of interruptions from jealous husbands or lovers.'

'Je-sus! You surely must be feeling your age then,' mocked Francine. 'I thought it was the thrill of illicit relationships and competing with jealous rivals that turned you on.'

'It used to be – but this little domestic idyll is such a novel experience it's thrill enough. I'm beginning to think I must be in love – I'll let you know when it starts to wear off.'

'Mmm. You do that.' Francine closed her eyes and stretched, cat-like.

Guy stroked her stomach, the slight bulge barely perceptible yet. 'How's this person in here been in my absence?'

'This person's been just fine. I keep thinking he or she might be starting to stomp around but I guess it's only peristaltic action after a good dinner. My grandmother told me it would be unmistakable when it happened for the first time – like the feel of a small bird fluttering inside a hatbox, so she informed me. Can't say that's a feeling I'm too familiar with so I guess I may miss the signal – never thought of myself as a hatbox before.'

'Was she much given to trapping birds in hatboxes then? Sounds a sinister occupation.'

'Not that I know of. Mmm . . . that's nice. Just keep on doing that, will you – it's very soothing.'

'Don't you go to sleep on me, Mrs Winston,' said Guy taking his hand away and tickling the end of her nose with another strand of her hair. 'I need to talk to you. Wives are supposed to be desperate to know everything their husbands have been up to when they've been away. Don't you want to know how I got on with Victoria?'

Francine opened one eye and gave him an amused look. 'Well, since you're so obviously bur-r-r-sting to enlighten me I guess you'll tell me,' she said, and closed her eye again. She knew it was her ability not to react as he expected that was an important part of her hold over Guy.

While he was away, she had thought a great deal about Victoria. Her feelings for the younger woman had never been straightforward, though she'd often been on the verge of liking her and was genuinely distressed for her now. She was appalled at what had happened, but this tragedy only added to the secret insecurity she felt about the deep childhood bond that existed between the two cousins. She knew that Guy cared deeply for Victoria – probably more deeply than he realised himself, she thought shrewdly. It had not only been Richard, so ready to flatter Guy, so anxious to fall in with his wishes, whom Francine found threatening. She had known that as Richard had become more and more demanding of Guy, so Guy had found his intensity increasingly claustrophobic. Victoria, however, had always been another matter. And now? Widows can be very threatening to wives, thought Francine, their vulnerability wrong-footing one so easily.

She had watched Guy come through the arrivals gate at the airport with the combined lifting of the heart and simultaneous stab of anxiety that had become familiar to her, and decided she must on no account let her husband know how absolutely her happiness depended on him. Never mind about the baby fluttering to get free – if its father ever felt trapped, she thought he would be all too likely to struggle out and fly away for ever. Francine did not intend to let this happen. She was aware that she had always cared more passionately for Guy than he did for her, but she had hopes that he might at last be beginning to love her too.

She had kissed him breezily, enquired after his grand-mother's health, and then moved swiftly to the topic of his interview with the budding diva at La Scala and her per-formance in the controversial production of *Ballo* that Guy had gone out to Milan to see. The fact that she was passionate and knowledgeable about opera herself made this easier – it was one of their many shared interests – but it had taken a real effort of will not to display curiosity about Victoria's reactions to the revelations regarding Richard. The fact that Guy guessed that Francine would be intensely curious did not lessen his pique that she hadn't yet asked about it. There'd been ample opportunity both on the way home and at dinner, and he'd been waiting for her to raise the subject – but she hadn't done so. It was like playing poker, Francine thought – but she knew that the stakes she played for were very high.

However, it was now quite obvious that Guy was itching to tell her about Victoria and she was very prepared to listen.

'OK then – shoot. I'm all ears,' she said, settling comfortably back against the pillows.

Guy lit two cigarettes, and leaned over to put one in her mouth – then took it away again. 'Sorry – you're not supposed to do that now are you? Do you want me to give it up too? Would it make it easier for you?'

She was surprised 'Would you do that . . . if I wanted you to?'

'Of course.'

'This baby's really important to you, isn't it?'

'Yes,' he said, and added lightly, 'but I'm finding its mum is quite important too. I have missed you, you know.'

'Thanks, darling.' Francine was touched. It was the first time he had said this to her, and she thought it marked a very important milestone in their relationship. 'You keep on puffing away for now – but I'll let you know if I need moral support. The amazing thing is, I don't really want to smoke at the moment. Lucky, isn't it? Now . . . run the whole drama past me. I hope you were gentle with Victoria?'

Guy told her about his visit to Vrahos: about the increasingly obvious dilapidation of the old Venetian House that he loved so much and his realisation that it was in an even worse state than he'd thought; about Evanthi's improving health and her pleased reaction to the news about the baby – and then about the picnic at Angelokastro and Victoria's horror at what he had to tell her. Finally he told her about the terrible fright she had given him in the boat.

'I made a proper cock-up of breaking it all to her,' he said soberly. 'I'd been dreading it but it was far, far worse than I thought. I longed for you to be there to talk it out with me and I drank a great deal too much afterwards as a result. Of course, I knew that what I had to tell her was going to be a shock, but somehow I hadn't expected her to have quite such a violent reaction . . . to be *so* stunned. Stupid of me. Richard was devoted to Victoria but, unlike me, he's never been the least bit interested in women sexually and he can't have been an ardent lover. She hinted as much. Victoria has known him for ever – you'd think she'd have picked up that he was gay after all that time, wouldn't you?'

'I guess that's exactly why she *didn't* pick it up – no first impression, no impact. When you've always known someone, and continue to see them all the time, you cease even to know what they look like any more. Victoria has always struck me as stuck in a sort of time warp anyway – so beautiful, and one would imagine capable of tremendous passion, and yet . . . curiously un-streetwise – not really having found herself yet.'

'My father, who's shrewd about people and who's particularly fond of her, has always called her the Sleeping Beauty.'

'Waiting for her prince?' asked Francine. 'Well, it clearly wasn't Richard.' She hesitated, then asked: 'How much will you mind, Guy, if that prince suddenly turns up for her one day?'

Guy drew on his cigarette and blew three perfect smoke rings in the air. 'I don't know,' he said slowly, taken aback by the question. 'In theory I'd be delighted, but I suppose if I'm honest, I might find it difficult.' He looked at her. 'Much less than I would once have done though,' he added.

Francine let this go, though she was secretly pleased. But I mustn't get complacent, she thought. Instead she asked: 'I just can't think how Richard could ever have imagined he would make a success of such a marriage – make her happy or find happiness himself. Well, he certainly didn't find that, poor guy. What actually pushed him into marrying her?'

'I suppose I did,' said Guy. 'I certainly didn't mean to, and I sure-as-hell feel guilty now. I was thinking about it on the plane on the way home. I tackled Vicky and asked her what she'd really thought and she admitted they drifted into marriage like a *fait accompli* – it was always a joke when we were growing up that they would marry one day. But it was something I said that actually tipped Richard into doing it. It was after we came down from Cambridge.' He gazed up at the ceiling, remembering vividly how Richard had started to get heavy and demanding, objecting to Guy's love affairs and general wild experiments with life and wanting to go back to 'how we used to be'.

'I wanted to end our relationship and move forward,' he said, 'but Richard wanted everything to stay as it always had been. I remember goading him with being stuck in the past and saying: "You'd better marry Victoria then – and we can all three have the best of all worlds," but I didn't mean him to take me literally. The next thing I knew they were engaged.'

'Did you tell Victoria that?'

'Not that bit – no, of course not.'

'What do you think she'll do now? Will she stay out in Corfu?'

'I think so – for a bit, anyway. She feels safe there and she's always adored being with Nonna. But she can't tread water for ever – she'll have to start swimming again sometime.'

'Perhaps she'll get bored,' suggested Francine, 'and need to get back where the action is.'

Guy shook his head. 'She's not a busy urban socialite like you. She could dream her time away out there for ages. Shall we go out for a week soon and you can see it for yourself? Would you like that? By the way, I promised Nonna we'd have the baby christened at Vrahos. I ought to have asked you first. I hope you don't mind?'

Francine had never been to Vrahos. In all the years of their on/off relationship, including her brief unsatisfactory marriage to a wealthy American banker – a gesture of independence to Guy, which had not been without its beneficial effect, though she had paid a price of considerable unhappiness for a few years, he had invited many other friends to stay in Corfu, but never her. Was it a sign at last of his acceptance of her in a part of his life that he had hitherto kept private? Or was it the lure of Victoria that made him want to go back now? Francine still felt uneasy but she also felt a flicker of hope for the future.

'That sounds a great idea,' she said, but all the same she felt he needed reminding of what she now expected of him, though she knew how much he disliked being pressurised or cornered. She sat up and the bedclothes fell away, revealing her nakedness.

'Listen, Guy,' she said. 'There is something I desperately need to say to you . . . and I shan't say it again so you darn well better take note.'

'You sound very serious all of a sudden.' He thought she was like a tigress with her bright hair and curiously flecked, tawny eyes. She looked dangerous and unpredictable – and infinitely seductive.

'I am. I'm deadly serious. I knew what I wanted when I married you and I was well aware that you hadn't exactly got a reputation for being reliable husband-material but I took a calculated risk. But being pregnant sure as hell changes one's attitudes on a whole load of things, and I realise now that it doesn't only affect me but that I've taken a risk for our baby too. Don't get me wrong – I'm thrilled about the baby and I love you. I know you're delighted too, but if you ever let this child down – that'll be *it* as far as I'm concerned. Curtains. So no more messing around and that doesn't just mean hands off other women – it means hands off the boys as well, Guy Winston – *for ever.*'

'Hell's bells! D'you want me to make *more* solemn vows or what?' asked Guy, trying to sound light-hearted, to disguise the fact that he was shaken by her sudden vehemence. He looked down at her with respect, aware that the outburst would have required courage.

'No. I don't want you to vow anything,' she said. 'I don't want to discuss it at all. I'm just telling you, Guy – you do anything to hurt our baby and there won't be any second chances with me.' She lay back against the pillows again and pulled the duvet up to her chin.

For answer Guy stubbed out his cigarette, turned towards her and slid his hand under the duvet.

Chapter Twenty-one

The following day, when Sam and Sophie emerged blearily from their rooms rubbing the sleep out of their eyes, Patrick had already been up for several hours and marvelled, as always, at the ability of the young to remain oblivious for so long to the miraculous sunlight streaming in through their windows. Sophie in particular looked decidedly the worse for wear. They had jaunted off after supper the previous evening to hit the night life of Kryovrisi, zooming away on the scooter in a cloud of dust and exhaust fumes, leaving their father feeling like an old hen whose chicks have disappeared.

'You're only just seventeen, Sophie. You probably won't be able to get in if you try to go clubbing,' he warned, secretly hoping this would be the case, 'in which case Sam must bring you back.' His daughter looked at him pityingly. 'Yeah, yeah, yeah, Dad! But I won't have any trouble getting in – don't *worry* about me.' She added soothingly, 'I've got my fake ID.'

'Why don't I find that reassuring?' asked Patrick. He wasn't at all sure whether to let her go or not. 'Would Mum let you go?' he asked.

Sophie rolled her eyes. 'You must be joking! Mum never wants me to go anywhere fun – not that she seems much interested in what I do any more.' She changed to a wheedling tone. '*Please*, Dad – it isn't as if I'd be on my own. I'm not going to do anything stupid, I promise.'

Patrick hesitated for a moment and then took a quick decision. 'All right then, Sophie. I know you worked extremely hard last term – but don't let me down. You know very well what my rules are.' Though Patrick gave the appearance of being so laid-back, he was capable of being formidable if he was roused and his children did not flout his few rules lightly.

Sophie, much relieved, beamed at him. 'Darling Dad, you're so *cool*! Trust me! I swear you won't regret it.'

'There won't *be* any trouble, Dad,' said Sam reassuringly. 'It'll probably only be the Harbour Lights again anyway. Don't think any of the clubs will have opened up yet.'

'Sure *you'll* be all right left on your own?' Sophie had asked, twining her arms round her father's neck, and giving him a fondly maternal look that made him feel about a hundred.

'Of course. You go off and have a good time – and thank you both for coming to Vrahos. It was great having you with me.'

Patrick thought wryly of the many times in the past when he had tried – and failed – to impress on Rachel that it was important to show Sam and Sophie that they were trusted and allow them more of the freedom they would undoubtedly seize anyway if it was unreasonably withheld. Now that the decisions were his alone, it was proving more difficult putting this wisdom into practice than he had anticipated. He checked that they had their mobiles with them, extracted a promise from Sam to drive with care, waved them off with apparent cheerfulness – and been dismayed to find how much he minded. He had then worked on the text of his book and made notes about his first impressions of The Venetian House, which he knew he was going to enjoy writing about as well as photographing, and hoped he could do justice to both house and owner. He found himself thinking not only about Evanthi Doukas but about her granddaughter as well, wondering what her husband had been like, what her future would be. The plan for tennis would be a good ploy for Sam and Sophie, and Patrick, a wily performer on the court himself, decided he was very much looking forward to it.

After a slight struggle with his conscience he rang Rachel – and then wished he hadn't. The minute he heard her voice he knew the call was not going to go well. Extraordinary, he thought, how revealing the telephone can be of the state of the person on the other end of the line, even before any real conversation has taken place. He enquired after her and Posy, then tried to tell her what good company he was finding their older children and about the lunch at Vrahos, hoping to interest her in both the place and the people – but though Rachel asked about Sam and Sophie she did not want to hear about his own ploys. She sounded as brittle as an icicle and was full of minor complaints about life at home, and martyrdom at having been left behind 'to cope alone', as she put it, while they enjoyed themselves on holiday.

'Don't give me that,' Patrick was goaded into saying. 'You could perfectly well be out here with us too – as you very well know.'

There was silence the other end, and it took him a moment to realise that Rachel had put the telephone down. He knew she would expect him to ring back immediately, to apologise, and tell her how much he wished she was with him. He did not do so.

At midnight he resisted the temptation to go and search for his young and had taken himself to bed. He heard them return in the small hours, much smothered laughter from the kitchen telling him that they were trying not to disturb him and that he would risk spoiling their efforts if he suddenly appeared enquiring about their evening. He had felt unexpectedly lonely and envious of their youthful high spirits, but berated himself for these signs of becoming a middle-aged curmudgeon.

'God! My head!' moaned Sophie now, clutching her tousled hair and collapsing on to a chair. 'I feel terrible.'

'Well, you were completely wasted when we got in last night,' said Sam unsympathetically. 'Take a couple of paraceta-mol or something – it's nothing some breakfast won't cure, anyway. God! I do need bacon and eggs – want some too?'

'Breakfast?' Sophie gave a dramatic shudder as she watched her brother rootling about in the fridge and then cracking eggs into the frying pan. 'Don't speak to me about food!' But after a mug of black coffee and a couple of large bowls of Greek yoghurt with honey and grapes she appeared to make a miraculous recovery and, unable to resist the enticing smell of sizzling bacon, felt well enough to sneak several rashers of bacon off Sam's plate and eat them in her fingers. In between restorative mouthfuls they told Patrick that they had met a party of other English teenagers, one of whom had been at school with Sam. It turned out that his parents, who owned a villa at Aghia Sophia, were friends of the Marshalls, and Sophie said they had all had a fantastic evening together and had made a date to meet again for lunch at the taverna at Aghia Sophia.

'We said we'd go round the headland in the RIB if the weather was OK and explained we might have you along with us, Dad. Want to come?'

But though touched at the offer, Patrick, who had no intention of cramping their style and no inclination to play gooseberry either, declined. 'Go and have a good time,' he said. 'I'll see you when I see you – but give me a ring if you don't intend to be back for supper. I shall wander round with my camera.'

After they had departed, he decided to go down to Kryovrisi, grab a bite of lunch, buy something for the Cunninghams to eat the next day and spend the afternoon taking pictures.

He was pleasantly surprised to be able to park so easily on the harbour front. When they had been to Corfu before, it had been in August and the pretty little town was a seething mass of red-fleshed tourists in clapped-out rental cars, all competing for the same space. Half the shops were shut now and the narrow main street looked not only deserted but curiously bare, lacking the lines of gaudy T-shirts, which were usually hung across the street from house to house like strings of bunting.

Along the edge of the quay, fishing nets, spread out for mending, were draped over bollards and upended boats were being repainted ready for the season. There was the usual gathering of men outside the harbour bar drinking coffee, playing cards and arguing fiercely about local politics, but there was a general feeling of anticipation of action to come, rather than action itself. It was like stepping into a video for a travel programme – on which someone had pressed the pause button.

The taverna overlooking the harbour was open, however, and he chose a table outside under the awning and ordered white-wine-and-fish stew with boiled potatoes – which proved excellent – followed by one of the tiny cups of thick, strong Greek coffee that never seemed to last long enough for his taste. He was not someone who needed constant company in order to enjoy himself and normally he would have enjoyed a pleasant meal in relaxed surroundings and revelled in that special luxury of feeling the perfect temperature: instead he thought of

Rachel and last night's unsatisfactory telephone call – and the light seemed to go out of the day. He had no idea what to do about his marriage – had it not been for the children he was no longer even sure that he wanted to save it.

He gave himself a mental shake. It was no good sitting here brooding on the situation – he would go and take some pictures. At least I'm good at that, he thought ruefully. When he had finished the coffee and paid the bill he decided to go to the small but well-stocked supermarket behind the taverna and get the shopping over first. While he was standing at the frozen-food cabinet wondering what to buy for the Cunninghams and doubtfully inspecting a pack of *kalamari*, which looked more like a bag of grey rubber tubes ready-sterilised for a sinister medical procedure than anything that might be turned into a gastronomic meal, a voice behind him said, 'Deciding on our lunch for tomorrow?'

He turned round to see Victoria Cunningham, a wire basket over her arm, regarding him with amusement. His pleasure on seeing her was sharp – it was as though just by thinking of her he had conjured her up.

'Hello there – how lovely to see you!'

Victoria thought he did indeed look delighted.

'What a nice surprise,' he went on, 'and you're quite right! I *was* wondering about your lunch.' He indicated the grey tubes. 'Not sure Sophie's and my combined culinary skills are up to dealing with those.'

'Mine neither – though Dora makes squid taste absolutely delicious.' She laughed suddenly and her face was transformed. 'You were peering so doubtfully into the freezer I nearly told you we couldn't come after all, just to let you off the hook. Why not just give us cold meat and salad? It's what Jake likes best and if we've been playing tennis you don't want to faff around with complicated food the minute we get back. Personally I could live on tomatoes out here. The ones at home always seem completely tasteless after these. Please don't go to lots of trouble – we'd be happy with bread and cheese. Couldn't we just have lovely pickings of this and that?'

'What a relief,' he said, laughing back at her. 'I'm not very good on the catering front. Help me choose your lunch then.'

They wandered round, picking out anything that took their fancy: a pack of salami, taramasalata, the inevitable Feta cheese, a cooked chicken still warm from the spit, and lots of wonderful tomatoes; the shopping, which a few minutes before had seemed a dreary chore, became an amusing and companionable jaunt. She was delightfully easy company, and he thought how much he had missed this easy camaraderie with Rachel for a long time.

When they got to the checkout Victoria was greeted with much enthusiasm by Dinos, the proprietor, and chatted away to him in rapid Greek while he totted up Patrick's purchases.

'Dinos met Sam and Sophie last night,' she informed Patrick. 'They told him they were staying at Petradi. Sam seems very popular with the girls, apparently. Dinos says he could tell you some tales about the English young who come out here that would make your hair stand on end! Everyone in Kryovrisi knows everything about everyone else – it's something you get used to if you live here.'

'Better not translate for me then, because I don't think I want to know too much about Sam's exploits! At least Sam can take care of himself – it's Sophie I worry about at the moment. You've no idea how deeply uneasy fathers feel about their teenage daughters. It seems only the other day that she was just a little girl. They've gone off in the boat we've hired from Petros to join some new friends they met at a bar last night. God knows what they'll get up to.'

'Sophie seemed pretty together to me,' said Victoria, 'much more than I ever was at her age. Anyway, Petros always checks up on where his boats are and makes sure everyone's accounted for if it gets rough.' She didn't want to tell him about her own folly in the boat. 'Are you going back to Petradi now?'

'I thought I might climb up to the old fort here and take some pictures – unless you have any particular suggestions?'

'I suppose you wouldn't like to come back to Vrahos and start on some of the photographs for the book?' she asked rather diffidently. 'It's just that you said you wanted to be able to prowl about and that might be easier when I'm around – in case you wanted anything but didn't want to bother Nonna. She'll be resting at the moment and Jake's gone off to Corfu town with

212

Dora and Yannis and their little boy, so I'm free this afternoon. But I'd leave you to your own devices. I wouldn't get in your hair or anything.'

'That would be marvellous,' said Patrick. 'I nearly asked if I could do that but I didn't want to impose on you. It would be a tremendous help to have you on hand. Luckily I brought one of the Marshalls' cool-bags to put the food in, so it ought to be all right for a bit.'

'We'll go in convoy then – follow me round to the right when we get to the house. You don't need to leave your car outside the courtyard like you did yesterday.'

She climbed into an ancient Ford, which looked as if it was entirely held together by masking tape and sounded, when she drove off up the narrow street, as if several old tin-cans had been tied underneath. Clearly the house was not the only thing belonging to Evanthi Doukas in need of restoration, Patrick thought. The day had been transformed for him.

After they had turned off the main road and rattled over the potholes down the long drive to the house, he followed her round to a side entrance.

'I'll just get my camera out of the back of the car,' said Patrick.

Victoria peered through the window. 'Is that all you take round with you?' she asked. 'I thought you'd have loads of equipment. How many different cameras do you use?'

'Most of the time I only use one – I'm very faithful to my old Bronica Gsi. I hate being laden down with too much stuff and everything goes into two bags – one for the cameras and one with the minimum lighting equipment and flashbulbs. I need a tripod too, of course.'

'So what would you like to do?'

'I'd love you to show me round outside – tell me if there's anywhere I shouldn't go – and then if it's all right with you I'd just like to explore on my own.'

'Fine,' she said. 'Come in this way and I'll show you how to get out on to the terrace where I'll probably be if you want me – we won't lock the door – and perhaps you might like to look at the chapel. I'll show you where the key is.'

She led the way through the door into a long stone passage and out on to the terrace at the back of the house below the balcony from which he had admired the view the day before.

'The chapel's under that,' she said, indicating a double bell tower, the top of which was on eye level with them. 'It hangs on the edge of the cliff and when the bells are rung you can hear them from miles away. The sound echoes round the rocks and over the sea.'

'That would make a fantastic photograph.' Patrick could see it in his mind's eye – the deep Venetian pink of the flaking plaster, the grey of the stone surrounds and the dark bells hanging in the tall arches against the bluest of skies. 'Is the chapel still in use?' he asked.

'Very much so. There's a service every month for which, by tradition, the local priest – the *papas* – gets free olive oil and then there are special occasions – festivals and village weddings and things. Jake was christened there, and my cousin Guy and his wife are hoping to have the christening of their first baby here later this year. I longed to get married in the chapel, I thought it would be terribly romantic, but Richard's – my husband's – family were against it.' She pulled a rueful face. 'They're equally mistrustful of romantic gestures and different denominations. Greek Orthodox comes under the heading of dangerous "smells and bells" in their book. They insisted on the whole big English country wedding bit with all their county friends, and the service definitely C. of E. As for Richard himself . . .' He thought for a moment she was going to tell him more, but she obviously changed her mind and added in a socially conversational tone: 'You really ought to talk to my cousin Guy about the house and its treasures – he'd be a mine of information. I think you know his father, who's married to my Aunt Toula?'

'I've met him – I liked him so much. We nearly did a project together.'

'Uncle Anthony's special. It can't have been easy for them to take me on aged seven after my parents were killed but he's always treated me as if I was his own daughter.'

'How are you coping now?' Patrick asked, thinking what a lot of trouble she'd had in her life.

'I don't really know – probably not very well but I don't have a yardstick. I suppose you could say I'm on the run by being out here – a way of putting my life on hold. Jake's my main concern, of course.'

'Surely putting your life on hold is the right thing to do at the moment,' he said gently. 'If you rushed into major decisions too soon you'd almost certainly make mistakes you'd regret later. Give yourself time. Jake's so young it can't matter if he has some time out from school now. You're not being pressed to make major decisions, are you?'

'N-no – not really.' He thought she sounded doubtful. 'Everyone treats me with great care, almost as if I wasn't capable of managing *anything* any more. I'm just aware of so many hidden agendas and all the very different opinions that Richard's family and mine have on many subjects. I suppose I'm being forced to think out all sorts of things for myself for the first time in my life – though it sounds ridiculous to say that at my age. Feeble.'

'You should do what you feel's right for you and Jake – not for anyone else.'

Victoria leaned against the stone wall at the edge of the terrace, gazing at the two great bells in the tower with intense concentration as though a prescription might suddenly appear on their weathered black surfaces that would miraculously give her all the answers.

'I really don't know why I'm telling you all this,' she said, picking with one finger at the yellowy-green lichen on the wall.

'I do,' said Patrick. 'It's much easier to talk to a stranger – someone who isn't involved with your life in any way and has no axe to grind. Sometimes just hearing yourself say something aloud clarifies your own mind – and you don't have to worry that it will seem too important or be taken up the wrong way.'

She looked up at him and gave him one of her brilliant smiles. 'Yes,' she said. 'Yes, that's it exactly. Thank you.' How perceptive he was, she thought, very aware of the connection between them that she had been conscious of the day before. She added in a lighter tone, 'I shall use you as my new sounding board then.'

'You do that,' said Patrick. 'Any time. The service is free.' He wanted to ask her more about her life, but didn't like to probe. Instead he said: 'Now – how about taking me down to the chapel? Then you can leave me to my own devices for a bit and I'll come and find you when I've taken a few experimental Polaroid shots and had a few ideas. OK?'

'Fine,' she said, grateful to him for breaking the rather intense moment so easily. 'Follow me and I'll take you on a conducted tour. Those ruins over there were once the tower of the old fortress – but we won't go that way because there's not much to see and, anyway, it's highly unsafe – one of the many things that needs money throwing at it. Watch how you go, though . . . the steps are very steep and can be slippery.'

The chapel was built on to the side of the rock. Victoria took a huge iron key from a nail at the side of the heavy wooden door and fitted it into the lock. 'You always have to give the door a bit of help,' she said, putting her shoulder against it, obviously accustomed to its resistance. It opened with a protesting creak. 'I'll show you inside,' she said, 'then you can come back or not as you want. Just lock the door after you leave and put the key back when you go.' Patrick couldn't help wondering why the chapel was locked at all if the key was kept in such an obvious place.

The chapel smelled of cold stone, candle-grease and incense – of sanctity and silence, thought Patrick.

'When I was a little girl I used to think prayer had this particular smell,' said Victoria voicing his idea. 'One whiff of this and the air always seemed reassuringly full of listening angels.'

'Harder to capture that vision as one gets older,' he said, smiling at her.

'Too right,' she said, and added sadly: 'Just when I need it most.'

Patrick was conscious of a lump in his throat.

Carved wooden stalls round the walls of the little chapel provided the only seating, and the flagged stones in the centre were bare. Sunlight, streaming down from one of the semi-circular windows, sent a shaft of dancing golden dust-specks across the emptiness – truly, 'dust glorified', thought Patrick. Life-sized paintings of saints and bishops dressed in colourful robes and standing against golden backgrounds, were mounted in a rood screen at the east end, lending colour and drama to an otherwise simple building. Victoria indicated a tooled silver casket set in a niche in the wall.

'Our personal family supply of relics are kept in that,' she said lightly. 'It always reminds me of the witches in *Macbeth*. You know – "eye of newt and toe of frog", not to mention the poor shipwrecked pilot's thumb – only in this case it's saints' toe-clippings and the scrapings off a bishop's shin-bone.'

'Very useful,' said Patrick.

Victoria took a taper and lit one of the candles on a stand by the door, which flickered and wavered in the draught from the open doorway but managed to stay alight. After a moment's hesitation Patrick, much moved, did the same, privately dedicating his candle to the future of this young widow and her child to whom he found himself increasingly drawn. He wondered if she had lit hers for her husband. Then, by unspoken consent, they stepped outside again into the sunlight.

They agreed that Patrick would come and find Victoria at the house later on, and would spend the rest of the afternoon making notes, taking shots and generally getting a feel for the place.

'Oh, by the way,' she said, 'I asked Nonna about the icon and she said of course you can see it. It used to be in the chapel but she keeps it upstairs now. I'll bring it down for you to look at when you come in.'

He felt absurdly pleased that she should have remembered his request when she had so much on her mind.

It was well over two hours later when he joined her on the terrace. She was writing letters.

'Am I disturbing you?' he asked.

She looked up with obvious pleasure. 'Oh, hi there. No, not at all – I'm delighted to have an excuse to stop. I'm having a go at replying to some of the letters of condolence I've had. People have been so incredibly kind but I get daunted by the ever-growing pile that needs to be answered. However, I've made a bit of headway this afternoon and done one or two difficult ones that I'd been putting off.'

'Have you hit on some sort of formula about what to say? I'm sure no one expects you to reply at any length – if at all.'

'I've worked out a fairly standard answer, but some people have written such remarkable letters I feel I can't just send a routine answer to everyone.'

'Don't rush at it. Time doesn't come into something like this. Do you want to go on while you're still in the mood, or have you done enough for the time being?' He thought she looked exhausted. 'That looks a fairly impressive pile of envelopes you've addressed there.'

'I've done enough. Tell me how you got on.'

'Really well. I've had a wonderful afternoon – I couldn't be more grateful to you for suggesting it and I hope I've taken some spectacular pictures. This is such a fascinating place – so full of wonderful architectural surprises in unexpected places, like that Venetian fountain for instance – I'd have to be a really bad photographer to fail completely. I just hope I can do justice to the magic of the place. The light's beginning to fade so I thought I'd pack it in for today. I've put all my stuff in the car and just came to say goodbye and thank you.'

'Come and have a drink before you go,' she said, suddenly wanting to delay his departure. 'I don't know about you but I could do with one.'

'Are you sure? Well, that would be lovely – just a quick one.'

'Let's go in, it's getting chilly. It's been a heavenly day but the warm evenings haven't started yet.'

She led the way through the Grand Salon. 'We'll go up to the little drawing room where you saw Nonna yesterday,' she said, and Patrick followed her, making mental notes of what pictures he would like to take when he came to do the interior shots of the house. When she opened the door at the end of the upstairs passage he was struck again by the cosier charm of the smaller room, and a feeling of dropping back in time.

'Come and look,' she said. 'I've put the icon out on the table for you to see.' She picked it up and held it out to him and he took it, very carefully, in his hands.

'I feel extremely honoured,' he said, gazing with admiration at the two angels depicted on the front against a gold background, automatically wondering what would be the best way to photograph it. 'Tell me about it.'

Victoria came and stood beside him.

'You probably know more about icons than I do,' she said, 'so I can only tell you what I know about this one. Those are the Archangels Gabriel and Michael on the outer panels. Aren't they splendid? Michael looks a real warrior, doesn't he – all ready to do battle with the devil – and I always think Gabriel's wings are specially beautiful.'

'May I open it up?'

'Of course. Then inside, you see, we have two bishop saints in their checkerboard robes standing either side of the Virgin and Child; each of them famous for being what Nonna would call a thaumaturge – a miracle worker. This one's St Gregory, and the one on the left is St Nicholas.' She laughed. 'Poor St Nicholas – I'm afraid when I was little he got inextricably mixed up in my head with Father Christmas and Enid Blyton's Big-Ears because Nonna taught us that we could always recognise images of St Nicholas by his curly beard and enormous ears – real jug handles! It made him seem wonderfully cosy and approachable, so not surprisingly, he was my favourite saint.'

'It's an amazing object. Those jewel colours against the gold background! Beautiful.'

'Yes,' she said. 'Nonna used to tell us that the gold is supposed to represent the light locked into the icon.'

'And your grandmother told me it was signed?'

'Mmm – you can *just* make out the Greek letters here if you look very closely.' She traced them with her finger and translated: 'BY THE HAND OF THE SERVANT OF GOD, ANDREAS RITZOS.'

'And is it dated?'

'So I've always been told, though I couldn't possibly work it out myself. Apparently they used letters to represent numbers and then the date was reckoned from the Creation of the World, which was thought to have happened 5508 years before the birth of Christ so you have to work the letters out first and then subtract that figure.' She laughed. 'Frightfully complicated – like those "take away the number you first thought of" riddles. Ritzos was born in 1422 and had a workshop on Crete but Uncle Anthony told me his works were much in demand not just in Greece but throughout Italy.'

'It's a real treasure. I can certainly see why your grandmother 'doesn't want to part with it,' Patrick said seriously, and added, 'or you either – I can tell you love it too. It'll be a shame if it has to go.'

'Oh, yes,' she said with great feeling and her eyes suddenly filled with tears.

He looked at her with concern. 'I'm so sorry – that was probably a clumsy thing to say.'

'Not at all – just horribly true,' she said in a choked voice. 'It's rather getting to me at the moment that everything's becoming so run down. Showing Vrahos to you, I keep thinking how decayed it must all look to anyone who doesn't know it and love it as I do.'

'You don't have to worry about that with me,' said Patrick, wishing he could comfort her. 'All I see is charm and magic and a very special atmosphere.'

'Thank you.' She made an obvious effort to recover and gave him a watery smile. 'I'll go and get that bottle of wine. Make yourself at home.'

'Can I poke around and think how I would like to photograph this room?' he asked. 'There's such a wealth of fascinating objects. Spoiled for choice indeed, as they say in Yorkshire, where I live.'

'Look at anything you like. I won't be a moment.'

He watched her go, and as she went he thought that he would be more than happy to go on looking at her.

When she returned, carrying a bottle of wine, Patrick was standing by the fireplace intently examining a small silver box, which he was holding in his hand. Something in the expression on his face made her wonder if he'd found another object of rare value.

'This is absolutely extraordinary,' he said. 'Can you tell me the history of it?'

She looked surprised. 'Not really. It's been by Nonna's chair as long as I can remember, but I didn't know it was anything particularly special and I can't say I've ever really examined it before. Awful how much you take for granted when you're a child. My cousin Guy's much more clued up than me – he knows far more about the treasures in this house. Is it a snuffbox?'

He handed it to her. 'Have a close look at it now – no it's not a snuffbox. Open it and read the inscription inside the lid and then tell me whose initials you think those are?'

'Well, *Pantotina* means Forever or Always – and the first set of initials E.V.M.P. must stand for Evanthi Victoria Maria Palombini. That was Nonna's maiden name. But it doesn't look like an antique box to me – that's a comparatively modern mark on the bottom – and the inscribed date on the top is October 1938. I'm afraid I've no idea who H.P.M. could be. What makes you think it's so interesting? Is it valuable?'

'Not in a monetary sense, though it's a charming object. It must have been specially commissioned, with its unusual border of bees and swallows round the top and the entwined hearts round the word *Pantotina* inside. No, the really extraordinary thing is that I've seen almost the exact replica of this box all my life. Except that the initials are the other way round – the one I know is inscribed *to* H.P.M and *from* E.V.M.P. – otherwise the two boxes are absolutely identical. And, you see, I *do* know who H.P.M. is.'

They were standing looking at each other in astonishment when Evanthi Doukas opened the door.

Chapter Twenty-two

'Good evening, Mr Hammond – *kalispera*.' Evanthi Doukas stood in the doorway and looked from Patrick to Victoria and back again . Her eyebrows shot up when she saw the silver box in Victoria's hand.

'Oh, Nonna, how lovely. Have you had a good rest?' Victoria gave her grandmother a loving look. 'Patrick's been taking pictures for the book all afternoon and I was just about to give him a drink. Now I can get you one too. He's interested in this little box.' Victoria held it up. 'But I don't know its history at all. Can you tell him about it?'

'I could, of course – but why should you be interested, Mr Hammond?' Evanthi looked at her most patrician and unapproachable. 'I would have thought you could have picked on many objects in this room of far greater interest than that,' she said crushingly.

'This one is of particular interest to me,' said Patrick, refusing to be intimidated.

She came slowly forward, using her stick but holding herself rigidly upright. She lowered herself carefully into her chair and then held out her hand for the box. Victoria gave it to her. She turned it over and over, opening and closing it and studying it intently, almost as though she was afraid it might have been polluted in some way. Then she snapped it shut and put it back in its habitual place on the table beside her.

'So,' she said at last, 'what is it that you want to know then?' Her face was as carefully closed as the silver box. Patrick guessed she was a woman of strong emotions who had long ago learned how to hide them when it suited her.

'I want to know the story of how you came by it, and also—' he broke off and looked up at the portrait of Evanthi hanging over the fireplace, and then back at the old woman in front of him. He continued slowly, 'When I saw your portrait yesterday I knew at once there was something familiar about it: something that might explain the extraordinary reaction of the old lady outside your front door when we arrived yesterday. When I met Victoria I was even more sure.' He looked at her and said, 'You're the original *Girl on the Rock* aren't you, Mrs Doukas?'

'And you,' she said very quietly, her expression still inscrutable but with no pretence of misunderstanding either, 'you have to be Hugh Marston's son. You are so very like him. I got a terrible shock when you walked in yesterday – as no doubt my old maid, Nafsica, must have done if she saw you too. But I thought your name was Hammond?'

Patrick nodded. 'It is – and I'm not Hugh's son,' he said, 'I'm his nephew. He's my mother's brother but he's always been more like a father to me.' He added gently: 'Hugh never married. My mother always told us this was because he'd had a great love in his life which somehow went wrong – but until the other week I never heard him speak about it himself.'

'Are you going to tell me what on earth you're both talking about?' Victoria was bursting with curiosity. 'What girl on what rock? Who is this Hugh?'

But Evanthi had eyes only for Patrick. 'Is he . . . still alive?' she asked.

'Oh, very much so! He's a bit immobile nowadays, what with arthritis and some arterial trouble from years of smoking and drinking – though I've never seen him appear drunk in my life – so, of course, getting about with an artificial leg is an increasing effort, but he's very much himself still: courageous and funny and impossible and irresistible as ever.' He looked at her sharply. 'You knew he'd lost a leg in the war?'

She shook her head. They can't have met for sixty years then, thought Patrick, astonished, and yet the mention of his name still has such power over her.

'Is he still painting?'

'Yes – as well as ever, though it's a physical struggle now. I think he'd die if he couldn't paint. He concentrates mostly on animals – particularly horses, which are what he's most famous for. He's just taken on a big commission for Prince Haroun – the owner of the famous Haroun stud, who's bred such a series of notable winners. My mother thinks he's mad to have agreed to do it, but I think it's wonderful and will keep him going. Hugh's pictures are tremendously sought after now. If they ever come on the market they fetch high prices at auction, but it doesn't happen often because people tend to hang on to them for posterity if they possibly can. He no longer accepts commissions for portraits of people, though he's promised to paint Sophie this summer. She's thrilled at the idea. My children all adore him.'

Patrick watched Evanthi's face. The tight control was slipping a little and a slow tear was rolling, unchecked, down her powdered cheek. He guessed that shedding tears in public was an extremely rare thing for her to do.

He said: 'Uncle Hugh told me the other day that he's never painted a better portrait than *Girl on the Rock*. He's always refused to sell it or exhibit it and we've none of us ever known who the sitter was, but an odd thing happened the other day. He suddenly found his original sketch for the portrait – which had apparently been lost for years – and told me that when he came across it he had actually been thinking of the sitter at the exact moment he found it.'

'I sent him a message when I thought I was about to die,' said Evanthi simply – as though this explained everything.

'You mean you've been in touch with him recently?'

'Not in the way you mean – but I sent him a message all the same. I'm glad he received it.'

'He told me he carried that sketch with him all through the war,' said Patrick, much moved by the look on her face. 'He said it helped him to survive when he was wounded.'

At that moment the telephone by Evanthi's chair started to ring. Victoria answered it.

'Oh, hello,' she said. 'Yes, he's right here. No, that's quite all right, of course you can't help it – mobiles don't work here; we don't get a signal. It's Sophie for you, Patrick.' She handed him the receiver.

'Do forgive me . . .' he looked apologetic. 'Hello? Sophie? Everything all right? Oh, for God's sake – you are both hopeless.' He sounded very irritated. 'I'll be back shortly. Well, you'll just have to wait till I come then – no great hardship and serve you right. OK. See you soon. Bye.'

He put the telephone down and turned back towards the room. Victoria was kneeling by her grandmother's chair. Patrick thought Hugh would have appreciated the picture they made together, and though there was still so much he wanted to know he also thought that perhaps it was as well that he should have to go now and leave the two of them alone together.

'I'm so sorry about that – my incompetent children forgot to take the spare key to Petradi with them and are locked out.' He grinned. 'Sophie sounded most aggrieved. "How were we to know you wouldn't be there when we got back?" was how she put it. But I must go anyway. I've taken up too much of your time already – not to mention giving you a shock. I'd love to hear more of your story another time – if you're willing to share it with me. And to talk about that wonderful icon.' He held his hand out to Evanthi and she took it in both hers.

'Hugh's nephew,' she said. 'Yes, I will share some of the story with you – but not today. I need time to think about a great many things from a very long time ago. But come back soon. Victoria will show you out – won't you, *chrysso mou*?'

'Of course, Nonna. I'll be back in a moment.' Victoria got to her feet and accompanied Patrick to the door and down the long passage again.

'Well!' she said as they went down the stairs together. 'How really weird! I'm utterly riveted. What an extraordinary coincidence – if it *is* a coincidence. Nonna won't think it is, I can tell you that. She's extremely fey.' She gave Patrick an amused look. 'She'll think you were "sent",' she said.

He smiled back at her. 'Perhaps I was! Certainly when I followed up my agent's suggestion to get in touch with your grandmother and come out to see Vrahos, I had no idea that I was going to stumble across a mystery connected with my own family. I nearly told you, when you were showing me round this afternoon, what an extraordinary reception we'd had yesterday from the old lady in the courtyard,' and he told her about Nafsica's reaction.

'I got quite a shock myself when I met you,' he added, looking at Victoria.

'Nafsica took to her bed after she'd seen you,' she said,

glancing up at him and then looking quickly away, not quite meeting his gaze. 'Apparently she's been carrying on as if you had horns and a tail, but I didn't like to tell you that. She's been badgering Dora to get the *papas* – the local priest – to come and hear her confession because she insists she has done something terrible. I think he's coming on Sunday. Meanwhile, Nafsica is driving poor Dora completely bananas saying she's going to die – and clearly feeling the hellfires licking round her – but refusing to explain. I think that's why Yannis offered to take Dora and the boys into town – to get away from all the weeping and wailing of his grandmother-in-law.'

'Did you tell *your* grandmother about that?'

'No – she was tired last night and I didn't want to upset her any more. But I think I must tell her now.'

She walked out with Patrick to where he'd left the car.

'Oh,' she said, 'you never got your drink after all. I'm so sorry.'

'I'll have it another time. There were more important things to occupy us,' he said gently. 'Will you be all right?' he asked, finding it hard to tear himself away. 'It seems to me you've got more than enough on your plate already, without having to cope with another family drama. Please don't feel you've got to come over to us tomorrow if you don't feel up to it.'

But he hoped very much that she would come.

'Of course I'll come. Besides, I shall have to bring you up to date with the next exciting instalment, shan't I? I may know a bit more by then. Shall you tell Sam and Sophie about it?'

'Would your grandmother mind?'

'Oh, I shouldn't think so – not now it's out in the open after all these years. Do tell them. Then we can all talk about it. I shall be bursting to discuss it.'

'All right,' he said. 'They'll be absolutely gripped too.'

He stood hesitating by the car for a moment as if uncertain whether to go or not, though he had struck her so far as being a decisive sort of man. Then he said: 'Well, goodbye, Victoria – see you at the Krokalia Beach tomorrow for some very family-standard tennis,' and he folded his long legs into the car and drove off rather fast down the pot-holey drive.

*

Victoria walked slowly back up to the little drawing room. Evanthi had not stirred and was sitting in her chair in the half-light of evening, apparently gazing into space or, more likely, thought Victoria, gazing inside herself, remembering Hugh Marston and making a journey back through time. She did not notice Victoria come in.

'Nonna?' Victoria said softly. 'Are you all right?'

Evanthi held out a hand. 'Yes, I'm all right, *agapi*. But I've got a lot to think about and I shall have to consider what, if anything, I am going to do now.'

'Do you feel you can tell me about it? You've never said a word before and yet it was clearly terribly important to you once.'

'For a long time it was too painful and too private to talk about and after I thought that it had ceased to matter to anyone else except myself, I suppose I got into a habit of silence. I don't agree with all these self-indulgent modern views that one should bare one's soul and tell everything to total strangers,' she said fiercely. '*Counselling* I believe it's called – very American and not one of their better exports.' She gave a derisive snort and Victoria thought it would be a brave therapist who took Evanthi Doukas on, though she could see the attraction of counselling for herself, and thought of what Patrick had said to her earlier that afternoon about it being easier to talk to a stranger. She had certainly found it easy to talk to him. When she lay awake at night, tormented by her own confused emotions, she longed to be able to discuss her relationship with Richard without the burden of feeling disloyal to the husband who could never now either defend himself or explain to her what his own feelings had really been. How could she explain to any of her family that mental images of Guy and Richard having sex together haunted her – filling her head with hateful thoughts by day and causing her to wake shaking and sweating in the night? How could she explain the terrible sense of betrayal that she felt against both Richard and Guy?

'Why should we any of us expect to be released from pain in this life anyway?' Evanthi continued severely, following her own train of thought. Then her face softened. 'But yes, I will share it with you, darling, and who knows? Perhaps we can help each other. I know I've grown into an arrogant, intolerant old woman in some ways – but I have to tell you that I don't come very well out of this story. I lost faith in someone else's solemn vow, and because I was hurt and angry, I broke a promise of my own. But I've learned today that perhaps that other person did keep their vow after all.'

'When I was a very little girl,' said Victoria, looking down and twisting her wedding ring round and round on her finger, 'you once told me that one should be struck by love like a bolt of lightning. I've never forgotten that. Was Patrick's uncle your bolt of lightning, Nonna?'

'He was, yes. Oh, he was. And however painful it has been all these years I can never regret what we had together for a very short time – because it was the real thing. If I had my life over again I would never cut that out despite all the anguish it has caused me.' Evanthi looked at her granddaughter with compassion. 'But you, *agapi mou* – you have not been struck by lightning yet and that is one part of your great misery now, isn't it? Not only what you have lost . . . but what you deliberately chose not to have. Neither to receive – nor to give?'

'Oh, Nonna,' said Victoria sadly, wondering how much Evanthi knew, and what, if anything Guy might have told her – surely not the whole truth? 'I am in such a muddle of sadness and anger. Partly against poor Richard who must have been desperately unhappy to do what I think he did, but also against my own stupidity . . . and . . . and my cowardice about life. An attempt to play for safety because I couldn't have what I really wanted. Please tell me your story to take my mind off myself.'

When Dora came in to say that she and Yannis and the little boys were back and she had put Jake to bed, she found grand-mother and granddaughter sitting together in the dark, both completely absorbed in a vanished world.

Chapter Twenty-three

Hugh and Evanthi had first met at a stiflingly grand dinner party at the house of Hugh's aunt, the formidable Lady Georgia Graham. She had invited her nephew – or rather dragooned him into attending – because the Brazilian Ambassador, who was to be the guest of honour, was a collector of contemporary art, and Lady Georgia, whose chief recreation was arranging other people's lives, considered it might be advantageous for a budding artist to meet him. She was devoted to The Arts in an undiscriminating kind of way, fancied herself greatly in the role of benevolent fairy godmother to the great names of tomorrow, but had strong – and often misinformed – opinions that did not always coincide with the aspirations of her protégés.

To balance the numbers at her table she had invited the daughter of old friends from abroad who happened to be visiting London that week, though she decided against placing the two young people next to each other at dinner. She recognised her nephew's considerable talent and meant to have a hand in fostering his career – if only to irritate her brother-in-law – but she also recognised Hugh's dangerous charm for the opposite sex, and had no intention of fostering any flirtation with an eighteen-year-old débutante, and a foreign one to boot. She was well aware that her erstwhile school friend, Contessa Palombini, of Greek nationality herself but married to an Italian, already had definite plans in mind for her daughter's future, which certainly did not include a wild young Englishman who was not only a younger son with no prospects, but was insisting on embarking on an unreliable career not of his parents' choosing. She was fond of her sister's son – admired the stand he had taken with his autocratic father in the cause of art – but she didn't trust him an inch.

Evanthi had not wanted to go to the dinner party, but her mother had insisted.

'Oh, Mamma! I won't know a soul there and there will be no one else of my age . . . and I haven't seen Lady Georgia since I was little anyway. I can hardly remember her.'

'All the more reason to see her now. It is extremely kind of her to ask you and it would be most ungrateful to refuse. Please don't be tiresome, Evanthi.'

Mother and daughter were often at loggerheads: they were too alike for peaceful co-existence, sharing the same mercurial temperament and both being extremely strong-willed, though Evanthi possessed the happy talent for making-up after quarrels whereas Maria Palombini could carry a grievance for weeks like the after-effects of a severe bout of flu. This time, however, knowing that if she refused to accept Lady Georgia's invitation an equally stuffy dinner party would be her lot in the house where they were staying, Evanthi gave way with reasonable grace.

They had a further disagreement about what she should wear, but she had out-manoeuvred her powerful parent by simply ignoring the demure dress of white lace, which her mother had instructed the housemaid to lay out on her bed, and opting instead for a clinging sheath of red beaded silk-chiffon, which had been a present from her father when they had visited Paris a few weeks earlier. Her mother, who complained that her husband spoiled their only child, had been furious that she had not been consulted about the gift. He had taken Evanthi off to Lachasse and they had chosen it together. Evanthi had been longing for an occasion to wear the dress, though she knew better than to ask her mother's permission. She was careful to make sure that by the time she knocked at her mother's bedroom door to say goodbye there would be no time to change – to be late would have been unthinkable – and she had the satisfaction of knowing that her mother considered she was most unsuitably dressed for someone of her age. Suitable or not, she knew she looked stunning – it was just a pity that the effect would be wasted on all the dreary old people at the dinner party.

Hugh had found himself placed between the Brazilian Ambassador's wife – whose mastery of the English language was not only tenuous but who clearly did not share her husband's interest in painting – and a buxom lady from Leicestershire with a dropped bosom and wonderful pearls, who knew his parents and whose conversational talents appeared to be restricted to the topics of family trees and foxes. Glancing across the table he had been immediately arrested by the striking-looking girl sitting opposite to him. Though at first glance she appeared to be listening politely to the florid-faced man on her right, who was giving her a cliché-by-cliché account of his latest speech in the House of Commons, Hugh thought she looked miles away and was probably every bit as bored as he felt himself. He decided she needed a diversion. He discreetly rolled a small piece of bread to a satisfying roundness between his finger and thumb and then under cover of wielding his table-napkin, and thanks to years of target-practice at his sisters, flicked it expertly across the table so that it hit her smartly on the throat. She looked up startled and, as he had intended, encountered his gaze. He gave an almost imperceptible wink that could have passed as a nervous tick. Evanthi, enchanted, winked back. Both knew immediately that they would have to see more of each other.

The rest of dinner passed in a flash as they engaged in a delicious flirtation by means of covert and inventive signals without rousing the suspicions of anyone else in the dining room.

When the women withdrew to the upstairs drawing room, leaving the men to their port and cigars, Evanthi went to sit next to the lady from Leicestershire, having correctly guessed that she would thus be able to discover the identity of the incredibly good-looking flicker of bread pellets. She learned that he was Lady Georgia's nephew, that his mother was a member of an aristocratic but impecunious family of Irish extraction – which accounted for his notorious streak of wildness, according to the lady from Leicestershire . 'Breeding always tells,' she informed Evanthi, producing a few enlightening examples of the hereditary behaviour of hounds she had known.

It appeared that his father not only had an estate in Yorkshire but was a Lord Lieutenant and an M.F.H. Evanthi, who had a hazy idea that a lieutenant was the most junior form of officer in the English army, and, not being conversant with English hunting jargon hadn't a notion what a Master of Foxhounds was, failed to be impressed – though clearly in her mentor's opinion both positions were guaranteed passports to the highest echelons of society. Finally she learned that he was called Hugh Marston, had been sent down from Cambridge for breaking the rules, was intent on becoming an artist in the teeth of family opposition and was generally considered rather Bohemian. 'Though I dare say there are some perfectly charming people living in Bohemia,' the lady from Leicestershire had added hastily. She hadn't the faintest idea where Bohemia was but could pick out a foreigner when she saw one and this very dark-haired girl with the not unattractive but definitely un-English accent might come from absolutely anywhere.

Evanthi was just starting to get worried that the car that was being sent to fetch her might arrive before the men returned to join them, when there was the sound of male voices and fruity laughter coming up the stairs and they appeared. By this time she was standing on her own near the window, Lady Georgia having borne her companion away to talk to someone else.

Hugh made an instant beeline to her side, introduced himself and kissed her hand with far more expertise than most Englishmen managed. 'I am our hostess's nephew,' he announced, 'so even though we haven't been formally introduced it is my absolute duty to look after you.'

'How convenient for you,' said Evanthi. 'But I already know who you are. The lady with a face like a peony has been telling me the history of your life.'

'That should have been interesting.'

'Oh, it was. Among other things she told me you are a notable shot – but I had learned that for myself.'

'A-h-h! That really was a brilliant shot, wasn't it?' His eyes were full of amusement as he looked down at her. He was extremely tall. 'That dress is the most sensational colour for you,' he said, 'but please turn round.' Evanthi raised her eyebrows but obligingly twirled about on her pointed satin shoes, which were dyed to the exact shade of her dress. 'Oh good,' said Hugh, 'that's all right then – what a relief! I should have had more faith.' The dress, which was high in the front, was cut extremely low at the back and was the very latest fashion.

Evanthi laughed. 'Do you always make such personal remarks to people you haven't met before?' she asked.

'Only to very special people. But we have to skip the formalities because we need to get to know each other very fast.'

'Oh, really? Why is that?'

'Because I'm going to paint you,' he said.

The following day Hugh had called with a huge bunch of flowers to invite her out to luncheon. By great good luck Evanthi's mother was out when he arrived, and her hostess – the delightful wife of the First Secretary at the Italian Embassy with whom they were staying, who had taken a great fancy to her young guest – was delighted to encourage such a dashing caller, though Evanthi had no doubt that her mother, who had antediluvian ideas about chaperonage, would be far from pleased when she heard about it.

'Colours seen by candlelight' are not supposed to look so good by the light of day, but Evanthi thought Hugh Marston's colours looked even more delightful in the morning than they had the night before.

He took her to L'Apéritif in Jermyn Street, and she was unsophisticated enough to be very impressed that the head waiter obviously knew him well and treated him with partiality, escorting them to their table himself. They drank White Ladies while they studied the menu and Evanthi thought it was the most delicious drink she'd ever tasted. Though she had been brought up to drink wine with meals since she was a child, cocktails were not served in her parents' houses either in Greece or in Italy. She felt fast and daring – and had the delicious sensation that she was on the brink of a great adventure.

She told him about her various homes: the house in southern Tuscany near Pienza, where as well as the terraced vines and olive groves, the countryside unrolled in great vistas of golden barley and scarlet poppies against a backdrop of mountains; where wild boar roamed and porcupines scuttled out of the undergrowth at dusk; about the flat in Rome with its views of ancient tiled roofs and the constant sound of bells – but even dearer to her heart, she told him, was the old Venetian House on

Corfu where she had spent much of her childhood while her parents travelled the world, and which belonged to her Greek grandmother. When her father had been posted to the Italian Embassy in Athens they had used it as a weekend retreat.

'It will be mine one day,' she told Hugh, 'because I am the only child and my mother's only brother was killed in the Great War. Mamma and I often fight about things but we both love Vrahos, and when we are there we are always at our happiest. My father doesn't love it like we do because it doesn't belong to him and he is very – how would you say it? – concerned with his own places?'

'Territorial?' suggested Hugh.

'Yes, thank you – territorial – and he doesn't like it that I have always felt more Greek than Italian, but I was born there – and it is the place where I would like to die. The Spirit of Place is very strong and is always with me.'

'The Spirit of Place,' repeated Hugh. 'I like the sound of that – like a guardian angel perhaps?'

'Perhaps. Where does your place spirit – your guardian angel – live? In Yorkshire?'

'No,' he said seriously. 'I love Yorkshire, but I don't think my angel is there. I think my "place spirit" is in the Alps – where you can put seal-skins on the bottom of your skis and climb for hours in silence with the sun on your back and the high peaks around you – and then take the skins off, stow them in a rucksack and hurtle down in an eighth of the time it took you to get up, making your own tracks, with powder-snow whistling round your knees. Where the snow can suddenly explode at your feet and turn into ptarmigan and fly away; where black game come booming over your head out of the fir trees and you may see roe deer and chamois.'

She had leaned her chin on her hand and listened entranced as he told her about his passion for mountains and animals – especially horses. Then he roared with laughter suddenly. 'How serious you're making me,' he said. 'I think I might order lots of these angels of yours – it would definitely be useful to have them around on a racecourse, for instance. Imagine the advantage of having one riding with you at a point-to-point or nudging you when visiting your bookie!'

'A *point-to-point*? A *bookie*? What are those?' she asked.

So he had told her about racing too, making her laugh at stories of his outrageous exploits. He was a born raconteur.

Then he had talked about his painting, and she had glimpsed the dedication behind the frivolity. 'Most of my family think I'm making an irresponsible choice with my career,' he said. 'They'd like me to keep my painting as a hobby, something I can do occasionally for pleasure while I carry on the real business of life in the City or the army or politics. I've no intention of joining the army, unless of course – Heaven forbid! – there's a war. Then I should join up at once. But I've managed to fob my father off by joining the Territorial Army, and as for politics!' Hugh made a frightful face. 'I could never toe a party line and I might turn out like that old windbag you were sitting next to last night! My family don't realise that I don't *have* a choice. I have to be an artist. For me it's like breathing.' He laughed. 'They can't believe I will make any money, you see, and my father has warned me that he won't subsidise me if I insist on defying him.' He added lightly: 'But I intend to become famous! I shall confound them all and sell my pictures for vast sums of money to rich bankers who will implore me to immortalise their plain, over-dressed wives for posterity.'

'Won't they be rather dull – these plain wives?'

'Of course. But they will make me rich enough to be able to paint the subjects I really want to. Horses, of course – my great passion – and,' he added looking at her, 'a few very beautiful women of my own choosing.' Evanthi had felt her colour rising and her heart had thumped in the most disconcerting way but she had looked right back at him, a challenge in her eyes.

'Now tell me more about you,' he said.

She had told him how much she wanted to go to university, but how her parents wouldn't even consider the idea. 'They want me to be a wonderful hostess – their perfectly prepared creation for a pre-ordained role with a particular person. You will think me very arrogant,' she said, 'but I have a good brain and I don't want just to be an ornament in someone else's life. And I feel so ungrateful because my parents are lovely and I know they think they have my best interests at heart, but I want to be someone in my own right as well.'

'You're that already,' he said. 'You could never be anything else. I thought that the moment I saw you across the table last night.'

'So you threw bread at me to prove how intellectual you thought I looked?'

And they had started laughing again, weaving in and out of seriousness and hilarity, sharing their hopes and ambitions, their love for their respective families but their equal determination not to follow meekly along the paths that had been mapped out for them. Both had the sensation that their worlds were expanding at incredible speed.

After lunch they had walked down St James's Street and into St James's Park and sat on a bench and lost all idea of the time. There were snowdrops out, and though it was only February a few early crocus clumped along the edge of the lake; willows were trailing their fingers in the water and birds were singing. They did not notice that it was getting both cold and dark.

The sound of Big Ben striking five o'clock brought them back to reality. 'Santa Ciela Bernadetta!' exclaimed Evanthi, leaping to her feet in horror. 'I must go immediately! Signora Mazotto was having some friends of my parents to English tea. My mother will be completely furious with me.'

'When shall I see you again?' Hugh asked.

'We're leaving for Italy tomorrow. My father has to get back to Rome.'

'Well, isn't that lucky?' he said, deadpan. 'What an amazing coincidence! I'm coming to Rome soon too – to work, you understand. I've . . . er . . . suddenly remembered that I have to do some painting out there.'

'Then we might encounter each other,' she said gravely, but her eyes were alight with amusement. 'You must come and call. I will give you our address.'

He delivered her back to Eaton Place in a taxi – too late for her hostess's tea party – and the moment Contessa Palombini met the dashing young man who had taken her daughter out to lunch and saw how they looked at each other, she knew that Evanthi was going to become extremely difficult to deal with and that a serious obstacle had arisen to her own plans for the future.

Chapter Twenty-four

Dora's arrival broke the spell. She turned on the light as she came into the drawing room and Evanthi and Victoria blinked as if they had just come out of the cinema and felt disorientated to find themselves sitting in their usual surroundings.

Victoria was horrified to discover how late it was – nearly nine o'clock. She had been so absorbed in Evanthi's story that all thoughts of time or of Jake's whereabouts had completely gone out of her mind. 'I am sorry if we are late,' said Dora, who had learned that one of the many eccentricities of the English – in which she included Victoria – was an extraordinarily regimented idea about the correct timing of children's bedtimes, 'but we stopped on the way back to see Yannis' parents. I have bathed both the boys and put Jake in his bed and now he would like you to say good night.'

'Oh, Dora, you are wonderful. Thank you so much. I'll go straight away.' Victoria stretched out her hand to her grandmother. 'Nonna – I'll come back and see you as soon as I've settled him. Are you all right?'

'Yes, *agapi*, bless you, I'm perfectly all right. But I'm tired with talking so much, and with old, old memories. Dora will help me up to bed, but come and say good night to me.'

Victoria thought Evanthi looked completely worn out, and gave her an anxious look. Then she flew upstairs and found Jake curled up in bed half listening to one of his *Harry Potter* tapes, but already nearly asleep – twiddling the tell-tale Tintin strand of hair – his eyelids drooping though he opened them wide when his mother came in and sat up briefly to give her a rib-crushing hug before snuggling down again. He said he'd had a wonderful day. After they'd done the shopping they'd gone to Kalámi, and Angelo's grandfather had taken him and Angelo out in his fishing boat and they'd helped put the nets out and then they'd had ice creams, and then . . . Jake's voice tailed off mid-sentence and his eyes closed. Victoria sat on the edge of his bed, stroking his hair until she was certain he was deeply asleep, her own mind whirling with its mass of new information. She couldn't wait to hear the rest of Evanthi's story, but when she went up to her grandmother's room she found her nearly asleep too.

'Don't you want anything to eat, Nonna? I could bring you up some supper on a tray.'

'No thank you, *agapi*. Dora has brought me a tisane and that is all I want. But you must have something.'

'Don't worry about me. I'll raid the kitchen,' said Victoria. 'Oh, Nonna! What a story! Will you tell me the rest of it?'

'Yes, I'll tell you – but not now. And, alas, it is not all so happy. Leave me now, *chrysso mou*. I have much to think about.'

Victoria kissed the soft cheek, which looked as pale and transparent as white tissue paper, and closed the door very softly behind her. 'Dear God! Don't let her die yet,' she prayed. She felt very moved by the intensity with which her grandmother had been able to recall that first meeting with her lost love – so many, many years ago. She shivered at the thought of the relentless passage of time. I shall be old too some day, she thought, and what will my memories be? What shall I tell Jake's children about their grandfather? What shall I tell Jake himself about Richard?

She wondered what Hugh Marston had been like. She couldn't imagine that Evanthi would have fallen so powerfully and immediately under the spell of anyone unless they had tremendous personal magnetism, and thought wistfully that it was a far cry from anything she had experienced herself. Obviously Hugh must have looked very like his nephew for Patrick to be so immediately recognisable to both Evanthi and Nafsica, but were they alike as people? Patrick certainly had charm too, but she thought he must be a more reserved character than she imagined his uncle to be and liked him the better for that. She had an urge to ring him up to share what she had learned of her grandmother's story so far, but decided it would be better to wait till tomorrow.

What was Patrick Hammond's wife like, she wondered. She

thought it surprising that he'd hardly mentioned her at all, though he obviously adored his children and seemed very much a family man. Had he rung his wife to tell her about the extraordinary coincidence of the silver boxes and share the experiences of his day with her? Victoria found herself longing for Richard to be on the other end of a telephone, interested in her life – the calm waters of their relationship unmuddied by all the doubt and anguish that had been stirred up recently. She realised that for the first time for weeks her mind had been completely taken off the turmoil of emotions that haunted most of her waking moments recently – and some of her sleeping ones too. She contemplated ringing Guy, as she would unquestionably have done only a few weeks ago, but at the thought of him the horrible burning lump seemed to rise up in her throat again and she felt choked afresh with hurt and anger.

That night she had the dream again. It started in her childhood. All was sunshine and serenity and she and Guy and Richard were playing together on a beach – as they had so often done in real life – when suddenly she became aware that the boys had disappeared and left her alone. She was sure they were somewhere near because she could still hear their voices, but she couldn't actually see them; then the voices changed to laughter, horrible mocking laughter and she knew they were deliberately hiding from her. She tried to call out to them, to beg them to come back, but no sound would come out of her mouth.

The scene changed and she was in a wood now, which got thicker and darker and kept closing in on her; the trees were doing a weird sort of dance, swaying on their roots while their branches stretched out twig-like fingers to try to clutch at her. She stumbled blindly through undergrowth, her breath coming in panicky gasps while all the time she tried to yell for the boys to come back and rescue her but was still unable to make any noise. She caught occasional glimpses of them peering out at her from behind trees and laughing, and though she knew quite well who they were, their faces had changed horribly and become grotesque – hideously menacing. She started to run, this time desperate, not to find them, but to get away from them because they had turned into monster-like creatures and were now chasing her. She could feel their hot breath on the back of her neck and knew they were just about to catch her when she caught her foot on a bramble and tripped. At the same moment all the trees suddenly shot into the air, their roots coming out of the ground with a great sucking noise. Then she was falling – falling into a black nothingness – and the scream came at last.

She woke sweating, panting and shaking, and it was a long time before she could shake the nightmare off. Towards dawn she dropped off into a heavy sleep and opened her eyes what seemed like only moments later to find Jake bouncing up and down on the end of her bed.

They set off after breakfast for the Krokalia Beach Hotel, a huge concrete block – much featured in tourist brochures – with excellent facilities but about as much charm as a multi-storey car park.

Jake, who had embarked on writing a novel in a new notebook, which he'd bought in Kerkyra the day before, was armed with his pencil case as well as a carrier bag containing his beloved hot-wheels cars. When the authorial mood came over him he would become completely absorbed by the writing muse for hours and Victoria knew that until the mood wore off he'd be blissfully occupied while she played tennis. Before breakfast he had got as far as writing the title on the first page in several different coloured pens, and then giving the as-yet unwritten saga some wonderfully complimentary reviews on the back page. '*Mr Shropshire – the story of a dragan* by Petros Drinking-Well' announced the title page in screaming pink and purple letters. Jake was greatly given to pseudonyms, especially the double-barrelled variety, and rarely wrote under his own name .

'Mr Drinking-Well has riten a reely good book,' announced the *Sun* on the last page, and, 'A hugly good reed,' gushed *The Times*.

'Very impressive. Have you thought of the plot yet?' asked Victoria as she strapped the budding author into the back seat.

'Not yet,' said Jake. 'It's best to think of the title first – but the trouble with this one is that the story in my head doesn't have much to do with dragons.'

'Mightn't it be better to write the story first then and choose a title later?'

'It doesn't work that way round,' said Jake scornfully. 'Stories don't come till you actually start on them – but I always get cool ideas when I do begin so I'm not worried.'

'Oh, good,' said Victoria, envying her son his certainties. 'Well, I shall look forward to reading it when it's finished.' She already had a drawer full of Jake's literary masterpieces in her desk at Manor Farm. He was nothing if not prolific.

The Hammonds were already knocking up when Victoria and Jake arrived at the tennis court, but broke off at once when they saw her and came to greet her with an enthusiasm that gave her a warm glow and made her feel as though they had all known each other for much longer than two days. A shady spot was found for the author within sight of the court and Sam obligingly went to get him a supply of Fanta orange to aid inspiration. It was decided that father and daughter should take on Victoria and Sam. It proved a good contest. Patrick and Sam were both good players and Sophie's wildness – punctuated by flashes of brilliance – was offset by Patrick's guile; Victoria, for all her apparent fragility, proved to have a sizzling forehand, though she was useless at the net, but Sam was well pleased with this arrangement for play.

He looked at his partner with open admiration. She really had got an amazing figure. He felt his father had stolen a march on him by spending the previous afternoon and evening at Vrahos, and determined to make him run about the court as much as he could. No quarter would be shown on the grounds of age and general parental decrepitude, decided Sam – who had only recently started to be able, occasionally, to beat his father at singles. After one set all, the competitive streak in father and son kicked in and both became determined to win. At ten-all in the third set their partners started to wilt in the fierce sunshine and Sophie announced that she was going to expire if they went on much longer.

'Get a grip, Sophe. Don't be so feeble,' said Sam bracingly, but Victoria said she was out of training and thought she would collapse soon too.

'Sudden death or tie break then?' asked Patrick.

'Tie break,' said Sam firmly, and was far from pleased when his father promptly returned his best serve down the line and then, at the end of a long rally, Victoria hit one out.

'Oh Sam! I'm sorry! I've let you down,' she cried.

'You know what they say about geriatrics,' said Patrick, amused by the expression on his son's face and well aware that Sam, wishing to be seen in a favourable light by his partner, was furious at having lost to his father in front of her. 'Old age and cunning can still triumph over youth and skill.'

'Wait till next time,' said Sam. 'Victoria and I will have our revenge.'

They collected Jake, who had moved on from literary pursuits and was busy racing the hot-wheels cars down the children's slide that the hotel had thoughtfully provided near the court.

'I've been timing them all. The red car's easily the champion and the silver one's the worst,' he told Sam. 'Do you want to have a go and we'll see whose car's best? You can choose any colour you like,' offered Jake generously, 'except red.' So Sam obligingly chose a battered blue mini that to Jake's disgust performed spectacularly well for its new driver and this time it was Jake who didn't like losing. He started to kick the ground with the toe of his trainer and argue about the rules of the game, which he'd only just invented. Victoria shot him a warning look, hoping he wasn't going to make a scene and shame her in front of her new friends.

'Don't forget we've got to have a football match later on,' said Sam diplomatically, and earned a grateful smile from his goddess. 'I'd better come with you, Victoria,' he said when they had all walked back through the hotel garden to the car park, 'then I can show you the way to Petradi,' and he shot his father a triumphant look as he climbed into the passenger seat of the dilapidated Vrahos car. Two could play at the guile game.

When they got to the house Patrick led the way to the kitchen. 'Now then, action, you two, please,' he said to his son and daughter. 'Sam, could you get the drinks and, Sophie, could you get the food out of the fridge and we'll put our scratch lunch together?'

'Hang on a mo,' said Sophie, who'd been fiddling with her mobile. 'I must just text Ellie back. She's really stressed out because she's going to this theme party tomorrow and doesn't know what to go as – and I've had the most brilliant idea.'

'Why doesn't she go as a Rubens nymph?' suggested Sam. 'She'd be perfect – all that bulging pink thigh – and then she wouldn't have to bother about clothes.'

Sophie gave him a withering look. 'It's got to have a horticultural theme.'

'A Desiree potato then?'

'Oh, very funny, humorous to a degree. No, she's absolutely got to go as Audrey Hepburn. Wouldn't that be amazingly cool?'

'*Ellie?*' Sam rolled his eyes. 'You must be off your trolley, Sophe! What's Audrey Hepburn got to do with horticulture anyway?'

'You're pathetically ignorant. Audrey Hepburn and horticulture are synonymous,' said Sophie loftily. 'I mean, you think *horticulture*, you think *Hepburn* – don't you, Victoria? Isn't she the very first thing you think of?'

'Well . . .' Victoria looked doubtful, but didn't want to hurt Sophie's feelings. 'I suppose I think of a wonderful actress, certainly she was the epitome of chic, but I'm not sure I knew that Audrey Hepburn had anything to do with gardening.'

'Exactly!' said Sophie triumphantly. 'The epitome of chic – *exactly* what I thought! Who said anything about gardening?'

Sam gave a shout of laughter and Patrick put his arm round his daughter. 'Oh, Sophie, darling, I do love you. Horticulture's the cultivation of gardens. You wouldn't by any chance mean *haute couture*, would you?'

Sophie peered at the text message on her mobile and let out a wail. 'Oh no!' she moaned. 'Why do I always read everything wrong? I thought that was just how the French pronounced it.' They all laughed and Victoria thought it was very much to Sophie's credit that she managed to join in.

'I'm awfully hungry,' announced Jake. 'Will lunch be soon?'

'Right now,' said Patrick. 'Get cracking, you guys. Shall we eat out – I think it's warm enough.' He started to put knives and forks on a tray while Sophie went to the fridge.

'Snag is, there isn't actually anything much *in* here, Dad,' she said. 'I thought you said you bought a whole lot of food in Kryovrisi yesterday?'

'I did. And when I got back yesterday evening, at your urgent request to come and let you in, if you remember, I asked you to unload the food out of the car and put it straight in the fridge while Sam carried the drink in and I unlocked the house. What did you do with it all?'

'Oh Lord! I sort of forgot.' Sophie guiltily remembered that the Petradi telephone had been ringing when her father drove up and she'd rushed to answer it as soon as he'd unlocked the door, thinking it might be Ellie Marshall. However – far more amazing and wonderful – it had been Sam's friend, the divine Matthew Burnaby with whom they'd spent the day – and indeed only parted from an hour before, a tremendously encouraging sign in Sophie's view. He'd actually wanted to speak to her, not Sam at all, a piece of information that she'd already relayed to Ellie. Naturally such an earth-shaking event had put all thoughts of food right out of her head.

'Oh, for heaven's sake! I'd only just asked you. How could you have forgotten?' asked Patrick. 'Where is it now anyway?'

'Don't panic, no one could possibly have pinched it,' said Sophie blithely, her mind running on the thrilling possibility of another call from Matthew. 'Relax, Dad. It'll all be in the boot.'

'That's what I'm afraid of. It doesn't do food much good to be baked for hours in a car that's been left in the full sun – even a cool bag can't deal with that. Will you please go and look *now*?'

'Don't be cross with her,' said Victoria, as Sophie disappeared hastily round the side of the house. 'It could happen to anyone.'

'Not to anyone – but all too easily to Sophie.' Patrick grinned and made a resigned face. 'I ought to have noticed myself, but we went out to dinner and I never checked the fridge.'

There was a shriek from the direction of the back door followed by violent slamming of the boot.

'Well?' he asked as Sophie shot back in, managing to look tragic and hold her nose at the same time.

'Disaster! Disaster! Oh, Dad, I'm really sorry. You've never smelled anything so rank in all your life.' Sophie wrung her hands and shuddered dramatically. 'The salad's a goner – all hot and limp – but the chicken and the taramasalata and stuff are positively heaving!'

'Can I come and smell it?' asked Jake, relishing the drama.

They all trooped out to the car, and Sophie dramatically flung the boot open again.

'Wow!' Jake backed away hastily. 'Do we have to eat that?'

'You certainly don't – trouble is, I'm not sure we've got much else except a few tomatoes.'

'Have you got any bacon and eggs?' asked Victoria.

'There might be some, unless Sam's scoffed them, but not enough for all of us.'

'Got any pasta?'

'I think so. I remember seeing a packet of tagliatelli floating around somewhere.'

'I'm sure Sophie and I could knock up something,' said Victoria. 'I'm not the world's best cook but Dora does a brilliant pasta carbonara, which seems to stretch bacon and eggs for miles – and the tomatoes will be a terrific bonus to go with it.'

'We can't have you cooking lunch for us,' protested Patrick.

'Oh, this is fun! Other people's domestic disasters are deeply reassuring to me – I have so many myself!'

'Good thing Mum isn't here,' said Sam. 'She'd have absolutely flipped by now. She doesn't think any domestic dramas are funny. You'd be mince by now, Sophe.'

'You don't have to tell Mum about forgetting the shopping, do you, Dad?' asked Sophie.

'No,' said Patrick, with feeling. 'I think we might keep this little episode to ourselves.' And Sophie appeared so relieved that Victoria couldn't help wondering again what Rachel Hammond was like.

'Come on then, Sophie,' she said. 'Let's see what we can produce and you can show me where everything is. Jake – you help lay the table.'

Sophie gave Victoria a grateful look and decided that she liked her very much as they went off together; Patrick, listening to the laughter that came from kitchen, couldn't help making some comparisons – and then felt deeply disloyal.

After a good deal of banging and clanging and dropping of saucepans the two cooks eventually emerged triumphantly bearing a dish of rather wet-looking pasta and a bowl of yellowish liquid with a few bits of chopped-up ham floating in it.

'There wasn't any bacon but we found a slightly manky-looking slice of ham instead. I think the eggs are really supposed to have cream beaten in to them so we've used a blob of yoghurt instead.' Victoria swirled the yellow liquid with a fork. 'I don't see why it shouldn't work just as well,' she added hopefully.

'It doesn't look anything like Dora's.' Jake was darkly mistrustful of his mother's domestic abilities.

'Oh – well, it may be a culinary discovery,' said Victoria cheerfully. 'Don't be boring darling – live dangerously.' She sloshed some pasta on to a plate and poured sauce over it. 'Come on, just try it.' Jake took a cautious mouthful and put his fork down hastily.

'It's *disgusting*, Mum – all slimy.'

'Are the eggs cooked – just as a matter of interest?' enquired Patrick, highly entertained by the proceedings.

'Well, no – we did wonder, didn't we, Sophie? – but I think they're supposed to cook as they meet the hot pasta.'

'That pasta looks awfully cold to me.' Sam peered at the dish. 'Not exactly steaming.'

Sophie and Victoria looked at each other and started to giggle.

'D'you think we should give it a burst in the microwave?' suggested Sophie.

'Brilliant!'

They bore the carbonara out again. A moment later there was a wail of laughter from the kitchen. The whole concoction had turned to a solid, lump more reminiscent of concrete than anything else.

'Sorry, guys! Death of carbonara,' said Victoria.

'Phew-ee! Saved from salmonella then,' said Sam, grinning.

Socially, if not gastronomically, lunch was a great success. The tomato salad, tasting wonderfully of freshly torn-up basil leaves was delicious, they found some cheese in the back of the fridge, which, together with crusty bread, filled the corners. As so often happens with entertaining, once the onus of striving to

246

make a good impression has been removed, they all relaxed and enjoyed each other's company.

Inevitably the conversation turned to the discovery of Evanthi's lost love, and Victoria filled them in with what she had gathered from her grandmother the evening before. Sophie thought it was too romantic for words.

'You'd love Uncle Hugh,' she told Victoria. 'He's wonderful – and he's the most amazing artist. Really famous.'

'So I gather. What's he like? I'm wildly curious.'

Sophie wrinkled her nose and considered. 'Well, he's hard to describe because he's so *different*. He makes Sam and me die of laughter, but some people do find him rather scary. Mum's a bit edgy with him because she always thinks he's laughing at her, but he's frightfully kind underneath. I suppose he's rather like Dad – only Uncle Hugh's *even* taller – and he's sort of . . .' she paused and looked at her father in a considering sort of way, 'he's sort of a louder and larger version of Dad really.'

'She means he's infinitely more talented and original than me – but drinks a lot more,' said Patrick, laughing and topping up their glasses with white wine. 'Besides, I'm a very ordinary bloke – and he most certainly is not. What am I going to tell him about all this? Do you think we should engineer a meeting between the two of them or would that be disastrous? Perhaps they'd rather keep their original memories of each other intact and not have them overlaid by all the cruel alterations of old age.'

'You can't just not tell him,' protested Sophie. 'Victoria's grandmother knows he's alive now, so it wouldn't be fair for him not to know she is too. Anyway, I think they both look rather wonderful still, in spite of being so old.'

'Good point, Sophie,' said Patrick. 'What do you think, Victoria?'

'I think Sophie's right – but it would be fascinating to hear his version of the story. Couldn't you ask him about it when you get home – and then decide how to play it, depending on what he says? But knowing Nonna I expect she'll have her own views – and no doubt she'll express them pretty pungently! As to a meeting . . . well, I've no idea whether Nonna could travel now. She certainly couldn't at the moment, but she's made such an amazing recovery already she might do anything.'

'Doctors say that if people who are terminally ill want to stay alive badly enough for a particular event, they often seem to manage it,' said Patrick. 'Your grandmother's not in such dire straits, and perhaps this might give them both a new lease of life.' He got up. 'I'm going to make some coffee – who'd like some? Just you, Victoria? Right. Coming up.'

Jake, who was getting bored with the conversation, asked if he could get down and pointedly started kicking a ball he'd found round the terrace, and since Sam was not nearly so interested in octogenarian romance as the other three and needed physical action at regular intervals himself, he readily agreed to go and play the promised game of football.

'You are a complete star, Sam,' said Victoria, and he felt well rewarded as he and Jake headed off into the olive grove together.

Patrick, emerging from the house a few minutes later, announced that he'd just answered the telephone.

'It's for you, Sophie – Matthew what's-it – son of the Marshalls' chums you went to yesterday – he wants you and Sam to go over again.'

Sophie flew off.

Patrick handed Victoria a mug of strong black coffee and sat down beside her.

'Jake's a splendid little boy,' he said. 'You're obviously making a great job of coping with him on your own – it must be so hard. How's he been affected by your tragedy? He must miss your husband terribly too.'

'Oh, he does – dreadfully. I can't bear it for him. He doesn't talk about it much, though I try to encourage him to, but he gets extremely uptight and cries easily over little things. He's always been highly strung but sometimes now he's really tricky – stormy and rude, which isn't like him at all. Richard absolutely adored Jake and was awfully good with him. It's hard to tell how it will affect him long term because being out here is like a holiday and he's having lots of lovely attention from everyone – especially me! That worries me a bit – little boys are so possessive about their mums, aren't they? It's very hard not to spoil them.'

Patrick didn't feel he could comment on this. Sam and Rachel seemed to have been at loggerheads since the day he was born. 'Oh, I shouldn't worry too much,' he said easily. 'Most things come out in the wash. In our family it's our younger daughter who's particularly hooked up on her mum. She's a bit of a pain at the moment – but I expect she'll turn out all right in the end.'

'Well, I should be very happy if Jake turned out as nice as Sam and Sophie. How much longer are you out here for?' she asked.

'Only two more days. We go home on Thursday. We slotted our visit in between the two Easters.'

Victoria felt a stab of disappointment. 'What a shame you won't be here for our Easter,' she said. 'Sam and Sophie would love all the colour and drama and processions – St Spirídon, our island saint, doing his circuit round the town in his silver casket and working miracles left right and centre to the blare of brass bands, not to mention the great plate-smashing ritual of chucking the crockery into the street. Jake absolutely adores that.'

'It sounds great stuff. I think I've read about it. What a brilliant way of getting rid of those chipped plates that breed in the back of cupboards. Isn't it supposed to symbolise the casting out of Judas Iscariot?'

'Yes, but there are other theories about the symbolism too – some Christian, some pretty pagan, but anyway to do with ceremonies about spring and new beginnings. I don't think people bother too much about the origins. It's just a glorious excuse for chucking things. Very liberating! Nonna has friends who have a flat over the Liston and we always used to go there and get a wonderful view of it all. We usually go to midnight mass in the main square on Saturday night, and it's all very joyful, with bells ringing and priests declaiming *Kristos anesti* and masses of fireworks everywhere. I remember when I was a child thinking my first English Easter was incredibly dull!'

'I wish we could stay for it,' he said, thinking how much he would like to be able to extend their time in Corfu, and not just because of the Easter celebrations. 'But, sadly, because Easter was early at home this year Sophie's school starts next week and Sam has to go back to Newcastle. Tell me more about the local customs. It sounds wonderful.'

'Well, Holy Week's a great orgy of white-washing houses and making *koulouri* – special Easter biscuits. You still see women in the villages carrying great trayloads on their heads going to put them in the oven of the local bakery. In Corfu there are traditional Easter cookies decorated with eggs and feathers.' Victoria pulled a face. 'But it's not all wonderful – lots of slaughtering of lambs goes on behind the local houses, which upsets Jake, and Dora's grandmother, Nafsica – the one who freaked at the sight of you – always insists on making a fearsome traditional dish called *mayeritsa*, which has to be consumed after midnight mass. It's a brew of lamb's guts and everything goes in, lungs, spleen, the lot. You might not fancy that too much. It smells awful, and I've eaten some pretty revolting brews in my time, though Nafsica manages to make it taste surprisingly good with lots of lemon and herbs and spring onions.'

'I think I'd certainly want to pass on that,' said Patrick, laughing at her expression.

'I don't know what we'll do this year,' she said sadly. 'Perhaps I'll let Jake go off with Yannis and Dora and Angelo. Nonna won't be well enough and I'm not sure I could face all the festivities at the moment – too many memories. I'll probably go to mass in Kryovrisi.'

Patrick thought she suddenly looked white and strained again, and he ached for her.

'I imagine you might want to do some more photography while you're here?' she said after a pause.

'Yes – I'd like to if it's possible. But you wouldn't need to bother with me. I could easily be left to my own devices if your grandmother would trust me to roam round the house. I don't want to be a nuisance.'

'Oh, you'd never be that,' she said quickly. He looked at her and their eyes met for a moment. Then they both looked away and there was a silence.

Suddenly the relaxed camaraderie between them seemed to have vanished and they were conscious of a feeling of constraint; each of them uneasily aware of the connection they were starting to make together, but uncertain if this was appropriate.

Victoria got up. 'We really must go. We've taken up far too

much of your day already – and I must get back and see how Nonna is. But we've had a lovely time. Thank you so much.'

Patrick smiled at her. 'It's been lovely having you both. Next time you come we'll do better about lunch! I'll go and find Jake for you.'

Victoria started to gather up their things. As she was having a final check to see that Jake hadn't left any of his cars lying about the terrace, Sophie emerged from the house, looking extremely pleased with life.

'Good telephone call?' asked Victoria, raising an eyebrow and grinning at her.

'Fantastic.' Sophie rolled her eyes. She would have liked to discuss the amazing Matthew Burnaby with Victoria, but the reappearance of her brother put a stop to that – Sophie would have died rather than enthuse about Matthew in front of Sam. He and Jake were both scarlet in the face, and Jake's dark hair was wet with sweat.

'Jake's the new David Beckham,' announced Sam. 'Expect a call from Sven-Göran Eriksson any minute. I'm completely shattered.'

'That was *cool*, Mum,' said Jake.

'Well, you certainly don't look cool,' she said, laughing. 'You've obviously had a lovely time, darling. What do you say to Sam for playing with you – and to Mr Hammond and Sophie for having us to lunch?'

'Thank you very much,' said Jake. 'Can we come again?'

'You certainly can,' said Patrick. But even as he said it, he wondered if there would actually be a next time, and was acutely conscious that the idea that there might not was a very unwelcome thought.

As the Hammonds walked out to the car to see their visitors off, Sophie's mind was occupied with thoughts of Matthew, and having kissed Victoria goodbye she rushed back to the house to send an urgent text to Ellie – but Patrick and Sam stood and waved as Victoria drove off down the track.

Chapter Twenty-five

Victoria and Jake arrived back at Vrahos to hear raised voices coming from the kitchen. Yannis and Dora, both clearly extremely heated, were having a furious argument, and Angelo, saucer-eyed, was sitting under the table looking unusually subdued. Dora had obviously been crying. Yannis looked mulish.

'Oh, Victoria, thank God you are back,' shrieked Dora. 'Now you will speak some sense into this stupid husband of mine! He wants me to do something that would kill Kyria! I have told him NO! NO! NO! On no account must these things be shown to her – she is not strong enough. She would die of shock – and then it would be my fault. As for my grandmother – words fail me!' said Dora – something that was patently untrue.

'And I say that it is her property so it's not for you to decide whether to give it her or not – or for Victoria either,' shouted the normally sunny Yannis, and he thumped the table so furiously with his great fist that the coffee cups jumped about in their saucers and a carafe of wine tipped over, staining the tablecloth a dark red. Wine spilled at table is supposed to bring good fortune in Corfu but Victoria thought it looked more as if it boded some terrible blood-letting. Normally Dora would have rushed to mop it up and pour salt on the mark but this afternoon she didn't even appear to notice.

'I can't make head or tail of what you're talking about,' said Victoria, though she had a shrewd idea what the connection must be. Perhaps another piece of the jigsaw puzzle was about to fall into place. 'Don't let's discuss this in front of the boys, whatever it is,' she said, and she shooed Jake and Angelo firmly outside.

It took some time to untangle the story because Dora and Yannis kept interrupting each other, but eventually she gathered that the priest had come to see Nafsica that morning and been with her for some time. As he was leaving he told Dora that she should go to her grandmother immediately – there was something important for her to see.

When Dora went upstairs Nafsica was sitting on the edge of her bed, keening away as if she was at a funeral wake and periodically repeating: 'And she trusted me,' like the response in some litany of doom.

'Kyria will never forgive me – never,' she moaned. 'I have kept them all these years, every one of them – never told anyone or shown them to a soul, and now the *papas* says I must give them back to her. And what will she think of me? All these years – and she has always trusted me! I told Pater it was not my fault and the Contessa made me do it.' There was a further outbreak of crying and then she burst out angrily, 'But he says I am still responsible for my own actions! Pater doesn't understand. The Contessa told me it was for Kyria's own good – that I had the power to save her from certain unhappiness. Then she asked me if I wanted to continue working for her and reminded me whom our house belonged to. What could I do? Pater says we are both old women now and I must tell her before it is too late and one of us goes to face our Maker. He says I may receive forgiveness when she forgives me, but I must tell her everything – but she trusted me – what will she say?' And Nafsica had started weeping all over again. 'I shall die and be punished unless she forgives me, and how can I expect her to do that?'

Eventually, after great efforts on Dora's part to calm her down, the old woman had got down painfully on her rheumatic knees and pulled a battered metal deed box from under her bed. She had taken a key from a thin chain round her neck, fitted it in the lock and flung the lid open. It smelled musty and dusty inside and was filled with rows of envelopes, the paper yellowed with age. All were stamped and addressed. None of them was opened. Dora looked at her grandmother, a huge question in her eyes. She thought that in the last few days Nafsica – always small and birdlike anyway – had shrunk to skin and bone and her face had the same yellowish appearance as the letters in the box.

'Yiayia, what is all this? Whatever did you do?' she asked in bewilderment.

'They are the letters the English gentleman wrote to Despinis Evanthi,' said Nafsica reverting to a style of address she hadn't used for sixty-odd years. 'The artist to whom she was secretly engaged – and who she loved so much. *O Panagia mou!* I had never seen such love as theirs! Every day they wrote to each other – and most of those letters in the box are from him to her – but some of them are from her to him.'

'Kyria? Had an English lover?' Dora was astonished. The idea that stately Evanthi, an admired and respected figurehead all Dora's life, should once have had secret assignations with a passionate Romeo set her not usually very vivid imagination racing with images of moonlight meetings in olive groves and snatched kisses in dark corners.

'But why have you got them?' asked Dora.

'Because I stole them,' whispered Nafsica. 'I had been her go-between, helped to cover their meetings and hide their letters from the Contessa, who was set against the match. And I betrayed them. When the family were here at Vrahos it was one of my duties to collect the incoming mail and put it out on the table in the Grand Salon, and then to take any letters the family had written and put them in the box at the end of the drive for the postman to collect. I used to collect any letters addressed to Despinis Evanthi from the Englishman and give them to her before her mother saw them, and she would give me her answers for the post rather than leave them on the table where anyone could see them. After the Contessa discovered they were still corresponding she made me promise that I would make sure Despinis Evanthi did not receive his letters any more – and I started to keep any of hers to him after I'd promised the Contessa.'

'But you have always loved Kyria,' said Dora, horrified at such disloyalty. 'How could you do that to her?' She knew her grandmother to possess the obstinacy of a mule and could not imagine her giving in easily to pressure – even from her employer.

'Yes, I loved her, but I agreed with the Contessa,' said Nafsica fiercely. 'It *was* for her own good! Her mother had arranged for her to marry a husband from a very good Greek family. She and Kyria Doukas had grown up together and had always planned for their children to marry each other – since they were babies. Why should she be allowed to throw herself away on a foreigner with no money – and she so clever and so beautiful? It would have been a disaster. I should never have helped them in the first place – but it was always hard to say no to her. She had such a way with her – she still has,' sobbed Nafsica, and added inevitably, '*But she trusted me.*'

Victoria looked from Dora to Yannis. 'Where are the letters now?' she asked. Dora pointed to a battered black tin box on the kitchen dresser where a collection of old majolica plates had been displayed for as long as Victoria could remember. Patrick Hammond might consider them excellent candidates for the plate-smashing ceremony, decided Victoria, noticing the chipped condition of many of them for the first time, pictures of Patrick still pervading her thoughts even at this time of domestic crisis. She looked at the tin box with foreboding. Then she took a deep breath.

'I'm sorry, Dora, but I have to agree with Yannis,' she said. 'Those letters belong to Nonna and we have no more right to keep them from her than Nafsica had to hide them in the first place. But I also think she should be prepared a little before we hand them over. As you say, Dora, it might be a terrible shock – but perhaps not quite so much of a shock as you think. I had never heard of her lost love before, but only last night she was telling me about it. Did Nafsica say what made her decide to speak after all these years?'

'She thought she had a vision of him the day Mr Hammond came to lunch. She thought Kyria's old fiancé must have died and come to haunt her out of revenge.'

'Patrick Hammond is the nephew of Nonna's English love – apparently they look uncannily alike. That's what made Nonna speak to me about it too. It was pure chance that he came here – though, of course, Nonna doesn't think so – but both your grandmother and Nonna recognised his face immediately. No wonder poor Nafsica thought she'd seen a ghost. You told me how strange she was but I didn't connect the two things then. She must have been frightened out of her wits.'

'So what do we do?' asked Dora. 'Yiayia won't go and see Kyria. I've already suggested it but she's too ashamed.'

'I'll tell Nonna about the letters and ask her what she wants to do. She'll have to talk to Nafsica eventually – perhaps when they've both had a chance to simmer down a bit? Nonna has incredible inner strength. I'm sure it will be all right.'

Dora and Yannis looked very relieved.

'I was going to get her tea-tray ready soon,' said Dora. 'Would you like to take it up if I give the boys their meal?'

'Fine,' said Victoria. 'Let me go and have a quick bath and put my things away and I'll come and collect it.' But for all her apparent confidence in front of Dora and Yannis, as she went up to her room she felt sick with misgiving about the effect this new turn of events might have on her grandmother's fragile health. How strange the connection with the Hammonds was, she thought. It was difficult not to imagine there might be some special significance about Patrick's arrival on the scene at this particular moment in her life, but she thrust the idea away, deeply bothered that it should even have entered her head.

When she carried the old silver tray, which she remembered so well from her childhood, into the little drawing room, Evanthi was sitting in her usual chair with a rug over her knees, even though Victoria thought it was very warm. Her face lit up when she saw Victoria.

'Oh, *agapi* – how lovely. Did you have a happy time? Tell me about your day.'

'Great fun, thank you. I must say, I do like the Hammonds.' She hesitated, as though she were about to say more but had changed her mind.

Evanthi shot her a sharp look, but didn't comment. 'How was the tennis?'

'Fine. My heart sank when I arrived because they were knocking up and I could see they were all rather good. But they were extremely nice to play with and I wasn't *too* bad. I think Guy would have been quite proud of me.'

Evanthi noticed that she didn't say Richard would have been proud of her. It had always been Guy's approval that mattered to Victoria – and apparently still did, thought her grandmother with anxiety.

'I kept wondering about you, and all you told me last night,' said Victoria. 'What have you spent your day doing, Nonna?'

'Thinking. I would like to see Patrick Hammond again before he goes back to England. Does he want to take more photographs before he goes home? When do they leave?'

'Yes, he does and he asked if that would be all right with you. They go back on Thursday.'

'Will you ring him for me and ask him to come either tomorrow or Wednesday then? I have an errand I want him to do for me.'

Victoria thought this was just the lead-in she needed for what she had to tell her grandmother. She took a deep breath. 'Nonna, I have something to tell you – and something to show you that may be a shock. Do you feel strong enough to face more from your past – something that may prove distressing?'

'I am quite good at facing things,' said Evanthi drily. 'I have had a lot of practice. Tell me.'

'It's about Nafsica.'

'Nafsica?' There was no doubting Evanthi's immediate concern. 'Is she all right? Patrick Hammond said he'd had an extraordinary effect on her when he arrived. Dear Nafsica – she's always been so devoted to me. It must have been a shock for her too – to see someone looking so like Hugh. Nafsica was our great ally for the whole of one summer in keeping our meetings secret from my mother. Don't tell me she's ill?'

'Not exactly. But perhaps not quite so much of an ally as you thought either – though apparently with what she perceived to be your best interests at heart. She's not ill yet – but I think she could easily make herself ill. She's very unhappy, very bothered and . . . and terribly guilty.'

'Whatever has she got to feel guilty about?'

Victoria hesitated, searching for the right words.

'Come along, *agapi*! If you have something to say, please come out with it and stop treating me as if I was mentally unsound,' said Evanthi sharply, with a steely flash of what Guy always called her 'Empress of India' look.

'All right then,' said Victoria, relieved to see this reassuring sign of Evanthi's imperiousness and feeling it would stand her in good stead. 'Nafsica asked for the *papas* to come and see her because she thinks herself in mortal danger of either Divine retribution – or yours. I really don't know which she would feel to be worse! Apparently Pater came today and Dora says Nafsica told him she'd been coerced by your mother into sabotaging your relationship with Patrick's uncle. Now she's produced a whole lot of his unopened letters that she's had hidden all these years – and a few from you to him that she never posted either. Dora says she's in a terrible state.'

Evanthi stared at her. 'Our letters! Where are they?'

Victoria went and fetched the box, which she had left outside the door. She carried it over and put it on a low stool by Evanthi's chair.

'Do you want me to open it for you?'

'Please.'

Victoria watched anxiously. Evanthi put out a hand and picked up one of the letters. Her face was expressionless – but Victoria saw that her hand was trembling as she turned the envelope over and over and just touched the handwriting, running a finger along the lines of the address as though she were reading Braille.

'*O Panagia mou!*' she said at last. 'I never thought to see that writing again. Oh, this might explain so much.'

'Are you going to open them?' asked Victoria, unable to bear the suspense.

'Yes. Yes, of course. But not now.' Evanthi held the letter as though she could not bear to part with it.

Victoria flushed. 'I'm sorry, Nonna! That was very insensitive of me. You want to be alone when you read them, don't you?'

'I think so. Not because there is anything I wouldn't want you to know, *chrysso mou*, but because I don't know myself how I am going to come to terms with what I may learn. Pour us both a cup of tea and then leave me to make a journey into the past.'

'Will you be able to forgive Nafsica, do you think?'

Evanthi sighed. 'Oh, I expect so, *agapi*. Yes, of course I will – I too am very conscious of Divine Judgement approaching and will need much forgiveness for myself.' She gave a wry smile. 'I don't want to tip the scales even further by bearing new grudges now. Poor Nafsica! It is not with her that I have a grievance – it is with myself, and my own pride and obstinacy. You think I blame her, but you didn't know my mother! She would have applied irresistible pressure to Nafsica, and besides,' she gave a wintery smile, 'they both achieved the outcome they wanted. Even when she was helping us Nafsica never approved of my liaison with Hugh. She is deeply xenophobic. She was furious when Toula married wonderful Anthony – in her view a foreigner and beyond the pale.'

'And when I married Richard!' Victoria pulled a face, remembering Nafsica's thunderclap reaction to the news of her engagement.

'Ah, yes indeed – and when you married Richard.'

'You weren't very pleased about that yourself,' said Victoria.

'No,' said Evanthi, and added before she could stop herself, 'but not because he was English.'

'Nonna?' Victoria plaited the fringe of the rug on which she was sitting, with great concentration, as she had often done as a small child. 'Can I ask you something?'

'You can always ask,' said Evanthi discouragingly.

'Did you realise that Richard was gay . . . homosexual that is?'

'I know perfectly well what gay means, thank you, Victoria,' replied Evanthi tartly. 'I may be old but just because my generation do not discuss sexual matters as freely as yours doesn't mean we are ignorant.' She added drily, 'There's not exactly anything new about the condition. But a lovely word has been hijacked to represent exclusively something quite different from its original meaning – that seems a pity to me and impoverishes the English language. I hate to think of all the beautiful lines of English poetry that I learned and loved as a child but are now read by schoolchildren with a smirk.'

'But did you know about Richard?' persisted Victoria, who was used to her grandmother's habit of trailing red herrings when she did not wish to pursue a particular line of conversation. Having steeled herself to ask the question, she was not to be put off.

'No, I didn't *know*. Since he was a boy I'd had a . . . a slight suspicion, more of an intuition, but nothing at all to go on. At the time you got engaged I thought that Guy would surely have known if it were true and would have told you himself.' Victoria concentrated on plaiting the fringe. 'It was just that I never thought Richard would be right as a husband for you. And I was right, though you appeared reasonably happy for longer than I'd dared hope. Certainly I never anticipated such a tragic end.'

'And what do you think about Guy and his marriage?' asked Victoria.

'Guy is different from Richard,' said Evanthi. 'He likes to indulge himself with whatever he fancies and he likes to experiment. And, of course, he has always been very spoiled – by his mother, by Nafsica – and I have to admit by me too. But I have hopes of his marriage. Francine does not sound as if she will give in to him too easily – and he tells me she never bores him. A good sign.' She looked at her granddaughter, so loving but, in her own way, so wilful too. 'I am sorry, *agapi* – I am not going to say what you want to hear about Guy. It would not ultimately be helpful. I understand more than you think, my little one, and I bleed for you. It is very lonely contemplating one's mistakes – I should know. I have had plenty of practice at that too.'

'How did you cope, Nonna?' It was a cry of desperation.

'You have to transform the mistake – to gain from it. I learned a terrible lesson about my own pride and hot-headedness. My marriage may not have been one of high romance – any more than yours was, though for different reasons – but in his way your grandfather was a good husband. If I hadn't married him I would not have had your father, who was the light of my life – or Toula or you or Guy – and if you had not married Richard, you, *agapi mou*, would not have had Jake. Hold on to that.'

Victoria got up. 'Thank you, Nonna,' she said. 'I'll take your tray now and leave you with your letters. It seems we have neither of us been very good at following advice.'

As she went downstairs she thought to herself that perhaps she and her grandmother were more alike than she had ever realised.

Chapter Twenty-six

❖

Sophie was in a trance of happiness. Not only had she and Sam been invited to spend Wednesday, their last day, with the Burnabys, but Matthew had told her they would be travelling back from Corfu on the same flight as the Hammonds. What was more, he'd indicated that he hoped to see her again after they got home. 'You might come for a weekend sometime,' he'd suggested. 'We could get Sam to come and perhaps Ellie Marshall too?' Sophie had loved that 'we'.

She said, 'Yeah, cool. Why not?' and wondered if this had sounded over-eager. She had gone over and over the conversation in her mind, analysing every little nuance and inflection of what they had both said, filtering it for hidden meaning. Then an ominous thought struck her. Would Mum be difficult about it? The answer was almost certainly yes. On the other hand, if Ellie were to come too and they enlisted the help of Ellie's mum, surely Rachel might see that it would be ridiculous to say no? Sophie knew Ellie had nurtured a secret passion for Sam for years and it would provide him with just the opportunity to see that Ellie was no longer just his kid sister's plump friend with railtracks on her teeth and a distressing tendency to the odd crop of spots, but a seriously fit girl with a fantastic figure and a wonderful complexion. High time Sam noticed Ellie's metamorphosis, thought Sophie, who had taken enormous satisfaction at her brother's surprise that Matthew should be paying her so much attention. 'Pretending to be grown-up, are we?' he had teased, but Sophie could tell he was impressed.

Sam, meanwhile, was in two minds about going to the Burnabys on his last day in Corfu. He had enjoyed their previous expedition – there'd been a fun crowd of people staying with them, the Burnaby parents were generous and glossy – in Uncle Hugh's parlance obviously not short of a bob or two, thought Sam. Mr Burnaby was a bit of a boring old fart, though he obviously still fancied himself no end as a player – on no very convincing grounds that Sam could see – but they were hospitable and friendly and knew their parental place which was to provide quantities of food and drink and not invade their children's space too much.

The question in Sam's mind was whether, if he decided to go with Sophie, he might miss a last chance of seeing Victoria Cunningham. Sam had fantasised about rescuing Victoria, or better still Jake – that might be even more effective – from some dire situation and thereby earning her undying gratitude. In this stirring scenario his father was always standing uselessly by, envious of Sam's quick-thinking effectiveness and there was also the thrillingly erotic post-rescue second act in which his father definitely didn't even have a walk-on part. Realistically Sam was aware that it would be difficult to think up an excuse for inviting Victoria to do anything without involving his father, though it would be annoying to find Patrick had gone off to Vrahos without him.

Sophie was desperate to see Matthew, though, and Sam was not only very fond of his sister but considered she got a raw deal at home on the social front; besides, thought susceptible Sam, one of the girls staying with the Burnabys showed considerable talent and might possibly repay further investigation. He graciously decided to accept the Burnabys' invitation – he really ought to keep an eye on Sophie.

On Tuesday morning Patrick decided to go up Mount Pantokrator, Corfu's highest point, to photograph the mass of spring flowers, which at this time of year transformed its grey lunar landscape into a veritable rock garden of colour. Somewhat diffidently he asked his son and daughter if they wanted to come too, not wishing to stop them from doing anything more exciting with their friends, but was delighted when they accepted with enthusiasm. They decided not to bother with a picnic but to find a taverna somewhere on the way back; Patrick put his camera and a light meter in a backpack, added a bottle of water and a bar of chocolate and they set off in the car in a cheerful frame of mind. He couldn't help reflecting how relaxing it was to be able to take off on a spontaneous expedition so easily: no arguments about what to take; no complicated preparations involving neat little jars of this and that and perfect bite-size sandwiches; above all, no accompanying martyrdom – that quality that is death to carefree enjoyment.

Once they left the main road and headed inland, the choice of route seemed to bear little relation to what was marked on the map and they missed their way several times. Somehow it seemed part of the pleasure and what would have been an irritation in England became part of the island enchantment. As they ground up the hillside in bottom gear any pretence of tarmac surfaces disappeared. After a bit they decided it would be more fun to abandon the car and walk, though they had trouble finding a bit of even ground where they could safely leave it.

'It feels as if we've dropped back in time,' said Sophie. 'It's like those illustrations in the old Bible-stories book Granny used to read to us. Even the sheep look biblical – hey, listen I can hear bells and – oh, *yuck*!' She suddenly held her nose. 'What's that awful smell?'

A herd of long-haired goats, apparently appearing from nowhere, chose that moment to saunter across the track, making it quite clear who had the priority of the road. The lead Billy, a magnificent but evil-smelling grey and white creature with long sweeping horns, gave them a malevolent stare before heading up the vertical hillside, leaping from rock to rock with the confidence of complete sure-footedness.

'Look at the babies!' Sophie was entranced. 'They're so sw-e-e-et! Oh, wicked! I'd no idea goats came in so many different colours. I like those little chocolate ones best.'

'Right,' said Patrick, who had been clicking away with his camera, as the troupe finally disappeared up the mountain, their blacks, greys and browns providing the perfect camouflage against earth and stone and shadows, the distant tinkling of their bells the only clue to their progress. 'That'll give me some splendid touristy pictures. Come on then, guys. We'll have a drink when we get to the top.'

As they tacked upwards, the wild gladioli, iris and lupin,

which made blobs of vibrant colour in a tapestry background of grass and yellow fennel, were joined by smaller species that thrived in higher altitudes. Sophie had stuck a polythene bag and a rubber band in her pocket in which to store any unknown flowers for later identification, an enthusiasm that she had shared with Rachel on previous Mediterranean holidays. It had formed one of the occasional bonds between them and she hoped she might be able to rekindle her mother's interest if she saw anything unusual. She was very excited when she found what Patrick thought was a Monkey orchid.

'But don't pick it,' he warned. 'They're quite rare and if we study it carefully enough we can memorise what it looks like.'

'Can't wait to tell Mum,' said Sophie, very pleased with herself. 'Then we can tick it off on our list in her *Wild Flowers of the Mediterranean* book.'

Patrick hoped that Rachel would at least make a show of being interested in Sophie's find when they got home, but he didn't feel very confident and he ached for Sophie's vulnerability.

Buzzards wheeled in leisurely circles above them and Sam spotted a peregrine. The little monastery at the summit – no longer inhabited but occasionally opened up by the priest from one of the villages below – was disappointingly closed when they got to the top an hour later. Sam and Sophie happily stretched out in the sun while Patrick wandered off with his camera.

'God! Look at all the flowers! And it's so *green* everywhere – I can't get over it. Which time of year d'you like best, now or July?' Sophie rolled over on her front and propped her chin on her hands.

'I suppose it's more beautiful now but I do miss swimming in the sea. It looks so tantalising it's hard to believe it's so bloody freezing. Still, it's been a great time. I'm glad we came. Dad's been in better form than he's been in for ages, don't you think, Sophe?' asked Sam, chewing a blade of grass and tipping his baseball cap over his eyes. 'I reckon it's done him good. Hope it'll last once he's home again.'

'It won't,' said Sophie gloomily. 'I do worry about him and Mum. But at least he's had a break from Mum's lethal mix of carping and indifference – it's all the fault of that Bronwen woman. Honestly, she seems to have taken Mum over completely. She practically lives with us now and I know Dad loathes her, for all he's so scrupulously polite. Can't think what Mum sees in her.'

'She makes her feel safe,' said Sam shrewdly. 'Mum's always had to have a guru. Think of slimy Dr Carstairs with his farcical diets, remember the strawberries and champagne one that infuriated Dad so?' Sam snorted derisively. 'Or grotty Father Stephan when she was going through her religious phase. Funny when you think how bigoted Mum can get, that she can switch tacks so suddenly and seems able to swallow other people's crankiness so easily. It's just that until Bronwen appeared on the scene Dad was a bit of a guru to her too – and none of the others lived on the doorstep. Cheer up, Sophe, she's bound to get sick of her soon.'

'Well, I hope you're right,' said Sophie doubtfully. 'Anyway, I'm glad the whole Vrahos thing for the book's worked out so well. Riveting about old Mrs Doukas and Uncle Hugh. I can't wait for Dad to go and tell him about her and get his side of the saga.' She giggled. 'I can't imagine that stately old bat being swept along by passion can you? Do you think they leaped into bed together? What do you suppose she was like?'

'Stunning, I should think – presumably rather like Victoria.'

'Ho, ho! You really have got the hots for her, haven't you?' teased Sophie. 'Perhaps you're genetically programmed to fancy her. You were certainly gawping at her all yesterday – positively star-struck.'

'Well, I wasn't the only one.' Sam flicked a pebble at his sister.

'I didn't gawp at her,' said Sophie indignantly. 'Why should I?'

'Not *you*, stooopid . . . Dad. He can't take his eyes off her. Surely you must have noticed?'

'No,' said Sophie. 'No, I haven't. Now *you're* being stupid.' But a small uncomfortable question had been planted in her head.

When Patrick wandered back to join them, having used masses of film, he was puzzled by a slight tension in the atmosphere, which seemed to have blown up like a small wisp of dark cloud appearing from nowhere in an otherwise blue sky. It wasn't enough to spoil the rest of their day but it was there – something and nothing.

They were having a drink on the terrace that evening, watching the sea darken to ink-blue and the sky turn almost imperceptibly from deepest azure to palest acid green behind the snowy mountains of Albania, and listening to the pair of swallows that had nested beneath the eaves of the house, chattering away to each other as they lay wing to wing in their marital bed, when the telephone in the house rang. With huge self-control, Sophie, hoping it was Matthew, managed not to rush to answer it, but yawned and stretched in a disinterested sort of way that deceived no one.

'I'll go,' said Patrick, getting up and taking his glass of wine with him. 'It'll probably be Mum.' Rachel had not rung them once during the week, and after their last unfriendly conversation Patrick had not rung her again either. Sophie, who often found her mother's critical inquisitions extremely hard to bear, could not believe that she could now be so uninterested that she didn't even want to know how her family were getting on. Had the beloved Posy been involved, thought Sophie resentfully, it would have been a different matter. As he picked up the telephone Patrick decided that for everyone's sake he must try to mend some fences before they arrived home.

He was gone for some time.

'So how are things back at home then?' asked Sam when his father returned.

'Well, it wasn't Mum so I'm afraid I don't know,' said Patrick. 'It was Victoria Cunningham. Her grandmother has asked to see me tomorrow. Victoria thinks she wants me to take a message to Uncle Hugh, which should be interesting. As you're both off to the Burnabys I said I'd go over for lunch and then I can finish taking pictures in the house and see what she wants as well.'

Sam and Sophie exchanged a glance that wasn't lost on their father.

'Oh, well, let's hope you enjoy yourself then,' said Sam huffily.

Patrick raised an eyebrow and shot his son an amused look. 'Yes, I expect I shall,' he said coolly.

'Aren't you going to ring Mum then?' asked Sophie.

'Not tonight. I'll ring her tomorrow night – if she hasn't rung me,' said Patrick. 'But in any case she has our flight times and knows when to expect us back,' and though this hardly seemed to be the point, something in his face prevented either his son or daughter from pursuing the matter.

Chapter Twenty-seven

❖

After Sam and Sophie had departed for the Burnabys, Patrick had worked till late morning and then driven over to Vrahos. Victoria was out when he arrived, as she had told him on the telephone she would be. She had a date to take Jake to see the local schoolmaster, to discuss whether he might consider letting Jake join Angelo for the summer term, but Evanthi had in any case made it perfectly plain to her that she would like to see Patrick alone. Victoria had also told him about Nafsica's acts of treachery and the box of letters, hidden for so many years. Patrick had no idea what his uncle would make of it, and hoped the shock of it all wouldn't be too much for the old man's system. He comforted himself with the knowledge that Hugh Marston had always been a great survivor.

Dora let him in. 'Come in, please. Kyria is expecting you,' she said, looking at him rather uncertainly, not sure if he knew about her grandmother's acts of treachery to his uncle. She was relieved when Patrick gave her his usual friendly smile and, if he knew, made no reference to it.

Evanthi was sitting in her usual chair. She wore a long black caftan, which, together with a black and purple scarf wound round her head in a turban and fastened with an amethyst brooch, gave her the look of an Eastern potentate. It was tremendously becoming to her. Patrick looked at her appreciatively, a twinkle in his eye. At eighty-two she could still use clothes to make a statement, he thought. 'Magnificent,' he said. 'Ready for another portrait – this time a photographic one, I think.' From the answering gleam she gave him he could tell he had interpreted her own thoughts correctly.

'Come in, Patrick – how nice to see you.' She held out her hand to him. It was the first time she had used his Christian name. 'Come and sit down. I know Victoria has told you about your uncle's letters.'

'Yes,' he said. 'It's an extraordinary story. I see now why I had such a dramatic effect on Dora's grandmother when I arrived, but it must have been very distressing for you.'

'Yes and no. Sad – but wonderful too,' she said. 'Because you see I know now what I have long suspected – that Hugh never broke his word to me. I can't tell you what that means to me. All those years ago, when he inexplicably stopped writing to me and my mother fed me all sorts of poison about him, I should never have believed that he would let me down. I was young and passionate and wildly in love,' she smiled ruefully, 'but "hell hath no fury" and all that – you know what they say about a woman spurned. I had a great deal of pride and a terrible temper. I have got a little wiser with age – not much but a little. I will tell you the story sometime . . . but now I want to ask you to help me with something – with two things in fact.'

'I'll do anything I can for you,' said Patrick, wondering what was coming.

'I would like Hugh to meet Victoria,' she said.

'Well, that would be very easy to arrange.' Patrick was only too delighted. He couldn't help thinking this would provide a wonderful excuse to see Victoria again, something he knew he badly wanted to do. 'Have you suggested it to her?'

'No. I wanted to talk to you first – to ask if you would prepare the way with Hugh. He may not want to be in touch after all these years.' She gave him a quizzical look: 'We can't recapture our lost youth – and you will be relieved to know that I have no false illusions,' she said drily. 'But it would be healing to be reconciled – a sort of tidying-up in preparation for dying. There are things I would like to take with me on the final journey – and the knowledge of Hugh's forgiveness is one of them. I was the guilty party in this break-up. I know that.'

She reached out and picked up the silver box from beside her chair, running her thumb round it, feeling the bees and swallows that flew round the edge. 'I've been wondering what to do,' she said, 'and I suddenly thought I'd like Victoria to take this to Hugh in person. I don't mean as a gift – I want it back – but I'd like him to see it as proof that I've kept it all these years and from what you say, it seems he has kept mine. I can't tell you how happy that makes me. I could trust Victoria to tell him things I'd like him to know. Writing long letters is an effort for me now, I'm not good at intimate conversations on the telephone – especially after all these years – and I'm not well enough to travel at the moment. Perhaps I never will be. I have to face that.'

'And the other thing? You said there were two?'

'Well, that's partly an extension of the first but to do with Victoria herself. I'm well aware that though this is the right place for her to be at the moment, she may not want to stay here indefinitely – much as I would love that. It's too soon after the tragedy for her to make major decisions yet, but sometime she will have to think whether to make a new life for herself here or in England. I've been struck by how good it's been for her to get out with you and your family and have her mind taken off her troubles. She has to go to England soon to see her lawyer and discuss family matters with her father-in-law, but when she does go I think it would be so nice for her to see you and Sam and Sophie again. She has obviously enjoyed your company so much – and of course,' added Evanthi as an afterthought, 'it would be nice for her to meet the rest of your family too.' Privately she thought it was a great pity that Patrick had a wife at all. 'I know you and Hugh both live in Yorkshire so if he agrees to see her would you have her to stay?' She gave Patrick one of the smiles that made her likeness to her granddaughter so marked.

'Yes, of course,' said Patrick. 'I'd be only too pleased and it would be nice for my wife to meet Victoria too.'

But even as he spoke, he was uncomfortably conscious that only one of these statements was true. He knew he would indeed be delighted to see Victoria again – but he couldn't imagine her visit would go down particularly well with Rachel.

'Has Victoria talked to you at all about Richard?' asked Evanthi.

'Not directly – no.' Patrick thought that if she had, he certainly wouldn't be prepared to discuss what had been said with her grandmother. He wondered what was at the back of

Evanthi's request. Was it really only to do with Hugh and herself – or had she other motives? The suspicion crossed his mind that she might be trying to encourage a relationship between himself and Victoria – though surely she would not approve of adultery, given that she was obviously aware that he was married.

'You think I'm an interfering old woman, don't you?' asked Evanthi, unnervingly perceptive.

'Well,' said Patrick, smiling at her, 'I expect you could be sometimes. Don't we all long to help with the lives of beloved children and grandchildren? I know I often do! And I can see you love Victoria very much. But I'll certainly talk to Hugh for you. I'd be very pleased to do that.'

'I get the feeling you don't want to discuss Victoria with me.'

'No,' he said, giving her an amused look. 'I don't think I do.'

I will not be beguiled into letting this fascinating old woman manipulate me, thought Patrick.

'I'll send you the proofs of some photographs and the text for the chapter on Vrahos as soon as I can,' he said. 'Victoria suggested that I ought to talk to your grandson about the house and the family. How would you feel about that?'

'Well, Guy is certainly extremely knowledgeable.' Evanthi was at her most urbane. But she doesn't want me to meet him, he thought, and wondered why not. It clearly wasn't because he was out of favour; he knew from Victoria how much her grandmother adored Guy.

'How would you feel about a photograph of the icon in the book?' he asked. 'It was so kind of you to let Victoria show it to me. I see why you call it "the jewel in the Vrahos crown". It's remarkable. Am I right in thinking it's very much in the Venetain style of icon painting?'

'Yes, indeed,' she said. 'So suitable for this house, don't you think? I would like you to photograph it. It has been in my family for four hundred years and there's a legend that if it leaves Vrahos, then the family will have to leave too.'

Patrick was immediately intrigued. 'Would you object to that being mentioned in the book? Those family stories bring a place to life. People love reading about legends.'

'I would have to think about that,' she said.

'You mentioned that you might have to sell it to save the house?'

Evanthi gazed towards the window but her eyes looked blank and Patrick guessed she was viewing some inner landscape that he could not see. 'Yes,' she said after a pause. 'That is the advice that I am constantly given. The trouble is that there's no other single item of comparable value. Guy would say what is the point of keeping the icon when the house may have to be sold, but I say what is the point of parting with the icon to save the house if by the very act of doing so the family will leave anyway.'

'You believe the legend then?'

'I don't disbelieve it,' she said enigmatically.

'What is the story behind the legend?'

She smiled. 'A romantic one, naturally, but I don't vouch for its accuracy! The eldest son of one of my ancestors is supposed to have fallen in love with the daughter of a rival family – a Romeo and Juliet situation. The two fathers were great, great enemies and, believe me, Greek family feuds are serious, so the young couple ran away and made a clandestine marriage. The daughter's parents disowned her and gave her no marriage settlement – a matter of shame for the young husband's family – but she managed to bring with her an icon for which she felt a great reverence. When her father discovered it was missing he demanded it back because he said his daughter had stolen it. But my ancestors refused to return it, claiming they were keeping it in lieu of the dowry they should have received. The girl subsequently gave birth to a son but died in childbirth, and in his rage and anguish her father put a curse on her husband's family: no male heir born within the walls of Vrahos would inherit so long as the icon remained as their property, but that if the icon left the house then the family would have to leave too. I believe that's called a "catch twenty-two" situation. It is certainly true that no male heir actually born at Vrahos has ever inherited. Generations of my family have gone to great lengths to avoid their sons being born in this house – including me – but fate has often intervened as it did with my son Constantine, Victoria's father, who was born here during the war.' She added drily: 'I was under house arrest at the time, and helping me avoid an old family curse wasn't a top priority with the Germans. As you may know, my son was killed in a plane crash thereby adding another name to the list of those supposedly affected by the curse. So you see I have no reason to doubt that the second part of the prophecy might be true too.'

'Yes,' said Patrick. 'I can see why you wouldn't choose to part with the icon.'

He wondered if Evanthi and Hugh had identified with the luckless couple of four hundred years earlier, and if this had added an extra edge of excitement to their own love affair.

'My grandson, Guy, thinks it's all complete nonsense,' said Evanthi, 'but quite apart from the legend, selling the icon will be a last resort as far as I am concerned because it is my most treasured possession – and I do not mean in the commercial sense, though I believe it may be quite valuable. My son-in-law, Anthony, certainly thinks so. But I may have to consider selling it for Victoria's sake.'

While they had been talking Patrick had got his camera out of its case and was unobtrusively checking the light meter.

'Will you go on telling me about the history of the house and family while I take a few photographs?' he asked, thinking this would be the perfect moment to get a picture of Evanthi.

When Victoria came in for lunch she found the photographic session just finishing, but Patrick and Evanthi still deep in conversation. Evanthi was telling him all sorts of stories about family history that Victoria had never heard before. She thought her grandmother had a new sparkle in her eye and looked better than she'd seen her look for a long time. Perhaps the discovery of her lost love really will give her a new lease of life, thought Victoria. She had been afraid Patrick might have gone before she got back, and was absurdly pleased to find him still there.

She shared the news that Jake was to be allowed to go to school with Angelo for the summer term. Victoria had thought the headmaster delightful. He spoke a little English himself but did not propose to speak anything but Greek to Jake; there were already two other foreign children in the school – one Italian, one German – who had blended in very easily, he said, and after all Jake already had some understanding of the language – a huge advantage. He did not foresee any problems. Victoria was mightily relieved and felt it would bring some routine and normality into Jake's life. While she was talking Patrick took a picture of her standing against the fireplace below the portrait of her grandparents and her father. 'Just finishing the film,' he said, smiling at her as she started to protest. 'If it comes out well I shall send you a copy,' but he knew that he was primarily taking it for himself.

After lunch they had coffee on the terrace and then Evanthi said she must go and have her rest.

'I shall be in touch as soon as I've seen Hugh,' said Patrick, getting to his feet too. 'I can't tell you how much I'm looking forward to telling him I've found you – and that you are still beautiful.'

'Thank you. I shall be looking forward to your call,' she said. 'Give him . . . give him my love. I can't imagine him as an old man.' She allowed Patrick to kiss her goodbye, and gently patted his arm. 'It has been wonderful to get to know you. There are certain differences, but in many ways you remind me of your uncle. I hope you all have a very good journey tomorrow. Say goodbye to Sam and Sophie for me and please don't feel you need to hurry away now just because I have to leave you. I am sure there are things you might still like to see here that Victoria could show you.'

But despite this suggestion, after Evanthi had made a stately exit, Patrick said he had work to do and resisted the temptation to stay and talk to Victoria – a temptation made all the more difficult because he couldn't help noticing her spontaneous look of disappointment when he said he must go. Both were aware of a strong current of attraction between them.

'Will you come and stay with us when you come over to England?' he asked as she walked downstairs with him. 'Your grandmother tells me she'd like you to meet my uncle. I think she hopes you could be a sort of envoy for her.'

'Oh, does she indeed?' Victoria laughed. 'Let's see how your uncle reacts first! I'd love to meet him but I'm not sure I fancy the role of go-between! I'd also love to come and see you all again too but I wouldn't want to impose on you and your wife.'

'You wouldn't do that. I'll be in touch and let you know how everything goes,' said Patrick. 'Thank you for making my visit to Vrahos so special.' He took her hand in his for moment and then gave her a swift goodbye kiss. 'See you again soon, then, Victoria,' he said.

'See you soon,' she replied.

When he looked in his driving mirror as he bumped down the pot-holey drive he could see her still standing in the archway outside the courtyard of the crumbling old house. He put his arm out of the window and waved, and saw her wave back.

She hated seeing Patrick go, while at the same time telling herself she had no right to such a feeling. She watched till the car was out of sight, and felt a terrible gloom settle over her.

Jake and Angelo were playing with the kittens and though she would have welcomed the distraction of Jake's bright company it seemed a shame to interrupt their game. She walked slowly to the viewpoint by herself and felt her aloneness close round her like an ice-cube.

Where are you now? Why did you do it? How could you leave us? she asked Richard for the umpteenth time. But as usual there was no response.

Chapter Twenty-eight

❧

A journey provides time for reflection, and flying some thirty thousand feet above ground level, suspended in the sky between Greece and England, between Vrahos and Kirkby Knighton – between Victoria and Rachel – Patrick did some serious thinking.

He was well aware that his marriage was in serious trouble – had actually been in trouble for longer than he cared to admit. It had been easy to blame the arrival of Posy as the catalyst for the deterioration in their relationship – and certainly that had played a part – but Patrick knew it was not the whole truth. He blamed himself for not being more assertive from the start, but the threat of nervous collapse can be a powerful tool for manipulation, and it was one Rachel had never hesitated to use. I should never have let it get to this stage, thought Patrick. When did I cross the divide between cherishing the ravishingly pretty, hypersensitive girl with whom I fell so deeply in love and over-protecting the demanding and neurotic woman she seems to have become? When did it become a habit to shield her from anything she perceived to be threatening, not because she really needed it but because it made life more peaceful for everyone else, including me? When, he asked himself, did I start to be so irritated by Rachel – to fall out of love with her? It was not a comfortable question.

Then there had been the arrival of Bronwen, who had wormed her way into their lives to such an alarming degree that Rachel now seemed incapable of making any move without reference to her. 'Bronwen thinks' and 'Bronwen says' had become words that set his teeth on edge. It had come home forcibly to Patrick over the last week just how much his two older children – Sophie in particular – distrusted and resented Bronwen. And, of course, there was Posy – a pocket version of her mother to look at, though no one could describe her as nervous. It's time I took much more part in her upbringing, whatever Rachel wants, decided Patrick. I love her too much to let her become a monster child whom everyone dislikes – and he made up his mind that he must force some sort of a confrontation on his wife.

But before he could do this he knew he had to examine something else – his feelings for Victoria Cunningham, because he was aware that for the first time he was now also in the throes of a really serious temptation. If I'm to start issuing ultimatums to Rachel in an effort to save our marriage, he thought, I owe it to her to try to banish Victoria from my mind – but he thought this might be impossible, and a part of him did not even want to try.

He wondered if he was leaving Corfu in the nick of time before his emotions got out of hand, while he could still recognise the possibility that his feelings might be a compound of sympathy for a tragic young widow and the attraction of a temporarily unattached male to a younger and outstandingly attractive woman. And yet, and yet . . . Try as he would to drive her out, Victoria kept appearing in his mind's eye: her expressive face and wonderful smile; the depth of pain in her eyes when she had lit the candle in the chapel; the way her nose wrinkled just before she broke into laughter. Laughter, thought Patrick. That's one of the things that's lacking in our marriage – we don't laugh together. Rachel had always had a quick tongue and in their early days he'd been proud of, and amused by, her quick wits and sharpness, so it came as a shock to admit to himself that Rachel really had very little sense of humour – certainly no sense of the ridiculous – and was completely unable to laugh at herself. It was a deadly realisation. He wished he hadn't thought of it.

He didn't see much of Sam and Sophie on the flight home. As soon as they clapped eyes on the Burnaby family at the airport they gravitated towards them like pins activated by a magnet. Patrick made polite conversation to Johnny and Petra Burnaby as they waited to board the small plane for Athens, but once they got to Olympia airport he declined their invitation to join them at the bar. He found Petra's gushing declaration that she was absolutely wild about all his books – a positive fan – and had been dying to meet him for ages, combined with her frank appraisal of his person too much to take so early in the morning, while her husband's back-slapping suggestion that it was never too early for a drink when travelling, sent him running for cover. He looked with deep distrust at Johnny Burnaby's white socks, disliked being addressed as 'old man' by a perfect stranger, was disinclined to cooperate in the social game of 'do-you-know-the so-and-sos' and felt himself growing more and more curmudgeonly with every breath.

Sophie, terrified equally about what her father might think of Matthew or Matthew might think of him, was agonisingly conscious of divided loyalties; having adored and admired her father for most of her life it was disconcerting suddenly to feel anxiously critical and protectively defensive of him all at the same time.

At Heathrow Patrick felt ashamed of himself for being so stand-offish and went over to make amends to his children's friends while they all waited at the carousel for their luggage to appear. He even heard himself saying, 'Next time you come and visit the Marshalls you must get them to bring you over to us,' an invitation he thought he would almost certainly regret. Disconcerting how often one's friends' friends turned out to be uncongenial, he thought, but was rewarded by a grateful smile from Sophie that was compensation enough. He realised with a pang how quickly his daughter was growing up. She's in love too, he thought with surprise, and wondered if the magic of Vrahos had cast a spell on them all.

'Don't you think Matthew's nice, Dad?' Sophie asked in what she hoped was an off-hand, disinterested sort of voice. 'But I mean *really* nice? It's a pity Mr Burnaby's such a creep and I feel quite sorry for Matthew's mum because,' she lowered her voice, 'though she's quite sexy too in a way, I think he might actually be an *awful* old philanthropist.' Patrick gave his daughter a very affectionate look.

In a surprisingly short time they had collected Patrick's car and were heading up the M25 towards the A1 and the North. On the way home they all three recaptured the happy companionship that had been such a feature of the first days of the holiday.

Just before they reached the turn for Ripon, Sophie suddenly asked: 'Did Mum ever ring you last night?'

'No – she didn't actually.' Patrick hoped he sounded casual. 'I tried her but she must have been out – probably giving the dogs a run or something. I left a message to confirm we'd be back for supper unless we got delayed – but we've done really well.' He glanced sideways at Sophie. She was biting her nails, something he hadn't seen her do for a week. As they turned in at the drive he was full of good resolutions. He took the left-hand fork, which led round to the back of the house, but not before they had all seen another car heading down the front drive: Bronwen's all-too-familiar red VW.

Sophie let out a moan. 'Oh no! Wouldn't you just know it! Mum's resident shrink! Now we really know we're home.'

'At least she's going not coming,' said Sam. 'Hope she doesn't turn back.'

Patrick said nothing, but the good resolutions did a sharp slither. He tooted the horn as they drew up at the back door and then looked at his watch. It was just before seven. He hoped he'd be in time to say good night to Posy.

There was no sign of life in the kitchen – no explosion of greeting from the dogs bursting from their baskets under the big table as they usually did, though barking could be heard coming from the direction of the stables where they were usually only put to dry off if they got wet and muddy. Sam pushed open the swing door that led through to the front of the house and as he and Sophie charged through, Sophie suddenly realised she was longing to share all their news with her mother and hoping desperately for a favourable reaction.

'Hi, there! We're ba-ack!' she called out.

As they reached the hall Rachel was coming down the stairs. 'Well, hello, darlings,' she said to her son and daughter. 'Lovely to see you.'

'Mu-um!' shrieked Sophie, bounding up the stairs towards her.

'*Shush!*' said Rachel sharply. 'Please don't yell like that, Sophie! You'll disturb Posy.'

279

She extended a cool cheek towards her daughter but Sophie pulled back as though she'd been stung. 'I think I'll go straight up,' she muttered, pushing past her mother, her head turned away, determined not to let her see the hot, hurt tears that had infuriatingly sprung into her eyes.

'No!' said Rachel. 'No – Sophie stop! You're not to go up!' And she grabbed hold of the back of Sophie's fleece and yanked at her. 'Please wait,' she said, 'because I've got something to tell you. I've . . . I've got a special surprise for you but I want to explain it first.'

Sophie paused uncertainly, but she turned round. Something in Rachel's voice made Patrick's heart sink.

'Don't I get a greeting?' he asked lightly, putting an arm round his wife. 'Hello, darling, how are you? Haven't we made good time?' And he bent to kiss her.

'Hi, Mum.' Sam gave his mother a cautious embrace, and she returned it with one of her cheek-meets-air kisses. Sam and Sophie had learned when they were very young that their mother did not like greetings that rumpled her.

'So how is everything?' asked Patrick. 'And how's Posy? Have you both been all right? Very hard to get hold of, you've been all week, I must say!' He smiled down at his wife, but she avoided his eyes.

'Yes – well, we've . . . I've . . . been very busy.'

'What's the special surprise for Sophie then? Are we allowed to know?'

'Yes of course. We-ell . . .' Rachel didn't seem in any hurry to burst the surprise on them. 'I've made the most of the time you've been away to do a few things in the house I've been meaning to do for ages. I hope you're going to be pleased, Sophie darling, because I think it's a big improvement,' she said and then went on in a rush. 'I've made a few changes.'

'What sort of changes?' asked Sophie anxiously.

'Well, for one thing I've redecorated your room. Made it really nice for you to work in now that you have so much to do at weekends and in the holidays – like a proper little study of your own,' said Rachel enticingly.

'Mum – you haven't thrown anything *away*? You haven't touched my things?'

'Well, of course I've had to *touch* things – don't be silly, darling.' Rachel sounded defensive. 'You can hardly redecorate without touching anything. I found the most heavenly wallpaper. I know you're going to love it.'

'Well, perhaps we'd better go up and look then,' suggested Patrick, giving his wife a quizzical look. 'And I want to say good night to Posy.'

'I'm afraid I've already tucked her down,' said Rachel quickly.

Sophie turned again to go up the stairs, but Rachel put a delaying hand on her arm. 'Wait a minute, Sophie. Don't go in to your old room – I've actually done a bit of swapping around. I've . . . I've changed you and Posy over.'

'You've done *WHAT*?'

'I've changed you and Posy over. It makes much better sense now that you're away so much more, and she needs more floor space to spread her toys out, and . . .' Her voice trailed away. Sam, who had been standing by, looked at his mother, appalled. Sophie's room had always been intensely important to her – her place of safety, her private world into which she could retreat if life became too threatening or difficult. She had always spent hours up there.

'Mum, how . . . how *could* you?' asked Sophie, her voice little more than a whisper. '*How could you?* Without even *asking* me?'

'This is my house,' said Rachel defensively. 'You seem to forget that. And anyway, I *thought* you'd be pleased.'

'No.' Patrick's voice was calm but very definite. 'No, I don't think so, Rachel. And actually it's not your house. It's *our* house, and you shouldn't have done such a thing without asking Sophie – and me. Sophie, you'd better go and look before you say anything more. I'm sure Mum will have made it lovely for you, whatever your first reactions are and you may even think it's much better – but if you don't like the exchange when you've tried it you can always have your old room back.'

'She most certainly can't,' said Rachel furiously. 'We've worked really hard to make it nice for her: new furniture, new curtains, new—'

'Who is we?' asked Patrick. 'I thought you told me you were giving Yvonne a week's holiday while we were away?'

'I did. She doesn't get back till Monday. Bronwen's very kindly been helping me. We've chosen it all and done it together. She has wonderful taste.'

There was a frozen silence.

It was broken by a wail from the top of the stairs. 'Mumm-eee! Mumm-eee! I want a drink of wa-a-ter.' Miss Posy Hammond, looking totally beguiling in her white nightdress, was standing at the top of the stairs, her mop of pale curls circling her head like a halo on a china angel. There was an excited sparkle in her blue eyes. Posy could sniff out drama with the enthusiasm of a police dog on the track of hidden drugs.

'Now look what you've done,' said Rachel, secretly thankful for the diversion. 'I'd just got her nicely settled before you came in. She'll never go to sleep now.'

'See Posy's new bedroom,' invited the angel who had an unerring instinct for inciting trouble.

Patrick picked his younger daughter up, tossed her in the air and then held her tight. She smelled deliciously of soap and baby powder and her soft hair tickled his chin as she buried her head in his neck in a fit of pretend bashfulness that deceived no one. Then she looked up under her unfairly long lashes. 'Daddy,' she said, stroking his face, '*my* Daddy.' And then hopefully: 'Presents?'

'What a little minx you are,' said Patrick, striving to sound normal. 'Perhaps presents – but only if you're a good girl and there's no nonsense afterwards. Come on, let's all go up and look at Mummy's handiwork.' He felt a terrible sense of outrage on behalf of Sophie, who looked as if she might be sick.

They trouped upstairs.

Sophie had slept in the sunny bedroom to the right of the stairs for as long as she could remember. Next door, in between her room and her parents' bedroom was a smaller one, which had originally been Sam's when he was a baby. He had long ago chosen to move to the top floor and occupied one of the large attic rooms – originally nurseries and servants' quarters to previous generations – where he could play his music as loud as he liked without causing aggravation to anyone else. There was nothing wrong with Posy's room – it made a charming night-nursery for a little girl – but it was considerably smaller than Sophie's so it was inevitable that she should have a sense of being down-graded, but worse, far worse, was the fact that it wasn't *hers*, her old familiar nest, and had she been offered a choice about exchanging with her little sister she would certainly have refused – indeed had already done so about six months earlier when Rachel had casually suggested it, a fact of which only she and Rachel were aware.

Rachel opened the door of Posy's old room with the look of one producing a very special rabbit out of a hat.

'*There*, darling,' she said brightly. 'See how nice I've made it for you. Built-in cupboards and bookshelves and a proper modern desk. Don't you adore the curtains? I got the material at Peter Jones, and Mrs Jefferson in the village has been working like a beaver to get them done for you. Bronwen and I only put them up this afternoon.'

Sophie stared and made a strangled sort of gasp.

'You must have been planning it all before we went to Corfu and you never said a word,' she said accusingly. 'But where are all my *things*?'

'Well, your clothes are all there – put away, for a change – though I really think you might have a good clear-out. I was very tempted to chuck some of them out but I hope now you've got everything new and fresh that you may start to take a pride in keeping things nice.'

'How can I have anyone to stay – there's no room for a second bed – and my posters and my ornaments, my old books, *my things*. Where are they?' She turned on her mother. She was shaking. 'You've given half of them to Posy, haven't you? Oh my God, Mum – you've never given her my dolls' house! But you have – *haven't you*? She'll wreck it.'

The dolls' house had once belonged to Patrick's mother, who had given it to Sophie for her fourth birthday. It had always played an important part in Sophie's life – she had peopled it with an imaginary family, constantly redecorated it and often taken refuge in its private world. Recently the redecorating had taken on a more serious turn, encouraged by Maggie Marshall, herself a serious collector of miniature furniture, whose own dolls' house was a work of art. Philip Marshall claimed it enabled the rest of the family to live without constant upheaval because it assuaged Maggie's passion for interior decorating, and her collection was quite valuable now.

'Why aren't there any dolls in your house?' Sophie had once asked her, and Maggie had answered: 'Because *I* live in it,' and watched the light of comprehension break over Sophie's face.

'Don't be hysterical, Sophie,' Rachel said coldly, now. 'You can't possibly play with dolls at your age. Now you're being completely ridiculous.'

The door to Sophie's old room was ajar where Posy had crept out of it a few minutes earlier. Sophie flung it wide open and switched on the light. She let out a bellow.

'I knew it! I knew it! You've given her *everything*. Sam – witness it. Those are all my things.' Posy's bed, never short of soft toys, was now covered in Sophie's beloved old crew of battered animals as well.

Sam peered in. He looked at his mother in wonderment. 'Jesus, Mum! How could you?'

'Don't swear, please, Sam!' Two bright spots of colour flamed on Rachel's cheeks. 'Sophie's very ungrateful. I've gone to endless trouble and expense to make her a lovely new room and she's behaving like a silly child.'

'It isn't my room at all – it's . . . it's like some horrible page out of a catalogue for office furniture. How could you? I hate it and I hate you!' Sophie shrieked at her mother, beside herself with misery and rage.

'Apologise this instant! Patrick, make her say she's sorry!'

'I won't!' shrieked Sophie. 'There's no way I'm going to sleep in Posy's room and you can't make me.'

Rachel whipped her hand out and dealt her daughter a stinging slap across the face.

For a moment it looked as if the whole family were playing statues.

'That was quite uncalled for,' said Patrick in a low voice to his wife. 'For God's sake, leave it off, both of you. Let's all go down, have a drink and calm down. Sophie, I won't have you speaking to your mother like that, no matter what your feelings are – clearly we shall have to talk this over tomorrow and sort something out. You'd better sleep in the spare room tonight.'

Only one person had been enjoying this scene and that was Posy, but spectator sports were not much in her line and it suddenly dawned on her no one was paying her the slightest attention. She opened her mouth and let out her best and most piercing scream – in her experience an infallible cure for this most unwelcome of situations.

'Stop that noise this minute unless you want to go straight back to bed,' said her father. To everyone's astonishment Posy's scream stopped as instantly as if Patrick had suddenly managed to punch in the correct code on an ear-splitting burglar alarm. The silence was electrifying.

Sophie turned, pushed past them all and rushed down the stairs.

'Go after her, Sam,' said Patrick wearily. 'We'll be down in a minute.'

Husband and wife stood and looked at each other. Patrick saw someone disturbingly familiar – but Rachel saw a stranger.

Chapter Twenty-nine

'How dare you side with Sophie against me?' hissed Rachel. She looked like a furious cat.

'And how could you do anything so bloody stupid?' said Patrick furiously, trying to hold his anger in check. 'You know what Sophie's room means to her – whatever possessed you? What a homecoming!'

He put his younger daughter on the floor and bent down to her. 'Now listen to me, Rosy-Posy. I *have* got a present for you and because you stopped that horrible screaming I'll go downstairs and get it for you while Mummy puts you back into bed, but any silly nonsense and I shall take it away again. Do you understand? Are you going to go to bed like a good girl and no fuss?'

Posy nodded enthusiastically. 'Posy *very* good today,' she said virtuously.

'Amazing what a little bribery will achieve,' said Patrick, but Rachel was in no mood for sharing parental amusement. She snatched at Posy's hand as though she were preventing her from drowning and glared at her husband.

'Right then,' said Patrick coolly. 'I'll be back in a few minutes, Posy – and I expect to find you in bed.' And he went downstairs without looking back at Rachel.

Sam and Sophie were in the kitchen. Sam was waiting for the kettle to boil to make his sister a mug of tea, and Sophie, her face blotchy and swollen with tears, was crouched in the corner of the squashy sofa at the far end of the room, talking into her mobile.

'Thanks,' she was saying. 'That's *so, so* kind – it would absolutely save me. You're a star. No, no . . . . really – I won't need fetching. I'll get Sam to bring me. See you later.'

Patrick cocked his head towards Sophie and raised his eyebrows at Sam.

'Maggie Marshall,' Sam informed him. 'Sophe rang Ellie and she's just put her mother on.'

Sophie switched off her mobile and looked at her father. She had never been pretty in the Meissen shepherdess style in which Posy and her mother were pretty, but lately her father had noticed with pleasure that she was growing into her very different kind of looks and that her amusing, bony face – always arresting but not flattering to a child – was becoming truly attractive; something to do with good cheekbones and a lot of animation, thought Patrick. His uncle, with his connoisseur's eye, had long seen her potential and always declared, to Rachel's disbelief, that the rather plain little girl who couldn't please her mother would one day break hearts. Now she suddenly looked peaky and plain all over again – and touchingly younger than her seventeen years.

Patrick sat down beside her on the sofa and put an arm round her. 'Now then, Sophie darling,' he said. 'Let's not over-react. I think Mum has made a bad mistake over this, but she won't have meant to upset you.' The look Sophie gave him cut him to the heart, but he went on firmly: 'We're all tired now and we can review things tomorrow. How would it be if we made a pact not to talk any more about who sleeps where tonight and stuck to the subject of Corfu?'

Sophie shook her head vehemently. 'No, Dad, I'm sorry. Mum's not the least bit interested in us, or Corfu – not even in your book – or anything. She hasn't even asked how we are. I am *not* going to sleep in Posy's room, I'm going to stay with Ellie – Maggie says I can.'

It was on the tip of Patrick's tongue to say she couldn't go, when the telephone rang. Sam picked it up. 'Oh, hi. Yes, he's here.' He handed the receiver to Patrick. 'Maggie – for you,' he said.

'Hi, Maggie,' Patrick said. 'I'm so sorry you've been embroiled in a bit of a storm-in-a-teacup. I was going to ring you later anyway to tell you how fantastic Petradi was and what a great time we've had. I must come over and see you sometime – we need to have a financial settling-up anyway.'

'Heavens! No urgency about that – but I'd love to hear how it all went. Now what's all this drama about Sophie?'

'Oh, just a bit of a family disagreement – you know how these things blow up out of nothing when everyone's tired,' said Patrick, not wanting to throw blame at Rachel in front of Sophie. 'I gather you've said she can stay? She's clearly very keen to come – perhaps it might solve a problem, just for tonight. Things have got a bit tense this end.'

'Sophie's welcome any time,' said Maggie, 'for as long as she likes. She knows that, but I wanted to check it was all right with you first. Why doesn't she stay for the weekend? Ellie'd be thrilled. We haven't eaten yet – do you want to bring her over and stay to have a bite of supper too? Phil can open a bottle of Corfiot wine and make you feel nostalgic for Petradi.'

It was tempting to accept. The cheerful Marshall household was just what Patrick felt like, but he also knew that he needed to have a few things out with Rachel first. It was agreed that Sam could borrow the battered family car to take Sophie over to the Marshalls and stay for supper with them.

'All right then, Sophie – cooling-off time,' said Patrick. 'I must go up and say good night to Posy – I promised I'd give her the present we bought before she goes to sleep – but I'll be down again in a minute. You'd better transfer your things from my car to the Polo.'

'Oh, we mustn't keep darling little Posy waiting, must we?' Sophie flung at him. 'Well, I won't be here when you come down so don't hurry.'

'Stop that, Sophie,' said Patrick sharply. 'Whatever your feelings, it's not Posy's fault that she's in your bedroom. I'm very sorry this has happened – but it has, and we'll have to try to sort something out. Now give me a good-night hug if you don't want to wait. We've had such a lovely time together. Let's not spoil it.' He went to kiss his daughter, but she jerked her head away and shrugged him off. Patrick gave her a long look then turned on his heel and went upstairs.

'Oh, for God's sake, Sophe,' said Sam, 'give us a break! Surely you don't need to take it out on Dad. I'll go and get the car.'

Sophie went to pick up her backpack with a stone in her heart.

*

Some time later, when Patrick and Rachel sat down to what an onlooker might have supposed to be an intimate little supper *à deux*, the atmosphere in the kitchen was so charged with carefully controlled ill-feeling that it felt as if a time-bomb might explode. Rachel moved about as if she had been switched on to auto-pilot, making it clear that though she might be going through the physical motions of producing food for her husband, it was all done by remote control and her essential self was playing no part in ministering to him. She gave mono-syllabic answers to questions about what she and Posy had been doing and stared abstractedly into space when Patrick tried to tell her about Petradi, his visit to Vrahos and his interview with Evanthi Doukas with regard to his book. He did not mention Evanthi's link with Hugh: somehow it seemed too sensitive a subject to be exposed to her chilling disinterest. And he did not mention Victoria at all. He knew from experience that once his wife settled into a sulk it could go on for days and he longed to shake her – literally – out of her martyred silence. Once, he'd had the ability to charm her out of her moods if he exerted himself, but this time he had no intention of smoothing her path back to amicable relations.

As he ate a perfectly cooked salmon fillet, topped with a pesto and parmesan crust, and served with new potatoes and tight lips, he found himself longing for failed pasta carbonara presented with laughter. If she expected him to apologise for his sharpness, sympathise about Sophie's turbulent reaction to the surprise her mother had sprung on her and then listen to a spiel about ungrateful teenage daughters, she would be in for a long fruitless wait. As they cleared the plates away and stacked the dishwasher together the distance between them seemed to stretch as far as Corfu.

Then the telephone rang. Patrick answered it expecting it might be Maggie Marshall again, or even Sophie herself. Unlike her mother, Sophie was not normally a bearer of grudges and Patrick guessed she would be feeling miserable about her parting words. But it was Bronwen Richards.

'Well, hello there,' she said in her huskily sexy voice. 'So the wanderer has returned, I gather?'

'Did you want to speak to Rachel?'

'Not really – it was you I wanted to talk to. I rang to know your reaction to her new decision. I hope you're pleased?'

The woman's a menace, thought Patrick – it's none of her business who sleeps in which room in this house. What a bloody nerve!

'If you mean Sophie's reaction to her change of room,' he said coldly, 'it wasn't very good, I'm afraid. She was extremely upset. I should have thought it might have been fairly obvious that she would be. But don't worry, it's nothing we can't sort out.'

'Oh, Sophie . . . no. I meant *your* reaction to Rachel's new enterprise.'

'What new enterprise?'

'Hasn't she told you yet? I thought she would have done.' Bronwen's words hung provocatively in the air. 'She's agreed to be secretary to my protest group. I think it's a splendid decision. As her friend *and* her therapist I think it's just what Rachel needs – a cause outside the home that she can really get her teeth into.'

'What cause? I haven't the slightest idea what you're talking about.' Patrick found himself gripping the receiver so hard in suppressed annoyance that it was lucky he didn't break it.

'Oh, she'll tell you all about it. Rachel's so wonderfully efficient and we hope to arrange some quite high-profile events.'

'What sort of events?'

'Oh, rallies – pressure groups – demonstrations. That sort of thing.'

'Demonstrations against *what*?'

'Against anything *we* think needs protesting about,' said Bronwen sweetly. 'There are so many important issues locally that want watching, about which Rachel feels as strongly as the rest of us. She will be a hugely important addition to our ranks. Rachel's generously suggested we can have our meetings in your house – so I'll see you around no doubt, Patrick.' And Bronwen rang off.

Patrick looked at Rachel, who had donned apron and rubber gloves like protective armour, and was assiduously wiping down the spankingly clean surface of the draining board with Dettox and drying the washing-up bowl.

'Oh, Rachel,' he said. 'What have you got yourself into?'

'Just because you don't like Bronwen—'

'No, I don't like Bronwen,' he said decisively. 'And I don't trust her either. I think she's trouble – deliberate, poisonous trouble. I'd be very unhappy to see you getting involved with any of her protests.'

'I don't have to agree with you about everything.'

'Of course not – it would be very dull if you did. But it sounds as if Bronwen just wants to stir up controversy for the sake of it – any old cause would do.'

'You don't know that.'

'Can you tell me what she's specifically against then?'

'Well . . . um . . .' Rachel cast him a look of annoyance. 'Oh, injustice . . . prejudices . . . the under-privileged . . . petty regulations. Well, lots of things,' she said feebly. 'Anything specific that crops up really.'

'Exactly. Can you tell me what she's *for* then?'

'I don't have to be cross-examined like this. You've been saying I ought to get a part-time job for ages – well, now I have. And I'm not giving up my friendship with Bronwen just because you're jealous of her.'

'Then there's no more to be said about it.' Patrick refused to rise to this jibe, which she'd flung at him before. 'But Sophie's another matter altogether. You know how important this term is for her with her ASs in June. She gets het up enough before exams anyway without a running battle going on at home. This has got to be sorted out. If you're so set on moving Posy, why don't we offer Sophie the chance to go upstairs with Sam? We're hardly short of space up there. She could have a wonderful big room with a fantastic view – a spare bed for when she has friends to stay – that old nursery sofa that's stored up there would be great too – and of course the dolls' house – that *must* go back. It was appalling to let Posy have that. My mother specifically gave it to Sophie.'

'Posy'll be terribly upset.'

'Tough. She'll get over it,' said Patrick unfeelingly. 'And Sophie should have grown out of it by now.'

'Nonsense. Anyway, we have to do something.'

'It's such a waste of money – all those fittings that I had put in specially – the wallpaper . . .' Rachel was beginning to sound whiny. Patrick shrugged impatiently.

'Well, that's your fault. It isn't about money – luckily for you. I'll give Sophie a reasonable cheque and she can do the attic up for herself, choose her own curtains and things. I'm sure she and Ellie would love to paint it together. As for all that soulless office furniture, you'd better use Posy's room as your own office if you're going to be so busy organising protests for duff causes.' He gave Rachel a shrewd look: 'And Sophie was certainly right about one thing: don't tell me you got everything chosen, delivered and organised in the week we were away because I wouldn't believe you. You must have planned it all before we went to Corfu. I'm fed up with the whole subject. I'll talk to Sophie tomorrow and if she's happy with that idea she can get on with it and then I don't want to hear any more about it. Now I'm going to get myself a drink and look at my post.'

And Patrick walked out of the kitchen and disappeared into his study, leaving his wife standing in the kitchen, once again, staring after him.

Chapter Thirty

When Sam returned at about eleven his mother had disappeared to bed but his father, nursing a larger than usual glass of whisky, was still dealing with his mail.

'Hi, Dad – working already? That's really pushing it. How's things?' He gave his father a commiserating look.

'Hello, Sam. Thanks for taking Sophie. That was a real help. Is she all right?'

'Yeah, she's OK. Sent you her love, by the way. Said she'd ring you in the morning.'

'Oh, good.' Patrick, much relieved, interpreted this to be both an apology and a message of reassurance and envied the amazing power of the young both to be overcome by, and then swiftly recuperate from, dramas. He felt dreadful himself. 'So – how were the Marshalls?' he asked.

'Oh – great. I hadn't seen them for absolutely ages. I'd forgotten what a yummy mummy Maggie was, and she still looks great for her age. We always loved it when she used to do the school run because she was such fun,' said Sam, and added casually. 'Ellie's not half bad now either. You'd be amazed how she's changed, Dad.'

'Good for her age too then?' asked Patrick.

Sam grinned. 'Bit young for me – but I might keep my eye on her. Has Mum chilled yet? She really lost it about Sophe, didn't she? Bet it was all the fault of that woman.'

'Yes – I could wring her bloody neck. Now she seems to have got your mother involved in some dodgy protest group she runs. I fear the worst.'

'Oh well, we can resort to sabotage too,' said Sam cheerfully. 'We'll think of a way to get rid of her, between us.' Patrick suddenly felt much better for his son's company.

'I see you've got the dogs back in.' Sam fondled the ears of

Patrick's two Labradors, Bullet and Swift, who were stretched out on the hearthrug. 'Where were they? Mum usually likes having them in as bodyguards if you're away. I suppose Bronwen persuaded her to banish them?'

'Yes – so I gather. More to bait me, I suspect, than anything to do with the dogs themselves.'

'How pathetic – she must loathe you as much as you loathe her. I bet she fancied you rotten and you blew her out,' suggested Sam light-heartedly – and could tell by the look on his father's face that he had hit on a hitherto unsuspected truth. 'Wow,' he said, impressed at this surprising evidence of parental pulling power. 'Poor old Dad. You'd better watch your back now. She really is pretty random, you know – the sort to slip dope in your drink.'

'Thanks!' Patrick laughed. 'I'll look to you to protect me!'

'Any time! I'll be off to bed then. I'm knackered. Night, Dad.' Sam put a hand on his father's shoulder for a moment before he breezed off. 'We had a great time at Petradi,' he said.

Patrick looked after his son with great affection. Sam would be all right, he thought. He'd had his own share of stormy times with his mother but his relationship with her was far less complicated than Sophie's, and in any case, Sam had been blessed with an easier temperament than his sister. Patrick trembled for Sophie. Despite Sam's light-hearted words about Bronwen, Patrick felt a frisson of disquiet all the same – though more for Rachel than himself. What was Bronwen really after?

After he'd let the dogs out and then shut them in the back room where they slept at night amongst the family's coats and boots, Sophie's riding paraphernalia, his own gardening impedimenta and a miscellaneous collection of rackets and golf clubs, Patrick went slowly upstairs. He hesitated for a moment on the landing, and then went into his dressing room via the landing door; but after he'd finished unpacking he did not go through the connecting door into his and Rachel's bedroom to join her in their king-size bed. He spent the night in the single bed in the dressing room without attempting to say good night to his wife.

Rachel, still awake, heard him come up, heard him moving about next door but did not call out to him either.

*

The next morning, Friday, was one of the two days a week when Patrick's secretary, Tania, came in. She was a cheerful competent young woman, who could be relied on to use her initiative if necessary but also knew when it was safer to refer to Patrick first. She was reasonably tactful with her employer's prickly wife but didn't allow herself to be fazed by her either. If Rachel occasionally chose to behave like a neurotic cow, then that, in Tania's opinion, was her problem and life was too short for everyone else to dance to her tune. She always described her employer as a lovely man, but was much too absorbed in her own hectic social life to nurture romantic thoughts concerning him; she was genuinely interested in his books, admired his talent, was conscientious about her work but would not have lost much sleep if Patrick had suddenly decided to dispense with her services: there were always other fish in the sea. After the tensions in his family life Tania's semi-detached friendliness suited Patrick perfectly and he enjoyed her undemanding company.

They dealt with the letters and telephone calls there'd been in his absence first.

'Miss Winterton rang,' said Tania. 'She wanted to know how you'd got on at Vrahos. I said you'd let her know. And she's got a new contact for you – some little-known château in France she thought sounded interesting – but she'll ring you about it next week. The Eagle Press want to discuss dates with you sometime and would like to talk about possible photographs for the cover. Could you do an article for the *Heritage at Risk Quarterly Review* on houses worth saving? I said you'd let the editor know. What else? Oh yes – Mr Marston rang. No drama, apparently. He said to tell you he's fine. I told him I was sure you'd ring when you got back.'

'I'll ring him now. I've got to go and pick Sophie up from the Marshalls so I'll try and go round either on the way there or the way back.'

'Oh yes, and Mrs Marshall rang just now while you were out with the dogs,' said Tania. 'She suggested you might all like to go over for kitchen lunch and tell her about Petradi, if you're picking Sophie up. But she said Sophie was welcome to stay for the weekend if it didn't suit you or Rachel to fetch her today.'

'I'll ring her too.'

He decided to accept Maggie's offer of lunch and picked up the telephone. Maggie, ever hospitable, invited the whole family to come. The more the merrier, she said cheerfully, but Patrick said no, it would just be him.

'I want to go and check up on old Uncle Hugh this afternoon. He'd love to see Sophie too and it'll give me a good chance to talk to her on her own after last night's spot of trouble.'

'Fine – whatever suits.' As usual Maggie sounded wonderfully relaxed. Sophie and Ellie hadn't surfaced yet, she said, so she hadn't had a chance to check things out this morning. 'See you when we see you then. Love to Rachel,' she said easily.

Next he rang Mrs Parkes, who was reassuring about Hugh's state of health. 'He's fine. Mr Marston will be around for a long time yet, you see if he's not.' Patrick said he hoped she was right – she usually was – and that he and Sophie would look in during the afternoon. He thought he could stop en route for the Marshalls and drop the films he'd taken at the photographic shop he always used in Knighton, since he no longer found it necessary to process his photographs himself, now that standards had improved so much. He settled down to work on the notes he had taken about Vrahos, thoughts of both grandmother and granddaughter filling his mind.

Later, before he left, he went in search of Rachel. They had been scrupulously, unnaturally polite to each other at breakfast. Neither of them had referred to the upset of the evening before – nor to the fact that they had spent the night apart.

'Just off to fetch Sophie. I thought we'd look in on Uncle Hugh – we'll be back sometime after tea,' he said, not mentioning that he was going to lunch with the Marshalls. If Rachel chose to assume that he and Sophie would be lunching with the old man – well, so be it. 'Do you want anything in Knighton?'

'No thank you. Posy and I are going out too.'

Rachel didn't say where she was going and Patrick didn't ask. Clearly the cold war was still on.

*

Maggie was picking daffodils at the far end of the garden when Patrick drove up to the back of the house. She waved a greeting and he walked across the lawn to join her.

The Old Vicarage was a gabled, Victorian house of solid grey stone, which made up in comfort and space for what it lacked in architectural distinction: a pleasant unpretentious house with large, light rooms and a happy lived-in feeling – a house where you wouldn't be afraid to kick your shoes off and curl up on a sofa with a book. A house that was not unlike its owners, thought Patrick. No one would have described Maggie or Philip Marshall as glamorous but it was difficult not to feel at ease in their company. Despite her wonderful auburn hair and amusing face, Maggie was too freckled, rangy and untidy for glamour; tall, bespectacled Philip looked what he was – a country solicitor who was used to dealing with people from all walks of life and was trusted with the confidences of many of them. Patrick liked them both enormously.

'You look very busy,' he said, kissing Maggie on both cheeks.

'Cynthia and I are supposed to be doing the flowers for a Golden Wedding lunch party on Sunday,' she explained. Maggie and a friend ran a garden designing service together, but were also much in demand to do the decorating for social functions. Patrick thought she was one of those rare and lucky people who manage to combine a naturally relaxed attitude to life with being highly efficient.

'Don't break off on my account. I know I'm a bit early – I'll wander round the garden until you've finished. It's looking fabulous.'

'Oh, I've finished – there's not much more I can do till tomorrow morning,' she said. 'It seemed a shame not to augment the bought stuff when we've got such loads of daffs ourselves – they've done specially well this year.' She picked up the two flat baskets, which she'd filled with daffodils. 'It's great to see you, Patrick. I was at the flower market at four o'clock this morning so I'm good and ready for a break. I'll just go and bung these in buckets of water and then we'll forage for some lunch. I'm longing to hear how you got on at Petradi. Sorry you got back to a bit of a drama, though – teenage daughters can be dreadfully volatile, can't they?'

She didn't say that she'd been really concerned about Sophie the night before. Sophie had arrived looking red-eyed and blotchy but had made valiant efforts to appear normal. They'd had an outwardly cheerful supper with a lot of light-hearted teasing by Sam about Sophie's conquest of Matthew Burnaby countered by spirited retaliation from Sophie with tales of Sam's hopeless passion for his Greek goddess; there'd been much swapping of stories with Ellie about the glitziness of the Burnaby life-style, the goings-on at the Harbour Lights bar at Kryovrisi and the lethal after-effect of Petros' cocktails, but Maggie's watchful eye noticed that Sophie's animation seemed hectic and forced, and that while she pushed the fish pie round her plate – unusual for Sophie who liked her food – she was drinking rather too many glasses of wine. After exchanging a look with his wife, Philip had quietly removed the bottle from Sophie's end of the table.

After Sam had left, the two girls had gone up to bed but an hour later Ellie had appeared in her parents' bedroom and asked her mother to come. 'It's Sophe, Mum,' she said. 'I don't know what to do with her. She's in an awful state and I can't stop her crying.'

Sophie had been incoherent with tears, but eventually the story of the dismal homecoming, Rachel's disinterest in their arrival and the discovery of the loss of her old bedroom had come tumbling out – together with her loathing of Bronwen, her resentment at Rachel's preoccupation with Posy and fears for the future.

'I can never do anything to please Mum, I don't think she's ever loved me,' she'd whispered at last, and Maggie sat on her bed, hugging her and rocking her as if she'd still been a little girl.

'Now come on, Sophie darling, that's enough now,' she said bracingly when she judged the crying had gone on long enough. 'You're very tired – you've been travelling all day, the lovely holiday with Dad is over, you're going back to school next week – and you've had a spat with Mum. But it will all look different in the morning.' She'd got her a drink of hot Ribena, given her a paracetamol and hugged her good night. When, half an hour later, Maggie – who by this time couldn't sleep herself

– had crept back to check on her, Sophie was asleep, curled tightly in a foetal position.

Maggie'd left the two girls to sleep but when they emerged at mid-morning she thought Sophie still looked wan and unhappy and it had taken all her powers of persuasion to get her to agree that when Patrick came to collect her she would at least go back home with him to discuss the situation.

'All right, I'll go for Dad's sake,' Sophie eventually promised. 'But I won't sleep in Posy's room – even for him.'

'I'm sure you'll be able to work something out once everyone's had a chance to cool down,' said Maggie to Patrick now, with an optimism she was far from feeling.

Patrick shot her a shrewd look. 'I don't suppose Sophie's too happy about it,' he said. 'I've got a suggestion to put to her, which I hope she'll accept – otherwise we're in trouble. I don't want to let Rachel down, but she's really messed up and I can't side with her over this.'

Their conversation was brought to a halt by the appearance of Ellie and Sophie.

Sophie rushed to hug her father. 'Sorry, Dad,' she whispered, and Patrick felt a surge of love for her.

Conversation over lunch centred on Corfu. Maggie and Ellie were satisfyingly fascinated to hear about the discovery of Hugh Marston's romantic connection with Evanthi Doukas. If Maggie noticed that the name of Evanthi's granddaughter seemed to crop up rather often in the saga, she kept her thoughts to herself.

'Phil and I met a grandson of Mrs Doukas once,' she volunteered. 'He's that journalist who's got a column in a very glossy American gardens magazine and occasionally writes for the *Spectator* too – he's pretty glossy himself! Guy Something-or-other.'

'Guy Winston. That's the chap – I'm hoping to meet him. What did you make of him?' asked Patrick.

Maggie wrinkled her brow. 'Glamorous. Amusing. Definitely attractive but slightly . . .' she groped for the right word, '. . . slightly *unsettling*. A dash of Mephistopheles. I was warned he'd got a reputation as a lady-killer.' She grinned. 'He's certainly got a great line in chatting-up – Phil watched me like a hawk all the time I was talking to him! Put it like this: he was huge fun to sit next to and I'd love to meet him again, but I don't think I'd trust him round the next corner! But what an extraordinary coincidence about Mrs Doukas and your uncle! When are you going to tell Hugh about it?'

'This afternoon as ever is. I thought Sophie and I would call on him on our way home – I need you as a witness, Sophie, and I want some moral support. I thought Uncle Hugh might not believe me on my own. Shall we do that?'

'Oh yes,' breathed Sophie. 'Cool!'

When they had finished lunch Maggie suggested that Sophie might like to come back the following day to spend the weekend with Ellie. 'You could get all your things for school collected and bring them with you and then I could take you and Ellie back together on Monday morning – how would that grab you?'

Sophie nodded violently. 'OK, Dad?'

'I think it would be an excellent plan.' Patrick gave Maggie a grateful look.

'Well, it would be great for us too because I'm going to be busy tomorrow with the flowers for this do on Sunday so it would be nice for Ellie to have company. She wants to go into Knighton to get some last-minute bits and bobs for school – don't you, darling? – and Phil said he'd take her, so they could pick you up, Sophie. Say about eleven?'

There was a feeling of constraint in the car after they had waved goodbye to the Marshalls.

'Dad?' As they turned out of the drive on to the road for Knighton, Sophie shot Patrick a look that was half anxious, half defiant. 'About my room . . .'

'Before you say anything I've got a suggestion to put to you.' Patrick felt it was important not to get into a confrontation from which it might become too difficult for Sophie to withdraw. He outlined his idea about converting the big room on the top floor. 'You could choose what you want for curtains and things, and have all your own old pictures and ornaments back . . .'

'The ones Mum hasn't chucked out already . . .' muttered Sophie.

Patrick ignored this and went on, 'And make it really nice – lots of room to have a friend to stay, and you and Sam would have the whole of the top floor between you. I'll foot the bill, but you must do the organising. If you paint it yourself I might even give you and Ellie some pocket money for doing the decorating, but you'd have to do it properly. How about it?'

'And would Posy have to keep my old room?'

'Well, you can't have both rooms,' said Patrick mildly.

'I hate the way Posy always gets away with everything. It's so unfair.' Sophie was picking the skin round her thumbnails.

'Is that your answer then? It's take it or leave it, Sophie.' He could see she was struggling with herself.

'All right,' she said at last – and then in a very small voice, 'Thanks, Dad.'

Patrick was greatly relieved. 'Good,' he said briskly. 'That's decided then. And you must make your peace with Mum. How you do that's up to you and her, but I'm not having an atmosphere hanging over us all.' Even as he said this he thought ruefully that he would need to take a dose of his own medicine because he still felt very angry with his wife.

He put out a hand to Sophie. 'Now,' he said, 'how do you think we should prepare Uncle Hugh for our news?'

Chapter Thirty-one

They found Hugh in his studio, about to have a post-prandial snooze, but he was obviously delighted to see them, and heaved himself up from his chair.

'Well, young lady,' he said, putting his hands on Sophie's shoulders and looking down at her appreciatively, 'you're looking very well. That suntan suits you. I seem to remember you agreed to let me paint you. When are you coming to sit for me?'

'Any time,' said Sophie promptly. 'If you really mean it. I go back to school on Monday – but I'm home most weekends. I could ride over on Punch any Saturday or Sunday . . . except,' she broke off uncertainly and looked distraught, 'what on earth would I *wear*?'

Hugh laughed. 'The burning question to all women! I wouldn't want you in a ball dress, if that's what's worrying you – you young things nowadays make yourselves look so out-landish when you dress up. Too much flesh and not enough glamour – it's not at all the same thing. No, I'll paint you in your jeans and T-shirt or whatever you wear to ride in everyday.' He smiled at her. 'It's your expressive face I'm after . . .'

'Huh!' Patrick grinned. 'Let's hope you don't pick one of the days when she looks like a thunderclap then!'

'She never looks like a thunderclap with me, do you, Sophie?' said Hugh, letting her go and steadying himself with one hand on the back of his chair. 'Mind you, I don't want any of those frightful spikes you sometimes put in your hair either. And why don't we have old Punch in the portrait? Would you like that? We could have you leaning against one of the apple trees in the orchard and the old rascal cropping the grass and doing his best to give himself laminitis.'

'Oh, wicked – that would be *really* cool.' Sophie beamed. 'I do love you, Uncle Hugh,' she said. Looking at her lit-up face, such a contrast to yesterday's look of woe, Patrick felt a rush of gratitude to the old man. He thought this was just the boost for morale that Sophie needed – the combination of admiration and teasing acting like the effect of water on a thirsty plant. His uncle always brought out the very best in her.

'Would you like me to take some photographs of the pair of them?' he offered. 'Then you'd be able to work on the portrait when Sophie's at school as well as at weekends.'

'That would be excellent. Yes, please,' he smiled. 'Now, tell me what you've all been up to.'

'Tania says you didn't know which day we were coming back. Rachel may have forgotten to give you my message, but I should have told you myself. I'm sorry.'

'I expect it was me that forgot – I don't think you told me where you were off to this time either – but I haven't spoken to Rachel for ages. She's all right, is she?' asked Hugh, giving Patrick a beady look.

'Rather busy at the moment,' said Patrick shortly, glad to be able to change the subject. 'Now before we fill you in with our news just tell me how you really are.'

'Not bad at all – quite pleased with myself, in fact. The quack's pills are working and I've nearly completed that commission for Prince Haroun. He came over the other day and seemed satisfied. Just as well – I shall charge him a packet.' Hugh gave a chuckle. 'He was staying with wicked old Rosamund Duntan. They had an off-and-on affair for years, you know, despite the fact that the little man only just about comes up to one of her new hips. Poor old Roz – she still looks pretty convincing from a distance but I think she's finally had a lift too far. She's got a permanent smile now like the smile on the face of the tiger – the back of her neck must be a positive cat's cradle of nips and tucks! I could tell you some tales about her – she was a stunner when she was young. Now come and look at my great work. I'd value your opinion.' He limped over to the easel, and leaning on his stick with one hand, twitched a sheet back with the other to reveal the big canvas. 'There you are,' he said, manoeuvring himself out of the way and standing back. 'I've finished working on Moonlight Flit and her latest progeny –

she's got a beautiful head on her, hasn't she? – and I'm putting the final touches to the other mares and foals, then it's done.'

Patrick came and stood beside him, marvelling at the quality of the painting and thinking that the impression of life and energy that had always been such a hallmark of Hugh's work was as potent as ever. He let out an appreciative whistle: 'One of your very best,' he said. 'How do you do it?'

Hugh gave him a wry look. 'You were going to say "at your age"! Makes me feel like Old Father William!'

There was a muffled squeak from Sophie, who had been wandering round the studio looking at Hugh's other pictures.

'*Dad!*' she hissed. 'Look – it's just like Victoria! I've seen it before but then I didn't know about—' She broke off and looked anxiously at Patrick, afraid of saying the wrong thing. 'Is it . . . ? She looked from her father to Hugh Marston, her eyes wide with questions.

She was looking at the portrait of *Girl on the Rock*.

Patrick gave her a nod. He thought she had just provided him with the perfect introduction to what they had to tell his uncle – but he also thought they had better get him safely back in his chair first. 'Come and take a look at this, Sophie,' he said. 'Then we want to tell Uncle Hugh all about our trip, don't we?'

Sophie looked at the big picture with awe. 'Oh, Uncle Hugh!' she said. 'It's fabulous – they're all so beautiful! And Moonlight Flit looks so thrilled with her foal . . . so . . . so *loving*. How do you manage to show so much expression on a *horse*?'

'Oh, it's just technique and long practice,' said Hugh, but Patrick could see he was pleased. 'Animals have tremendous expressions, though not always facial ones – it's partly in attitude: mostly the way they move and stand – though I painted a pair of stallions fighting once and there was no doubt about the look in their eyes – but when I was in India as a young man before the war I remember seeing a very ancient carving in a cave at Mahabalipuram near Madras of a cow looking at her new-born calf, and being amazed at the impression of tenderness those ancient craftsmen had managed to convey in stone. I wanted to be able to do that too – in paint.'

'Won't it be an awful come-down painting me and Punchy

after Prince Haroun's beautiful thoroughbreds?' asked Sophie doubtfully.

'Not a bit of it. Punch may not be much of a looker but, like his owner, he has personality – and one day soon you *are* going to be beautiful, Miss Hammond. I've always said so.' He laughed at the expression of disbelief on her face.

'It'll be like taking pictures of a room in the middle of a make-over – before and after,' teased Patrick.

'Or a butterfly emerging from a chrysalis,' said Hugh. 'That's a better analogy. Now let's go back to the house, and we'll get Mrs Parkes to rustle up some coffee.'

Sophie exchanged a look with her father, and he felt relieved that they seemed to have recovered the companionable relationship of the last week.

When they had settled Hugh back in his favourite chair in the cluttered drawing room and Mrs Parkes had brought a pot of lethally strong coffee for him and Patrick, and a glass of Coke for Sophie, Patrick stretched out his long legs from the chair on the other side of the fireplace and Sophie curled up on the hearthrug.

'Sophie and Sam and I've been out in Corfu for a week,' said Patrick.

Hugh Marston lit one of his inevitable cigars. If Sophie expected a visible reaction at the mention of Corfu she was disappointed, but Patrick, who knew that his uncle had often won serious sums of money playing poker, was not surprised when he merely flicked a match into the fire and said casually, 'I haven't been there for years – it used to be a beautiful island, but I expect it's changed a bit since I knew it. Were you researching for the book or just having a holiday?'

'We had some holiday too but I was mainly researching for the book. Saphira got me an introduction to go and look at an old Venetian house near Kryovrisi and meet its owner. Does the name Vrahos mean anything to you?'

Hugh looked from Patrick to Sophie. 'From your faces I think you know that it does,' he said. 'What have you been digging up about my past?'

For answer Patrick felt in the inside pocket of his jacket and handed Hugh an envelope. 'I have a letter for you,' he said.

Hugh took it and stared at it for a long time in silence, as though by doing so he expected to see the contents without opening it. 'I never thought I'd see that writing again,' he said at last, just as Evanthi had said to Victoria. Sophie, who had not known that Patrick had the letter, could hardly bear the suspense.

'Aren't you going to read it?' she blurted out.

'Yes, of course.' But Hugh put the letter in his pocket. 'Most certainly I shall read it – but not just yet. I'm sorry, Sophie – forgive me for being so disappointing and dull – like Lear, I've become "a very foolish, fond old man" . . . and I need to be alone when I read this letter.' He concentrated on his cigar for a long moment, then said: 'I take it Evanthi Palombini is still alive then? Is she all right? Please tell me all you know.'

So Patrick told him about the visit to Vrahos, about his surprise at the old servant's reaction when she first saw him and then the obvious shock his appearance had given Evanthi. 'To start with I had this odd feeling that I'd met her somewhere before,' he said, 'but it wasn't till I saw a portrait of her as a young woman that things started to add up. It wasn't a particularly good painting – not in the same league as yours – but there was no mistaking the face. It was your *Girl on the Rock*, which I'd known all my life. Do you remember in February when I came over one day and you showed me the original sketch, which you'd suddenly come across?' Hugh nodded and Patrick went on, 'So it was fresh in my mind, you see, and it seems such an extraordinary coincidence that I should have met the original sitter so soon afterwards – especially when I had no idea of any Corfu connection before we went out there. You'd never told me the original story.'

Sophie opened her mouth to ask about the silver box and tell him more details about their visit to Vrahos but encountered a warning look from her father, who shook his head slightly. He wasn't sure how much of the story Evanthi might have revealed in her letter and decided not to mention at this stage either the silver box or Nafsica's hiding of the letters. If Evanthi wanted Victoria to bring the little box over, perhaps she intended it to be a surprise. He wished he'd taken fuller instructions about how much to say to Hugh and decided he must ring up Victoria and ask her to find out before he disclosed more than Evanthi intended.

While Patrick was talking about his lunch with Evanthi, telling him about Victoria, describing the guided tour she had given him, and of his own enthusiasm for doing a chapter of his book on Vrahos, Hugh got himself out of his chair again, limped over to the window and stood gazing out into the garden with his back to Patrick and Sophie.

'Believe it or not I've thought of Evanthi every day of my life for sixty years,' he said fiercely, as though daring Patrick and Sophie to disbelieve it, and as he looked out of the window he was not seeing his Yorkshire garden with the mass of daffodils in the long grass under the cherry trees, but a kingfisher sea and a small bay in a rocky landscape. He saw again a curious shaped rock like a crouching dinosaur on which sat a dark-haired girl dangling her bare brown legs in the water and laughing; he saw a young couple dancing to a wind-up gramophone in the Grand Salon of an old Venetian house under the stuffy gaze and gimlet eyes of portraits of Greek ancestors, while the strains of 'Night and Day' and 'Dancing Cheek to Cheek' echoed up to the coffered wooden ceiling. He saw the full moon making a silver path across the sea all the way to the coast of Albania and heard the night noises of cicadas and tree frogs, and the monotonous calling of a scops owl.

'I think you said something about the war intervening in a relationship?' prompted Patrick after a long pause, feeling the silence might go on indefinitely.

'Did I?' Hugh's voice sounded as if it came from a long way off and he continued to stare out of the window, in a private world. Then he gave himself a slight shake as though he was trying to surface from a dream. 'Well, yes, in a way I suppose it did,' he said. 'But something went very wrong between us that had little to do with war – and somehow we failed to sort it out before it was too late. I made one last attempt to set things right after the war. I went over to Corfu to try to find her but when I got there I discovered she was married with a child.'

'Did you actually see her?'

'No. I wrote one last letter – after many other unanswered

307

ones – but she still didn't answer it and I couldn't risk wrecking her life by turning up uninvited and causing trouble, so I came home and got on with mine. I've often wondered if I was right – or merely disastrously stupid. We had more rigid codes of behaviour over breaking up marriages in those days. I don't think it would happen quite like that today – different standards and customs and who's to say which is right? But I swore I'd never marry anyone else and I haven't.'

He turned round. 'Don't look so tragic,' he said to Sophie. 'I've had a terrific life in many ways – and a lot of fun. Ask your father! He would tell you that I haven't exactly been noted for wearing the willow, and many people would say I've broken every rule in the accepted code of conduct.'

'But not your personal code of honour,' suggested Patrick.

'I hope not that – no. Now cheer up, young lady, and stop that snivelling,' he said briskly, more touched at tender-hearted Sophie's brimming eyes and stricken expression than he was prepared to admit. 'You might get a permanent red nose – and then I won't paint you. No *Girl under the Apple Tree* to hang alongside *Girl on the Rock* – and that would be a loss to posterity!'

'Oh, Uncle Hugh,' she said, fishing in her jeans for a tissue. 'It's *so* sad – but it's not too late to put some of it right. Mrs Doukas is wonderful – perhaps not exactly beautiful any more,' she amended, honesty getting the better of her, 'but you can tell that she once was. And you could see each other again . . . think of that. She must want to meet you or she wouldn't have written.'

Hugh looked sadly at Sophie. 'Trying to put the clock back can be a terrible mistake. It might be better to hang on to the original vision. Old age creeps up so that you hardly notice the alteration in people you see all the time, but to see someone you have loved very much a long time ago and suddenly find them totally changed – that could be devastating. I'm not sure I could face it – for either of us. What if some depressing geriatric image overlaid my memories, and I couldn't get them back? What if she just saw a sad old wreck – a peg-legged one at that – and could find no trace of the young chap she fell for at a stuffy dinner party when he had the impertinence to flip a bit of bread across the table at her many years ago? That would be too much of a risk.'

'I think that's rather cowardly,' said Sophie indignantly. 'Think what you might be missing.'

'Uncle Hugh's been accused of a lot of things in his life but I don't think cowardice has ever been one of them before,' said Patrick.

Sophie stuck her chin out. 'Well, that's what I think it would be.' She felt she couldn't bear the romantic story, which had so captured her imagination, to have such a tame ending.

'That's a bit harsh, Sophie.' Patrick frowned at her warningly.

'No, not at all, she's right to say what she thinks.' Hugh gave her a reassuring look. 'She may even *be* right, and anyway, I value her opinion, but I need time to think about it, and I have a letter to read first. I know your eyes are burning a hole in my pocket, Sophie, and I promise I'll tell you more another time.'

'Would you tell me the story of what happened when I come and sit for you?'

'Yes,' he said. 'I'll do that. I'll regale you with the drama and immortalise your expression of burning interest – and you'll be the first person I've ever told.'

'And would you see Victoria if she came over?'

'Oh, I'd certainly do that,' he said. 'I'd very much like to meet Evanthi's granddaughter.'

And with that Sophie had to be content, because Patrick thought the old man suddenly looked extremely tired and decided they ought to leave him to have a rest.

When they got home Sam was practising putting while his small sister peddled busily round on her tricycle pretending to be his caddy. She had no idea what a caddy was, but Sam had told her it was a very important job, which meant retrieving all his golf balls from the little holes in the lawn and zooming round in a special car called a golf buggy. Posy adored Sam and, provided they were on their own, always behaved impeccably when she was with him; if she started to be too demanding, Sam simply sloped off and took no further notice of her – not Posy's idea of fun at all. She enormously admired her big sister and they occasionally had their times of happy rapport together too, but the quickest way to get Sophie's full attention was to do something really provocative, at which Posy was extremely accomplished.

Patrick dropped Sophie off at the front to join Sam, and Posy, abandoning her caddying duties, climbed into the car with her father while he went round the back to put it away.

'Hi there, Sophe. How did you get on then?' Sam asked.

'Brilliant. Dad gave Uncle Hugh a letter from Mrs Doukas and he was absolutely gob-smacked.'

'What did it say?'

'I don't *know*.' Sophie pulled an agonised face. 'He wouldn't open it while we were there. I nearly burst with curiosity!'

'I bet you did,' grinned Sam. 'So have you sorted out your sleeping arrangements?'

'Oh, that! Yeah – thanks for yesterday. Dad's had quite a cool idea, actually.' Sophie shrugged and tried to sound nonchalant – she did not feel ready yet to talk about her emotional reaction the night before, her feelings still raw. 'Bad luck for you Sam,' she said. 'I'm probably coming upstairs to invade your domain. Dad says Ellie and I can decorate the other big room. It'll be great.'

'Oh God,' said Sam. 'I suppose you'll hog the bathroom for hours and have Ellie up there shrieking and giggling with you all the time.'

Sophie gave him a sly look. 'You rather fancied Ellie last night. Don't pretend you didn't – I could tell.'

'Well, she's improved a bit since I last saw her,' said Sam defensively, 'and there was certainly room for it. I just thought she needed a bit of encouragement, that's all.' He changed the subject hastily. 'Guess who's been here for lunch.'

'Not the dreaded Bronwen?'

'Got it in one.'

'Dad will do his nut,' said Sophie. 'What did she want this time?'

'She and Mum were discussing some sort of protest about proposed improvements to the village hall.'

'Why should they mind about that?'

'God knows – except perhaps that Dad's on the Parish Council and has backed the idea. I don't think Bronwen gives a damn. I think it's just a general wind-up.'

'But what's it got to do with Mum?' asked Sophie.

'Nothing,' said Sam gloomily. 'Absolutely nothing, but anyone would think it was going to turn into an international incident. She's starting to talk in jargon-speak like a political tract. Know what I think?'

'No – what?'

'I think it will drive Dad straight into Victoria's arms – and I wouldn't blame him one bit.'

Sophie looked at her brother, appalled. 'I know what you said in Corfu – but it can't be that serious. Dad would never *leave* Mum. I know she's giving him a hard time at the moment – he's not the only one – but if Bronwen would just vanish, I'm sure they'd be OK again. You're not suggesting they might actually split up?'

'Bet a lot of your friends' parents have split up,' challenged Sam.

'Well, a few have – but the Marshalls – and, oh . . . lots of others are still together.' Sophie thought wildly of several of her friends whose parents had been divorced and looked extremely bothered. 'Anyway, Dad's *different*.'

'Course he's not. Grow up, Sophe,' said Sam – lofty, worldly-wise, Sam, teaching his younger sister a thing or two. 'Bet you anything he won't be able to resist ringing Victoria up soon,' he goaded. 'You see if I'm not right. I give it a week at the outside.'

Patrick coming out of the house to join them, wondered why Sophie suddenly looked at him as if he'd grown a tail and horns between the garage and the front door.

Later that evening, when Patrick said good night to his younger daughter, she was sitting up in Sophie's old bed looking like one of Raphael's baby angels.

'Have you had a lovely day, Rosy-Posy? What have you been doing?'

'Helping Mummy.' Posy oozed virtue.

'That was nice.' Patrick sat on the edge of the bed and wound one of Posy's fat, fair curls round his finger. 'What did you help her with? Were you picking flowers?'

'No. You guess.'

'Were you drawing . . . or cooking . . . or putting things away for Mummy?'

'NO! Silly Daddy!'

'I give up. What were you doing then?'

'We was takin' down the notices.' Posy's eyes sparkled.

'What notices?'

'They was gree-e-een,' said Posy, drawing the word out with relish. 'Lubbly gree-e-een notices.'

'What did you do with the lovely green notices?' asked Patrick, baffled by this information.

'We tared them up,' said Posy importantly, 'and then we throwed them away,' and she made tossing movements with her delectable chubby arms. She gave Patrick a cosy, conspiratorial look. 'It's a secret,' she said impressively. 'Mummy says it's Posy and Mummy's secret.'

Patrick planted a kiss on top of Posy's shining hair, every fibre of him alerted to trouble. 'Well, you tuck down now,' he said firmly. 'Who's coming to sleep next to you tonight?'

There was hardly room for Posy in the bed, surrounded as she always was by her collection of Beanie Babies. She was a tartar for discipline and the Beanies received the privilege of prime positions in the pecking order only according to her iron whim. Tonight Spike the rhinoceros and Stretch the ostrich were the lucky ones. Bones the dog was out of favour and was ruthlessly cast out on to the floor. Patrick was conscious of a fellow feeling for Bones, 'Get a grip, Bones. Stand up for your rights. Bite her toes,' he advised, sticking him firmly back on the bed.

'Night-night, then, Posy. Sleep tight.' And with that Patrick turned off the light, put a bedroom slipper in the door to keep it ajar – and went downstairs to confront his wife.

Chapter Thirty-two

The school that served Vrahos and several neighbouring villages was perched above the main road to Kérkyra. The approach was up steep steps, which led into the playground area in front of the small single-storey building that was all the school consisted of. Two old motor-tyres suspended from the branches of a plane tree provided swings, there was an ancient wooden seesaw, and hopscotch was marked out on the concrete. Inside there were two classrooms divided by a tiny office, outside were two old-fashioned privies of the squat-and-footplates variety – and that was it.

It was a far cry from the PNEU in Toddingham, with its up-to-the-minute equipment, football field, netball courts, school hall and computer room – not to mention all the trendy parents doing the school run in their Subarus and Discoveries. Victoria had lain awake worrying that she was doing the wrong thing by sending Jake to a little local school in a rural area of a Greek island for an unspecified length of time, where he would not only have to cope with unknown children and a completely different syllabus but a different language as well. She reassured herself by remembering how much she had liked the village schoolmaster, whom both Dora and Evanthi assured her was a brilliant teacher who achieved first-class results with the thirty children in his care – but a disapproving letter from her eldest sister-in-law had added considerably both to her anxiety about what she was about to do – and her determination to do it anyway.

Meriel Hawkins wrote to say how deeply distressed Richard's father was to hear that Victoria was intending to send Jake to a FOREIGN school. Did Victoria think this was wise – did she really think Richard would have been happy about it? Of course, she announced magnanimously, she realised

Victoria must still be upset – as indeed they all were (*Upset!* thought Victoria) – but Meriel begged her to think of Jake's future and put his interests first – hadn't he been through enough traumatic experiences? In Meriel's view it was high time he came home again – he'd already been abroad for a whole month and might LOSE TOUCH. If Victoria couldn't cope with him at the moment and wasn't ready to return to England herself, then Meriel and Stafford would be prepared to have him for a bit. It wouldn't be exactly convenient, of course – leading the kind of hectic lives they led! – but luckily she had good domestic help and there was nothing she wouldn't be prepared to do to put Richard's son back on the RIGHT TRACK. She added that she would be ringing up to discuss plans when Victoria had had a chance to think it over.

There were, of course, other options, the letter continued. Had she considered sending him to boarding school early? She knew Victoria was anti boarding school but it would surely be a better option than a Greek Village School!! She knew of an excellent prep school nearby which occasionally took children before they were eight to help out with family circumstances – fathers stationed abroad, for instance – and Jake would, after all be seven next birthday. 'Worth thinking about!!!' wrote Meriel, heavily underlined and with rows of the exclamation marks with which her letters were always littered. She seemed to be under the impression that if she used enough shriek marks, her interfering suggestions would somehow be rendered less offensive.

Back on track indeed, thought Victoria furiously, smarting at the insinuation that she was deliberately putting Jake through yet another damaging ordeal. And what right had Meriel to question whether Richard would have approved of any decisions she now took when he himself had deliberately abandoned his wife and child? Victoria seethed. She wondered if any of his family had the slightest idea that he might have taken his own life. She thought Meriel might have an inkling, but would certainly never admit to the possibility.

She had received many tiresome letters from Meriel over the years, but as they usually ended up being a source of jokes to share with Guy and Richard, they had often seemed hilarious rather than infuriating. Now there was no one to laugh with and this particular communication incensed her to such a degree that she felt like tearing it up and stamping on the pieces. She was determined to keep in close touch with her father-in-law, but wished she hadn't mentioned the subject of schooling in her last telephone call to him. Bill's views on education were confined to the conventions of his upbringing, though he was more tolerant – within narrow limits – than his manipulative, control freak of an eldest daughter. He had not been enthusiastic about Victoria's suggestion – she hadn't expected him to be – but neither had he seemed distressed; but then, she reflected, it was hard to tell with Bill Cunningham. She always had a shrewd notion what his opinions were likely to be because they'd never varied in all the years she'd known him, but she had very little idea about how he felt on an emotional level: he kept his heart firmly zipped in a secure inner pocket and preferred other people to do the same.

She supposed it was a case of like father like son – though she had never thought of it like that before. Every day seemed to bring her a new, unwelcome revelation about how little she had really known her husband. How can we have lived so closely together for eight years and turned out to be such strangers? she asked herself a dozen times a day. It haunted her. There had been a series of advertisements on television recently in which well-known broadcasters announced a forthcoming channel and then appeared to peel off their faces like rubber masks to reveal a different TV personality beneath. Victoria thought there was a nightmare quality to this particular gimmick and wondered how many more masks were going to be peeled off Richard. Would she ever discover the identity of the real person? Had Richard been unhappy all through their marriage?

It was a huge relief when Jake bounced back from his first day at school and showed no signs of being traumatised by the experience.

With Jake at school and no household responsibilities, she had more time on her hands – time to grieve, time to review the past and think about the future; time for loneliness to sink its sharp teeth into her and get a grip.

Despite her pleasure in her grandmother's company, she

wished the Hammonds were still at Petradi. It would have been fun to show them something of the hidden Corfu still existing beneath the tourist façade. She would like to meet Sam and Sophie in the Harbour Lights for a drink in the evening after Evanthi had retired for the night, or take Sophie on a shopping jaunt to Kérkyra and introduce her to the charms of the network of narrow streets and little squares with their old Venetian houses. After showing Patrick their own Vrahos treasure, she would like to have seen his reaction to the effect of golden light in the cathedral, reflected from the mass of sacred paintings, which seemed to cover every inch of wall and which always gave Victoria the feeling that she had actually stepped inside an icon. She kept noticing people and places, grand views or small details on buildings that she thought would make wonderful photographs and wished she could point them out to him. There had been a feeling of independence – almost a sense of adventure – about her friendship with the Hammond family. Most of her friends up to now had first been the friends of Guy and Richard and many of her activities had centred round them – but Patrick and his children knew nothing of her husband or her cousin and had, she felt, liked her for herself.

Thoughts of Patrick alone, however, were unnervingly disturbing and led down avenues where it seemed dangerous to venture. It is far too soon, she told herself, concerned at the way her mind kept returning to him; it is not six months since Richard's death and I can't get him out of my head . . . and anyway, she added to herself censoriously, he is married. She wondered if critical Guy would approve of him – and with this query came the acknowledgement to herself that Guy had for too long represented the yardstick by which she measured everything and everyone. But Richard has gone for good and Guy belongs to Francine now, she thought forlornly – and she had to face the fact that her long-time idol had toppled off the pedestal where she had placed him so long ago, and now she just couldn't trust him.

I must learn to make up my own mind about things and people, she resolved.

She had not spoken to Guy since the Hammonds' visit, though she knew from Evanthi that he'd gone off to the States for one of his periodic trips to see the editor of *Capability* and discuss ideas for future articles. Francine had gone with him, and was intending to see her family and friends in New York – and no doubt tell them the news about the baby, thought Victoria with an envious pang. She was full of conflicting emotions about Guy. It seemed wrong that he knew nothing yet about the discovery of Evanthi's lost love, but though part of her ached to tell him, she still felt too raw and hurt to attempt reconciliation.

Anthony and Toula rang often. She longed to see them but dreaded the trip to England that she must shortly undertake; dreaded the many decisions she would be called on to make, the confrontations she would be forced to have with Richard's family. It all seemed terribly threatening – then she remembered the proposed mission to visit Hugh Marston and felt a spark of excitement at the thought of it – and of seeing Patrick again. That would be something to look forward to.

She spent hours with Evanthi, piecing together more of her life: it was like listening to a gripping serial story on the radio, she thought, and couldn't wait to hear the next episode.

'So tell me what happened after Hugh had taken you out to lunch. Was Great-grandmother Palombini furious? When did you next meet?' she asked as she and Evanthi lunched together on Dora's delectable spicy meatballs in red sauce accompanied by tiny courgettes and fried potatoes.

'He followed me out to Italy,' said Evanthi. 'Of course I had hoped he would come – I *knew* he would – but all the same you can imagine my delight when he turned up in Rome. He pretended he'd come to Italy to do some commissions and it didn't take long before he really got some. And, yes, my mother was incandescent with fury. She set her face against Hugh from the start, not on grounds of personal dislike – at least not to begin with – but because she was so determined I should marry into a good Greek family. My mother, who had married a foreigner herself!'

'Wasn't she happy with your father then?' asked Victoria, helping herself to salad.

'Oh, it was no reflection on my parents' marriage. She adored my father but I have noticed that people who feel free to break

317

with tradition themselves can often be the most rigid in applying those rules to other people. She and Calliope Doukas had planned the match when Stavros and I were in the cradle – my mother was obsessed with the idea. She felt it would ensure the future of this house, and what my mother wanted she usually got.'

'You say it wasn't personal dislike to begin with,' said Victoria, 'did it become personal later?'

'Oh, it did indeed, yes. Because Hugh thwarted her, because he refused to kowtow to her, because she said he stole my heart and she knew she was powerless to change that. But he didn't *steal* my heart,' said Evanthi, her great eyes flashing: 'I *gave* it to him. My mother could be a fiercely loyal friend – but a terrible, unforgiving enemy. She didn't brook opposition and she was not above taking revenge. In many ways she was a very primitive personality – what she made Nafsica do over the letters was absolutely in character. I can't think why I didn't suspect it at the time – but I didn't.'

'So go on. Did Hugh just turn up and ring the doorbell?'

'He was too shrewd to do that – he would have been shown the door on my mother's orders. No, he enlisted the help of his aunt Lady Georgia – my godmother. Hugh could charm the birds off most trees if he tried, and he persuaded Lady Georgia that she must act as fairy godmother to us both. She had a great many influential friends in diplomatic circles and got him invited to social gatherings that my family were asked to as well, so it was difficult for my mother to stop us meeting. And all the time we fell more deeply in love. We were both completely bowled over. Every day was as exciting as the evening we met for the first time and yet we felt we had known each other for ever. No matter what else has happened to me in life, it has all been worth it just to have had that.'

Victoria was conscious of a stab of pure envy. 'Nonna, you weren't lucky later, but oh, you were lucky then,' she said wistfully, then added almost inaudibly, 'I was never hit by anything like that kind of *coup de foudre* . . . that passion. Perhaps I wouldn't even recognise it.'

Evanthi looked at her with compassion. 'You are still very young, *agapi*. Don't rule it out. It may yet happen – age has nothing to do with love, anyway. And I'll tell you one thing for certain – if it happens you will know.'

Victoria shook her head. 'I don't feel young any more,' she said soberly. 'I feel Richard has taken my youth with him.'

'Don't be utterly ridiculous!' Evanthi was at her most forceful. 'I have no sympathy for such a silly statement. I shan't tell you any more of my story if this is how it affects you.'

'I'm sorry – please go on.' Victoria, amused and comforted by her grandmother's astringent attitude, did not want to stem the flow of reminiscences. 'So what happened then?' she prompted.

'Hugh did some remarkable paintings and was becoming very sought after. You might have thought that would bring my mother round to him – it certainly made him a better prospect financially – but it had the reverse effect. I suppose it made her regard him as a serious threat instead of just a nuisance. Anyway, despite her efforts to prevent it we managed to see each other most days – and I showed him Rome . . . my city. He looked at all the wonderful treasures through my native Italian eyes and I looked at them as though for the first time through his observant artist's eyes. It was a revelation and a privilege. He used to say that we must train our eyes to *look* at things.'

'Oh, Nonna – that's what you always used to say to us! Guy and I were only talking about it the other day – saying what an influence it had been on us both. Patrick Hammond said much the same thing to me when he was talking about his photography and how he chooses what to take.'

'Ah well, no doubt he got that from Hugh too. Hugh was the sort of person who changed one's whole outlook – one of those special people who lights you up with their enthusiasms instead of killing you with boredom. A rare gift, indeed,' said Evanthi.

'You have it too.' Victoria looked at her watch and realised that she must go and collect Jake and Angelo shortly and that she would have to wait for the next instalment till another time. 'What did your father think of Hugh?' she asked, as she started to clear their plates away. 'Did he disapprove too?'

'Hugh and my father got on well – what little they saw of each other – but things were not easy politically, you understand, and Italian relations were strained with both England

and Greece. My father never approved of the *Fascisti* but he thought Mussolini had done some good things for our agriculture and the running of the country. Then Italy invaded Albania and he could see that trouble was coming in Europe. Ugly things were happening.' Evanthi stopped and shifted stiffly in her chair. 'Now you must go, *agapi*. I will have a rest – but I am beginning to feel so much better it gives me hope that I have a little time left after all!'

Victoria gave her hug. 'You hang on in there, Nonna,' she said. 'I couldn't cope with losing you.' And she went off to meet the boys and take them for a swim and an ice cream.

As she bumped down the drive, she hoped desperately that somehow they could find a way to hang on to the house without parting with the icon and that she would gather the strength and resolution to face the difficulties that lay ahead.

One evening, about two weeks after the Hammonds had returned to England, the telephone rang after dinner. Evanthi had already gone to bed but Victoria was still sitting on the terrace watching the fireflies flickering in the darkness and wishing she had someone to share the magic with. She went inside to answer it, glad to be jerked into action. She picked up the receiver. '*Herete?*' she said, automatically answering in Greek.

'Is that Victoria?'

'Yes it is. Who's that?'

'Hello, Victoria – this is Patrick Hammond here. I hope I'm not disturbing you?'

'Oh, hi there.' She had recognised the voice immediately but for some reason hadn't chosen to disclose the fact. 'You're not disturbing me at all – it's lovely to hear from you. I presume you got back all right then – how are you all?'

'We're fine. Sam's back at Newcastle and Sophie's started school again – but she can come home most weekends, which is nice.'

'I did like them both,' said Victoria. 'I shall be pleased if Jake grows up as nice as they are.' Then she said, 'We missed you all dreadfully after you'd gone.'

At the other end of the line Patrick's heart did a somersault.

'Well, I certainly missed you too – we all did – and Jake, of course. How's he doing? Has he started at the local school?'

'Oh, it's a wonderful success.' She was touched that he had remembered. 'He started last week and went off happy as a lark with Dora's little boy. It seems to be going really well.'

'You must be very relieved. It's always an anxiety when they start a new school and under your circumstances doubly so, I imagine.'

'I must admit I was terribly bothered – especially as I've had a lot of criticism from my in-laws for even thinking of it.'

'But now you feel triumphantly justified?' he teased.

She laughed. 'Well, I suppose I do rather – though it's early days yet. I've still got my fingers and toes crossed. Now do tell me what I'm dying to know – have you been to see your uncle yet and told him about Nonna?'

'I have indeed. It's part of the reason I'm ringing up – my excuse, if you like, because I really wanted an excuse to talk to you and find out how things were going for you.'

Victoria felt a rush of pleasure. 'Tell me about your uncle's reaction to the voice from his past,' she said, dodging a verbal response to the second of his reasons, but none the less happy. 'I've been absolutely dying to know.'

'He's told Sophie that he's replied to your grandmother. Did you know she had written a letter for me to deliver to him? Sophie nearly died of curiosity when we gave it to him because he stuck it in his pocket and didn't open it while we were there. Has your grandmother had his answer yet?'

'Not as far as I know – but posts can take ages out here. She hasn't said anything to me about it, but I didn't actually know she'd given you a letter – quite secretive of her, really. It shows how important it still is to her. After all the dramas over their original correspondence you'd think they might fight shy of letters as a means of renewing contact, wouldn't you?'

They chatted on, and it seemed wonderfully natural and easy to Victoria, as though she was talking to a friend of many years' standing.

'I must let you go,' Patrick said at last. 'I ought not to have rung so late, but I wanted to be sure of speaking to you and not just leaving a message with your grandmother or Dora. When are you coming over to England? I know Uncle Hugh would really like to see you – and I have a suggestion to put to you.'

'I do have to come back to deal with business affairs,' she said, intrigued. 'I haven't got a date fixed yet – to be honest I'm dreading it so much I've been putting it off – but now that Jake's settled so well I could easily leave him with Nonna and Dora and I'd love to meet your uncle too . . . so what's your suggestion?'

'Well, Uncle Hugh has to be in London in late June. The Crompton Gallery in Brook Street is holding a major retrospective of his work and they want him to be there for the private view. I have to be south then anyway to see my publishers, so I've offered to drive him up to London. We've got a small flat in Warwick Square so I'll stay there but I expect he'll prefer to be at his club where they always make a terrific fuss of him. If you happened to be in London you might like to come and meet him then? I'm hoping to persuade him to let the gallery borrow *Girl on the Rock* for the exhibition – it's never been shown before because he's always refused – then you could see why it made such an impression on me. I thought it might be easier for you than coming all the way up to Yorkshire to see him. What do you think?'

'Oh, I'd love that,' said Victoria. 'If you give me the dates I'll see if Richard's lawyer can give me an appointment that week and find out if it would suit my father-in-law as well.'

'Would you be staying in London?' asked Patrick.

'I shall have to go home to Baybury – it's one of the many things I need to do, but I'll probably spend a few days in London first. Richard and I looked on my cousin Guy's house as our London base – a second home – but he's just got married so I can't assume I can turn up any old time without warning like I used to. I'll have to sound his wife out – but I expect they'll have me.' She wondered what it would be like to stay with Francine and what it would be like, now, to stay with Guy. Could she face it?

'Wonderful,' said Patrick. 'Let me know if you can arrange your other dates to suit. That would be great. And,' he hesitated for a moment, 'could I take you out to dinner one night?' But before she could answer he rushed on, almost as if he were afraid she might refuse, 'Please remember me to your grand-mother and tell her she still casts a spell on Uncle Hugh. I'll be in touch again very soon.'

After he'd rung off Victoria felt as if she had been given an injection of new energy and resolution – and hope.

She realised that she had no idea what the Hammonds' telephone number or even their address was so she would have to wait till he made contact again. He hadn't mentioned his wife at all – would she be coming up to London too? There seemed to be a lot of things Victoria didn't know – but she didn't care because she knew one thing for certain: she would go to London at the end of June whether the dates suited Peter Mason and Bill Cunningham or not.

A few days after Patrick's telephone call, Guy rang to say that he and Francine were back from the States and to enquire after everyone at Vrahos. Victoria had not intended to speak to Guy yet and when Dora told her there was a call from England, assumed it was Patrick again. For the first time in her life she was conscious of disappointment at hearing her cousin's voice, while at the other end of the line Guy was disconcerted to hear the chill that was in hers.

They'd had a great trip, he said in answer to Victoria's distantly polite query: Francine's family had been thrilled about the baby, and the editor of *Capability* was renewing Guy's contract to write on whatever topic took his fancy for another year; another magazine wanted him to do a series of articles on flowers of different mountain ranges, which would provide a good excuse for some interesting trips.

'So how've you been, Vicky darling – and Jake? How's Nonna – tell me all the news.' Guy felt desperate to mend his fences with the little cousin he'd always loved but taken for granted.

Despite her confused feelings about Guy, Victoria couldn't resist telling him about the Hammonds' visit and the intriguing link to Evanthi's past. Guy was immediately intrigued. Typically, he knew all about Hugh Marston's paintings, of which he said he was a great admirer. Discussing anything with Guy was like rummaging in a fascinating lumber room, thought

Victoria: you never knew what you might come across because he was such a repository of miscellaneous information.

'Nonna wants me to meet him,' said Victoria. 'Patrick Hammond says he's having a London exhibition soon.' Out of habit she heard herself asking: 'Could I stay with you if I came over for it?'

'Of course. That would be fantastic. When do you want to come?'

'I'm waiting to hear the exact date. Are you sure that would be all right with Francine?'

She heard him call out: 'Darling? Victoria wants to know if she can come and stay with us?' and Francine's voice replying: 'Sure – tell her just to say the word. I need loads of advice about the baby. Come for as long as she likes – bring Jake – whatever. Say I shall look forward to it.'

That's generous, thought Victoria. She means to be welcoming. I must try to respond to her in kind – but the prospect still seemed threatening.

For his part, Guy immediately wondered what Patrick Hammond was like, because on hearing Victoria's studiously casual mention of him he had known with absolute certainty that there was something going on between them and he had felt all his hackles rise.

Chapter Thirty-three

❖

In the weeks following Patrick's return from Corfu, he and Rachel had a monumental row – two monumental rows to be exact – which resulted in Patrick banning Bronwen from coming to the house or having any contact with Posy. He had been overwhelmed with anger to discover that during his absence Rachel had not only been engaged in a campaign to take down any statutory notices that had been posted outside properties in the area for which planning applications had been made, but had taken Posy with her. It seemed to Patrick such a completely pointless exercise anyway – not apparently targeted against any particular building, just vaguely against the Planning Department of the Council, since Rachel had gone round removing green notices anywhere she saw them in quite a large area. When challenged as to what, exactly, she objected to, Rachel would only say vaguely that the protest group were against 'petty bureaucracy' and muttered about rights of the individual. Patrick looked at her in baffled incomprehension.

'You told me the other day that individual rights had to be sacrificed for the greater good. We live in exceptionally beautiful countryside – it's rightly a preservation area. Would you want anyone to be able to put up unsuitable, hideous buildings wherever they liked?'

Patrick couldn't contain his exasperation; his voice rose in anger. 'You made enough fuss about that frightful extension the new owners of the Glebe House wanted to build last year and were pleased it wasn't allowed. Now you seem to be against the fact people even have to ask permission. Have you lost the plot completely, Rachel? This protest group would be laughable if I didn't suspect the ideas behind it were so unpleasant. I can't stop you making a complete fool of *yourself*, but what the hell did you mean by taking Posy with you?'

'Please don't shout at me, Patrick.' Rachel stood up, looking defensive.

'Then answer my question. How *could* you involve Posy in acts of meaningless vandalism? What sort of behaviour is that teaching her for the future? It's monstrous of you.'

'Oh, don't be such a pain, Patrick!' Coming from Rachel, who had always been a stickler for the proprieties and anxiously conventional in all her views, this enraged Patrick even more.

'That's rich coming from you,' he said, looking at her in disbelief.

'Hang on,' said Rachel defensively, 'Yvonne was away, you'd gone jaunting off to Corfu, Bronwen was busy and I had no one to leave Posy with. What was I supposed to do, for heaven's sake?'

'Not go round the countryside tearing down notices, for a start. If you're short of things to do get yourself a job, if that's what's wrong – but don't take Posy on any of these crazy protest outings. I'm warning, you Rachel, I've had it up to *here* with your contrariness. You've been completely impossible ever since Posy was born and we've all tried to make allowances up to now – but this is something else. We absolutely cannot go on like this, for all our sakes.' And he turned on his heel and left her.

Rachel was taken aback. There was something about the way he had looked at her – exasperation, bordering on dislike – that was new, and gave her pause. What did she really want from her marriage? Rachel wasn't sure herself; she decided to consult Bronwen.

But there was worse to come.

Some years earlier Hugh Marston had set up savings accounts for Sam and Sophie and, more recently, for Posy too. Every time he sold a picture he paid something into their accounts. Sam had been allowed to use some of his money on his gap year before he went to Newcastle, and Sophie was hoping to do the same, though Patrick insisted they should both earn some of the money for their travels too. Only recently Hugh had given Patrick three cheques and Patrick had asked Tania to pay them in to the children's accounts.

A few days later Tania came in search of him. 'What would

you like me to do about Posy's share of the money?' she asked. 'I've paid in Sam and Sophie's but you didn't tell me you'd closed Posy's account.'

Patrick looked blank. 'I haven't closed it. What are you talking about?'

'They rang from the bank to say Posy's account had been automatically closed because all the money had been withdrawn from it.'

'There must be some mistake,' said Patrick. 'I've got to go into Knighton this afternoon so I'll look into it.'

When he got back he found Rachel at her desk in the small sitting room, which they always used when they were on their own. He tossed her a printout of the closed account.

'What does this mean? There was five thousand and seventy-five pounds in Posy's savings account a month ago and it's all been withdrawn. Only you or I could have done that – and it certainly wasn't me.'

Rachel looked disconcerted. 'Oh – that,' she said with an attempt at nonchalance; not looking at him; busying herself with papers on her desk, shrugging her shoulders.

'Yes,' said Patrick. '*That*. So what's the explanation?'

'I couldn't know they'd close the account – that's ludicrous. I shall complain. It's only for a temporary thing anyway. I needed the money for something.'

'*You needed the money*? For what?'

'It's none of your business – and I've only borrowed it anyway.'

'Don't give me that!' said Patrick furiously. 'Of course it's my business. You had no right to take Posy's money. What the hell have you done with it?'

'It was just a loan for someone.'

Patrick looked at his wife with horror. 'Don't tell me you've lent Posy's money to that woman?' he exploded.

'If you mean Bronwen, what if I have?' Rachel tried to sound indifferent but only succeeded in sounding sulky. 'It's in a good cause. And I've just told you, Posy'll get it back eventually.'

'*Eventually!* What's that supposed to mean? There's a nasty word for what you've done. It's called embezzlement. You bloody well cancel the cheque you gave Bronwen NOW.'

Patrick picked up the telephone and handed it to Rachel. 'Go on – get your cheque book now, look up the number of the cheque and ring the bank.'

'I can't,' said Rachel, 'I didn't write her a cheque. I gave her cash. Stop getting at me, Patrick. It's only a *loan*, for God's sake!'

'A loan of something that wasn't yours to lend! Why on earth did you have to use Posy's savings anyway? You've got your own money and we've got a joint account.' Rachel did not meet his eyes and turned her head away. Two bright spots of colour flamed on her cheeks giving her normally pale, almost translucent, skin the look of painted porcelain, like the face of a Victorian doll. Her mouth set in an unattractively tight little line as though it had been zipped up. To Patrick her expression told a tale.

'You've lent Bronwen money before, haven't you?' he said accusingly. 'Possibly a lot of money, but at least your own – and now you've used Posy's because you've run yourself short and didn't want me to find out. Oh, Rachel, what the hell have you got yourself into?'

'You're making a huge mountain out of a molehill,' said Rachel coldly.

Patrick felt as if he was looking at a stranger. He was so angry with his wife that he could hardly trust himself to speak. 'What has happened to you?' he asked at last. 'Does our marriage mean nothing to you any more? You seem prepared to put everything we've achieved together at risk. You've made it fairly plain lately that you don't care for me any more but don't you care about our family either? Have you any idea how much you hurt Sophie by what you did over her room? Now you seem prepared to defraud Posy. You wouldn't have done either of those things once. Bronwen appears to have cast a complete spell on you. It's intolerable. Are you going to ask her to return the money or am I going to have to do it – or is the possibility of getting it back already a lost cause?'

'Of course it's not a lost cause! Don't *fuss* so. I'll talk to Bronwen about it myself if you're going to be so paranoid about it.'

Patrick walked towards the door. 'I'll give you two days to sort it out and get the money returned,' he said icily. 'I can't stop you seeing Bronwen, but I'm telling you, Rachel, I don't want her in this house, I don't want her anywhere near Posy and I don't want Posy taken on any more cranky expeditions.'

He stood for a moment in the doorway. Then he said more gently: 'Rachel – are you *frightened* of her? Has she got some sort of hold over you that I don't know about? If she has, tell me now and I promise I won't blame you any more and I'll help you all I can. But I must know.'

It was a defining moment. Then Rachel said disastrously, 'Don't be utterly ridiculous, Patrick. Bronwen is one of my closest friends – one of the most important people in my life. Of course I'm not afraid of her. Just because you don't like her, you choose to blame her for anything and everything that doesn't suit you – and anyway, let *me* tell *you* something . . .'

But Patrick didn't wait to hear what that was. 'Suit yourself. But on your own head be it,' he said over his shoulder as he walked out of the room.

He went into his study, closed the door and sat at his desk with his head buried in his hands.

Then he took a decision: later that evening he would make a telephone call to Corfu.

Rachel was tempted to take Posy straight to Bronwen's house just to spite Patrick, but she was sufficiently unnerved by his anger not to do so; also, since Yvonne had now returned from her holiday, she could hardly use the excuse that she had no one with whom to leave Posy, so she drove down to the Old Chapel House on her own, despite the fact that though Bronwen reserved the right to turn up at Rachel's house without warning, she discouraged unannounced visits to her own house.

Bronwen had just finished giving a class on self-assertiveness to a mixed group who were leaving as Rachel drove up. They were a meek-looking bunch, who all appeared terrified of Bronwen. It didn't look as if the assertiveness training had taken effect yet; certainly none of the class seemed prepared to practise on their teacher the theories she had been trying to instil into them.

'See you all next week then. Same time – and please bring

notebooks and pens next time and wear loose clothes.' Bronwen ushered them out.

'Oh, Bronwen – I don't think I'm going to be able to manage Wednesday next week,' said an overweight young woman in tight floral shorts that did nothing to minimise her hips. 'I'm afraid my husband wants me to go to London with him.' She gazed anxiously at Bronwen. 'Will it matter if I miss one class?'

Bronwen gave her a scornful look. 'It's entirely up to you,' she said. 'If you can't make the commitment then I can't do it for you.'

Floral Shorts looked like a rabbit hypnotised by a stoat. 'I'll see what I can do,' she said. 'I'll ask my husband what he thinks . . .' She glanced hopefully at Bronwen for signs of understanding but none was forthcoming.

Bronwen rolled her eyes at Rachel, expressing her opinion on clients in general and subservient women in particular.

'Hello, Rachel – I didn't expect you today,' Bronwen, wearing a white tracksuit and clutching her trademark bottle of water had a length of scarlet silk bound round her head so that her wild hair was temporarily invisible; her feet were bare. One of the things that Rachel found both fascinating and alarming about her friendship with Bronwen was that you never knew from one day to the next who she was going to be – Lesbian Rights Upholder or Man-eating Vamp; Nun or Stripper; dedicated Vegan or rapacious Carnivore. Today the look was not so much fierce High Priestess as ascetic Spiritual Director crossed with PT instructor.

'That one won't be back,' prophesied Bronwen, nodding at the departing posterior of the woman in the flowered shorts, and added scathingly. 'She'll be too scared to tell her husband that there'll be no refund if she cancels the rest of the course and too scared of me to tell me she's not coming any more.' She looked pointedly at her watch. 'I'm afraid I've got a client coming shortly but you can come in for ten minutes if you like. You look very agitated, Rachel. What's up?'

'I'm sorry to burst in on you but I need to see you. I'm having trouble with Patrick about the money. I know it's absurd and he's being a pain but he's found out about Posy's savings account and he's absolutely livid.'

'So?' Bronwen raised an eyebrow.

'So I'm most terribly sorry, but I'm going to have to ask you to return the money . . . just for the moment. I'll try to think of something else.'

'That's a pity,' said Bronwen sharply. 'I thought you were really with me over this.'

'Oh, I am, I am,' said Rachel hastily. 'It's just that I suppose I shouldn't really have borrowed from Posy, and Patrick's being tricky about it. Will getting the money back be a problem?'

Bronwen hesitated for a moment, and then shrugged. 'Oh, I don't think so – but I'll need a little time. I'll see if I can get it back for you in a couple of weeks.'

'Patrick did say something about two days . . .'

'Two days is impossible. Get real, Rachel! Tell him I'll try to have it in a week,' said Bronwen.

'You're not angry with *me*, are you?' Rachel looked distinctly anxious.

Bronwen imitated Rachel's rather high, breathless-sounding voice: '*Oh, Bronwen, please don't be cross,*' she mocked. Then she added in a more conciliatory tone, 'Surely a week would be no problem?'

Rachel flushed. 'Well, I suppose a week can't matter,' she said doubtfully. 'It isn't as if Posy could possibly want it. I thought it might be a good idea to let Patrick cool off for a bit, so I'm thinking of going down to my parents for a few days. Perhaps I could get my father to lend me five thousand? That would save a lot of bother. It's worth a try and he needn't know what it's for – I don't think he'd be too keen on the protest group idea. He's a bit conventional – ex-army and all that.' She laughed nervously, and threw an appeasing look at Bronwen, who shrugged.

'Well, I'll have to hope you can fix something,' she said coolly. 'See you when you get back then.'

'I suppose I'd better be off if you're busy.' Rachel was unwilling to go but knew Bronwen would be irritated if she stayed. 'In case Patrick wants to know, what did you actually *do* with the money, Bronwen?' she asked. 'Did you open an account for the group? Have you banked it already or what?'

'Don't you trust me then?' Bronwen was at her most sphinx-like.

'Of course I do! It was just that I wondered why it was so difficult to get hold of the cash when I only gave it you the other day . . .' Rachel's voice trailed away. She hated it when Bronwen was in one of her scornful moods and lately they seemed to be getting more frequent. Rachel, who had been indulged and protected all her life, was not used to being made to feel either foolish or superfluous. At the start of their friendship Bronwen had made her feel wonderful but now she was sometimes disconcertingly dismissive, though she still seemed to want to be involved with Rachel's every move. Recently she had taken to hinting that she thought it was high time Rachel took a long cold look at her marriage and asked herself if she couldn't find a more fulfilling relationship.

Bronwen looked at her watch again, and Rachel got back into her car. She drove home in an anxious state of mind. She had always taken Patrick's devotion for granted. Ought she to be more conciliatory towards him – or had they come to a parting point?

Patrick felt a sense of relief when Rachel departed to her parents, taking Posy and Yvonne with her. At least it would get them both away from Bronwen for a bit. He planned to pay Bronwen a visit himself and have a few things out with her, and thought it would be much easier if his wife were out of the way. But he had to admit to himself that this wasn't the only reason he was pleased to see her go. He knew he had some big questions to face and despite all his resolutions on the aeroplane to try, for the children's sake, to make his marriage work, there was nothing about his homecoming to encourage him to stick with his wife.

He was working on the book one morning when Tania came in to say that Philip Marshall was on the telephone.

Phil came straight to the point. 'Maggie told me you wanted to know if I could dig up any information through my legal contacts about that Richards woman Rachel's got so involved with. I've been asking a few questions. You're not going to like what I've come up with.'

Patrick groaned. 'I knew it! She's a dreadful woman – and she really seems to have got her claws into Rachel. I wouldn't trust her further than I could spit. She's managed to get Rachel to lend her quite a large sum of money – not, I think, for the first time.'

'Well, get it back damn quick if you can. Bronwen Richards has got a record for this sort of thing. She's a con artist and a fraudster who got a suspended sentence some years ago for similar offences and was lucky not to go inside. Also I gather her dodgy boyfriend is suspected of drug dealing and the police have been watching him. Between you and me, I think they may be planning a raid on Bronwen's house next time he shows up – not to mention the fact that she shouldn't be practising as a therapist. Her qualifications were perfectly genuine once but she's been struck off the register. She's using a different name now, of course. Get Rachel out of her clutches – Bronwen Richards is bad news and you don't want her round your kids. Oh, and, Patrick . . . don't say anything to Rachel about the drugs at this point. If the police are planning something it wouldn't help if Bronwen was warned. Not that I'm suggesting Rachel would say anything if you asked her not to,' he said unconvincingly, 'but you know how easy it is to let something slip by mistake.'

Patrick's heart sank. 'Oh my God! That's really serious. I've known for ages that Bronwen was extremely bad news but this is much worse than I thought. She can be horribly plausible, but I hadn't picked up on the drug aspect. That's extremely worrying. At least I've got something to go on as far as Rachel's concerned over the money aspect. God, what a mess! Thanks, Phil. I'll keep in touch.'

Later that day, when Philip got home, he said to Maggie: 'What do you think the odds are of Patrick and Rachel's marriage surviving?'

'Not good,' said Maggie, who was sitting at the kitchen table surrounded by garden catalogues and graph paper, drawing up plans for a client's new herbaceous border. 'The odds wouldn't be brilliant even if no one else was involved, but Ellie's let it slip that Sophie thinks Patrick's fallen for someone else – and if he has, it won't just be a jolly little flutter, it'll be really serious. Rachel's a fool.'

'She's also unbelievably selfish and one of the most tiresome women I know,' said Phil, exasperated. 'I've never understood why Patrick's put up with her all these years. I couldn't have done it.'

'I'm not quite sure what to make of that,' said Maggie, laughing at him. 'Do I take it you'd get rid of me without a qualm if I got up your nose, but that luckily you haven't found me quite that infuriating yet?'

'Oh, you can be infuriating too,' said Philip with a grin, 'but you're not even approaching Rachel's league in tiresomeness.' And he gave his wife a very loving kiss on her wide, slightly crooked mouth that always looked as if it was about to break into a smile.

After four days, Rachel telephoned Patrick to say that she had decided to stay on with her parents for a bit longer. They were not getting any younger, she said, and added that one never knew how much longer their good health would last. If Patrick thought this decision had less to do with his in-laws' age than the fact that so far there had been no sign of any money being returned by Bronwen, he didn't say so. He had a chat with Posy, who was clearly revelling in grandparental adulation and made no comment to his wife about her arrangements. He told her that he would have to go up to London on business, but only for one night, and would speak to Sophie to let her know there would be no one at home on Wednesday in case she rang. Had Rachel told her that she was with the grandparents? Yes, of course, said Rachel huffily – that is, she hadn't actually spoken to Sophie but she'd left a message with the school. The house telephone was permanently engaged, she complained. But not, said Patrick coldly, Sophie's mobile, which she was allowed now that she was in the sixth form. He thought it was too bad of Rachel not to have spoken to her elder daughter. She seemed to be allowing the feud over the bedroom to simmer on.

He left the car at York station and caught the early train to King's Cross. He had originally planned to spend the night in the flat, but when he got to London he discovered that his meeting the following day had been cancelled so he decided to return home the same evening. The extra time would give him a chance to visit Hugh next morning.

He wasn't late getting home; it was only about nine when he turned into the drive, having had a highly satisfactory day and seen both Saphira Winterton and the publishers to discuss not only the present book but also future projects. He drove straight round to the back of the house. There was no barking from the dogs as Tania would have been in earlier and taken them home with her for the night – an arrangement that was wonderfully useful. As he unlocked the door there was not the usual beeping from the burglar alarm, but neither was there any sinister message flashing in the little window above the keypad indicating an intruder or a false alarm. All was in order. Tania must have forgotten to set it, he thought, and felt ashamed of his momentary annoyance because this was unlike her – though she was breezily laid-back over many things she was usually punctilious about security. He made a mental note to mention it to her the following morning and went on through into the hall. And then a sixth sense alerted him to something unusual and he froze.

Nothing was out of place and no doors were open. The grandfather clock ticked away as peacefully as it always did and there were no extraneous sounds, but there was some quality in the silence that made him suddenly certain he was not alone in the house. He stood in the dusk without turning on the lights – listening intently, and found that he was holding his breath. It seemed as if the whole house was holding its breath with him. He must have waited for a least a minute before he flung open the door to his study and turned on the lights.

Bronwen Richards was standing by his desk.

Chapter Thirty-four

They stared at each other for a moment in silence. It would have been hard to know who was the more startled.

'What the hell are you doing here?' asked Patrick.

'Hi there, Patrick – I've come to pay you a surprise visit,' said Bronwen coolly, making a lightning recovery. 'That's not a very friendly greeting.'

'It wasn't intended to be. How the devil did you get in?'

Bronwen looked at him provocatively. She leaned back against the desk with a display of nonchalance that might have won her an Oscar if it had been filmed – but it was not lost on Patrick that with one hand behind her back she was surreptitiously trying to close one of the drawers of his desk.

'Please stand away from my desk or I shall call the police.' There was a flicker of anxiety on her face, quickly replaced by her usual arrogance. 'I repeat,' said Patrick, 'how did you get in?'

'Oh, I wouldn't call the police – they might be too interested in some of your wife's recent activities,' Bronwen's voice was silky sweet, but she stepped away from the desk, leaving the top drawer slightly open. 'You can't accuse me of breaking in because I used the key Rachel gave me herself ages ago – as I've often done before. In case you're wondering, I also know the code for your alarm.'

'The hell you do!' Patrick wondered how many other times she'd snooped around, what she might have seen and what she might have taken. 'I suppose it's too much to expect that you've come to return the money you conned Rachel into lending you?'

'I didn't con her. Rachel wanted to lend it. But I gather you want it returned. I've told her it will take a week or so to get the cash back.' She shot him another provocative look. 'You'll just have to be patient, Patrick.'

'I don't have to be anything of the sort. The alarm code will be altered and I shall have the locks changed tomorrow – and may I have that key back now, please?'

She laughed mockingly, throwing an unmistakable challenge and an invitation at him. 'Would you try to get it off me by force?' she asked softly.

'No, Bronwen, I wouldn't. I'd leave that to the police.'

'That might be a mistake. I could tell them a lot of things your wife's been involved in lately and I don't think you'd like that much, Patrick.'

'I don't suppose I should like anything you've involved her in,' retorted Patrick, 'and for Rachel's sake I hope I don't have to call them – but don't make any mistake: I will if I have to. And it would give me great satisfaction to see you arrested. Give me that key now and then go.'

'And if I don't?'

For answer Patrick walked over to the desk, picked up the telephone and started dialling.

Bronwen took the key out of her pocket and tossed it at him. He put his foot on it, and held the receiver out so that she could hear the ringing tone before he replaced it.

'That was wise of you,' he said, pocketing the key. 'And please remember I won't hesitate to call them again – only next time I'll make sure I don't ring off before I get through – Rachel or no Rachel. She may have torn down a few notices, and signed her name to some nonsensical petitions connected with your bogus protest group but I know her too well to think she'd knowingly get involved in anything really serious. Whatever you've got on her must be very minor – and far more incriminating to you than her.'

They eyed each other across the room. Patrick was tempted to tell her that he knew about her record but, mindful of Philip's request, didn't want to alert her to police suspicions.

'We could deal with each other better than this, Patrick. I've always thought so.' Bronwen came slowly towards him. 'I admit I didn't think you'd be here,' she said. 'Rachel told me you were in London – but now that you are here it seems a pity not to make the most of it.' She stopped in front of him, suggestively fingering a button on her shirt and stood there –

too close for comfort. 'I could give you a great time,' she said. 'You're far more interesting to me than your wife – you always have been.'

'I'll give you one minute to be out of here,' said Patrick icily, 'and don't ever come back.'

He held the door open. She gave him a long speculative look, but he stared her down, determined neither to retreat from her nor show the slightest flicker of response. Then she shrugged her shoulders. 'Oh, well – your loss,' she said. He followed her into the hall and escorted her to the unlocked front door in silence. He watched her get into her red car and drive off, very fast, down the front drive.

It was only after the tail-lights of the car had disappeared from sight that he realised he'd failed to discover what she had come for – and whether or not she had found what she wanted and managed to take it away with her right under his nose. He could smell her musky perfume lingering in the air. There had been something sinister and unpleasant about the episode that made him very anxious for his wife. He might not feel for Rachel as he used to do, but he still felt protective towards her. He also felt sullied by the encounter with Bronwen.

He looked all through his desk – in particular in the drawer he'd seen Bronwen fiddling with – but all appeared to be in order. He never kept cash there anyway – though he knew there was some in the safe in the cellar; he checked to see if the safe key was missing – but it was there in the centre drawer. What could she have been after? He went through the house, checking for signs of disturbance, but couldn't detect anything untoward anywhere. In the sitting room the flap of Rachel's bureau-type desk was closed up and all the drawers were neatly shut: it was all apparently just as Rachel, a dedicated tweaker of cushions, aligner of ornaments and closer of cupboards would have left it. All the same, he must get her to check that there was nothing missing as soon as she returned.

The answering machine was flashing and he pressed the button to hear his wife's voice.

'Patrick – it's me. I know you're in London tonight but just to let you know I've decided to come home on Friday. I'm going to leave Yvonne and Posy down here for a bit longer and they can come back by train later. My ma seems keen to have them for a few more days and you've been saying for ages that we ought to have some time on our own – so I hope you'll be pleased. Night then – see you Friday.'

But Patrick's heart sank. He found himself not at all keen for his wife's return.

Down in Surrey, in her parents' trim house near Chobham, Rachel had encountered unexpected criticism from a source that had hitherto been dotingly compliant of her every whim. Her parents liked their son-in-law; indeed, though they might not have admitted it, they'd been quite relieved when he'd taken the responsibility for their difficult daughter off their hands, because Rachel had always led them a terrible dance. They had initially been disappointed that, once she was married, their clever daughter had never shown any further inclination to pursue the career possibilities that had cropped up during her time at Oxford, or made apparent use of her undoubted brains, and perhaps they would never have considered anyone quite worthy of their only child, but over the years they had come to think Patrick came close to qualifying for his position. Recently, however, they had not been blind to the tensions in the marriage and had hoped Rachel's obsession with her third child would lessen to a more normal state of affairs as Posy grew older. Like Patrick, they had initially thought the new therapist, on whom Rachel had become so dependent, had wrought something of a miracle in her approach to motherhood; but this gratitude had waned as they witnessed their daughter's emotional pendulum swing from one extreme to the other. They were fearful about what might happen if it suddenly swung back. They admired Patrick's loyalty to his demanding wife but were anxiously aware that his forbearance was wearing threadbare.

They were also troubled about the effect that Rachel's dissatisfied carping might have on her older children and thought the entrancing Posy was in danger of becoming a perfect pain. But this awareness had been tempered by their habitual fear of putting Rachel under pressure – a fear that had its roots in the anxiety they had felt for her since the day she had so unexpectedly appeared late in their married lives, after they had given up all hope of conceiving a child.

After several nervous conferences they decided for once to express their views – to which Rachel's reaction had been predictably prickly. In reality she paid more attention to their warnings than she was prepared to let on. Despite Bronwen's frequent suggestions that she should abandon her marriage, she wasn't sure she wanted to part from her husband. She drove north in the expectation that she would only have to show him how much she still needed him to be welcomed back with open arms. She wasn't sure she actually wanted to *be* in his arms any more but she certainly required them to be ready to receive her.

On the way home Rachel decided to call on Bronwen to test her reaction to this proposed *rapprochement* with her husband. If she explained that it would be in Bronwen's financial interest to get Patrick on side again, surely she would agree? The thought of Bronwen's disapproval of any of her actions made Rachel nervous. Also, without the stabilising influence of either Patrick or Yvonne, she was not finding the two-year-old passions of her small daughter easy to handle.

The red car wasn't parked outside the house so she assumed Bronwen must be visiting a client. However, since it was already after one o'clock and she knew Bronwen rarely made appointments after twelve on a Friday, she decided to wait. She left a message on Bronwen's mobile, turned the radio on and settled down to listen to the news. After half an hour when there was still no sign of her it occurred to Rachel that Bronwen might have driven round to the back without her noticing, so she got out of the car and went down the side of the house. She glanced through the windows of the main room as she passed and then peered in.

What she saw – or rather didn't see – stopped her in her tracks. The room was completely empty. There was not a stick of furniture to be seen – not a picture on the walls. Rachel couldn't believe her eyes. She dashed round to the front again, peered in all the windows and rattled the door. Nothing. She went round the house, looking for an open window, but they were all were closed. The house appeared to be deserted. The back door was locked and she had to stand on tiptoe to see into the kitchen window.

She nearly jumped out of her skin when something soft pressed against her leg from behind. It was Bronwen's goat. The door to her shed was propped open and she had been turned loose. Rachel peered cautiously into the shed but there were no clues there. She can't just have *left*, thought Rachel wildly – not without saying a word to me. Her heart started to thump. Perhaps the house had been broken into – but there were no signs of any break-in. Was Bronwen all right – could she be lying somewhere in a pool of blood having been attacked? Rachel didn't feel strong enough to force an entry and go inside. She sat down on the doorstep because her legs felt so shaky. I couldn't manage my life without Bronwen, she thought. I *need* her.

She looked up to find Bronwen's nearest neighbour, toothless old Mrs Boothroyd from the row of cottages up the hill, standing in front of her.

'You'll be wanting the Richards woman, I dare say,' said Mrs Boothroyd. She had her bedroom slippers on and her stockings were rolled down round her ankles, exposing a terrifying display of varicose veins writhing round her legs like copulating snakes.

'Where is she?' Rachel looked up hopefully, averting her eyes from the unlovely legs, thankful that someone – even Mrs Boothroyd – had appeared on the scene.

'Well, you'll not find her,' said Mrs Boothroyd with satisfaction. 'She's flitted.'

'You mean she's moved?'

'Like I said – she's flitted.'

'Did she say where she was going?'

'She didn't say owt,' Mrs Boothroyd, clearly enjoying the situation hugely, sniffed disparagingly. 'But then I didn't ask her owt neither,' she informed Rachel, adding self-righteously, 'Me, I was allus one to mind my own business.'

'When did she go?' asked Rachel, ignoring this patent untruth.

'It were Wednesday night – I know it were Wednesday because that's my Arthur's darts night and I happened to be having a look to see if he were coming up lane when I seen her getting into that rubbish car of hers. She took off like she was Jehu in the Bible come to drive in the Knighton Hill Climb,' said Mrs Boothroyd, allowing her imagination full rein. 'Then that fancy fella of hers – Milo or some such name – he come last night with a couple of lads in a great white rent-a-van and flits all her furniture. They was at it best part of the night. We could hear them ferkling about inside, but they never come out nor said nowt to us.' Mrs Boothroyd sounded outraged at this lack of consideration on the part of Bronwen's lover and his minions.

She settled back to her tale. 'Whiles later they starts loading up van, and my Arthur, he looks out of bedroom window and he says to me: "By jingo, our Doris – they'll not get all that lot in there" – but they did.' Mrs Boothroyd paused for breath. '*Then*,' she said impressively, 'this Milo drives off in the small hours. So now they've gone – lock, stock and barrel – and I don't suppose we'll be seeing hide nor hair of them again. My Arthur allus said she were a fly-by-night sort of person as would bugger off one day without a word of warning. And she has.' Mrs Boothroyd looked triumphant.

'You don't know if they left a forwarding address with anyone, do you?'

'Not with me she hasn't.'

'Who would have a key to the house?' asked Rachel, realising that she had no idea if Bronwen had actually owned the house, and if not, to whom it might belong.

'Couldn't say, I'm sure.' Mrs Boothroyd having used up Rachel's potential as a listener, lost interest in her and slopped off uphill in her bedroom slippers.

Rachel felt frantic. She fetched her mobile and dialled first their home number at Wytherton House, where the answering machine kicked in, and then the phone in Patrick's study. To her great relief he answered.

'Patrick? It's me. Oh, thank goodness you're there. I'm at Bronwen's house. Something awful has happened.'

'Have you had an accident? Just tell me calmly.'

'She's gone. Bronwen's gone.'

'But are you all right? Are you hurt? What's happened?'

'Yes . . . NO. No, of course I'm not *hurt* . . . but I'm not all right either.' Rachel sounded hysterical. 'I've had a dreadful shock. The house is completely cleared out. Mrs Boothroyd saw them

drive away. Oh, Patrick, I couldn't cope without Bronwen –
what shall I do now?'

'Get in the car and drive straight home, I should think. I'll see
you shortly,' said Patrick unsympathetically, and rang off.

Patrick had been standing at his desk when the telephone rang.

He had got hold of the security firm and had the code number
on the alarm and the locks on the doors changed – thoughts of
shutting empty stable doors came to mind. He was not looking
forward to the confrontation he intended to have with Rachel.
Would she be able to throw any light on what Bronwen had
been looking for? He went over the scene again and again in his
mind. And then suddenly a thought struck him. What if instead
of trying to take something out of his desk drawer, she had in
reality been putting something back? What if she had already
used the key to the safe and had been about to slip it back in the
drawer when he had walked in on her? He went into his study
to get the key and it was at this moment that Rachel had
telephoned. Once he'd established that Rachel was unharmed,
his first reaction to her information was not surprise so much as
relief that Bronwen should have departed – but this was
followed swiftly by irritation at Rachel's querulous voice. He
was well aware that she wanted him to treat her as if she had
just been dealt a major personal tragedy but he couldn't help
comparing her spurious helplessness to the memory of Victoria,
struggling with real tragedy. He put the key in his pocket and
as he heard her car on the drive he went to meet his wife.

He recognised her expression as soon as she got out of the car
– nobody could make herself look more wan and pathetic than
Rachel when she required sympathy, but Patrick was not in the
mood to dispense it.

He gave her a statutory peck on the cheek, and she leaned
against him. 'I'm so upset,' she said. 'I've had such a horrid
shock.'

'Yes, you said – well, brace yourself because you may be
going to get another.' Patrick pushed her upright. 'Come with
me,' he said. 'We have to make a little trip down to the cellar.'

'To the cellar – *now*? Whatever for? I need to lie down.'

'It won't take long. We have to check something first, you can lie down for as long as you like after that.' He was not going to tell her about Bronwen's visit until they had inspected the contents of the safe: he did not trust her to give truthful answers if she thought Bronwen was under suspicion. She followed him to the stairs that led to the cellars, keeping up a stream of complaints.

The large old-fashioned safe was hidden behind a door at the bottom of the steps. Patrick inserted the key. He noticed immediately that the wad of notes that he kept for emergencies was missing – about three hundred pounds as far as he remembered. Near the front of the safe were several old leather cases mostly containing items of jewellery, which had once belonged to Patrick's grandmother, and which Rachel occasionally wore for grand events; they had been earmarked for the future ownership of Sophie and Posy.

'We'll just check everything together,' said Patrick.

'Oh, for heaven's sake!' Rachel exclained, but something about his expression stopped her from arguing.

The first two cases they opened were in order. The third was empty.

'What was in this one?' asked Patrick – although he knew.

'That diamond and emerald brooch of your grandmother's – the one that unscrews and becomes a pendant and two clips. I've never worn it because it's so heavy. Odd it isn't there – I know it was in its box not long ago because when I was showing all the jewellery to—' Rachel broke off.

'When you showed it to who?' demanded Patrick sharply.

Rachel looked flustered. 'Look what is all this?' she asked. 'Are you suggesting we've been burgled?'

'Yes – that's exactly what I'm suggesting. Who did you show the jewellery to, Rachel, and why?'

'Well, certainly not to any burglar!' said Rachel sarcastically.

'So – who then? Come on.'

'Actually I showed them to Bronwen – if you must know.' Rachel looked defiant but Patrick could tell she was rattled. She went on with an unconvincing show of bravado, 'She'd been showing me some of her own Celtic pieces – silver bracelets and crosses and things – Bronwen's always been interested in jewellery design – and I happened to mention that some of your family bits were beautiful and offered to show them to her. That's all.'

'Did you bring her down here to the safe to show them?'

Rachel shrugged. 'I may have done.'

'Did you or didn't you?'

'Oh, *Patrick*! Don't bully me! I can't remember . . . well, all right, yes, I suppose I did. So what?'

'So you might be interested to know that I found your friend in my study at ten o'clock on Wednesday night when I got back from London. I thought she was taking something out of the drawer but I now realise she was actually putting the safe key back – having used it. Funny that all the cash and the most valuable brooch have disappeared from the safe, and that Bronwen appears to have done a bunk. Did you know she had a record?'

'Don't be ridiculous! You're making it up just to spite me.' Rachel spat the words at him.

'I'm afraid I'm not. Phil found out.' Patrick looked at his wife with a mixture of pity and exasperation. 'He ran a check on her for me. I'm going to telephone the police now. I should have done it when I caught her – but for your sake I didn't.'

Rachel caught at his arm. '*No*, Patrick, *no*! You mustn't! You're making me ill. There must be some perfectly good explanation!'

He shook her off as gently as he could and headed for the telephone in his study. 'I'm sorry, Rachel, my mind's made up. I may be too late already if she's done a runner – fool that I am.'

Rachel ran after him. 'I shall never speak to you again if you ring the police,' she screamed hysterically. 'I shall . . . I shall leave you, Patrick. I really mean it.'

She waited for his instant rush of contrition, for him to reason with her, reassure her. It did not happen. Unbelievably, he took not the slightest notice – and this time when he dialled the police he waited for an answer.

After he had spoken to them, Patrick rang Philip Marshall, who immediately offered to be present when they came to take a statement from Rachel – just in case there was any what he called 'awkwardness'. Patrick had accepted thankfully. He couldn't help feeling sorry for his wife, but at the same time he realised sadly that his feelings of pity no longer included love, and that she quite obviously had ceased to care for him.

Philip arrived just before the police.

At first Rachel announced that she wasn't going to speak to the two officers from the local CID but Philip managed to convince her that this was a very unwise attitude. Luckily they weren't much interested in the activities of the protest group, about which, to Rachel's astonishment, they had been well informed on the local grapevine. They seemed to think Bronwen had formed it more as a means to manipulate Rachel and the other groupies than because she was involved with any cause – but her other activities, such as the stealing of the brooch and the money and possible drug charges, were another matter.

Rachel had been shaken to discover how much the police knew about Bronwen, but in answer to polite but searching questions insisted that she had no idea where Bronwen might have gone. Neither Patrick nor Philip got the impression that the police found her vehemence very convincing. Patrick didn't feel convinced himself – but was thankful that the police seemed to regard Rachel as a foolish, gullible woman, rather than an accomplice, and made it clear that they had bigger fish to catch. Rachel was by no means the first client Bronwen had taken for a ride, they said; she had done similar things before under a different name. She was no longer licensed to practise as a therapist and should never have treated Rachel – or anyone else in the area. They said they would let Patrick know if there were any developments about the brooch and might need to ask Rachel further questions.

'Just let us know if the woman tries to get in contact with your wife at all, will you, sir?' said the sergeant as he climbed into his car.

As the police drove away, Philip said he'd better be getting back to his office too.

'I don't think you need worry too much about any repercussions over Rachel's petty activities,' he said as Patrick walked out to his car with him, 'but don't hesitate to ring me if there's any difficulty – and try to drum it into her that she'd better not have any more contact with Bronwen Richards.'

'I certainly will! I can't tell you how grateful I am to you for coming, Phil. You and Maggie are a huge support. Life's a bit tricky on the home front at the moment, as you know – and you've been fantastic to Sophie too.'

'Sophie's a great girl. By the way, Maggs suggested you might like to come over for a meal at the weekend as the girls are home? We're on to do either of the school trips, so perhaps you or Rachel could give us a ring about arrangements for collecting them tomorrow?' Philip privately thought it would be a real turn-up for the books if Rachel went to fetch the girls.

'Sure. I'll let you know this evening – when the dust has settled a bit,' said Patrick making a rueful face. 'Bye then, Phil – and thanks.'

He went back to find Rachel furiously hurling armfuls of clothes into her car.

'What on earth are you doing? I came to see if you wanted me to help unload the car,' he said, 'but it looks more as if you're packing it up.'

'I told you I'd go if you called the police in. I'm leaving you, Patrick,' she announced dramatically.

'Where do you intend going?'

'I'm going straight back to my parents where at least I seem to be more appreciated than I am here. I've had enough – and you can't stop me.'

'I wouldn't dream of trying to stop you,' said Patrick coldly. 'I've had more than enough too. Have you given any thought as to what I'm to tell Sam and Sophie? Sophie's coming home tomorrow morning. She's going to wonder where you are. Had you forgotten it's her long exeat or doesn't that matter to you? She's got a sitting with Hugh in the afternoon – but I don't suppose you're interested in that either.'

'Tell them anything you like. Tell them the truth – say that without Bronwen to help me through everything I can't cope with family life any more.' She flung the words at him.

'Oh, don't be so bloody dramatic. And don't think you can just take Posy away from home indefinitely either because I won't stand for it. For heaven's sake, go and sort yourself out, Rachel. We'll review our situation in a few weeks when we've both had a chance to cool off and think about the future.'

Patrick turned on his heel and walked back into the house. He knew Rachel expected him to stand on the doorstep and watch her go and had no intention of giving her that satisfaction.

All the same he was sufficiently concerned about her welfare to ring his mother-in-law and warn her of her daughter's return and ask her to let him know when she had arrived safely. He felt truly sorry for Norma and Howard Ingfield and thought it was hard for them in their late seventies to be landed with a full-blown Rachel crisis.

As he went into the kitchen to make a mug of coffee before going back to work he was saddened to find he felt nothing but relief at the prospect of his wife's absence.

Chapter Thirty-five

When Sophie appeared in his studio on Saturday afternoon, Hugh Marston could tell at once that there was something amiss. He thought she looked wretched – not at all the bright companion who usually bounced in and whose visits had always caused him much amusement and enjoyment. He was too old a hand to ask what the matter was straight away, he just gave her a delighted greeting and an extra big hug, and called for Mrs Parkes to bring Sophie some of her home-made lemonade after the hot ride over from Wytherton House.

Mrs Parkes, not so reticent, took one look at Sophie and asked what she'd been doing with herself because she looked right peelie-wallie, and added with a disapproving sniff that she blamed junk food and all these exams they did nowadays. 'Os and As and what-have-yous – what a fool carry-on! No one's ever asked me for any certificates of education – which is just as well,' she said with a cackle, 'because I haven't got any and I've managed very well without them, thank you! There, you drink that up, young lady, and have a slice of my gingerbread – that'll put roses back in your cheeks.' There were not many troubles, in Mrs Parkes' opinion, that couldn't be alleviated by a bite of her home cooking.

'Thank you, Mrs P. You make the best lemonade in the entire world,' said Sophie.

'Now don't you go tiring her out with all this posing lark,' said Mrs Parkes to her employer, 'or I shall have something to say to you.' With this dire threat she withdrew and left them to it. She thought Sophie's visits did Hugh a great deal of good. He seemed to be having a particularly good summer. She had noticed an energy about him lately that had been missing for some time. If it hadn't been for what she always referred to as his wooden leg, she'd have said he had a new spring in his step.

'I've turned Punchy loose in the paddock, Uncle Hugh. Is that all right?'

'Fine. You must have had a beautiful ride over. My favourite time of year, with all the beeches at their best. Did you come by the river?'

'Umm, we did – there's a perfect fallen branch for Punch to jump and all the bluebells are out in Wytherton Wood. It smelled heavenly. Can you still get down there to fish?'

'I can on the quad. Don't tell Mrs P., though – she doesn't like me going to the river on my own any more. Thinks I'll drown if I catch a fish, or tip the bike over on that steep bit getting there.' He grinned at Sophie.

'Have you ever tipped it over?' asked Sophie. She and Sam had always adored going on the back of Hugh's bone-shaker of a quad bike, roaring across the fields at full throttle and taking the most impossible gradients at breakneck speed. Now that he couldn't ride any more he said he still had to have some physical excitement in his life. He had never let his artificial leg stop him from partaking in any of his favourite sports but, since the hip operation two years previously, he'd had to give up hunting and shooting and content himself with fishing, which he could still manage. The quad bike represented his much-valued independence.

Hugh shot her a conspiratorial look. 'I did have a little spill the other day,' he admitted. 'I suppose I was at rather an unsafe angle. Anyway, the quad tipped over and my leg shot off! I had to crawl down the hill and fetch it, but luckily there was no one about to see and I managed get the quad up and put myself back together again like Humpty Dumpty – nothing worse than a few bruises so I didn't have to confess to my keeper, bless her!'

Sophie giggled. 'I won't tell her,' she said. 'I think I'd better not tell Dad either – he worries about you too.'

'Good. We'll share our secrets then. Now hop up there and I'll get to work while you fill me in with all your news.' Hugh indicated the small platform in the middle of the studio and Sophie went and leaned against the chair, which had to stand in for an apple tree. Patrick had taken some stunning photographs of her in the orchard at home and blown-up versions of these were stuck up on the studio wall. Even Sophie, constantly dissatisfied with her own appearance, had been secretly pleased with them.

'You promised you'd go on telling me your love story,' she reminded him.

'So I did! That was rash of me. Just fill me in with your news first and then I'll go on with my saga. How's school and what are you up to this weekend? Anything special on?'

'School's OK. This is my last exeat before my exams so I'm home for a week. Dad and me are going to the cinema with the Marshalls one night, and Ellie's coming over to me – otherwise nothing much. Pottering about with Punch and doing some revising . . .' She hesitated, and seemed to become extremely absorbed in fiddling with the mass of narrow bracelets on her wrist. 'Did you know that Mum has gone?' she asked in a low voice.

'Gone where?'

'Only to Granny and Grandpa at the moment. But I mean gone like in left,' said Sophie. 'Like in she's *left* Dad.'

'No,' said Hugh, looking extremely surprised. 'I didn't know. Are you sure that's right, Sophie? Who told you?'

'Dad did. He collected Ellie and me from school and after we'd dropped Ellie off he said there was something difficult and important he had to tell me. He said I was old enough to know the truth and he felt he should be honest with me. Then he said Mum wouldn't be at home at all this exeat. She came home yesterday and then just went off again. I mean, she knew it was my half-term and everything.' Sophie's voice wobbled ominously and Hugh could see she was struggling with herself. Then she went on in a rush: 'Dad says Mum's sort of flipped because that ghastly Bronwen woman's done a bunk with some of her jewellery or something – but he also said that he and Mum haven't been getting on for ages and they're going to have a trial separation.'

Sophie struggled with tears before she could go on speaking. 'They both need a bit of space from each other – oh, and a lot of stuff about how if they do split it will all be very civilised and he'd never try to cut us off from Mum and . . . blah, blah, *blah*,' said Sophie angrily, wrapping a rather grubby handkerchief round her thumb, which had started to bleed where she'd picked off a bit of loose skin. 'That's what *all* parents *always* say at first, but it's not what happens. I know that from some of my friends at school. 'I mean, I know Mum can be difficult, but . . .' She looked at Hugh with troubled eyes. 'I do love her,' she muttered.

He wanted to say that it was no good carrying on with the sitting in her present state; he didn't want her anguished expression to creep into the portrait, but he felt she would be more likely to open up and talk if he at least made a pretence of continuing to paint. He said carefully: 'That must have been an awful shock for you. What do you feel about it, Sophie?'

She gave a gulp, then blurted out: 'Oh, Uncle Hugh, I feel perfectly terrible because I think it may be my fault.'

'Fiddlesticks,' said Hugh briskly. 'How could it possibly be your fault? Of course it's not! What on earth put that into your head?'

Sophie told him about their homecoming and the row over the rooms. 'I made an awful fuss,' she said miserably. 'I was so hurt and so jealous of Posy, who's Mum's favourite by miles. And I felt furious with both Mum *and* Dad – even though it wasn't his fault – and I said awful things. I told Mum I hated her – and now I think I may have made her go away.' Her voice rose to a wail.

'What absolute rot.' Hugh filled in a bit of background. He thought Sophie looked very near to an edge – too near. He felt desperately sorry for her but decided too much sympathy might tip her right over. 'Listen to me, Sophie,' he said firmly. 'When a relationship between two people comes unstuck, *they* are responsible for what happens, not anyone else. There may be other factors involved, of course – but what happens, how they deal with it, is up to the two of them. It's never entirely one person's fault anyway – and passing blame to and fro's a fruitless exercise. I understand how tough this is for you but if your mother walks out on her marriage because of a row with a bolshy teenager or because some nut has nicked her jewellery then there must have been things wrong with the marriage anyway that have nothing to do with either of those incidents. And if your father lets her go it can only be either because he doesn't feel he *could* save the relationship, *or* – and I'm really sorry about this, Sophie – because he doesn't any longer want to save it. It may be very painful, but you have to accept that.' He smiled at her, and added in a lighter voice: 'Don't be a drama queen, darling girl. It'll be very sad if they split but it won't be the end of your world and certainly won't be your fault. Better to part than destroy each other. Stop beating yourself up and let them get on with it.'

'Do you think they might get back together?' she asked, calmed by his robust words despite herself.

'I wouldn't like to bet on it. They *might* – but not because of anything you do or don't do. I have to say I'd put it at six-to-four against. It's been obvious there was trouble brewing for a very long time. They've grown apart – don't ask me why. Sadly it happens, and you're old enough to know that. I'm surprised their marriage has lasted as long as it has – they don't have enough in common.'

'When you and Victoria's grandmother split up you weren't either of you responsible for it,' objected Sophie. 'It was all the fault of her domineering mother and that wicked old maid who threw such a megga wobbly when she saw Dad.'

Hugh shook his head. 'I grant you we had some bad luck,' he said, 'and I've learned a lot in the last weeks that I never knew before – but I still think we were ultimately responsible. We were young and hot-headed and angry and proud and – like you've just said about yourself – very hurt. If Evanthi and I'd kept faith in each other, our split needn't have happened.'

'But stealing your letters – that was just *so* unfair,' said Sophie, wondering how much Hugh and Evanthi had communicated since Patrick had delivered the letter.

'Life *is* unfair. You'll think I'm an awful old cynic but the sooner you realise that, the better – which doesn't mean one shouldn't do one's damnedest to try to make it more fair. It's easy to moan on about injustice, but I'll tell you something else: moaners are no bloody fun to be with! No fun at all!' He cocked his head at her and she gave him a watery smile.

'OK, Uncle Hugh. I'll try not to be one.' Then she said suddenly: 'Do you think you'd have stayed together if you'd married – you and Mrs Doukas?'

'I don't know, Sophie,' he said soberly. 'That's a fair question.

I've often asked myself the same thing. But I'd like to think so – though the fact remains, we fell at the very first fence.' Then he added with a gleam: 'But no other woman's come even near matching her in my view, and I've been able to make quite a few comparisons!'

Sophie blew her nose violently. 'Go on with your story,' she said. 'Tell me about your split.'

'Where had I got to?' he asked, glad that he'd diverted her.

'Where you'd followed her out to Italy, and had a wonderfully romantic time looking at ruins by moonlight and painting and having secret assignations to dodge her mother. I think you were going to go out to Vrahos.'

'Ah – Vrahos! Now there's a magic place. Evanthi adored it. She was steeped in it: in the island, the estate and the family history. I'm glad she's been able to make her life there – that's some compensation. If she'd married me I don't think that would have happened; her mother would have seen to that. Cut her out of her will or something. What did you make of the old place?'

'I thought it was like walking into a picture in some old fairy-story book – all dusty and mysterious. Full of secrets and cobwebs and clanging bells. You wouldn't be surprised to find the Sleeping Beauty snoozing away on a sofa, or a dragon setting off a smoke alarm. Was it like that when you were there?'

Hugh laughed. 'Well, certainly no cobwebs – I suppose there was an army of hidden retainers to sweep them away. Floors and furniture and everything gleamed and the whole house smelled of beeswax and lavender. If I ever smell real beeswax polish it takes me right back there even now. But I know what you mean – there was always a timeless feel about it, as though nothing had altered over centuries, and I dare say not much has changed even now.'

'I don't know,' said Sophie doubtfully. 'I think you might find it all a bit sad now if it was that well cared for when you knew it. I adored it and it's still quite grand in a way – but it's awfully dilapidated. No hidden army – just the granddaughter of the old woman who hid your letters; she has to do *everything* and the whole place is falling to pieces. Some of the ceilings look as if they might collapse any minute – they sort of sag like

354

school beds. Tell you what, though – Dad's taken the most stunning pictures so you'll be able to see it again. So when did you first go out there?'

Hugh sighed. 'Well, I couldn't stay on in Italy indefinitely and Evanthi's mother carted her off on some trip to relations – largely to get her away from me – so we planned to meet in England later with the help of my aunt. And we wrote to each other. We wrote every day, and we got to know each other even better like that. This *texting* and e-mailing and telephoning you all do is not the same as proper love letters – not as permanent; not as *revealing*. I can see that it's wonderfully speedy – but it's not the same. We shared our thoughts and hopes with each other – and fears too. Not just about our own future – we never doubted we'd be together – but about the dark shadows that were hovering over Europe. Evanthi wrote wonderful letters. She poured the words out on paper full of dashes and under-lining and exclamation marks. It was like talking to her. I still have all her letters.'

'And did you draw her lots of little pictures in yours like you've always done for us?' asked Sophie.

Hugh smiled. 'Of course,' he said.

'How awful she never got them!' Sophie could hardly bear it.

'Oh, she got those early ones all right. And with each letter we fell more in love. We managed to meet a few times – I went over to Rome again and she came to England and stayed with my aunt, and I got her up to Yorkshire once or twice. My father'd been deeply disapproving about our friendship, muttering that her diplomat father must be a bloody fascist if he worked for Mussolini. I'd warned Evanthi that my father could well say some very outspoken things to her about Italy's invasion of Abyssinia and might not seem too friendly – but of course he fell for her at once. It only took her one evening to charm his boots off! We didn't hear any more about "Mussoloving Eye-ties" after that – not in her presence anyway.'

'What about your mother?' asked Sophie. 'Dad says he always adored his grandmother. She sounds lovely.'

'Oh, my mother was an angel,' said Hugh. 'She and Evanthi got on splendidly. You get your looks from her. I've always thought so.'

Sophie was enchanted. 'So then what?' she asked.

'Then we had a bit of luck. Evanthi's father was sent to Washington, and naturally her mother went too. Evanthi managed to persuade them that she ought to go to Vrahos to be with her grandmother who always went there at weekends in the summer.' Hugh gave Sophie an amused look over his half-spectacles. 'Of course, I went out to Corfu too but her grand-mother just thought it was nice for her to have a young friend in the neighbourhood and her mother didn't discover about it for sometime. Look – I'll show you something.' He went over to a cupboard and eventually pulled out an old sketchbook. 'Ah – this is what I'm looking for. Let's go into the garden. It's too good a day to be in all afternoon and I think I've done enough standing for the moment.'

They sat outside on a seat together and he showed her the sketchbook. There were drawings and watercolour sketches of places and people, plants and animals – melons growing on a compost heap; a cat stretched out in the sun on a doorstep; an old man riding on a donkey while his wife trudged along behind; sheep with bells round their necks under the olive trees; tall cypress trees standing sentinel against an impossibly blue sky. There were places Sophie recognised: the bell tower of the chapel at Vrahos; the great front doors with the lion-mask knockers; the view from the terrace. There was one loose sketch Sophie particularly liked of the old house perched dizzily on the rock, its Venetian pink plaster standing out against the bluest of skies. A marmalade cat, which obviously didn't suffer from vertigo, was stretched out along the balustrade, sunning itself and Sophie thought you could almost feel the heat beating down.

'Where did you paint that from?' she asked. 'From a boat?'

'Ah, that's a bit of a cheat – artistic licence, if you like. I'd have had to be hovering in a hot-air balloon to get that exact view,' said Hugh. 'You can see the house like that from a boat, of course, but not so close. I did that from memory after the war.'

'You ought to send that one to Mrs Doukas,' said Sophie.

He looked as if an idea had struck him. 'I might just do that,' he said.

Turning a page Sophie came across a sketch of a comely, round-faced young woman with a basket on her head.

'Oh there's Dora!' she exclaimed. Then: 'But it can't be . . .'

'Dora? I don't remember any Dora . . . no, that's Nafsica – who later sabotaged our romance so successfully.'

'Goodness! You wouldn't recognise her now. We only saw her once but she looked like a skinny old witch.'

'This was sixty years ago, don't forget. She was a pretty young woman then.'

'Did you realise she was against you?' asked Sophie.

'I don't think she was originally. She thought it was very romantic and acted as our go-between during that late summer and early autumn. Tourists flock to the island in the high season but September and October in Corfu are incomparable – fresh mornings and evenings, but never too hot, and the sea a perfect temperature for swimming. There is a breathtaking quality to the light at that time of year and I've never seen more spectacular sunrises and sunsets anywhere.' Hugh glimmered at Sophie: 'I have special memories of moonlit evenings too and even stars reflected in the water. Nafsica helped to cover up for us – to hide our meetings from Evanthi's grandmother. There was only one extremely unreliable telephone at Vrahos – pretty public too, it was, in the hall – and Nafsica used to take messages when we made arrangements to meet. Evanthi trusted her completely. I suppose it must have been after we announced our determination to get married that Contessa Palombini really put the frighteners on Nafsica and the guerrilla warfare started. The Contessa was a very powerful and manipulative woman. The staff in both Italy and at Vrahos were absolutely terrified of her – and of course Nafsica approved of the Contessa's own choice of bridegroom for Evanthi anyway – Stavros Doukas – a young lawyer who'd grown up with Evanthi. He had a distinguished international career after the war. I used to read about him in the papers from time to time.'

'Did you ever meet him?' asked Sophie curiously.

'Only once. He came to call when I was there – a stuffed shirt of a chap who looked as if he'd swallowed a poker – though I believe he was very brave in the war. In my youthful arrogance that autumn I remember thinking he wasn't much of a threat – so wet you could have shot snipe off him. I was wrong.'

Sophie could imagine the scene. She thought her great-uncle

must have been irresistible. 'Bet he didn't think the same about you, though!' she said.

'Perhaps not – but he had the last laugh all the same, didn't he?' He added, 'Probably the only time he laughed in his life. Fella certainly wasn't a bundle of fun.'

Sitting in the late May lushness of his green, very English garden, with wallflowers and pheasant-eye narcissi scenting the air and blackbirds and thrushes singing from the rhododendrons, he took Sophie back to the dryness and heat of late summer in Corfu – a long-ago Corfu with few made-up roads or tourists; no luxury modern holiday villas with swimming pools; no concrete block hotels – no lager louts. Through his eyes she saw two young people, passionately in love, revelling in the freedom of an unsophisticated, rural way of life. They had spent two months exploring the island, often on foot but sometimes sailing round its rocky coast in an old caique, discovering secret bays; picnicking on the little island of the swallows that Evanthi loved – swimming by moonlight. Dancing.

'Evanthi danced the best charleston of anyone I knew,' he said. 'I was pretty hot stuff myself before I got this peg leg, but she was sensational!' He was amused at Sophie's look of disbelief.

All the time, wherever they went, he told her, he had sketched and painted – for pleasure but also as a way of building up a portfolio. And all the time, with the optimism and naivety of youth they had been convinced that despite her mother they would be together for the rest of their lives.

And then he had painted Evanthi – Evanthi sitting laughing at him from the dragon-shaped rock in one particular little bay they came to think of as their special place. 'The best portrait I've ever done or ever will do,' Hugh said. 'I have high hopes of this one of you – perhaps the last one I'll paint – but it won't match that one. I've had many offers for it over the years but I've never even contemplated parting with it.'

Sophie felt tears pricking at her eyes. She couldn't bear to think he might never paint another portrait.

'Of course we were lotus-eating,' went on Hugh, turning the page to reveal a watercolour sketch of scarlet hibiscus against a whitewashed wall, 'and that's an irresistible diet – but not one you can live on for ever. I asked Evanthi to marry me and she accepted. I knew we wouldn't get instant approval but I wanted to show her parents I was serious and I was full of youthful confidence. My work was beginning to be successful; I was getting commissions and my paintings were starting to sell. Even my father was becoming resigned to the idea of me having a career as an artist, and I'd been offered a one-man exhibition in London the following year. I wanted to speak to her father before it was discovered – as I knew it surely would be – that we'd more-or-less spent late summer together at Vrahos. Not that I actually stayed in the house itself – we'd never have got away with that. I rented an apartment in Kryovrisi.'

Hugh paused. Sophie felt he was talking to himself as much as to her now. She was dying to know if they'd become lovers, but couldn't quite summon up the nerve to ask. 'So . . .' she prompted. 'Go on.'

'Evanthi didn't want me to speak to her parents so soon; she knew better than I did how her mother would react – but I was adamant. I knew her father was going to be in Rome for a few weeks in October and I caught the ferry to Brindisi and went to ask his permission to marry his daughter. Of course he refused – but he was reasonable. He said that if we would agree not to see each other for at least six months and if we were still of the same mind the following year, then he might – *might* – reconsider. Of course he was well aware that when Evanthi was twenty-one she wouldn't need his consent legally but she was still only nineteen. But all hell was let loose when he told his wife he'd left us a chink of hope.'

'She sounds a frightful old bat,' said Sophie.

'She was a beautiful woman with passionate views on absolutely everything, who was used to getting her own way. She could be very charming, but she lacked Evanthi's great warmth and humour and I didn't trust her an inch. I rushed back to Corfu – with the Contessa, intent on removing her precious daughter from my contaminating presence, hot on my heels! Evanthi wanted us to run away together, but I didn't want her to have that scandal hanging round her neck – attitudes to women were very different then from what they are

359

today – you've no idea – and especially in Greece. We exchanged solemn vows and we had two little silver boxes made in Corfu town to our own design to symbolise our love and commitment – for ever. I still have mine,' said Hugh. 'It's in the drawing room – you must have seen it hundreds of times – but I don't suppose Evanthi has hers any longer.'

Sophie opened her mouth to tell him, and then shut it again, remembering that Victoria was going to bring the box over. 'So go on,' she prompted him

'Then I went back to England and we started the letter writing again. You must remember that all this took place against the threat of war between England and Germany – and, of course with Italy too; between my country and Evanthi's. That period of my youth is now a history lesson to your generation. This was just after the Munich crisis when our Prime Minister, Neville Chamberlain, negotiated with Hitler for what some people thought was a brilliant reprieve and others considered was a dishonourable peace. Anyway, war was postponed. My father had a lot of contacts in the army and the polo-playing world, and through him I got a marvellous commission to go to India for six months and paint the polo ponies belonging to a maharaja pal of his – ponies and palaces and wild life in every sense! Right up my street! It was a wonderful chance to travel round India too and I was convinced that if I could make my name as an artist, Evanthi's mother would come round eventually – but of course it was while I was in India that the missing-letter trouble started. There's not much more to tell you, Sophie. You know what happened.'

'Oh, you must finish the story properly,' she begged. 'You can't leave it there. Didn't you ever meet again?'

'We met one more time – in late November. I went out to Vrahos on my way to India and we managed to steal a last weekend together. To begin with I put the obvious gaps in our correspondence down to the combined efforts of the Greek and Indian postal systems – entirely possible, believe me, and I imagined she would realise that too – and, of course, I was on the move a lot of the time, following the maharaja on his travels. But I started getting frantic about the gaps in our correspondence. Some of her letters to me were so obviously missing and those I got were full of reproaches that I hadn't written, but with the blind optimism of youth I never doubted Evanthi for a moment, or realised what an awful effect it must be having on her. Looking back I think it was very arrogant of me. I'll never forget the shock of my arrival back in England in the summer, knowing we had achieved the six months' separation demanded by Evanthi's father and pretty pleased with myself that my reputation as a painter had gone up several notches. I was all set for a wonderful reunion with Evanthi and totally confident that this time we would be able to get married. I'd cabled Evanthi I was coming home and I went to stay in London with Aunt Georgia, intending to go straight out to Greece before going home to Yorkshire . . . and heard that Evanthi had married Stavros Doukas.'

'How *ghastly*! What did your aunt say?'

'She wondered if the news about Evanthi had been a surprise to me and said she'd always thought we had something serious going between us and asked what had gone wrong. Of course I had no idea what she was talking about. When she told me the bottom dropped out of my world.'

He smiled at Sophie. 'So now we are corresponding again after sixty years, and gradually filling in the many missing bits in our jigsaw puzzle,' he said. 'Life is really extraordinarily strange.'

'I can't bear it. It's an *awful* story. Such a waste. Did you never try to see her again?'

'Well, the war came next and that altered everything. England was at war with Italy as well as Germany – and they were both at war with Greece. Because I was a Territorial I was called up immediately and sent to France. Then came Dunkirk and the miraculous rescue off the beaches and back to England for the lucky ones including me.'

'But that wasn't where you lost your leg and got your medal, was it?' asked Sophie.

'No, no, that was much later, and by then I'd been transferred to the K.D.G. – the King's Dragoon Guards. I got my MC in the desert in North Africa – all a lot of nonsense; I was no braver than hundreds of others. To be honest, Sophie, when the war started I didn't really care whether I lived or died, but it's amazing how precious life seems when it's really threatened, no matter how miserable you are. I actually lost my leg and was taken prisoner in Italy on the way to liberate Perugia – but that's another story.'

'But I thought you were a prisoner in Germany?' objected Sophie.

'I was eventually – I was taken there from a transit camp in Italy. But first, because I was wounded, I was taken to a hospital at Bologna. Luckily for me it was a first-rate hospital, too, with a bloody good surgeon.' Hugh added drily, 'Fella was doing up to fifteen amputations a day so he got plenty of practice.'

Sophie shuddered. 'What was the worst thing you remember about it?' she asked ghoulishly.

'The over-inflated tyres on the ambulance,' said Hugh promptly. 'They blew them up to the maximum because it was supposed to make accidents marginally less likely on the appalling roads, but it also made for a hellish bumpy ride! Not too comfortable if you've just had your leg blown off. It was fifty miles from the field hospital, where I was first taken, to Bologna.'

'Did you ever wonder if Evanthi might actually be somewhere near?' asked Sophie.

'I certainly did. I thought about her endlessly – was she in Italy or was she in Greece? Above all, was she safe? I reckoned she would be having a very tough time wherever she was, but I felt in my bones she was still alive – I thought I'd know if she'd been killed. I suppose a reprehensible bit of me secretly hoped something might have happened to Stavros Doukas and I fantasised that if Evanthi and I both survived the war, we'd get back together again, this time for good. It's what kept me going. All the nurses at the hospital were nuns. They were wonderful – changing dressings one minute, down on their knees praying, the next. I spoke a bit of Italian and one of them tried to make enquiries for me but, of course, communications were hopeless.'

'Did your parents know what had happened to you?'

'Not for a bit. I was reported "missing, believed prisoner" to start with. Later they heard through the Red Cross.'

'So when you finally went to Germany, what then?'

362

'Then Colditz – via Munich.'

'*Colditz?* Like all those old telly films?' Sophie was impressed.

'Well . . . fairly like,' said Hugh.

'Was it terrible? Were you tortured?'

'Oh, not tortured or anything like that . . . but it wasn't exactly a picnic. You could easily get a month in solitary confinement just for calling a guard a rude name, for instance – as I discovered to my cost – but I suppose cold and hunger were the worst things really.' Hugh could see Sophie was dying for details. He continued, 'We were hungry enough to scavenge round the camp kitchen's rubbish bins and re-peel the peelings of a vile vegetable called kohlrabi to make soup, and I remember most of us were unable to go up more than a few steps of the stairs without having to stop and recover – or else black out.' He laughed. 'But I used to come downstairs extremely fast because I was so unsteady on my one leg that I usually fell down them!'

'How awful!' She looked at him, round-eyed. 'You must have been literally starving. So when did you first get news of Evanthi again?'

'Near the end of the war the Regiment were ordered to Greece to combat the communist attempt to take the country over, and a friend and brother officer – who'd met Evanthi with me and knew all about us – tried to get news of her for me. But he heard she was still married and had a child. That was the end of hope.'

Hugh looked across the garden but Sophie knew he was seeing a very different scene.

After a moment he went on: 'I made one last attempt to talk to her. I just wanted to know what had caused her to change her mind, and I wanted her to know that I'd never wavered. After I'd been demobbed – as soon as it was possible to travel to Europe again – I went out to Greece. I turned up at Vrahos without warning, not knowing what I would find, but thinking I'd have a better chance of talking to her if I surprised her. It was Nafsica who opened the door. She was horrified to see me – and it was from her I learned that Evanthi had been caught in Corfu at the outbreak of war and been trapped there for the duration. Both her parents had been killed in Italy – bombed, I think. I scribbled a note and asked Nafsica to take it to her but she returned to say Evanthi wouldn't receive me. I now know from Evanthi that Nafsica never said a word about it. She never knew I was there and never got that note either. I see why Nafsica must have been spooked when your father turned up.'

'What did you do next?'

'I went home. Perhaps it was as well. I'd selfishly wanted her to know that I'd thought of her every day throughout the war and would never marry anyone else – but who knows? If we'd met again we might not have been able to resist each other. I always went on loving her – and, do you know, Sophie, despite her marriage I never really doubted that she loved me too. Rum, isn't it? So there you are – what a tale of human folly! Now I think we'll go and get Mrs P. to give us some tea – and I need a dash of something a bit stronger in mine after dredging up all those ghosts. Give me a hand up, there's a good girl. I'm a bit stiff.'

He got slowly to his feet and they walked back to the house in silence. Sophie felt there was nothing she could say.

Tea broke the spell, and they talked about things unconnected with either Rachel's defection or Hugh's love story.

Just as she was saying goodbye Sophie suddenly said: 'Uncle Hugh, can I ask you something?'

'You can always ask. I don't guarantee to answer.'

'What was your first reaction after you were wounded and they told you they'd have to amputate your leg?'

'I thought I'd never be able to dance with Evanthi again,' he said promptly, 'and it seemed unbearable.' Then he laughed. 'You crafty puss! What a trick question. I also thought it was bloody unfair – that's what!'

'Oh, Uncle Hugh, I do love you,' she said. 'But I bet you didn't moan, anyway.'

'I hope not,' he said soberly. 'I'd seen too many people killed by then – many of them my friends. That concentrates the mind wonderfully on priorities. I was lucky to be alive.'

He watched Sophie walk across the garden to collect the old pony, and wondered what the future had in store for her – for all of them.

Chapter Thirty-six

Francine glanced round the spare bedroom that overlooked the garden and checked to see whether she had forgotten anything. There was a carefully chosen selection of books by the bed including the latest prize-winning biography, a literary novel, a couple of nail-biting thrillers and the poems of Walt Whitman, together with several glossy magazines catering for tastes ranging from fashion to the arts; interior decorating to high society – and, of course, this month's issue of *Capability*, though she guessed Victoria would already have read Guy's latest column. In the bathroom she had put some timeless classics – *Elizabeth and her German Garden* and Gwen Raverat's incomparable *Period Piece.* There was Jo Malone bath essence and a huge bottle of soothing lavender aromatherapy oil. In the bedroom there was mineral water, an electric kettle and the wherewithal for making cups of tea. The walk-in cupboard had a plentiful supply of padded coat-hangers and the drawers in the bow-fronted mahogany chest were freshly lined with delicately scented paper.

Francine had just redecorated this bedroom and bathroom in a restful blue toile de Jouy and hoped it looked fresh and welcoming but not too glaringly new – setting her own seal on the house that had for so long been Guy's bachelor pad, without proclaiming the change of regime in a too in-your-face a way to be acceptable to those of his friends who still regarded her with suspicion.

Having Victoria to stay was a challenge – for all three of us, thought Francine, though she wasn't sure how much Guy was aware of this, and suspected it might actually prove more difficult for him than he anticipated. He had not approved her choice of room for Victoria.

'Why have you put Vicky in here? You ought to put her in the green room,' he had objected. 'She and Richard *always* slept in the green room. I'm sure she'll expect to be there because they really looked on it as theirs.'

'Exactly,' said Francine. 'I didn't think she'd want to be in the room she always shared with Richard – and I'm not going to put her there.'

'Oh, well – if it makes you feel insecure . . .' Guy had shrugged and given her one of his enigmatic, taunting looks, but she had merely laughed at him and taken no notice of the displeasure that followed and which could come over Guy with the suddenness of a thunderclap and deaden the atmosphere. This mood will blow off again without a storm breaking, she told herself. She was getting rather good at weather forecasts – good, too, at not allowing the uncertain climate in which she now lived to affect her decisions too much.

She had gone off to a monthly meeting of her book club with every outward appearance of unconcern and not gone looking for Guy when she came back in. Sure enough he had come up behind her and put his arms round her when she was changing to go out to dinner.

'Would you like to come with me to Heathrow tomorrow when I go to meet Vicky?' he had asked.

Francine knew it was his way of apologising for his ill temper. She allowed herself to relax against him for a moment and closed her eyes. Then she pulled away and went and sat down at her dressing table and started expertly applying make-up, achieving an effect of naturalness that was both a brilliant deception and a work of art.

'Sure I'll come, if you like,' she said, concentrating on outlining her left eye, 'but I think she'd rather have you to herself. I know I would in her shoes.'

Guy watched her as she finished doing her eyes and started dusting blusher over her cheekbones with a soft brush.

'Shall we not go to the Heathcotes after all?' he asked softly, putting his hands on her shoulders. 'I'll ring them and say . . . say something unexpected and very urgent has just come up.' He glinted at her in the mirror.

'Certainly not,' said Francine severely. 'Go take a cold shower, Guy Winston. Maddie Heathcote will have been counting the hours till she sees you again. She thinks you're God's gift to women and I couldn't be so cruel as to deprive her of a treat. This dress is getting real snug. I don't think I'll be wearing it again for a while. I must get some reinforcements for my wardrobe. Do you think Victoria would like to come on a spending spree with me? She might feel ready for some new clothes herself.'

'She might.' Guy took his hands from her shoulders. 'I'm not sure what her financial situation is at the moment, though. She may be a bit strapped for cash.'

'Isn't it lucky no one could say the same of you,' said Francine, laughing at him. 'It's one of the attributes that drew me to you in the first place. But perhaps we could help over the money thing. You can be so tactful if you set your mind to it, honey – I'm sure you'll think of a way to get over that.'

'Good idea. I'll see what I can do,' said Guy, who enjoyed playing Mr Bountiful. He was aware that he was being managed – a novel experience – but Francine's mixture of teasing and flattery was done with such a light touch that he found it surprisingly acceptable.

'Well, I suppose if you insist on denying me an evening of domestic bliss, I'd better hurry up and change,' he said. 'I'll go and have that shower.'

Victoria had decided to go to England for a fortnight. She dreaded telling Jake she was going, but his only reaction had been to say, 'Need I come with you?' He had settled into the local school like the proverbial duck to water and went off happily with Angelo each morning as if he had lived at Vrahos all his life.

'Children don't half cut one down to size,' Victoria said to Evanthi with a rueful smile. 'There was I, worrying myself sick that he'd be dreadfully upset at me leaving him behind and wondering if I ought to go! What a waste of energy on my part. He doesn't give a stuff!'

'It shows how secure you've made him feel, despite all the dramas in his life,' said Evanthi comfortingly. 'He knows you would never abandon him. He looks a different child from the white-faced little boy who arrived four months ago. Don't worry about him, *agapi*. It will do you good to get away for a bit, although I'm aware that you're partly going for my benefit. It means so much to me that you are going to meet Hugh and will report back to me, and tell me everything about him. Jake will be fine – he has dear Dora and Yannis and Angelo . . . and for what it's worth he has me too. I may not be very active but I'm always here.'

'Darling Nonna! It's worth everything,' said Victoria. 'You are the linchpin for us both. And, of course, I'm longing to meet Hugh!'

In fact, Victoria was becoming apprehensive about the whole trip. She was uncertain quite what Evanthi expected her to achieve on her behalf. Suppose she gets wounded all over again, she thought, and this time it's my fault? Suppose I don't like him – how shall I tell her? And what will *his* expectations of such a meeting be?

She was longing to visit Anthony and Toula, but was not looking forward to meetings with Richard's family, and wondered how she would cope with the memories and emotions that would inevitably be stirred up by going back to Manor Farm.

It was my home for eight years, she thought: surely I ought to want to be there – what does that tell me? What sort of person does that make me?

Out here at Vrahos it was possible – part of the time – to achieve some semblance of normality, but back in England there were things to be faced from which she could not go on hiding. Nor could her complicated feelings about Richard remain unresolved and she realised also that she was dreading seeing Guy again. I don't know who I am any more, thought Victoria.

She wondered what it would be like to stay with Guy, now that so many things had changed. The house, which for years she had almost treated as her own, was now Francine's home. There were dark questions, not only of Victoria's own feelings for Guy – something she had never liked to examine too closely – but also of Francine's reactions to the relationship between Guy and Richard and herself to be faced.

Sitting high above the sea among the ruins of Angelokastro, after the never-to-be-forgotten picnic when Guy had dropped the bombshell about Richard, he'd assured her that Francine knew all about it, but she couldn't help wondering what she *felt*. Is she really as cool as she looks, she wondered, or is she as nervous about me as I am about her?

And now there was also Patrick. Victoria's feelings were in turmoil. She was both longing to see him and dreading it too, increasingly disturbed by the realisation that she was in the grip of a powerful sexual attraction quite different from anything she had ever felt before, an attraction for which, coming so soon after Richard's death, she felt very unprepared. What, she asked herself, if, in her present unbalanced emotional state, she had misread the signals she thought she had received from Patrick? What, indeed, about his marriage? Their next meeting would not be on reassuring home territory but in the more sophisticated setting of London and without the easy company of Sam and Sophie to make everything casual. This suddenly seemed unnerving too.

Patrick had rung her again – ostensibly to keep her informed about arrangements for attending the preview of Hugh's exhibition but also to renew his invitation to take her out to dinner. 'Then we can catch up on each other's news before your meeting with Hugh,' he had said easily. She had enjoyed chatting to him on the telephone, but going out to dinner was another matter. She was afraid her ordinary social skills might have deserted her during the last difficult months and wondered if she could still sustain a conversation *à deux* for a whole evening, especially with someone whose good opinion she so badly wanted, but whom she did not really know at all well.

It's ridiculous to be so lacking in confidence, she told herself sternly – like being eighteen again. She wondered if her uncertainty was another effect of bereavement and if she might be going slightly mad. Hadn't C. S. Lewis written of his surprise that grief felt so very like fear? It all seemed horribly complicated, and if she allowed herself to dwell on any of it for too long, Victoria felt physically sick.

She decided to go to London first, before going to Baybury.

She had to see Peter Mason anyway – not something she was looking forward to either – and there was a meeting with Meriel Hawkins to be endured at some stage.

As she packed for the journey she realised how inadequate her wardrobe was for a week in London that would include the sort of social occasions she hadn't attended since Richard's death. It had been March when she left England – now it was June. She had brought only the minimum of clothes with her, and all those had been casual ones: there had been no need for anything more formal at Vrahos. Though Evanthi habitually changed for dinner, it was only into something comfortable such as one of her collections of caftans. I shall feel a frump, thought Victoria gloomily, visions of the glamorous Francine cat-walking alarmingly across her imagination. And what shall I wear for dinner with Patrick?

Guy was standing at the rail to meet her when she arrived at Heathrow. She was relieved to see that he was alone, but her usual surge of joy on meeting him was missing.

'Well, you certainly look better than when I last saw you,' he said after he had kissed her. It was not lost on him that there was no responding kiss. I am not forgiven, noted Guy.

Victoria thought of the many times when Guy had met her off aeroplanes or trains, and of her usual uncomplicated delight at the first sight of him, her joy at his welcoming hug. Now she was only conscious that she did not want him to touch her. Would it always be like this, she wondered sadly.

'Vrahos must have worked its usual magic. Living in Greece suits you,' he said.

Victoria gave a slight shrug. 'I feel like Timmy Willie the country mouse coming to stay with Johnny Town-Mouse in the big city! So – how are you, Guy? You look much the same.'

'Good God! What on earth did you expect? It's only a few months since we were last together! What's that supposed to mean? I think you might notice a change in Francine, though – the baby's beginning to show now – but surely expectant fathers aren't supposed to change too?'

'No, of course not. I didn't mean that. It's just that everything seems different at the moment. Perhaps it's me that's changed.'

He laughed uneasily. 'Not you! You never change – thank goodness!' He gave her one of his swiftly appraising, critical looks. 'Your hair needs cutting, though – you look like a shaggy little dog! Come on, let's get the lift to the car park and I'll have you home in no time.'

Home? thought Victoria. I don't know where home is any more. Certainly not Guy's house.

Cruising up the M4 in Guy's open-topped BMW they talked about safe subjects like the family. Guy brought her up to date with the latest news about Toula and Anthony, about Francine and the plans for the baby, and she told him about Jake and Evanthi and Vrahos; they talked about the coincidence of getting to know the Hammonds and finding out about Hugh Marston. Victoria told him about her impending dates first with Patrick and then with Hugh himself. Guy said he had received a letter from Patrick asking if they could meet sometime to talk about Vrahos.

'I'd like to meet him anyway,' he said. 'Not just because of Vrahos, and certainly not because of Nonna's old romance – which you seem to have got so dewy-eyed about – but because I think we might be useful to each other in the future. He takes fantastic photographs. I've seen his work and like his stuff very much. Why don't I invite myself to come along too if you have dinner with him? Wouldn't that be good?'

But the last thing Victoria wanted was for Guy to join her and Patrick. 'I don't think that's at all a good idea,' she said coolly. 'I'll suggest he gives you a ring and you can do that some other time.'

Guy shot her a curious look and raised an eyebrow. There was a little silence between them and both were aware of constraint. Damn, thought Victoria. Guy's going to be watching my every reaction to Patrick like a hawk now. She thought her feelings were complicated enough as it was, and certainly didn't feel ready for family speculation – least of all Guy's.

As they approached the turning to The Boltons from the Old Brompton Road she began to feel her stomach muscles contracting.

Added to her nervousness about meeting Francine and coping for the next week with the choking resentment she still felt about Guy, was a new concern: the thought of living for the next few days under the microscope of his discerning scrutiny. She gave herself a stern mental shake, and determined not to let Guy's curiosity rattle her as they pulled up outside number forty.

Chapter Thirty-seven

Francine's greeting – much warmer than Victoria expected – had come as a pleasant surprise. It had been a comfort too to find she had not been put in the room she and Richard had always shared. Francine had come straight to the point when she escorted Victoria upstairs.

'I do hope I've got this right,' she said, pausing before she opened the door of the blue bedroom. 'Guy was mad as a hornet at me for putting you in here, but I felt you might not want to be in your old room. It would be the easiest thing in the world to change if I've guessed wrong,' and she gave Victoria an enquiring look. She added with a deprecating little shrug, 'I've hedged my bets – though I haven't admitted as much to Guy – so the beds in the green room are made up too. You've only got to say if you'd be happier there. I shan't mind.'

Victoria was touched. 'Oh, what a relief! You've guessed exactly right. How clever of you,' and she smiled at Guy's wife. 'Oh – you *have* made this nice,' she exclaimed as they went in together. 'It used to be rather a gloomy room. Blissful books too – my favourite thing in other people's spare rooms. And you've put *The Young Visiters* by the loo! How brilliant – Daisy Ashford is just what I feel like reading. You must have gone to a lot of trouble.' On an impulse she went and gave Francine a hug and was surprised to see the older woman's eyes fill with tears.

'Is it difficult having Guy's old friends and family to stay?' she asked.

'Well, I guess I'm kinda jumpy,' admitted Francine. 'And specially with you, because you're just so important to Guy.' She laughed and said, 'But I've no intention of letting Guy know I'm nervous. I like to keep him guessing about my reactions – so don't you tell on me!'

'I won't. Nobody can boost one's morale more than Guy if he

wants to – but no one can put the boot in more accurately either – and I should know after a childhood of being inflated or deflated by your husband!' There! she had said it – 'your husband', and it had come out quite naturally.

She went over to the dressing table and peered at her reflection in the mirror. 'He says my hair needs cutting,' she said. 'I had thought I might grow it a bit but Guy's just told me I look shaggy! I haven't been near a hairdresser since I left England. What do you think I should do with it? Your hair always looks so fantastic.'

Francine looked at her consideringly. 'I don't think it's so much the actual length as the shape,' she said seriously. 'You've got such great bone-structure I think you could have it cut much shorter near your face – at the sides but not necessarily at the back. I suppose you wouldn't like to let my lovely Lennie loose on you? He's coloured me when I've been in England for years but he's ace with the scissors too – and he absolutely never turns you out with anything you're not comfortable with.'

'That would be great,' said Victoria. 'I don't suppose you'd come with me and give me moral support?'

'Sure. I'd love to – I have designs on you anyway to help me get new clothes to cover this bump. Let's have a shopping spree. I'd already asked Guy if he thought you might be up for that. Now I'm going to leave you to unpack and freshen up – take a tub, put your toes up – anything you like, and be as long as you want. Come down any time. Then we'll have dinner in the kitchen. Guy says he's cooking in your honour.'

After Francine had gone Victoria took several deep breaths of relief. One dread less, she told herself. Getting on with Francine was not going to be a problem – but how she was going to deal with her feelings about Guy she didn't know.

When she went down to the kitchen, scene of many of Guy's renowned bachelor parties, delicious smells were wafting up the stairs. Guy, an inspired cook when he chose, was making paella and Francine was lolling on the huge squashy sofa that took up the whole of one wall, chatting to him, a glass in her hand while he played about with saffron and rice and hurled bits of chicken and shellfish into a huge pot. They looked so companionable that Victoria felt a wave of desolation wash over her. That used to be me – gossiping to Guy while he cooked, she thought: funny how loneliness could strike hardest in the company of other people rather than at times of genuine solitude. Living with Evanthi for the last four months, with Jake as the focus for her attention, she'd forgotten about the feeling of being a gooseberry in the company of married friends. She gave herself a fierce mental shake. I must get used to being solo, she thought, because this is how things are going to be – and she felt a stab of guilt that recently – since Guy had burst his bombshell – she had not allowed herself to appreciate the many good things there had been about her marriage but had fed her feelings of hurt and betrayal till they had become as bloated and unwieldy as Strasbourg geese. I must remember the happy times too, she thought, even if it makes the loneliness worse. Waddle off, she instructed the overfed grievances, and aloud she said brightly: 'That smells good! I'm starving.'

'Hi there. We're using you as an excuse. Francine's not really supposed to drink at the moment but champagne's medicinal and I know you love it.' Guy handed Victoria a glass. 'It'll do you good too. My gastronomic brew can bubble away on its own for a bit, so come and sit down and relax and let's plan your week. Tell us what you've already arranged and which of your special mates you'd like to see and what you'd like to do for the rest of the time. We want to see as much of you as possible – so I'm warning you we're going to be jealous of sparing you too much to other people, though maddeningly I have to be away for a couple of days. I gather you two are going to have a wickedly expensive outing together one day. I might even foot the entire bill for you both, I'm feeling so expansive! Don't say no,' he said, as Victoria started to protest. 'I'm cele-brating three very important things – impending fatherhood, your arrival and a fantastic new deal with *Capability* – so I can well afford to be generous and my very expensive wife says she'll feel inhibited if you don't spend as much as she does.' He rolled his eyes. 'I couldn't face her in thwarted-shopper mode at the moment – she's really scary then – so you'll be doing me a kindness to indulge me.'

'I'll certainly go on a shopping spree,' said Victoria, feeling reckless, 'but even as a payback for your rudeness about my hair I couldn't accept hand-outs. Thank you, Guy, that's a generous offer but I'm well able to fund myself.' After which lie she felt a great deal better. 'Francine can supervise my make-over and I'll be able to stun boring old Peter Mason with my new sophisticated image.'

'Now that really would be a wicked waste of money – but is he the only person you want to stun?' asked Guy slyly, riled at having his largesse spurned. He encountered a warning look from his wife. 'Go look to your cauldron, da-rr-ling,' she suggested. 'It sounds to me as if it's bubbling way too fast.'

'As if you'd even know if it had boiled away completely – oh thou-who-hast-never-stirred-a-pot-in-her-life!' mocked Guy. But he got up all the same and made a play of switching down the heat.

Francine's look was not lost on Victoria. They've been discussing me, she thought and I was right to think Guy would add two and two and make a dozen. She wondered what he had said to Francine but to her relief he let the subject drop – a surprise in itself – and the rest of the evening passed without too many uncomfortable moments. Guy, at his entertaining best, regaled them with hilarious stories about eccentric characters from the three very different worlds in which he moved on both sides of the Atlantic – opera, journalism and gardening. Victoria was aware that he was both trying to reassert his hold over her and to beguile her into forgiveness, but though she couldn't help laughing at some of his confections of storytelling, she did not feel inclined to accept olive branches yet. She wasn't sure that she would ever be able feel the same about Guy again; to her own surprise she wasn't sure she even wanted to.

The shopping trip was a success. They had gone first to Francine's hairdresser, Lennie's, in the Old Brompton Road. Lennie himself, a wonderfully camp East-Ender with a shaven head, an armoury of gold jewellery and a sharp cockney wit, was clearly a great fan of Francine's and greeted them with enthusiasm. He studied Victoria from all angles, ran a comb through her thick dark hair, pushed it this way and that, and then announced that he knew just what he wanted to do. 'Will you trust me, darlin'?' he asked and Victoria recklessly agreed that she would, suddenly enjoying being in London once more.

'I'm fed up with myself at the moment,' she said. 'So . . . transform me!'

'No problem. We'll get Rosa to shampoo you and then I'll murder these layers,' he said cheerfully. 'You won't know yourself – but I guarantee you'll like what you see.'

And he was right. 'Oh, *thank you,*' she said, extremely pleased with what he'd done. 'You're a genius. I feel I can face the world again.'

'My pleasure,' said Lennie. 'You've got wonderful hair.'

She had a nasty moment when she looked at the bill, however.

'That was one of my brighter ideas,' said Francine as they left the salon. 'You look fantastic.'

'Oh Francine, *thank you.* Isn't it extraordinary what a haircut can do for morale? Now where?'

'Now,' said Francine, 'for serious temptation, which I have every intention of giving in to. Let's go to Midas down the Fulham Road. Kate Morley, who owns it, is married to a friend of my parents. She has these fantastic embroidered jackets and tops in the most heavenly materials, and silk trousers to die for.'

The temptation turned out to be very serious indeed – an Aladdin's cave of colour where they went wild trying on exotic clothes in silks or velvet, many of them covered in glittering hand embroidery.

'Just what I need – something dramatic to cover the bulge,' said Francine, twirling in a long gold organza coat emblazoned with startling reds and oranges. 'I shall definitely get this – and that black Nehru jacket with the embroidered cuffs was real neat on you. You *have* to have it, Victoria.'

'I don't think I'd get enough wear out of it. I've no idea what my social life is going to be from now on.'

'Oh, come on – haven't you just gotten an invitation to attend a glamorous private view? Get the green silk trousers and the camisole top that goes with them *and* the black jacket – you'd look stunning. Then you could wear the jacket open with plain black trousers and a white T-shirt to make it more casual and it would take you absolutely anywhere – out to dinner, formal or informal. Whatever – you'll be sorted for anything. *Do* let Guy give you the jacket at least, I know he'd like to.'

'No, no, absolutely not.' Victoria was adamant. 'I'll get it for myself if you really think it's right.' She was still in a defiantly reckless mood, pushing anxieties about her bank balance to the far corner of her mind, cocking a mental snook at Peter Mason and Meriel.

Francine could see she was longing to be persuaded. 'I don't just *think* it's right, I know it,' she said firmly, and bought herself a skirt on an elasticated waistband, which would accommodate the bulge to perfection, and then chose a couple of wildly expensive tasselled silk scarves for them both. 'If you won't let Guy buy you a present you must indulge me,' she insisted. 'It's bad for me to be thwarted right now!'

'You're very generous, Francine,' said Victoria, touched, and meaning it in more ways than one.

'What's the point of having money if you don't have fun with it? It's great to have you keep me company.'

They staggered out of the shop laden with enormous glossy carriers, feeling very pleased with themselves, and headed for the baby department at Peter Jones where they had an equally happy time looking at cots and prams and tiny nighties.

When they got back to number forty The Boltons, Tessie, the Filipino housekeeper who had worked for Guy for years and had given Victoria a great welcome earlier that morning, said there had been several telephone messages for Victoria.

'Mrs Winston senior – she rang. She say she longing to see you. They be with you eight this evening. She say you should stay with her and not go to your old house next week. Then Mr Mason's secretary rang – he see you tomorrow like you suggest, and like to give you lunch also. Oh, and a Mr Hammond rang. Can you ring him, and I written down the number,' and she handed Victoria a piece of paper.

'You didn't tell me Toula and Anthony were coming. How lovely.'

'It was meant to be a surprise,' said Francine, getting them each a Diet Coke out of the fridge. 'Of course, Toula wanted to be here to greet you and we had great difficulty putting them off till this evening. Guy told a white lie about the time of your flight because we wanted you all to ourselves last night – you know how Toula always takes over wherever she is. We wouldn't have got a look in. You're much in demand, Mrs Cunningham! Is Patrick Hammond the man who's doing the book on Vrahos – Hugh Marston's nephew?'

'Yes, that's the chap.' Victoria took the Coke, thankful Guy wasn't there. 'Thanks, Francine – lovely – just what I needed. I suppose I'd better ring him.'

'Make any plans you like,' said Francine. 'Guy's away tomorrow and the next day, but I'm here all week so come and go as it suits you. Help yourself to the phone.'

'Thanks, but I can use my mobile.' Victoria didn't particularly want to ring Patrick in front of Francine, but neither did she want to give the impression that there was anything private about the call. She dialled the number Tessie had written down.

'Yes? Patrick Hammond here.' The voice sounded brisk – slightly intimidating.

'Hello, Patrick,' she said, trying to sound equally matter-of-fact, but feeling anything but, inside. 'It's Victoria. I believe you rang me.'

'Victoria! How lovely to hear you.' His voice changed completely. There could be no doubting his pleasure. 'When am I going to see you?'

'What were you suggesting?' she asked, her heart singing.

'I'm suggesting you let me take you out to dinner. When might you be free?'

'Um . . . would tomorrow be too soon?' she asked, longing to see him and thinking that it would be much easier to meet Patrick when Guy wasn't around to make assumptions or put her through an inquisition.

'Tomorrow would be wonderful. I thought it would be good to meet before you come to Hugh's do on Friday. There's a little local restaurant where I often go when I'm in London. It's not specially glamorous but it has very good food.'

'That sounds perfect. Tell me where to come and what time you'd like me to turn up?'

'Wouldn't you like me to pick you up?'

'It might be easier if I met you there because I'm not sure where I'll be coming from,' said Victoria who didn't want Patrick turning up at Guy and Francine's.

'Right, why don't you come here first for a drink – say about eight – and we can walk round to Merlin's when we're ready. It's only just round the corner from here.'

'That sounds fine. See you tomorrow then.'

After he had rung off, she realised that she still hadn't discovered if his wife would be with him. Somehow she didn't think so, but this was something that needed clearing up. She had sensed a reserve when Rachel's name had been mentioned in Corfu that had made her curious, yet nothing had been said that gave her any real clue as to whether there were problems in the marriage. Would Rachel Hammond be at Hugh Marston's private view? Victoria told herself that she would like to meet her.

She said to Francine, 'I've fixed for tomorrow evening with the Hammonds, if that's OK, but can I come back here first to recover from my session with Peter Mason?'

'Of course you can. I'll give you a key. I shall be waiting to revive you with tea and sympathy and expect you to tell me all the latest gems of "Masonese". Since you first told me about that I've actually met Peter – not to mention Clutterbuck – with Guy, and had hard work to keep a straight face. Now let's have something to eat.'

Francine might become a real friend, thought Victoria with surprise, so why didn't I even like her when she was just part of Guy's groupies? And then she thought, of course, because Richard was always so disparaging about her – so bitchy really. Unlike Guy, Richard had usually been kind about people, but whenever they met Francine he'd always done a character assassination job on her afterwards. Victoria supposed he must have been insanely jealous – and I was jealous of her too, honesty forced her to admit to herself. Somehow this jealousy seemed to have fallen away but whether this was due to her present anger with Guy, the loss of Richard or to Francine herself she didn't know.

That evening she had a wonderful reunion with Toula and Anthony. As usual Toula arrived like a whirlwind, all flailing arms and trailing scarves. Victoria was overjoyed to see them both. She thought Toula's attitude to Francine had mellowed since she'd last seen them together, doubtless due to the prospect of a first grandchild but she guessed that Anthony must have had a go at Toula about not interfering about the baby. To those who knew her well, it was obvious that she was making efforts to ration her pearls of advice on every aspect of child-rearing, though Victoria thought this might not be too obvious to anyone not familiar with her normal output. Francine seemed to be bearing up well, however, and caught Victoria's eye once or twice when Toula started to hold forth on the layette she thought essential. Naturally she didn't consider any of the purchases Francine and Victoria had made for the baby that morning were at all practical, but Francine just laughed and seemed unfazed. 'I guess you and I can go shop together any time, Toula,' she said easily. 'I'm always up for that – but we don't get the chance of doing things with Victoria too often.'

Toula was spiky about Evanthi's rediscovered love. She had greatly admired her austere father, and the idea that her mother might have been hankering for someone else all through the marriage offended her. 'I've never heard anything so ridiculous – I think it's all a lot of moonlight,' she said scornfully, and Anthony gave Victoria a surreptitious wink. 'What a nerve for this man to come hanging round after my mother again after all these years!' Toula's eyes flashed. 'I think my grandmother was absolutely right to send him packing in the first place – he was probably a goldminer. Anyway, he sounds most unreliable and if I ever meet him I shall tell him so. I never got on with Nafsica when I was a child but my opinion of her has definitely gone up.'

Victoria, who had been on the point of suggesting she and Anthony might like to come to Hugh Marston's private view with her, thought better of the idea.

Before Anthony and Toula left, Anthony took Victoria on one side. 'Would you like me to come with you to see Peter Mason tomorrow?' he asked. 'He's a pompous ass and a bit of a bully too but he wouldn't try to force you into any decisions if I was with you.' It was tempting to accept, but Victoria felt that if she was going to run her own and Jake's lives with any degree of success then she needed to be able to cope with the Peter Masons of the world.

'You're a darling,' she said, 'but no thank you. I must learn to stick up for myself, for Jake's sake.'

Anthony nodded approvingly. 'Good for you,' he said, thinking that something positive had happened to Victoria since he'd last seen her. He thought he detected signs that the Sleeping Beauty was waking up. 'Just remember I'm there if you need me. I'll be at the gallery all day so ring my mobile and I'll leap on my white charger and come galloping to your rescue.'

Toula promised to meet Victoria at Toddingham station on Monday morning and drive her over to Baybury. 'Violet has been busy getting the house ready for you – but I shall still make up a bed for you with us too, so you needn't decide now whether you'll sleep at Manor Farm or not,' she said, with an uncharacteristic display of tact.

The following day Victoria arrived at the offices of Mason, Whitaker & Ziegler and was pleased to discover how much less intimidated she felt than the last time she'd been there. She could hardly believe it was only four months ago. It felt like a lifetime. Francine insisted on lending her a crisp linen suit from Bloomingdale's, which she could no longer get into herself, and together with the new haircut Victoria felt she looked both expensive and efficient – and hoped this false impression would send a 'don't mess with me' message to Peter Mason. When Guy said goodbye before going off to interview the owners of a famous garden in Provence he had raised his eyebrows in semi-mocking appreciation.

'Well, well, little cousin! What a vision! You look as if you're off to negotiate an important take-over.'

'I am . . .' said Victoria '. . . of my own life.'

'Well, please don't change too much, Vicky,' he said. 'I wouldn't like to lose you.'

'I think you should have thought of that a long time ago,' she answered, and was conscious that she'd shaken him.

Francine, witnessing the little scene, felt an unexpected surge of sympathy for her husband. She knew he deserved his comeuppance and that he had hitherto sailed through life doing what he pleased without taking heed of the possible effects of his self-indulgence – but suddenly a lot of consequences seemed to be winging back like boomerangs.

Peter Mason kept her waiting for the statutory twenty minutes and then swept in full of apologies. 'So sorry to have kept you – pressure of business, I'm afraid. Life doesn't get easier.' She imagined him standing in his office, a large man balancing on the balls of his disconcertingly small feet, watch in hand, whiling away the appropriate amount of time dependent on the standing of each client, before he deemed it suitable to appear. Whereas he was obviously surprised at her change of image, she thought that apart from the fact that he appeared to have added yet another chin to the collection that rolled smoothly down towards his collar like sand-dunes, he seemed depressingly as she remembered – sleek, prosperous and very well satisfied with himself.

'I must say you're looking remarkably well, Victoria,' he said, squeezing her forearms as though to test her potential for tossing cabers. 'Remarkably well. Much better than I expected.' He sounded almost affronted. 'And how is that young man of yours? I presume you've brought him home with you?'

'Actually I've left Jake in Corfu with my grandmother. It seemed a pity to disrupt him when he's settled so well at school there.' Victoria thought it was better to bring up the subject of Jake's schooling straight away.

'Hmm, hmm.' Peter Mason pursed his lips and turned the corners of his mouth down in a disapproving little moue. 'Bill will be disappointed. I gather you are going down to see him next Tuesday. Jake's education is, of course, one of the things on our agenda for discussion today,' he said. 'Let's go along to a boardroom and get the business talk out of the way – and then perhaps I can give you lunch afterwards.'

During the next hour he painted what seemed to Victoria a discouraging picture of her future. Richard had had losses on the stock exchange about which she had known nothing. She gathered that Jake's education could be paid for out of the family trust – provided, of course, that Peter Mason and her father-in-law as co-trustees approved the choice of school. 'Which I'm sure we shall,' said Peter smoothly, eyeing her over the top of his spectacles.

Victoria said nothing. There seemed no point into getting into an argument at this stage before she'd even been back to Baybury.

'Now as to your house – by which I am, of course, referring to Manor Farm,' continued Peter – as though, thought Victoria, she might not remember where she'd been living for the past eight years – 'that's a trifle more problematical.' He took his spectacles off and polished them carefully. 'I doubt if you would have sufficient income – unless you have assets undisclosed to me – to go on living there as things stand at this moment in time. But I'm happy to say there are one or two other interesting alternatives which Bill has come up with, and you wouldn't want to stay at Manor Farm now anyway.'

'What makes you think that?' asked Victoria.

Peter looked disconcerted. 'Oh, um, well . . . associations with the past for one thing. Fresh starts and all that.' He gave his glasses an extra rub and then held them up to the light for greater scrutiny as though he might suddenly see something unexpected through them. 'And, ah . . . then the size of the house is another consideration, of course. You don't want to rattle about.'

'It's not *that* big,' objected Victoria, determined to make Peter come clean about whatever he had in mind for both her and the house.

'Not for a family, no, I'll grant you that – it's an ideal family-sized house, but I think . . . that is, Bill thinks . . . that perhaps . . . under the, ah . . . circumstances . . .' He let the sentence trail away.

'What you really mean,' said Victoria, 'is that Meriel wants Manor Farm as a second home and has already fixed it with Bill. She always has wanted it. It caused a bit of friction in the family when Bill let Richard have it, but for once he stood up to her.'

There was an uneasy pause. It struck Victoria that the mention of Richard's name made Peter uncomfortable, but he made a quick recovery. 'I'm glad you've brought up the idea of Meriel having it because that is a possibility, as it happens.' Peter Mason was at his blandest. 'Bill thinks it would be very suitable for them. It's reasonably near Stafford Hawkins' constituency, Meriel would be able to keep an eye on her father – important for both of them – and, of course, the Hawkinses could well afford it. Stafford's a warm man, you know. I have a lot of time for him.'

Victoria remembered Richard telling her that when Meriel had got engaged to Stafford, he had not been considered good enough for her. It had comforted her when the Cunningham clan had equally disapproved of her own engagement – though for very different reasons. Guy had joked that Stafford had been looked down on for being nouveau riche and Victoria for being nouveau pauvre – and foreign to boot. Now Stafford had made even more money and was an influential MP – but I've remained a disappointment, she thought.

'Are you saying I definitely couldn't afford it – even if I wanted to?' she asked.

Peter put his fingers, which reminded Victoria of uncooked sausages, carefully together and then interlocked them as though he were about to play 'Here's the church and here's the steeple' with a very small child. She thought he needed to have his heavy signet ring made a size larger; it bit into the flesh of his little finger.

'Not unless you have a secret supply of money that I know nothing about.' He clearly expected her to share this joke, not believing such an unlikely scenario for a moment. 'But there's no need to worry, my dear,' he went on, twinkling at her cosily. 'Naturally no one is going to turn you out at short notice! Believe me, we shall all take very good care of you and Jake. As I say, Bill has already thought of two possibilities for you, either of which I think might suit you very well.'

'And those are?'

'Well, one possibility would be to make a charming little flat for you and Jake in Bill's house. That would have considerable advantages for everyone concerned. After all, quite soon Jake will only be there during the school holidays and I'm sure he could have the run of the garden.' Victoria thought he made it sound as if Jake was a puppy undergoing house-training. It wasn't difficult to detect Meriel's hand behind this particular suggestion.

Peter cocked an enquiring eyebrow at her but she was determined not to react and just said, 'And what was the other idea?'

'You might prefer to have the cottage at Manor Farm itself –

I know the farm manager and his wife live there now, but I gather that's not an insuperable problem. The cottage would have advantages for you too. Meriel and Stafford could keep an eye on Jake and he'd be near his cousins. I realise the Hawkins children are older but they'd supply some family life for him. It won't be easy for you bringing up the boy alone and you're going to need all the help you can get.' Clearly the Cunningham family intended to keep her under close supervision.

'What about the farm?'

'Ah. Well, Bill's taken on the running of that again for the moment – but I think Stafford Hawkins may have helpful ideas for the future reorganisation of that too. You don't want to worry your head about the farm.'

'I see. Suppose Jake wanted to farm, later?'

'Then I'm sure Stafford would be an excellent person to advise you.'

Suddenly Victoria felt she could bear Peter's heavy company and patronising manner no longer. She glanced at her watch. It was already after one o'clock.

'Thank you, Peter. You've given me an idea of how things are – and much to think about. I'd like you to know that I'd never dream of cutting Jake off from Richard's family – especially not from Bill – but I haven't made up my mind yet where Jake and I will live or what I shall do with my life. You spoke about fresh starts and I may well decide to live in Corfu – that's where my real roots, are after all – but I need to go back to Baybury next week and take stock of our situation. I'll let you know when I come to any decision.' She got up and held out her hand, forestalling a kiss. 'Thank you for sparing me your time, Peter, and for giving me your views. I shall bear in mind what you've said. It was very kind of you to offer lunch but I have a lot to fit in while I'm over here and this week is getting rather hectic so perhaps you'll forgive me if I don't take you up on your offer this time.'

Peter looked as if he was about to protest but changed his mind. Victoria thought he was probably as relieved to see her go as she was to say goodbye to him. She hoped she had given him a few things to think about and guessed he would be on the telephone to Meriel the minute she was out of the office.

Chapter Thirty-eight

❧

Patrick's flat was on the second floor of one of the tall white stuccoed houses in Warwick Square. The day before his call to Victoria, he'd driven Hugh up to London and deposited him at Boodle's in St James's Street, where he'd gone off in fine fettle to seek out various old cronies in the bar. Hugh was greatly looking forward not only to the prospect of a few days socialising in London with his many friends, but to the small family dinner party he'd planned on the ladies' side of Boodle's after his exhibition, to which – via Patrick – he had invited Evanthi's granddaughter. That should prove extremely interesting in more ways than one, he thought. It had not escaped his notice that her name seemed to crop up in Patrick's conversation with some regularity.

They'd had an enjoyable drive together discussing their many mutual interests, ranging from sport to architecture; religion to painting – and, of course, family. As always, Patrick had been entertained by his uncle's fund of anecdotes, the recent disclosures about his past unleashing a whole lot of reminiscences that were completely new to his nephew. Inevitably they had also talked about Vrahos, and Patrick found it fascinating to speculate on how different his uncle's life, and therefore perhaps his own, might have been if he'd married Evanthi Palombini – as she had been some sixty years ago.

'Do you want to talk about Rachel?' The old man had asked at one point, apropos of nothing obvious, though Patrick could follow the train of thought rather too well for comfort.

Patrick hesitated. He did not feel it was the right moment to discuss her, and anyway a habit of loyalty, connected with the knowledge that Hugh had never liked her, also held him back. 'I would like to talk about her sometime,' he said, 'but I need to sort a few things out first. Meanwhile, as I gather Sophie told

387

you, Rachel has announced she wants a trial separation. I've talked to Sam and Sophie about it.'

'How did you feel they took it?'

'Hard to tell with Sam. I think he minds more than he lets on, but Sophie took it badly.'

Hugh nodded. 'She would, of course. Not much I can do to help,' he said, 'but you know you can use me as a sounding board if you need one.'

'Thanks. I may take you up on that sometime.' And Patrick had changed the subject.

He had a busy schedule ahead with several appointments to be fitted in. First he intended to go to the Crompton Gallery in Brook Street, where Hugh's retrospective exhibition was to be held. They'd brought the portrait of *Girl on the Rock* with them in the car, and Hugh had asked Patrick to deliver it to the gallery. It seemed a considerable responsibility and he thought the sooner he got it into the safekeeping of Jeremy Crompton, the better, but as he was about to carry it downstairs, hail a taxi and set out for Brook Street he changed his mind and decided to deliver it the following day instead. He just *had* to show it to Victoria that evening. He didn't want her to see it for the first time in the thrust and throng of the party on Friday night with a mass of people crowding round it; besides he wanted to enjoy her reaction to it and share the moment with her. He was enormously looking forward to seeing her, but was not without some apprehension. He hoped she had felt some attraction to him, but was well aware that so soon after the tragedy in her life she must still be in a highly emotional state and he had no wish to upset her by rushing things or to take advantage of her vulnerability.

He propped the portrait up on a chair in the sitting room, still swathed in its wrappings, and went off to catch a tube to Leicester Square to see Saphira Winterton in her office in St Martin's Lane. Saphira had been gratifyingly enthusiastic about the Vrahos photographs. They'd spent a profitable session discussing the present book and then tossed around ideas for future ventures. Several publishers had approached Saphira about possible commissions.

*

The front doorbell went at five past eight and Patrick answered it immediately. 'Victoria? Come on up – second floor. No lift, I'm afraid.' He pressed the buzzer and the door downstairs clicked open. He was waiting at the top of the stairs for her.

Once inside the flat they looked at each other in some surprise. Neither saw quite what he or she had expected.

Patrick recovered himself first. 'It's just *so* good to see you, Victoria,' he said, smiling at her with an obvious pleasure that made her heart lurch. He seemed even taller than she remembered and every bit as good-looking, but smoother, somehow, and much more glamorous in his London clothes – immaculately cut dark suit, expensive-looking shirt and tasselled black loafers – than in the casual holiday clothes she had seen him wearing in Corfu.

'You look utterly wonderful,' he told her.

'Well, don't sound so astonished!' she said, laughing at him, hoping her face didn't betray her sense of excitement.

'Oh, I'm not surprised that you look beautiful,' said Patrick, 'because I've never seen you look anything else – it's just that I hadn't met this soignée version before. A fascinating new insight! What a sensational jacket.'

'Thank you,' she said, sending a fervent mental vote of thanks to Francine.

Francine had insisted that she wore the new black silk jacket with all the colours of a bird of paradise on its cuffs. Victoria had been doubtful. 'Don't you think it's a bit too smart? I don't want to look overdressed.'

'Why ever not?' asked Francine.

Victoria looked nonplussed. 'I suppose I don't want to give out the wrong message,' she said doubtfully. Francine rolled her eyes despairingly. 'Oh, you English women – always so afraid of dressing to please. I just don't get it. He hasn't asked you out to dinner for a tramp over the moors or to grab a takeaway, for God's sake! What sort of message do you want to give out then?'

'I don't really know,' said Victoria truthfully, and added: 'And anyway, I'm not English.'

'Well, act Continental then! I don't particularly know about the Greeks but French and Italian women don't suffer from this dressing-down hang-up. Surely you just want him – or anyone else come to that – to think you look terrific and have taken a little trouble. It simply seems good manners to me – what's wrong with that?'

'Nothing, if you put it like that,' said Victoria, laughing.

'Well, go for it then,' and Francine had also insisted on making up Victoria's face before she went out. She always had the latest supply of samples that had been sent by famous cosmetic firms, hoping she would write about them for the American fashion glossy for which she did shopping reviews: 'Face Facts with Francine'.

'Amazing,' said Victoria, gazing at her reflection with surprise. 'I hardly look made up at all but it certainly improves matters!'

'*C'mon* Victoria! Did you think I'd turn you out looking like the Scarlet Woman?' smiled Francine. 'Do I usually look so over-made up myself then?'

'No, never. You always look wonderful.'

'Well, thanks – but if so it's because I make darn sure I do!' Francine made a self-deprecating face and grinned at Victoria. 'I don't have all your natural assets – but I sure as hell try to make the best of those I have,' she said. She surveyed her handiwork with satisfaction. 'You really don't know how lucky you are, Victoria,' she added seriously. 'So go have a fun time. There's a charge for this service, though – you gotta tell me all about your evening when you come back!'

'What would you like to drink?' asked Patrick now, going over to a table in the window. 'Wine or something stronger? We've got most things.'

'Wine would be great, thank you. What a lovely room – are the pictures by your uncle?'

'They are indeed,' said Patrick, opening a bottle of wine. 'I've always loved his charcoal drawings. They're so bold – so immediate. Such a lot of energy packed into a few lines. I'm glad you like them. I think they look rather well in here. You'll see them again on Friday night because I'm lending them for the exhibition – but I also have something here I particularly want to show you.' He handed her a glass of chilled chablis and went over to the chair where he had propped the picture. 'Shut your eyes,' he said. He pulled off the cover, and went back to stand beside her. 'Now look.'

Obediently she looked.

'Nonna's portrait!' she exclaimed, and then: 'Oh *wow*!' No more words were needed – her face said it all and he felt hugely pleased with her obvious delight.

'We brought it up to London on Monday but I particularly wanted to show it to you before it goes to the gallery tomorrow.' Patrick looked from the picture to Victoria. 'I think Hugh's going to get quite a shock when he sees you,' he said. 'There are obvious differences – you're a pocket version for one thing – but you must look unnervingly like his memories of your grandmother. Not just your colouring but something in your expression – and, of course, those eyes.' He added quietly, 'No wonder he fell for her.'

Victoria felt herself flushing. She could feel her heart bumping so hard she was afraid he might hear it. She felt on fire, charged up as if sparks could be coming out of her ears, and thought that if she accidentally brushed against him she might well give him an electric shock. She went to examine the picture more closely and then stood back again.

'It's sensational,' she said at last. 'To think Nonna hasn't seen it since it was painted! And that rock she's sitting on – I know *exactly* where that is, it's unmistakable. We called it the dragon rock when we were children – you can see why – but Jake thinks it looks more like a dinosaur. It moves me so much to think of Nonna and your uncle all those years ago, I'm absolutely fascinated by it. Sometimes when I ask too many questions she'll suddenly clam up on me for a bit – and then she'll come out with another bit of information so that I feel as if I keep finding new clues. Their story's like a sort of treasure hunt, don't you think – an ongoing one apparently?'

'Yes,' he said. 'I've been piecing bits of the saga together too. Let's compare notes over dinner and see if we can fill in a few blanks for each other. Sophie's been sitting for him and he probably tells her more than he'd ever tell me – she's a mine of information on the subject.' He grinned at Victoria. 'You can imagine how she laps it all up! She sent you her love, by the way. I hope you'll see her and Sam on Friday night.'

'Oh, good,' said Victoria, genuinely pleased. 'How are they? What's Sophie's portrait like – does it do her justice?'

'I haven't been allowed to see it yet – very tantalising. It's being unveiled at the preview and the gallery already have it, so you'll see that too. But I can tell Hugh's pleased with it, and the fact that he wanted to paint her is doing wonders for her confidence. He's always been so good with the young. Now I have something else to show you.' He handed her an A4 size cardboard-backed envelope. 'It's a present,' he said quietly.

'A present for me?' she asked. 'Whatever is it?'

'Open it and see. I very much hope you approve.'

Victoria drew out two photographs of Evanthi. She gave a little gasp of pleasure and Patrick could see she was extremely pleased. The first was the one he'd taken of her in her purple turban and black caftan – Evanthi at her most regal, sitting in her winged chair by the fire in the drawing room. She looked as if she might be defying marauding pirates, or quelling a riot. The second photograph had caught her standing in the doorway of the open French windows that led on to the terrace, gazing out to sea. Patrick's lens had spared no detail of her finely lined face, or the shredding tatters of the faded, once beautiful curtains against which she stood. Her silver hair was piled up in its usual knot and she was leaning on her stick. He had captured vividly a moment in the present . . . but the foreground and the details of the room behind, were gently fading into a blur. She looked proud and patrician but also tired and frail – and vulnerable.

Patrick saw Victoria's eyes filling with tears. She laid the two photographs side by side on the table and examined them in silence. Then she went and put her hands on his shoulders and looked up into his face. '*Thank you*,' she said. 'Oh, Patrick thank you *SO* much.' His arms went round her and he held her tightly against him and in that instant something that had been hovering between them became much stronger for them both: a flare of hope – but suddenly something much more than a possibility. Victoria gave herself up, for a moment, to his embrace, then forced herself to pull away. Images of

Richard flashed into her mind . . . and Patrick has a wife, she thought.

But her grandmother's words came winging back to her too: 'If it happens – you will know.'

He slackened his hold immediately, but just touched her face, very gently, with his finger before he let her go – acutely conscious both of her instinctive, quick response to him and then her sudden uncertainty. She looked at him anxiously, afraid he would misunderstand the reason for her withdrawal.

'It's all right,' he said reassuringly. 'I understand. Is this all too soon for you?'

'Perhaps. A bit soon,' she echoed in a shaky voice. 'But don't be sorry, either!' She went back to the table where she had put the photographs, not trusting herself to stay too close to him.

'These are *brilliant*,' she said, glad to have a chance to compose herself. 'Oh, Patrick! You have caught Nonna's essence at the end of her life with your clever, clever camera just as surely as your uncle did with his brush when they were young. I shall treasure these photographs all my life.'

There were things he longed to say to her, but in the meantime her reaction to his embrace had told him what he needed to know.

'Did she realise you were photographing her?' asked Victoria, turning to the photographs again, still trying to recover her equilibrium.

'She did for the formal one.' He smiled at the memory: 'She had every intention of posing for me and as you can see with that amazingly becoming turban and the jewellery, she was dressed up for it too – but I don't think she had any idea I'd taken the one in the window. That was done on a different day when I was prowling round taking shots of all sorts of objects in the room and I caught her unawares. I think the first one would be good in the book – every inch the chatelaine of Vrahos – but the second one is specially for you. I haven't sent either of them to your grandmother yet. In fact, there are lots more to choose from and you may like others better, but these are the two I thought were the best myself.'

'Are you going to show them to your uncle?' she asked, sipping her wine.

'I thought I might, but I wanted you to be the first to see them. What do you think? Should I let him see them too?'

'Oh, I think you must. After all, he knows his "girl on the rock" is an old lady now so that it wouldn't exactly be a shock, and there's surely much in these photos that's instantly recognisable as the person he must have loved so much.'

'I'm glad you think that. I had a strong feeling at the time that the reason she wanted me to photograph her had far more to do with Hugh than for any illustration for my book!'

At that moment the telephone rang, breaking the spell between them. Patrick answered it.

'Oh, hello, Saphira. Well, I'm just about to go out,' Victoria heard him say. 'Would it keep till tomorrow? Oh, I see. Well, hold on a moment then.' He made an apologetic face at Victoria, and put his hand over the receiver. 'Sorry about this – I'll go and take it in the other room. I'll be as quick as I can.'

'Don't worry about me,' she said. 'I'm very happy and I've got lots to look at.'

She wondered who Saphira was, and realised how little she knew about Patrick's life. She got up to study the portrait again, thinking how wonderfully the artist had conveyed the clarity of the Corfiot light, the colour of the sea and the rocky headland that she knew so well, with the dark cypress trees standing tall against the sky. She wandered round the room looking at Hugh Marston's powerful drawings, mostly of horses in action – a marvellous one of a stampede, and another of two stallions fighting – but there were a couple of sketches of people too, one, above the fireplace, of a good-looking boy in an open-necked shirt, whose face was familiar. There was a look of Sam, but she guessed it was actually Patrick aged about fourteen. On a chest of drawers between the windows were framed photographs: it was easy to recognise a small Sam and Sophie wielding buckets and spades, standing beside a sandcastle on a beach; then there was a more recent group in which they sat on a rug in a garden on either side of a spectacularly pretty fair-haired woman with a small girl on her lap. Rachel! Unable to resist a closer inspection, Victoria picked the photograph up at the exact moment when Patrick came back into the room. She felt her colour rising.

'I'm afraid I'm being nosy about your family,' she said, trying not to sound guiltily apologetic like a child caught raiding the sweetie cupboard. 'This must be your wife and your younger little girl. How . . . how stunning your wife is.'

'Yes,' he said, watching her. 'Rachel has always been ravishing to look at,' but somehow he did not make this sound like a compliment. Victoria felt she couldn't leave it there; there were too many things she had to know. 'Am I going to meet her on Friday night ?' she asked. 'You said Sam and Sophie were coming – will Rachel be there too?'

'Sam and Sophie are both desperate to come – nothing would keep them away! Sophie's just finished her exams so she's already broken up. She's been working really hard so it will be great for her to have some fun. She and Sam are coming down on the train from York.' He paused for a moment. 'But no, you won't meet Rachel. She isn't coming.'

He walked over to the window and stood looking out, hands thrust in his trouser pockets. Victoria waited anxiously for what he had to say, realising how important this was to her. Then he said abruptly, 'Rachel and I seem to have come to a parting of the ways. It's been on the cards for quite a while, but after we got back from Corfu something happened at home that has suddenly brought matters to a head for both of us. Rachel's suggested a trial separation and I've agreed. I want that too.'

'I'm sorry,' she said, not feeling sorry at all, but not knowing what else to say. She wanted to ask if he still loved his wife; what had triggered the break; whether there were other people involved.

He turned round and raised an eyebrow at her. 'You have a great big "think bubble" coming out of the top of your head with a huge question mark in it,' he said, smiling at her.

'Yes,' she said truthfully. 'I expect you think I was snooping just now – and I was – but I can't help being curious, and if . . . if we are going to see any more of each other I need to know a lot of things. Do you want to talk to me about it?'

'Yes,' he said. 'I very much want to tell you about Rachel and I agree we need to talk about her and about our families and about your marriage too – about many, many things – but do you know what I'd really like now?'

She shook her head.

'I'd like to go out to dinner together and just enjoy each other's company. Let's be light-hearted this evening, without trying to go into all the difficulties and dilemmas – and in your case tragedy too – which we have in our lives. Would that be selfish?'

Suddenly Victoria felt extraordinarily happy – happier than she'd been for ages – perhaps for years, she thought in surprise.

'I'd love that too,' she said, with relief.

'Drink up then,' he said smiling at her, 'and let's go.'

It was a lovely warm evening. Four people were still playing tennis on the court in the square gardens; swifts were swooping and a blackbird was singing. 'Isn't it heavenly being *exactly* the right temperature?' said Victoria as they walked together to the restaurant for dinner. 'I think it's one of the great physical pleasures. Part of the reason I adore being in Corfu in the summer is the whole barefoot way of life – not fussing about the wellies and waterproofs and the might-I-need-an-extra-jersey syndrome. When I was at my most distraught after Richard's death, my grandmother told me to try to use these small moments – sighting a kingfisher, the first cyclamen, a spider's web, the sun on one's back – like a stepladder to help me climb up again, help me survive.'

'*Thank you* moments,' he said, thinking that for him walking beside her was just such a one.

She thought, as she had done in Corfu, how joyful it was to find someone who seemed to understand so completely her point of view.

The food at Merlin's was as good as Patrick had promised, the service friendly and the setting unpretentious and easy, but they were so absorbed in each other that they hardly noticed their surroundings.

Over dinner they returned to the topic of Evanthi and Hugh.

'What amazes me,' said Patrick, 'is that your grandmother married your grandfather so quickly. It must have been shattering for her to get no answers to her letters from Hugh and she must have felt desperately hurt and let down – but it seems extraordinary to have actually *married* him without seeing Hugh again and trying to discover what had gone wrong when he was in India. Did she tell you her side of that?'

Before Victoria had left Vrahos, she had extracted another piece of the story from Evanthi, but she sensed an implied criticism in Patrick's question that made her feel very protective of her grandmother. 'Yes, she did indeed,' she said defensively, 'and it certainly seemed a good enough explanation to me.'

'No need to bristle,' said Patrick, thinking how beautiful she looked when her eyes flashed. 'I'm not making an accusation! Of course there has to be an explanation – I'm just intensely curious. What did she say?'

'I'm sorry,' said Victoria, mollified. 'I didn't mean to snap. I've got so involved with the whole story I feel as if it's still happening. Well . . . after Hugh'd gone off to India, Nonna discovered she was pregnant. It wouldn't be so terrifying today – and probably wouldn't have happened anyway, with the pill and everything – but it was obviously shattering then. I had longed to know if they'd become lovers but I have to say I was still surprised when she told me about the baby because somehow you never think of your grandmother in that particular way.'

'Ah,' said Patrick, taking a mouthful of wine, 'I had wondered about that too. But then human nature doesn't change – only the attitudes about what's socially acceptable and the ways of dealing with it. So . . . go on. What happened next?'

'Nonna said the baby must have been conceived during a last, vividly happy, snatched meeting just before Hugh left for India,' she said, glancing at Patrick and then looking away again, disturbingly aware of the strong physical connection that there was between the two of them as well. 'She didn't know for sure till Christmas-time. At first she was appalled and terrified – and then suddenly absolutely thrilled. She wrote to Hugh at once to tell him. To say to hell with her mother and all the opposition! Surely now they'd be allowed to marry – and please could he come back? She was convinced he'd be overjoyed too. But, of course, she waited and waited for his answer – and wrote again and waited – and tried and failed to get through to him by cable and telephone . . . getting more and more desperate. It was awful just hearing her talking about it all these years later. I could feel her panic and anguish, and all the time her mother was feeding her lies and telling her she'd heard from Lady Georgia that he'd got another girl – and, well you can imagine it all.'

Patrick could see that Victoria was living through the story herself, her eyes wide with distress, her voice tight with emotion. He touched her hand briefly and refilled her glass.

After a sip of wine she got herself back in hand and went on with the story. 'Then her mother discovered about the baby,' she said, 'and all hell was let loose. Nonna'd confided in Nafsica, who must have reported straight back to my great-grandmother. There was no point in denying anything because her mother was bound to discover soon anyway. Nonna was left in no doubt that Hugh was more unacceptable than ever and that under no circumstances would she be allowed to keep the baby. That's what did it, of course. If she'd been in touch with him, all would have been different and she'd have gone off with him and kept the baby.

'Her mother offered her a choice: have the baby adopted the moment it was born and never see Hugh again – or marry Stavros Doukas and pass the baby off as his. Of course, time was of the essence because if she left it any longer everyone would know. She told me that if she couldn't have Hugh she didn't care who she married – but his unborn baby became the most precious thing in her life and she knew she'd do anything to keep it. Apparently, my grandfather proposed to her at regular intervals and had told her he'd never give up until the day she went to the altar with another man. She accepted him.'

'But surely he must have been extremely surprised at the idea of a wedding at such short notice?' objected Patrick. 'They seemed to go in for long engagements in those days and you'd have thought he might have expected quite a grand affair anyway.'

'Don't forget the horrors of probable war were looming,' said Victoria, 'but I asked her that too. It seems fate really played into my great-grandmother's hands then. Old Mrs Doukas – my other great-grandmother – had had a stroke a few weeks earlier. It wasn't a bad one and she made a good recovery later but they didn't know that at the time. She was desperate to see her only son married to the girl of her choice and a very quiet family wedding, as soon as possible, seemed the perfect answer, in case she died.'

'I bet Evanthi's mother had put a spell on her,' said Patrick. 'She sounds capable of anything. You have ruthless blood running in your veins, Victoria Cunningham! Who'd have thought it?'

'Ah well – you must never underrate me,' said Victoria, laughing at him across the table.

'I'll watch my step!' He thought, as he had the first time they met, what a wonderfully alive face she had, and imagined Hugh had once got as much pleasure from watching Evanthi as he himself was getting now just from looking at Victoria.

'And your grandfather never knew – never even guessed – about the baby?' he asked.

'He didn't have to guess because Nonna told him. She said my grandfather was an honourable man who'd been in love with her for years and when it came to the point she couldn't bring herself to deceive him.'

The arrival of their main course interrupted the conversation for a few moments while the waiter removed the bone from the Dover sole Victoria had chosen and then served Patrick with rack of lamb. 'How scrummy this looks,' she said, 'one of my favourite things.'

'So go on,' he prompted when the waiter had withdrawn. 'I'm enthralled.'

She said seriously, 'I can't tell you how relieved I was to hear Nonna say that – it would have been so out of character for her to do anything shabby. Impulsive, passionate, pig-headed, arrogant – any of those – but shabby, no. I think she half hoped he'd call the wedding off and fling her out. Apparently he was devastated – but he was also generous. I have to say my grandfather comes well out of this story. He must have loved her a great deal because things were different then and it was still very much a man's world; also Greek men have a lot of family pride. He agreed to take the baby on as his own but insisted that she would have to promise never to try to get in touch with Hugh again. At this stage, of course, she thought

Hugh had let her down but, even so, it was a hard promise to give – and later she said, an even harder one to keep.'

'Do you remember your grandfather?'

'Not really – I have a shadowy image in my head of an alarming figure looming over me in my pram – but it may have come from a photograph. Guy remembers him very well, though, and says he was very forbidding.'

'That can't be the end of the story. What happened to Hugh and Evanthi's baby?'

'That's the bitter thing. I could hardly bear it when Nonna told me, because as it turned out it was all for nothing – two months after the wedding she had a miscarriage. She felt she'd lost everything then.' Patrick saw there were tears in her eyes. 'Don't judge Nonna too harshly for not keeping faith with your uncle,' she said sadly. 'She paid a heavy price and no one could judge her more harshly than she judged herself. She was desperately tempted to break her promise to my grandfather after she lost the baby – but she didn't.'

'I wouldn't dream of judging either of them,' said Patrick, touched by her championship of Evanthi, 'and I agree with you – it was brave and honourable of her to tell your grandfather the truth.'

He told her Hugh's side of the story, as regaled by Sophie, and added: 'But no one can take away what they had, and I can't help being glad that she and Hugh were lovers and had their moments of joy together before it all went so horribly wrong.'

'I'm glad about that too,' said Victoria.

'Do you think she's told Hugh about the baby?' asked Patrick, but Victoria didn't know and they both felt they needed to move on to other topics.

They didn't talk about their marriages or their future, but about their respective childhoods; about their children; about their loves and hates, discovering a shared passion for opera and travelling – and that the same ridiculous things made them laugh. The time went so fast that they were amazed to find it was midnight and the restaurant was about to close.

They walked to Patrick's car and he drove her slowly home. When they turned right off the Fulham Road, up Gilston Road and into The Boltons, Victoria felt they had got there much too soon.

'I can't wait for you and Hugh to meet on Friday,' Patrick said. 'Wonderful to think I'll see you again so soon, Victoria.'

'I'm longing to meet him too, but I've had a wonderful evening with you, Patrick.'

She lifted her face to his and he kissed her good night – a swift but by no means an impersonal kiss. Then she ran up the steps to the front door and, after fitting her key in the lock, turned to look back at him again.

He was still standing at the bottom of the steps, watching her. She gave him the sudden vivid smile he'd come to look for and paused for a moment longer.

Then she called: 'See you on Friday,' blew him another kiss and turned and disappeared quickly into the house.

Chapter Thirty-nine

❧

The following morning Victoria wandered down in her dressing gown, having slept extremely well, better than she had done for ages, to find Francine sitting at the kitchen table drinking tea and reading the paper.

'Hi there.' Francine looked up. 'I didn't want to wake you – I thought you needed a lie-in, but I'm glad you've come now because I'm dying to know whether your clothes were right last night and I have to go out soon. The kettle's just boiled – tea or coffee?'

'Coffee, please, if it's easy.'

'Sure – I'll go green with envy while you're drinking it. The baby doesn't seem to appreciate coffee and it's always been my essential morning fix before I can get going. I make do with tea at the moment which I don't usually like nearly as much.' Francine spooned coffee into the espresso machine and switched it on. 'So – how was the evening then?' she asked, though one look at Victoria's face already told her that it must have been special. She thought she looked transformed.

'The evening was great and the jacket was duly admired. Your ears must have burned – I sent you grateful thoughts for making me wear it.'

'And did the distinguished photographer achieve a leap from mere holiday acquaintance to serious new friend?'

'Oh, yes,' said Victoria, helping herself to a croissant and drizzling honey on to her plate, 'he achieved that all right. He passed with flying colours. The crucial question is . . . did I?'

Francine gave her a quizzical look. 'I'll bet you did! You're so attractive, Victoria, but you need to have more faith in yourself. If Patrick Hammond can give you that, I'll be his champion. So – come on! When are you seeing him again?'

Victoria laughed. 'Tomorrow!' she said, her eyes alight. 'I'm having dinner with the family after the preview party. It's the great meeting with Nonna's old boyfriend, if you remember.'

'Of course it is! Gee – Toula was a bit iffy about him, wasn't she?' Francine widened her eyes. 'And Guy's jealous as hell because he likes to think he should have been asked too, so your reporting on the event is going to be tricky!'

'Oh dear.' Victoria pulled a face. 'I did wonder. Perhaps I ought to ask if you can all come?'

'Certainly not – that'd be asking for trouble! You leave Guy to me.'

'Francine . . .' Victoria turned the remains of her croissant into crumbs, 'there's something I want to say to you. You've been so welcoming – so lovely – to me. You do know there's nothing . . . absolutely nothing . . . . between Guy and me, don't you? Yes, I've always adored him – and I probably always will, though I'm finding it hard to forgive him about the whole Richard business. But I'm not *in love* with Guy. For years I suppose I thought I was – in a hero-worshipping sort of way – and it's a relief suddenly to find he doesn't exert that hold over me any more. Perhaps I've belatedly grown out of a childhood passion. It's awful that it's taken a tragedy to make that happen.'

If Francine thought this might have as much to do with Patrick Hammond as with the tragedy, she didn't say so. 'Thank you for telling me,' she said, touched.

'That day I came to see you before I went to Corfu, suggesting you'd had an affair with Richard,' said Victoria in a low voice, 'you must have thought I was completely mad and very offensive. It makes me cringe to think of it.'

'I didn't think you were *mad* – I just had no idea what to do or say. I guess I was terrified of making things worse, but I suppose they couldn't have gotten much worse for you really.' There was a silence between them, and then Francine said, 'If I'm honest I did feel threatened about you and Guy – but it's OK now.'

'If you were worried about *me*, whatever did you feel about Guy and Richard? I should have thought that must be infinitely worse?'

Francine shook her head. 'Unlike you, my eyes were open from the start and anyway I knew that relationship had been over for a long time as far as Guy was concerned. He should have had the courage to be straight with Richard ages before, but it was difficult, and as things turned out, he was right to be afraid of the effect it might have on him. You may think I'm arrogant but I've always felt convinced I could make things work between Guy and me.'

'He told me in Corfu that he thinks it will work too,' said Victoria. 'I never thought I'd say this but I really think he loves you – and I'm glad. And he's entranced about the baby, isn't he? I truly hope you'll be happy.'

'Let's put all these old agonies behind us and start again together,' said Francine, reaching across the table and giving Victoria's hand a reassuring squeeze. 'I guess I didn't realise how much I'd miss my New York women friends and I'm just loving having you here. You've no idea how pleased Guy was that you asked to come to us despite everything. He'll be back this evening so let's go do a movie or something. Would that be good?'

'That would be great. I haven't been to a film for ages. I'd love it.'

Victoria was extremely relieved to have had this conversation with Francine and felt a sense of light-heartedness she hadn't had for a long time. They agreed to go their separate ways during the day, and Victoria said she'd be back at teatime. She'd arranged to meet Romie Constable for lunch, the friend from Baybury with whom she'd shared the school run at Toddingham and who had promised to come up to London to see her. She had been much looking forward to seeing Romie, but now her head was so full of Patrick that it was hard to concentrate on anything else. She certainly didn't feel like telling Romie about him yet. She might be a loving friend, but she was also incapable of keeping anything to herself and Victoria knew that by the time Romie'd told several other friends – in strict confidence, of course – about Victoria's budding romance, it would be all round Baybury and into the ears of the Cunningham family in no time.

The party at Brook Street was in full swing by the time Victoria got there on Friday evening. She showed her invitation card to the glamorous woman sitting at a table just inside the door who checked her name and then handed her a glossy catalogue – from the cover of which her grandmother's face looked out at her. Victoria wanted to shout out loud and wave the catalogue at everyone – and longed for Evanthi to be with her to share the moment. The portrait was reproduced again inside the catalogue: '*Girl on the Rock* – Portrait of Evanthi Palombini, 1938' read the caption.

Victoria accepted a glass of champagne and then looked at the sea of people milling round her, and couldn't see a single face she recognised. She had a moment of panic when she felt like bolting back out into the street again, until across the room she saw the back of Patrick's head sticking up above everyone else's – and at the same moment he turned round and saw her too and his face lit up. He came over immediately.

'Wonderful!' he said. 'I was so afraid you might not make it at the last minute. It must have been daunting to arrive into this mêlée on your own, but now you've come I promise we'll look after you. I am so very pleased to see you.'

'Me too,' she said, hugely pleased to have found him. 'But oh, Patrick! You didn't tell me about the catalogue cover. It's sensational!'

'I had a pile of them in the flat the other evening, but I wanted it to be a surprise for you so I hid them away. I've got some for you to take to your grandmother or give to other members of your family. Now come and say hello to Hugh – he's being lionised by everyone and loving every moment of it, but he's longing to meet you. Obviously you won't get a chance to talk about Evanthi here but there'll be lots of time for that later and you'll be sitting next to him at dinner.'

He led her over to the far side of the room.

'You certainly don't need to tell me which he is,' said Victoria, laughing. 'I see why poor old Nafsica freaked at the sight of you. Except for that mane of white hair you really are uncannily alike!'

'I'll probably have the white hair all too soon myself – though I think I'll keep mine a bit shorter than his,' said Patrick. Hugh was standing by the portrait of *Girl on the Rock* talking to an eminent art critic from Washington. When he saw Victoria he held out both hands to her, dropping his stick and nearly falling over in the process. Luckily Patrick and the art critic fielded him just in time to prevent him crashing to the floor.

'Evanthi's granddaughter!' he said, beaming at her, once they'd straightened him up and he'd recovered his balance. 'What a wonderful moment! If you come and stand here everyone will think you've just stepped out of the frame.' He turned to the art critic. 'Just look at her,' he said. 'Can't you see the resemblance? This is the granddaughter of Evanthi Palombini.'

'I certainly can. You must tell me more about this.' The critic, sensing a story, looked extremely interested, but someone else came up at that moment to claim Hugh's attention and he had to turn away. Victoria felt a tentative touch on her sleeve and turned to find Sophie standing beside her – a Sophie who at first glance looked unrecognisably groomed and sophisticated in smart black trousers and a black top, but who smiled a trifle uncertainly at Victoria as if she wasn't sure how to react.

'Oh, Sophie, how *lovely*! How great to see you.' There could be no doubting Victoria's pleasure as she gave Sophie a hug. 'Will you take me round and tell me about all the pictures?' she asked.

'That's an excellent idea,' said Patrick. 'Sophie darling, why don't you and Sam look after Victoria for me? I think perhaps I'd better stay fairly near Uncle Hugh to catch him when he next falls over! Take Victoria to look at *Girl under the Apple Tree* and introduce her to anyone you know, and I'll come and collect you all later. Would that be all right, Victoria?'

'Lovely,' she said, touched by his concern. 'I can't think of anything nicer.' So Sophie bore her off to inspect her own portrait, gathering Sam en route, who seemed gratifyingly pleased to see his Corfiot goddess again.

Victoria stood in front of the portrait. 'Oh, Sophie!' she said. 'You must be absolutely thrilled. It's *fantastic*! What's so fascinating is that it's *so* like you now – yet somehow it shows what you're going to be like in a few years' time too. Did you enjoy sitting for it?'

Sophie nodded, very pleased at Victoria's reaction. 'It was really cool. Uncle Hugh told me all about him and your grandmother while he was painting me. It was *so* sad I could hardly bear it! I'm glad you like it – I can't really believe it's me,' said Sophie. 'Dad's only just seen it because Uncle Hugh wouldn't let him look before and he seems really pleased too.' Then she looked at Victoria and a shadow crossed her face.' I just wish Mum could be here too,' she muttered. 'It seems all wrong to be showing anyone my picture before she's seen it.'

Victoria was uncomfortably aware that though Patrick had told her Rachel would not be at the party, he had not told her why or what the trigger for their decision to separate had been. To her embarrassment, she felt herself flushing and wanted to say that whatever the reason for Rachel's non-attendance tonight, it was not because of her.

'I'd gathered she wasn't here – I'm so sorry,' she said awkwardly. 'What . . . what had luck she couldn't come.'

There was an uneasy little pause. Sam gave his sister a cautionary look.

'Great picture, isn't it?' he said to Victoria. Then he grinned at his sister. 'But Sophe's been insufferable ever since it was finished,' he teased. 'Horses are really Uncle Hugh's forte, though, so I think Punch is the best part of the picture!'

'Huh! You're just jealous,' said Sophie. 'Don't listen to him, Victoria!'

Their usual affectionate banter seemed to be restored, but Victoria felt she had received a warning.

'Come on,' said Sam. 'If we can drag Sophie away from her own image we'll show you some *really* beautiful creatures.'

They were obviously enormously proud of their great-uncle and knowledgeable about his paintings. Victoria recognised the charcoal drawings she'd seen in Patrick's flat, but there were many others too. Looking at some early watercolours of India she felt sure they must have been done during the ill-fated trip that had been the trigger for his misunderstandings with Evanthi. The bulk of the paintings were of animals but there was a selection of wartime sketches too, some of which were deeply disturbing.

'They all look so *young*,' she said sadly, looking at a drawing of a wounded soldier, 'but I suppose he was very young himself when he did those. What an amazingly versatile artist he is –

some of those big oils are extremely powerful! I love the one of the leopard stretched out in the tree. It looks half asleep but you feel it could move like lightning any moment.'

'That's been lent by Prince Haroun, who's a patron of Uncle Hugh's. Uncle Hugh's just finished a huge picture of his mares and foals. It's in the next room. You must see that too.'

By the time they'd got round all three rooms in the gallery the majority of people were starting to leave and the throng had thinned out, so it had become easier to study the exhibits in comfort. Victoria was thoroughly enjoying herself, feeling how natural and easy it was to be with the Hammonds again, when she saw a portentous-looking figure bearing down on her and realised it was Peter Mason.

'Victoria! What a very unexpected pleasure,' he said, emphasising the unexpectedness more than the pleasure she thought, but helping himself to the kiss she'd managed to avoid on Wednesday all the same. 'You never told me you were coming.' He made it sound like an accusation, so that she half expected him to demand to check her invitation. 'What brings you here? Not ideas of buying a picture, I trust!' and he laughed uproariously at such a ridiculous suggestion, rocking like a chair that has lost a castor.

'Oh, don't worry – nothing so above my touch. I've come to pay homage to my grandmother's portrait,' said Victoria sweetly, indicating the glossy cover of the catalogue. 'You probably didn't know Hugh Marston was an old family friend of hers, did you? Sadly my grandmother couldn't come herself so I'm representing her.' She had the satisfaction of seeing she had disconcerted him and felt he was hastily reassessing her for possible upgrading to a more important category in his mental filing system, but all the same his rather prominent eyes kept swivelling away while they talked – as she remembered they were inclined to do at any gathering, in case someone more influential than the person he was currently talking to might appear. He reminded her of a lizard, ever watchful for juicy prey, and when he suddenly focused over her shoulder she half expected to see him shoot his tongue out and catch a celebrity on the end of it. But: 'Ah . . . Patrick!' he said, his mellifluous voice sounding particularly well-oiled. 'My dear chap, how good to see you. I was hoping to have a word. What a talented family you are! I've been hearing great things about your forthcoming book – Saphira's a long-standing friend – and now you must be delighted at the success of dear old Hugh's retrospective evening. I predict rave reviews tomorrow. Oh – do you know Victoria Cunningham?'

'Indeed I do,' said Patrick, giving Victoria the ghost of a wink. 'And I've come to collect her because she's having dinner with us, so I'm afraid I'm going to take her away from you, Peter.' To Victoria he said: 'I think Hugh's stood for quite long enough. He may feel he can't leave till everyone's gone but they all seem to be on the move now. We've got a car coming to pick us all up and take us to Boodle's. Sam, will you go and see how Hugh's doing and bring him along when he's ready? Bye then, Peter – glad you've enjoyed the evening,' and he started to shepherd Victoria and Sophie towards the door.

'We must meet sometime,' said Peter, not wanting his quarry to escape him so easily. 'Have lunch . . . discuss a few things . . . I might have some ideas to put to you . . . I'll get my secretary to give you a ring.'

Victoria could see his antennae working overtime, assessing the situation, speculating on her connection with Hugh Marston and Patrick Hammond. She had no doubt that by the time she got to Baybury on Monday the Cunningham family would have had a full report of her social activities. Luckily at that moment Peter caught sight of Prince Haroun, who was just leaving. The prince was surrounded by his usual retinue of aides and bodyguards, most of whom were sporting dark glasses as though they were contending with the blazing desert sun rather than the discreet lighting of a Mayfair picture gallery. Peter, moving with surprising speed for one so ponderously built, tried to intercept the prince before he got to the door, but was headed off by the bodyguards, who bowled towards him like an army of red ants.

'I didn't know you knew that self-important old windbag,' said Patrick, watching this manoeuvre with much amusement.

'He's my trustee,' said Victoria, pulling a face. 'He was Richard's godfather. He doesn't approve of me and I think I'm about to have a major tussle with him about Jake's education and where I should live and a few important things like that. But perhaps he'll get shot by one of those trigger-happy assassins,' she added hopefully. 'That would solve my problems!'

'I fear Peter was born in a bullet-proof vest,' said Patrick, laughing. 'Don't you let him bulldoze you – you stick out for what you want. Ah, here comes Hugh. Let's go.'

The car dropped them in St James's Street, and while Patrick and Sam escorted Hugh through the main entrance to avoid him having to negotiate too many stairs, Victoria and Sophie went up the stone steps by the *Economist* building and then down to the Ladies' Entrance opposite, to tidy up before dinner.

'You look very sophisticated, Sophie,' said Victoria, spraying herself with Chanel No. 19. 'Very chic trousers, and I *love* your hair knotted up like that.'

'Dad said he'd pay for something new but that I had to look smart – and it must be what *he* called smart, not just what I thought was trendy,' said Sophie with a giggle. 'As Mum was away I enlisted the help of my friend Ellie's mother, who always looks pretty cool herself for someone her age, and she took us shopping to the Harvey Nick's in Leeds. You look *amazing* yourself, Victoria.'

'I had a sinful shopping spree too – it's eating into my conscience!' Victoria wondered how Rachel Cunningham could have borne to let someone else have the fun of choosing her daughter's outfit for such an important family occasion. 'I got my cousin's American wife to act as my fashion consultant and I'd never have bought this outfit without her. Glad you approve,' she said as they went to join the others.

They had a wonderful evening. Victoria sat between Hugh and Patrick, with Sam and Sophie opposite. Though Hugh obviously wanted to know every detail about Evanthi, his manners were clearly much too good to allow him to monopolise Victoria to the exclusion of his other guests, and she liked the way he made a point of including Sam and Sophie in the conversation.

'Perhaps you and I can get in a huddle together after dinner and you can bring me up to date about your grandmother and tell me how she really is,' he said to her, beaming. 'There's so much I want to ask you that I hardly know where to begin. I can't tell you what it means to me to be in touch with her again after all these years.'

So they talked about Vrahos in a general way, Victoria telling them about her childhood there and Hugh describing what the island had been like when he knew it, while Patrick, occasionally catching Victoria's eye and smiling at her, was delighted to see how well they got on together. They discussed Patrick's book and he told them about some of the other houses he was hoping to include; they talked about Sophie's forthcoming exams and Sam's plans to go to Thailand in the summer vacation. They had a hugely enjoyable post-mortem about the exhibition and the people who'd been there. Hugh was full of stories connected with his various patrons – some of them wildly indiscreet – and they discussed the two portraits that had been such a talking point to everyone earlier in the evening. Hugh proposed a toast to Evanthi and Sophie – his two beautiful models.

'Just look at your daughter's face,' said Victoria to Patrick as they got up to leave the dining room and have coffee next door. 'Doesn't your uncle make her spark? He really is a very, very special person. I could fall in love with him myself.'

'Don't do that,' said Patrick, 'or I might shoot him!'

Victoria shot an apprehensive look in Sophie's direction, but she did not appear to have heard.

'I've got the silver box in my bag,' she whispered. 'Would now be a good moment to show it to him, do you think?'

'Perfect. I hoped you might do that.'

So Hugh and Victoria sat together on one of the sofas against the wall at the far side of the room.

'I have something I'd like you to take to your grandmother,' he said. 'It was partly Sophie's idea. I hope Evanthi will like it.' And he handed Victoria a flat, oblong packet.

'Nonna asked me to bring you something too,' she said. 'She wants it back, but she thought you might like to see it again. She asked me to tell you that she has kept it with her wherever she's been for the last sixty years. I remember it when I was a child but until the day Patrick came to Vrahos I never knew its

411

history,' and she placed a small packet wrapped in tissue paper on his knee.

He opened it. When he saw what it was he took Victoria's hand in his and gripped it tightly for a moment. Then he felt in his pocket. 'I have its twin right here,' he said huskily. 'I put it in my pocket this evening partly to bring me luck because I was exhibiting Evanthi's portrait, and also because I wanted to show it to you.' He sat holding the two almost identical little boxes, one in each hand, staring at them. She could see that he was very moved.

'Tell me about the bees and swallows,' she said. 'Are the swallows anything to do with Helidonia – the little island you can see from Vrahos, where Nonna used to take us for picnics when we were children? We always knew it was a special place for her. My son, Jake, loves to go there now.' And she thought of her own near-disastrous attempt to get to the island and of Guy and Petros coming to her rescue. How things have changed for me since then, she thought.

'Yes,' said Hugh. 'That island was where I proposed to Evanthi and she accepted me. I'm glad you like it too. I painted her a picture of two swallows, lying wing to wing in their nest – she called them Hugh and Evanthi. Swallows are supposed to symbolise the bringing of good news – did you know that?'

'Of course,' she said, smiling at him, 'Nonna taught me that. This spring, when I was at my lowest ebb, I used to watch a pair of swallows who were renovating an old nest above the terrace at Vrahos lying wing to wing like that – chat, chat, chat – they never seemed to run out of things to say to each other and I used to feel envious of them because they were together and I was alone – and yet in a funny way they cheered me up too. I was brought up with that little picture, it's always been in Nonna's bedroom, but I had no idea it was by you. I loved it when I was a little girl and used to make up stories about them. And the bees?'

'Bees were an important part of the Vrahos estate in those days. They produced the best honey I've ever tasted and there were something like sixty swarms, if I remember right. Nafsica's father, Socrates, who ran the farm, looked after them. Do they still have those distinctive blue-grey beehives with the flat tops?'

'They do indeed – you see them all over Corfu – and the honey's still wonderful though sadly there are only three swarms left at Vrahos now.' They were both lost in a different world, miles away from Hugh's London club, but both thinking of Evanthi. 'So go on,' she prompted.

'Well, apparently there'd always been wild bees living in the roof of Vrahos and Evanthi insisted they were the guardians of the house. She maintained that if you have the honour to share your house with bees you must respect them, and communicate with them – and keep them informed about major changes in your life.'

Victoria laughed. 'That sounds very like Nonna! We were brought up to talk to those bees. I still do it. But I'll tell you something strange – whenever anything of note happens to the family those wild bees swarm – and that's a fact. I could tell you some fascinating stories about them.'

'Well,' Hugh went on, 'Evanthi decided they were also the guardians of our love and insisted on telling them about us.' He laughed. 'I teased her about it, but she was perfectly serious – so that's why we had them put on our silver boxes.' He looked at Victoria, serious now, not laughing any more. 'I'm afraid those bees didn't do a very good job,' he said.

'Don't say that,' Victoria said fiercely, something in his voice catching at her heart. 'Lots of people stay together for years in a state of mutual indifference. Not many can be parted in the way you were and still keep their love strong for sixty years without contact with each other as you have done. I think they did an *amazing* job. Can I look at your box?'

He handed it to her. 'They're nearly identical,' he said, 'except the inscriptions are the other way round.'

She traced the word *Pantotina* with her finger, 'And it *has* turned out to be for ever, even if not in the way you originally hoped.' She hesitated, and then asked diffidently, 'I know you're in touch with each other . . . but do you think you and Nonna will actually meet again?'

'I don't know,' he said slowly. 'I ask myself the same question and I'd like to think so. If the occasion presents itself I hope we'll be able to manage it. I've become something of a fatalist nowadays – *what will be, will be*. I used to want everything to happen immediately but I've acquired more patience with old age. Which is bloody silly when you come to think of it because I also know, all too well, that my time is running out!'

'Don't say that,' she said again. 'I can't bear it. Since Richard – my husband – died I feel life is terrifyingly uncertain at *any* age, held together by only the thinnest of threads. Gossamer thin. It haunts me.'

'You've just had a big tragedy in your life,' he said, 'but you have youth and strength on your side, beautiful Victoria, and you have a lot more living to do – I know it – so don't waste your life by being afraid to go forward.' He leaned down and reached for his stick. 'I must go,' he said gruffly. 'It's past my bedtime and I've had a long day. Give Evanthi my love. I hope she likes my present. May I keep her box for a while? Tell her I'll return it to her when I see her, and in the meantime I'll lend her mine.' He looked at Victoria with a twinkle in his eye. 'You see, I can still be romantic, even at my age,' he said. '"My true love hath my heart and I have his . . ." and all that.' He pocketed the little box Victoria had brought and handed her the other one, and she took it from him and put it carefully in her bag, too moved to trust her voice to say anything more.

Patrick, who had been watching this exchange with a lump in his own throat, helped the old man get slowly to his feet.

'I'm staying in the club,' Hugh said, 'but the rest of you needn't feel you've got to rush off just because I'm taking to my bed.' He turned to Patrick. 'I'll get you to walk me over to the other side if you will, dear boy. Good night then, Evanthi's granddaughter – it's been wonderful talking to you. I hope I'll see you again very soon. Tell your grandmother that the *Girl on the Rock* stole the show as she always did. Good night, darling Sophie – my other beautiful model. I was proud to have you there too. Good night Sam, dear boy. Come and see me at home soon.'

Victoria went and put her hands on his shoulders. 'Nonna has silver hair like yours now,' she said as she kissed him good night. 'But apart from that I'll tell her I don't imagine you've changed very much. Thank you for letting me join your family party and giving me such a special evening.'

'I won't be long – don't go yet,' Patrick said to her as he took his uncle's arm.

'Thanks for looking after me at the gallery,' said Victoria to Sam and Sophie. 'I wouldn't have missed meeting your Uncle Hugh for anything in the world. He's a very special person. No wonder my grandmother fell in love with him.'

And the three of them stood in silence and watched the two tall figures walk slowly together towards the lift.

When the Hammonds got back to Warwick Square after putting Victoria in a taxi and hailing another for themselves, the answering machine was flashing.

'Shall I see what the messages are, Dad?' Sophie asked. She wondered if there might be a message from Matthew Burnaby to whom she had sent a text two days ago, informing him that she and Sam would be in London at the weekend.

'Oh, do, thanks. Can't think it's anything urgent – probably Saphira,' said Patrick, pouring himself a small whisky and water. Do you want a drink, Sam?'

'Got a Bud?' asked Sam

'I think so – yes, there's one left. Sorry, I meant to stock up. We'll get some more tomorrow. What would you two like to do over the weekend?' Patrick had a clear idea of what he would like to do himself if Sam and Sophie turned out to have plans of their own, but they came first and he didn't feel inclined to suggest it until he knew how they wanted to spend their Saturday.

'There's a message from Granny,' announced Sophie. 'Can you ring her? She needs to speak to you. She tried home earlier and left a message but as you haven't rung back she thinks you might be here. Will you ring tomorrow if you're too late tonight. She said it's not a drama but she sounded rather twittery.'

'Your grandmother always sounds twittery,' said Patrick. 'I've never known her sound anything else – her life is one long twitter. But Mum certainly knows we're all here because I told her.' He didn't add that he'd thought it monstrous of Rachel, staying within such easy reach of London, not to have made the effort for Sophie's sake to come to the party and see Sophie's portrait exhibited for the first time. He had told her so in no uncertain terms – but it hadn't made any difference. 'Oh dear. Wonder what Granny wants.' He looked at his watch. 'It's too late to ring her back now, they'll have gone to bed.'

'Are Mum and Posy coming up at all over the weekend?' asked Sophie, trying to sound casual.

'I'm afraid not, darling. Have you spoken to her lately?'

'She rang me at school to ask how the exams were going. I specially asked her to come tonight – but she said she couldn't make it – not that I mind or anything,' said Sophie undoing the knot on top of her head and tossing her hair back in a very nonchalant way to emphasise the depths of her not caring. Patrick ached for her.

'Were there any other messages?'

Sophie brightened up. 'There was one from Matthew. He wants Sam and me to go down to Maidenhead to his parents tomorrow and spend the day with them all.'

'Would you like to do that?'

'It seems rather mean to go off and leave you all on your own,' said Sophie, and Patrick was touched because he could see she was longing to go.

'Don't you worry about me. You go off and enjoy yourselves. I've got loads of things I might do,' he said.

'I bet I know what one of them is,' said Sam.

'What?' asked Sophie.

'He wants to ask Victoria Cunningham out to lunch – don't you, Dad?' teased Sam.

Patrick took a quick decision. 'Yes,' he said. 'If you go off to the Burnabys I might well try to do that – though I've no idea if she's free – but if there's anything special either of you want me to do with you, that has priority.' They both looked . . . guarded, thought Patrick.

'Listen,' he said, hoping desperately to hit the right note, wanting to be honest but afraid of saying too much. 'I very much like Victoria. I think you know that. She's on her own now. I enjoy her company, and this link with Hugh and her grandmother is a shared bond, but please don't go reading anything more into it at the moment. If there ever were to be anything more – with her or *anyone else* – I promise you'd be the first to be told. And you two and Posy come first. OK?'

'OK,' muttered Sam, looking uncomfortable and wishing he hadn't brought the matter up.

'Sophie?'

'I suppose so,' she said in a tight little voice, shrugging one shoulder.

'I thought you liked Victoria,' said Patrick, and then wished he hadn't.

Sophie punched one of the cushions of the sofa. 'I *do* like her, Dad – it's not that. It's just that it's . . . well, it's all so *difficult.*'

'I know,' said Patrick. 'I know it's hard for you. I do understand that and I'm very sorry.' He tried to put his arm round his daughter but she jerked away. Patrick stood up. 'Well, I'm off to bed now,' he said. 'It was great to have you there this evening supporting Uncle Hugh and sharing in his reflected glory. I felt so proud of you both. He was on cracking form, wasn't he? I'll ring Granny in the morning and find out what the latest drama is – if anything. She's probably mislaid her car keys!' He hesitated for a moment longer, hoping for a softening in Sophie's attitude, but she started flicking through the pages of a magazine in an ostentatiously bored kind of way.

'Night then, both of you,' said Patrick.

He felt he should have been able to salvage what had been such a happy evening, but at the same time he was conscious of a sense of relief at having the subject of Victoria raised openly and was aware that had Sam not brought it up he would have felt uncertain whether or not to mention possible future meetings between him and Victoria – meetings that he had every intention of trying to arrange.

'Poor old Dad – let him have his fling, you can see he's up for it,' said Sam, feeling sorry for his sister but not knowing what to say to her, not really sure how to react himself. He turned the television on for the sport results. 'He's probably missing Mum.'

'Well, he has a funny way of showing it,' said Sophie in a strangled voice, her lovely, sophisticated evening, her new black trousers and all the compliments about the portrait suddenly besmirched by dust and ash. 'A *fling* – why should he have a fling? It makes me feel sick.'

'Oh, come on – be fair.'

'I don't want to be fair,' wailed Sophie, childishly. 'I don't suppose it's in my genes to be fair. After all, Mum's about the most unfair person I know.'

'Oh, Sophe! Play something else for a change, will you?' Sam looked at his sister helplessly.

Sophie stumped off to the slip of a room next to her parents' bedroom, which she shared with Posy if they were all in the flat together – at least she could have the bottom bunk for once. Just as she was dropping off to sleep she heard the sound of her father's voice from next door. Talking to Mum, she thought drowsily. Then she sat bolt upright, listening intently – of course he wasn't talking to Mum! She couldn't quite hear what he was saying but it was enough for her to know with absolute certainty that he was telephoning Victoria.

Sophie flung herself back on the bed, buried her face in the pillow and pulled the duvet over her ears.

Chapter Forty

❖

There had been a fraught atmosphere recently at Pinewood Lodge, the gabled house backing on to Chobham Common where Colonel and Mrs Ingfield had lived for the last thirty years since the colonel retired from the army.

The common, with its birch and fir trees and the sandy stretches of grassland reaching right up to their garden, gave them a spurious feeling of living in the country: nothing too wild and threatening and so conveniently near London. They enjoyed seeing the many Thelwell-type little girls from the neighbourhood tittupping through the bracken on their stout ponies or, at weekends, their sleeker fathers – intent on destressing after the tensions of a week in the City – thundering about on more mettlesome steeds; there was polo to be watched in nearby Windsor Great Park – treading the divots suited Norma to perfection as a form of exercise. The real countryside, with its roaming livestock and tendency to mud, was not to her taste. The house suited them perfectly – it was easy to manage, not too big when they were on their own but large enough – for a limited time – to accommodate the Hammonds if they came to stay *en famille* – not something that happened very often.

The Ingfields had many friends in the area and normally led a well-regulated existence, which Norma felt she had earned after years of following the flag in uncongenial parts of the world and putting up with army quarters. Norma ran the house with clockwork efficiency and Howard organised the garden with all the military precision of which he was capable, a field marshal of the flowerbeds. It would have been a daring tulip that sneaked out of line in the spring border, and the lawn was as carefully tended as a municipal bowling green.

Now, however, the even tenor of their ways had been interrupted and everybody's nerves were on edge. Howard

419

took refuge at the golf club whenever he could, but Norma found herself having to forgo many of her regular commitments – the Ladies Flower Club, the meetings of N.A.D.F.A.S. – even her crucial Thursday morning hair appointment – all had been disrupted by the demands of her daughter and granddaughter. Looking after the two of them seemed to have become a full-time job, and one for which Norma no longer had either energy or inclination.

Since Rachel had returned from Yorkshire announcing that she would be seeking a divorce from Patrick on the grounds, she said vaguely, of incompatibility, things had become increasingly tense. When she and Posy had first descended on her parents for a supposedly short visit, with the laudable intention (so Rachel said) of checking on their welfare, the bouncy and invaluable Yvonne had accompanied them, but now Yvonne, who hadn't bargained on being banished for more than a couple of weeks from Yorkshire to darkest Chobham, had returned north. She had told Rachel she missed her boyfriend, the weekly quizzes at the pub at Kirkby-Wytherton and the meetings of the Young Farmers' Club, but had not said that she also found the atmosphere of the Ingfield household stifling to a degree.

To start with the Ingfields had not taken their daughter's pronouncement very seriously. However, as the weeks passed it became clear that the rift in the Hammond marriage was not just another of Rachel's attention-seeking dramas, but might be serious; the truth started to sink in that Patrick was no keener for Rachel to return to him than she was to do so. Since Yvonne's departure, Posy had trailed round the house grizzling disconsolately while her army of Beanie Babies appeared to have bred indiscriminately all over their hitherto uncluttered house; even the drawing room had been invaded by dolls' prams and cots. Back under her parents' roof again after so many years, Rachel, so obsessively tidy in her own house, so overly wrapped-up in her youngest daughter, seemed to have lost interest in childcare or domestic issues and left it to her mother. She was always going off for trips to London to see friends from university days about whom she had not bothered for a long time. Sometimes she dragged Posy with her, sometimes left her at Pinewood Lodge, but neither Norma nor Posy seemed to be enjoying such exposure to each other's company as much as Rachel felt they should have done. She was uncommunicative with her parents about what she was doing or who she was seeing on her trips.

'D'you think she's picked up some fella?' the colonel asked his wife uneasily.

'Oh, I don't think so, dear. I think she's just catching up with old friends,' said Norma, soothingly, but privately Howard still wondered. It would at least be better than all the strange interests Rachel seemed to have got caught up in lately. Since the arrival of Bronwen in her life, to the colonel's baffled incomprehension his daughter had developed a line in psychobabble that sent him speeding to his study for a gin and tonic at the most inappropriate hours of the day. Anything would be preferable to tripping over Rachel on the landing in what he considered 'dodgy positions', practising yoga on a little rubber mat or plugged into a CD player meditating to the music of copulating whales.

'I don't know what's got into her,' he complained to his wife. 'She's always been difficult but she used to be *normal*. No wonder Patrick's had enough! If I have to hear the opinions of that Richards woman much more I shall blow a fuse. Rachel told me yesterday she believes they were lamas together in a previous incarnation, for God's sake!' The colonel had had an absurd vision of his daughter and Bronwen Richards, not dressed up in saffron robes in a temple, but cropping grass together side by side somewhere in the Andes. Not normally given to whimsy, he was unnerved by such a flight of fancy. 'According to Rachel this frightful pseud – who sounds like a criminal if Patrick's to be believed – has freed her from the inhibitions and hang-ups which *we* apparently gave her in her childhood. All I can say is that I wish she'd bloody well get some of them back again.'

Howard Ingfield gazed gloomily at his gleaming brown brogues as though he sought a revelation in their ultra shiny toecaps. He'd been driven into a state of near apoplexy by the sight of Rachel doing what she called her 'Indian energising exercises' on the patio that morning – after which she was so exhausted that she didn't feel up to giving Posy breakfast.

It was therefore with a sense of foreboding that they heard Rachel answer her mobile one evening (right in the middle of dinner too) and shriek *'Bronwen!'* in a tone of high excitement. She had rushed out of the dining room and not returned for nearly half an hour, when she appeared to be in a state of euphoria.

'Wonderful!' she announced. 'Bronwen's gone to Spain and has suggested I go out to visit her!'

'Whatever for?' asked Norma, her heart sinking.

'Just for a little holiday with Posy at the moment, but possibly to see if I might like to help with a new centre she and Milo are setting up together. It sounds a wonderful venture.'

'A centre for what?' asked Howard, chomping up his steak and kidney pie.

'Oh, therapies and things,' said Rachel vaguely. 'Bronwen thinks I might be a terrific asset in getting it off the ground.'

'I'll bet she does!' growled her father, 'so long as you take your cheque book with you.' He'd been very uncooperative when Rachel suggested he might like to lend Bronwen money.

'I'm amazed she has the nerve to ask you,' said Norma indignantly. 'It's lucky you can't go.'

'What do you mean?' asked Rachel. 'Now that Patrick and I are splitting up, I'm free to do anything I like. Bronwen's been saying for ages that I've been a slave to his lifestyle for far too long. There are other possibilities that have come up lately about what I may want to do with my life, but this sounds interesting – the sort of thing I could really get my teeth into. A challenge. Anyway, I need advice from her about my future.'

'Have you taken leave of your senses, Rachel?' Norma couldn't believe what she was hearing. 'The school holidays are about to start. I know Sam's off travelling but what about Sophie? And I don't think Patrick would be too happy at the idea of you taking Posy to stay with the woman who stole your jewellery. I thought the police told you to let them know if she made contact? That's very serious.'

'Oh that . . .' Rachel waved her hand dismissively. 'Bronwen says that jewellery thing was all a ridiculous misunderstanding. Patrick wouldn't let her explain properly. She says she only borrowed it as security for a loan . . . just to tide her over . . . apparently she'd mentioned it to me, but it must have slipped my mind. I'll get it all back when she redeems it. Now that she's got over the shock of Patrick losing the plot in that ridiculous way, she thinks it's all a bit of a joke.'

'If you swallow that you'll swallow anything,' exploded her father. It was clear to him that this woman was capable of making his daughter believe any amount of dangerous moonshine. 'For an intelligent woman you can be remarkably stupid sometimes, Rachel,' he said testily.

'If you're going to persist with this idea of a separation, you'll have to get it all put on a proper footing, Rachel, darling,' said her mother nervously. 'Your father and I love having you and Posy to stay – of course we do – but we're not getting any younger and we can't go on indefinitely like this, for all our sakes. You and Patrick will have to sort out some more permanent arrangement soon.'

Which was exactly what Patrick had said to his wife on the telephone only a few days before.

Rachel's pretty face set in the mulish look her parents knew so well. 'Well, Patrick will have to cope with Posy for a change if he doesn't want me to take her to Spain,' she said, conveniently forgetting that for the last two years she'd been doing her best to shut her husband out of his daughter's upbringing. 'I'm sure Yvonne would go back to Wytherton – it's only coming south she doesn't like.'

'What about Posy's feelings? She's such a mummy's girl.'

'Posy's growing up. She'll have to adapt – as we all will – to change,' said Rachel loftily. Without the back-up of Patrick and Yvonne she was not finding the sole charge of her small daughter as easy as she expected. The beguilingly dependent toddler was turning into a strong-willed little person whose wishes by no means always coincided with her mother's.

Her parents stared at her. 'Well, you certainly can't leave her here with us,' said Howard Ingfield decidedly. 'It's too much for your mother.' He thought the time had come, belatedly, to take a stand with his daughter. He was beginning to think his son-in-law must have been little short of a saint to put up with her for so long.

'For heaven's sake! I'd only be gone for a week or two! Anyone would think I was doing a runner, from the way you're talking.'

'Like Bronwen Richards did,' said her father disagreeably. 'Well, don't come to me for help if this con-artist gets you into trouble. I shall wash my hands of you. They tell me Spanish gaols are exceedingly uncomfortable.' And the colonel had stalked angrily out of the room, knowing perfectly well that he would never be capable of carrying out this threat but feeling a great deal better for having uttered it.

'Why don't you sleep on it, darling?' said Norma soothingly, the old habit of trying not to upset Rachel kicking in, but deciding that it was time she spoke to her son-in-law herself and alerted him to his wife's latest idea. 'It may all seem different to you in the morning. It's never a good idea to make impulsive decisions,' she added – not that she'd ever tried it herself.

When Sophie emerged blearily into the kitchen at Warwick Square at nine thirty on Saturday, her father was sitting at the kitchen table drinking coffee and reading *The Times*. Nothing except the prospect of seeing Matthew Burnaby would have made her surface so early, but for Matthew she had set her alarm and intended to rouse Sam in time to get a mid-morning train down to Maidenhead.

'How's my Sophie?' asked Patrick cheerfully. 'Did you sleep all right after that great party last night?'

Sophie grunted and glowered at him through her hair, every movement expressing reproach. Patrick gave her a questioning look and went back to his paper. He had a shrewd idea what was eating into his daughter and felt very sorry for her, but he wasn't going to play guessing games with her.

'So – did you ring Granny last night then?' she asked eventually, finding his lack of reaction maddeningly frustrating.

'No – as I said it was too late. I tried this morning but they were engaged so I'm just about to try again.'

'Oh – funny. I could have sworn you rang last night.' Sophie's voice was loaded with accusation. 'In fact,' she said provocatively, 'I know you did because I heard you.'

'No, you didn't, Sophie,' said Patrick evenly. 'You heard me ringing Victoria – as I think you very well know.'

'How on earth was I supposed to know that?'

'Partly because I told you I was going to, and presumably because – as you've just told me – you could hear the conversation?'

There was an uncomfortable pause. Sophie stared defiantly at her father and encountered a look that didn't appear very often but which she recognised all too well. She dropped her eyes first.

'Now listen to me, darling. I know how hard all this is for you but . . .' Patrick, who was determined not to be goaded into a row with his daughter, was about to try to talk to her about the whole Rachel situation when the telephone rang. He picked it up.

'Hello? Oh, hello, Norma. I gather you tried to get hold of me yesterday, but I didn't get your message till late last night.'

Sophie felt grateful the call would give her a chance to recover from a loss of face. She didn't really want to have a confrontation with her father either.

Then she heard him say: 'She's thinking of doing *WHAT*? She can't be serious? That's so bloody stupid!'

Sophie nearly exploded with curiosity.

Patrick said: 'I see. No . . . no, of course you can't. Yes, I fully understand that. Can I speak to her? Is she there now? Oh . . . well when will she be back?' Sophie could hear her grandmother's voice wittering on. Then her father said, 'Of course. Right. Are you sure she'll be there on Sunday if I come down? I'll do a bit of reorganising and ring you back. No, of course you were right to tell me. Sunday lunch would be very helpful, thank you, Norma. Perhaps we could all three come? I'll let you know. Bye then – speak to you shortly.'

'Dad, what's happened?'

'That bloody Bronwen woman again!' Patrick looked angrier than Sophie had ever seen him. 'And I thought we were shot of her at last! Your mother wants to go off to Spain to see Bronwen Richards – that's what.'

'*No!* What are you going to do?'

'Go down to Chobham on Sunday and try to sort things out

with Mum. I suggested I should go today but Granny says Mum's not there anyway and they're taking Posy out to lunch with friends. I'm damned if I'm going to let your mother take Posy anywhere near that frightful woman. I'd rather call the police.'

'Do you think Mum might still go even without Posy?' asked Sophie.

'Let's hope not, but apparently she told your grandmother it was high time I took my turn with Posy – and Posy would just have to get used to it,' said Patrick wryly.

'Oh, Dad – that was a mean thing for Mum to say. You've always been great with Posy. Lucky Yvonne's there.'

'She isn't,' said Patrick grimly. 'It appears Yvonne went back to Yorkshire but Mum never told me that.'

'I don't believe it! Granny and Grandpa are *hopeless* with Posy – she's quite scared of them. Sam and I used to be scared of them when we were little too – Granny never thought anything was funny and Grandpa always seemed so cross. Poor Pose will be miserable.'

Patrick put his arm round his elder daughter. 'You're very generous to your sister, Sophie. I know you find her a torment sometimes. I'm going to be in London most of next week because the Heritage at Risk people have asked me to photograph a couple of properties in the south. Mum and I urgently need to get the plans for the summer holidays sorted out so I think it would be good if you and Sam came down to Chobham too. I know you both want to go to the Marshalls on Sunday night but I could put you on a train to York later in the day. For the next couple of months I'm afraid this upheaval is going to affect you most of all, Sophie, so I think you should be involved in any discussions about holiday plans. What do you think?'

'I'd like to come – but, oh Dad! – how can Mum bear to see Bronwen again?' Sophie had a lot to think about.

'I really can't imagine,' said Patrick despairingly. 'Better wake Sam if you're off to the Burnabys at eleven – and you'd better tell him the latest developments in the Hammond family crisis too.'

'Gosh, yes!' Sophie got up from the table, taking her piece of toast with her. She didn't dare ask if Victoria had accepted her father's invitation but as she got to the door he took pity on her. 'In case you're wondering,' he said 'Victoria *is* coming out to lunch with me. I would have put her off if Mum was at Chobham, but as it is I'd like to stick to the plan. I thought we might go to the Hind's Head at Bray or somewhere round there – is it any good offering to pick you and Sam up from the Burnabys on our way back? We wouldn't be that far away if it would help.'

Sophie came back and flung her arms round her father. 'Thanks, Dad. Thing is – it might be a bit *soon* to be picked up after lunch . . . depends on how things go. You know how it is?'

'1 know,' said Patrick. 'Tell you what, I'll keep my mobile switched on for once and if you want collecting you can ring me. If not you and Sam can make your own way back – but let me know if things go *so* well that you intend to stay with the Burnabys for dinner as well. How's that?'

'Cool,' said Sophie. Then she added: 'Sorry I was such a pain. Everything seems such a muddle at the moment . . . but you really are the best father in the entire world.'

'Hmm,' said Patrick laughing. *'Sometimes!'*

Chapter Forty-one

Patrick arrived to pick Victoria up soon after eleven. Guy answered the door and the two men eyed each other with interest and a carefully disguised suspicion, which deceived neither of them.

Over kitchen breakfast in their dressing gowns, Victoria had regaled Guy and Francine with an account of her meeting with Hugh the previous evening, of the party at the Crompton Gallery and, above all, of the portrait of Evanthi. She showed them the cover of the catalogue and could see Guy was impressed.

'You just *have* to go and see it,' she told them. 'I think the exhibition's on for a month and you'd love some of the other pictures too – but seeing Nonna's portrait is an absolute must. There's a stunning one of Sophie Hammond – Patrick's daughter too – interesting to compare Hugh's style as a young man and now.'

Guy already knew and admired Hugh's work though he'd never actually met him, and he and Francine promised they would go the following week. It was fun telling them about everything and they made a very satisfactory audience, being full of curiosity about what she had thought of Hugh.

'Could you understand what your grandmother saw in him?' asked Francine. 'He must have been quite something for her to have carried such a torch for him all these years.'

'Oh, *absolutely*,' said Victoria unguardedly. 'I thought he was irresistible. I could easily fall in love with him myself!' Guy gave her a sharp look.

'You said Nonna and Nafsica both thought Patrick Hammond was incredibly like his uncle when they saw him at Vrahos, so perhaps you could fall for the nephew just as easily as for the uncle?' he suggested – joking, but with an edge to his voice.

428

'Oh, definitely!' By admitting such a possibility so airily Victoria hoped she would allay any suspicion Guy might have that she had already done so, but when she announced a little later that she was going to lunch with the Hammonds, deliberately not specifying that it was with Patrick alone and not with the rest of the family, he gave her a very beady look. She was thankful that he and Francine had gone to bed when she'd got in the night before and did not know that her mobile had rung just as she was getting into bed herself. She had been very surprised.

'I just wanted to check that you'd got back all right,' Patrick had said. 'I can't tell you how lovely it was having you with us and watching Hugh enjoy your company too. Victoria . . . I'd hate you to feel I'm crowding you but is there the slightest chance that you'd be free tomorrow? Sam and Sophie are unexpectedly going to some friends – the famous Matthew she was so hooked on in Corfu – so I've got the day to myself to do what I like . . . and what I'd like more than anything would be to see you again.'

She had hesitated for a moment, and Patrick, at the other end of the line, held his breath for her answer, but, 'I can't think of anything I'd like more either,' she said happily.

'Wonderful. For an awful moment I thought you were going to say no. Shall I pick you up mid morning and we'll go off somewhere for lunch?'

'Guy and Francine are having a dinner party for me in the evening so that I can see various friends while I'm over here – but I'm sure they haven't arranged anything in the middle of the day. I'd adore to come. I'll look forward to seeing you very soon, then.'

'Me too,' he said. 'Good night. Sleep well.'

After he'd rung off she had lain awake for a long time wondering what was happening to her and where it might be taking her. It seemed disturbingly soon after Richard's death to be feeling any of the emotions she was conscious of, and she was half horrified at herself, and yet she also had a sense of rightness, almost of inevitability, that would not allow for guilt. What had Hugh said last night about fate? *What will be, will be.* She felt a *frisson* of excitement.

*

'You must be Patrick Hammond,' said Guy now, holding the door open. 'We've corresponded. I know you want to talk to me about Vrahos and I have a suggestion of my own I'd like to put to you so we must get together soon. I've been hearing all about this portrait of my grandmother, and my wife and I intend to go and see it next week. It's an extraordinary story about my grandmother and your uncle and it's lost nothing in the telling by Victoria, I assure you! Come along in and I'll give Victoria a shout. I think she and Francine may have gone into the garden.'

He stood back and Patrick went into the hall, his photographer's eye automatically taking in the details: Continental furniture; modern sculpture; black and white Italian marble floor; dark green walls, white paintwork – very smart, very striking; an interesting collection of drawings – cleverly hung, he noted approvingly.

'Is that an Ayrton?' he asked looking at a drawing of Icarus flying too close to the sun.

'It is indeed. One of the first drawings I ever bought.' Guy made a wry face: 'Victoria likes to pretend it's a picture of me,' he said, lighting a cigarette and then went on, 'I think it's high time I added a Marston to my collection. I'm familiar with his oils, but Vicky was telling me this morning how much she admired some of the drawings you've lent for the exhibition. I shall look forward to seeing those too.'

'Well, I like them – though I'm biased, of course! Hugh's work has increased amazingly in value lately – not that I think market value is a good criterion for buying pictures. I do enjoy your comments in *Capability*, by the way, on all sorts of subjects. I never miss your column if I can help it.'

Under cover of this studied politeness they assessed each other. To Francine and Victoria, appearing at that moment, they seemed like two dogs walking round each other stiff-legged, not exactly unfriendly, but sniffing for potential animosity.

Francine was immediately struck by how Victoria and Patrick reacted to each other – not because of any outward demonstration, though they exchanged a social kiss of greeting, but because of an unmistakable feeling of electricity between them. Francine thought she had never seen Victoria illuminated in this way before – as if an inner light had been switched on.

She shot a glance at her husband, very sure that he would have noticed it too; anxious as to how he might react.

'Hi there, Patrick, I'm Francine Winston,' she said, holding out her hand. 'Good to see you. I'd offer you coffee but I know you want to hijack Victoria for the day and I guess you'll be wanting to get off. Why don't you drop by for a drink when you bring her back, if you've got time? Have fun both of you.'

She and Guy stood together on the steps and watched as Patrick and Victoria drove off. Guy put his arm round his wife as they walked back into the house.

'That was very adroitly stage-managed, Mrs Winston, wafting them away so speedily,' he said, glinting at her sardonically. 'You were afraid I might behave badly and antagonise him, weren't you?'

'I sure was,' she said, 'BUT you didn't. And that was pretty big of you, darling, because I have a gut feeling this is really important for Victoria and I guess you picked up on it too. I know you won't find it easy, but you have to let your little cousin go – and if you do, you're actually much less likely to lose her. I guarantee that.'

'I'll take note of your pearls of wisdom then, oh wise-one,' he said lightly, the half-mocking expression that she knew so well on his face. He looked at her, suddenly serious. 'And I get your message loud and clear – so don't think I don't know what you're not quite saying,' he said: 'that I've done enough damage already and mustn't wreck her life any further. It's all right, Francine. I can't put the clock back, and it's too late for poor old Richard – but I know what I've done to Vicky and that I'm not forgiven yet. She's made that pretty clear lately.'

'Tell you what,' said Francine, on the whole not dissatisfied with his reaction, 'I've just had a smart idea. Why don't we go off to the Crompton Gallery and see the famous portrait this morning? Then you can give your grandmother your reaction next time you ring her? I'd love to go.'

'Yes, great idea,' said Guy. 'Let's do that.

Patrick took Victoria to the Hind's Head at Bray where they sat outside drinking Pimm's and rejoicing in each other's company. Though the food at lunch was delicious, Victoria was in such a trance of happiness that she might have been given blotting paper to eat for all that she would have noticed. She couldn't believe she'd ever been worried that she might find conversation difficult. She felt not only could she talk to Patrick with the ease that normally only comes after knowing someone for years, but with an added excitement that lent wings to everything they said to each other.

Sophie had rung in the middle of lunch to say she and Sam had been invited to spend the whole day with the Burnabys and Matthew's father had offered to give them a lift back to London after supper. Was that all right, she had asked anxiously. Patrick said it was very much all right and switched off his mobile with a feeling of relief.

'Shall we take a boat and go on the river?' he suggested after they'd had coffee, longing to get her away from their fellow diners, with no fear of interruptions. It seemed a perfect idea to Victoria.

Chugging lazily up the Thames with nothing more adventurous than a few locks to negotiate seemed the ideal occupation for a perfect English summer afternoon. Of course they discussed the previous evening, and talked about Hugh's paintings.

'You made a big impression last night,' Patrick told her. 'I had Hugh on the telephone before I came to pick you up. He sent you his love.'

They laughed together about Peter Mason's obvious big-game hunting of the physically tiny Prince Haroun round the gallery and she told him about her misgivings over Peter's suggestions for her future and her anxiety about going back to Manor Farm the following week. 'It's something I've been able to put off while I've been at Vrahos,' she said. 'But I know I have to get it over and face my demons. I'm hoping going there may exorcise a few of them.'

'Have you given much thought to where you want to live?' he asked.

'I know what I *think* I'd like to do – but it's difficult. One moment people tell me it's foolish to take any decision in under a year after a bereavement, and the next there seems to be pressure to fit in with what everyone else thinks I ought to do. And I'm very conscious that whatever I decide

I have to get it right for Jake.'

'And what do you think *you'd* like to do?'

'I think I'd like to base ourselves at Vrahos for the next two or three years. Jake adores the school – every evening when I ring up he's full of what he's been doing and he's rapidly becoming bilingual. But he's not seven yet so I feel there'd be plenty of time to reconsider if it doesn't work out. We can keep Nonna company, which would mean a lot to her and to me. I have to face the fact that it may not be possible to keep Vrahos when she dies but at least I'll be learning about it and can help her with the administration of the estate now – or what's left of it. It doesn't look as if I'd be allowed to stay in our old house at Baybury even if I wanted to. Richard and I didn't actually own anything ourselves. It all belongs to a family trust.'

'That sounds eminently reasonable to me. You can surely do all that without having to make irreversible decisions too soon.'

'Ideally I suppose I'd like to have a small pad in England too but I doubt if I'll be able to afford that and I can always stay with Guy's parents. Yes, you're right. I don't have to burn any boats. Perhaps I've been getting in a state about nothing.'

'Sometimes it takes an outsider to see these things,' he said gently. 'Take it as it comes. See how you feel next week – and don't let anyone rush you.'

Once more she was struck by his kindness and concern, but how did he really feel about her? She thought she knew, but hardly dared to trust her instincts, terrified that she might make another mistake in her life and get mortally hurt again. Tentatively she asked him about Rachel, and Patrick found himself acknowledging things that he'd hardly dared admit, even to himself. Victoria listened quietly, occasionally prompting him with a question, but building up a picture of a marriage that had started to fray at the edges a long time ago. He told her about Bronwen and his fears that Rachel might still do something foolish and get badly hurt herself in the process.

'What has really shaken me,' he said, 'which I only discovered about this morning, is that she's proposing to swan off to Spain after this woman, and was prepared to take Posy too. Luckily her mother rang to warn me. I have to face the fact that Rachel really only thinks about herself.'

'Might you ever get back together, for Posy's sake, do you think?' asked Victoria.

'No,' said Patrick with great finality. 'Not now. When I went home after Corfu I made up my mind to make one last effort to sort out our marriage – though it's not what I wanted for myself for . . . well . . . for various reasons.' He looked at Victoria, and she dropped her eyes and looked away. Patrick went on: 'But Rachel wouldn't have it and when she announced she wanted a separation I have to admit I was relieved. Surprised and saddened, but hugely relieved. What I heard this morning is the final straw. I'll always help Rachel if I can and do my best to keep on good terms with her because of the children – but live together again . . . no way. She may change her mind – she usually does – but it's too late for me. I'm sure about that now.'

'How will Sam and Sophie feel about it?'

'Sam will mind – but he'll be all right. He's nearly twenty and very happy at Newcastle. He's always been gregarious and has lots of friends. Sam's a great extrovert and he and Rachel have been at loggerheads since the day he was born. But Sophie's another matter altogether, because underneath all the froth and giggles she's much more insecure. All her life she's longed to please her mother – and mostly failed. She's often deeply resentful of Rachel but she won't find a parting between us easy to accept. Also she's always been jealous of Posy – with good reason – and I don't know how she'll react now that I'll have to be more hands-on with Posy myself. I suppose Posy will need to be based mainly with her mother, though. I shall really mind that,' he said, and Victoria thought he looked very sad.

'I was surprised this morning,' Patrick went on, 'because Sophie's first reaction was to feel sorry for her little sister and I thought it was pretty big of her under the circumstances.' And Patrick told her about the saga of the bedrooms when they had got back from Corfu.

Victoria felt furiously indignant on Sophie's behalf.

'How will you cope with Posy when you do have her on your own?' she asked.

'I don't know. We've had wonderful help from a very nice local girl up to now, but she obviously hated being with my in-laws and she's just left. She might come back, though – I hope so. I just pray Rachel and I will be able to work things out in a reasonably civilised way. Luckily our lawyer is a great friend – the one who owns Petradi – and I'm going to suggest to Rachel tomorrow that we consult him and get him to come up with some suggestions. I don't suppose it'll be easy, though.'

Victoria thought this was probably an understatement to say the least, but it was not something she wanted to dwell on at the moment.

It was very hot and they decided to pull into the bank and tie up under the shade of a willow tree. There were cushions in the boat and Patrick had brought a rug, so they stretched out on the bank where they could watch other boats going up and down, and the occasional swan gliding along the green surface of the Thames.

'Tell me about Richard,' said Patrick. 'What really happened?'

Haltingly at first she told him about her own marriage; starting with the shared childhood and the bonds forged between three children; about her reliance on Richard and how they were both in thrall to Guy; of how they drifted into marriage, and continued to do things as a threesome. He got the picture of a marriage based on friendship, and if he privately thought that no fires had been lit, that was something of a relief. She told him of Richard's unexpectedly violent reaction to Guy's marriage and Jeff's terrible discovery: finding him near the wood after his gun had exploded; of her growing conviction that he had intended to take his own life. Finally she told him of the day when Guy had confirmed her suspicions, and had then told her why, sitting among the ruins of Angelokastro high above the sea, and of her feelings of shock and outrage; the sensation that her life was in ruins too – and not just the future but the past as well. Sometimes her voice was so low – scarcely more than a whisper – that he had to strain to catch what she said. He was horrified at what he was hearing, both explicitly and in what she left unsaid.

'I felt as if all my married life had not only been taken away but had been . . . tarnished. Had been a sham all along only I'd been too blind to see it,' she said. 'And I felt so betrayed – by *both* of them. But just lately I've thought that I was terribly at fault too and that I short-changed Richard as much as he short-changed me. I married him for all the wrong reasons – and a bit of me always knew it. I'm not proud of that. I've felt so bitter towards him, but unlike Guy, Richard was basically a good kind man – actually a loving person – and he must have been desperately unhappy to do what he did, even if I never understand how he could possibly do such a thing to Jake. I need to feel I've mourned him properly – I owe him that at least – but how do you mourn for someone who wasn't who you thought they were?'

She shivered and gripped her hands tightly together in an effort to stop them trembling.

'Don't make it so complicated,' suggested Patrick. 'Grieve for the person you thought he was at the time – the kind protector; your childhood friend; someone who loved you very much in the only way he could; Jake's father – your companion. *That* is the person you have lost. Just mourn for *that* loss – God knows it's enough. The other Richard was outside your knowledge or control.'

'Yes,' she said at last. 'I suppose you're right. Thank you – that helps.'

'And what about Guy?' he asked, gazing up at the sky, concentrating on watching one particular cloud change shape, very much needing to know what her real feelings for her cousin were now.

'Ah . . . Guy. That's complicated – or at least it used to be. But something surprising has happened lately. I was dreading coming to stay with him and Francine. Dreading what effect it might have on me to see Guy with a wife; dreading my own jealousy – especially because she's going to have a baby and I so longed for another one myself. But it hasn't turned out like that. I shall always love Guy as a cousin, but in an extraordinary way I feel as if I've been released from him. I still feel sick when I think of him and Richard, and I still feel terribly angry with Guy but I no longer feel in his *power*. If I'm honest there's a bit of me that's quite enjoying the feeling that for the first time in my life it's him that wants to make peace with me – not me endlessly waiting for his sun to shine on me again. For as long as I can remember I've tapped the barometer of Guy's moods. Stormy? Take cover. Changeable? Walk carefully. Set fair? Oh bliss, enjoy it while it lasts! Now, suddenly it doesn't matter. It's like being cured of a drug addiction.'

'He sounds an absolute shit to me,' said Patrick frankly.

'He's not really,' she said quickly. 'He *can* be – but he has another side to him too, I promise you.'

'I'll have to take your word for it,' he said. For someone who'd just been cured of an addiction he thought she sounded very defensive of her cousin. 'He's certainly a talented journalist. Will he be able to make Francine happy, d'you think?'

She looked rather surprised. 'How awful – I've never really thought of that,' she admitted. 'He's certainly capable of inflicting wounds on anyone who loves him, but I've always thought of her as being well able to look after herself. Guy may have met his match with Francine in every sense. I think she's actually helped to free me from my fixation on him.'

'I liked the look of her,' said Patrick, privately hoping that he might have contributed a little himself to the fraying of the bonds that had bound Victoria to her cousin. 'She's very glamorous and she was extremely friendly. I had a feeling she was trying to support you.'

'Well, she's certainly gone out of her way to be nice to me. Do you think she's very attractive then?' asked Victoria, plucking a piece of grass and winding it round her finger.

'Oh, yes,' he said, 'I can see she's got quite a message but I only met her very briefly and she's not really my type.' He sat up and studied Victoria's face and was amazed at the look of uncertainty he saw on it. 'But she could never even hold a candle to you,' he said softly, 'and I think you must know that.'

'No,' she said forlornly. 'I don't know that. People always think I'm sure of myself, but I'm not inside. Since we were first married I've always felt Richard's lack of passion was somehow my fault – that there had to be some lack in me that made him seem so . . . so unresponsive. Do you know what that's done to me?' She looked distraught. 'It's taken away any confidence I ever had in myself,' she said fiercely, 'as a woman, I mean.'

'That's ridiculous! You of all people! Surely after all these revelations about Richard, and now that you *know* how he felt about women sexually, you can't still feel it was because there was anything lacking in you?'

She said nothing but he could see she was close to tears.

437

'I don't think you're being quite honest with yourself,' he said. 'I think you must have an idea how I – for one – feel about you. I've fallen in love with you, Victoria. I didn't mean to, or want to but I can't believe you aren't aware of it. I think you're the most beautiful, desirable woman I've ever met, and I was beginning to hope that you might feel something for me.'

'I do,' she whispered. 'Oh, I do. I didn't want to, but I can't help it. Do you think it's disloyal of me to feel like this – so soon after Richard?'

For answer he drew her into his arms and kissed her and this time she did not pull away and it was as though all her pent-up passions were suddenly released.

When some minutes later he released her for a moment in order to hold her away from him and try to read her face, she suddenly started to laugh. He looked at her questioningly.

'After all these years of envying other people and wondering what it would feel like and whether I'd know if it ever happened to me – do you know what you are?' she asked.

Patrick shook his head. 'Tell me.'

'You're my bolt from the blue,' she said triumphantly. 'And I've been struck at last, just as my grandmother always told me I ought to be. I felt it the first time I met you, but I daren't admit it even to myself. How does it feel to be a bolt of lightning?'

'I can't think of anything I'd rather be,' said Patrick, enchanted.

'And shall I tell you something else?'

'Go on then.'

'Did you hear your uncle and me discussing the wild bees at Vrahos and how they're supposed to swarm when anything important happens to someone in the family?'

'I did – hence the bees on the silver boxes.'

'Exactly! Well, while I was talking to him about them I suddenly remembered something extraordinary.' She looked up at him, her enormous dark eyes full of amusement and delight. 'They swarmed the day you first came to Vrahos. The day we *met*,' she said jubilantly. 'How about that?'

'Oh well,' said Patrick, 'that clinches it. If the bees approve . . . who are we to argue?'

Chapter Forty-two

It was with reservations that Patrick agreed to go in for a drink when he dropped Victoria back with Guy and Francine early on Saturday evening, but she was so keen for him to accept the invitation that he hadn't the heart to disappoint her. Victoria, wildly in love as she had never been before, not only longed for an excuse to stay together a little longer, but couldn't wait for Guy and Francine to get to know Patrick better. Her pleasure swiftly turned to unease, however, when she recognised that Guy had undergone one of his mercurial changes since the morning and was at his most provocative – asking Patrick's opinions and then deliberately disagreeing with them. The barometer of Guy's moods definitely read stormy.

'Oh Lord – whatever's got into Guy now?' Victoria asked Francine after Patrick, who had no intention of allowing Guy to play verbal games with him and who couldn't bear the anxiety on Victoria's face, had asked to be shown the garden.

'The green-eyed monster, I guess,' said Francine with a slight shrug, conscious of a sharp little pang herself at this sign of her husband's possessiveness over his cousin. 'He's been in great form all day – but then you waltz in smelling of dew and roses and looking like you'd just been given the crown jewels and I guess he couldn't hack it. Men! They're all so darn territorial and Guy's used to seeing a "Keep off the Grass" sign on your lawn. But for heaven's sake relax, Victoria. Your friend doesn't look the type to be scared off easily and they're both big boys. Let them sort it out.' She smiled at Victoria. 'I don't need to ask you if you've had a good day, do I?'

'The best! Oh, Francine, you don't know what an incredible time I've had!'

'C'mon then – tell me about it. I'm all ears.'

It was as well they didn't know that as the two men toured

439

the garden, Guy's demon had impelled him to say with his most sphinx-like expression, 'I hope you realise what a special person my little cousin is and how much she's been through lately. She's very vulnerable and I'd hate to see her hurt again. If you have intentions in her direction I trust they're strictly honourable?'

Patrick had looked his host up and down and raised an eyebrow. 'A lot more honourable than I gather yours were to her husband,' he answered equably – but there was no mistaking his menace.

For a moment Guy looked as if he'd been stabbed. Then he raised his hands in mock surrender. '*Touché*,' was all he said.

'Just so long as we understand each other.' Patrick looked at his watch. 'I know you've got a dinner party – and I must be going anyway. Thanks for the drink.'

When they walked back into the house, discussing the history of Vrahos and apparently making plans to meet in the future, Francine and Victoria were both relieved to see that Guy's mood seemed to have switched again and that he and Patrick appeared to be perfectly amicable.

Patrick rang Victoria on Sunday after taking Sam and Sophie to catch the train for York to stay with the Marshalls. Victoria had just finished her usual pre-bedtime call to Jake when her mobile rang. It was wonderful to hear Patrick's voice. She felt as if her whole life had been transformed, as if she had been given a transfusion of energy and optimism.

'How did you get on with Rachel?' she asked after he'd enquired about her own day.

'Well,' said Patrick, 'it wasn't the easiest day, but it might have been a whole lot worse. We got a few things sorted out and it was lovely to see Posy. We got a terrific welcome from her. I think Sophie was touched at how thrilled the tiresome little sister was to see her.'

'And what about Spain?'

Patrick groaned. 'Rachel's still insisting she's going out there. She can't – or more likely won't – see what terrible bad news that woman is. Despite what happened Bronwen still seems to have an influence over her. Rachel can be incredibly stubborn sometimes but at least she's agreed to leave Posy with me if she does go. And I think we've sorted out the summer holiday dates reasonably amicably so that Rachel and I can play Box and Cox at the flat and Wytherton House and Sophie'll get some time with her mum as well as with me, which is important. At least Rachel's parents were trying to be helpful.'

'I'm so glad,' said Victoria, feeling a surge of relief that Rachel was going to be off the scene for a bit.

Patrick said: 'Victoria, I've got a suggestion to put to you. How long are you planning to spend at Baybury before you go back to Vrahos?'

'Well, it rather depends on how I find things when I get there and how much there is to do. I've got to sort out Richard's clothes and things, which I'm dreading, and I've no idea how long that will take. And then there are various people I must see, including Richard's father. I wouldn't want to be away from Jake for more than another week but I haven't actually fixed a definite day yet – it partly depends on flights and things too. Why?'

'I've been asked to do an article for the *Heritage at Risk Quarterly Review* on houses worth saving . . . ones which aren't in the first league but whose owners would like to open to the public if they could get some sort of grant towards repairs and maintenance. It would involve taking some photographs, possibly going round the gardens, talking to a few people and getting a general feel – that sort of thing. I've done it once or twice before.'

'That sounds interesting,' said Victoria, wondering what was coming.

'Yes – it's usually great fun,' he said, 'but thank goodness I don't have to make any decisions, or even specific recommendations. I just have to present a picture for the members of HAR. There are two particular houses I've been asked to look at while I'm in the south. They're both within reach of London so I was going to do it from here, but I just wondered . . .' He paused.

'Yes?' she said, holding her breath in anticipation of what his suggestion might be.

'Could you possibly come with me?' he asked. 'It would be so wonderful to have more time together – just you and me – without either of our families or anyone else. We could stay somewhere really nice for a night? Don't misunderstand me . . . no pressure for anything you didn't want or feel ready for . . .' He paused, then added: 'I don't feel I can bear not to see you again before you go back to Corfu. Any hope?'

'Oh, Patrick,' said Victoria, her heart singing. 'I can't think of anything I'd like more.'

'Fantastic.'

Victoria did some quick thinking. 'Toula and Uncle Anthony are expecting me to stay tomorrow night but I feel I need to be at Manor Farm by myself at some stage, so I plan to go there on Tuesday. I have to try to lay some ghosts and I must get the sorting-out done. If I said yes, could it be towards the end of the week?'

'It could be anything that suited you,' said Patrick, overjoyed at her response. 'I wish I could help you over all you've got to face, but I think I get the message that this is something you have to work out for yourself?' He was aware of how overprotective he had been in his relationship with Rachel and didn't want to repeat the mistake.

'Yes,' she said, unconsciously echoing his thoughts. 'I feel I must stand on my own feet now or I'll be going backwards and not moving on.'

'I'll get Tania, my secretary, to see if she can arrange the two visits on Thursday or Friday and I'll get on to finding somewhere good for us to stay. I can't tell you what it means to me that you'll come. I won't ring when you're with your aunt and uncle but shall we talk on Tuesday evening?'

'That would be perfect,' said Victoria, privately thinking that forty-eight hours would seem a long time. 'Till Tuesday evening then. I'm going to have to go now, Patrick, or Guy and Francine will wonder what's become of me. Good night. And thank you for . . . everything.'

'Good night . . . darling Victoria.'

Toula was at the station at Toddingham on Monday morning to meet Victoria. They exchanged a huge hug before Toula drove her back to Durnford House for lunch, accelerating thrillingly round corners and overtaking lorries with unfounded confidence.

It felt extraordinary to be back, almost as if the last six months had not existed. With the telepathy that some dogs have for their owners' arrivals, Teal was already waiting at the front door when they drew up. 'Now isn't that uncanny?' said Toula. 'He never comes to the door when I come home.' The old dog went wild when he saw Victoria.

'People say dogs have no sense of the passage of time,' said Victoria when the first frenzy of his welcome had abated slightly, 'but they're wrong. This is beyond any greeting he gives if I've only been away for a few days. Poor old boy – he's getting awfully ancient. D'you think he's missed us?'

'Oh, yes. He hasn't actually *pined*, but he's missed you dreadfully all the same,' said Toula, 'Luckily he gets on fine with our two but I'm afraid he's getting awfully rheumaticky. His poor back legs let him down sometimes. He spends a lot of time sitting in the window of Anthony's study watching the drive, and Anthony's convinced he's hoping for one of you to arrive home.'

'And now it's the wrong one who's come,' said Victoria sadly. 'He'd so much rather have Jake – or best of all, of course, Richard. I've always been third best for Teal. He's regarded me as a sort of trusted family retainer – fine to get meals, go for walks when there's no shooting and dry him when he's been in the pond – but not in Richard's league.'

'Well, you'd never guess from the way he's carrying on now! He's having an ecstasy,' said Toula. 'Like Bernini's St Theresa greeting the angel.'

'Goodness,' giggled Victoria, thinking this was a typically far-fetched Toula comparison. 'Do you think St Theresa dribbled and panted and licked the angel's knees? My skirt's sopping already. I'd love to take him back to Vrahos to Jake, but I don't know if it would be a good idea.'

'It's so lovely to see you, darling,' said Toula. 'Have you really made up your mind to stay at Vrahos then?'

'I shall definitely go back till the end of the summer. Then, unless anything crops up this week to make me change my mind, I'd like to make our base there for the foreseeable future. It wouldn't be fair to make a final decision until I've talked to Bill. I owe him that. Do you think I'd be mad, Toula?'

'It's certainly what Anthony thinks you should do. I'm not so sure, myself.'

'What Uncle Anthony thinks means a lot to me – and what you think too, of course,' she added hastily.

Though darkly suspicious about Hugh Marston, Toula was dying of curiosity about him and wanted to hear every detail about Victoria's meeting, critical Guy having given his parents an extremely enthusiastic account of Evanthi's portrait on the telephone.

'I've brought a catalogue of the exhibition for you and Uncle Anthony.' Victoria bent down and grovelled in her tote bag. 'There you are.'

'Hmm. I suppose we shall have to go and see it now,' said Toula grudgingly, impressed in spite of herself. 'But I certainly don't want to meet the artist. How did the dinner party with Guy and Francine go on Saturday?'

'Wonderful – lots of old friends. I had a lovely time. They really pushed the boat out for me.' She wondered if Guy had also reported on her day with Patrick and whether the family tom-toms had been beating out information. From the look on Toula's face she guessed they had.

Although it was less than a week since she'd seen her in London, Toula had noticed immediately that Victoria looked as if she'd undergone some sort of change. She looked ironed out – happier, thought Toula, than she'd been for a long time, and she was even more curious to know about Hugh Marston's nephew than about the artist himself. As Victoria rightly guessed, Guy had not been silent on the subject. 'Looks as if history might be repeating itself,' he had told his mother. Primed by Anthony, to whom she had reported this interesting bit of speculation, she had managed, with rare reticence, not to ask about Patrick Hammond in the first minute of reunion with her niece. She hoped Victoria would bring the subject up herself – though Toula had every intention of finding out more, whatever Anthony thought.

After lunch they took the dogs for a walk, Toula and

444

Anthony's Jack Russells racing on ahead and Teal lumbering along behind.

'Why don't you think it would be a good idea for me to live at Vrahos?' asked Victoria. 'Is it because of Jake and his schooling?'

'Oh heavens, no . . . Jake would be fine. You don't want to pay attention to Cunningham theories about education.' Toula snorted derisively though her own son could hardly have had a more conventional English public-schooling. 'The Cunninghams would probably like all small boys to do National Service in the army from the age of six. Meriel's been brainwashing Bill about the need for Jake to grow up in what she calls a properly structured environment – whatever that means. Her own children are a very poor advertisement for her theories. They're dreadfully spoiled – I gave her a little hint about that the other day. Anthony was very cross with me.' Victoria laughed: she knew the size of her aunt's 'little hints' of old.

'No, it's you I worry about,' went on Toula. 'You're happy at Vrahos *now* because it's an escape, but what will happen when Nonna dies? You might give up several years of your life to her only to find there's no money left for you to live on there afterwards – and I worry that you'd never *meet* anyone if you were buried out there.' By which, of course, Victoria knew her aunt meant a suitable future husband. Toula threw her a gimlet look.

'I don't want to live at Vrahos just in order to inherit it,' said Victoria, ignoring the unspoken invitation to confide: she didn't feel ready to talk to Toula about Patrick yet. 'I know the house is in terrible shape and the money's run out,' she went on, 'but what matters is that Nonna shouldn't have to face changes in her lifetime – but that's not unselfishness. It's just that I love her and the place so much I want to make the most of what time they've both got left. But I'll talk to Uncle Anthony about it – and I promise I'll think about what you say too.'

Anthony got an early train from London, and was home in good time. There was much to discuss. As she went to bed in the little room that had once been hers at Durnford House, her brain was so full of questions that she expected to lie awake for ages, but in fact she was asleep within minutes of switching her light out, and only woke when Anthony, in his dressing gown, came in with a mug of tea before he got the train to London.

Later in the morning Toula drove Victoria over to Manor Farm and unwillingly left her there.

'Anthony came and gave your car a run the other day,' she said, 'so at least we know it will start. If you change your mind you can drive back to us any time. I think it's ridiculous that you should stay here at all but he says I must respect your wishes and let you do things in your own way. Cra-a-zy!' Toula threw up her arms in a gesture of incomprehension at the ridiculous views of husbands and the waywardness of nieces and then gave her a fierce hug.

'Thank you, darling Toula – you're both angels.' Victoria hugged her back. 'This is something I have to do, but I'll give you a ring tonight and I promise to come straight back if I find I can't cope.'

She waited till her aunt drove off and then took a deep breath, put her key in the front door and flung it open.

She dumped her case in the porch, deciding to take it up later and opened the inner door into the hall. Everything looked the same – and yet Victoria had a sense of unreality as though she might be viewing a film. She half expected ghosts of herself and Richard and Jake to float before her and start playing their parts in the daily life that had once been so familiar. Teal, whom she had brought with her for company, went round the hall sniffing and whining with the hackles on his back raised.

'It's just you and me here now, Tealy,' she said aloud and her voice echoed in the silence.

She was glad that she had not been tempted to bring Jake with her and thought he would have found it very unsettling.

She forced herself to fling open all the doors and go into each room. When they got to the boot room Teal made straight for the corner where his bed had always been, but it wasn't there because Anthony had taken it to Durnford House, thinking it might help the old dog to settle in new surroundings. He slumped on to the flagged floor, puzzled, thumping his stump

446

of a tail and waiting expectantly for Victoria to conjure up some normality for him. Then he heaved himself up on his shaky legs and padded after her into the playroom. It looked unnaturally clean and tidy – no Lego strewn about the floor, no open books or half-finished drawings. Clearly Violet had kept everything spotless. Victoria had wondered if she would sink back into the house with a sense of homecoming – but instead she felt like an intruder.

She beat a retreat back into the hall, thankful that Anthony had arranged for her post to be delivered to Durnford so that at least a landslide of junk mail and brown-enveloped letters had not greeted her. The drawing room and dining room brought back memories of the last time they had been used for entertaining, after Richard's funeral. When Victoria finally braced herself to go up to her bedroom, Teal acknowledged defeat and collapsed at the foot of the stairs, knowing he could no longer make it to the top.

'What really happened, Tealy?' she asked, sitting on the bottom step and fondling the old dog's ears. 'You were the only witness. What do you know that no one else does?'

She remembered how convinced she had been, when the suspicion of suicide had first been put into her head, that Richard would have left her a letter if it had really been so. He had always been a great writer of loving little notes, perhaps, she thought now, because he had found that an easier way to express his love than by physical demonstrations. She had searched first his desk, then his office for a letter. Finally, in a frenzy of despair, she had taken the house apart in her search for some last communication from him. She had found nothing.

She got to her feet, but Teal remained where he was, gazing mournfully up at her and despite her new-found hopes, tears trickled slowly down her cheeks.

There was a little vase of roses on her dressing table which she knew must have been put there by Violet. Because she felt a deadly lethargy creeping over her, and could imagine Evanthi's voice, at its briskest, warning her against falling prey to the sin of accidie, Victoria decided to walk down to see Violet straightaway.

*

447

When she arrived at the Burrowses' cottage, which was situated at the back entrance to Manor Farm, Violet was on the lookout for her. The two women embraced each other wordlessly and then exchanged a long look.

'Oh, it is good to see you,' said Victoria, eventually.

'The kettles on the boil – you'll have a cuppa won't you? And I've made one of my cut-and-come-again cakes specially.' Violet's affections were always expressed through baking, no matter what time of day it was.

There was much news to be exchanged but both women were aware of skirting round the subject of the future. Violet was the first to broach it.

'I don't know how I'm going to say this after the years we've been with you and Richard,' she said at last, after pressing more cake on Victoria, 'and it seems a shame to greet you with this – given as how you've only just come home and all you've been through lately – but Jeff says I must tell you straight.' She took a deep breath. 'We're thinking of making a change,' she blurted out.

'Oh, Violet,' said Victoria. 'Thank you for telling me. You're braver than me – because I'm thinking of changes too and I was trying to find the courage to talk to you about it. You've put me to shame. Tell me about your ideas first and then I'll fill you in about mine.'

'It's that Meriel – or Mrs Ha-a-w-kins, as she says I ought to call her now,' said Violet drawing the name out as though she was loading a crossbow. 'Me and Jeff were always ever so happy working with you and Richard, but I gather that husband of Meriel's may be taking the farm over now and he's all hot air and theories, like most politicians. Jeff's been in farming all his life and he can't be doing with the likes of Stafford Hawkins giving him orders and then swanning off to Parliament. Old Mr Cunningham's all right – he's never been a bundle of laughs but at least he is what he is and never tries to be anything different.' Victoria thought this was quite a good description of her father-in-law. 'And I couldn't stomach working for that Meriel,' went on Violet. 'The truth is, Jeff's been offered another job the other side of Toddingham and we're minded to take it.'

'You must do whatever's best for yourselves and the family – and I completely understand because I can't take the Hawkinses either. June Cunningham's OK, but Meriel's always got up my nose. Mr Mason tells me they want to live in Manor Farm so I'm thinking of staying out in Corfu.'

It was an enormous relief to be able to talk about it openly. Violet said indignantly that Meriel had several times come to get the keys to the house at weekends. 'She pretended she needed to fetch papers or some such for her father,' sniffed Violet, 'but I could see the measuring tape in her pocket and I wasn't born yesterday! Measuring up is what she was doing, but I measured her up in no time. She wanted to keep the keys but I wasn't having that. "You'll bring them back to me, *if* you please, Mrs Ha-a-w-kins," I told her. "Victoria entrusted them to me, and no one but me is having the charge of them."' She added with satisfaction: 'She didn't like that. Good job she'll be in London till Friday night.'

'That's a relief! I'm seeing Richard's father for lunch tomorrow – but I suppose I shall have to face Meriel sometime.'

They made a date for the following morning for Violet to come and help her start the disturbing task of sorting out Richard's clothes.

Victoria walked slowly back to the house, with Teal pottering along behind her. The garden was looking surprisingly good – the border, which had been Richard's especial pride, was full of colour, the lawn had been mown and there was hardly a weed to be seen. She was touched that it had been so carefully tended in her absence and thought she must remember to ask Jeff who was responsible. Am I right to contemplate leaving all this? she asked herself. Then she remembered Peter Mason's words. It seemed unlikely she would be allowed to stay anyway, but for Jake's sake, ought she to put up more resistance even though it had never felt like home to her in the way Vrahos did? Pondering all this she let herself back into the house, leaving Teal in the porch.

More from a sixth sense than because she could hear anything unusual, she knew immediately that there was someone in the house. She froze and stood listening intently then went through the swing door to the back. There was no one there but the back door was open and a blue Vauxhall car was parked in the yard outside; in the kitchen someone had left a handbag on the table. Clearly whoever the intruder was, they saw no need to disguise their presence. Then she heard footsteps overhead. Very quietly Victoria went up the back stairs and along the passage. There was a rustling sound coming from her bedroom and the door was ajar. She pushed it open and stood contemplating, at eye level, the bulging backs of two very stout legs.

'Hello, Meriel,' said Victoria.

Later that evening when Patrick rang she told him she had almost committed the perfect murder because Meriel Hawkins had been so startled that she'd fallen off the stepladder on which she'd been standing, busily Sellotaping samples of wallpaper above Victoria's bed.

'Luckily for her, she fell on the bed so she wasn't even bruised – but I never saw anyone look so shifty in all my life,' she told him. 'What a nerve!'

'But I think you enjoyed yourself, didn't you?' asked Patrick, much amused by her account of the drama.

'Well, I did,' she admitted. 'It was so funny! And, what's more, it's given me the moral high ground. Do you know she even had the gall to suggest it might be better if I didn't tell my father-in-law tomorrow about her being in the house in case it upsets him! She'd come all the way down from London with her rotten old samples and wasn't even going to look in on him. She really is an insufferable cow.'

'And will you tell him?'

'Probably not,' admitted Victoria. 'He's a bit of an old stick but I'm desperately sorry for him and he's the only member of Richard's family I'm really fond of. But the point is that Meriel *thinks* I might tell him – and I shall keep her in suspense!'

'And are you going to fight her for the house?'

'Again, probably not. She wants it so desperately . . . and I don't. I've decided it would be a purely spiteful thing to do. There's nothing for me here any more. But Meriel's no longer in a position to try to dictate to me where Jake and I should live or lecture me about how I ought to bring him up. I almost feel grateful. It's sort of freed me in a way to do my own thing and start a new life.'

'Good,' said Patrick, relieved. 'Now then . . . plans. Tania's managed to arrange both my visits at the end of the week: one for Thursday afternoon and one for Friday, and I've provisionally booked us in for Thursday night to the Old Priory at Hettington, which is about halfway between them. It's quiet and has lovely grounds and good food, and we could be really peaceful there. Does that sound all right?'

'It sounds perfect.' She was longing to spend time alone with him – whatever it might bring.

'Shall I come and pick you up?'

'I think I'd rather meet you there.'

'I thought you might say that. I'll send you the directions. Do you feel you've managed to lay any of your ghosts?'

'I think so – at least I'm glad I came. After Meriel left I went up through the wood to where the accident happened. It's the first time I've managed to do that, and I sat there for ages thinking about Richard.'

'That was brave,' he said, thinking that under her gentleness she had great strength and courage. 'Did it help?'

'I think it helped me to make a certain peace with myself. I just felt incredibly sad and wished I knew what had really happened. I said a few things I needed to say out loud – funny what a powerful thing that is to do. Luckily there was no one around to hear me.'

'I wish I was around you now,' said Patrick quietly.

'I wish you were too,' she said.

Chapter Forty-three

On Wednesday morning, with Violet's assistance, Victoria managed to start sorting out Richard's possessions, putting anything especially personal or valuable aside for Jake, allocating suitable gifts for relations and close friends and dividing his clothes between members of the family and various charities. The furniture could wait till another visit when she might be more certain about the future. Without Violet's kind but unsentimental help she knew she would have sat despairingly amongst piles of clothes, succumbing to sadness and indecision, but even with Violet's cheerful company she found it a horrible job and was glad of the excuse to take a break at lunch time and go over to see her father-in-law.

'You're an angel,' said Victoria, giving the older woman a grateful hug. 'Thanks to you, we've got on much better than I expected.'

'I'll come back later this afternoon and start getting all the clothes for the charity shop packed up,' said practical Violet. 'You go off now and see the old man.'

The shock of his son's death had aged Bill Cunningham considerably since the spring, but Victoria thought he was pleased to see her in his restrained way. She took her latest photographs of Jake to show him.

'He doesn't look at all like Richard,' he said at one point. 'But then he never has.'

It was hard to know what the right response was. 'Perhaps not obviously,' Victoria said, aching for him. 'Mostly because he has my dark hair and Richard was so fair – and, of course, Jake's very brown at the moment after a summer in Corfu, which accentuates the difference – all the same he is like him in some ways. I often see a resemblance to Richard, a fleeting expression or the way he walks with his hands behind his back – you do that too Bill; his eye for a ball and his love of games; the way he likes to organise his things – he has Richard's meticulous streak and he certainly doesn't get that from me. If he grows up to be as kind as Richard I shall be pleased.' But she couldn't help thinking painfully that under the everyday thoughtfulness and courtesy that had been such a part of Richard's make-up, he'd proved himself capable of an act of such massive lack of consideration that the repercussions of it would go on echoing for years.

Bill stared out of the window. 'You don't really want to live here any longer, do you Victoria – not after what happened?' he asked abruptly. 'You want to take the boy abroad.'

'I think so – at any rate, for the time being,' she said, steeling herself to be truthful. She put a hand on his arm. 'But nothing's final. I want you to know I've no intention of losing touch with you – not just because of Richard or for Jake's sake but for mine as well. You'll be very welcome to stay with us as often as you like – wherever we are – and I shall bring Jake to you. I shall have to come over again soon and I promise I'll bring him with me next time. I don't want Jake to lose touch with his English roots any more than you do and I shan't make decisions about his future without consulting you – I give you my word on that, Bill. But it will be *you* I consult – not Peter Mason or Meriel or Stafford.'

'I understand,' he said, 'and I don't blame you.' She had a feeling that he understood all too well. 'I think June may be interested in coming to live here with me and, as you may have gathered from Peter, Meriel and Stafford might take on Manor Farm – that is, if *you* don't want to stay there. It goes without staying it's yours for as long as you like.' This was a very different way of painting the picture than the version that had been presented to her by Peter Mason and she was deeply touched. She thought that dreary June, with her dipping hems and droopy cardigans, would at least look after her father.

She felt very sad when she said goodbye. As she drove away she could see him in her driving mirror, still standing on the steps of the house – a lonely, aloof, inhibited old man whose world had literally been blown apart.

She looked in on Toula on the way home to cheer herself up

with a gossip and a cup of tea. Toula was always a mine of information about local tittle-tattle, and the fact that her version of events was usually inaccurate and always highly prejudiced didn't make it any less enjoyable.

'So what's the news locally?' asked Victoria.

'Well, can you believe it?' said Toula 'Meriel Hawkins has announced to the Toddenham W.I. that she's been on a course so that she can demonstrate marital arts to us all.'

'You mean *sex instruction* – from *Meriel*?' Victoria had a mind-boggling vision of her sister-in-law and bossy Mrs Banham entwined in a complicated Karma Sutra clinch.

Toula gave a scornful snort. 'Don't be absurd, Victoria. Of course it's nothing to do with sex! It's an exercise regime based on movements Chinese warriors make or something. Anthony says I need to lose weight but I don't see myself prancing about in the Parish Room with one of those funny curved swords. I'd rather go on a diet. You must have heard of it – I believe some people call it t'ai chi.'

Victoria shrieked with laughter. 'I think you mean martial arts, not marital ones.'

'That's what I said.'

'Oh, darling Toula, you have perked me up,' said Victoria, feeling much better. 'And you might take a quick swipe at Meriel for me if you decide to join!'

When she got back to Manor Farm it was after five o'clock, and Violet was about to go home. 'I'll be off now to get Jeff's tea,' she said. 'But I'll be over again in the morning and I reckon we'll get everything finished in a couple of hours. Oh, and Guy rang. I told him I thought you'd be back by five and asked if he wanted you to ring him, but he said there's something come up as he needs to talk to you about so he's coming down this evening. He'll be with you about six.'

'Goodness,' said Victoria, 'how peculiar. I only left him and Francine on Monday and they're off to Italy first thing in the morning. Did he say what it was about?'

Violet shook her head. 'No – just that there was no point in you ringing him because he'd already have left. Bye for now then. See you tomorrow.'

Victoria couldn't imagine what could have cropped up to make Guy drive down the M4 to see her again so soon. She tried to tell herself that if there had been a drama at Vrahos it would surely have been Toula or Anthony who would have been called; if it was something to do with Francine, then Guy surely wouldn't be leaving her now. Her mind churned with possibilities and she felt deeply uneasy.

Earlier that day, in London, Guy had sat at the kitchen table opening his post before packing for a trip to Verona the following day. Francine had slipped out to get new batteries for the pocket fan, which she hoped would help her survive if the heat wave currently afflicting the Continent got too oppressive. For the first time in her life she was finding high temperatures a problem and was afraid that the crowds in the Arena and the oppressive atmospheric conditions might cause her to faint during one of the operas. Guy had suggested she should stay quietly at home but she desperately wanted to attend the three open-air performances that he was due to review, so that she could discuss the productions with him afterwards. Also, because his job took him away so much, Francine had every intention of accompanying him whenever it was possible to do so. She thought it might be her last chance to go on one of his assignments before the baby was born.

The week before, Victoria had suddenly asked her if she trusted Guy, and Francine had pulled a comical face, laughed and answered cheerfully: 'Good heavens, no! I just plan to make it as difficult as possible for him to stray!'

Nothing had alerted Guy to the possibility that the thick, white A5 envelope, which had come by recorded delivery, might contain anything out of the ordinary. But when he'd opened it and read the brief covering letter enclosed with the two other packages in it, the colour drained from his face.

He was still sitting staring at it when Francine returned. She was shocked by his appearance.

'I thought you'd gone shopping,' he said. 'You're back very quick.'

'I only went to the corner shop. What on earth's up with you? You look *awful*.'

Then her eyes widened. 'Guy . . . isn't that Richard's writing?' she asked, looking at the two unopened, hand-addressed envelopes on the table.

Guy nodded. 'Read this,' he said, handing her an official-looking typed letter. 'It's from some firm of solicitors in Reading that I've never even heard of.' He got up and paced restlessly round the kitchen, picking things up and putting them down, and jingling the change in his pockets.

'Dear Mr Winston,' Francine read, 'Our late client, Richard W. Cunningham, of Manor Farm, Baybury, Berkshire has requested that, in the event of his death, we should forward the enclosed letters to you six months after his demise. He further requests that if, after reading the letter addressed to yourself, you should decide it to be appropriate, you will then, in person, deliver the other letter to Mrs Victoria Cunningham.'

'Oh my God,' said Francine, 'so Richard did leave farewell letters after all!' She looked at the two envelopes on the table. One was addressed to Guy Winston Esq, 40 The Boltons, London SW7, the other just said 'For Vicky'. Both were written in Richard's neat, rounded hand.

'Aren't you going to open yours?' she asked.

'I suppose so,' he said, not making any move to do so.

'Do you want to be alone when you read it – shall I leave you?'

'No. Please stay.' He put his hand on hers for a moment, and then picked up the envelope with his name on and opened it as cautiously as though it might contain an explosive device. He drew out a single sheet of paper with the Manor Farm heading. When he had read it he handed it to Francine. She thought he looked shell-shocked.

Guy – If you get this letter I shall have been dead for six months. I can't go on – and you of all people will know why. It's taken me long enough to accept, but you've made your-self clear and there's no more to be said on that score. But between us we've completely messed up Victoria's life and none of this is her fault. For her sake and Jake's, I hope I can make it look like an accident and she need never know anything different – in which case destroy the letter I've written to her. But if she has discovered or guessed the truth, then please give her the enclosed. Either way she and Jake will be better off without me. I have failed them dismally. Please do all you can for them both. You owe us all that at least – Richard.

Guy gazed at Francine. Then he said – and the words came out in a series of jerks as though they were being forced out of him: 'I know it only confirms what we knew . . . but somehow seeing it in his writing . . . it's so sad, such a terrible affirmation of what happened . . . of his despair; of the awful waste . . .' His voice trailed away and Francine could see he was struggling for composure. He went on in a rush: '. . . of my own contribution to the whole business, my treachery to Vicky. I should have put a complete stop to our affair years ago at Cambridge. Oh God! It was such a shock suddenly seeing his writing that for a mad moment I almost thought . . .' He did not complete the sentence. Then he went on: 'What the hell am I to do? Just when Vicky's beginning to get over things a little, it'll knock her right back.'

Francine handed the letter over and went and put her arms round him. She said: 'I think it may help her – Richard must have intended his letter to be of comfort to her. And, anyway, you have no choice, darling.'

She thought there was no grain of comfort for Guy in his own letter from Richard, but perhaps he neither expected nor felt he deserved one.

'Darling,' she said, giving him a little shake, 'you need to talk about it. You've been trying to blank it all out but now you'll have to face it. You have to give her the letter but you can also do the other thing he's asked – make it your cause to see that the future's as easy for her and Jake as it can possibly be, given their circumstances. That might help you too.'

He took her face in his hands. 'You're so good for me, Francine,' he said. 'You see things so clearly. Don't think I don't know what a shit I can be. You're right, as usual. I've got a meeting at lunch time but I think I should go straight down to Baybury this afternoon and see Vicky before we go away. I suppose you wouldn't like to come too?'

Francine shook her head decisively. 'I think it should be between the two of you.'

'You're probably right. I'll try not to be too late back, but don't wait up for me.'

Driving down the M4 later that afternoon, Guy felt as if he had a time-bomb in the car. What effect would the letter have on Victoria? What did it actually say?

Victoria was upstairs when Guy drew up at the front door of Manor Farm and as soon as she heard his familiar four toots on the horn – three short, one long – she rushed downstairs, feeling sick with apprehension. What new drama could have caused him – Guy of all people, not normally given to quixotic gestures that inconvenienced him – to come all the way down from London to see her rather than speak on the telephone?

'What's happened?' she asked as soon as he got out of the car. 'Is it Jake? Is it Nonna? Is it Francine?'

'It's all right, Vicky,' he said. 'It's nothing to do with any of them. Something has turned up unexpectedly which I have to show you. Where shall we go?'

'Let's go in the garden,' she said. She led the way through the house and out of the French windows in the drawing room. She had put a bottle of wine and two glasses on the old white garden table, and poured them each a glass. 'So . . .' she said, sounding more controlled than she felt, 'tell me what's happened.'

He told her about his unexpected post that morning and showed her the letter from the solicitor. When he gave her the envelope addressed to her, she went very white and her hands shook as she slit the envelope open and pulled out two sheets of paper in Richard's writing.

Guy hardly dared to look at her and for a moment there was complete silence between them while she read it. It was not a very long letter – it barely took her a couple of minutes – but to Guy they seemed to go on for ever. He waited for her to pass it to him when she had finished it, but she did not do so. Instead she folded it very carefully and deliberately, slid it back in its envelope and put it in her pocket. Tears were coursing down her cheeks and she couldn't speak.

458

When she finally got herself under control, she said in a choked voice: 'To think he must have been so desperate but so deliberate – planned it all so carefully – and I had no idea, not a clue that he might attempt anything so dreadful.'

'I know, I know. You don't need to tell me that. I knew and didn't believe him.'

'Oh, Guy, how *could* he do it?'

He forced himself to meet her eyes. 'I don't know, but I'm certain you couldn't have prevented it, Vicky. I might have been able to, but not you. I have to live with that. You needn't. The question is: can you forgive us for what it's done to you?'

'I hope so. I think so,' she whispered. 'I do so badly want to.' She went on hesitantly: 'As you've probably guessed, something quite unforeseen has happened to me in the last weeks. I think I've found someone else – someone very special. It's been so unexpected and seems much too soon but I've been struck by lightning, just as Nonna always said I should be, and . . . oh, Guy . . . I can't tell you how wonderful it feels or how much it terrifies me because if anything went wrong with it now I don't think I could bear it.'

'It won't,' he said. 'If anyone deserves happiness, you do.'

'I don't deserve anything, but deserving never seems to have much to do with good or bad. But I've lost the confidence to expect things to go right. And think what happened to Nonna and Hugh. All those terrible misunderstandings!' She looked at him with such anxiety in her eyes that he felt as though he was being flayed.

'Don't think like that,' he said, and then: 'I really liked Patrick, Vicky. Francine and I both did, and of course we guessed. Anyone who saw you together couldn't possibly mistake the fact that you're both head over heels in love. When are you next seeing him?'

'Tomorrow. He's got to photograph some houses and we were planning to snatch a little time alone together to talk about things before I go back to Vrahos. But I'm not sure what I ought to do now.'

'Well, go for it. Don't let what's happened hold you back,' said Guy emphatically, thinking of Richard's request to him and Francine's instructions. 'Think what it would mean to

Nonna if you and Patrick got together – a sort of compensation for all that went wrong for her. Don't let anything muck it up for you. Have you talked about Patrick to Mum and Dad?'

'No, not yet . . . but I have a shrewd idea that you must have done,' she said. 'Toula was bursting with ill-disguised curiosity. I hadn't wanted to say anything to anyone at this stage, it seems too like tempting fate, but I'd decided that I must talk to them before I go back to Vrahos because I'd hate them to feel hurt or shut out.'

'Are you going to show me Richard's letter?' Guy hated himself for asking, but couldn't resist it. He felt desperate to know what Richard had written.

Victoria shot him an enigmatic look. She thought of his dual ability, experienced so often in the past, for occasional wanton cruelties and sudden redeeming kindnesses; of his capacity to give generous and unstinting help when the fancy took him and his destructive tendency to cause trouble when it didn't; she also thought of Francine's realistic and unequivocal answer to her own question about trusting Guy.

She shook her head. 'No, Guy. I don't think so. It was a very personal letter to me.' She added, to soften the rebuff : 'You haven't shown me what he wrote to you – and I don't want to know. It's better for us both that way.'

It was on the tip of Guy's tongue to ask if she intended to let Patrick see her letter, but he bit the question back and thought that at least he had thereby kept a shred of self-respect intact. He recognised sadly that his relationship with the little cousin he loved but had taken too much for granted, might be patched up but would never be quite the same again. He had fallen from grace.

'I shall have to go back to Francine soon,' he said, looking at his watch, 'but I don't like leaving you. Why don't you go back to Durnford House tonight? Mum and Dad would be only too delighted.'

But Victoria was adamant that she would be all right. 'I can ring them if I change my mind, and I'm going to them on Friday night anyway before I fly back to Corfu on Saturday.' She wanted to be alone: to read and reread Richard's letter, ponder on its contents and think about the future.

'Thank you for coming, Guy,' she said as he kissed her goodbye. 'It must have been a hard thing to do and I truly appreciate it. This is a tough time for us both, but at least we know something definite. Give my love to Francine – and I really mean that. See you both when you come to Vrahos.'

'See you at Vrahos,' he echoed. 'And, Vicky . . . good luck tomorrow. Promise me you'll still go?'

'I promise,' she said, and she stood and watched his car go down the drive before she turned and went back into the house, glad to have faithful Teal to keep her company, who neither asked questions nor required complicated emotional reactions from her.

Patrick got to the Old Priory Hotel at about six o'clock and was relieved that he had arrived before Victoria.

He had booked separate but adjoining rooms, hoping this might not be required but not wanting to put Victoria under any pressure. Both rooms overlooked the garden – a garden that Patrick had photographed in the past as part of a promotion for the hotel. The ruined arches of the old priory cloisters now provided a framework for climbing shrubs and rambling roses, and there was a formal rose garden too, enclosed in carefully clipped yew hedges with garden seats positioned at strategic intervals; statues of nymphs and shepherds in floppy hats conducted asexual flirtations among the rose beds; there was a lake with real swans admiring their own reflections in its calm green waters; in the surrounding parkland there was a view of a Palladian folly, built long after the priory had ceased to be a religious foundation, which invited exploration and suggested pleasant strolls. It was all suitably romantic.

Patrick got himself a drink from the bar and found a seat under a huge cedar tree to one side of the house where he would be able to see any car coming up the drive, and thought about Victoria. He knew himself to be deeply in love, hoped and thought she felt the same – but wondered if she had fully realised the difficulties she might be facing if they got together. He thought wryly that his two elder children were nearer to Victoria in age than he was himself and he couldn't see Rachel going out of her way to be cooperative about family life, even though it was she who had asked for a separation in the first place.

The previous Sunday his father-in-law had let slip that he thought Rachel might be involved with someone else herself – and had then tried to gloss it over. It would not be the first time Rachel had trodden Shakespeare's 'primrose path of dalliance' during their marriage. Several years previously Patrick had been shattered to discover his wife was having an affair with an old flame from university days. Nothing had come of it because it turned out that Rachel's lover was simply amusing himself between marriages and had no intention of letting anything serious develop. Rachel had been hurt and humiliated, Patrick had been hurt and angry, but ultimately the Hammonds had patched their marriage up. The Marshalls had supported them through this difficult patch and Maggie had been helpful in bringing about a reconciliation. It was ironic, Patrick thought, watching for Victoria's arrival, that he should once have been so appalled by Rachel's unfaithfulness, whereas now he would be far from heartbroken if she were to fall for another man. Had she not been so intent on going out to Spain, he might have taken Howard Ingfield's suspicion more seriously, but as it was he thought it would be quite in character for Rachel to be winding her father up.

The sound of tyres crunching over the carefully raked gravel interrupted these reflections and with a lifting of the heart he saw Victoria getting out of her car. She was wearing a white T-shirt, and a short red linen skirt, which showed off her long brown legs to perfection. He waved delightedly and walked swiftly over to fold her in his arms. But when he held her away from him to revel in the pleasure of looking at her again, he was dismayed to see she seemed drawn and unhappy – very different from when they had parted less than a week before.

'Victoria? What's the matter?' he asked, searching her face. 'It's so very good to see you – but have you had a change of heart about coming here with me?'

'No, oh, no,' she said, but he could feel her trembling.

'Something's happened all the same.'

'Yes,' she said, and then blurted out: 'I've had a letter from

Richard. I wasn't going to tell you yet, but it's completely thrown me.'

'A letter from *Richard* – after all this time?'

'Yes,' she said. 'It was sent to Guy. He brought it down last night – it's come through a firm of solicitors. A complete shock for both Guy and me.'

'Come on,' he said. 'Let's check you in and then you can tell me about it. I'd been going to suggest we had a drink on the terrace but it's a bit public there. Let's go straight upstairs.'

It didn't seem the moment to discuss sleeping arrangements. After the porter had taken her case up and left them, Victoria, feeling as if her legs might buckle under her, perched on the edge of the enormous four-poster bed. Patrick could see she was deeply troubled.

'Now tell me,' he said.

For answer she opened her bag and produced Richard's letter. 'Please read it,' she said, holding it out.

'Are you quite sure you want to share it with me?' he asked.

'Quite sure.'

He took the letter and went over to the window.

Darling Vicky,

I want you to know that none of this mess is your fault. There is *nothing* you could have done or said that would stop me doing what I intend to do – pray God I succeed. I am no good to anyone in my present state and I am convinced that you and Jake will be better off without me.

I cannot – I absolutely *cannot* – carry on living a lie. The deception is entirely of my own making and if I was a better, stronger person I might be able to do things differently – but it's just no good. Dearest Vicky – I really have tried. I am not ashamed of the way I am – only of my failure to acknowledge it, and of the way I have deceived you and tried to shelter behind you. I do love you very much, but not in the way which is your right, and which you deserve. I have always been desperately aware that you've often felt unhappy and frustrated about our relationship without realising the true cause of it. There has only ever been one person for me and I can't face the fact that he has finally rejected me and chosen someone else. Guy has never felt the same about me anyway, and I have at long last accepted that he never will. You have every right to be desperately angry with me both for Jake's sake and your own, but all the same I ask you to forgive me. Because you are *you* and such a generous, loving person, I believe in time you may be able to do so. If you get this it will be because you know what I have done and why. I can't leave a letter for you to read at the time of my death because I don't want to affect a coroner's verdict. It will be so much better for Jake if everyone thinks it's an accident.

Call what I'm going to do the coward's way out, but don't pity me. I've had a marvellous life and you have given me a son of whom I am so proud. Neither you nor I could regret that ever. I trust you completely to bring Jake up in the way you think best.

Perhaps you will find and marry someone special who can be a better husband than I have been – a proper husband. You have my blessing if you do.

Goodbye, darling Vicky, and thank you for everything you have given me. For my sake, try to be happy again and God bless you always.

Richard

Patrick came over and sat beside her on the bed and held her, rocking her gently as though he were comforting a child, and she leaned against him and wept, months of hurt and misery spewing out in releasing tears.

'I'm so sorry,' she blurted out between her sobs. 'It's so wonderful that you're here, but what a way to greet you.'

'Darling Victoria,' he said eventually, as her tears began to subside. 'It must have come as a terrible shock, but in some ways you must be relieved to get his letter too? However dreadful it was, it's over now. No more pain for him and nothing you hadn't faced already for you. And it sets you free. You have his blessing – *we* have his blessing. Isn't that rather wonderful, coming just now? And he tells you how much he loved you. It's a good letter – a healing letter.'

'*Healing?*' She looked at him, her almost black eyes looking enormous in her troubled face. 'Whatever he says about loving me and Jake it's clear we neither of us counted for anything compared with Guy. To have meant so little – how am I supposed to live with that?'

'Because he couldn't help it,' said Patrick, desperately wanting to comfort her. 'Because he was a man in the grip of an obsession and a terrible burden which he couldn't bear any more. Don't you see that? And he's given you a wonderful parting gift – he's released you to enjoy *our* love. And I do love you, Victoria. I love you very much. I love you in every way a man can possibly love a woman.' He took her face in his hands and started to kiss her, very gently at first and then as he felt her response, with increasing passion.

'This isn't a time for any more words,' he said softly. 'Let me show you, Victoria. Let me show you what it can mean.'

Chapter Forty-four

It was in a very different state of mind from the one in which she had arrived at the Old Priory the previous evening that Victoria drove to Durnford House on Friday afternoon. She felt so lit up that it occurred to her that her car might easily run on the energy of her happiness without any need for petrol, and when she passed other vehicles she half expected to take off and fly over the top of them.

'I didn't know it could be like that,' she had whispered to Patrick as she lay in his arms after their first lovemaking. 'It's a complete revelation.'

Then she started to laugh.

'A funny one too?' Patrick raised an amused eyebrow at her, delighted at her reaction.

'Umm . . . I was thinking you must have had lessons in the marital arts from my sister-in-law,' she said, and told him about Toula's latest malapropism.

Before a late dinner they had walked hand in hand round the gardens, with swifts swooping across the lawn, a wood pigeon crooning and a late thrush singing. Victoria thought she would never hear that particular carillon of birdsong again without remembering this place and this evening. Later they had made love again.

After a leisurely breakfast she accompanied Patrick to the house he was due to photograph the next morning. It turned out to be a late Victorian monstrosity of such a bizarre blend of styles that it had a certain perverse attraction, like an aesthetically hideous woman whose fairy godmother had waved a wicked wand over her cot but repented at the last minute and thrown in charm as a redeeming christening gift, suggested Patrick. It was certainly more like a castle in a Disney cartoon film than a Cotswold country house, and he had enjoyed photographing it, picking out details from turrets to minarets, galleries to gargoyles to convey its eccentric character. The owner, who had recently acquired it, plus contents and was deeply in love with the whole unwieldy edifice, turned out to be a bachelor millionaire who had made his fortune out of bathroom fittings and wished to share the allure of his new home with the public. Unusually, he did not require financial help from Heritage at Risk so much as their validation that the house was worth opening and he was pleased when Patrick told him he thought the public would greatly appreciate it.

Victoria hadn't enjoyed a morning so much for ages and thought Patrick the most entertaining of companions.

The owner of the house had given them lunch in a vast baronial dining room decorated with suspect suits of armour and a moth-eaten display of the taxidermist's skill that would have turned the stomach of a conservationist, but the menu, unlike the interior decoration, was light and delicious and their host unpretentious and interesting. The only thing he'd altered in the whole house, he told them proudly, was the plumbing. He had tactfully offered Victoria the chance to 'freshen up' before she left, and she had accepted with alacrity though more, as she told Patrick afterwards, to satisfy her curiosity than any call of nature.

'You were in there for ages. I was beginning to wonder if you'd been taken ill.'

'I was playing with all the gadgets,' she said, convulsed with laughter. 'It's like walking inside an oyster shell – everything's pearlised and shimmering, water gushes out of the mouths of dolphins when you press the right button – the only snag is you need to belong to Mensa to work out how to empty the basin afterwards. And imagine! When you flush the loo it plays "God save the Queen" so you feel you have to stand to attention until it's finished.'

They had returned to the Old Priory to go their separate ways, as Patrick was driving straight back to Yorkshire and Victoria was going back to Durnford House for the night. They would both have found it very hard to say goodbye if he hadn't suggested, as they had lain together the night before, discussing their hopes for the future, that he might come out to Corfu in a fortnight's time to stay with the Marshalls with Sophie and Posy, when Rachel took off to Spain. 'I can take the pictures I want of the island in high summer and perhaps some shots of the Venetian architecture in Corfu town itself, to put Vrahos in its context,' he said.

'Are you going to say anything to your children about us . . . about me?' Victoria had asked rather apprehensively, conscious of how desperately she wanted to be accepted by Patrick's family.

'Well, I'm not going to spell it out to Posy yet, she's too little, but I think I should be open with Sam and Sophie, don't you? Put them in the picture, tell them how we feel about each other – though I think they have a pretty shrewd idea about that already. It affects their future after all.'

'I suppose so,' she had said rather doubtfully. 'It's just quite a daunting thought. We all got on so well in April and I like them both so much, but though they were lovely to me at Hugh's exhibition I felt Sophie was a bit suspicious of me too, and I'm worried about how she may react if she thinks I'm a threat to her mum.'

'You can't expect to be instant best friends with Sophie,' said Patrick realistically. 'It will take time, but it wouldn't solve anything to make her feel shut out or give her a real cause for grievance. Sam may have a few problems too.' He grinned at her. 'He fancied you rotten himself last April.' Then he went on seriously: 'Don't look so worried, my love. What we have between us is so wonderful, don't let's spoil it now with anxieties we can't do anything about yet. Let's cope with the problems as they come along.' He had kissed her very tenderly. 'You'll need to think what line you're going to take with Jake though. He may well resent having to share you,' he added . . . but the kiss had taken both their minds off family issues and they let the subject drop for the time being while they explored other, more exciting, aspects of love.

Back at the hotel they said their farewells, knowing that they would be together again very soon.

'I'll see you at Vrahos then, my darling. I can't wait to talk to Hugh when I get home because I know he'll be so delighted.

Give my love to that special grandmother and I'll ring you later tonight. Will you be all right now?'

'I shall drive all the way on cloud nine,' she promised, laughing.

Victoria arrived at Durnford House soon after four to find Anthony and Toula having a cup of tea in the kitchen. After so determinedly putting off any mention of Patrick to them so far, she could now hardly wait to tell them about their relationship and talk about her hopes for the future. She didn't even mind that it clearly came as no surprise to them.

'At last you tell us!' Toula swept her into a wild embrace, scarves tangling and windmill arms flailing. 'Oh, *agapi mou*! I am so, so thrilled for you. Now we must meet this paragon for ourselves, because I suppose,' she added rather grudgingly, 'Nonna will claim all the credit for introducing you and I don't want her telling me what he's like until I've decided for myself!'

Anthony winked at Victoria and went to get a bottle of champagne from the cellar to drink before dinner. He thought he had never seen his niece looking so happy or so beautiful.

Later he drove her to Manor Farm to lock up the house, say goodbye to Violet and give her the keys. They took the three dogs for a last walk together. She had decided it would be wrong to transplant Teal to Vrahos, and though she hated the thought of parting from the old dog again and felt a traitor, she knew it was better to leave him with the Winstons where everything was familiar to him and where he was loved. In the pack order at Vrahos he would inevitably be subservient to Rocky and Tomasina and she thought that would be an indignity to inflict on him. They stopped to lean on a gate and give him a chance to catch up with the two terriers. It was a beautiful evening, all soft summer light and feathery clouds. The English countryside looked as peaceful as a painting by Constable and she thought it was hard to believe in the act of violence that had taken place six months before.

Anthony had walked round to the Crompton Gallery earlier in the day to look at Hugh's exhibition – though he knew his work of old – and had been greatly impressed.

'That portrait of Evanthi is really stunning,' he said. 'What a strange coincidence it is about their romance and now yours. Always fascinating when the threads in the tapestry are woven into such unlikely patterns. It makes one wonder about an overall design.'

'I can't imagine what the next stage is for Hugh and Nonna, though – if there is one,' said Victoria, tucking her hand through his arm. 'We know they're in touch but they're both quite secretive about it. Do you think I ought to engineer a surprise meeting between them?'

'Oh, I'd wait and see what develops,' answered Anthony shrewdly. 'You women always want to rush in and play Cupid but they're quite capable of organising themselves if they want to.'

'They made a right old mess of it last time,' objected Victoria.

'All the more reason not to rush in now and interfere,' he said. 'Concentrate on your own life, Vicky darling. I can't tell you how happy your news makes me, but don't *you* go missing opportunities yourself now that they have come your way.'

'No,' she said. 'I don't mean to. It would be my dream if Patrick and I could divide our time between England and Vrahos – but we haven't really got that far yet. I couldn't give up Vrahos. Uncle Anthony – can I ask you something?'

'You're obviously going to! But yes, of course.'

'What did you really think of the coroner's verdict on Richard?'

'I thought he gave the right verdict – the only possible one, given the evidence.'

'And it never crossed your mind that Richard might have meant to do it?'

Anthony looked at her. 'Well, it *crossed* my mind, yes. Richard was a very experienced shot – a safe and careful shot – so it was extremely surprising. But accidents always *are* surprising and anyone can have one at any time. What are you trying to tell me, Vicky?'

She gave him an edited account of Richard's letter, being open about Guy's long-standing knowledge of Richard's homosexuality, admitting what a bombshell it had been to her, but carefully avoiding any mention of Guy's own affair with him, though she wondered if Anthony suspected more than he let on. Despite her new-found happiness she still found her voice cracking when she spoke of it.

'Let it all rest now,' Anthony said firmly. 'There is absolutely nothing to be gained from picking this tragedy over and over. Give yourself a chance to enjoy your new relationship and when you're ready, move on. And, above all, don't feel guilty about happiness. Now come along and we'd better lock up and find Violet, or Toula will wonder what's happened to us.'

Anthony and Toula planned to come over to Vrahos in September, which made the goodbyes less painful. Anthony privately decided it was time he took a hand in affairs at Vrahos and intended to talk seriously to his mother-in-law about the future of the house and estate with regard to Victoria and find out just how things were placed. He'd always got on extremely well with Evanthi and knew she trusted him, but her relations with her daughter were more complicated and up to now Anthony had tried not to get too involved.

Victoria arrived back at Vrahos to a rapturous welcome from Jake. He had so much to tell her about the daily goings-on in her absence that he could hardly get the words out fast enough and had to stop and do a few somersaults mid-sentence to let off steam.

She felt as if she'd been away much longer than a fortnight but it was wonderful to be back; wonderful to see Jake looking so well – he hadn't had an asthma attack for weeks. Evanthi also looked less frail – indeed, she seemed to have taken on a new lease of life. Dora reported that her own grandmother and Evanthi had been truly reconciled but that though Nafsica had received generous assurances of forgiveness from her old mistress she was unwilling to be cheated of suitable martyrdom and still indulged in occasional noisy bouts of self-reproach that were becoming very trying for everyone. Dora said with a grin that Kyria was getting bored with Nafsica's wailing and had started to be very bracing with her and Victoria thought it sounded as if both old ladies were behaving entirely in character.

Evanthi was avid for details about Victoria's meeting with Hugh and wanted to hear all about him. She looked at the catalogue with pride and delight but couldn't help noticing with loving amusement – and considerable pleasure – that Victoria found it impossible not to keep reverting to the subject of Patrick. As Toula had predicted, Evanthi took full credit to herself for playing Cupid to this development.

When Victoria delivered Hugh's silver box to her grandmother, Evanthi, after holding it for a long time, put it carefully down on the chest beside her chair in the little drawing room, where its twin had always resided, but kept putting her hand out and touching it as though to check that it hadn't suddenly vanished, or perhaps, Victoria thought, because she felt it gave her a contact with Hugh. 'Do open your present too, Nonna,' urged Victoria, longing to see what was in the flat package Hugh had also entrusted to her. Evanthi gave her an amused smile and with maddening slowness opened it very carefully, smoothing the layers of tissue paper until from between layers of bubble wrap, she drew out the little watercolour of Vrahos, now beautifully mounted and framed, that had so taken Sophie's fancy. She looked at it with delight.

'Oh look . . . there's something on the back,' said Victoria.

Evanthi turned the picture over. Three verses were written in Hugh's spiky, forward-sloping hand.

> A watercolour
> turns a rusty key.
>
> Pink house, blue shutters
> – bluer sky – stray cats;
> a bougainvillea
> lolling down one wall;
> geraniums, stiff,
> in terracotta pots:
> and oh, you're there again,
> . . . still there with me.
>
> Kingfishers borrow
> feathers from the waves;
> a gasp of dolphins
> arrows past our bay.

Cicadas, beat out
rhythms to the heat
and, tireless, shake maracas
all the day;

Through star-long nights,
the scops owls call
as secrets rustle
in the olive leaves; then
when a pewter pathway
crosses moonlit sea
. . . I feel you there once more,
still there with me.

Grandmother and granddaughter looked at each other with tears in their eyes.

'Oh Nonna! He must still love you very much,' whispered Victoria.

Will Patrick and I be like that, she wondered – still in love in old age?

The summer season was now at its height. Huge water lorries ground up and down the hairpin bends of the island's main roads by night to cater to the requirements of modern plumbing and *de rigueur* swimming pools, and it was far too hot in the middle of the day to contemplate any but necessary trips in the Vrahos old banger of a car; the accident toll to scores of inexperienced scooter drivers (burning up not only the road miles but acres of perilously exposed flesh as well) was unacceptably high; the sea was the perfect temperature for swimming and provided a paradise for wind-surfers, water-skiers, and amateur sailors, and the many small shops did a roaring trade, as did the tavernas; the beaches at the main resorts were crowded with oily bodies, ignoring health warnings, lying thigh-to-thigh in the full glare of the midday sun. But it was still possible to dodge the down side of the twenty-first century up in the hills; still possible, if you hired a boat, to find deserted coves where you could picnic and swim in peace – except for the age-old enemy of wasps, which miraculously appeared from nowhere at the first whiff of a fizzy drink.

Jake and Angelo concocted endless jam-jar traps on the terrace and became fiercely competitive about the rival merits of Coke or Fanta, honey or jam as bait for attracting the striped terrorists to their doom. They had had gruesome body counts and kept a tally of their respective scores.

A stream of Evanthi's friends and acquaintances of varying nationalities arrived to stay either at Vrahos itself or in rented villas on the island; as usual Evanthi engaged a temporary cook for July and August to ease things for Dora – who would have preferred to keep her kitchen to herself but enjoyed sabotaging the efforts of a culinary rival. This season's specimen was a jolly Australian whose main aim in her free time was to sneak off to the Harbour Bar and try to go to bed with Petros – not a difficult ambition to achieve. As Petros' wife was a friend of Dora's, a happy time of guerrilla warfare was guaranteed, in which Jake and Angelo were enthusiastic double agents, changing allegiance with fickle frequency.

Guy and Francine came on from Verona after their week of opera. Guy usually avoided the height of summer but with Francine's baby due in October it seemed wise to come earlier this year. Victoria knew Francine was apprehensive about her first visit to Vrahos but, contrary to expectations, Evanthi and Francine took to each other immediately. They appreciated each other's outspoken strength of mind and clear-eyed realism; they enjoyed each other's sense of humour; they were absorbed by the prospect of the baby – and they were united by their feelings for the talented, tricky, unreliable man they both adored. Guy, on his best behaviour, was at his most beguiling: teasing his grand-mother as only he was allowed to do; chatting-up old Nafsica (who forgot to wear her hair shirt in his company), flirting with Dora and taking Jake on endless boating expeditions. He introduced his wife to all the places on the island he had most loved as a boy and was very solicitous about her welfare.

Though Victoria was counting the days till Patrick came out, she couldn't help being relieved that he and Guy would not overlap this time.

Unbeknownst to his cousin, Guy had raised the subject of

selling the icon with Evanthi when he went to have one of his long, gossipy, good-night sessions with her.

Of course they had discussed Victoria's involvement with Patrick and for the first time too, Guy had heard Evanthi's account of her blighted love affair from her own lips. 'It is my great hope that Hugh's nephew and Victoria may round the arc of the rainbow we fractured so wantonly all those years ago,' she said. 'It would be my prayer answered.'

'If you want Vicky to live at Vrahos with Patrick one day, Nonna, you will have to make it possible for her to do so,' said Guy, seizing on the Patrick issue to raise a taboo subject. 'You always taught us when we were children that it was no good praying for a miracle if we weren't prepared to help make it possible. I think you will have to face financial necessity and sell the icon.'

'So your father keeps telling me.' Evanthi, looking down her patrician nose at her grandson, was at her most quelling.

'And?' persisted Guy, not one to be quelled.

'And I have almost made up my mind at least to *consider* it – for Victoria and Patrick. . .but . . .'

'Almost but not quite? You could have a wonderful copy of the icon made, you know, if you can't face the thought of being without it.'

'*A copy?*' Evanthi was outraged, as he had known she would be. 'If I decide to part with it, I shall do so as an offering of love,' she said grandly. 'I wouldn't want any *copy*.' She made it sound like a dirty word.

'Oh, well then,' said Guy, 'you'd better hang on to the real thing since it's obviously so important to you. Dad always said he doubted if you'd ever actually bring yourself to part with it – even for Vicky and Vrahos.' Which was very crafty of Guy, if not quite accurate.

He got up. 'Good night, darling Nonna. It's wonderful to be here and I'm so pleased you like Francine. I can't tell you what that means to me. I must go and see if she's all right.' He kissed his grandmother good night and took himself off before she could enter into any further discussion on the subject, and was well satisfied that he had prepared ground for his father to cultivate later on.

'I've just been incredibly clever,' he told Francine, who was reading in bed. 'You're going to be so proud of me.'

'I think it's your amazing modesty that's one of your most endearing qualities,' said his wife, glinting at him over her book.

Patrick was as good as his word and when he got home he tried to talk to his son and daughter about his feelings for Victoria.

They listened uneasily, not sure how to respond. 'Isn't there any chance that you and Mum might get back together then?' asked Sophie in a small voice.

'I'm afraid not,' said Patrick. 'We've both got beyond that point and she wouldn't welcome it any more than I would. But you know that because we talked about our divorce at Granny's the other Sunday. Nothing will change at home yet – it's just that Mum and I won't both be here together very often, but we'll still try to do all the things together that affect you – parents' days at school and things like that. You'll enjoy having next week with Mum in London, Sophie, and then when she goes off to Spain, I've said I'll have Posy. Maggie and Phil have asked us out to Petradi again. You'd like that, wouldn't you?'

'Will Victoria be there?'

'Well, not actually at Petradi but she'll be at Vrahos, naturally. She does live there, after all and I have to go there again anyway to finish the book.'

'How very convenient for you,' said Sophie with heavy sarcasm, 'and what a treat for the rest of us!' and she banged out of the room, hating herself for her ungraciousness but unable to stop the unwanted, babyish tears from brimming down her face. She rushed across the garden to the paddock to catch Punch and go for a long angry ride.

'She doesn't really mean it, Dad,' muttered Sam awkwardly, thoroughly uncomfortable himself, torn between loyalty to his sister and affection for his father. 'Go a bit easy on her.'

'Thanks, Sam, I'll try to,' said Patrick, aware how embarrassing to the young any thought of sex in connection with parents always is. 'I know this is all very difficult for you both. Probably a good thing you're off on your travels.'

Sam was going to Thailand and Vietnam for two months with

a party of university friends, so Patrick had accepted the Marshalls' invitation for Sophie, Posy and himself with alacrity. He knew Sophie would miss Sam terribly and thought it would help her to have Ellie's cheerful company, and knew how devoted she was to the whole Marshall family. Yvonne, who had taken on a temporary job for August, had promised to come back to the Hammonds for the autumn to help them sort their lives out with as little disruption for Posy as possible – on condition, she had said, pulling a frightful face and grinning disarmingly at Patrick, that she didn't have to spend too much time at Chobham.

Both Patrick and Sophie had used Maggie as a sounding board for their different takes on the same story. Because Philip was not only his lawyer but had been his friend since schooldays, Patrick felt he could safely confide in both the Marshalls. Though Rachel had behaved badly last time the Hammond marriage had been in trouble, Maggie had still felt some sympathy for her, but this time her allegiance was firmly with Patrick.

Sophie, of course, also poured out her heart to Ellie, who lapped up the tales of the Hammond family's dramas and could hardly wait for the next exciting instalment. She regarded her own parents' lives as abysmally dull by comparison.

'Poor Sophe! Her mum's really only just left and her father's *already* got another woman,' she announced dramatically to her mother.

'You won't be doing Sophie any favours if you encourage her to feel more ill used than she already does,' said Maggie. 'The marriage has been foundering for ages and, sad though the break-up is in many ways, Sophie's going to have to accept Victoria. Personally I'm delighted Patrick's found himself someone else and hope he can have a bit of fun for a change.'

'Do you think they'll get married?' asked Ellie, but Maggie refused to be drawn.

'It's too soon to talk about that,' she said firmly. 'Patrick and Rachel are only just starting divorce proceedings so he isn't even free yet. Lots of things can happen in the meantime. Now, Ellie, do encourage Sophie to be civil to Victoria Cunningham while we're out in Corfu, even if she doesn't like her, otherwise everyone will be in for a miserable time, including herself.'

'Oh, but she does like her,' said Ellie. 'Actually she likes her a lot and says Victoria's always been absolutely sweet to her, but she feels it would all be much simpler if she hated her.'

Maggie groaned. 'Well, tell her to take a pull then,' she said bracingly. 'She's lucky if she does like her father's girlfriend and she's nice to her. It isn't always so, I assure you.'

But despite these words to Ellie, Maggie knew from Patrick that as far as he was concerned he was already quite sure what he wanted. He was longing for Philip and Maggie to meet Victoria.

'I told you that if Patrick fell for someone it would be really serious,' Maggie informed Philip as they lay in bed one Sunday morning. 'He's worried because she's so much younger than him – but he's absolutely crazy about her.'

'I don't think the age-gap should be a problem,' answered Philip. 'I'd be more worried that after the tragedy she's been through, it might be a case of "on the rebound" for her and then Patrick will get his fingers badly burned.'

'I'd be amazed if Victoria isn't bowled over too,' said Maggie. 'She's landed herself about the most attractive man I know.'

'Thanks!' Philip grinned at his wife. 'You're so good for one's morale, darling.'

'Oh, well – I said 'about' – and present company's excepted, of course,' said Maggie, laughing and snuggling up to her husband. 'Do put the Sunday papers away, Phil – you've got all the rest of the day to read those, but I've got to go and look at a garden later.'

The Marshalls travelled to Petradi a week before the Hammonds, and Philip went to meet them at the airport. Victoria had longed to go herself, but she and Patrick were determined to play their relationship in as low a key as possible and had agreed that for Sophie's sake it might be more tactful to postpone their own reunion till later. Patrick had promised to come over to Vrahos the following morning, and make any plans after that.

Despite Patrick's warning words, however, Victoria had been

unable to stop herself indulging in fantasies as to how things might develop. She visualised building a relationship with Patrick's little girl and thought it would be lovely for Posy and Jake to make friends. This, however, proved to be an unrealistic scenario, and though the reunion between Patrick and Victoria, to which they had both been looking forward with such intensity, was every bit as rapturous as either of them could have desired, the friendship between their younger children did not start well.

Jake and Posy, neither of them used to competition from other pebbles on their respective beaches, did not take kindly to one another and from the outset were at their worst in each other's company. Jake, disappointed at the absence of Sam, considered Posy, at nearly three, a very poor substitute for his hero and made no efforts to conceal his feelings. He didn't want any three-year-old – and specially not a mere girl – tagging along on expeditions, bidding for the limelight, and would much have preferred to stay at Vrahos in Angelo's congenial company than go on outings with his mother's new friends. Posy's far from artless prattle drove him mad but he got his revenge by pretending he couldn't understand a word she said and only addressing her in his newly acquired Greek. Posy used every wile she knew, including her tin-whistle scream, amongst her repertoire of ploys to attract his attention. However, having failed to engage his interest one morning, she deliberately stamped on the manuscript of Jake's latest novel, which he'd been composing under the shade of one of the Petradi olive trees. 'Boy's story gone,' she announced with satisfaction, grinding the illustrated masterpiece into the dusty earth with her small canvas shoe.

'No swimming for you today then, Posy,' said Patrick as he bore her off, screaming and kicking, to her room until such time as she could say she was sorry. He then settled down, apparently unruffled, in a deck chair to do *The Times* crossword, impervious to the bloodcurdling noise from overhead.

When the novel had been dusted down and a torn page carefully Sellotaped together, it proved not to have been as badly damaged as it might have been – but after that it was open warfare as far as Jake was concerned.

Sophie, while feeling surprisingly defensive of the little sister who often provoked her so much, couldn't help feeling sorry for Victoria at the same time. Longing for Patrick to be impressed by Jake, Victoria was furious with her son for making himself as objectionable as any six-year-old boy can be and what made it worse was that she knew she was not dealing well with the situation herself while Patrick, accustomed to the choppy waters of family life seemed to her to take it all with maddening calm.

'Don't get so worked up about it, darling,' he said when they eventually managed to steal off for a walk together, after Posy had made a pragmatic apology that Jake had accepted with a bad grace. 'The more notice you take, the worse they'll both be.'

The day after this altercation, the Petradi party came over to lunch at Vrahos and to Victoria's pleasure, not only were the Marshalls enthralled by the house, but Evanthi had been greatly taken with them – especially with Philip, whose knowledge of the island's history was a passport to her favour. She had glittered away from the head of the table and Victoria felt equally proud of her ancestral home, her grandmother and her new friends. Patrick brought his photographs of Vrahos, plus the text he'd written, to show Evanthi; Sophie and Ellie had been natural and delightful, and Posy for once was on her best behaviour. At Jake's request Angelo had been allowed to come to dining room lunch too, everyone seemed animated and happy, and Victoria started to relax and enjoy herself.

Before they arrived she had been nervous of meeting the Marshalls, about whom she'd heard a great deal – but from the outset they had been charming to her and she felt Maggie might become an ally. After Dora had brought in the coffee, she removed Angelo to go off with his father and escorted Evanthi to her rest while the rest of them went out on the terrace marvelling at the view and discussing what they would all like to do in the afternoon.

The sight of Jake and Posy sitting together on the edge of the terrace encouraged Victoria into thinking their relationship had undergone a thaw. She was soon disillusioned by paroxysms of weeping from Posy. Jake, bent on reprisal, had put his story-telling talents to deadly use by inventing a gripping saga about

Posy's Beanie Babies in which the ostrich, Stretch, had been gobbled up by Scoop, the pelican; the beloved Spike had turned malignant and put a spell on Bones and the whole lot had been abducted by Aliens. Posy hadn't the faintest idea what Aliens were, but as told by Jake, in grizzly detail, the Beanies' fate was clearly the stuff of nightmares.

Victoria had flown at Jake and banished him to his room in his turn.

'Stop trying so hard to make them be friends, Victoria,' said Patrick, when the ensuing pandemonium had been sorted out. 'You can't expect them to have much in common at their ages and the crosser you get the worse they'll be. They've got to learn to behave in a civilised way but it doesn't really matter whether they *like* each other at this stage.'

'It matters to me,' said Victoria stiffly.

The Marshalls looked on sympathetically as storm clouds floated on the horizon of the budding romance.

When the Petradi party decided to collect their boat from Kryovrisi and go down the coast to Aghia Sophia to do some water-skiing and windsurfing, Victoria declined Patrick's suggestion that she should grant Jake a reprieve and go with them.

'Do come too – both of you,' he said persuasively, smiling at her, while everyone else was collecting their belongings. 'To please me. It won't be the same if you don't come.' But Victoria remained obdurate. She felt as if a lump of something hard had formed in her throat, which prevented her from accepting. She said her goodbyes with a falsely bright smile and watched them disappear, miserably convinced that she had lowered herself in Patrick's eyes.

She went slowly upstairs and along the passage to Jake's room. He was lying on his bed with a book and didn't look up when she came in. She went and sat on the end of the bed; she could tell from his eyes that he'd stopped reading although he went on turning the pages with studied indifference to her presence. She waited.

'Have they gone?' he asked at last.

'Yes.'

'*Good,*' said Jake. Victoria sighed.

'Darling, Posy's so much younger than you and you really *frightened* her – and don't tell me you didn't mean to because I know you did. You're a big boy now – nearly seven – why did you have to be so unkind?'

'You know why. And she's a horrible little girl anyway. Why do we have to have them around all the time?'

'Because they're friends of mine and they're only here for a short time. I know it was awful about your story, but her daddy was very cross with her, she wasn't allowed to swim all day and she said she was sorry. You liked the Hammonds all right when they were here in April – I seem to remember you wanted to be with them all the time then.'

'Sam was here then and Posy wasn't. It's different now. She spoils everything.'

'Well, I know she's tiresome,' admitted Victoria, and then added unwisely, 'but she's missing her mummy so you must try to be nicer to her.'

Jake hurled his book across the room with such violence that several pages flew out when it hit the wall. 'And I'm missing Daddy,' he shouted at her, 'even if you're not.' He turned his face into the pillow and burst into tears.

Victoria tried to gather him into her arms but he fought her off.

'What do you mean, Jake?' She felt winded. 'Of course I miss Daddy too.'

'You don't, you don't,' yelled Jake. 'Angelo says you're going to marry Mr Hammond.'

'Angelo is a very silly little boy,' said Victoria furiously. 'He knows nothing whatever about it.'

'He heard Dora telling Yannis.'

'Well, Dora doesn't know anything either. She had no right to say that and I shall tell her so.'

'Then you're NOT going to marry Mr Hammond?'

Victoria could see a chasm opening beneath her feet. 'Listen, darling,' she said warily, 'I may marry again sometime. It wouldn't be honest to promise I wouldn't because people often do marry again and we none of us know what's going to happen in the future. We didn't know Daddy was going to be

482

killed. That was awful – it *is* awful – but we can't bring him back. I do promise that if I decide to marry I will tell you first. And it would never make any differences to you and me. All right?'

Jake looked at her challengingly. 'Has Mr Hammond asked you to marry him?'

'No,' said Victoria, thankful that she could be at least be truthful about this, 'and I'm not ready for that yet anyway . . . but I'm warning you, Jake, if you go on being so rude and behaving so badly there will be big trouble because I won't have it.'

Jake gave his mother a speculative look, and decided it was not the moment to push his luck. 'Sorry,' he muttered.

'All right,' said Victoria, sitting down on the bed and giving him the hug he had spurned a few minutes before. 'But don't let me down again. Now let's forget about it and go and swim together – just you and me.'

But as they went down to the bay she felt that Patrick's visit to which she had been looking forward so passionately was becoming fraught with anxiety.

Chapter Forty-five

Later that evening, Sophie and Ellie sat by the Petradi pool painting their toenails an alluring shade of purple and reviewing their day.

On the way back from the water-skiing, which had been a huge success, they had dropped in at the internet café in Kryovrisi to see if there were any e-mails; Sophie had received one from Sam in Thailand to say he was having a *fantastic* time, absolutely *everybody* was out there and they'd just been to the elephant sanctuary at Chang Mai. 'You and Ellie'd go wild over the baby ones,' Sam had put, and added, 'Love to Ellie and tell her I'll take her clubbing when I get back. How's Dad's romance?!! Go easy on Petros' Aphrodites at the Harbour Bar and don't do anything I wouldn't do!' As Sophie had just had a text full of hearts and kisses from Matthew Burnaby who was in Scotland fishing with his father, both she and Ellie were lit up by this evidence that they had not been forgotten by the two people who occupied most of their thoughts, despite the rival attractions of elephants and salmon.

'As for the big romance, poor Dad,' said Sophie, in an expansive mood, mellowed by this communication from her beloved, 'I'm afraid things aren't going so well for him and Victoria. Jake and Posy are both being poisonous at the moment and it seems to be getting to Victoria, big time. She's really stressing – had you noticed? I could see Dad was gutted that she wouldn't come to Aghia Sophia – I heard him asking her to, but she said no and looked all distant.'

'Perhaps they need to get away and be alone together,' suggested Ellie, waving her feet in the air to speed the drying of the varnish. 'That is, unless you still want to try to wreck their relationship like you once said you did?'

Sophie considered this. 'I have thought about it,' she

admitted, 'but I couldn't really do that to Dad. Victoria was nearly in tears after he was a bit sharp with her for getting so worked up with Jake and Posy – she pretended she'd swallowed a mozzie, but I knew she was trying not to cry. I'd been hating her just for being there – and then I suddenly felt dreadfully sorry for her. You can see she longs for us all to get on happily and for everything to be perfect – and it's not. What does your mum think about her?'

'Mum likes her a lot and thinks they'd be great for each other. But she also thinks Victoria would need to toughen up to cope with all the agro. She's had a terrible time already about her husband, poor thing – but that's different. Mum says it's always the little things that cause trouble. Perhaps we ought to help them along a bit? Would you feel disloyal to your mum if we did?'

'I don't *know*,' said Sophie, applying a second coat of purple with great concentration. 'I'm in such a muddle, I keep changing sides. One moment I feel completely furious with Mum for causing all this in the first place – the next minute I can't bear the thought of her and Dad splitting up. Part of the week in London with Mum was fun – we went shopping together and she was really great and bought me a slinky skirt to die for, and then she started getting all critical again and I really can't hack it when she's like that. I *like* Victoria and she's always been sweet to me and never tried to take over or anything like that, but I do find it hard to be with her and Dad. They try to include me, but they're so wrapped up in each other it's like they're joined by an invisible thread, and when one moves it sort of tweaks the other. I just know they're conscious of each other all the time and I feel shut out. Do you think I'm awful?'

'N-no-o.' Straightforward Ellie, not prone to such complicated feelings herself, sounded doubtful. 'Not awful . . . but everything always has to be such a big deal with you. I suppose you and Posy are very alike in some ways.' Sophie looked horrified.

'By the way,' went on Ellie, 'what did Matthew say in his text?'

They moved on to safer topics and were soon shrieking with

laughter again. When Maggie came out to join them and cautiously suggested they might offer to take Posy off to one of the sandy beaches on the west side of the island one day and give Patrick a chance to be free of nursery duties, she was pleasantly surprised when not only Ellie, but Sophie too, agreed with enthusiasm.

'D'you think we should offer to take Jake too?' asked Sophie, ripe for a bit of martyrdom.

'No way!' said Maggie, laughing. 'I agree with Patrick – no point in forcing those two on each other more than is necessary. We don't want actual bloodshed! I'm sure Jake would rather spend the day with his little Greek friend anyway, and I don't blame him. I'll go and see how Patrick reacts to the idea. I think he'll jump at the chance. We'll play buckets and spades with Posy and it'll be fun to show you the other side of the island, Sophie. I have to say, I think that's very generous of you to agree.' Sophie beamed.

There was general cause for celebration later. The two girls rang their school for the results of their AS exams. Sophie's yell of excitement brought everybody running.

'Dad! You'll never guess! I've got an A and three Bs!' She hugged her father wildly.

'Oh, Sophie darling, *well done*! I am proud of you.'

Ellie, as expected, had managed to get three As and a B, but with her dyslexia, Sophie's result was far better than had been predicted.

Evanthi had gone to bed when Patrick rang Victoria later that evening. Victoria was so relieved to hear his voice, she felt she could have taken a leaf out of Jake's book and turned a few cartwheels to express her feelings. She was delighted to hear of the girls' results, sent them her congratulations and when he told her of Maggie and the girls' proposal she was touched.

'Oh, Patrick, that would be so lovely. How very nice of them.'

'Not still huffed with me then?' he teased.

'No,' she said. 'I promise I've got over my huff and I'm sorry I've been so edgy – but it would be blissful to be on our own.'

'That's what I thought.' He was well content with her

486

reaction. 'We'll leave our horrible children behind. Where shall we go? Shall we go off in the boat?'

'Great idea,' she said. 'Let's go to Helidonia, Hugh and Nonna's special island, and I'll show you the actual rock in the portrait. I'll bring a picnic.'

'Wonderful.'

'Do you think it might be a good gesture in return if I suggested a girls' morning in Corfu town tomorrow?' asked Victoria. 'I could show Sophie and Ellie the best shops, which are sometimes quite hard to find amongst all the tourist tat and then if Maggie's never been there before, I could take her to the beautiful library of the Reading Society in the Liston, which Nonna could easily arrange. We could take Posy with us and have lunch in town and you and Phil could have a lovely woman-free time – no frictions!'

'I think that would go down very well,' said Patrick. 'Not with me, I hasten to say – I can't get enough of your company, as you very well know – but Sophie and Ellie are dying to hit the shops. Hang on while I take instructions.' He came back a moment later to say it was a very popular idea and he and Philip would commission her and Maggie to get celebratory presents for the girls because they'd both done so well.

'Good night then . . . darling Victoria . . . I do love you,' he said.

'Good night, Patrick,' she answered softly. 'I love you too.'

There was a new moon, and one star in the sky. Victoria wished on them both.

The shopping trip proved highly successful. Posy, unthreatened by a rival, was as good as gold and they all enjoyed each other's company. Philip and Patrick had played golf at the Corfu Club in the Ropa valley and it was in a much more relaxed atmosphere that they all joined up for dinner.

As Patrick was tying up the boat at the Vrahos landing stage the next morning, having brought their hired boat round from Kryovrisi, he could see Victoria coming down the steep, rocky path from the house, laden with the impedimenta for a day out. He stood on the little landing stage watching her, a slender figure in frayed pink shorts and a faded blue shirt, and thought with a pang that she didn't look much older than Sophie at that distance. When she got to the bottom he opened his arms and she dropped all the baggage and ran straight into them. Paradoxically it felt to Victoria both the most natural thing in the world – and the most exciting. When she surfaced from his kiss he slid his hands down her bare, brown arms and held her away from him, looking at her – drinking her in; relieved to see that she no longer looked like a teenager but like a woman, the woman he loved.

'I think we'd better get in that boat and get going,' he said, grinning at her.

'And then we've got all day together,' she said, laughing up at him.

'Yes,' said Patrick. 'That thought had occurred to me too.'

It was a far cry from the last time she had come to the little island in such misery and desperation, only months before, and the sky and the sea and the wind might all have belonged to a completely different world. And I am a different person too, thought Victoria.

'Are there likely to be other seekers of solitude on this island?' asked Patrick as they headed down the coast.

'Very unlikely – Helidonia belongs to Vrahos so the locals don't usually come and most holiday-makers find it too difficult. There's only one place where you can land and you have to know where it is. It's a bit tricky.' She told him about her last, nearly disastrous trip: 'I was a complete fool. Fortunately Guy and Petros guessed where I'd gone and came to rescue me.'

'Ah – lucky Guy and Petros,' he commented, pulling a wry face. 'I envy them that!'

'You have rescued me too – in quite a different way – from all sorts of things,' she said seriously. 'You'll never know what that means to me.'

They had an idyllic day. They swam, and sunbathed and explored; they built a fire and barbecued swordfish, skewered on spikes of rosemary, as Hugh and Evanthi had once done; they drank the dry white wine Victoria had brought and ate the large black olives, which Patrick said were like Victoria's eyes. 'What a very unromantic description,' she complained, expertly flicking an olive stone at him between her first finger and thumb.

She showed him the dragon rock, and he took a photograph of her sitting on it, dabbling her feet in the water, just as Evanthi had sat all those years before.

'History repeating itself,' said Patrick. 'But it's *my* girl on the rock this time! We'll show this to Hugh and compare the two portraits when we get back to England.'

They dived, naked, off the rocks into the amazingly clear water, the colour of kingfishers' wings, and watched a shoal of small silver flying-fish bow-and-arrow over the sea in front of them as they swam.

Later, history repeated itself again, as they made love with as much joy and abandon as two other lovers had shared together over sixty years ago.

'We won't ever let anything come between us like Hugh and Nonna did, will we?' asked Victoria, as she lay in his arms afterwards. 'Not even our beloved, tiresome children?' And for answer he started to kiss her again.

As usual, a stiff little wind got up suddenly in the middle of the day but died down again as softly as the ending of a sigh later in the afternoon. By the time they left the island it was only enough to ruffle the sea and feather through Victoria's hair as she sat in the bows on the way home in a trance of happiness.

'Have you time to come up and see Nonna for a moment?' she asked when they got back to Vrahos. 'I know she'd love to see you.'

'Of course,' he said. 'Maggie didn't know what time they'd get back – and anyway Sophie promised she'd start putting Posy to bed if they returned first. I'd just like to be back in time to tuck her down.'

Evanthi was reading on the terrace. One look at Victoria's face was enough to tell her what sort of day they'd had and she felt as if she was looking in a crystal ball but that, instead of glimpsing the future, she was seeing backwards in time. She held out her hands to them both, and they each took one. Victoria bent down to kiss her.

'Where's Jake?' she asked.

'Dora and Yannis have taken him off with Angelo to see

Yannis' parents. You know how he loves going there. She said to tell you they might be late back and she'd put the boys to bed if you weren't here.'

'Could I kidnap Victoria for dinner tonight as well, then?' asked Patrick.

'I think I might just spare her to you for a bit longer,' said Evanthi, smiling at them both.

He cocked an eyebrow at Victoria, but her assent was a foregone conclusion. 'I'll need to go back to Petradi first,' he said, 'but we'd planned to have dinner at Kryovrisi anyway tonight because we've promised Ellie and Sophie they can go dancing afterwards. If you don't mind coming back with me now, Victoria, I could run you home after dinner. Old Lefka who caretakes Petradi is coming in to baby-sit for Posy, and I know Phil and Maggie would be delighted if you joined us.'

While Victoria went to have a shower and change, he sat and talked to Evanthi.

'How difficult do you think it would be for Hugh to get out here again?' she asked abruptly. 'He never says anything about his health or mobility, and he brushes all my enquiries about his infirmities aside.' Which was the first indication either Patrick or Victoria had had that they must have spoken to each other on the telephone.

'I'm sure he could manage it with a bit of assistance,' said Patrick, pretending not to notice this riveting piece of information but longing to pass it on to Victoria. 'If I could get him to agree to a wheelchair at the airport, the journey ought to be a piece of cake. Shall I try to bring him over at the beginning of October?'

'Well, do sound him out,' said Evanthi. 'I felt afraid at the thought of meeting again when he first suggested it, but now I think I would be brave enough. I would so like to see him before I die – which I may tell you,' she added briskly, 'I have no intention of doing yet awhile!'

She laid her hand on Patrick's arm. 'I want you to know that you are making me very happy,' she said quietly. 'I have never seen Victoria like this. It is what I have wanted for her for a long time.'

*

'Having this evening together as well is an extra bonus,' said Victoria as they drove back to Petradi. 'Oh, Patrick – I can hardly bear to think you've only got two more days here. It's gone so horribly fast. I have never, ever felt as happy as I do today. I think it's the best day of my life.'

'Mine too,' he said, very touched.

They drove up the rough track to the house, churning up the dust. An ancient man, wearing baggy trousers and sporting long mustachios on his nutcracker face, was meandering through the olive grove leading five sheep on five separate bits of frayed rope, their hefty, teenage-looking lambs bouncing along beside them. It looked a very complicated manoeuvre like an unsuccessful rehearsal for maypole dancing at a village fête.

'I love the sheep out here,' said Victoria. 'With their long legs, they're so much more elegant than their English relations and I always think they look as if they've outlined their eyes with kohl, like Elizabeth Taylor playing Cleopatra. This is the real Corfu – not the concrete blocks and the crowded beaches. I'm so glad you love my magic island too. Doesn't everything look extra beautiful in the evening light?' And she sighed happily.

'Extra beautiful,' said Patrick, laughing at her, and giving her a very loving look. 'Even the sheep – but especially you.'

They were guiltily relieved to find the Marshalls' car was not yet back.

'Good – a little more time to ourselves. Let's go and sit outside and have a drink and make the most of it before the hordes return.'

It seemed very dark in the house, all the shutters having been closed against the fierce midday sun by Lefka when she'd come in to clean, earlier in the day, so that Patrick and Victoria had to grope their way through the big sitting room, laughing and clutching on to each other as they bumped into bits of furniture. They blinked, blearily, as they walked, hand in hand, out into the light again.

It took them a moment to see that there was someone lying on one of the sun-beds.

'Hello, Patrick,' said Rachel Hammond. 'I've come back to you.'

Chapter Forty-six

For a moment Patrick and Victoria froze as though they had been turned to stone. They stood there, still hand in hand, rooted to the spot, but Patrick felt Victoria flinch as though she'd been physically assaulted.

He recovered first. 'What the hell are you doing here?' he demanded.

Rachel swung her elegant legs over the side of the chaise longue, got languidly to her feet and advanced towards her husband. 'Not a very enthusiastic welcome, darling,' she drawled. 'Aren't you going to introduce us?' She looked Victoria up and down as though she were a bit of flotsam that had been washed up on the beach and should be disposed of as soon as possible. 'I'm Patrick's wife,' she explained unnecessarily. 'I don't think we've met.'

The shock of seeing her was total. For an awful moment Victoria thought she might be sick. Her legs felt shaky and, despite the warmth of the evening, she shivered, but pride helped her to pull herself together. Patrick kept a grip on her hand.

'Stop playing games, Rachel,' he said shortly. 'This is Victoria Cunningham – as I think you know very well. Explain what you think you're doing here.'

'I've come to join you,' she said. 'I decided not to stay on in Spain after all – I thought you'd be pleased. After all, you begged me not to go. Aren't you going to kiss me hello – or do you feel embarrassed at your age at being caught out holding hands like a schoolboy?'

Victoria wrenched her hand out of his and went and stood by the low terrace wall, looking over the olive groves to the sea – to Helidonia, the little island of the swallows. She couldn't have borne Rachel to see the infuriating tears that had sprung to her eyes. She had seen photographs of Rachel in the flat in Warwick Square so she'd known she was pretty, but she was far better-looking and much taller than she'd imagined, and had that quality of groomed elegance that has more to do with hair and make-up than actual clothes and much to do with time and trouble taken. Rachel Hammond never looked a mess.

At that moment there was the sound of the Marshalls' car arriving at the back of the house, the slamming of doors and cheerful chatter and then round the corner of the terrace came the rest of the party – led by Posy. When she saw Rachel she let out a screech of joy: 'Mummy, Mummy, Mummy!' She hurled herself at her mother and Rachel opened her arms to receive the onslaught and bent down to hug her. Victoria looked round then. Over the top of Posy's golden curls, so exactly the same colour as her mother's, the two women's eyes met and in Rachel Hammond's there was a look of triumph.

'Good God! What a surprise!' Philip, loaded with picnic paraphernalia, voiced the feelings of them all. Maggie and Ellie looked stunned, but Sophie just stood there for a moment and said '*Mum!*' on a note of wonderment – half horror, half delight. Then she too rushed to her mother.

Rachel tilted her face up from her embrace with Posy to present her elder daughter with a cool cheek to kiss. 'Hello, darling,' she said in her high, rather carrying voice. 'As you see, I've taken your advice. You suggested it might be a good thing if I came out here. It looks as if you were right.'

All the colour drained from Sophie's face as everyone's eyes turned towards her. She gave a strangled gasp, then turned and rushed back into the house and they heard the door of the bedroom she was sharing with Ellie bang shut.

'Go after her, Ellie,' said Maggie to her daughter. 'Stay with her. I'll come and find you later.' Knowing Rachel's talent for spin she didn't believe that Sophie's suggestion would have been quite as reported, but that trouble of all sorts was looming was all too obvious.

To Rachel she said, raising a quizzical eyebrow: 'Well, hi there, Rachel – this *is* an unexpected visit. You might have telephoned to let us know you were coming. It's a bit awkward really, because I'm afraid we haven't actually got a room for you. Posy's on the camp-bed in the ironing room as it is.'

'Oh, don't worry,' said Rachel airily, straightening up and going over to give Maggie a kiss-in-the-air greeting. 'I'd booked a room at the Corfu Palace just in case you were away or anything – but I don't need an extra room anyway because I'll go in with Patrick.'

'Oh no you bloody won't.' Patrick looked as if he would like to shake the satisfied expression off his wife's face. 'Let me remind you,' he said in a low but deadly voice, 'that *you* left *me* in the first place, Rachel. You've asked for a divorce, and I've agreed. We're not going back on that.' Then he suddenly observed his small daughter who, thumb in mouth and not fully understanding what was going on, was nevertheless standing drinking in the drama with absorbed fascination. He gestured towards her. 'This is not a suitable time or place to discuss things,' he said. 'We'll have this conversation later.'

Victoria had remained completely silent. Now she said: 'I think I should go back to Vrahos, but I haven't got my car. Please . . . could someone drive me there?'

'Don't go,' said Patrick, putting an arm round her. 'That's really not necessary.'

'I'd rather go. Please.'

'All right,' he said, unwillingly, wretched at her distress but thinking that if Rachel got going with one of her full-blown scenes, then Victoria, for her own sake, would be better out of the way. 'Of course – if that's what you want, then I'll take you back and come with you.'

'Please, no,' she said quietly, disengaging herself from him. 'I think you should stay here and sort things out – but I'd like to go home now.'

Patrick was about to protest, but Philip cut in. 'I'll take you, Victoria,' he said, taking the car keys out of his pocket and walking towards the back of the house. She threw him a grateful look, and followed him out to the car, her head held high, without even a glance at Rachel. Philip thought she had enormous dignity.

Patrick went with them. 'God! I'm sorry about this.'

'It's not your fault.' She was just in control of her voice.

'I'll come over later,' he said.

'No, Patrick.' She looked at him with very troubled eyes, so different, he thought, from how she had looked such a short time before, and shook her head. 'Not tonight. Come in the morning if you can. And better not ring tonight either because the telephone rings by Nonna's bed, and you know there's no signal at Vrahos so the mobile won't work.'

He held her closely to him for a moment. 'This is just a ridiculous farce,' he said. 'A typical dramatic Rachel gesture but it will all be *all right*. Good night, my little love. Don't forget that I love you.'

'Good night,' she whispered. 'And, Patrick?'

'Yes?'

'Be gentle with Sophie,' she said.

Philip felt desperately sorry for her as they bumped down the dusty track in the evening light.

'That was horrible for you, Victoria,' he said. 'But as Patrick said, Rachel's always been a drama queen. Don't take it too much to heart, and you were absolutely right to leave them to it. Let Patrick sort her out.'

'I thought it was all over between them. I didn't know she still wanted him.'

'I don't suppose she does,' said Philip. 'I expect things went wrong with that ghastly woman she went to see in Spain so she turned tail and came home. But Rachel wouldn't be one to stay at home by herself with no audience and even though she may not want Patrick she probably doesn't want anyone else to have him either. Rachel's used to getting her own way.'

'And Sophie? We'd all had such fun yesterday – I loved my day with Maggie and the girls. Sophie and Ellie were hugely good company. I understand how she must feel about me and Patrick warned me to take things slowly and not expect too much, but I'd hoped it was getting easier for her.'

'Ah,' said Philip, negotiating a hairpin bend. 'Poor Sophie. That's difficult. I know from Ellie that she likes you, Victoria, so you mustn't be hurt on a personal level, but naturally she'll still be doing her best to stop her parents splitting up. I'm a family solicitor – I see this sort of thing all the time. Children –

especially teenagers, full of raging hormones and volatile emotions – often go to great lengths to try to prevent a break-up, even when their parents' wrangles make them miserable. Rachel's always blown hot and cold at Sophie – mostly cold, it has to be said – and it's always made Maggie furious, but when she does blow hot, Sophie can't resist her and wants to please her all the more. God knows what Rachel will have said to Sophie when they were in London together. Listen, Victoria . . . Patrick's my oldest friend and I know him very well. Maggie and I can see he adores you and we both think you're made for each other. Don't let it get you down. Don't give up.'

'I'll try not to,' she said, touched and comforted. 'Thanks, Phil.'

She had grown to like Philip Marshall very much, a kind man with a dry wit – a wonderful foil for his equally kind but more flamboyant wife. It was the longest speech she'd heard him make.

He dropped her at Vrahos and watched her go across the courtyard and up the stone steps to the massive oak doors with the lion-mask door knockers. He thought the old house, with its flaking pink walls, so enchanting and romantic in the sunshine, looked huge and forbidding in the fading light. Victoria looked very small. He saw her take the massive iron key out of her bag and fit it in the lock and then she turned and waved. He raised his hand in a return salute and waited till she disappeared inside before he drove back to face the situation at Petradi.

It was Dora who answered the telephone when Patrick rang first thing the following morning. He left a message to say he'd be at Vrahos as near midday as he could manage and hoped to take Victoria off somewhere for lunch.

They needed to be alone, he thought, without fear of interruptions, but first he had to drive Rachel and Posy down to the Corfu Palace Hotel where they were going to spend the day before catching a flight together to London in the evening.

The night before, tired and over-wrought after a long day out making castles on the sandy beach of Ágios Geórgios on the west of the island, gorging ice creams, dodging wasps and jumping the waves with Sophie and Ellie, followed by the excitement of her mother's arrival, Posy had become completely hysterical when Rachel announced that since she obviously wasn't welcome at Petradi, she would go back to the hotel immediately. She had clung to her mother and screamed and sobbed, initially milking the situation for all she was worth, but eventually simply too exhausted and strung-up to stop. Patrick offered grimly to sleep on the sofa in the sitting room and let Rachel have his bedroom, an offer that she graciously accepted. As Maggie went to get clean sheets for Rachel, she reflected crossly that – as she'd witnessed so many times in the past – Rachel had got her way in the end because nobody else had the stomach to upset her children any further.

Having left his wife and daughter at the hotel, Patrick stopped at Petradi before going on to Vrahos. He wanted to talk to Sophie before he saw Victoria. Philip and Maggie had gone to the supermarket in Kryovrisi and the two girls were by the pool. One look at Patrick's face sent Ellie speeding back to the house on the pretext that she'd just finished her book and wanted to look for another.

Patrick sat down beside his daughter. She looked at him, half scared, half defiant, expecting anger, but he didn't speak for a few moments. Then very quietly he said, 'Just tell me your side of the story, Sophe. Did you know Mum was going to turn up like that?'

'No! I promise I didn't. You must believe me!'

'Of course I believe you,' he said. 'But did you really suggest she should come out here and see what I was "up to", as she put it to me last night?'

'No! Yes . . . well, sort of,' Sophie clenched and unclenched her fingers. 'I suppose I did in a way – but I never expected her to turn up like that. I swear I didn't.'

Patrick waited. Sophie appeared to be engrossed in the progress of a tiny spider along the slippery plastic arm of the sun-bed. He thought she looked agonised.

'After you talked to me and Sam and told us what you felt about Victoria, I did tell Mum what you'd said about her, when we were in London,' she whispered at last. She felt weighed down by the fact that whichever parent she was with, made her feel like a traitor to the other. 'She wouldn't believe it was serious at first and accused me of making it up and I suppose I did say something like, "Well, you jolly well ought to come and see for yourself then if you won't take my word for it." Oh, Dad, I'm so sorry.'

'It's not your fault. *I'm* sorry that inevitably you've got dragged into it.'

'Can I ask you something?'

'Of course.'

'It's truly not that I don't like Victoria, but . . . is there no chance that you and Mum might get back together?' she asked desperately.

'Oh, Sophie darling, I'm afraid not.'

'Because of Victoria?'

'Well, partly because of Victoria, of course. It wouldn't be honest if I pretended otherwise because I do love her very much, but for many, many other reasons too. It's a long time since Mum and I've been happy together – you know that. And Mum left me before Victoria and I got together.'

'But not before you *met* her,' said Sophie shrewdly. 'Mum wants you back now. She told me so last night.'

'I don't think she does really, Sophie.' Patrick sighed. How could he tell his daughter about Rachel's complete loss of interest for the last three years, certainly aggravated, but not initially caused by Bronwen Richards; of his growing weariness with her moods and obsessions and blinkered self-centredness? How could he tell her about Rachel's own past love affair?

'I think you could at least *try* again,' muttered Sophie. 'If Mum's prepared to try again, I think you could too.' Patrick ached for her. He admired her bravery in facing him with her opinions – but he knew he couldn't help her.

'I'm sorry, Sophie,' he said getting up. 'I can't do it. Thank you for your honesty but it's too late for Mum and me now. It won't ever make any difference to what I feel for you and Sam and Posy, I promise you that. I'm going over to Vrahos to see Victoria now . . . .and I'm not going to give her up.'

Sophie stayed by the pool, staring out at the arid, rocky Albanian mountains, and listening to the sound of the car as Patrick drove off. Because everything else was so quiet with only the breeze whispering in the olive trees, the steady background drone of cicadas and the occasional bray of a donkey or crow of a cockerel to break the sleepy midday silence, she could hear the noise of the engine chugging down the track for a long, long time – it seemed to Sophie to go on for ever – taking her father away from family life as she had known it up till now. Sophie curled up in a tight little ball and wept.

Chapter Forty-seven

It was Dora who let Patrick in at Vrahos.

'My husband has taken Kyria down to Kryovrisi to the bank,' she said. 'Jake's gone with her and Victoria has walked up to the viewpoint with Rocky. She asked if you'd go and join her there as soon as you got here.'

He walked along the path. Victoria was sitting on a boulder, looking out to sea, the big dog leaning against her. When Patrick called out to her she looked round and got to her feet, but she didn't run into his arms. She came to meet him so slowly that it appeared to be an effort to walk. He seized both her hands and gazed anxiously down at her. She looked so distraught that he wondered if some new disaster had struck.

'What is it, my sweet?' he asked tenderly, full of love for this beguiling, vulnerable woman to whom he had given his heart. 'Tell me. Has anything else happened?'

For answer she just shook her head despairingly and leaned her forehead against his chest and stood there in his arms, unspeaking. Then she leaned away from him, still saying nothing, but she staring into his face with such a look of torment that he could hardly bear it.

'Don't look like that. It's going to be all right, darling,' he said reassuringly. 'There's no need to be so anxious. I've made our position abundantly clear to Rachel . . . and to Sophie. I'm desperately sorry you should have had to go through that awful scene last night. It was monstrous of Rachel to turn up and behave like that, but it will all get sorted out. I promise.'

'No, Patrick . . . it's over,' she said very quietly, her voice hardly more than a whisper. 'I've done some very serious thinking and I can't go on seeing you.'

'What are you talking about?' He looked at her in horror. 'Of course you're upset – you have every reason to be, but it's absurd to say that!'

'No,' she said bleakly. 'It's true. You have to accept it.'

'Darling love, you're over-reacting,' said Patrick, thinking the strain had all been too much for her. 'What happened last night doesn't make any difference to you and me – it may serve to bring everything into the open, which will be a good thing. It was only Rachel making dramatic gestures, as usual. She's the queen of the big scene!' He took her face in his hands, trying to win a smile from her, but she didn't react to his touch and he had a nightmare feeling that she was hardly even hearing him. He slid his hands down her arms to take her own hands in his, but she pulled them away and stepped quickly back from him. He felt as if she was putting an electric fence between them.

'Look, darling,' he persisted, 'I've told Rachel exactly where she stands and she's going back to London this evening. She's insisting on taking Posy with her even though Sophie and I are going home tomorrow anyway. Typical Rachel contrariness!' He smiled at her, trying to introduce a lighter note, but there was no answering glimmer from Victoria and Patrick was deeply disturbed by her stillness and her ashen face.

He said, 'I've just got back from driving them both to Corfu town. I would have come sooner but I wanted to talk to Sophie first. I remembered what you said and I didn't get angry with her.' He willed her to respond, desperate to get through to her. 'Sophie's very upset too and feels terribly guilty because she thinks it was her fault that Rachel turned up – which in a way it was. I'm extremely sorry for Sophie, but she'll come round and I left her in no doubt that there's no question of her mother and me getting back together again.'

He wondered if Victoria was hurt with him for not coming to her first, though he thought such pettiness would be out of character. 'Did you get my message from Dora?' he asked.

'Yes. Yes, I did,' she said. 'It's not that.

'What then? There *is* something else, isn't there?' He tried to read her face 'There has to be – but whatever it is we can talk it over. There's nothing we can't sort out between us.'

He felt furiously angry with Rachel, and conscious of some change in Victoria that he couldn't fathom.

'What we have together is *wonderful*, Victoria,' he said fiercely. '*I* know it is . . . *you* know it is. We love each other, for God's sake!'

She looked at him with an unreadable expression – an almost blank look on her face.

'But not enough,' she said, and the words were like icy drops of water. 'And I can't do it, Patrick.'

'*Not enough!* How can you say that? What can't you do?'

'I can't break up your marriage.'

'Oh for God's sake! Our marriage was on the rocks long ago. You know you haven't broken it up.'

'Rachel thinks I have.'

'Rubbish! She knows very well it isn't due to you. Stop imagining things,' said Patrick impatiently. 'You can't possibly know what she thinks . . . half the time she doesn't even know herself.'

'I've just been talking to her,' said Victoria.

Patrick looked thunderstruck. 'Talking to *Rachel*?' Victoria nodded. 'Yes. She rang me after you'd left her. It's finally made me realise that it has to be over between us, Patrick.'

'Don't be bloody ridiculous! What the hell's she been saying to you? How dare she ring you! Tell me exactly what happened.'

'No,' said Victoria, raising her chin at him, with an expression on her face that he had not seen before, but which reminded him forcibly of her grandmother. 'I don't want to talk about it. It's over, Patrick.'

She steeled herself to say the one thing that she knew might make him go away, frantic to get the parting over before her resolve weakened – the parting that she had determined was vital for everyone's sake.

'I can't take all this any more,' she said with a despairing little shrug. 'I'm sorry, but I've been through too much already. I thought I loved you – I really did think so – but obviously not enough to cope with all these problems. I want you to go away. I don't want to see you again.'

Patrick stared at her in shock. 'I don't believe you! That can't be true – not after what we've come to mean to each other in the last few months. Not after the way we were together yesterday. You can't just wipe that out.'

Victoria looked back at him in silence, reliving her conversation with Rachel.

She had been walking through the hall at Vrahos, when the telephone rang and she had automatically picked it up.

'*Herete?*'

'Is that Victoria Cunningham?'

She had known immediately who it was and her mouth had gone dry.

'Yes it is,' she had said, trying to sound calm. 'Speaking . . .'

Now, as she relived the shock of that moment, she felt numb with grief, but the force of her anxiety made her implacable. 'Don't ask me to explain any more,' she said, 'because I don't want to talk about it. Please just go.'

'Oh for God's sake! You can't possibly mean that. What we have between us is special, you know it is,' said Patrick furiously, really angry now. 'I've no idea what Rachel's said to make you behave like this, but it has to be complete, bloody nonsense. I'm amazed you can suddenly be prepared to throw everything we have together away on a whim. Tell me what she said!'

To Victoria, already near breaking point, the word whim made her dark eyes blaze.

'No!' she shouted back at him. 'It doesn't matter what she said! You'd never understand and if you really loved me you wouldn't put me through this inquisition! I can't take all this hassle. You'll have to accept that whatever we had together was just a holiday romance and now it's *over*. I don't want you any more. *Please go!*'

Without another word Patrick turned on his heel and strode off down the hill.

Had he looked round he would have seen a stricken look of absolute longing on Victoria's face – but he didn't even glance back.

As she watched him go, tears coursing down her cheeks, she felt she had been given a glimpse of wonderful happiness, only to have it cruelly snatched away; and the big dog, sensing a terrible distress he couldn't understand, raised his nose to the sky and howled, setting up an echo that reverberated across the sea and round the rocks.

*

Later in the afternoon Evanthi was resting on her bed, tired after her expedition to Kryovrisi, when there was a tap on her door. She had heard from a miserable Victoria the night before about the drama at Petradi following what had obviously been an idyllic day for herself and Patrick, the two lovers about whose future Evanthi cared so passionately. Knowing Victoria was expecting Patrick to come over, Evanthi had decided that she and Jake should be well out of the way when he arrived. She profoundly hoped that Victoria – who had not appeared for lunch – was now coming to tell her that Patrick had dealt with his dreadfully tiresome-sounding wife and that all was once more set to rights. Yannis, at Dora's suggestion, had taken the two little boys off in the boat.

When Victoria put her head round the door Evanthi was holding the icon in her hands. The panels were open, hiding the Archangels on the outside, but displaying St Nicholas and St Gregory on either side of the Virgin and Child.

'*Agapi!* Tell me what has happened?' But one look at Victoria's face told her enough to make her heart fail.

Victoria sat down on the edge of the big bed. 'Were you praying, Nonna?' she asked, indicating the icon.

'I was just having a word with the saints – there were a few things I needed to speak to them about.' Evanthi sounded for all the world as if she'd just been ringing the builders.

'Ah – the so-called Wonderworkers.'

'Yes,' said Evanthi.

'I wish they could work wonders for me now,' said Victoria, looking at her grandmother with a defeated look that despite all her previous troubles, her grandmother thought was disturbingly different from before. Evanthi put the icon into her hands. 'Try them,' she suggested gently.

'What – pray to the little saint in the hope that he might suddenly make everything better for me and fill my Christmas stocking with goodies?' Victoria sounded bitter.

'That's not how I think of – or use – the icon, as you very well know, Victoria,' said Evanthi austerely – though she could hardly bear the misery on Victoria's face.

'I'm sorry. I know it's not. *Help* me, Nonna.' It was a mere whisper. '*Help me*. How did *you* manage? I've lost everything and I can't even pray any more. I've lost that too.'

'Then don't try,' said Evanthi briskly. 'There are times when you just have to let other people do the praying for you. I agree it's no good demanding lists of *wants*, but one can always ask for *help*. The icon is not *God*, it's a tool – one that I love, one that happens to suit me, but just a tool all the same.'

'But it means a great deal to you, doesn't it?' asked Victoria, tracing the patterns on the chequerboard robes of the bishop-saints with her finger.

'I've revered it all my life but nothing is indispensable – it's a prop I could manage without if I had to. I suppose . . .' said Evanthi, not wanting to pressurise Victoria with questions, hoping to give her time to say whatever she needed to '. . . I suppose that I use it like water-diviners use their rods or some people dowse for information with pendulums – as a way of seeking knowledge or wisdom that's locked inside me all the time, but that I'm finding it hard to access.'

'You always make prayer sound so easy,' said Victoria.

'*Easy?*' Evanthi was scornful. 'Don't be foolish, Victoria! Of course it isn't *easy*. But it can be *simple* – if you allow it to be.' She watched her much-loved granddaughter and thought she looked just as she used to when she was a child – sitting on the end of the bed, desperate for comfort but closed in, not able to express the full extent of her unhappiness.

'Talk to me about Patrick, *agapi*,' she said. 'I can't help you if you won't tell me.'

'Darling Nonna – you help me just by being you and being here. But you can't alter what's happened. Patrick's wife returned. She wants him back. Full stop.'

'Surely he doesn't want her back?'

'No. It was the last thing we either of us wanted. He's very, very angry with her . . . and now he's very angry and hurt with me.'

'Then . . . ?'

Victoria stared blankly at the icon, not seeing it any more. She was in the hall again, answering the telephone, hearing Rachel's taunting voice.

505

'Nonna, if I tell you what she said, will you swear not to tell Patrick?' she asked, at last.

'I swear,' said Evanthi, but even as she said it she had a feeling she would regret making such a promise.

After Patrick had dropped her and Posy at the hotel, Rachel had sat in the air-conditioned, marble coolness of the Corfu Palace, so convenient for the town centre or the airport, so spacious and soothing to bruised spirits, sipped an iced lemon pressé and considered her options.

Could Patrick be serious about the dark-haired young woman who had turned up at Petradi with him? Though one couldn't help noticing her amazing eyes, she had looked almost scruffy by Rachel's standards, with no make-up, hair still damp from either a swim or a shower and very casually dressed: surely no real competition if Rachel chose to take her on. But despite her confidence in her own charms and her scornful words to Sophie on the subject in London, having now seen Patrick and Victoria together, Rachel had no doubt that her husband not only *could* be serious about this young woman, but clearly already *was* – and Rachel had good reason to know just how committed, loving and faithful Patrick was capable of being.

Had she completely forfeited his allegiance? Bitter words had been exchanged the night before as Patrick set out to make his position plain. Rachel was far from sure she wanted to go back to him and to Yorkshire – she had never really liked living in the country – but his serious involvement with another woman was a slight to her pride that made her boil with resentment.

She'd had a horrible time in Spain – not that anyone at Petradi, least of all Patrick, seemed interested.

She couldn't avoid the realisation that she'd been thoroughly misguided about Bronwen, but considering the sensitivity that had always made her – in her own opinion – especially in need of cherishing and protection, she thought such a mistake was hardly surprising. She chose not to think about the many warnings her husband had given her.

Nothing about her trip had been what she expected: the therapy centre proved to be a shabby, rented apartment with peeling paint in an insalubrious suburb; Bronwen and Milo, once she had signed a document stating that the 'borrowed' jewellery – which they'd already sold – had been a gift, hardly bothered with her at all. The vision Rachel had briefly toyed with, of herself as the charming co-owner and receptionist of a glamorous clinic for Spanish socialites, had evaporated. In fact there didn't seem to be any patients at all, let alone rich and interesting ones. She had also been counting on therapy sessions for herself, Bronwen's advice having become as addictive as a drug over the last three years, but Bronwen had lost interest in her and took little trouble to disguise it. As for Milo, whose drinking bouts Rachel had not previously experienced, she had actually been frightened of him.

Brooding angrily about all this, Rachel left Posy in the care of an obliging waitress – whom she tipped handsomely – and went to make a telephone call.

She had felt a surge of triumph when Victoria answered herself.

'I am just ringing,' said Rachel Hammond, 'to warn you to leave my husband alone.'

'I'm afraid it's too late for that,' Victoria's heart had thumped so loudly she felt it must be audible over the telephone. 'You left him . . . and I love him.'

'Well, I'm telling you,' Rachel's voice was edged and clear as cut glass, 'to think very carefully before you try to steal my husband and wreck my children's lives. If you do, you'll have to take the consequences and live with your conscience after-wards.' She paused. 'Can you really cope with that?'

As Victoria opened her mouth to retort, the full impact of Rachel's words hit her. Suddenly, horrifyingly she perceived a hidden threat – the horrible insinuation that what had happened to Richard could happen again. She gave a strangled little gasp, dropped the telephone and just stood there in the hall, completely horror-struck.

'Well?' challenged Rachel from the Corfu Palace Hotel call-box, wanting a response – any response. She had waited for Victoria to say something, but there was total silence.

'Are you still there?' she asked, but there was no reply.

Eventually Rachel was forced to put the receiver back, feeling cheated of a grand scene.

'And did Patrick think Rachel meant that as a serious suicide threat?' asked Evanthi shrewdly, when Victoria had finished telling her side of the story.

'I didn't tell him,' said Victoria, bleakly. 'He'd have tried to talk me round and convince me she was just being a drama queen. So I knew it had to be my decision and I also knew I couldn't possibly risk it. Not for him. Not for myself. Not for anyone.'

'O Panagia mou! But he might have been right?' exclaimed Evanthi, recognising with a sinking heart the mulish expression on Victoria's face and conscious of an alarming sense of déjà-vu.

'Perhaps – but once I'd never have dreamed Richard could do such a thing either,' countered Victoria unanswerably. 'A year ago, if anyone had suggested it to me, I'd have denied any possibility of it – and look what happened. Even Guy, to whom Richard actually made the threat, didn't believe him and he was dreadfully, horribly wrong. I could never, ever have that on my conscience . . . no matter what the cost.'

She looked at her grandmother with an expression of such finality that all argument died on Evanthi's lips.

'No one who hasn't been through it can have any idea what it's like to live with the knowledge that someone you've loved, someone you've been married to and had a child with, has been driven to commit such an act of desperation,' said Victoria, passionately. 'Nobody can bring Richard back for Jake, but I couldn't chance the same thing to happening to Patrick's children. I couldn't. You must see that, Nonna.'

Evanthi saw it all too well.

'So I've told Patrick I won't see him again – that I don't love him enough to take on all the complications,' said Victoria, getting to her feet. 'Perhaps it's a judgement on me for daring to think I could have such happiness so soon after Richard's death. Now I've lost them both.'

She handed the icon back to Evanthi. 'I know what Uncle Anthony thinks you should do about this,' she said. 'And I have a feeling Guy's been getting at you about it too. Don't listen to either of them, Nonna. I'd *hate* you to part with it for my sake – and I envy you your faith. You brought me up to have such a strong one myself but I can't hang on to that any longer, either. It's gone.'

'Oh well, it's notoriously easy to have faith so long as things are going well for you, but it's a monstrous arrogance to think God only exists as long as you're getting what you want.'

Anguish for those she loved always made Evanthi especially astringent, but this was the grandmother Victoria knew and loved and felt safe with, and she found this squirt of lemon juice reassuring.

Once she would have looked forward to sharing such a tart Evanthi-ism with Guy. Now she only longed to share everything with Patrick, and the thought that she might never see him again felt unbearable.

Evanthi held out her arms to her and Victoria collapsed back on the bed and buried her head in her grandmother's shoulder, her thin shoulders heaving with sobs.

'Don't despair,' Evanthi said, stroking the dark hair as she had done so often when Victoria was a little girl, but now deeply disturbed herself. 'And don't worry about your faith, *chrysso mou*. I have enough for us both.'

Chapter Forty-eight

No one at Petradi was in any doubt about Patrick's state of desolation when he returned from Vrahos. He told them briefly, with a grim-faced aloofness that precluded questions or expressions of sympathy, that Victoria had broken their relationship off, and then took himself off to walk up Pantokrator at a breakneck speed. He was gone for the rest of the day, only reappearing in time to do his packing.

No one had any doubt either that Victoria's decision must have been triggered by the sudden reappearance of Rachel, but they were stunned at the news all the same.

Philip and Maggie, deeply distressed for Patrick, but conscious that it was Sophie's last day, took the two girls out in the boat for the rest of the afternoon but no one felt able to enjoy the trip.

Sophie was in torment.

'I feel so guilty,' she kept saying to Maggie. 'I desperately didn't want Mum and Dad to split up but Dad says they're going to do that anyway and now he hasn't got Victoria either.' And then like a litany she kept repeating: 'He's so unhappy and it's all my fault.'

Eventually Maggie was driven to saying bracingly: 'Now stop it, Sophie. You can't be responsible for other people's decisions, we none of us can. This really is something between the three of them. It *affects* you, of course, but it's entirely up to them to work it out. There may be more to this decision than we know about, and you are *not* to blame. Your father told you that this morning and I know he meant it.'

Perhaps it was as well that Patrick and Sophie's flight left early the next morning so there could be no hanging about or prolonged farewells. The Marshalls were staying on for another week, but the joy had gone out of their holiday this year.

*

Rachel and Patrick now started to divide their time between Yorkshire and London, mostly avoiding each other, but on the occasions when they had be under the same roof, leading separate lives in an atmosphere of cold politeness.

Patrick informed Rachel briefly that Victoria had broken off their relationship, refusing to give her the satisfaction of discussing the reasons, but giving her a look of cold contempt that was far more cutting than any tirade. Even Rachel could see that there would be no point in trying to woo him back, whether she wanted him or not. She half-heartedly toyed with the idea of taking just enough tranquillisers to give him a fright – as punishment for his lack of interest – but as Patrick would certainly have predicted, had he known about Victoria's interpretation of Rachel's telephone conversation, the thought that she might misjudge the dose prevented her from even coming close to making an actual attempt.

For the last weeks of the school holidays Sophie found herself basking in unaccustomed attention from her mother. Rachel made an unusual effort to treat her daughter as a friend, and though Sophie was initially mistrustful, she had just begun to wonder if they might, perhaps, achieve a more amicable relationship, if not perhaps the light-hearted, bantering companionship that Ellie and Maggie enjoyed, when the honeymoon period came to an abrupt end due to a minor tiff over clothes and the dissatisfactions that Rachel had always felt about her elder daughter resurfaced. The effect on Sophie was devastating, and without Patrick to smooth things out, she was really unhappy.

It was a relief when term started and for the first time in her life Sophie couldn't wait to go back to school.

It was into this tense atmosphere that Sam, in bouncy form and full of traveller's tales, returned from his trip in late September. He thought his mother and younger sister were quite unchanged, was horrified at how tense and withdrawn Sophie seemed most of the time, but was really shaken by the look of his father, whom he had always considered impermeable.

Sophie poured out her account of the family dramas to her brother and it was deeply comforting to share it with him.

Sam, who to his own surprise had found himself thinking a

great deal about Ellie while he was away, had taken himself off to see the Marshalls at the earliest opportunity and got a version of events from Ellie, inevitably with a slightly different slant from Sophie's.

'Victoria and your dad were just *so* happy together it was lovely being with them,' Ellie said to him as they sat entwined on the sofa after Maggie and Philip had gone to bed, 'but poor Sophe found that very tough to cope with. I've never seen anyone look as dreadful as your dad did after Victoria broke it off. We'd just had a happy girls' shopping trip the day before, celebrating our AS results and Sophe had said for the first time that she could see that she might feel OK about Victoria in time. I know it seems awful to say this, but I hope your parents *do* split up. I don't see how they could possibly be happy together again after this. Mum says your father's utterly devastated, but she thinks your mother will swan off easily enough when a new craze hits her.'

'What does your father think my parents should do?' asked Sam.

'Daddy thinks they should go for a divorce even though Victoria and Patrick have split up – have it all legal and tidy. You know Dad – not a lawyer for nothing!'

'How devastated would you be if *your* parents split up?' asked Sam, not sure what he really felt about the prospect.

Ellie sat bolt upright with a look of horror. 'Don't even go there! I'd be gutted!' she said. Then she cuddled up to Sam again, enchanted that since his return their relationship appeared to have moved up several very exciting gears. 'But then I simply can't imagine it,' she said. 'The thing is, that unlike your parents, Mum and Dad actually enjoy each other's company. They make each other laugh. They *do* things together. How do you think your father's coping now?'

'Awful,' said Sam. 'I've never, ever seen Dad like this – he's usually such good company and always interested in every-thing we do, but neither Sophe nor I can get through to him at all. It's as if he's not *there*. He asks me about my trip, and he's like, "Oh, great, do tell me more about it," but he's not even *listening*.'

To everyone's secret relief, Rachel, hitherto the least

clubbable of women, announced that she was going to Oxford to attend a reunion at Trinity.

'These reunions don't come round very often and our year hasn't got together for ages,' she said, explaining to Sophie and Sam why she couldn't possibly be with them after all, at a weekend for which they'd both be home and after she'd told Patrick she wanted to be at Wytherton. 'There are one or two old friends I particularly want to see. I shall drop in on Granny and Grandpa for a night or two on the way back and probably spend a night in London. I badly need a break.'

Neither Sam nor Sophie felt brave enough to ask if the time in Spain had counted as a break but there was a palpable lightening of the atmosphere after she had departed.

At least Yvonne was back, which everyone, especially Posy, was pleased about – a new Yvonne who had become better able to stand up to her small charge's temperamental mother, and having negotiated new employment terms with Patrick, was more sure of her ground when Rachel made impossible demands.

One Saturday Sophie rode over to visit Hugh and they had tea together, toasting crumpets on the ancient brass toasting fork that hung from a bit of string in front of the drawing room fireplace. Mrs Parkes was out, but Hugh remembered that she'd bought chestnuts in Knighton market to cook with a brace of partridges for his Sunday lunch, so they decided to roast the chestnuts too, balancing one of Mrs Parkes's gleaming baking tins on top of the smouldering logs. This proved to be a less successful operation since they forgot to pierce the skins, with the result that the chestnuts exploded round the room like incendiary bombs, adding a good many new holes to the already much singed carpet and completely blackening the tin. They were lucky to escape any injury to themselves and became hysterical with laughter as Sophie leaped about the room, dodging chestnuts and whacking smouldering upholstery, while Hugh tried to poke the tin off the fire with his stick.

'That was just like the war again! I must say, you're good under fire, Sophie,' he said, as he wiped his eyes – streaming from the combined effects of smoke and laughter – with one of the flamboyant silk handkerchief that always cascaded from his top pocket. 'Don't know what I'd have done without you.'

'You wouldn't have been roasting chestnuts for a start!' Sophie pointed out.

After this exciting episode she felt more cheerful than she had for weeks. Though Hugh had already heard about the break-up between Patrick and Victoria, he listened attentively while she regaled him with her version of the events in Corfu: about her mother's unexpected arrival at Petradi, for which she felt so responsible, and which in Sophie's view had effectively put an end to her father's romantic dream with Victoria. It was a huge relief to Sophie to talk to someone who understood.

'What your mother needs is an outside job that really interests her,' proclaimed Hugh, making one of the new holes in the carpet much worse by rubbing at it with his stick. 'I've always said so. She's got a good brain and never used it since she married your father. Rachel's always been in thrall to a vision of herself that doesn't match reality. She saw herself as a clinging old-fashioned wife and mother – God knows why – because she wasn't suited to being a domestic paragon and didn't enjoy the things that went with the job. She'd have been a better mother to you and Sam if she hadn't seen so much of you – unless circumstances had forced her to buckle down and *do* more for you as well. She likes to pretend she's a shrinking violet,' Hugh snorted derisively, 'but I've always thought she was as tough as old boots!'

He grinned at Sophie's surprised expression and went on, warming to his theme: 'I suppose she might have been good as a pioneering wife in the Wild West – toting a gun on one hip and a baby on the other and shooting a few Red Indians occasionally to slake her killer instinct.'

'*Mum?*' Sophie, reared on the doctrine of her mother's extreme sensibility, was stunned by this novel appraisal of the parent around whom the family had always pussyfooted with such care. 'Goodness! So do you think she and Dad ought to split up, even if he and Victoria can't get together?'

'I'm afraid I do,' he said. 'They'll destroy each other other-wise. You don't look too happy yourself at the moment, Sophie. What's happened to my bright *Girl under the Apple Tree*?'

'She's gone missing,' she said dolefully. 'You see, it was my

fault. I told Mum about Victoria and that's why she came back.'
She added, 'I still don't quite see why Victoria had to make such
a big deal about it – after all, she already knew Dad was
married. Ellie says she thinks her parents know more than
they're letting on but they won't discuss it. Have you gathered
anything, Uncle Hugh?' she asked, wondering if her father had
talked to him.

But if he had, Hugh was not going to be drawn. 'I don't
suppose it had anything to do with you,' he said. 'If your mother
didn't know about Victoria already – and you can bet your boots
she did – then she soon would have done, and the result would
have been the same in the end. Rachel's an unfulfilled woman
who needs to turn her critical faculties on something other than
her family. She'd probably have been happier married to a man
whom *she* had to try to please, rather than one who always tried
to please her, like your father did when they were first married.
I used to think he was hopeless with her. Surprising really,
because he's usually very good with people, but he had a blind
spot about it. It might not have mattered, but your mother got
greedy, so whatever he did was never enough for her. A craving
for approval's an insidious thing and can have very damaging
consequences. Rachel might have been better off with that shit
who let her down a few years ago.'

'What shit?' asked Sophie.

'Oh God! I shouldn't have said that!' Hugh felt the scales that
were falling from Sophie's eyes would soon be littering the
carpet. He looked at her consideringly. No bad thing perhaps,
he thought.

'You're almost grown up now, darling girl, perhaps you
should learn another side of the story?' he suggested. 'Your
mother had a fling herself a few years ago, but your father
forgave her then – so, you see, it's six and six. Don't start
judging either of them. But I'm a sentimental old fool and I was
very taken with Victoria Cunningham – and not just because
she's Evanthi Palombini's granddaughter either. I hadn't seen
your father look so happy for years.'

They sat in silence for a bit, while Sophie digested this
information and pondered on the unexpected complexities of
adult life.

'What do you want to do with *your* life Sophie?' Hugh asked after a bit.

'I know what I'd *like* to do – but I'm not sure I could,' she said cautiously.

'What's that?'

'Well, I've struggled so hard with my dyslexia, and I got much better grades than anyone expected in my AS results, so I'd like to go to uni first and then do a teacher training course and help children who have the same condition – if I could get accepted that is.'

'Excellent. Go for it.' He said abruptly: 'Concentrate on your own life, Sophie. Your parents must sort theirs out for themselves.'

'That's what everybody says, but how are you sorting yours out, Uncle Hugh?' asked Sophie slyly, thinking she might turn the tables on the old man and give him a bit of advice about his own future. Nobody had the faintest idea what the situation was between himself and Evanthi and everyone was curious. It was one of the things they'd all happily speculated on at Petradi.

He looked at her over the top of his spectacles, with a gleam of amusement. 'Evanthi and I are in touch, if that's what you mean,' was all he would say – but she thought he looked rather pleased with himself.

She rode home with a lot to think about.

The following weekend, when Rachel returned after the reunion, Sam and Sophie braced themselves for her to be at her most difficult, but to their relief she came home in a mood of excitement bordering on euphoria. She had met an old friend, now a well-known biographer, and there was a chance she might be offered a job as a research editor. She was fired with enthusiasm.

'So what's new?' Sophie asked Sam gloomily. 'Same old difference: for Bronwen read Old Uni Friend, the latest in a long line of gurus.'

At Vrahos, Victoria existed in a sort of limbo, feeling less than half alive and dragging herself through each day. She tried to throw herself into the running of the estate, where it became increasingly obvious that the income from the farm was no longer even beginning to keep pace with the needs of the house, and that everything on the farm was outdated too.

She often thought about Richard and reread his letter with sadness and gratitude, hoping that somehow some part of him – a surviving consciousness – might know what the letter had meant to her: she no longer felt tormented by the bitterness that had disturbed her previously, though her feeling that Richard had granted her permission to be with Patrick now seemed terribly ironic. But the letter had also helped her to talk to Jake about his father, and thereby, she hoped, cement some happy memories of Richard in his son's head, which he would be able to look back on with pleasure when he was older.

But if she thought about her husband frequently, she thought about Patrick almost constantly, and was uncomfortably aware that her grief for Richard had not approached the despair she was experiencing for the quite different loss of Patrick. She felt as if she had undergone an amputation. The pain was sometimes so acute she could hardly bear it. One evening, in the little drawing room, intending to throw another log on the fire, her eye had been caught by Hugh's watercolour, where Evanthi had propped it against the wall on the chest by her chair, near the silver box. Foolishly, Victoria had taken the picture in her hands, turned it over and reread the poem on the back and the longing that it should have been written not for Evanthi by Hugh, but for her, by Patrick, was almost overwhelming.

One day, soon after the Hammonds had returned home, she saw Maggie in Kryovrisi. Victoria had panicked and fled down a side road, feeling unable to face her, but Maggie bravely chased after her and gave her a swift hug. The two women clung to each other for a moment.

'Please don't say anything nice to me,' begged Victoria, tears filling her eyes as she returned the hug, afraid she might break down completely if Maggie was too sympathetic. 'I don't think I could take it. Just tell me if Patrick is all right.'

'Oh, Victoria, *of course he's not all right*. How could he be?' said Maggie sadly. 'Any more,' she added pointedly, 'than I imagine you are. He was devastated by your decision. But I'm not going to go on about that. I only want to say two things to you and then I'll go. One is that Phil and I are more sorry than we can say, and if he or I can do anything at all – ever – to help, then give us a ring, any time. I'll send you our home address. And the other is . . . *don't give up on Patrick*. See you, Victoria, please don't lose touch.' And she whisked away.

Patrick had telephoned as soon as he got back to England, bitterly regretting his angry departure; determined to put things right with Victoria and find out what had really caused such an apparent change of heart, but Victoria absolutely refused to speak to him, telling Dora to say she was unavailable. She was afraid that if she heard his voice she would be quite unable to keep up her principled stand – but she immediately regretted this high-minded course of action and longed and longed for him to ring again.

He didn't do so. Instead he wrote her one precious letter to tell her how much he would always love her. 'You may think me arrogant, but I can't believe you don't still love me,' he wrote, 'and I think I could have made you happy. I want you to know that my feelings for you will never change.' He said that the book on Vrahos would be out before Christmas, and that of course complimentary copies would be sent to her and Evanthi. Along with the photograph he'd taken of her on Helidonia, it would become his most treasured possession. He was starting on his new book and would be away most of October in Italy, Hungary and Spain, doing research. He signed the letter '*Pantotina*, Patrick.'

Though in one way it told her the most important thing she could want to know, in another way it told her nothing: not how he was, or what was happening in his marriage, or even how his children were. It was a brief letter. Victoria cried so much when she read it she was thankful that the brilliant sunshine gave her an excuse to wear dark glasses for the rest of the day. Over the next weeks, she read and reread it so many times – searching fruitlessly for hidden meanings to reveal themselves – that eventually the paper split in half where it had been folded. She composed countless answers in her head – but she did not send them.

Jake went happily back to school and continued to fill out and look more robust, though he still suffered from occasional nightmares, and there were times, usually in the evening, when he still wept inconsolably for his father. Those were the times that stiffened Victoria's resolve not to weaken and ring Patrick, as she often longed to do.

As promised, Anthony and Toula, who had been appalled to hear Victoria's news, came out to stay at the end of September. Separately, they each tried to talk to her about Patrick, but neither met with any success.

'She is such an oyster,' wailed Toula to her husband.

'Clam,' said Anthony automatically. 'Give her time, darling.'

'Time!' Toula snorted, scornfully. 'I've never had any use for that!'

On this occasion, Evanthi listened to Anthony's advice regarding the future of both Victoria and Vrahos and, without actually agreeing to a sale, greatly to his surprise, allowed him to take the icon away at the end of his visit so that he could show it to a friend of his in Athens – an acknowledged expert on Byzantine icons who had a particular interest in Andreas Ritzos and the Cretan School. Evanthi told Anthony tartly that the combined pressure from Guy and himself was getting very trying and she was only playing along with their ideas to keep them both quiet. Since giving in to keep anyone quiet was not at all in his strong-minded mother-in-law's nature, Anthony was well satisfied with her reaction, and took it to be, if not a green, then at least an amber, light to the idea of a possible sale.

'I have a shrewd idea what the icon might fetch at auction,' he told Evanthi, 'but Kristos will be much more accurate in his valuation than I can be and might even know of a suitable private buyer. If you do finally consider selling, I think you might find that a more acceptable option than putting it on the open market.'

Evanthi had made no comment, but Anthony thought she was not averse to this suggestion.

After the main tourist season finished at the end of September, the island settled down to its age-old rhythms. Piles of nets started to appear ready for spreading under the olive trees – for, unlike the mainland, the olives on Corfu are not picked off the trees, but are allowed to fall as they ripen.

The plants in the ridged terracotta pithoi on the terrace at Vrahos were a riot of colour – hibiscus and plumbago, geraniums and cannas and the delightful little pointed chilli peppers that Jake thought looked like multi-coloured Christmas-tree lights.

October, when the crowds had gone, was normally one of Victoria's favourite months. The sea, baked by the heat of summer, was the perfect temperature for swimming, but the mornings and evenings were delightfully fresh. It was a month of spectacular sunsets and sunrises, the pink and purple folds of the Albanian mountains melting into the clouds so that it was often hard to distinguish sky from land, and always, during the day, there was the incredible clarity of the early autumn light.

Little pink and purple cyclamen sprang up everywhere and brilliant yellow sternbergias looked like patches of sunshine on the baked earth. She tried to savour these delights but longed so badly to share them with one particular person that the pain of his absence became a permanent dull ache.

One day she and Jake drove up in the hills to the deserted village of old Perithia with its derelict Venetian houses and romantic air of mystery. The road became ever steeper as they hair-pinned thrillingly round corners to gaze at the sheer drops and dizzying views that stretched out below them.

'Are those tombstones?' asked Jake, fascinated by the extraordinary white slabs of natural rock sticking up all round them like jagged teeth.

Jake was at his most companionable, chatting happily away to her and interested in everything she could tell him about the island. It should have been an idyllic day, but all the time a part of Victoria was thinking of Patrick, imagining his reaction to everything she was showing to Jake. When they suddenly passed a little oasis of cultivated ground in the rocky terrain, covered with vines and square blue beehives like those Hugh had once asked her about, Hugh and Evanthi sprang so vividly to mind that the realisation that she and Patrick, despite all their resolutions, had failed to avoid the same awful wastage of a special love filled her with depression all over again.

'Mum – you're not *listening* to me,' complained Jake, and she was guiltily conscious that she was short-changing him of her attention.

'I'm sorry, darling,' she said. 'I've got boring grown-up problems in my head but I'll try to banish them and do better,' and she made a big effort to concentrate her whole mind on her young son and forget about the invisible other passenger in the car.

Two events of great family significance occurred that October. Francine gave birth to a stillborn son and Corfu was hit by a violent storm.

Chapter Forty-nine

It had been Toula who telephoned Vrahos with the news about the baby. Later Victoria had spoken to Guy at the hospital.

Francine had apparently gone into labour ten days early. 'They couldn't find the baby's heart-beat,' Guy told her, his voice breaking. 'Francine had a very rough time – and so did he, but by the time they got him out he was already gone.' Victoria had never heard Guy sound so wretched. All past resentments and anger fell away from her.

'Shall I fly straight over?' she asked. 'Would Francine like me to come – would you? I'll do anything – or nothing. Whatever helps.'

'Come a bit later,' he said. 'I think that would be great for us both, but not quite yet. I'm terribly worried about Francine. She's being incredibly brave but she's totally devastated. We both are. I think we need to be alone together and try to take it in – and Francine just wants to hold the little chap while we still can. They're being wonderful here, but we have to face letting him go soon. Oh, Vicky, he looks so perfect, but so small – so still. And we can't *give* him anything or do anything for him. We'd promised Nonna that if the baby was a boy we'd call him Constantine after your father but . . .' Guy's voice cracked and disappeared for a moment, 'but we thought perhaps as things are, we'd save that for . . . for another time. We've decided to call him Stavros after Grandfather Doukas.' Then he said huskily, 'Francine was going to ask you to be his godmother . . . I suppose you couldn't face coming to his funeral?'

'Of course I'll come.' said Victoria, touched to the core. 'I'll still feel I'm his godmother – always. And please tell Francine I'm honoured. I won't intrude – I'd just like to be there with the three of you. Nonna and I are sending you both our special love. She's desperately upset for you.'

'Tell her I'd like to talk to her soon. I don't think I could face it today.'

'She'll understand,' said Victoria. 'She always does.'

Guy and Francine's baby was buried in the churchyard at Durnford, with just his parents, his paternal grandparents and Victoria present. Guy carried the heart-rendingly small coffin himself and placed it in the earth. It was an October day of stiff breeze but Indian-summer sunshine and an almost Corfiot-blue sky. Beech leaves swirled down, supposedly carrying magic wishes, but no one felt like trying to catch one; a few remaining swallows, who had left their autumnal departure dangerously late, swooped round the church, practising their aerobatic skills and strengthening their wings for the long flight ahead. Perhaps, thought Victoria, they would break their journey to Africa on Helidonia? But thoughts of Helidonia inevitably brought thoughts of Patrick and there was enough sadness to be coped with today. She tried to shut him out of her mind.

Before she left Corfu she had cut a few sprays from the Vrahos olive trees and dug up clumps of wild cyclamen, never giving a thought to the restrictions on importing plants. Earlier in the day she and Guy and Francine had planted the cyclamen round the little grave and lined it with the silver sprays. 'You were a bit lucky not to get stopped taking all that through customs,' Anthony told her and she was thankful it had not occurred to her that she might be breaking the law because she knew she would have done it all the same.

Guy and Francine stood very close together throughout the short, simple service and when it was over, by unspoken agreement, Anthony, Toula and Victoria slipped quietly away and left them alone to take a last farewell of their baby son.

Later Anthony drove Victoria to Heathrow to catch a flight to Athens. She clung to him for a moment as she said goodbye – a strong and comforting presence all her life. Now he had tears on his cheeks himself.

The storm came the evening after Victoria got back. The wind, which had been rising throughout the day, whipping the olive trees to a frenzy, churning up the sea like a boiling cauldron, suddenly moved into another phase altogether as though it had acquired the strength of a demented giant bent on destruction. The islanders were used to equinoctial gales, but this was something different. All along the coast, awnings outside tavernas were torn down and ripped apart, beach chairs and tables were lifted into the air and smashed down again often fifty metres from their original position; walkways were ripped up as if they had been made of matchwood; boats were wrecked and power cables brought down. Bits of masonry rained down in the streets as though the buildings from which they came had been blown up in an explosion; chimney pots rolled about in the streets and fallen trees and branches blocked many of the roads. The noise was horrendous. It was impossible to be heard without shouting – it seemed almost impossible to think. When the rain finally came it seemed to pour down in solid walls of water.

No one could stand against the gale. Early on, Yannis had tried to go outside to bring the furniture in from the terrace and been knocked clean off his feet. He managed to crawl back on all fours, but was badly bruised and shaken. There was nothing to do but go to bed by the light of a torch and cower in the darkness. Dora kept a stock of candles for the not infrequent occasions when the electricity went off and there were several Calor gas lamps, but such were the draughts in the old house that with the wind shrieking through it, the candles either blew out or became a fire hazard, and with no way of knowing how long it might be before power lines could be repaired, they decided to conserve the gas as much as possible. Jake and Victoria curled up together on the big sofa at the foot of Evanthi's bed.

By the early hours of the morning the worst of the storm had abated – but the devastation not only outside but, more alarmingly, inside as well, soon became apparent. Victoria crept downstairs at dawn to make a cup of tea – forgetting that there would be no way of boiling a kettle – and looked in to the Grand Salon on her way to the kitchen. Even in the half-light of early morning, the sight that met her eyes filled her with horror. Part of the famous coffered ceiling had collapsed and there was a pile of rubble in the centre of the room completely burying an eighteenth-century table on which precious vellum-bound books belonging to Evanthi's family were always displayed. Water was dripping down the outside wall, drenching the pictures between the windows and saturating the furniture beneath. It was too soon to know how much damage had been done, but Victoria knew it must be considerable. She gazed about her in a state of shock.

Her first instinct was to rush upstairs to break the news to Evanthi, but as the old lady had only dropped off to sleep after the storm started to abate, fear of the effect it might have on her health held Victoria back. Was this the end of Vrahos? She opened one of the French windows on to the terrace and, hugging her dressing gown round her, went barefoot outside. The wind was dropping but huge black clouds still billowed over the sea, staining it the colour of purple grapes – Homer's famous 'wine-dark sea', she thought. The sky to the east was lightening and a great flame-disc rose from behind the mountains to balance on the edge of the horizon, touching everything with fire. She watched, breathless, until, in what seemed an extraordinarily short space of time, the sun had risen clear of the skyline as though it were conquering the last remnants of the storm and a fierce determination came over her not to be defeated by all the damage and decay – not to be defeated by anything.

Things may have to change, she thought, but we can't just let this beloved old house – this *home* – crumble away. There have to be solutions.

She went back into the house to find that Dora had got a fire going in the old kitchen range and was boiling a kettle, and Yannis had been up for ages inspecting the damage to the outside of the house – but it was the havoc that the smashed shutters and broken windows had caused to the inside by letting in such a weight of water that Victoria guessed was going to prove so terribly costly. The three of them sat at the kitchen table and drank cups of coffee and held a council of war. Then Yannis went off to get help from the village and Victoria went upstairs to face Evanthi.

Evanthi took the news with her usual outward fortitude, the

challenge seeming to give her renewed energy too, though Victoria was not deceived about the effort it cost her to show such a brave face. She knew her grandmother had not only been deeply saddened by the loss of her beloved Guy's baby, but extremely hard hit by her own parting from Patrick. Though Evanthi had understood Victoria's initial reaction to Rachel's call, as the weeks went by she made no bones about the fact that she thought Victoria was being needlessly destructive of her future happiness, an attitude that Victoria found difficult to bear.

'How fortunate, under the circumstances, that I've instructed Anthony to go into the question of selling the icon,' said Evanthi now, for all the world, Victoria thought, as if it had been her own proposal – ignoring the vehemence with which she had resisted the idea for years. 'The sale of it may prove to be the salvation of Vrahos and if I hadn't asked Anthony to take it away with him, it might have got damaged too.'

'Perhaps St Nicholas was doing some wonder-working,' suggested Victoria drily.

'Certainly. If you remember I recommended that you should consult him yourself, *chrysso mou*. One must always be open to new initiatives,' said Evanthi blandly.

With the help of a local building firm and many willing volunteers from the village, the house was soon made temporarily weatherproof – probably more weatherproof than it had been for years, according to Yannis. Sheets of plastic and boarding covered the worst trouble spots and the rubble was cleared away. The following week Anthony flew over from England to help assess the extent of the damage to the more valuable objects, and to give his opinion on the possibilities of restoration. He had so many contacts in the art world that he could be relied upon to know the best experts to call in.

It was no surprise to anyone to learn that the insurance had not been updated for years.

'I know you and Guy have both told me constantly that I should see to it,' admitted Evanthi with painful honesty, when she was alone with her son-in-law. 'But it seemed such a colossal sum of money to find every year and I knew if I told you I hadn't done it you'd have offered to pay – which I certainly couldn't have accepted. I'm afraid I gambled on getting away without a major disaster. Now I bitterly regret that I didn't listen to you and try to take some action. My poor Victoria! What a legacy of trouble I shall be leaving her. I am an arrogant, foolish old woman.'

Anthony looked at his usually imperious mother-in-law with great affection. 'It's always difficult to know what, if anything, to do about insurance for art treasures and old houses,' he said gently. 'Plenty of other people in similar positions decide to do nothing too, and quite often they're right. Don't blame yourself – that would upset Victoria more than anything. And it's not all hopeless. I have some news for you. I showed your icon to my friend Kristos as I said I would.' He paused, studying her face. 'And Kristos gave it a value of a quarter of a million in sterling – conceivably more if it went to auction and there was more than one buyer who intended to get it.'

Evanthi looked out of the window. He could see she was struggling with herself. Then she said, 'You did mention that Kristos might know of a private buyer?'

'Yes,' said Anthony. 'I was coming to that. As a matter of fact it seems there *is* a possible potential buyer – someone who knows all about Andreas Ritzos and who would want the icon for his own private collection – would really value it. I said I thought you might consider such an offer.'

'What do you advise me to do, Anthony?' she asked. 'In the future, Victoria may not be able to manage the burden of keeping the house going, but at the moment she seems to think she would like to live here and of course that would be my dearest wish – especially now when she needs to make a new life for herself. I wouldn't want her to start off with a millstone round her neck. I have thought a great deal about it and I am ready to part with the icon, if it is the right thing to do for her and for Jake. I would greatly prefer it to go to someone who I know would appreciate it – but if you think I should sell it on the open market, then, for Victoria's sake, I would do that too.'

'I think you should accept this offer,' said Anthony decidedly, greatly relieved at her reaction, but knowing how hard it was for her. 'I'm told the buyer would pay the full price

– even possibly a little more. You might do better at auction but I very much doubt it, and you might easily do worse. There are several other things I think you and Victoria may be able to do too to help with the finances in the long term, but to have a large sum immediately available to stop any further deterioration would be a good start. The advantage of a private purchase would be that you could have the money relatively soon. If it were to go to auction you would have to wait until a really important sale came up and it would all take much longer. But in the long run I'm convinced the key to keeping this house going and making the estate viable again is to diversify and think of new ways of using all the assets. The tourist trade is an obvious example and I believe it would be good for Victoria to get her teeth into a new project. But that's for later. Meanwhile, two hundred and fifty thousand pounds would put you well on the way to saving the house. Would you like me to set it up for you?'

'Yes,' said Evanthi. 'Yes, *dear* Anthony, please arrange it for me. Don't ask Victoria – she might feel impelled to say no for my sake. Just go ahead and do it.'

They talked of other things then: of Guy and Francine and their future. 'I've grown very fond of Francine,' said Anthony. 'I always liked her, though Toula certainly didn't to start with.' He smiled ruefully at Evanthi. 'Toula was never going to take kindly to any daughter-in-law but I think in the long run there's a better chance of her getting on with one who can stand up to her, as Francine undoubtedly can. They've come together over this. Apparently there's no reason why Guy and Francine shouldn't try for another child in due course, though of course she's thirty-eight – so biologically that tips the scales against her. Let's hope things work out better next time. Guy's a tricky chap and always will be, but she seems able to cope with him and I must say he's been wonderful over this. I only hope he won't let her down in the future.'

'I don't think he will,' said Evanthi, 'though you can never quite tell with Guy. I think this shared sadness will bring them closer together. And perhaps mourning for the baby will have enabled Guy to mourn also for Richard – something I have a feeling he needed to do.'

'Interesting you should say that,' said Anthony, thinking that not much got past Evanthi's shrewd observation. 'That's what Toula feels. How do you think Victoria is now?'

'Ah – that's an awful worry. She's been a tower of strength over this last disaster, but I know she's still desperately unhappy. I am so distressed that her relationship with Patrick Hammond broke up, not just because it's history repeating itself, but also because they were so *right* for each other. I can hardly bear to see Victoria going through what I went through all those years ago and it seems so unnecessary. I could murder Patrick's wife for turning up like that. You realise what Victoria thought Rachel Hammond was threatening to do?'

Anthony nodded. 'You told me. Do you think she knew what an Achilles heel she was aiming at?' he asked. 'Surely she couldn't have known about Richard? His actual death, yes, of course – but I mean about the suicide question?'

'Oh no, I think she was just troublemaking generally, but the idea has lodged in Victoria's mind and she's paranoid about it. I can't talk sense into her. If Patrick really knew the truth he would never have let her go. I long to write to him but Victoria made me promise not to tell him and now she won't even talk to me about it any more. You do like Patrick, don't you, Anthony?'

'I've only met him professionally so I don't know him all that well – but certainly well enough to think it's a crying shame they broke up. I'd never seen Victoria so lit-up and happy. I can't bear it for her after all she's been through over Richard. At least it's good for her to be here with you.' He added soberly, 'We must pray that her luck changes.'

'Or that she comes to her senses,' said Evanthi.

The next day Anthony went home, promising to get in touch the moment he had any news about the icon.

Victoria busied herself sorting out the storm damage and the affairs of the house and farm. Every day she wondered what the post would bring, half hoping and half fearing there might be a letter addressed in Patrick's distinctive handwriting: desperately longing for some communication – any communication – from him, but at the same time dreading that if there was a letter she might not have the strength to stick to her resolve, still convinced she was doing the right thing. She knew he was probably out of the country but as the days went by and turned into weeks she tried to resign herself to the fact that their painful goodbye had indeed been final, but the longing she felt for Patrick didn't lessen; she wondered if it ever would.

Guy and Francine decided to go out to the States for a bit. Francine had made a good physical recovery but was very low and Guy thought it would do her good to be on her home territory and meet her old friends. They were considering letting the London house and going out to live in New York for a year – it would be as easy for Guy to work from there as from England – but they'd promised whatever happened to come out to spend Christmas at Vrahos together with Anthony and Toula, and, to Victoria's surprise and pleasure, Bill Cunningham had accepted an invitation to come too. It had been Evanthi's suggestion to ask him.

In the middle of November Anthony rang Vrahos and spoke to Victoria.

'I have important news for you,' he said.

'Yes?' she asked, suddenly breathless.

Anthony had rung to say the icon had been sold and that a cheque would shortly be in the post.

'How . . . how wonderful!' said Victoria, her heartbeat returning drearily to normal. Anthony reported that the buyer was delighted with his purchase and wanted Kyria Doukas to know it would be greatly valued and that he did not intend to resell it – a possibility that had not occurred to Evanthi. He had informed Anthony that, when he was next in Athens, he would like to come over to Corfu and would consider it a great privilege if Evanthi would agree to see him and tell him personally all she knew of the icon's history and the legends attached to it. He was considering writing a book on Byzantine icons and their use as an aid to contemplation.

Victoria was doubtful about this idea. 'Oh, Uncle Anthony, I'll ask her of course, but don't you think it might upset her? I know she misses it dreadfully though she never says so. I'm not sure I could bear it either. I'm terribly conscious that she only parted with it out of love for me.'

However, when she rather cautiously put this suggestion to her grandmother, Evanthi's reaction was more favourable than she expected. 'I might consider that,' she said. 'I think I ought to know what sort of person the new owner is and I'd like to feel he knew everything I could tell him about the icon. I shall want to know if he intends to use it as an aid to his own personal worship.'

Victoria's heart sank slightly; she could foresee the meeting being extremely awkward if Evanthi disapproved of the new owner's views, regretted letting him have the icon and tried to get it back.

'He has just paid an enormous sum of money for it. You don't think it might be taking a bit of a liberty to quiz him about his faith?' she asked.

'Certainly not. If he's writing a book on contemplation he will surely want to hear my views on the subject,' said Evanthi. Victoria thought wryly that if the purchaser ventured to visit Vrahos, he would probably hear her views on a good many other subjects as well, whether he wanted to or not.

One morning at the beginning of December, Victoria was out when a visitor unexpectedly called at Vrahos. She had gone into town with Jake to do some Christmas shopping. They'd revived themselves with lunch in a restaurant and got back home early in the afternoon. Victoria was surprised, and dismayed, to see a car parked outside the courtyard. It was not one she recognised, but as it had a local number plate, she assumed it was some elderly friend of Evanthi's come to pay a pre-Christmas call.

'Oh dear,' she said to Jake, 'I don't at all feel like making conversation to any of Nonna's old cronies. They look at me with their beady, knowing eyes and I hate the inquisition they always put me through about my life.'

'Need we see them?'

'Well, *you* certainly don't need to. You scoot off and play with Angelo. I'll try to slink upstairs without being caught.' On her way up she put her head round the kitchen door.

'Who on earth has Nonna got with her?' she asked Dora.

'The dealer man who bought her holy picture.'

'*What?*' Victoria was indignant. 'You mean he's just turned up without asking? What a nerve! Why ever did you let him in?'

'He telephoned and you weren't here. Of course I asked Kyria first and she said she would see him.' Dora spread out her hands. 'What was I to do? I hoped you would be back before he arrived. Kyria wants you to go up and meet him.'

'Oh, I'm sorry, Dora – of course it's not your fault. I just think he might have had the decency to give us a bit of warning. I was very much against her seeing him. I suppose I shall have to go and make polite noises at him. I hope he won't upset her and tire her out. I shall try to speed him on his way.'

She didn't bother to tidy up but went straight up to the little drawing room, which had mercifully been unaffected by the storm, feeling tired, ruffled and in no mood for strangers.

But it was not a stranger who was sitting on the sofa with Evanthi.

It was Hugh Marston.

Victoria stood in the doorway with her mouth open, her astonishment almost visibly hanging in the air like the bubble above the head of a cartoon character.

Hugh and Evanthi both looked up – then they looked back at each other, her stunned surprise obviously affording them huge satisfaction. Hugh started to struggle to his feet to greet her but Evanthi laid a restraining hand on his arm.

'Well, *chrysso mou*,' she said to Victoria, a brilliant sparkle in her eye, 'you see we have an unexpected visitor! I made Dora promise not to tell you.'

'Hugh! How absolutely *wonderful*!' Victoria came over to kiss him, lit up with pleasure, thrilled for her grandmother. 'I thought you were going to be the collector chap who's bought the Ritzos,' she said, 'and I was going to be really grumpy and try to get rid of you!'

Then she saw what Evanthi was holding on her lap, and looked from one to the other of them, with dawning comprehension.

'And you *are*!' she exclaimed. 'You *are* the buyer! Oh, Hugh!'

'And I am,' said Hugh, laughing at her and looking extremely pleased with himself. 'I have brought a present for your grandmother, and nothing I have ever bought has afforded me anything like so much pleasure. I shall be eternally grateful to your uncle Anthony for informing me that it was coming up for sale – but it seems I also have his son Guy to thank.'

'*Guy?*'

'Yes,' said Hugh, looking searchingly at Victoria. 'Guy Winston suggested that his father should telephone Patrick and tell him about the terrible storm you've had and mention in passing that as a result of it your grandmother was having to consider selling the Vrahos icon.'

At the mention of Patrick's name all the colour drained out of Victoria's face.

Hugh went on: 'Apparently Patrick and your uncle then hatched the idea of sounding me out as a possible buyer. Of course I jumped at the chance . . .' He looked at her with a twinkle in his eye, and added, 'Having always wanted to own a genuine Ritzos, you understand, and being interested in the use of icons for worship.'

'You do realise, *agape*, what this means?' asked Evanthi. 'Now that the icon is back at Vrahos, it means – according to the legend – that the family won't have to leave after all! The storm was probably just a warning to us. Think of that!' But Victoria wasn't listening to her grandmother. She was staring at Hugh and twisting her fingers together in a state of great agitation.

'How . . . how is Patrick?' she managed to ask.

For answer, Hugh got slowly to his feet; Evanthi handed him his stick and he limped stiffly over to the window, flung it open and stepped out on to the balcony. 'Come over here,' he said, holding out his hand. Victoria went over to him, her heart suddenly thumping so loudly she thought it might shake the foundations of the old house more than any storm had done.

'Why don't you ask him yourself?' asked Hugh. She looked down. Leaning on the low wall surrounding the terrace, far below, was a tall figure.

Victoria stepped sharply back into the room, as though she'd touched a live wire.

'Oh God! What shall I do?' she asked wildly.

'Stop being so foolish and obstinate, I hope,' said Evanthi sharply.

Hugh shot his long-lost love a look of amusement, but to Victoria he said, very gently, 'If you *really* don't love Patrick, then stay up here and I will tell him you don't wish to see him and he'll go straight back to the airport. But if you do still love him, I suggest you go down and try to sort things out between you.'

She didn't wait to hear any more. She shot out of the drawing room and hurtled down the stone stairs so fast that afterwards she had no recollection of how she got to the bottom. She ran through the shuttered Grand Salon with its piled-up furniture and plastic sheeting and the all-pervading smell of damp. At the half-open French windows, she checked.

Patrick had turned and was watching as she came out on to the terrace, but he didn't move or come towards her and they stood gazing at each other, eyes locked.

'Why have you come?' she asked at last, her voice very shaky.

'Did you really believe I would give you up so easily?' he countered. 'I've come to ask you some questions, darling Victoria. If you truly don't love me then I promise I'll walk away and never bother you again . . . but you'll have to convince me, and this time I want more of an explanation.'

'What . . . what about Rachel . . .?' She hardly dared to ask. 'Has anything changed?'

'No, not really,' he said, looking at her with a challenge in his eyes. 'I always told you it was finished between Rachel and me. We're still going for a divorce, as we'd already decided, but she'll have to make her own life from now on. I can't take responsibility for her future decisions – and neither can you.'

She wondered if he knew about the telephone call.

He walked slowly towards her. 'But I haven't come to talk about Rachel. I've come to talk about us, my darling,' he said softly. 'I've come because I love you, because I can't live without you – and because I still dare to hope you feel the same way. These last months have been hell. Shall I go away or shall we try again? It's your choice. Which is it to be?'

He opened his arms, and Victoria walked straight into them.

After they had held each other for a long time, she looked up at him from the depths of his embrace. Falteringly she told him of her conversation with Rachel and her terrible fear of Richard's tragedy repeating itself.

'Something your uncle said when we met to plot this reunion

for Hugh and Evanthi gave me a hint of this,' he said, 'but I'm so glad you've told me yourself. I could have told you Rachel would never have done anything like that – but I don't suppose you'd have believed me at the time.'

'How could I have been so stupid as not to share it with you?' she asked. 'To think I nearly lost you! I've come to see that I had no right to force that decision on you without even explaining, but oh, Patrick! I was just so afraid.'

'It was a brave and unselfish thing you did,' he said, looking down at her with great love, 'but we both got things wrong. I knew Rachel must have made trouble, but when you suggested that what you and I had together could just have been a holiday romance I was so hurt and angry I let my pride get the better of me. Then when you wouldn't either speak to me or answer my letter, I admit doubts crept in and I was afraid you meant what you said about not loving me enough. Let's make a vow never to let misunderstandings come between us again. We'll take our decisions together in future.'

They walked, arms round each other, to the edge of the terrace, the winter sunshine and the clear sky still painting the water with kingfisher colours – one of the true halcyon days.

'I don't suppose life will be easy for either of us,' he said, 'but whatever happens let's face everything together, my darling. We shall have a lot of problems to sort out, and our respective, maddening, much loved children to consider and contend with. There are many possibilities of what we might do – but for me, being apart isn't one of them.'

She rubbed her cheek against his sleeve. 'Not for me either,' she whispered.

'And Hugh and Nonna?' she asked, after he'd kissed her again. 'It's *so* amazing that he's bought the icon – I can't take it in. What a wonderful idea of yours.' She looked up at him, laughing. 'But you and Uncle Anthony and Guy won't get any credit from Nonna, you know, either about the icon or about getting us back together – all the glory will go to St Nicholas and St Gregory, I can guarantee that! Talking of Hugh and Nonna – do you think we should go back upstairs to them now?'

'Certainly not,' he said, laughing back at her. 'They've waited over sixty years to see each other again. They won't want us barging in on them yet – they will have many private things to talk about together . . . and so have we, my darling. So have we.'

And they stood together looking out to sea.